# PRAISE FOR EQUILLIAN'S KEY

## BOOK 1 OF THE ARCHIVES OF THE NIGHT-WATCHERS SERIES

"K.L. Harris is a fiercely talented writer, and her debut proves she is an emerging talent on the fantasy scene. She deftly balances breath-stealing action with grounded emotional resonance between the characters in this fun, epic ride."

—Eric Praschan, author of the bestselling James Women Trilogy

"This is the best fantasy fiction I have read in a long time! The plot was well imagined. The World Creation was very creative-with bits of steampunk added (like flying ships). The characters were believable. And the book kept me riveted. It was a page turner of the best order."

—IndieBRAG

# STAR-LOCKED

ARCHIVES OF THE NIGHT-WATCHERS

BOOK TWO

# STAR-LOCKED

## K.L. HARRIS

Make-Believe Press

www.make-believepress.com



Library of Congress Control Number:   2024911764
ISBN: 978-1-7323686-2-0
First Edition, August 2024

Cover illustration © Carlos Quevedo
Title page compass illustration © K.L. Harris

*Dedicated in loving memory to **Derek***


*Also, to **The Dame Good Writers**
And me beloved hearties—**Kyler, Arya,** and **Ben***

*On the day you came to be*
*The Stars aligned themselves in greeting,*
*Watchers of the night—*
*Composers of our dreams.*
*Guiding you as you grew,*
*They led you to your destiny.*
*So must it be—you cannot flee from the fate for which you came,*
*For you are naught but an interlocking cog in empyrean's machine.*

The Words of the Watchers: Article 7

CONTENTS

# ASH

Master Coada drummed his fingers on his large oak desk as he stared at the white opalescent stone in front of him. It was a beautiful piece of work, perfectly round with flecks of gold, red, and green that shimmered when they caught the light. It took most graduate alchemists years to be able to make something as masterfully done as this, but Patrick had a knack for alchemy. He'd excelled in all his studies from the start, making child's play of some of The House's most advanced practices. Patrick sat before Master Coada on the other side of his desk, his shoulders slumped and his knee bouncing up and down. He was a young man of seventeen, though in that moment he looked more like a boy. He was nervous because he was in trouble. It was Patrick's initiation, his night to create the very first enchanted object of his own design, which would qualify him as a senior alchemist of The Alchemists House of Discovery. He had submitted drawn schematics months before, outlining the object he would make, along with written essays posing a convincing case of why the object should be made and how it would contribute in a positive way to society. All of which had been considered and weighed by the board and finally approved by The House's headmaster, Master Coada.

Patrick had spent months making his object by hand, carving it out of Dragon's Milk stone, sanding it, polishing it to a sheen. But when it came time to imbue it with its enchantment, Patrick didn't give it the ability approved by the board — he gave it a different one. Master Coada knew he should strip Patrick of his titles and expel him from The Alchemists House of Discovery for what he'd done, but the boy was too damn brilliant. Coada was worried his talent would be a greater risk out in the world unsupervised than in here, despite any trouble he might cause. Coada rubbed his brow.

"Patrick, why? Why in the stars didn't you make what we'd planned, what's been approved by the board?"

"I'm sorry, Master Coada. I honestly thought you'd be pleased. I only came up with the new plan last night. I couldn't sleep because of the anticipation I had for today, and it just sort of popped into my head. I think it's much better than my original idea. But I knew if I mentioned it, I would've had to go through the whole process of writing papers and the like all over again before I could ever make it. The whole thing is such an ordeal. I thought surely it would get approved in the end anyway…I really thought you and the board would be pleased…" Patrick rambled, trailing off at the end under Master Coada's stare.

"Have you ever considered there might be a reason why the whole thing's such an ordeal?" Master Coada asked, putting his fingers to his temple.

"No sir," Patrick admitted ashamedly.

"We have these practices in place to prevent the very thing you've done. You've created an object with the potential to do harm. You must understand—with the power to create enchantments comes a great responsibility. You have taken a vow to use that power for the benefit and well-being of humanity as a whole and to under no circumstances ever abuse that power or use it for the power of one, have you not?"

"Yes, of course, but this does benefit humanity! I don't see how it could even be used for anything harmful. All I've done is create an object that can house all one's enchantments—making them portable and readily accessible. Imagine being able to use the Impeccable Rhythm Enchantment with any shoes of your choice, instead of needing to change into the enchanted ones. Or if you're a chef, wouldn't you want to be able to transfer the Eversharp Enchantment to any of your knives, instead of being limited to only one design? What if—"

"What if someone were to use the Eversharp Enchantment to gain an advantage in battle?" Coada interjected.

Patrick laughed. "A lot of good that would do! The Eversharp Enchantment makes it so the blade can cut anything but human skin."

"Precisely. It could be used on the weapon of one's enemies, making them useless."

"Isn't that a good thing?" Patrick asked.

"Not if the one using the enchantment is the greater threat to humanity. Imagine how powerful it could make someone if they have all the enchantments accessible to them through your object. All it would take to gain an advantage for a sinister purpose is a little imagination. The potential your object has to do harm is monumental. There's never been one made more powerful or dangerous than the one you've created today," Coada concluded.

"Right," Patrick gulped nervously.

"You don't understand these things because you're inexperienced. You've rushed into something without thinking it through, which is exactly why it must be approved by the board and not an individual. You're very talented, Patrick, but you don't have the benefit of the wisdom that can only come from a lifetime of experience."

Before Coada could say another word there was a heavy knock on the door.

"Can it wait? I'm in the middle of a meeting!" Coada called out in irritation.

"Sorry sir, it's urgent."

"Come in, if you must."

The door cracked open and Coada's assistant, Devin, poked his head in.

"Sorry for the intrusion, sir. A Sendsong's just arrived with an urgent message from Detective Chief Inspector Miles. He's requesting your presence."

"Requesting *my* presence, at this hour? Whatever for?—Alright, I'm coming. Just give us a minute and I'll be right behind you."

Devin nodded and gently shut the door.

"I do apologize for the interruption, Patrick, we'll speak more on the matter tomorrow. It's late at any rate—we'll all have clearer minds in the morning. Head back to your room and get some sleep. I'll keep the object until we decide what's to be done."

"Yes, Master Coada...for what it's worth, I had the best of intentions—honest."

"I know," Master Coada acknowledged with a caring smile. He opened his desk drawer and placed the white stone ball into it and then locked it, dropping the key into his pocket. He patted Patrick's shoulder as he passed and left the room.


Master Coada walked down the hallway of The Alchemists House of Discovery towards the roosting house. Devin was already there waiting for him. He handed Coada a folded letter. Coada recognized the Sendsong pruning its feathers comfortably on a perch by his side. Its longest tail feather was painted red, marking it as an official government messenger. It was the one The House had donated to Detective Chief Inspector Miles as a gift—to help in criminal cases. The mechanical enchanted birds were designed by the original alchemists and had never been successfully replicated. They were Coada's favorite enchanted object. Since he was a child, he'd always loved birds, and the original Sendsongs had intrigued him most of all. He consumed stories about them, fiction or fact. Large blue-black birds with long tail feathers and milky white eyes blind to sight, but keen and piercing to the vibrational signature of everything, allowing them to find anyone from anywhere. The alchemists' mechanical replicas were just as effective messengers, with beautifully polished white porcelain exteriors. After The Last War, Coada donated a Sendsong to every governmental body across the united world, with the hopes it would improve Equillian's system of government with better communication—as well as create an alliance between the governmental bodies and The Alchemists House of Discovery. And it had. In fact, it had helped a great deal—only it had been a long time since he'd seen one of those Sendsongs come here. Coada opened the message that Devin handed him.

*Master Coada,*
*Rupert Finley is dead. There has been an incident involving an*
*enchanted object. I request your presence at 4 Wyndelwhere Place*
*immediately.*
*—Detective Chief Inspector Miles*

Coada was paralyzed by the words in front of him. *Rupert Finley, dead? Surely not*—Coada had an appointment scheduled with the optician in two days' time. Rupert had requested the meeting himself only just last week, insisting he had something to show Coada that would be of great interest and mutual benefit for them both. Coada had been looking forward to the engagement. He'd always respected and admired the Finleys; their family had created optical instruments for The House for generations. And an enchanted object involved? Such a thing was preposterous! But if one of their objects had any connection to the incident, then Coada wanted to be the first to know. He made his way to The House's grand entrance with Devin close on his tail. He collected his heavy wool coat and bowler hat from the stand near the door and turned to his assistant. "Hold The House, Devin. I'm going out," he announced, and stepped into the night.

When Coada arrived at Wyndelwhere Place, it was a mess. Black smoke billowed from the charred skeleton of Finley's residence. Coada couldn't believe it—the last time he'd seen the place it was a charming building with white smoke streaming peacefully from its chimney stack, such a juxtaposition to the black cloud before him now. The building was a smoldering shadow of its former self, charred black and broken from the fire that had consumed it. The whole area was roped off and crawling with officers from the Bureau. They parted to let Coada through. He quickly found his way to Detective Chief Inspector Miles.

The Chief Inspector was a middle-aged man with a long face and deeply furrowed brows that showed he'd seen too much of the dark side of humanity to have any optimism left. He was reading from a clipboard with a lit puff-stick between his teeth. He looked up as Coada approached.

"Coada! Thanks for coming out at this hour," he greeted, putting down the clipboard to shake Coada's hand.

"How are you, Miles? It's been a while."

"Too long. I'm sorry it's not under better circumstances."

"Next time," Coada returned with a warm smile. "What's happened here?"

"Come." Miles motioned for Coada to follow him towards the burning remnants of Rupert Finley's residence.

"One of the neighbors notified the fire department a few hours ago. They came out as soon as they could, but the fire'd already done its worst. Thankfully, they were able to prevent it from spreading to the other residences. Now, here's where things get weird. When the smoke cleared, the fire department found this." Miles pointed to an area above the rubble. Coada looked up from the broken bricks he'd been navigating. There in the center of what had once been the living room, floating in the air above burnt furniture and ash, slightly obscured from the grey smoke still rising from the scene, was a deconstructed enchanted object. It was the inner pieces of a natural orrery, called an Ethereal Globe—a glass ball housing a perfect scaled-down working copy of Equillian's solar system. It was designed by a female alchemist named Indigo Evans. The exquisite piece was created not only to study the cosmos, but also to enjoy its beauty.

Coada couldn't believe what he was seeing. It was as if the glass had simply disappeared and all the cosmic elements inside had taken up residence in Finley's home—suspending a miniature replica of the solar system in the middle of the man's living room. Coada stepped closer to inspect the small stars, sun, moons, and planets peacefully moving in their natural rotations. He reached out and touched one of the stars, quickly pulling his finger back in searing pain. The star had singed his finger, as if it were *real*.

"Careful, three of the Bureau's men are already nursing injuries from that thing," Miles warned.

"Incredible," Coada whispered. He'd never seen anything like it. He held his open palm towards the sun and felt heat emanating from it. The inner workings of the artefact hadn't been made with the usual safety requirements, because the outside had been secured with an Anti-Tampering Enchantment. The enchantment should've made it impossible for this to happen, yet here it was, deconstructed before his very eyes.

*What had Finley been working on?* Coada wondered. There was only one thing in existence that he knew of that made it possible to interact with the structure of an enchanted object—and it belonged to him. Given to the alchemists two decades before by the most infamous Finley brothers themselves—Remi and Morris Finley, grandfather and granduncle to Rupert Finley. Morris worked in the Finley family trade—creating unique lenses that founded the foundation of their family's legacy, revolutionizing the optics industry; and Remi, a renowned explorer known mostly for researching and documenting the Dreg Islands that inhabited the fringes of the Desert Ocean. The brothers had given The House a prototype called the *Astra Lens,* a lens created from a green crystal discovered by Remi on one of his expeditions. According to their report, Remi found the crystal embedded in a fallen star that crash-landed on one of the Dreg Islands, and Morris made it into a lens because the crystal's flawless clarity and surprising properties were superior to glass for the purpose. It wasn't until after the crystal lens was made that its true capability was revealed, making the crystal it was made from far more valuable than simply a glass alternative. The Astra Lens prototype was gifted to The Alchemists House of Discovery to inspire funding for another voyage to recover the rest of the cosmic mineral. Remi and Morris hoped to procure the remaining shards of the crystal to create more lenses. The House did fund their voyage, but Remi and Morris never returned. And as far as Coada knew, that was the end of the Finleys' creation. The single lens had been passed down from the last headmaster to Master Coada, and it was his understanding that it was the only one in existence—as well as the only thing that made it possible to achieve the feats the original alchemists had accomplished unaided. But even with the lens, Coada had never been able to bypass any of the Safety Enchantments once they'd been fused into an enchanted object. Coada only wished Rupert had lived long enough to show him what it was he'd been working on. Coada never heard him mention anything about the Astra Lens; Rupert was only a boy when his grandfather and granduncle set off on their expedition. Coada had no idea if Rupert had any knowledge of the optical device and its ability—the headmaster had sworn not to discuss the lens with anyone. But if Rupert had successfully re-created it and knew how to use it to do this, then Coada wanted to know how. He looked around at the remnants of the fire. A slew of lenses and scientific instruments were scattered amongst the debris, all to be expected for an optician of Finley's caliber. His vast collection of books stacked on the blackened shelves behind the charred desk were all but destroyed. Except the middle shelf, which was simply…empty. That immediately struck Coada as odd. It felt like only yesterday he was standing in the very same spot talking to Rupert about the books on that shelf. Rupert had told him that if it hadn't been for his family's pooled knowledge through generations of detailed notes, the Finleys never would've revolutionized the lens industry. The optician always carried two or three books with him, one he used to take notes of his own findings and others which were documents of his family's work that he used as a reference. Coada hadn't thought much of it at the time, but if Morris Finley had documented his work with the Astra Lens, then Rupert most likely had his granduncle's original formula. Coada could still recall the worn leather bindings on the books' spines. He stepped closer to the charred shelves and scanned the volumes flaking to ash upon them. From what he could tell, the only books still haunting the shelves consisted mostly of scientific publications on lenses, light spectrums, and the like, but there were none of the Finleys' family logs. He kicked around the ash on the floor but couldn't find any hint of pages or leather bindings.

"Is this the way the room was found?" Coada inquired.

"It's the way I found it. Unfortunately, I wasn't the first one here," Miles admitted, carefully stepping over a fallen blackened chair to stand beside him.

"And you're certain Finley's dead?" Coada asked, the words feeling strange to say out loud.

"Yeah, real shame. Still waiting for the coroner to collect him. I was hoping you might be able to identify the body. I heard you two knew each other?" Miles asked, nodding towards a black blanket covering the shape of a body on the floor.

Coada nodded solemnly.

Miles walked over and uncovered the face. Coada shuddered. It was Finley alright, or at least the vessel he'd occupied. "It's him," he confirmed somberly.

"Thanks." Miles replaced the blanket.

"They think the Ethereal Globe had something to do with it?" Coada asked.

Miles motioned with his head for Coada to follow him around the corner, away from the rest of the officials combing the scene. Once they were some distance from everyone, Miles stepped close to Coada and lowered his voice. "There's something off about this case. I mean outside the bizarro mobile hovering over there, it's clear there's been foul play involved with Finley's death. Only, for whatever reason, that's being covered up. All the witnesses I've spoken to have given me obviously fake statements, and men I've worked with for years in this department are skipping over evidence like it's not even there. But I can't do anything about it—the General immediately took this case off my hands. And all he seems to care about is an enchanted object doing something it shouldn't next to a corpse. It looks to me like he's treating it like a golden opportunity."

"A golden opportunity?" Coada asked.

Miles scanned the crime scene. "Look around, the press are here from every corner of the united world—swarming like bees to honey. The local journos are always circling around a corpse like buzzards, but we'd hardly roped this place off before everyone in reach was here acting like it's the event of the century. Someone's obviously tipped them off, and it's not Finley they're interested in, it's that deconstructed globe."

"But why?" Coada asked.

"The press spins stories in favor of their coin purses. And there are people in high places who've been feeding their pockets—and ones in this department—for years. I don't know what their motive is, but I get the impression they want to bring down The Alchemists House of Discovery."

"That doesn't make any sense. All we've ever done is enrich lives with our objects. We've gone to extensive lengths to ensure they can never be manipulated or become too powerful," Coada objected.

"Maybe that's the problem."

Coada digested that.

Miles sucked in the last of his puff-stick, then dropped it to the ground and lit another.

"You know how these bigwigs work, they're only at the top because they don't play fair. If one of them wants your technology for themselves, it's in their best interest to cut you down until you're forced to sell." Miles took another drag and then looked around to make sure no one else was listening in. "Look, I brought you here tonight for two reasons—one, as a friend it's my duty to advise you lie low for the next few weeks—if they're after The House, no doubt they'll be after you. And two, I need to know if you know anything. If I want to get to the bottom of this, it's looking like I'll have to do it alone—and you're one of the few I can trust."

Coada chewed his bottom lip. What Miles was saying disturbed him. Not only because of what it meant for The House and the implications it would have on the world, but because Rupert deserved so much better. He wasn't only an icon within the scientific community, he was a good person and the last of the Finley line. It wasn't just a man who died tonight. It was a legacy.

"Surely the department cares that a man of Finley's standing was murdered?"

"Finley's been out of the limelight for years. If you think about it, he's the perfect candidate for this—known well enough to make a big impression, but not current enough for his death to outshine the incident with the enchanted object. I wouldn't be surprised if this whole thing's a setup. You think someone from The House could've been paid off to tamper with the object?" Miles inquired, while looking warily at the other officials combing the crime scene in the distance.

"No," Coada replied frankly.

"How can you be so sure?"

"You have to understand, what happened to the Ethereal Globe is supposed to be beyond the bounds of possibility—even I can't disassemble an enchanted object. Every artefact made is carefully safeguarded against this very thing. Until tonight, I would've said it was impossible."

After a few moments of thought Coada added, "I think Finley is the only one who could've done this."

"How could Finley be capable of such a thing? He worked with optics, not enchanted artefacts."

"I'm not sure," Coada admitted.

"What makes you suspect it was him then?"

Coada hesitated. "He and I had a meeting scheduled two days from now. Finley was going to show me something he'd been working on, he hinted it was something big. I think whatever happened to that object is connected to whatever that *something* was."

"If you're right, then maybe someone else got wind of it and killed him for it? Took it for themselves and burned the evidence," Miles suggested.

Coada frowned. "Stars, I hope not. That would mean this tragedy's only the beginning."

"How do you mean?"

"Enchanted objects have always been harmless because they're impossible to alter. We purposely make them that way. We have strict procedures in place to prevent them from being tampered with or used for anything injurious. But if someone out there has the power to bypass our safety measurements, then there's no telling what else they can do. I need to get that globe back to The House as soon as possible, so I can figure out what went wrong and how to stop it from happening again. For the sake of us all," Coada exhorted.

Miles's brow furrowed. "There's no way the department will let you take that thing, not when it's evidence in a crime case. They're already trying to figure out how to transport it to the lab at the department—and they're excited about it. They've always wanted to know how your objects work, and now they've been handed one with its guts exposed. They're not going to give that up."

"They can't possibly understand what they're dealing with without me! Surely they'll want my help on the case?"

"On the contrary, having The House's object involved makes you a possible suspect. Guaranteed, they'll hire every self-proclaimed expert on Equillian before they come to you or The Alchemists House of Discovery."

"But that's preposterous! It's our product!"

Miles put a comforting hand on his friend's shoulder.

"This is bigger than you and me. The truth is, they won't come to you because you walk a straight line. They can't have that if they're trying to do something crooked. If you want to help in this case, the best thing you can do is lie low and trust no one. I called you here tonight as a favor to us both. Your opinion on this matter is the only one I trust—those of us who still care about what's right over our coin purses have to stick together. There's not many of us left, and I'm afraid our days might be numbered. Once the press tells the world your objects are unstable, The Alchemists House of Discovery will go under investigation. It's possible The House could be accused of Finley's murder. My advice is go home and pack your bags. Have someone at The House cover your absence for as long as possible until you're somewhere out of reach."

"If I run, I'll be condemning myself!" Coada objected.

"If you don't run, you'll be condemned anyway. We need you, Coada. If there really is someone out there with the ability to alter enchantments, then you could be the only one capable of stopping them."

Coada turned that over for a moment. "Can I have one of those?" he asked, motioning towards the puff-stick burning in Miles's hand.

"Course." Miles handed him one freshly lit.

Coada accepted the puff-stick with shaky fingers and sucked in a long, steady drag before coughing several times. Miles hit him on the back. Coada smiled weakly and took another puff. He couldn't remember the last time he'd had one, nor could he remember ever needing one so desperately. After he'd taken the edge off his nerves he said, "The original alchemists worked so hard to prevent this—we've kept their secrets from the beginning in order to stop this very thing from happening. And now, it seems the precautions we've taken to prevent our fears are the very things which have caused them to manifest."

"You can't blame yourself for this, Miles. As long as the world turns there'll be scumbags trying to take advantage of a good thing—spoiling it for the rest of us. All that matters is that they don't succeed in the end. For us to have a fighting chance, I need you to stay in the game. Send me a Sendsong when you're able and let me know you're safe. In the meantime, I'll find out what I can."

Coada nodded and snuffed out the puff-stick on the lamppost beside him before tucking it away in his pocket. "You're a true friend, Miles, thank you," he said, and shook the detective's hand.

"Avoid saying anything to the press on your way out, they'll take whatever you say and find a way to spin it against you. Better to give them as little ammunition as possible," Miles advised.

Coada nodded and turned to leave. After three steps he paused and turned back. "Say, Miles, what happened to Rupert's son?"

"What son?"

"Rupert had an adopted son; it was his sister's kid. She died a week after childbirth, a result of complications, I think. He should be five or six by now," Coada said.

"I had no idea. There's no sign of a boy."

The tension in Coada's shoulders relaxed. "Thank the Stars for that. Name was something like Casper or...Casio. Casio, that was it. And he'd taken his father's surname...O'Reilly, I think it was. Rupert was all he had."

"Thanks, I'll look into it," Miles assured him.

Coada nodded and then turned back, stepping out into the lamplit street.

# DREAM WAKING

Bastian turned his charcoal pencil on its side and began shading the reflection of a setting sun sinking into a calm ocean. He was sketching the view of Westdock's coastline from the roof of the Star Temple—he loved that view. It was his favorite place to watch the sun dip into the sea and the stars emerge from its fading light. He paused in his work and looked up at the front of the classroom. Sister Strata was preparing for her lecture. She was a plump woman, dressed in the long dark-blue gown that was signature to the ecclesiastics of the Order of the Stars. The dress had embroidered gold stars rising up from the hem of its skirt and a single larger seven-pointed star embroidered over the wearer's heart. Sister Strata's eyes and demeanor were like steel. Bastian could never get anything past her—she always seemed to know what he was going to do before he did It. Luckily, her classes were generally engaging enough to keep him from looking for alternative ways to entertain himself.

Felix was in the seat directly across the aisle from Bastian. He was helping Lisa Woo make a sacred geometry flower out of paper. It was a complicated design that involved forty-two different folds, demanding incredible patience. It also happened to be something Felix was quite good at. Lisa was obviously enjoying his attention—she was gazing at his face dreamily without paying any mind to what he was doing.

Bastian readjusted his sitting position and returned to his drawing. He hated the small wooden chairs at the Order. He could never understand how the sisters expected them to stay still for the long duration of their lessons in such uncomfortable seating.

"Welcome to the middle grade," Sister Strata began, stepping out from behind her desk.

She took off her glasses and let them hang by the thin silver chain around her neck as she scanned the room, looking into the faces of the children in front of her,

"The middle year is the year of the Seeker constellation. As you all know, the Seeker is the mother of questions. Do any of you know what's earned her that title?" she asked.

June, a small girl with dark skin and a galaxy of freckles across her nose shot up a hand. Sister Strata nodded to her.

"She's called the mother of questions because she never stops asking them, even when she's already gotten an answer."

"That's right, and why do you think she does that?" Sister Strata asked the class.

"To annoy everyone?" Robert answered from the back. He was a stout boy with bright red hair and cheeks as round as apples. His answer incited snickering and giggles throughout the class. Sister Strata quieted them with a single glance.

"Anyone else?"

The class replied with silence.

"She continually asks questions because she's seeking truth. When she finds answers, she asks questions of those answers, because she knows there's never only one answer for anything—and the one way to guarantee you never find the real and full truth of this world is if you stop looking for it. The Seeker's continual pursuit of knowledge and her humble understanding of her own ignorance is what makes her the wisest and most knowledgeable of all the constellations. And yet—if you ask her, she'll tell you she knows nothing."

"How can she be so wise if she doesn't know anything?" Robert interjected.

"Because the more you learn, the more you uncover how vast our lack of understanding truly is. To be fully certain of anything is ignorance in itself. You can easily spot the most naïve in a room—just look for the one making the most noise, feigning answers for that which they know nothing about," Sister Strata stated, looking pointedly at Robert.

The children laughed and Robert shrunk in his seat. Sister Strata waited for the laughter to die down before she continued.

"The Seeker is the chosen constellation for the middle grade, because this is the year you'll begin to ask big questions. Questions such as 'Who am I?' and 'What is my place in this world?' You might be asking yourself where you came from, thinking the answer to that question will give you the answers to the others. You might be wondering why the Order withholds your past from you?"

She looked around the room inquiringly and several of the children nodded back at her. "You may even feel cheated or upset by it," she surmised.

There were more nods, and those who were occupied with creative activities put them down and gave her their full attention. Sister Strata looked into each of their faces.

"I assure you, it's for your greatest benefit. We humans have a habit of categorizing people—even ourselves. And most of the time we identify using the past rather than the present. It's a disservice both to individuals and to humanity as a whole. Your ancestors will not provide you with the answers you're looking for. It doesn't matter where you came from. Whether royal blood runs through your veins or you were born in a gutter and came from a cwipless beggar—it makes no difference. You are all children of the Stars. Your past and your heritage does not define you." She looked into the eyes of her captive audience to make sure each and every one of them heard and understood her.

"As Star Children, you have the privilege of starting your life with a clean slate. You will not be held accountable for the actions of your forefathers, only for your own actions and the choices you make in this life—your life. Not only are you freed from the stigma of your family tree, as Star Children, you're also freed from their titles. Those with titles feel bound to them and are unaware they have a choice. A soldier dutifully sacrifices his or her life for a queen without question, because they've been told they are a soldier and that's their duty. A queen stands back and commands others to sacrifice themselves for her, because she's been told she's a queen and that's her duty. They act according to what's expected of their title, instead of acting according to what's better for the greater good and true to themselves. Convinced they are robbed of choice, they've become prisoners of false ideology, unaware that the key to their freedom is to simply ask questions. Why am I sacrificing my life for this person or this cause? Is it worth it? Why am I commanding these people to die? Is there another way? I ask you, does a queen's life have more value than a soldier's?" Sister Strata inquired.

The children looked around at one another. A couple nodded hesitantly.

"When a queen and a soldier are stripped of their titles and laid bare side by side, there's only one thing differentiating them—their individual character. It's the choices we make and who we are that define us, not titles. The world out there doesn't want you to know that. They don't want you to ask questions. They don't want you to discover your true potential. They want you to know your place by the title they give you, and they want you to think you're bound to it. This is a lie, a fallacy, and a handicap to anyone who believes it. The gift you have as Star Children is to have that handicap removed. You are your own leader, you define your own limits, and the only titles you'll bear are the ones you choose and define for yourselves."

⌁

"Dodger, Dodger! Wake up!"

Bastian's eyes shot open. Cricket was holding him by his jacket, shaking him vigorously. "Thank the Stars. I need ya ta stay with me, mate. We 'ave ta get down from 'ere. Can ya stand?"

Cricket's voice sounded a million miles away. Bastian's head throbbed. There was a high-pitched whine ringing in his ears. A loud crackle sounded above them, and Bastian could feel heat radiating down — it was nice. He looked up. The sails overhead the crow's-nest were ablaze with bright red and orange flames dancing fiercely in the wind.

*That can't be good.*

His vision tunnelled, his consciousness seeping away from him like a receding tide.

⌁

Dodger's head slumped against Cricket's chest.

"No, no, no, Dodger, ya 'ave ta get up, mate!" Cricket called above the freezing gale. The thief didn't stir. "Shick!" Cricket looked down at his hands — they were covered in Dodger's blood. There was a gash above the thief's left eyebrow where his head had collided with the mast. Cricket looked down to the main deck. The crew were calling out to one another, running across the boards in desperation as they worked to put out the fire engulfing the ship. A loud splintering crack rang out over Cricket's head. He looked up at the blazing Moonraker and Skysail above them. The length of mast between the two sails had split open. They were running out of time. Cricket looked at the crashing waves far below. He took off his and Dodger's jackets and wrapped them both around his rifle.

"Heads!" Cricket called and dropped the bundle to the deck. He bit down on his sleeve at the shoulder and tore it free from his shirt, then wrapped it around Dodger's head to compress his wound. Next he untethered a glass float hanging from the crow's-nest. He pulled a dagger from his boot and cut the line running alongside the mast, then used it to lash the float across Bastian's chest. "Alright Dodger, time ta do what ya do best — dodge death." Cricket wrapped his arms around the thief's chest and heaved him over the side of the crow's-nest, casting him as far as he could into the ocean below. Then he rang the alarm bell fiercely and cried, "Man overboard!" He grabbed the line above him, pulling himself up onto the top edge of the nest, and leapt.

Bastian felt a hard stinging slap against his back a millisecond before plunging into icy cold water. The ocean surged him to the surface, and he gasped in surprise. His mind whirled in panic, trying to make sense of his surroundings as the ocean swelled and heaved him to and fro. He struggled to stay above the waves as he looked around. The Black Mary was only a few meters beside, rocking dangerously low from one side to the other. The pirate ship was alight—the top of the main mast and the crow's-nest he'd been in only moments before were completely engulfed in flames.

A wave passed over Bastian. He spluttered and coughed as cold salt water forced its way up his nose and down his throat. He recovered just before another wave hit him from the side, splashing over his head. Bastian took a breath and tried to dip beneath the waves for some relief, but the float lashed to his chest kept him from going under. Another wave hit him, and then another. Bastian gulped for air and seawater rushed inside his mouth, making him cough violently. Clawing at the waves, he fought against the tide until he was almost too numb to move. He forced himself to hug the float strapped to his chest before his arms and legs stopped obeying his command. Then he stared up at the star-studded sky and relaxed into the cold. His eyes closed and the intense feeling of panic subsided. Bastian held his breath as he was tossed this way and that, only catching a quick gulp of air when there was a moment of respite. He prayed to the Stars and hung onto the float for dear life as the churning sea tossed him like a piece of driftwood.

Sister Strata had the class's full engagement now. Even Bastian's pencil sat idle in his hand, and Lisa Woo's attention had transferred from Felix to the front of the classroom.

"Now that you've passed your childhood years and are transitioning into young adults, it's my duty to prepare you for what lies ahead," she announced. "It won't be easy. The world is a battlefield, everything in it is fighting for its life, and you will be fighting for yours until the day you die."

Cricket's feet hit the freezing water and he vanished under the surging waves like a torpedo. He spread out his limbs to stop his descent, then kicked towards the surface. His head broke through, and he gasped for air. He looked around for the thief as the heavy surge pushed him to and fro, but he couldn't see him anywhere. Then he spotted Dodger bobbing in the bright reflection of fire on the water's surface two meters out. Cricket started towards him with big, long strokes. He dove underwater, swimming against the surge with all his might, then came up beside Dodger and turned him onto his back. Wrapping one arm around the thief's chest, Cricket pulled him towards the Black Mary.

Three men were leaning over the guardrail of the main deck shouting and pointing towards them. As soon as Cricket was in range, they tossed out a line. Cricket grabbed hold just before a swell pulled him and Dodger to the side, and the men tugged them towards the ship. Cricket grabbed onto the Black Mary the moment he reached it, tying the line around Dodger's waist with numb fingers. The sailors above heaved the rope up towards the main deck.

Rhino yanked Bastian over the ship's side. The burly pirate set him on his feet and Bastian collapsed to the floorboards, barely managing to catch himself with his cold, stiff arms before vomiting seawater across the deck.

"Oi! Watch the boots!" Rhino exclaimed.

Bastian's lungs and throat burned, and his head throbbed. He was numb with cold. He rolled over onto his back and lay on the deck, taking large, raspy gulps of air. The sounds of crashing waves, shouting men, and hurried footsteps pounding across the boards swirled around him.

Cricket was pulled onto the deck a moment later. He doubled over with his hands on his knees, coughing. He spit salt water on the deck, then looked to the surrounding sailors and addressed the one nearest,

"Ink, I dropped our jackets from the main mast wrapped around me rifle."

The tall, slender man had a bald head completely covered with tattoos, he grunted and nodded before hurrying off to find them.

Rhino put his hand on Cricket's shoulder. "Ya alright? Yer drenched through."

Cricket nodded. "We need ta get Dodger dry an' warm as quick as we can, 'es in a bad way."

"What 'appened?"

"'e decided ta play chicken with the mast—guess who won?"

Rhino laughed, "Ha! Can dodge death, but not poles, eh lad?" he jested, thumping Dodger on the shoulder. He pulled his hand away in surprise and turned to Cricket with concern.

"'e's shiverin' like mad! We'd better get 'im below an' warmed up fast. With that 'ead injury, 'is body will be strugglin' twice as 'ard."

"Aye, not ta mention the amount o' piss 'e's consumed tonight. The man 'asn't stopped drinkin'."

"At least 'e still be shiverin', it's when 'e stops we 'ave ta worry."

"I'm not far behind, I can already feel me limbs beginnin' ta lock up."

"Right, down we go," Rhino asserted, and positioned himself to lift Bastian.

Cricket turned to a plump man beside them. "Guts, grab as many blankets as ya can, an' notify Doc that Dodger be needin' immediate attention. See if ya can make a bed ready fer 'im."

The man nodded vigorously and headed for the stairs, his round belly bouncing as he ran. Ink returned with the jackets and Cricket's rifle.

Cricket took them in hand. "Good man. Let's get Dodger out o' that shirt before takin' 'im below. No need ta bring the stench o' 'is stomach with us."

Rhino took a dagger from his boot and cut the float free from Bastian's chest. He worked with Ink to pull off Bastian's shirt while Cricket took off his own. Cricket put on one of the jackets and passed the other to Rhino. Bastian shivered uncontrollably as the men dressed him. He stared distantly towards the burning sails high above their heads. The top quarter of the mainmast was tilting dangerously to one side. There was a loud crack as the remaining splinters holding it together snapped, and the top fell. Bastian stared transfixed at the flaming pillar as it plummeted towards them, the tattered, blazing sails streamed behind it like the wings of a dying phoenix. It was beautiful. Exhaustion washed over him, and his lids grew heavy. He was too weak, too broken, and too tired to fight the oncoming wave of sleep.

"Heads! Mainmast!" Cricket yelled.

Rhino scooped Bastian into his arms and leapt out of the way just before the flaming top of the mast hit the deck where they'd been standing. Burning embers showered around them. The crew yelled and scattered as the flames spread outward across the deck.

"Stay yer courage men, it be nothin' but fire! We just defeated a kraken fer Stars sake!" Snibs, the quartermaster, cried. "More water!"

"Come on lads, let's get ya both below," Rhino asserted. Cricket nodded and followed Rhino as they pushed through the chaos and down the companionway into the belly of the Black Mary. The mess was alive with activity. The tables were turned into makeshift beds occupied by injured men, groaning in misery. Guts was standing by an empty space at the far table with several blankets laid down and several more in hand.

Cricket patted the plump man on the shoulder. "Well done."

Rhino laid Dodger on top of the blankets. Doc was there a second later checking Dodger's pulse. He slapped Dodger across the face. The thief groaned weakly, barely opening his eyes.

"Get 'im awake! An get 'im out o' the rest o' these wet clothes. 'e needs ta be under the blankets as quick as 'e can," Doc demanded. Then he grabbed one of the passing men. "Bring me a 'ot tea from the galley."

"Aye, aye, Doc." The sailor headed for the ship's kitchen.

Doc turned on Cricket next. "What in the nine realms o' darkness are ya doin' standin' about 'ere drenched!? Go change before I 'ave the pair o' ya on this table!"

Cricket smiled. "Aye, aye, Doc," he returned, and headed for his locker.

⌒

Rhino and Guts pulled the rest of Bastian's wet clothes off and piled blankets on him, propping his head up with blankets from behind. Rhino leaned towards his ear. "Ye'll get through this mate, just don't stop fightin'," he said, then he and Guts hurried back up top to help with the fire on the main deck.

"Oi!" Doc called after them, but it was too late, they were already gone. Doc shook his head and turned to Bastian. "They're supposed ta be keepin' ya awake, the task be on yer shoulders now, lad. There be too many men needin' me. Don't let yerself drift off, I need ya ta remain conscious fer as long as ya can," he said, then he turned towards his other patients and left Bastian alone.

Bastian looked around him, trying to keep his attention engaged. There was a man to his left who was missing the lower half of his right leg. There was a tightly wrapped bandage around the stump drenched with blood, and the man was biting down on a piece of rope, whining and moaning through his pain, tears silently streaming from his eyes as he muttered prayers to the Night-Watchers. Bastian looked away, diverting his attention to the ceiling, which doubled as the floorboards for the deck above. He could hear the thumping footsteps and distant shouts of the men as they worked to put out the fire. The mingled sounds of the chaos above, the misery below, and the creaking and swaying of the Black Mary turned into a wash of noise that felt far away. His whole body ached with cold, and his head pounded. More than anything, he was tired, so very, very tired. Bastian closed his eyes.

Sister Strata walked with the posture of a commanding officer, her hands clasped comfortably behind her back as she strolled up the aisle between the attentive children, continuing her lecture.

"The most difficult trials you'll face will not be physical ones, or even ones with other people, but the ones you face inside yourselves. Trials that take place within your own minds as you fight against the shadows of self-doubt and fear. And others that will take place in your hearts, when emotion clouds your judgement and makes you lose sight of what's right or true. Victory or defeat teeters on a single decision—will you make yourself an ally or an enemy? You'll find no better ally than yourself, nor will you find a more formidable foe. Arm yourself with the greatest weapon you have by learning to trust yourself. Your whole self, giving both your head and heart equal value. For you will be your strongest when they are united. Allow them to show compassion towards each other and look out for one another. When your mind reaches its darkest places, your heart must flood it with compassion to chase the darkness away. When it becomes stuck on a problem it can't solve, your heart must guide it with intuition. And when your heart becomes lost or broken, your mind must help to guide it with logic and reason..."

Snibs weaved his way through the tables of groaning men in the mess hall until he reached Doc. The large dark man looked exhausted, but still he moved purposely from patient to patient, calling out orders to the able seamen lending a hand.

"'ow's the lad doin'?" Snibs inquired.

"Which one?" Doc asked, wiping the sweat and exhaustion from his brow.

"The thief."

"Not well, 'e's warmed up a bit at least, but I can't get 'im ta stir."

"This be no place fer 'im, 'e needs a warm room an' proper attention. The cap'n wants 'im brought ta 'is quarters."

Doc raised his eyebrows. "All these men need proper attention an' a warm room, an' most are in worse condition than 'e is."

"Are ya questionin' the cap'n's orders?" Snibs asked threateningly.

Doc stared at him, aghast. "No, course not." He looked around the room at the tables covered with injured men and shrugged. "Alright, could use the extra space anyways. Let me stitch 'im up an' then ya can take 'im where ya will."

"Ya can stitch 'im up there, Cap'n wants 'im moved immediately, an' 'e wants ya ta attend ta the lad personally."

"I've never 'eard the cap'n request such a thin' fer anyone! What could 'e possibly want with the lad?"

"Not me place er yers ta ask," Snibs growled.

"An' what—I'm supposed ta leave the rest o' these men 'ere, unattended?!"

"Quicker ya get the thin' done, the quicker ya can get back ta 'em."

Doc stared at Snibs in disbelief, then he huffed in anger and moved to Dodger, scooping him up into his large black arms like a babe. "This better be fer good reason," he grumbled, before heading down the corridor towards the captain's quarters.

⌒

"…Believe and trust in yourselves, even when no one else does—especially when no one else does. For you are your greatest asset. When you step out into the world, step out with an open mind filled with questions and never stop asking them. By accepting your own ignorance, you create the opportunity to learn. Accomplishing anything only takes the five P's—Patience, Persistence, and Practice, Practice, Practice. Be ambitious and put the work in. Taking the time to gain knowledge and master new skills is worth every effort. Having extra capabilities can mean the difference between success and failure, the difference between life and death. Knowledge is your shield and a mastered skill your sword—arm yourselves with as much as you can and you shall rise above kings and queens on life's battlefield, to the place of dragons. Never forget, even though the Stars lay the paths that are before us, it's your choice which one you take. For you are the true helmsman of your fate, the sovereign of your destiny," Sister Strata concluded fervently, finishing her lecture.

Bastian suddenly realized his socks were wet. That's odd, he thought, and looked at the floor. The classroom was flooded with water, and it was steadily rising. He raised a hand. "Sister Strata?" he asked uneasily. But when he looked up, his classroom and everything in it was gone—replaced by the open ocean as far as the eye could see. Bastian found himself transported from the classroom at the Order of the Stars to a small lifeboat rapidly taking on water. The ocean was as still and reflective as black glass, the moon full and bright. Its light shimmered on the water's surface with a fierce brilliance. Storm clouds brewed distantly on the horizon, churning in a dark, brooding mass that lit up with the electric flicker of lightning. The large cracking boom of thunder followed a second after. Bastian looked around him, desperately searching for the source of the leak in the boat. There was a hole in one of the floorboards at the bow. Bastian pulled off his socks and stuffed them into the gap. He took an oar out of its ring and began using it to bail the water from the craft.

A faint breeze picked up, disturbing the ocean's smooth surface. Floating on the wind came a haunting melody. Bastian stopped to listen, straining his ears to make out the words.

*The night was clear when the ships drew near*
*Attackin' from behind.*
*They were no match*
*Fer the Black Mary lads*
*Who finished 'em in stride.*
*We finished 'em in stride.*

*But barely were the colors high.*
*When another foe did rise.*
*Another foe did rise.*

*A mountain from the deep she was,*
*With glowin' eyes an' boilin' blood,*
*Eight limbs, an' swirlin' skin,*
*Comin' ta avenge 'er kin.*
*'Twas none other than the Queen Kraken.*

The words of the song and the voice singing it felt familiar somehow, but Bastian couldn't put his finger on why or who it was. A shadow passed over the boat. Bastian looked up. The sky above him was quickly being covered by heavy dark clouds. Thunder rumbled and a streak of lightning branched down from the sky into the water in a blinding flash. It began to rain.

Bastian sat back in the small vessel feeling defeated. He turned his head to the sky and closed his eyes, letting the water droplets wash away his troubles. But his tranquility only lasted a moment before he felt the presence of something looming above him. He opened his eyes to see a silhouette of a gargantuan suckered limb rising out of the ocean like a giant sprouting vine. It began weaving its way towards him as another limb came out of the water beside it, both writhing like black snakes. The creature's mountainous head followed, ascending from the depths to reveal two monstrous green eyes with black, slitted pupils that turned and locked on Bastian. The creature's skin was rapidly changing color, swirling from dark blue to sea green, before settling on a deep red.

*The Kraken*, Bastian thought in horror.

He retreated as far as he could to the back of the lifeboat. He pressed himself up against the stern, petrified. The Kraken's arm wrapped itself around the front of the bowsprit and pulled. Bastian and his small vessel sped through the water towards the creature's head. The beast turned its underside to the dark churning sky and opened its beaked mouth encircled with row upon row of jagged teeth —and shattered the night with a blood-curdling scream.

Bastian flung his eyes open and sat up with a gasp.

He was sitting in a plush velvet armchair. A roaring pain rushed through his head—his brain was throbbing in time with his pounding heart. He put his hand to his forehead and winced. There was a line of stitches across his left eyebrow as neatly done as Gwena's stitchwork.

"Easy lad, yer alright."

Bastian turned to find himself face to face with the most feared man on the seven seas—the captain of the Black Mary, Muerte Tormenta. The pirate captain was sitting beside him holding a vial filled with something pungent. Bastian could still feel its scent burning in his nostrils. He looked around, feeling incredibly disoriented. He was in a dimly lit room he didn't recognize, and he had no idea how he'd gotten there.

He leaned back in the armchair and closed his eyes. His heart was still racing from the dream he'd only just escaped from. It'd felt so real. He tried to recall his last moments of consciousness. A series of images rushed back to him like the passing pages of a flip-book. The battle with Lord Bardviss's galleons, the monstrous Kraken, Boom throwing one of his explosives into its gaping jaws as it dove beneath the ship, and then… nothing. It was like turning a page to find the rest of the book had been torn out.

"Drink."

Bastian opened his eyes. The captain was offering him a black leather stein.

Bastian's throat was as parched as sandpaper. He took the Black Jack in both hands and drank eagerly. It was filled with the familiar taste of grog— one part rum, two parts water. Bastian had become accustomed to the drink during his time on the Black Mary. It was all there was besides alcohol of a different nature that was reserved for special occasions. He drained every last drop and felt better for it as the pain in his head subsided.

"Do ya know where ya are, lad?" The captain asked.

"The Nine Levels of Darkness," Bastian muttered.

Half the captain's mouth curled into smile. "Glad ta see ya still 'ave spirit."

"What happened?"

"Yer 'ead collided with the mast. Cricket kept ya from burnin' ta death—but in place, ya almost drowned. Yer body 'as been through quite the ordeal. Ye 'ave been sleepin' like a babe ever since. Ya 'ardly even stirred while Doc stitched ya up."

Bastian's hand moved to the stitches on his forehead. He ran his fingers across them lightly and counted sixteen. A stitch for every year he'd been alive. That was fitting, he thought. A memento to mark his coming of age. As if everything he'd been through since his birthday wasn't enough to scar him for life.

"How long have I been out?"

The captain produced a gold pocket watch with a clipper ship engraved on its cover.

"Eighteen 'ours er so."

"Eighteen hours?!" Bastian exclaimed.

"Would 'ave slept till the break o' dawn no doubt if I 'adn't woke ya."

"I'm glad you did, I was having a horrid dream" Bastian confessed, putting his hand to his head.

"The Kraken?"

Bastian nodded.

"I imagine many o' the men will be 'avin' night terrors o' that beast fer a time."

"Not you?" Bastian asked.

The captain's mouth turned into a sad smile, his eyes shining dark pools of mystery that whispered *I've seen far worse.*

Bastian took in the chamber. It was small, but lavishly furnished. There was an alcove to one side with a bed in it. A piano was built into the wall in the corner and next to it was a dressing table with an oval mirror above it. There was an Everfire hearth burning steadily, keeping the room at the perfect temperature—as signature to its enchantment. On the opposite side of the chamber was a large oak desk covered with disheveled maps, papers, and various nautical instruments. Behind it was a built-in bookcase filled to the brim with leather-bound books of various sizes and colors, locked behind glass doors. And the back wall of the quarters was made up of thousands of small windowpanes, making a mosaic of the dark waves and bright stars dusting the night sky beyond.

Sitting in front of the window on a tall wooden perch was a mechanical bird looking out. Most of its feathers were glossy black porcelain, with a scarlet one curling out behind its head and a long shiny metallic gold one hanging down from the center of its tail. Bastian recognized the Sendsong from a book he once read on enchanted objects. The original birds that the mechanical versions were modelled after were blind, but they were highly attuned to the language of songs. The Order described the language of songs as the language of truth—a sort of vibrational frequency emitted by everything on Equillian, revealing their true nature. Every individual had a unique frequency, a vibrational signature. The original birds were incredibly sensitive to these vibrations and could find anyone in the world with nothing but their name. Sendsongs couldn't understand words, but they knew the intention behind them as clear as if they'd been spoken in their own tongue. The birds knew instantly whether words were being spoken dishonestly or with sincerity. If they were spoken to help or do harm. If the speaker was in love with the person they were speaking to or if it was lust, hate, indifference, or whatever else. Everything said was laid bare before them as if they could see and read a person's very soul. The birds were commonly seen in the decor of seers and fortune-tellers. Bastian had even seen them worked into illustrations inscribed in some of the old books in the library at the Order. But real Sendsongs had been extinct for centuries. They were large black birds with milky violet eyes. The one before him now was clearly mechanical—the glossy porcelain and the faint click-clicking of gear-work gave it away, but it was incredible craftsmanship. The bird was so lifelike. Bastian couldn't help but think how much he would love to take it apart. Unfortunately, enchanted objects were impossible to disassemble.

*Well, unless you're Rupert Finley*, Bastian thought, remembering the article of the optician who'd been found dead next to a disassembled Ethereal Globe—igniting the ban of enchanted objects. The ban that had transformed the world. Bastian wished he knew what really happened that night.

The Sendsong tore its gaze from the ocean and turned to Bastian. Its eyes were remarkable. They stared intently at him with the intense spark of a sharp living thing. Instead of being milky, they were metallic violet—clear and piercing. Bastian instantly felt exposed, even embarrassed, as if the bird had caught him without his clothes on. Only he found himself transfixed and didn't want to look away. The bird's eyes were so mesmerizing, so intriguing. His self-doubt melted, and it felt as if he was looking into the heart of the universe—it was intoxicating. His pain and fear subsided, and a deep calm and clarity washed over him. He felt stronger, wiser, all knowing. It was as if his true self was casting off the cloak of human foibles—the self-doubt, the anxiety, the senseless mind chatter, and warped misconceptions all falling away to reveal his true nature. Then the bird blinked and looked back out the window, and the moment was gone. Bastian looked after the bird curiously, then shook himself free of its lingering trance.

"I call 'er Pitch," the captain said.

"Pardon?"

The captain nodded towards the Sendsong. He stood up and walked to a cupboard where he retrieved a small oil pitcher and used it to pour some oil into a coin-sized bowl. Then he brought the bowl to the bird and held it out to it. The Sendsong drank the oil eagerly.

"I plucked 'er whistle from a dead man and made a few alterations. I could never understand why the alchemists made their version o' the birds white. I like 'er much better this way, don't you?" the captain asked.

"I don't know what she looked like before; I've never seen one outside illustrations. But she's beautiful."

"Did ya 'ear that, Pitch? The lad thinks yer beautiful."

The Sendsong cocked its head and made a little melodic chirp.

"Are we in your quarters?" Bastian inquired.

"Aye, ye'll 'ave ta excuse the mess, I'm not accustomed ta company."

Bastian recalled Cricket's warning he'd given during his tour of the ship— *"never go up there unless ya 'ave been invited mate, seems ta be a bad omen when yer summoned ta the cap'n's quarters."*

"Why am I here?" Bastian asked.

The captain walked over to the other side of the room and refilled his glass and another from a cut-crystal decanter. He sat back down next to Bastian and handed the other glass to him, then took a drink from his own.

"Ya opened the chest," he answered at last.

"The chest? But Snibs said opening the chest wasn't worth anything."

"'e's right in a way, there wasn't anythin' in the chest, never was."

"Nothing in the chest?! Then why did you stake my life on opening it?!" Bastian exclaimed.

"I've been waitin' seven years fer someone ta open that box. Watched countless try an' fail. Includin' every man in me own crew. An' then out o' the blue, a thief shows up on me ship, a Star-brat from Westdock—barely old enough ta be a man, an' the contraption's open in five minutes."

"You only gave me five minutes!"

Half the captain's mouth curled into a smile. "Ya stowed away on me ship."

"Fair point," Bastian admitted. He recalled the way the captain had kicked the lid shut before anyone could view the chest's contents, and suddenly it dawned on him. "You didn't want the crew to know it was empty, that's why you took it away so quickly, wasn't it?"

"They wouldn't understand."

"I hate to disappoint you, but it wasn't my skill that opened the chest, it was pure luck. In my desperation I touched every part of it and somehow activated the enchantment revealing the key."

The captain's eyes twinkled with amusement.

"What's so funny?"

"It wasn't the enchantment that revealed the key."

"It had to've been, no one else could see it."

"Precisely. The key 'as been sittin' in plain sight at the bottom o' that chest fer the last seven years, and no one 'as ever noticed it but yew. Ya see Dodger, I 'aven't been searchin' fer the person who can use that key, I've been searchin' fer the one who can see it."

Bastian digested that. He recalled that first day on the Black Mary, how the key had emitted bright gold light. How Cricket had thought he was crazy when he'd mentioned it. It was the first time Bastian had seen anything like it, but it certainly hadn't been the last. The very next morning the entire top deck shimmered with the same gold glow, and that shimmer had been haunting him ever since.

*Could the strange stuff actually be real?* he wondered. At least then he could stop worrying about his sanity.

"Right…well, whatever I was seeing, it's gone now. Maybe a good hit to the head was exactly what I needed," he jested.

The captain walked to the door and flipped a switch on the wall. The sound of gear-work started click-clack-clicking, and four black bags were mechanically lifted off Everfire lanterns in each corner of the room illuminating the chamber. Bastian closed his eyes and held up an arm to shield himself from the light.

"Still gone, is it?" the captain asked.

Bastian cautiously opened one eye, and then the other. Both eyes widened in wonder. The entire room was saturated with fine gold dust gleaming and twinkling brilliantly. It was on absolutely everything and on the captain most of all. The glimmering smoke-like powder was being drawn to Muerte Tormenta, wafting up and around him, spinning and curling in fine tendrils and then looping back to him again. Bastian opened his mouth to say something, only nothing came out. The captain smiled, and then he held out his hand with his palm up and swept it casually through the air, turning it in a wide circle. The gold dust began to rise from the floor and swirl with the motion. The captain tightened his circle and so did the dust below it, twisting into a column like a tornado, until it was a dense swirling mass suspended in the air. Then he clenched his hand into a fist, and instantly the column of glittering dust condensed into a floating rod of solid gold.

Muerte snatched the rod out of the air and twirled it in his hand like a baton, then held it out to Bastian, who stared at the object in front of him like it was a phantom spirit. He cautiously took it into his hands. It was heavy and solid, and cool to the touch. He inspected it closely. It looked and felt as real as any gold he'd ever come across.

Surely it was a play of the light and some masterful sleight of hand. He'd seen a similar trick before, where a rod seemed to appear out of thin air. It was in Madam Pomphrey's magic show. Gwena told him afterwards how the trick had been done. How the rod wasn't solid at all, but a spiral of thin metal that contracted into itself and then sprung out with the turn of a latch. It looked completely solid from a distance, but Gwena insisted its false nature would be obvious with closer inspection. This rod was clearly a more clever design. Bastian couldn't find a single fault—more to the point, he couldn't understand why the captain was conjuring up such a spectacle in the first place. He handed the rod back to him.

"A fine trick. How'd you do it?"

The captain laughed. "This be no parlor trick, lad." He twirled the rod around his hand again. This time as it spun, it disintegrated back to gold dust until it was nothing but a billowing cloud. Bastian stared at the evaporated object in disbelief.

"We 'ave somethin' in common, ye an' I," the captain said, "we're both adept at gettin' through locks—only ya pick man's base contraptions, an' I pick the laws o' our reality."

"Are you telling me the gold dust I've been seeing allows you to do that?" Bastian asked.

"It's called Equillian's Key. More commonly known as the Ghost Element."

"The Ghost Element? Ha! I'm still dreaming." Bastian hit the side of his head with his palm in an attempt to wake himself, and instantly regretted it. A sharp pain rang through his temple confirming just how awake he was.

The captain may as well have said pixie dust and elephants were real. The Ghost Element. What a hoot that was. Bastian had read recently in one of Felix's books that the Hall of Scientific Study had discredited and removed one of their lead scientists for his obsession with the Ghost Element, and his insistence it was real without offering any scientific basis. The book was called *A Walk Through the Hall of Scientific Study*. It had a write-up on everyone who had ever worked there and all their major discoveries and achievements.

The captain replaced his mocking expression with a serious one, and Bastian realized he wasn't joking.

"If it's real, then how come you and I are the only ones who can see it?" Bastian queried.

"In yer case, a birth defect, I imagine. Luckily, one that 'appens ta be incredibly useful."

"For what?"

Muerte Tormenta studied Bastian with his strange blue and green eyes, "I 'ave an assignment fer ya," he proclaimed. "Ye'll master this new talent o' yers, an' when we reach Jaxland, we'll put it ta test."

"And what, if I pass I get to keep my life?" Bastian scoffed.

"I'll do better than that. If ya pass, I'll award ya yer freedom," the captain offered.

Bastian perked up suddenly. "My freedom?"

"That's what ya want, isn't it?"

"Yes, yes it is. Just to clarify, you're saying if I learn to use this dust, and use it to pass this test of yours, I can go free at the next port?"

"Ya can go wherever ya like."

Bastian studied Muerte Tormenta, looking for any sign of dishonesty.

"If I do, will you kill me?" he asked.

The captain raised an eyebrow, "Is there any reason why I should?"

"No. I have absolutely no desire to involve myself with your business once I'm back on the mainland. I want nothing more than to seek out the life I'd abandoned when I boarded this ship."

"Do we 'ave an agreement then?" the captain asked.

"How do I know I can trust you?"

Muerte smiled. "That's an interestin' question, comin' from a thief."

"Good point. I suppose we'll both just have to trust one another. Alright, I'll learn to use this Equillian's Key, as you call it. I'll pass your test, and in exchange I'll take my freedom," Bastian proclaimed.

"Splendid!" The captain held up his glass. Bastian clinked it with his and they both drank.

Then the captain stood, "Snibs will fill in the details shortly. Get some rest, ye'll start yer trainin' on the morrow," he declared, and left the room.

Bastian watched him go. It was only once he was alone that he realized he'd just agreed to do something without having a clue what it was.

He looked out through the windowpanes towards the night sky. "Shick have mercy," he muttered.

Dread washed over Bastian as it dawned on him that he'd most likely just signed his life away. Still, he didn't regret it. He imagined that in truth, he had little choice anyway—besides, life wasn't worth living if he couldn't get back to Gwena. He'd do anything to win back his freedom, just for the chance to see her again.

"Maybe we'll be reunited after all, Gwen," he whispered to the stars. Then the thought struck him—the Sendsong. The enchanted objects were created as messengers—maybe he could use it to get a message to her. Bastian felt his pockets, hoping to find his notebook with the letter he'd written to Gwena his first night on the ship. It wasn't there—of course it wasn't there, he was wearing a whole new set of clothing, he didn't even know who they belonged to. He looked around and spotted a feathered quill and inkpot on the captain's desk. He rolled out of the chair and stood up. After only a couple of steps his head swam and a dark border circled his scope of vision, threatening to swallow him whole. He felt uncomfortably light-headed and knew in that moment, if he didn't sit down, he would end up on the floor involuntarily. Bastian sat where he was. After several deep breaths he regained himself and stood again, walking the rest of the way to the desk. The black Sendsong was staring down at him curiously. Bastian parked himself in the captain's chair and scanned the desk's surface for a piece of blank parchment. It was a mess. He finally found a piece under a pile of other papers and quickly started to write a letter.

*Dear Gwena,*

Bastian paused, finding himself suddenly at a loss for words. Now that he had the opportunity to write something that might actually reach Gwena, he had no idea what to say to her. So much had happened since they last saw each other—what, four days ago was it? It felt like a lifetime. He didn't know where or how to begin.

*Dear Gwena,*

*I'm so sorry I couldn't be there to meet you. I've been held up outside my control. But please know I'm alright and doing everything in my power to find my way back to you. Thinking of you always. -B.*

Bastian read over the letter. Bloody rubbish! he thought and tore the paper in half. Why is this so much harder when I know she'll be reading it? he wondered and began again.

*Dear Gwena,*

The door to the cabin opened. Bastian quickly and silently slipped both letters into his pocket and picked up a navigational book from the desk just as Snibs, the ship's quartermaster, stepped inside.

"What are ya doin' at the cap'n's desk?" he growled. He walked over and grabbed the book out of Bastian's hands and looked at the title. "*Star Navigation?*"

"I used to study it at the Order. Maybe it's something I can contribute to make myself a little more useful around here?" Bastian offered.

Snibs narrowed his eyes at him, "If ya want ta be more useful, then get off yer arse an' back ta yer swabbin' duties!"

"Right. Don't say I didn't offer."

"Back ta where we put ya! I need a word."

Bastian pulled himself up with support from the desk and made his way back to the chair he'd woken in.

"Now, glue yer arse down an' make sure it sticks," Snibs commanded, sitting across from him.

"Nice to see you too," Bastian returned with a small smile.

Snibs nodded to Bastian's scar. "How's yer 'ead feelin'?"

"About as good as yours looks. Been missing out on your beauty sleep?"

"Ta say the least," Snibs grunted.

"How's the crew?" Bastian asked in earnest.

"As good as can be expected. We're lucky ta be alive—the lot o' us."

"Yeah, I'm grateful for that. By the sounds of it, I had the opportunity to die several times."

"Ya 'ave Cricket an' the cap'n ta credit fer yer sorry arse still bein' 'ere. Ya be indebted ta 'em both fer that. Make sure ya let Cricket know 'ow grateful ya are."

"I will, I was well indebted to him already. I would've frozen to death before last night if he hadn't lent me his rags," Bastian confessed.

"Yes, I noticed ya were wearin' 'is garb. Well—ya can consider what ya be wearin' now as yers, I pulled those from ones unclaimed. When we get ta Jaxland, ye'll 'ave the opportunity ta acquire more."

"I don't have any coin."

"Yer the thief, I'm sure ye'll figure it out."

"I would've thought stealing from other pirates was against the code or something?"

"Ha! As long as they're not from our crew, take as much as ya like. We 'old little loyalty ta those bottom-feeders. Just make sure not ta get caught, er ya might lose one o' those slippery 'ands o' yers," Snibs warned.

"Thanks for the advice," Bastian replied dryly.

Snibs picked up Bastian's glass and drained what was left of it.

"Now, ta business. Because ya 'it yer 'ead rather 'ard, I'm goin' ta fill ya in on what ya've missed—so listen closely. Yer visions ya reported 'avin' were due ta exhaustion, nothin' more. They stopped once ya 'ad a good rest. Ya were brought ta the cap'n's quarters fer questionin' due ta suspicions o' ya bein' a spy fer Lord Bardviss."

"A spy for Lord Bardviss?! I would never work for that son-of-a-codfish!"

"Shut yer trap an' let me finish!" Snibs growled.

Bastian held his tongue.

"As I was sayin'—that son-o'-a-codfish 'as been tryin' ta eliminate piracy due ta the nuisance they cause 'is merchant fleet. Ya stowin' away on the ship an leadin' 'is galleons ta our back 'as roused suspicion."

"I suppose that's fair," Bastian admitted.

"Ya think?" Snibs walked over to the captain's liquor cabinet and refilled Bastian's glass, then took a long hard drink.

"Lucky fer yer sorry bones, after a long unpleasant conversation with the cap'n, 'e now be satisfied ye're no friend o' the bastard lord."

"That's a relief."

"But 'e's not convinced yer worth keepin'."

"Right."

"As discussed before the fray, the cap'n 'as arranged a special task fer ya on Jaxland, one that if accomplished will satisfactorily prove yer as good as yer claims an' show where yer true loyalty lies. An' if ya fail, it will mean ya lost yer life tryin'—an' the cap'n will be conveniently rid o' ya. Do ya 'ave any questions?"

"Yeah. What's the special task I'll be doing on Jaxland?"

"That's on a need ta know basis. Currently, ya 'ave no need ta know."

"Do I have a chance?" Bastian asked in earnest.

"Ya wouldn't be doin' it if ya didn't," Snibs stated plainly.

Bastian guessed the odds most likely weren't in his favor, but the quarter master's words still brought him comfort.

"Any other questions?"

"No." Bastian knew full well how these sorts of games worked. He was relieved to adopt the story. If any of the men knew Bastian was getting special treatment from the captain, it would quickly isolate him from the rest of the crew. And he couldn't tell anyone in their right mind he was seeing the Ghost Element.

Snibs drained what was left in the glass.

"Very good. If fer any reason ya think things 'appened different, it be a side effect o' yer injury—savvy?"

"Perfectly," Bastian agreed.

"Now, the cap'n wants ya ta return ta yer duties as soon as yer able. If ya need ta rest further, ya can do so in yer old sleepin' arrangements, 'e needs 'is cabin unoccupied. As part o' yer daily chores from now on, ye'll be assistin' Tink in 'is workshop. 'e'll prep ya fer the task at 'and. Yer expected ta work 'ard an' do everythin' 'e asks without question. That be clear?"

"As a summer's day."

Snibs nodded satisfactorily.

Bastian hesitated before saying, "I've no doubt you played a part in me still being here, Snibs, thank you," he said sincerely.

Snibs rose from his chair and leaned over Bastian. "I was only followin' orders. Speakin' o' which—I'm sorry fer this."

"Sorry for what?"

Snibs backhanded Bastian across the face. Pain ripped through his skull.

"Shick! What in the nine realms was that for?!" Bastian held his throbbing cheek. He could taste blood and felt the tenderness of a bruise already forming.

"The story won't stick unless ye've been knocked around a bit," Snibs explained.

"Right. Remind me to thank you later," Bastian remarked coolly.

Snibs opened the cabin door and turned to Bastian expectantly.

"I'll be right behind you, I need another minute to settle my head. My consciousness was already threatening to abandon me before your meat racket decided to play ball with my face."

"Stop yer whinin', ya only suffered a mild concussion when yer 'ead split. Ya need food be all. Don't think I'm givin' ya another minute alone ta snoop around in 'ere. I'll 'elp ya along if needs be. Out ya go," Snibs commanded.

Bastian's spirit sank, he had been so close to getting a letter off to Gwena. He didn't know if he would get another opportunity. Either way, it was clear he'd lost this one.

He pushed himself up from his chair and followed Snibs.

— 36 —

# SKY VIEW

Felix watched the last stars fade with the morning's light outside the porthole in Lilliana's quarters. The duchess was sleeping soundly in her bed beside him. They'd spent most of the night entangled together with an unquenchable thirst for one another, drinking each other in until the first signs of daybreak. The whole thing felt surreal. Felix couldn't believe the Jewel of Westdock pulled him into her bed. After the night at the Wendrians' castle—when Lilliana humored his advances only to escape Lord Bardviss—Felix was convinced he never actually stood a chance. But this time, Lilliana had not only been the instigator, she'd also given him a night he'd never forget. The duchess bedded him with an intimacy, a passionate fervor he'd never experienced with professionals or one-time flings, elevating his favorite sport to a whole new pinnacle. The problem was it spoke of real emotion behind the physical pleasure, and that was…dangerous. Now that the night had come to an end, the reality of their unfavorable circumstances was rising with the sun, and Felix was beginning to feel the weight of his predicament. He knew full well his and Lilliana's time together couldn't last beyond the dawn. The ship's pilot and Lilliana's surrogate uncle, Roy, was in the room next door. Lilliana had already informed him that Felix was common born. If he found Felix and Lilliana in bed together, he would most likely throw Felix over the side of the airship—or worse. Finding the two of them like this would be enough to make the blood boil in any father figure, but the fact that Lilliana was a duchess and Felix was a commoner made it at least a hundred times worse. There was a wedge so thick between their classes that anyone who openly crossed it was marked, their family's name smeared like they'd dragged it through dragon manure. Felix had enjoyed enticing the highborn across that line on countless occasions, except he'd insured he was long gone before ever having to face the consequences. Something that wasn't an option thousands of feet above the ground in an airship.

Felix ran his eyes across Lilliana's sleeping form. Her thick cherry curls cascaded across her supple walnut skin, covering her bare chest in a sea of red. Her lips were turned up in a dreamy smile. He wanted to kiss her awake and rekindle their passion once more, only he was incredibly aware that Roy might rise at any moment, and he couldn't be in Lilliana's quarters when he did.

Reluctantly, Felix silently rolled off the bed. He found his various items of clothing spread across the floor and dressed. He combed his hands through his short black hair in an attempt to remove the evidence of the passionate night they'd had. Then he grabbed his blanket and slipped out of the room, closing the door gently behind him. He thanked the Stars that Roy was a deep sleeper as he tiptoed past his chamber door and climbed the companionway to the upper deck of the airship.

Felix sat down in front of the large Everfire pillar housing the enchanted flame that kept the airship's balloon afloat. He wrapped his blanket around his shoulders and checked his pockets. He was pleased to find his puff-stick case still there from the night before. He pulled out the slender silver box Bastian had acquired for him from some blue-blood's pocket. Inside were a stack of razor-thin Tymetree paper and a purple leather pouch filled with Spice leaf. The paper made from Tymetree bark had a natural subtle flavor—both salty and sweet, with a hint of lavender. The Spice leaf came from Westdock's signature spice plant that grew wild among the hills looming around the horseshoe cove. The plant's large broad green leaves turned vibrant orange when dried. The flavor was unique. A little sweet, smoky, and musky with a bit of a bite, with undertones of citrus, honey, cinnamon, cardamom, and turmeric. The spice and the many spiced products Westdock made from it were the town's largest exports. The shredded dried leaf had a naturally sticky texture that made it easy to form into puff-sticks.

Felix shaped some of the Spice leaf into a thin log with his fingers before rolling it in Tymetree paper. He rolled several puff-sticks and stowed them away in his case for later. Then he lit one up with the floating enchanted flame in his Everfire Box. He savored the puff-stick's flavor as he watched the horizon become crowned in molten gold.

It was Twinsday, the second day of the week. Named after the constellation representing the twins Mi and My. They were brother and sister—two opposite halves of the same whole and opposite in every way, representing the dualities in the world and in ourselves.

The ship was bound for Sky View—the wealthiest precinct on Equillian, made up of twenty-one floating islands named the Windswept Isles.

They were suspended thirty thousand feet above the mainland. Made of light, porous volcanic stone that absorbed and trapped elevator gas like water in a sponge, which had caused the islands to rise out of the ocean into the sky millions of years before, eventually coming to rest at an altitude that gave them equilibrium.

As the sun continued to ascend, its light scattered across the curve of the atmosphere, igniting the clouds with bright shades of pink, orange, and gold. Felix's eyes widened as the islands came into view. At first, he thought they were clouds in the distance, but as the airship drew closer he could see a few of the smaller islands in detail. They were large chunks of floating rock with long steep cliffs jutting down beneath them. Their tops were covered with lush grass meadows and babbling brooks cascading off the cliffsides into glittering waterfalls that dropped into the open sky.

One small island held nothing but a shed and a large flock of sheep grazing happily on a field of wildflowers around a crystal-clear lake. Another small island had a chateau surrounded with magnificent gardens and two small jetties protruding from its sides docking lavish airships. A flock of white and yellow birds was flying around it.

Felix could see several more airships busying about between the islands in the distance. The vessels were ornately painted with bright colors and had large billowing blue sails.

"You're up early."

Felix turned around to see Roy coming up onto the deck behind him. The aviator was wearing his thick brown leather jacket and drinking a large cup of tea.

"I didn't want to miss this," he said.

Roy came to stand beside him and gazed out at the view. "It doesn't matter how many times I see it, I'm still awestruck every time I come to Sky View. It's by far Equillian's most beautiful precinct."

"Have you seen them all?" Felix asked.

"The ones worth seeing."

Felix pointed towards a large swirling black mass of clouds on the outskirts of the westernmost islands. "What's that over there?"

"The Everstorm," Roy stated sourly, as if it were an uninvited guest.

Felix walked to the port railing to get a better view. He'd heard of the eternal tempest, but didn't know much about it. He was sure Bastian would've known. His brother loved geography and the wonders of the world outside Westdock. Felix, on the other hand, had honed his education on subjects useful for blending in with aristocrats and plundering their pockets.

The huge raging storm funneled down from the upper atmosphere in a spiraling, churning mass of dark billowing clouds that dissipated before reaching the ocean thousands of feet below them. From what he'd heard, the storm hadn't changed its location or ceased its fury since recorded time began. It was far from the ship, but he could clearly see the electric light show dancing inside the clouds like a firework display behind a curtain.

"Is that what the duke disappeared into?" Felix queried, recalling the story of Lilliana's father's disappearance.

"So they say. Flew his own airship into the storm after the death of his brother. But I don't buy it," Roy told him, walking over to join Felix at the railing.

"No kidding. I don't even know the guy and I don't buy it. Who in their right mind would fly into that?"

"Precisely."

"Do you have any theories?"

"None. There's only one thing I'm certain of—everything we've been fed on the matter is utter hogwash. I know Drake Wendrian wouldn't have flown into that storm unless he had a damn good reason. And if he did, I intend to find out precisely what it was," Roy proclaimed, taking a sip of his tea while gazing out at the Everstorm.

After a moment of silent contemplation, he turned to Felix. "When you're ready, come below. I could use your help readying the ship for our descent." He glanced at the crushed silk pajamas he'd loaned Felix before adding, "After we settle in at the estate, I'll take you to buy some new clothes."

"Brilliant. I'll come down with you now," Felix replied. He extinguished his puff-stick and stowed it away for later, taking one more look at the dark looming storm before following Roy below deck.

⌒

Lilliana was sitting at the table in the main cabin of the airship. She was smartly dressed in a white silk blouse and high-waisted tan trousers, with her cherry curls pulled back in a neat knot. She had her attention glued on one of her books while enjoying a cup of tea.

"Morning, Everspark, have you packed? We'll be at your family's estate in less than an hour," Roy asked her.

"Not yet, I'll get right on it," she said, without so much as a glance towards Felix or Roy. Then she stood from the table and headed towards her chamber humming a tune.

"She appears to be in better spirits," Roy remarked.

"Yes, she does," Felix agreed, reflecting his bemusement.

"The kettle's still hot if you care for a cup," Roy offered.

"Thanks." Felix quickly diverted his mind to making tea.

"Oh, and before I forget, take this." Roy handed Felix a large purple pill.

"What is it?"

"Altitude medicine. It'll adjust your body to the high altitude—the air's a lot thinner up here," Roy explained.

"I noticed that." Felix studied the pill. "Any side effects I need to worry about?"

"It might disturb your sleep. Some find it hard to sleep at all when taking the stuff, but the only alternative is to wear one of these." Roy pulled what looked like a gas mask from one of the cupboards.

"What's that?"

"An oxygen mask."

"I suppose I'll take my chances," Felix said, and knocked back the large pill with his tea. He quickly cursed himself for not waiting for it to cool.

Roy chuckled and patted him on the shoulder, then sat down at the table. Felix joined him. There was a map of Sky View laid out. It was the first time Felix had seen a map of the islands. On the larger world maps, the illustrations of Sky View were merely a distant representation to mark their place in relation to the mainland, and nothing more. It was fascinating to see a picture of the islands in detail from a bird's-eye view. The Windswept Isles had once been a single rock that split into twenty-one pieces. Each looking like a puzzle piece that could slot into the ones around it. There were seven main islands, referred to as the Prime Islands. They stood suspended at the center of Sky View, with the diamond-shaped capital island—Drago Prime—at the heart. The capital was surrounded by the four largest of the Prime Islands. Each of these encircled one of the capital's four points—each named after a guiding constellation—Ariya Prime, Faya Prime, Gumption Prime, and Pansophy Prime. Each had a triangular gap in its surface where it had once been connected to the capital island. The remaining two Prime Islands were below them on the south side, stretching skinny and long on either side of Gumption Prime below the capital. These twin islands were named after The Twins constellation—Mi and My. Scattered around the main islands were fourteen smaller ones known as the Fragments. None of the Fragment Islands had individual names on the map. Roy informed Felix it was because they were all privately owned. At the western edge of the map was an illustration of a black swirl marking the Everstorm. Most of the islands had a body of water on them—even if small. Felix remembered reading an article about the Windswept Isles once. They had been collecting water and plant life, uninhabited until they were discovered by Richard Meers, the famous explorer who created the first maps of the precinct from the back of a dragon. It was a true paradise, populated by the elite and out of grasp for everyone else—except the hired help. But even to be a servant on Sky View you needed to pass a strict screening process before your name could be presented for consideration by the residing aristocrats. After that, all anyone could do was pray to the Stars they were chosen. To even visit Sky View cost a fortune. It was intentionally designed that way, to keep it inaccessible to the common born.

Roy pointed out the island belonging to the Wendrians on the map.

"Each of the Fragments are owned and inhabited by a single family, whereas the Prime Islands are home to hundreds of residents. The Wendrians have had their Fragment for generations. Their family was one of the original settlers of Sky View," he explained.

The island Roy was pointing to was a nice-sized Fragment just off the western side of the capital city. Felix couldn't even imagine how much it must be worth. There probably wasn't a household on Equillian—bar the emperor's palace—with enough coin in their coffers to afford such a thing.

"Join me in the control room. You can get a nice view of the islands from there as we come into port," Roy invited.

"I'd be delighted."

Felix stood behind Roy in the control room while the pilot operated the control station. Roy pulled on several cranks and turned a few dials, and the airship began to lose altitude. Now that Felix could see land again, his fear of heights returned. He tried not to think about it as they navigated through the Fragments' morning traffic. Soon the first of the Prime Islands came into view. It was covered with vast fields of rich green grass surrounded by rolling hills and mountains. There were waterfalls cascading from the mountain cliffs into rivers channeling into a large sparkling lake with a charming town bordering its edges. Felix was amazed at how much unpopulated space there was. Every now and again he could see a large estate or a chateau tucked into the land. But for the most part, it was untouched.

Felix stepped closer to the window. There was some sort of creature flying in the distance. It had two large leathery wings and brightly colored scales that gleamed in the sunlight. "Is that what I think it is?" Felix asked.

Roy followed his gaze. "If you think it's a dragon, then yes."

"A dragon?" Felix whispered in disbelief.

As they came closer, he could see it in detail. The huge lizard-like beast had massive, expansive wings. It was bright blue with a gold underbelly that shimmered in the sunlight, and despite its size flew as gracefully as a bird. Behind the dragon's large horned head was a rider mounted on its back. The woman was sitting in a saddle, guiding the dragon as casually as if it were a horse.

"How can she control it?" he asked. He'd always thought of dragons as wild, ferocious beasts from the tales he'd heard of The Last War. Lord Balthazar had conquered Equillian when he was only nineteen—the first person in history to be successful in uniting the world under a single banner. It was said he never would've been able to defeat The East if it weren't for dragons. Sky View had cultivated a ferocious breed specifically for war that was virtually unstoppable. It was their alliance that ultimately won Balthazar his supreme power. As soon as he took the throne, he declared War Dragons illegal and ordered them all to be put down. He told the people it was the only way to preserve world peace. Felix imagined he was right in a manner, though he doubted world peace motivated his actions more than his desire to maintain the throne. To repay Sky View for their sacrifice, Lord Balthazar made it illegal for any of the remaining breeds to be bred or born outside their borders—giving Sky View a monopoly on dragons.

"They're quite tame. They breed them that way and break them in early. Highly intelligent animals. As long as you treat them with respect, keep them fed, exercised, and mentally stimulated, they'll be respectful in return," Roy assured him.

"What happens if you don't?" Felix asked.

"Let's just say it wouldn't be in your best interest."

"Right. What type of dragons are those? I've only seen Pet Dragons."

"I couldn't tell you. I don't spend enough time up here to be familiar with the various species. Besides, they're continually creating new breeds, so it's difficult to keep track. Lilliana would be able to tell you. Her family's one of the top breeders up here. My best guess is that's some sort of riding dragon bred for human transport. They're all bred for a particular purpose. Racing Dragons are bred for agility, stamina, and speed, and—"

"Racing Dragons?" Felix interjected.

"Dragon racing is Sky View's most popular pastime."

"Of course, it is," Felix muttered into his cup, still feeling like this was all part of some elaborate waking dream.

"The Wendrians changed their house's specialty from War Dragons to Racing Dragons after Equillian was united. The ban was a hard hit for their family. They were the prime supplier for the war—known for having the most deadly breed. Lord Balthazar compensated them generously for putting down their prize stock, but it still took the Wendrians a while to reestablish themselves as breeders. Now Drake's family has a reputation for producing the fastest dragons. I've been told their prize mare's won the racing championship at the Sky Cup Derby the last two years in a row," Roy told him.

Felix nodded absently as he watched the dragon glide between the islands in front of them. The sun reflected brightly off its vivid metallic scales. He hadn't done any research on dragons—he'd never had a reason to. They were hardly seen on the mainland these days. He'd only encountered small Pet Dragons perched on the shoulders of the occasional merchant, and wanderers passing through Westdock. The small dragons were roughly the size of house cats and came in a variety of shapes and vibrant colors, like strange exotic birds. Wanderers liked them because they could easily light campfires and help to catch a meal, and merchants used them as a sort of guard animal because they tended to be fiercely loyal—only most ships refused to have them onboard for fear they might burn it down. Now, Felix found himself wishing he had educated himself on all the various varieties of dragons. Seeing the larger ones before him in all their splendid glory made him want to know everything about them.

"We'll be setting down soon. Could you shut the Everfire vent up top?" Roy asked. "We'll have to do it manually; the dial doesn't seem to be working. If we can get it closed, then the hot air that's left in the balloon should be sufficient to get us to our destination."

Felix nodded. "Happy to."

Felix stepped onto the top deck of the airship. It was warmer in Sky View than Westdock, with only a mild chill in the wind—making it feel more like spring than winter. The sun was shining brightly, highlighting the colors of everything around them against the stark robin's egg blue sky.

Felix stayed well away from the ship's edge as he walked over to the glass column housing an enchanted flame jetting through its center. He found a red crank below its base and pulled it across. A sheet of thick metal slid over the vent at the bottom half of the Everfire, trapping the flame in the large box below it. Everfire couldn't be extinguished. Once it came into existence it burned forever. Felix chuckled to himself—remembering when Bastian was determined to test that theory. His Star-brother tried everything he could imagine to snuff out the light in the Everfire lamp at their flat. To no avail, of course. Felix smiled at the thought of Bastian. His brother had an innate curiosity of the world and took apart every piece of technology he came across just to figure out how it worked. But you couldn't do that with Everfire or anything enchanted—there was no way to uncover its secrets. You needed a special box just to contain the enchanted flame if you wanted its heat and light to be blocked out. The only other way to hide its radiance was with a specially woven bag that could be put over the lanterns and torches.

Felix took in the view of the islands. The Windswept Isles were a paradise he never thought he'd see. "Thank you, Serendipity," he whispered.

He kissed the number seven tattooed on the back of his right hand. It had been ornately drawn in black ink on the space between his thumb and his pointer but had faded to a blue-green with time. It represented the Time Keeper of the seventh hour, and the daughter of Lady Luck—Serendipity. She was Felix's favorite constellation. A beautiful young woman bringing luck and good fortune to those who were less fortunate. Felix got the tattoo after his first brush with death. He'd beaten an old sailor at a game of cards and the man had pulled a pistol on him. Felix's heart raced, but he felt calmer than he should've in that moment. When he looked down the barrel of the gun, he knew his life stood on a knife's edge and whatever he did next would decide his fate. Somehow, he managed to talk the man down. He'd told him, "There's no shame in losing a few coins in a game, mate. But if you fault me for playing my cards right and pull that trigger, then you'll never live that shame down—it'll follow you for the rest of your life."

The man had lowered his pistol after, and Felix offered to buy him his supper and a drink. The man accepted and by the end of the night, they were almost friends.

That moment was life-changing for Felix. He suddenly stopped taking things for granted. He was grateful for what he had and endeavored to make the best of it. The experience made him acutely aware of two things. One, life was a gift that could be taken away at any moment. And two, words held true power. Felix knew Serendipity had been standing by his side that day and he owed his life to her. He got the tattoo on his hand the following morning, choosing her as his guardian on the path to changing his and Bastian's stars. Felix wished Bastian could be here to see Sky View with him. His brother loved dragons. Felix had fond memories of Bastian pretending to be one when they were very young. He'd coax Felix into joining in on the game of make-believe. Bastian had such a vivid imagination in those early days—if only those simple times of happiness hadn't ended so soon. Felix took a final look out at the horizon and then returned below deck.

Felix stepped back into the control room and found Roy where he'd left him.

"Thanks, champ," Roy said.

"Don't mention it. Can I help with anything else?"

Roy smiled. "Yeah, get dressed."

Felix looked down and realized he was still wearing Roy's silk pajamas. "Right."

"While you're at it, gather together whatever you want to take off the ship. Ideally, we should be ready to disembark as soon as we reach the estate. Won't be long now."

Felix nodded and headed out of the control room.

"And champ?" Roy called after him.

Felix poked his head back in.

"When you're finished, check in on Lilliana to see if she needs a hand, will you?"

"Sure." Felix headed for the sleeping quarters.

Felix looked at his reflection in the long mirror behind the wardrobe door in Roy's quarters. Felix had shared the chamber with the pilot for the duration of their journey, sleeping on a stiff pull-down cot he wouldn't miss. He was dressed in the rich blue and purple suit Gwena had made for Lord Bardviss. She'd loaned it to him for the masquerade at the Wendrians' castle on the night he was kidnapped by Lilliana. He was supposed to return it to her the following morning, only things didn't quite go as planned. Even though Felix had been wearing the suit for the last three days—and part of him wished he'd been stuck with something more comfortable—he was still glad to have it. It was a masterful piece of work that fit him beautifully, and more important, it did a fine job of transforming his appearance into that of a lord. In Sky View, if you weren't highborn you were a servant. And Felix certainly didn't want to be mistaken for the latter.

Satisfied with his appearance, Felix gathered his few belongings and put them into his suit pockets: his puff-stick case and Everfire Box, his pocket watch, his lucky deck of cards, his black leather coin pouch, and the Lady Luck charm Gwena had given him as a belated birthday present. The only thing he couldn't fit was the four bulging bags of duckets Lord Bardviss had sent him to get rid of Lilliana—or rather, sent "The Debt Collectors"—the fictitious organized crime group Felix had created for his ransom negotiations with Lord Bardviss. Felix had originally requested a down payment as security for Lilliana's safety. Only, instead of paying the amount requested, Lord Bardviss had sent him far more to ensure Lilliana never returned to Westdock. It surprised them all, and Felix realized there was something much larger at play with Lilliana's arranged betrothal and slimy fiancé than they'd anticipated. According to Felix's and Lilliana's verbal contract, the coin was his. It was his payment for posing as Lilliana's kidnapper. Which was ironic, considering she was the one who'd kidnapped him—the important thing was he got to keep the ransom, but with the abundant coin came the problem of storing it. It was too much to keep on his person, so he'd stashed it behind the toilet in Roy's privy.

Felix checked on it now. He wasn't worried Roy or Lilliana would take any of it, but some habits die hard. And he hadn't even counted it yet—he didn't have the heart to count it in front of the other two. He couldn't help feeling guilty he was profiting from Lilliana's dismal situation. But he also wasn't willing to turn the coin down when it could secure for him and Bastian the way out of poverty they'd always been looking for. He pulled out one of the bags and transferred fifteen duckets into his coin pouch, hoping that would hold him over for a while in Sky View. Then he stashed the bag back behind the toilet's pipework. Once it was safely out of view, Felix left Roy's quarters and headed for Lilliana's chamber.

<br>

The door to Lilliana's cabin was open. Felix could hear her singing inside as she packed her bag. She had a beautiful singing voice. It didn't surprise him because most nobles did. Singing lessons in their circles were considered as important as arithmetic.

Felix stopped in the doorway holding onto the top of the doorframe as he watched her work with her head in the clouds.

*"Lips of cherry, hair of soot, skin of ivory..."* she sang.

Felix smiled to himself. He recognized the melody. It was a common upbeat tune played frequently in pubs by wandering minstrels.

*"...Her love rides the wind, never changing with the tides, no matter how far..."*

"It always finds me," Felix finished, completing the verse.

Lilliana almost jumped out of her skin.

"You shouldn't creep up on people like that, you nearly scared the starlight out of me!"

Felix laughed. "I would hardly call that creeping. Mind if I come in?"

Lilliana cocked an eyebrow, "Can I help you with something?"

"Actually, Roy sent me to see if I can help *you*," he said, and stepped inside her quarters.

"Roy sent you? You mean, you aren't coming to help out of the goodness of your own heart?"

"Course not. I've no doubt you're perfectly capable of packing your own belongings."

Lilliana looked at her bag with its contents overflowing onto the bed and sighed with a subtle frown. "In truth, I could use a hand. I don't know how my handmaiden packed all this in the first time, it's like some sort of puzzle box from the Southern Isles," she confessed.

Felix came and stood beside her to assess the bag. It was filled to the brim with loosely folded clothes, books, shoes, jewelry boxes, and the like spilling out all around it. "Hmmm, maybe I've overestimated you."

Lilliana pushed his shoulder. "Oh, shush!"

"Have your things multiplied? I think they've fallen in love with one another and had little clothes babies," Felix diagnosed in a serious tone.

Lilliana laughed. "It's not that bad!"

"Have you considered lightening your load? I think you'd find throwing a few things overboard liberating," he suggested.

"I thought you were supposed to be helping?"

"I'm not?" Felix asked innocently.

"No! All these things were in my bag when I arrived. If they could fit then, they can fit now. Please help," she implored.

"Hmmm, what sort of man would I be if I ignored a damsel in distress?" Felix picked up her bag and dumped it out on the bed.

Lilliana gasped indignantly. "How dare you!"

Felix ignored her protest and continued, "First of all, your technique's all wrong. You'll never fit everything in that way. If you roll your clothes, you'll double your space and save your wardrobe from creases. Now, for your books—might I suggest you leave them on board? Not only will it greatly lighten your load, all your newly attained knowledge will be much more impressive if the source you acquired it from isn't seen," he advised.

"You call that helping?"

"Very much so. You clearly wouldn't have had a chance at being successful otherwise."

"Aren't you going to at least put back the contents you just emptied out?"

"And rob you of the hands-on experience and practice? I wouldn't dream of it! That's no way to truly help anyone, my lady—haven't you heard the saying? Give someone a fish and you feed them for a day, teach them how to fish and you feed them for life," Felix imparted.

"I would've thought teaching someone involved some sort of demonstration," Lilliana argued.

Felix smiled. "Observe." He picked up one of her dresses and smoothed it over before rolling it into a tight log and placing it in her case.

"How impressive. Can show me again? You do it so well," Lilliana commended, batting her eyelashes prettily.

Felix smirked, "Buttering me up won't work, I'm immune to flattery."

"I'm just not quite sure I understand the technique," she replied innocently.

Felix laughed. "Come on, my lady, a little work won't ruin those soft hands of yours. In fact, I think it'll do you good."

"Oh? How so?"

"Character building, a sense of accomplishment, maybe even a little humility. We can all do with a little humility now and again."

"You make it sound like it's so much more than packing a bag."

"Maybe it is. An old sailor told me once that life's greatest wisdom can be found in the most mundane activities."

"Is that right? I've clearly been depriving myself then."

"Clearly," Felix agreed.

Lilliana smirked. "At the very least, keep me company, won't you? These shoes make terrible conversation."

"Now that I can do. In fact, I might even lend a hand if you ask real nice," Felix offered, sitting down on the bed beside her bag.

"Please sir, won't you be so kind as to help a poor woman in distress?" Lilliana implored with exaggerated sweetness.

Felix smiled. "I expect you to match every object I place in this bag, like for like."

Lilliana shrugged. "I'll take what I can get."

Felix reached into her pile of clothes and picked up a short black slip fringed at the top and bottom with fine lace the color of Lilliana's ruby hair. He raised his eyebrows, "What occasion did you bring this for?"

Lilliana snatched the night dress from him, "My handmaiden thought I was packing for my honeymoon. I had to make it convincing. Besides, it's Demure silk, I wear it without occasion."

"Really?" Felix queried with intrigue, "I can think of many words to describe that dress, but none of them are *demure*."

Lilliana scoffed, "You have no respect for propriety, do you?"

"None whatsoever."

"Unbelievable!" Lilliana laughed.

"Speaking of disrespecting propriety, you threw it out the window yourself last night…are we going to talk about what happened?"

Lilliana's mirth disappeared, she kept her attention on her dress, rolling it to put in her case and then picking up a shirt. "Nothing happened, we talked on deck and then went our separate ways, end of story."

Felix bit his lower lip and studied her. "That's not exactly how I remember it…"

Lilliana stopped packing and looked at Felix with a life-threatening glare.

Felix held up his hands in defense. "Right. Nothing happened," he agreed promptly.

Lilliana nodded with satisfaction and returned her attention to her things.

Felix cleared his throat and lowered his voice. "Just for the record—which of course will be burnt after it's verbalized—I highly enjoyed last night and would happily do '*nothing*' with you again anytime."

Lilliana didn't say a word. But as Felix picked up another item of clothing, he saw her lips curl into the slightest hint of a smile.

# THE HEARTLAND

Gwena stared out the window of her first-class train cabin on the Equillian Express. It was Twinsday. It had been a little over a day since her departure and she'd spent most of the journey glued to that window, feasting on the visual splendor of the world outside as she passed it by. It was Gwena's first time outside Westdock, and she found every bit of scenery beyond its borders absolutely fascinating and wonderful. Her favorite had been passing through the Harvest Lands, the agricultural belt that spanned the center of Equillian's mainland east and west of the Heartland. It was flat countryside made up of rivers and farmland that yielded ninety-eight percent of the produce for Equillian. But it was also incredibly beautiful beyond anything Gwena had imagined. They passed through fields of golden Sunflowers, purple Bell Stalks and orchards of Winter Star Fruit and Ice Apples. There was so much color contrasting starkly against the sparkling white winter frost, it made her wonder what the place might look like in spring.

When Gwena tired of sitting, she went for a walk through the elegant train carriages of the Equillian Express. In the evening there was a pianist who played classical music in the cocktail car, and the dining car was always serving. Gwena had eaten the best meals of her life in the last twenty-one hours, all included with her first-class ticket. But now they were nearing the Heartland, she found she no longer had an appetite. She could see a vast city in the distance covering the land like an industrial spider. Even from afar the size was intimidating. All of her courage and excitement was quickly disintegrating into anxiety. Where would she go? What would she do once she got there? She tried to formulate a plan, something she could hold onto to ground herself. First, she decided she would need a place to stay. Somewhere within walking distance of the Central Posting House so she could check for letters from Bastian and Felix on Phendays—as promised in the letter she'd left for them with their old landlord. Maybe a small apartment or a room for let in someone's house? A guesthouse was probably best to start with. Then she could orient herself to the neighborhood and take her time in choosing where to live more permanently, at least until she was reunited with

Bastian and Felix. She imagined lodging in the city would be expensive. She didn't know how long the boys' stash of coin would last. She would have to find work as quickly as possible. Gwena pulled a little notebook and pencil out of her bag and began making a list.

*Find temporary accommodation near Central Posting House.*
*Find accommodation to let month to month.*
*Find work.*

Gwena bit the end of her pencil in thought. She'd have to get some new clothes. She only had two decent dresses, both of which had been her mother's. It was like that old saying "the cobbler's children have no shoes." Here she was, daughter of an acclaimed tailor and a skilled seamstress herself, without a single dress made for her. Next to the aristocrats on the train she felt shabby and old-fashioned. If she wanted to be able to present herself professionally for a new position in the city, she was going to have to acquire something a little more refined. She drew an arrow between numbers 2 and 3 on her list and added *Get new clothes.*

Gwena's attention was drawn to something moving in the corner of her eye. She looked up at the windowsill to see a fuzzy blue spider the size of her thumbnail.

"A Ghost-Iron Spider! What are you doing here, my friend? Surely you must be far from home," Gwena asked the creature conversationally.

She carefully reached into the bag at her feet and pulled a bare wooden spool out of her sewing kit. She put the spool in front of the spider, which started to crawl around the obstruction. She moved the spool to block its new route, and the spider crawled onto it. Gwena lifted it up and the spider fell, catching itself by a thread of its thick spider silk and spinning more of the filament in an attempt to lower itself to the ground. Gwena started slowly turning the spool, collecting the silk as the spider spun it. She was elated by her luck. Ghost-Iron Spider silk was incredibly useful—and incredibly difficult to come by. The spiders were named for the unique nature of their webs. The silk was practically invisible, sticky, and stronger than iron. Individually the spiders were small and harmless things, but they were social arachnids that lived in colonies in groups of anywhere between two hundred and five thousand spiders, and in those numbers they were lethal. A bite from one might make you queasy for several minutes, a bite from two hundred could kill a large bird, and a bite from five hundred could kill a medium-sized dragon and put a full-sized one in a weeklong coma. The Ghost-Iron Spiders primarily targeted birds for their prey. They wove vast and elaborate webs between trees, their soft blue coats camouflaged against the sky. When a bird was caught in their trap, the spiders swarmed it all at once—putting it under with their venom and then wrapping it into a silk cocoon, which they then collectively fed on for the next week or three. Gwena was surprised to see one in the train and especially one on its own. She imagined the train must have passed through its colony's web and scattered the spiders. As soon as Gwena had a generous amount of silk thread wrapped around her spool, she let the Ghost-Iron Spider reach the floor, where it detached itself and scuttled off to find a dark corner to hide in.

Gwena stowed her treasure away in her pocket and looked out the window at the approaching city. A moment later the train entered the mouth of a tunnel. Its entrance was covered completely in bright fuchsia moss and hanging green ivy. The plants became a blur of color as the train swept past them into inky darkness. For a moment everything was black, and it felt like the train wasn't moving at all. Then an Everfire lantern flashed into view, revealing another momentary blur of fuchsia moss before it was swallowed by darkness once more.

"Next stop, Heartland Central Station!" the conductor announced.

Gwena's gut tightened. She grabbed the packed quiver travelling bag at her feet and slung it across her shoulders, then headed for the dining car. Hungry or not, she didn't want to lose her last opportunity for stocking up on free food. She passed from one elegant carriage to the next until she reached the one with lavishly set tables. There was a food cart at the end that welcomed guests to help themselves between meals. She took a plate and piled it high with several spiced sweet buns, a couple of Star Fruits, some stuffed dates, and a whole bowl of roasted chestnuts. A plump woman watched her disdainfully from one of the tables while finishing off a plate of jammed scones and a pot of tea. She was the only other person in the dining car. Gwena stared back at her challengingly. The woman made a little "humph" and turned her attention to the dark tunnel view.

Gwena took her plate back to her room and wrapped the food carefully in napkins before storing them in her bag for later. She looked out the window just as they exited the tunnel and passed onto a stone bridge that curved over a winding river, bringing them face to face with the Heartland. The capital was a magnificent city full of tall buildings that seemed to rise as they grew nearer, like shadows in the late evening. It reminded her of a pop-up book her aunt had given her, a fairytale about an enchanted city. When she turned to the illustrations, the buildings would rise from the pages. She felt she was inside that book now.

Soon the buildings were all around her. Tall giants made of crème-colored stone bricks and ivory plaster with long windows and high, red-tiled roofs. The streets were all neatly laid with grey cobblestones and lined with ornate lampposts burning brightly with Everfire. The Equillian Express dipped into the station, and the train slowed in a cloud of steam before coming to a stop.

"Heartland Central Station!" the conductor cried.

Gwena's heart leapt into her throat. She stood with quivering hands as she threw on her travelling cloak and shouldered her mother's bag. She straightened her back, lifted her chin, and took a deep breath, pushing the air out sharply before resolutely opening the door to her cabin.

"Thank you for having me," she whispered to the room, before making her way towards the exit.

Gwena waited patiently behind a queue of passengers before following them out onto the station's platform. As she stepped off the train her eyes widened with wonder. The station was huge and crowded with people bustling on platforms striped between row upon row of train lines filling the station. Steam billowed up from three black engines purring on their tracks beside them, the vapor rising into the high glass ceiling.

None of the other trains were as large or as striking as the bright blue Equillian Express. It was the only train line that travelled from one end of the united world to the other. The smaller trains were used to transport passengers and cargo throughout the Heartland and to neighboring cities. Seeing so many well-dressed people all in the same place was a marvel. It was all so grand. Nothing like Westdock, where the crowds were predominantly merchants and sailors. Gwena held tightly onto her bag and cloak as she followed the school of pedestrian traffic in front of her. She couldn't have felt more out of place. Everyone around her moved with purpose and was so beautiful. Most dressed in fashions she'd never seen before. The women had gorgeous dresses with fine patterned fabric and large decorative hats, and the men wore handsome suits in different textures and colors with matching top hats, bowlers, or fedoras. Some held decorative canes made of hardwood with silver handles in the shapes of animal heads. In contrast, Gwena felt drab and plain and thought she was the only one without a clue as to where she was going. The stream of pedestrian traffic swept her through a large archway and into the heart of the station. She stopped next to a large clock tower to take it all in. The place was enormous. People detoured around her from all directions like water flowing around a stone. She was standing in a wide-open space lined with tellers along one wall and arching entrances to the different train lines on another. The opposite side was lined with doors to the outside, and above those were huge stained glass windows depicting the different landmarks of the Heartland. There was one for The Emperor's Palace, one for The Hall of Scientific Study, another for The Alchemists House of Discovery, and one for each of the most prestigious universities and grandest theaters. The late afternoon sun was pouring in through the tall windows, creating stark rays of colored light that streaked through the station. Gwena spied a large map of the Heartland on the wall secured behind glass. Underneath it was a wooden holder on a stand with the words *Free Maps* engraved on brass plating, only the holder was empty. She studied the large map on the wall behind it until she found the Central Posting House. She pulled out her notebook and drew a little map for herself with written directions. Then she stepped out onto the street.

Immediately Gwena was bombarded with the loud hum of the city—overlapping conversations, clacking horse hooves on cobblestone streets, closing doors, buskers and sellers hawking their wares, and pedestrian traffic accompanied by a gust of icy wind that passed straight through her. She pulled her cloak tightly around her shoulders and stepped into the wave of pedestrians flowing past.

Buildings towered above Gwena on both sides of the main street. The walkways were crowded with people hurrying in all directions, and the road was alive with horse-drawn carriages trotting up and down.

Gwena looked at her little map and went left, hurrying to keep pace as people shouldered past her. There were shops lining the way whose front windows glowed brightly with the welcoming light of Everfire lanterns. Gwena passed a perfumery abundant with ornate bottles filled with perfumes of all colors, a watch store with a giant clock in the window with an intricately detailed face, and a florist shop filled with giant bouquets. Their window displays were so beautifully and artfully decorated she wished she could step into them simply to soak up the magnificent visual splendor of their merchandise. But the day was waning and the last thing she wanted was to be stuck out on the streets at nightfall without accommodation.

Gwena followed the steps of her little map until it brought her to a crossroad. She could just make out her next turn on a signpost across the street. But getting there would be quite the challenge because the road had carriages passing up and down without pause, as well as a strange steam-powered vehicle—the likes of which she'd never seen before. She waited patiently for several minutes, hoping for a gap in traffic or for one of the carriages to stop. Then a woman came up beside her and stepped into the road without hesitation. Gwena gasped, but each of the horse-drawn carts immediately stopped, as if it was a perfectly normal practice. Gwena lifted her skirts and hurriedly followed behind, barely getting to the other side before the bustle resumed. She walked to the signpost and looked up. It matched the next turn she had listed on her map, Batemans Alley. But when she looked down the small street, it looked more like a formidable tunnel between buildings. Her instincts immediately spiked *warning*. Gwena hesitated—she was running out of daylight and needed to make her way to the other side of the laneway. She hadn't drawn any alternative routes on her map, and she was hesitant to ask for directions for fear she might reveal just how lost and alone she was. She decided resolutely that it was better to choose to go down a dodgy alley than to be sent down one maliciously. She took a deep breath and turned down the street. The small pass smelled potently of urine. She wrinkled her nose and walked brusquely towards the other side. When she finally reached the end she was met by a locked metal gate.

"Shick," Gwena muttered, eyeing the thick chain wrapped around it.

She looked at her hand-drawn map and her shoulders deflated. Her directions were telling her to go through the gate as if it wasn't there at all. What was she supposed to do now? She wondered. *Stars, help me.*

"You look lost, little lady," a voice announced.

Gwena turned around sharply to see a man approaching. He was skinny and tall, dressed in a black overcoat and a dirty top hat, wielding a thin cane he clearly had no need for.

"I'm fine. Just waiting for a friend," Gwena returned curtly, stepping back to keep distance between them.

The man smirked, "You're waiting for a friend, *here*?"

Another man stepped out from the shadows to join him.

"Who're you meeting in a place like this?"

"Snuff?" the first man jested, and both men laughed.

Gwena felt sick. Snuff, The Snuffer, or The Death Bringer as some called him, was the constellation for the Seventeenth hour—the hour of the setting sun. He was known for snuffing out daylight and the spark of a person's life. When someone died it was said they were "snuffed out."

Snuff was also responsible for love ceasing to burn in one's heart, or the fading of any other passion. There one day and snuffed out the next.

Gwena recognized the men before her immediately. They were predators—they preyed on fear, fed on it, and no matter what happened, Gwena was determined not to satisfy their appetite.

"I warn you, it would be wise to leave me alone."

The man with the cane gave a vile smirk. "Unlucky for you sweetheart, my friend and I have never been very wise."

The two ruffians laughed, and Gwena's stomach twisted. The second pulled out a switchblade and began flipping it around playfully, stepping closer to her with every turning cycle. He stopped directly in front of her and looked her up and down.

"Shame, you would be a pretty little thing if it wasn't for that line down your face," he remarked. Then he lifted her pearl necklace with his blade. "That's nice."

Gwena stepped back out of his reach and met the locked gate behind her. Her heart fluttered. She cursed herself for being so stupid as to wander down this path alone. She had no defences, and they had her completely cornered. Out of pure instinct she raised her arms out to the sides as if she was a powerful sorceress and began chanting in elaborate gibberish.

"Ownshacka Jhay falla foonta, ba sanga say, mallicoata falla may…" she called out powerfully, progressively raising her voice and its intensity with confidence and determination.

The men paused, thrown off by something so completely unexpected, their own confidence faltering. The one closest to her hesitated and stepped back. "What's she doing?"

"I don't know, I can't tell what she's saying. What language is that?"

"No idea, sounds ancient."

Gwena turned dramatically to the side, and with the hand obscured from view she reached inside her cloak pocket, wrapping it around her Everfire Globe and the spool of Ghost Iron Spider silk. Without ceasing her chanting, she stuck the end of the sticky invisible thread to her globe and palmed it so that it couldn't be seen. Then she raised both her arms towards the men once more.

The men stared at her, paralyzed with confusion and curiosity.

Gwena shouted an untranslatable command and launched the globe towards them. The Everfire torch shone brilliantly in the dwindling daylight, rocketing forward like a perfect fireball.

The men leapt out of the way in surprise.

"Shick! What was that?!"

But when Gwena pulled back the globe by the invisible thread and began swinging it in elaborate patterns around her as if by magic, the men's eyes widened in mesmerized wonder.

"Shick! She's a magi!"

"Don't be stupid, magi aren't real," the other scoffed, but it was without conviction. They both stared at her and the globe, transfixed in terror.

Gwena began chanting again and made a show of preparing for another attack when a swooshing sound cut through the air behind, and a dagger lodged itself in one of the men's shoulders. He yelped in pain, swinging around in panic. There was another swoosh and the other man sunk to one knee with a dagger sunk into the back of his calf. Gwena looked around, ready to face her new assailant. It was a woman walking towards them in a billowing naval jacket and a tricorn hat. She was an inch or two shorter than Gwena, with a pale round face and a head of thick black curls that cascaded over her shoulders. She was dressed in rich blue fisherman's pants tucked into high dark leather boots and a low-slung wide leather belt housing a row of daggers and two holstered pistols with mother of pearl handles, one on either side.

"Looks like yer in over yer 'eads, boys! Upsettin' a magi?" the woman shook her head while clicking her tongue. "I 'ear a single curse from 'em can tie yer balls in knots," she warned in a rich sailor's accent.

One of the men looked over at Gwena nervously, while the other squinted at the approaching woman.

"How dare you put blades in us, wench! We ought to snuff you out!"

"Chivalry be the only thin' ya boy's be snuffin' out tanight. Where be yer manners? This sorceress is goin' ta think the 'eartland doesn't know the meanin' o' 'ospitality. She could curse the whole city—ya damn fools!"

"Bonnie? Are you the one sticking blades in us? We don't deserve that, do we?" one of the men asked, sounding more emotionally hurt than physically.

"From what I've seen, ya deserve every bit an' more," the woman proclaimed.

"Come on, Bonnie, there's no need for all this. We were just after her coin purse, nothing more—honest."

"A man's got to eat—you understand?" the other implored.

"Ye've caught me in a good mood, so consider this a warnin'. But if I ever catch either o' ya slimy worms liftin' a finger ta a woman again, ye'll be twice as sorry. Savvy?"

"Yes ma'am."

"Now scurry out o' 'ere before me mood changes!"

The men quickly began to retreat into the shadows.

"Oi!"

The two men froze.

"I believe ya 'ave somethin' o' mine," the woman said.

The ruffians barely hesitated for a fraction of a second before pulling the daggers from their wounds with a whimper. They dropped them to the cobblestones and hobbled off as quickly as they could.

The woman smiled at Gwena as she picked up the daggers and cleaned the blood off with a rag before returning them to their sheaths.

"That was quite the performance. I think ya about 'ad those two pissin' themselves. I 'ope ya can forgive the intrusion? Couldn't 'elp meself, I 'ave been lookin' fer an excuse ta put 'oles in those boys fer a while now. Name's Bonnie," she greeted, holding out her hand.

Gwena shook it cautiously, "Nice to meet you—and not at all, I appreciate the help. My name's Gwena."

"Gwena, it's a nice name. Us gals 'ave ta stick together, eh? If ya don't mind me askin, what brings ya ta this formidable place?"

"I'm afraid I'm a bit lost. I'm trying to reach the Central Posting House," Gwena confessed.

"The Central Postin' House? It'll be closed this time o' day."

"That's no problem. I'm only hoping to find accommodation nearby."

Bonnie looked at her in surprise. "Ya don't 'ave anythin' booked?"

"No... Is that a problem?"

"There won't be anythin' available this end o' the city. Not with The Science Fair on."

"Pardon, the what?"

"The annual Science Fair. Don't ya know? It's a 'uge event. The 'all o' Scientific Study puts it on every year. People flood in from across Equillian ta attend. I would 'ave thought everyone knew it," Bonnie said.

"Right. Just my luck." Though Gwena knew bad luck most likely had nothing to do with it. The event was probably why the train tickets were bought by the original owner in the first place, before Felix won them in a game of cards.

"Well, ya are in luck, in fact. There's a few people in town who owe me favors. Come, I'll see what I can do fer ya," Bonnie offered, and she unwrapped the chain that was around the gate and opened it.

"You're joking, it was unlocked this whole time?!" Gwena exclaimed.

"It's the only reason I come down this way, makes a nice shortcut," Bonnie admitted, holding the gate open for her.

"Thank you!" Gwena picked up her skirts and stepped through. She followed Bonnie onto a path that wove through a park with neatly trimmed green lawns surrounding duck ponds and towering trees that cast long shadows across the cobblestone pathways. As the sun's light faded, the warm luminance from the Everfire streetlamps lit their course. Gwenna followed Bonnie through the park and onto winding streets, breathing in the views around her.

"So, if ya aren't 'ere fer The Science Fair, then what brings ya ta the 'eartland?" Bonnie inquired as they walked.

"I suppose I'm looking for a fresh start."

"Ah, a fresh start. Let me guess, yer a performer, 'opin' ta make it big on the city stage?"

Gwena laughed, "Haha, hardly."

"No? I would 'ave thought it was yer profession after yer performance back there."

"Magic has always been a hobby of mine, nothing more. I figured the element of surprise was the best chance I had."

"Very clever. Ya had those boys fooled good."

"I didn't fool you though?" Gwena asked.

"Fer better er worse, I'm well acquainted with the art o' trickery. So, if yer not a performer, an' yer not 'ere fer the fair, what made ya choose the 'eartland then?"

"I suppose you could say the Stars chose it for me. The only real choice I made was to leave the life I had behind. I'm hoping to find work here and stay for at least a time."

They were crossing over a large stone bridge that spanned a wide river. The night had blanketed its shadow across the landscape and the pedestrian traffic had died down. There was a violinist on the bridge playing sweet music by the light of an Everfire Box lantern at his feet. Bonnie dropped a few coins into his violin case as they passed. Lovers walked hand in hand lost in quiet chitchat, and a few young boys and girls with dirt-covered faces huddled around an upside-down milk crate, spinning dice.

"What kind o' work ya be lookin' fer?" Bonnie asked.

"I was a tailor in Westdock. I'll probably look for more of the same here—at least for a start. Though, to be honest, I'm hoping for something a little more exciting this time around. Maybe making costumes for one of the theaters, or coming up with my own designs—something like that."

"Ye're from Westdock, ya say?"

"Yes."

"That's a beautiful part o' the world."

"Have you been?"

"Once when I was a child. I still remember the rising 'ills an' the spiced pies. Don't think I 'ave ever 'ad anythin' more flavorful."

"It is nice, but nothing compared to this place." Gwena looked around her at the tangle of lamplit streets. She couldn't believe the sheer size of the buildings around her, and the number of people out after dark. The night was buzzing with activity. Restaurants were full, musicians played instruments on the sidewalks while lovers danced, artists were drawing pictures in chalk on the streets under the glow of the Everfire lamps, and the sound of laughter and boisterous voices rang all around. There was a vibrant nightlife that seemed to have more spirit and energy than the daytime hustle and bustle Gwena had witnessed earlier. It was so different from Westdock, and so absolutely wonderful.

"Are ya hungry?" Bonnie asked.

"A little. I must admit, I haven't had any dinner."

"Well, I can't say the 'eartland's pies are as good as Westdock's, but this fellow's selection be surprisingly palatable." Bonnie motioned to a small wooden food cart on the side of the road. There were several people waiting in line to be served one of the vendor's pies.

"Sounds brilliant!" Gwena exclaimed, and her and Bonnie joined the queue.

Gwena noticed a tall, well-dressed man approaching them. He was the most flawless man Gwena had ever seen. His smooth dark brown skin covered a clean-shaven and perfectly proportioned face with defined cheekbones, making him look more like one of the marble statues from the great stone masters than a real person. He caught Gwena looking at him and smiled, revealing two rows of sparkling white teeth before undressing her with a glance. Gwena blushed.

"If it isn't the venerable Castaway Bonnie, fancy seeing you here," the handsome man greeted, coming to join them.

Bonnie nodded to him. "Rafael, what are ya doin' 'ere?"

He held up a dry cleaning bag, "Picking up my suit."

"What happened ta Foible?"

"Madam Rouge fired him last Thrixday. He was getting too touchy-feely with some of the girls—Joyce complained."

"Good fer 'er, I never liked 'im er 'is work," Bonnie scoffed.

"I don't disagree, except for the fact that now we're left without a tailor. I've been waiting three days for this order. I went all the way across town to pick it up, only to find out it's not even done right. Madam Pomphrey has her new show going up at the end of next week, and they don't have costumes. It's a mess. And you know how long it will take to replace him. It's not like Rouge can hire just anyone for the club."

"Madam Pomphrey? She's performing here?!" Gwena exclaimed.

The two looked at her as if they'd forgotten she was there.

"Sure, ya 'eard o' 'er?"

"Have I ever! I've seen her perform, she's magnificent!"

"Who's this charming creature?" Rafael inquired, smiling invitingly at Gwena.

"Never ya mind. I'll see ya back at the club, Rafael," Bonnie said.

"I'm in no rush. Wouldn't mind having one of Joe's pies."

"See ya, Rafael," Bonnie emphasized with a threatening glare.

"Alright, alright, I'm off. See you later then." He winked at Gwena before heading down the street whistling a tune.

"That's Rafael, 'e flirts with anythin' that 'as two legs," Bonnie remarked.

Gwena blushed. Soon they reached the front of the line and the salesman greeted them with a smile. "Good evening. What can I get for you two ladies?"

"Two o' yer finest, Joe."

"Got two left with your name on them, Bonnie," the man returned warmly, and handed over two hot pies held in wax paper.

Bonnie paid the gentleman and stepped aside as she handed one of the pies to Gwena.

"So, yer a tailor in need o' occupation an' lodgin', who wants a bit o' excitement in yer duties—an 'as an interest in magic, eh?" Bonnie asked.

"Um…yes," Gwena admitted.

Bonnie smiled. "By Serendipity. I think we were fated ta run inta one another. I believe I 'ave just the job fer ya."

# THE PRISONER

Bastian held his throbbing head as he followed Snibs down the hall-way from the captain's quarters. He could hear Dagger's song float-ing up from the mess hall, growing louder as they went. It was the same song Bastian had heard in his dream. He wondered if the half-man had been singing it earlier and it found its way into his subconscious or if it had come there by premonition.

Bastian was disoriented, his surroundings felt surreal—like the land-scape of a waking dream. The one he woke from not an hour ago felt more tangible than his current reality. So much had happened in such a short time, his brain was having trouble comprehending it all.

*How did my life get here?* he wondered. Just last week things were simple. His biggest concerns were gaining coin and winning Gwena's heart. It had all felt so monumental and important then. But now, after having several brushes with his own mortality—and knowing full well they wouldn't be his last—he realized just how small those problems truly were and wished he could have them back again.

If it wasn't for his friends being in danger, he could've laughed at the macabre humor and complete ridiculousness of it all, only Bastian was worried sick for Gwena and Felix. As far as he knew, Felix had a dank dungeon cell waiting for him at the Wendrians' castle as punishment for running away with the duchess—that was, if he wasn't rotting in it already. And Gwena was most likely stuck in Westdock hating Bastian's guts for running out on her, and worse, suffering further abuse from her father.

He wanted to ensure their safety more than anything. His own pre-dicament was particularly excruciating because it was preventing him from being able to do anything to help them. Getting back to them was the burning beacon that guided his sole direction and purpose. He'd felt lost and powerless when he couldn't see his way off the Black Mary. But now he had the captain's own promise of freedom. All he had to do was survive. That was something he was good at, something he had plenty of experience in. It was something he could focus on and channel his ener-gy into, and if he succeeded, then perhaps he could be back with Gwena and Felix as soon as next month—out of this madness and back on track with the rest of his life. The idea made Bastian feel elated, it made the pain in his head subside. It didn't matter how bad things were, because there was finally a light at the end of the long dark tunnel he ventured.

Soon the hallway opened into the mess hall and Bastian heard the familiar sound of men's boisterous voices overlapping one another in conversation amidst Dagger's song. Bastian immediately noticed the crew was smaller than it had been the day before, and once again he was reminded of how truly lucky he was to still be there. His eyes scanned the tables looking for the few men he could dare to call friends amongst the rough rogues and was relieved to see Cricket, Stork, and Rhino all sitting together in their usual spot at the middle table.

Cricket saw Bastian first. He stopped mid-speech and hit Stork with the back of his hand. Stork looked over, saw Bastian and smiled. The rest of the men in the mess hall fell silent, their conversations paused to stare at him and Snibs. Dagger's song ended and everyone gave their attention to the quartermaster.

Snibs scanned the crew before announcing, "I know there 'ave been a few rumors goin' around about Dodger. So I'm goin' ta set 'em straight. The thief was brought ta the cap'n's quarters fer questionin' due ta the galleons that attacked us. Turns out they belonged ta Lord Bardviss," Snibs scowled, and the crew scowled in return.

"Dodger was on the run from the bastard lord, which is why 'e stowed away on the Black Mary, an' why the galleons pursued us. The cap'n needed ta be sure Dodger wasn't in cahoots with the enemy—but after a thorough examination, 'e's come up clean. Turns out 'e 'ates Bardviss as much as we do! The cap'n 'as found use fer The Death Dodger, but ta be sure o' 'is loyalty, 'e's organized a test fer 'im on Jaxland. Until then, 'e's ta be treated like one o' us. Ye'd all be wise not ta 'old a grudge. I know we lost two good men ta those galleons, even though they hadn't been with us long, two good men all the same—but truth be told, if it wasn't fer those ships at our back, that could 'ave been us the Kraken dragged down ta Davey Jones. Ya all know she's been tailin' us fer some time. An' despite it all, we're still 'ere— be grateful fer that. I'll 'ave no trouble. We need ta stick together—what's left o' us. If any o' ya 'ave a complaint, ya come see me, savvy?"

Most of the men guarded their reactions as closely as a hand of cards. Only a few nodded in agreement.

Snibs scanned them looking for potential trouble and then nodded with satisfaction before turning to Bastian. "In ya go then. Make sure ya get a good feed. Doc knows yer comin'." Then he turned back down the hall leaving Bastian alone.

Bastian felt like he'd just been released into a tank of sharks. He nodded to the men still staring at him.

Then Cricket stood up on the bench with his Black Jack raised high.

"The Dodger o' Death 'as managed ta give Snuff the slip yet again, lads. Thank the Stars such a slippery soul be on our side!" he declared.

To Bastian's complete surprise the men raised their black steins and cheered. There were only two in the hall who didn't: one with his head in his arms in what looked to be a bad way, and Spits—the pirate he'd beaten at Spitting Daggers the day before. Spits was sitting alone in the corner glowering. Bastian walked over to him, and Spits looked up and scowled. The room fell silent once more as everyone watched them.

Bastian offered Spits his hand. "I'm sorry for any offense I've caused you. I'm game to have a fresh start if you're willing?"

Spits eyed him warily, then he spat on the floor. "I s'pose there's enough arseholes out there already without us joinin' 'em, eh? It's water under," he declared, and shook Bastian's hand.

The crew raised their glasses and cheered.

Bastian grinned and nodded respectfully to the pirate before weaving his way through the tables towards Cricket and the others.

Cricket took a drink before slamming his stein on the table and jumping down to greet Bastian. "Glad ta 'ave ya back with us, mate!" he exclaimed, clasping Bastian's arm.

"Not nearly as glad as I am."

Stork, the tall red-headed pirate, slapped him on the back. "Cricket named ya well, laddy, ya be surprisingly good at dodgin' Snuff. An' I couldn't be gladder fer it," he said with a grin.

Rhino, Stork's huge twin, stood and pulled Bastian into a bear hug. Bastian laughed and returned the hug wholeheartedly.

"It's a relief ta see ya alive an' intact."

"I was about to say the same about you lot."

"Ya might be good at dodgin' the Death Bringer, but we're well seasoned at fendin' 'im off," Rhino declared.

"Someone get this man a drink! Can't ya see 'e's thirsty?" Stork proclaimed.

"On it!" Rhino volunteered, disappearing towards the galley.

Stork moved into Rhino's spot, offering his space on the bench to Bastian. " 'ave a seat," he invited, and Bastian sat down beside him.

Rhino returned a moment later with a fresh Black Jack brimming with grog and a bowl of hot stew.

"Doc gave me this fer ya." He set the meal down in front of Bastian before noticing his seat had been taken.

"Oi, brother! I go ta do a man a favor an' ya take me spot?" he exclaimed indignantly.

"It was only proper ta give Dodger mine."

"Course it was. It also would've been proper ta not take mine—ya scrote!"

Bastian started to stand and Rhino pushed him back down.

"Don't ya move yer arse, me gripe be with this sorry bag o' bones," he said, pointing accusingly at Stork. Then he grabbed his stein and stormed to the other side of the table muttering, "Clearly, I'm the only one who soaked up any manners from our muther."

"Ha! Yew, manners? Bah! That's a joke if I ever 'eard one," Stork laughed. "Ya 'ave the same relationship ta manners as a dog ta trees. If yer not ignorin' 'em entirely, yer pissin' all over 'em!"

"Speak fer yerself, ya uncultured swine! Ya know what, Dodger? Ye've done me a service, now I don't 'ave ta sit next ta that stinkin' maggot."

Bastian chuckled. "I'm glad to see you lot haven't changed."

"But ya 'ave. That shiner an' scar-maker be a nice addition ta yer face there, Dodger," Stork remarked.

"Aye, adds a bit o' color," Cricket said.

"'ow many stitches did Doc give ya?" Rhino asked.

"Sixteen," Bastian answered, before spooning in a mouthful of Doc's stew.

"That's nothin', only 'alf Rhino's record. Doc stitched 'im up last year from a blade—thirty-two stitches. Isn't that right, brother?" Stork said.

Rhino put his leg up on the table and pulled up his pants to reveal a long dark purple scar. Bastian raised his eyebrows.

"Every scar 'olds a story, an ya can't get one better than the night ya received yers. Personally, I'm jealous, wish I 'ad somethin' ta mark that night's 'appenin's. Think I might get a tattoo at Jaxland ta mark the occasion," Stork proclaimed.

"Yeah? What will you get?" Bastian inquired.

"Good question. Yer certainly spoiled fer choice—an attackin' galleon, a screamin' Kraken, a ship blazin' with sea fire. What'll it be?" Cricket asked.

"Not sure yet, there's almost too much ta choose from."

"Perhaps you can combine all three and have a flaming ship being pulled into the storming depths by a Kraken?" Bastian suggested.

"Er, maybe somethin' more symbolic, like a finger ta Snuff—tellin' the Death Bringer ta go shick 'imself!" Cricket proposed.

"Now, that I like!" Stork bellowed, and all three pirates laughed.

"Though admittedly, ya don't need ta give the Death Bringer any more reason not ta like ya, brother. I imagine we're all on 'is list already," Rhino cautioned.

"Everyone's on 'is list already! Death be the one thin' we can all truly be certain of. It's not a question o' if, only when," Cricket declared.

"True! An' I fer one am not willin' ta give 'im the satisfaction o' quiverin' at 'is name. Do yer worst, ya mangy shadow dancer, ye can snuff me beatin' 'eart, but mark me words, me name will be immortalized in legend before the end!" Stork proclaimed.

"Aye!" the pirates and Bastian cheered, holding up their steins enthusiastically. The four of them clinked their Black Jacks and drank.

"Yer braver than I, brother," Rhino said.

"Er, perhaps 'es just full o' gypsy courage," Cricket suggested, nodding towards Stork's stein in good humour.

"Speaking of gypsies, how about Falgo the other night? I've never seen a man with more courage or skill with a sword. The way he cut through the limbs of the Kraken," Bastian gave a low whistle, "that man's fit for legend!"

At the mention of Falgo's name, his companions went quiet.

"What?" Bastian wondered what he'd said wrong.

"Falgo's been in a bad way since that night," Rhino told him in a hushed tone.

"Why? Did he get injured?"

"Not exactly," Stork confessed, sharing glances with his comrades.

"Snibs discovered Falgo's been keepin' 'imself watered with the ship's storage goods. 'e's drained all the barrels o' 'ard drink that were stored in the 'ull fer trade, an' even 'ad 'is own supply o' rum stashed down there. Snibs only found out cause Falgo's supply caught fire. If Tails's furry friends 'adn't made Tails aware when it 'appened, it would've been the end o' us," Rhino told him.

"Can ya imagine? Survive two galleons, a kraken, an' wretched sea fire—only ta go down from Falgo's rum stash?" Stork said.

"What's wrong with Falgo then?"

"As punishment, Snibs 'as ordered Falgo not take a drop o' anythin' 'arder than grog until we return ta the mainland. The man 'asn't been sober fer as long as I've known 'im—an' the lack o'drink be puttin' 'im in a bad way," Cricket explained.

"Ta say the least," Stork muttered, nodding towards a shape in the back corner of the room.

Bastian glanced over and immediately recognized the shadow of a man he'd seen earlier, with his head buried in his arms.

"But that's ridiculous! We would all be dead if it wasn't for Falgo. He practically took on the Kraken single-handedly," Bastian objected.

"Come now, we all played our part," Stork asserted.

"Of course, and you were all brilliant! But you must admit, Falgo's sword bested the firearms when it came to the Kraken. He sliced through its limbs with single blows!"

"Falgo fights when it pleases 'im. Most o' the time 'e be content ta watch the show, while the rest o' us do the work," Stork stated.

"Though, ta be fair, when 'e does decide ta come ta the party, 'e be a storm ta be reckoned with—an' this time more so than ever," Cricket acknowledged.

"I don't think I've seen 'im more ruthless an' focused," Rhino admitted.

"Surely his contribution outweighs a hidden drinking habit? I mean come on, the man's only hurting himself!" Bastian protested.

"I'm not condoning Snib's decision—I 'ate ta see Falgo this way as much as anyone, but what do ya expect 'im ta do? Rules be rules. If 'e doesn't punish Falgo fer breakin' 'em, then what's goin' ta stop anyone else? I'm sure ya can imagine 'ow many men 'ere would keep themselves plied with piss if only given the chance," Cricket stated.

"Besides, it be fer 'is own good. 'e was killin' 'imself with that stuff, Doc said so 'imself!" Rhino said.

Bastian nodded but didn't utter another word about it. He knew full well alcohol was a dangerous poison when abused. But he also knew from his days at the Order it was even more harmful to make someone with an alcohol dependency snuff their habit dry. It didn't matter how much the private medical sectors argued against it, Bastian had seen it firsthand at the Star Temple. The Order held vast knowledge on the subject for two reasons. One, their main service to the community was tending to the sick and elderly free of charge—which meant they never had a shortage of patients to study. And two, because they kept excellent logs and records of their practices and the results that followed. More so, they shared those results with every branch of the Order across Equillian, pooling their knowledge. And alcoholics and people with other dependencies were something they dealt with on a regular basis. Helping in the medical branch of the Order was a regular part of being a Star Child. When Bastian was young he used to hate it when it was his turn to help with the addicts. They scared him. They were so miserable, so crazed and desperate. But as he got older and more used to them, his fear turned to pity and compassion. And there was certainly nothing more effectual in steering him clear of acquiring his own dependency. Bastian often wondered if the sisters of the Order had planned it that way.

Bastian didn't dare take another glance at Falgo while the others could see him, but the image of the broken man weighed heavy on his mind.

"What else have I missed?" he asked, changing the subject while taking a long drink from his stein.

"We 'ad a meager wake fer the men lost. Sent the ones recovered up ta the Stars on a floatin' pyre made from the wreckage an' some respectful silence fer everyone down with Davy Jones," Rhino said.

Bastian shuddered to think how many must be lost to the sea. He dearly hoped his body would be burned when his time came. He would far rather end up amongst the Stars than as one of Davy Jones's horde—condemned to the old world sunken beneath them. "How many were there?" Bastian inquired.

"It's 'ard ta say. We lost five all up. All newbies that 'ave only served under our flag fer the last few months er so. A couple went in the first fray, an' three o' 'em were ended by the Kraken—either taken er injured beyond repair by the beast. I 'ave no idear 'ow many men were lost amongst our foes, though. We've pulled out a lot o' bodies. Doc tried ta fix up the ones still breathin', but only one o' 'em survived," Cricket recounted.

Bastian fell silent. He couldn't help thinking he was responsible for their deaths—at least in part. If it wasn't for him, the galleons wouldn't have even been there.

"But the best part be yet ta come. As soon as we reach Jaxland we can celebrate the lives they lived with a proper carouse in the true Black Mary fashion!" Stork proclaimed.

"Aye, nothin' better ta show our respects an 'onor the dead than with a proper drinkin' bout in their name," Cricket concurred, holding up his stein to the deceased.

"Ya also missed most o' the 'eavy liftin'," Rhino told him.

"Yeah. Yer timin' be impeccable, ya sure ya didn't plan it that way?"

"Trust me, I'd rather be working than dealing with this headache," Bastian assured them.

"We still 'ave the bulk ta do. Now the lumber's down we can properly tuck into it. Should be finished by the end o' the week, I reckon," Cricket estimated.

"Where are we?" Bastian asked.

"Two day's out from Jaxland, anchored on a floatin' Dreg."

Bastian looked up from his stew. "We're on a floating Dreg?"

"Aye, blew east from the Desert Ocean in the gale," Rhino confirmed.

"Someone's in bed with Lady Luck, I tell ya. Not only did the thin' show up in the nick o' time, the Dreg be covered in a grove o' Mast Trees," Stork remarked.

"That is lucky. I look forward to seeing it. I've never seen a Dreg Island before."

"Don't get too excited, ye'll only be settin' yerself up fer disappointment."

"Aye, once ye've seen one, ye've seen 'em all."

"Sounds like you've been working hard. Felling Mast Trees is no easy task," Bastian commended.

The trees were as tall as giants and straight as arrows with only a small tuft of branches and green foliage on the very top, like a dandelion seed-puff, making them perfect for masts. Bastian had tried to carve Mast wood once in Westdock, but the wood was so hard and dense, it was as if it were petrified—making it incredibly difficult to work with.

"Not as 'ard as ya may think. Boom be fellin' the trees with those boom-sticks o' 'is. It's why we've been able ta make such good progress. But there 'as been no shortage o' thin's ta do. I must admit, I'm ready ta 'it the sack," Rhino confessed. He stood and drained his Black Jack, then slammed it on the table. "It's good ta 'ave ya back, Dodger. I'll see ya scallywags at dawn," he declared, and headed towards the sleeping quarters.

Stork drained what was left in his stein before saying, "I'm glad yer still with us, mate, ya 'ad me worried there fer a wee minute." He clapped Bastian on the shoulder, then followed his brother.

Cricket watched them go and then turned to Bastian and pulled a puff-pouch full of Spice leaf and Tymetree paper from his pocket. "Care fer a puff?"

Bastian's eyes lit up. "Where'd you get that?!" He'd finished his own supply the night of the battle and had been itching for one ever since he'd gained consciousness.

"Traded it with our sole captive from the galleons."

"We have a prisoner from Lord Bardviss's crew?"

"'e's one o' the Royal Navy's men. The only one who pulled through. Snibs as 'im locked up in the 'old," Cricket said.

"Was he really the only survivor?" Bastian asked.

"A few left on the lifeboats—the cap'n likes ta let enough get away ta tell the tale. But in truth, they'll be lucky ta make it back ta the mainland from this far west without supplies."

Bastian hurriedly spooned the last of his supper into his mouth. "I would love a puff!"

"Good, cause I 'ave no bloody idea 'ow ta roll the damn thin's," Cricket confessed with a grin.

Bastian and Cricket stood on the poop deck of the Black Mary, each with a puff-stick in hand. It was a crisp, clear night. A blanket of bright stars dotted the sky and the waves washed on the shore in a gentle lullaby. The ship was half beached on the floating Dreg Island, with its anchor stuck in the sand.

It was a small island, made of the same volcanic pumice stone as all the islands on Equillian, spewed out from some huge ancient volcano after the seas drowned the old world. White sand covered the Dreg's surface, and a thick grove of Mast Trees stood Just beyond the beach—their tall looming trunks and dense bushy tops looking like strange giants in the darkness.

It was no surprise to Bastian that this particular Dreg traveled so far in the storm. The wind would've caught the tree tops like sails and pushed the island along. Because the Dreg Islands weren't lashed to the sea bottom by thousands of years of sea growth like all the main islands of Equillian, they drifted around the ocean haphazardly, pushed by the wind and tide. Their porous structure had large pockets of air keeping them afloat. Though they always appeared to be small, the Dregs could be as large as mountains, with the majority of their bulk looming under the water's surface. No one knew how many there were, because the majority of them were in uncharted water, drifting in the Desert Ocean.

The ship's main deck was a construction site. The main mast had already been replaced with a fresh trunk. Its wood was stripped of its bark, giving it a warm golden hue that could be seen by the gentle glow of the Everfire lanterns. Bastian was sad to see that all of Whittler's intricate carvings decorating the last mast were gone. Not only had the carvings been beautiful, they'd captured the history of the Black Mary. Now that history only existed in wisps of memory. Bastian was grateful he'd had the opportunity to see it. The totem had been a masterpiece. The carvings had mostly depicted the story of the Kraken, how it had haunted the Black Mary's wake. Now the Kraken was gone, bringing that story to its end. The new mast was as bare as a blank page, marking the beginning of a new chapter for the Black Mary. Bastian wondered if anyone would take on the task of recording it.

"I like this stuff, I can see why ya make a 'abit of it," Cricket remarked as he took a drag from his puff-stick.

Bastian shrugged. "For better or worse. I never realized how much I rely on it until I ran out. Spice leaf is so easily accessible in Westdock. It grows wild in the hills. My brother and I can pick it from pretty much anywhere. Well, *could* anyway…" he amended, trailing off in thought.

"Ya 'ave a brother?" Cricket asked.

"Yeah," Bastian admitted after a beat.

"Where's 'e now?"

Bastian hesitated before answering, "Probably in the Wendrians' dungeon." He laughed dryly.

Cricket smirked. "Ah, so trouble runs in the family then?"

"I guess you could say that. Though we attract it in very different ways."

"Yeah? So what earned yer brother lodgin' in a noble's cell then?" Cricket queried, taking another drag.

"He courted the Duchess of Westdock at her own engagement party and convinced her to run away with him."

Cricket raised an eyebrow. "Is 'e a commoner?"

"Yup."

"Were they previously acquainted?"

"Nope."

"Is she decent lookin'?"

"She's known as the Jewel of Westdock."

Cricket whistled. "Shick! Yer brother clearly got all the charm in the family."

Bastian smiled, "It's always been a particular knack of his, and one I've never cared to strive for."

"Are ya worried about him?" Cricket asked.

Bastian looked out across the ocean and took a drag. "Yeah."

"Is that why ya want ta get back ta Westdock so badly?"

"Partially. He's the only family I've ever had. He would do everything in his power to save me if things were turned around. It kills me that I can't be there for him," Bastian confessed.

"Do ya know he's locked up fer sure?"

"No. He never came home from the castle that night. I didn't even know the duchess was missing until I was being chased by the castle's guard and accused of taking her myself."

Cricket knocked the ash from his puff stick. "Is that why ya stowed away on the Black Mary?"

Bastian nodded.

"Ha! Well, ya clearly 'ave nothin' ta worry about."

"What makes you say that?"

"Why would the castle's men be chasin' ya down if they already 'ad yer brother?"

"It's only a matter of time. They'll be throwing all their resources into finding them."

"Yer presumin' the castle knows 'e's with 'er," Cricket pointed out.

Bastian paused. Cricket was right, he'd been making that assumption all along. But Lord Bardviss had seen *him* fleeing from the Wendrians' personal quarters, not Felix. And they were chasing Bastian the following day, which meant he must be their only lead to Lady Lilliana's disappearance. And if the castle didn't know about Felix, then there would be no evidence tying him to the duchess's disappearance.

"Even if they find 'em, the duchess won't turn 'im in—she's most likely runnin' from 'er own betrothal. If she doesn't care about yer brother, then they've most likely parted ways already. If she does, then they're probably tucked away in some 'idden corner wastin' their time consumed with one another without a care in the world. I know that's what I'd be doin'," Cricket said.

"That's a good point, I hadn't thought of that."

"If 'e's 'alf as crafty as ya be, then I wager ya 'ave nothin' ta worry about. Lucky 'e doesn't know yer predicament, eh? Can ya imagine the state 'e'd be in if 'e knew ya were on the Black Mary? An' yet, what good would it do either o' ya? Yer still kickin' despite it all, aren't ya?"

"Yeah…" Bastian admitted, suddenly realizing the real thing he should be worrying about wasn't rescuing Felix, it was Felix trying to rescue him. If his brother ever found out what happened to Bastian and where he was, then any attempt at rescue would be disastrous. He could only hope his brother's attention was and would continue to be capitalized by the duchess. That at least would leave Bastian with only Gwena to worry about. "Do you have any family?" he asked Cricket.

"Ya mean, besides this sorry lot?"

Bastian smiled. "Yeah."

"Not as far as I can remember. When the cap'n found me, I was livin' on the streets workin' as a lookout fer a gang o' petty criminals on the mainland. I was the youngest o' the lot. They liked usin' me cause I was easy ta 'ide an' could whistle a masterful tune."

"Is that why they call you Cricket?"

Cricket nodded while blowing out a steady stream of smoke.

"How old were you?"

"Four er five maybe. Can't be sure."

"Four or five! How long ago was that?"

Cricket scratched his chin, "Fourteen years, I think."

"How old was the captain then? He doesn't look like he's old enough to have taken a ship fourteen years ago."

"I think 'e was thirteen er fourteen then. Pretty sure 'e was thirteen when 'e first took over the Black Mary."

"Thirteen!" Bastian exclaimed.

"Aye. We were all so young back then. There's only a small 'andful o' us left who 'ave been 'ere from the start. Far too many faces 'ave come an' gone. But that's enough about that. Looks like ya got slapped around a bit in there. Ya alright?" Cricket asked.

Bastian shrugged "Could've been a lot worse, considering."

Cricket took a drag from his puff-stick. "Is it true the cap'n wants ta test yer loyalty on Jaxland?"

"Yeah. I think there's something he wants me to take."

A spike of interest flashed in Cricket's eyes.

Bastian knocked the ash off the end of his puff-stick. "I start training for it with Tink tomorrow at any rate. He's the ship's tinker, right?"

"Tink? Aye…. Though, I 'ardly ever see 'im these days, keeps mostly ta 'imself. Never 'eard o' 'im trainin' anyone fer anythin'," Cricket replied absently.

"I have no idea what I'll be doing. Hopefully I'll be finding out more about it tomorrow."

"Right…" Cricket said skeptically.

"You don't believe me?"

"First ya open the cap'n's chest that no one else 'as been able ta crack. Then ya played Spittin' Daggers without consequence. An' after bringin' two galleons on our tail, yer still kickin'—even more so, the cap'n brought ya ta 'is own quarters ta 'question ya', conveniently when ya needed special medical attention. Now, 'e's 'avin' ya trained by Tink— one o' the most valuable members o' our crew, who 'ardly 'as time fer even us seasoned sailors. The cap'n an' Snibs might be able ta fool the rest, but I've been sailin' under this flag with Muerte from the start. It be clear 'e wants ya kept alive. I don't know why, but fer some reason yer unexpendable," Cricket concluded.

"At least until I recover what he wants on Jaxland. After that, I'm not so sure," Bastian said.

Cricket squinted his eyes at him. "I think I know what yer task be."

"What?" Bastian asked.

"Drax took somethin' from us a while back—only we couldn't prove it was 'im. The cap'n was outraged, but there was nothin' we could do about it."

"Why not?"

"Drax founded Jaxland. The island's a sanctuary fer pirates. Every ship that flies the black flag pays tribute ta Drax, an' in return we're protected by the pirate code. Which means none o' the other pirate crews can touch us. The second we get on Drax's bad side, we lose that protection—an' accusin' 'im o' stealin' practically be treason. The cap'n's been looking fer a way ta recover the stolen object ever since—it's an incredibly delicate situation," Cricket said.

"What did he take?" Bastian asked.

Cricket took a drag on his puff-stick before answering, "If ya don't know already, then the cap'n 'as reason fer that. It doesn't really matter anyways, does it? Ya still 'ave ta carry out the task regardless."

"I suppose. I'd still like to know."

"And I'd like ta know why the cap'n finds ya so valuable. But yer not gonna tell me that, are ya?" Cricket posed.

Bastian answered with silence.

"Didn't think so." Cricket gave Bastian a searching look, snubbed his puff-stick on the ship's railing, and then tossed the butt into the ocean. "It's gettin' late, best we get some rest. Will be another long day tammara."

"Cricket," Bastian called, searching for his next words, "I wish I could tell you more, I really do. I only remember pieces from last night, but I know I would be long gone if it wasn't for you...I owe you my life—you'll always have my loyalty."

Cricket nodded. "I'm glad ta 'ear it, mate. It's important ta be able ta trust one another out 'ere. Without it, we're all doomed."

Cricket tossed Bastian the puff-pouch filled with the rest of the Spice leaf and Tymetree paper, "Take it. I can't roll one without ya anyways. Just make me one when I ask, a?"

"Done!" Bastian exclaimed enthusiastically, then watched Cricket return below deck.

Bastian leaned on the ship's railing and looked out across ocean waves dimly lit by the pale moonlight and the star peppered sky. He wondered how much Cricket knew about the captain. By the sounds of it, he'd been on the Black Mary since Muerte first took control of the ship. No wonder Cricket had such a tough skin under his bright, grinning exterior. Bastian could only imagine the things he'd seen. The pirate certainly saw straight to the core of the situation. Which was going to make things difficult. The last time Bastian mentioned the strange gold dust to Cricket, he thought Bastian was high on hallucinogens. Either that or insane. Not to mention Bastian was under strict orders not to tell anyone. He only hoped Cricket wouldn't hold it against him. He valued his friendship—pirate or not—and Bastian would be sorry to lose it.

There was a gentle breeze tousling Bastian's hair and he couldn't help but think how grateful he was to still be alive to enjoy it. After such sobering brushes with death, life had taken on a whole new value, and he felt incredibly lucky to have it. Despite the hour, he was wide awake. His internal clock was completely skewed from his long sleep, but being well rested had made the world a brighter place. His agreement with the captain filled him with optimism. It was like a beacon of light guiding him to land after years at sea. He started to roll himself another puff-stick when a thought struck him. *Cricket said he'd got this from a survivor from Lord Bardviss's galleons. A man from the Royal Navy. If he was stationed in Westdock then he might know something about Felix and the situation at the castle.*

Bastian pocketed the puff-pouch and headed back below.

Bastian made his way silently down the ship's corridor. All the sailors besides those on watch duty were asleep in their hammocks. The mess hall was empty and except for the gentle creaking of the rocking ship and the distant sound of crashing waves, it was eerily quiet. Bastian listened intently as he passed the first floor to the ladderway and climbed down to the gundeck. The holding cell was in the center, flanked by a row of cannons on either side. It was a square metal cage made of crisscrossed flat iron bars that stretched from floor to ceiling. A young man was sitting in the corner of the cell with his head and arms slumped over knees drawn up to his chest. Bastian approached him cautiously, resting his hands silently on the bars to peer in at the young man bathed in the gentle glow of the firebeetle lanterns. He looked to be a couple years older than Bastian. He was dressed in the uniform of the Royal Navy—a long, thick, green felt jacket with shiny brass buttons lining either side, a blue and red vest over a white shirt, and billowing green pants tucked into tall black boots.

The young man opened his eyes. He saw Bastian and retreated to the opposite side of the cell. "What do you want?!" he asked anxiously. He had a handsome brown face, dark, brown curls neatly tied back in a knot behind his head, and warm brown eyes. There was something familiar about him.

Bastian raised his eyebrows in disbelief. "Dylan?"

The young man squinted at Bastian and recognition bloomed across his face. "Bastian?"

Bastian laughed. "By shick! I never would've imagined I'd see you here!"

"Nor I, you!" Dylan stood and walked over to the bars. He stuck his hand between them, and Bastian shook it like they'd been old comrades. Dylan was a boy from the Order. He'd been in the class above Bastian. They'd never been friends, for no reason other than lacking anything in common. But seeing him now felt like running into family.

"You're a sight for sore eyes," Dylan said, "I didn't think I'd be seeing anyone I know ever again. Are you a pirate?"

"Ha! So they tell me. And you're part of the Royal Navy?"

Dylan looked down at his uniform as if forgetting it was there.

"I signed up when I graduated from the Order, about two years ago now. I thought it might help make something of myself, maybe attract some girls—and the coin's not bad. Of course, I would've changed it all in a heartbeat if I'd known where it would lead me. Bad luck eh?"

"It could be worse, at least you're still here. The rest of your crew weren't so lucky."

Dylan nodded somberly. "There weren't any other survivors, then?"

"I heard a few got away on the lifeboats," Bastian said optimistically. "Was there anyone else I know on the galleons?" he asked.

Dylan shook his head, "Russel joined at the same time I did, but he wasn't assigned to this one."

"Why was the Navy sent out on Lord Bardviss's galleons anyway?" Bastian inquired.

"It was a mixed crew. Lord Bardviss sent his own ships, and the castle sent some of us along to lend a hand. What happened to you?" Dylan asked, pointing to the stitches on Bastian's brow and his bruised cheek.

"Nothing interesting. I was sitting in the crow's-nest during the fray and hit my head on the mast."

Dylan nodded. "Would've had a good view from up there. Tell me, was there really a kraken, or did I only imagine it?"

"It was real alright. But we won't be seeing it again. The master gunner fed it one of his combusting experiments. Would've blown the thing to bits," Bastian assured him.

"I suppose that's comforting. As long as none of its friends come looking for it. It doesn't even feel real. I keep thinking I'm going to wake up and this will all have been some terrible dream."

Bastian gave Dylan a sad smile. "Tell me about it."

"How did you end up here, anyway?" Dylan asked.

"Me?" Bastian cocked his head. "What do you mean, don't you know?"

Dylan smirked. "I suppose I should've guessed you would've become a pirate, it's fitting. Only—the Black Mary? The most feared pirate ship of our time? Even for you that's ambitious. I bet there's a good story there. And is Felix here too?" he asked, looking around as if he might find him lurking in the shadows.

Bastian blinked. "Surely you're having me on? I thought I was the whole reason Lord Bardviss's galleons came after us?"

Dylan stared at Bastian confused, then his eyes widened in realization, "You're the one who stole the golden egg?!"

Bastian jerked his head back. "The what?"

"The egg from the castle, it's the Wendrians' most prized artefact. Lord Bardviss sent us to retrieve it," Dylan explained.

"Wait, what?! That's the reason you came after this ship? For an egg?"

"Yeah, someone stole it from the castle's keeping room at the duchess's engagement party. We were told the culprit escaped on this ship."

Bastian's blood ran cold. He scratched his head and began pacing the deck, the gears of his mind a whir. "I may have taken something resembling that. But there isn't anything special about it—surely it's not worth sending two galleons to recover it?"

"Wait, you're telling me you stole the egg and you don't even know what it is?!" Dylan asked.

Bastian stopped dead in his tracks. "Hold on a minute, I thought Lord Bardviss sent you because he thought I'd kidnapped the duchess?"

Dylan snorted. "Hardly, he doesn't actually care about the duchess as much as he'd like everyone to believe. The betrothal is more of a business arrangement. You know how the nobles do things, Lord Bardviss wants to be Duke of Westdock and Lady Everitt needs his coin. Lord Bardviss sent us out here only to retrieve the egg. It's an enchanted War Dragon's egg, the last female in existence. Apparently the male one's kept somewhere at the duke's estate in Sky View. Together they have the potential to bring back War Dragons. If they fall into the wrong hands it could be catastrophic."

"Are you saying the egg I stole from the castle is a *War Dragon's* egg—and it can be hatched?" Bastian asked carefully.

"I presume so, the way they've been acting about it."

"And that's what all this is about? A dragon's egg?! What the bloody shick are the nobles doing with War Dragons' eggs in the first place?! There's a reason those things were snuffed out!" Bastian exclaimed with growing panic.

"The Wendrians were Lord Bardviss's top supplier of War Dragons during the war. They have a hatchery in Sky View. They had the most deadly breed, that's how Duke Drake became duke in the first place. Lord Balthazar arranged a marriage between Drake and his cousin Everitt to reward the Wendrian family for helping him win the war. The way I heard it, the Duke's grandfather had the two eggs preserved in gold by the alchemists after the dragons were banned—as a family heirloom," Dylan explained.

"Bloody shick! Why didn't they have it locked up in a case or something? It was sitting right there on a table in the center of the room—practically asking to be taken!" Bastian protested.

"Probably because they didn't anticipate anyone breaking into their locked keeping room inside a guarded castle," Dylan suggested.

Bastian ran his hand through his hair anxiously. "By the Watchers—if it was a commoner who'd preserved a War Dragon's egg, you know they would've been hung for it!"

"Of course. Nobles get away with murder, we all know that."

Bastian began pacing again. "I don't understand, on the dock Lord Bardviss said he'd kill me if I laid a hand on the duchess…"

"A show for the public, no doubt. He knows you didn't kidnap the duchess. He would've been using that as an excuse to go after you. The nobles don't want it known the eggs exist, let alone that one's been stolen. Can you imagine what would happen if that got out? The public would be outraged!"

"For good reason. I'm outraged!!"

"I still can't believe you're the one who took the egg—and you really didn't know what it was?" Dylan asked.

"It's just a gold egg! It wasn't labeled or anything. It was sitting, quite invitingly, in the middle of the room. How was I supposed to know it was the Wendrians' most prized artefact, let alone a real dragon's egg, let alone a War Dragon's egg?!" Bastian objected defensively with animated gesticulation.

Dylan looked at him for a beat and then he burst out laughing. "You know, when I heard someone stole the egg at the engagement party, I imagined some sinister, well-seasoned professional pulling off an elaborate scheme—something months in the making. But the fact it was you—thinking you were stealing a simple gold trinket—actually doesn't surprise me. Next, you're going to tell me Felix was the one seen following the duchess to her personal quarters."

Bastian returned his mirth with a telling stare.

Dylan's eyes widened in surprise, and then he laughed so hard tears streamed down his face. "Classic! You two haven't changed a bit!"

"I'm glad you find it so amusing," Bastian remarked dryly.

"I wish I could tell the other Star-brats back home. You know, you two are practically legend at the Temple."

"Really?"

"No joke! There isn't a student at the Order who doesn't know your names. And I can't imagine that changing anytime soon. Every time I hear someone retell a story of your shenanigans, it's more elaborate and embellished than the last."

Bastian smirked. "Felix would get a kick out of that."

"Speaking of which, where is that rogue? I still can't believe he picked up the Jewel of Westdock—that bastard always did have a way with women."

"That's actually why I'm here, I was hoping you might know what happened to him? He never returned from the castle. When I found out the duchess was missing, I feared the worst," Bastian confessed.

"Your guess is as good as anyone's then. Word is the man who followed her to her quarters disappeared when the duchess did. By the sounds of it, they probably left together," Dylan said.

"Is the castle looking for him?"

"Doubt it, they don't even know Lady Lilliana was with anyone before she vanished. No one would dare suggest to Lady Everitt or Lord Bardviss that the duchess was being disloyal."

"What do they think happened then?" Bastian asked.

"Word is, she simply disappeared. Most of the upper-crusters suspect a kidnapping. Most of the staff think she went on the lam to avoid her betrothal. Her handmaiden said she helped Lady Lilliana pack a bag only a week before. She thought it'd been for the duchess's honeymoon, only it went missing when the duchess did. The detective is keeping all possibilities open. Either way, her disappearance is strange. There's no evidence of how she left her bedroom. She was there one minute and gone the next."

"Didn't they leave through the window? I heard it shatter on my way out," Bastian said.

"What, from that height? If they had, their corpses would've been found at the bottom. The window was shattered alright, but there was no evidence anyone went through it."

Bastian scratched at the stubble forming on his chin. Sloppy misdirection, that didn't sound like Felix. *Maybe a secret passage?* he wondered.

Bastian felt a weight lifted from his shoulders. "It's a relief to hear he's not wanted by the castle."

"If you ask me, the two of them are probably shacking up together in one of the Duke's holiday homes in the Cathedral Mountains, or Everlast, maybe even Sky View. Lucky bastard," Dylan remarked.

Bastian hoped he was right. As long as Felix wasn't being hunted by the castle's guard, then Bastian was sure he could handle just about anything else on his own. It was a huge relief. He could only hope the duchess would keep him distracted long enough to prevent Felix from doing anything stupid in an attempt to rescue him.

"I wonder what Lord Bardviss will do when his ships don't come back," Dylan said absently.

"You think he'll send another one after us?" Bastian asked.

"I don't know. He was definitely more concerned about recouping the egg than the duchess. There's a hidden agenda there. I've never liked the man—he acts as if he's the emperor himself when he's not even duke yet. I tell you what, if I was the Duchess, I would've run away at the first opportunity."

"If he's that bad, then why's Lady Everitt allowing the betrothal?"

"Because they need his coin. Their Keeper swindled most of their fortune after the Duke went missing, and then disappeared himself. Lady Everitt hasn't been able to trust anyone since. She's tried to take over the Duke's work, but she's been struggling to pick up all the strings he left untied. Their family is on a sinking ship, and Lord Bardviss is the only one throwing them a lifeline. For his own benefit, of course, but that's of little consequence considering they're short on options. But enough from me, how in the Stars did you get recruited by the Black Mary?" Dylan asked.

"Ha! Funny that. The castle's men cornered me in the harbor the day after the masquerade. My only chance of escape was to stow away on the one ship leaving port."

Dylan looked at Bastian and blinked in disbelief, "And that ship happened to be the Black Mary?"

Bastian nodded.

Dylan's jaw dropped. "You're joking? You mean to tell me you didn't jump on this ship on purpose? I thought surely you must've already been part of their crew."

Bastian gave Dylan a look that clearly stated he hadn't.

Dylan laughed. "That's too much! First the egg, and then the Black Mary. What did you do to upset the Stars so badly?"

"Ha! I'd be asking yourself that question. At least I'm not the one behind bars."

"Speaking of which, why is that? If you stowed away on this ship, then why are you out there instead of in here?" Dylan asked.

"I convinced the captain I'm worth keeping—at least for now. I had to pick an old chest to keep them from feeding me to the sharks. Now, for better or worse, the captain's found a use for me. I'm just trying to stay alive long enough to find a way back home," Bastian confessed.

"Do you think you could help me out of here? Maybe convince him there's a use for me?" Dylan asked.

"Sorry mate, I don't have that kind of sway here. But I'll put in a good word. I can't imagine they'll get rid of you. They lost men the other night and need hands to replace them," Bastian assured him.

Dylan nodded. "Thanks, that brings me hope. I thought I was a goner for sure, especially being from the Navy. Truth be told, I'm surprised they haven't snuffed me out already. Regardless, I don't know if I'll last too long in here even if they don't kill me. I feel like I'm going mad."

"Course you will. Hang in there. I'll come down and visit when I can."

"Thanks," Dylan replied in earnest.

Bastian turned to go.

"Hey, Bastian. What happened to the egg?"

"The egg?"

"Yeah, the egg."

Bastian cleared his throat. "The captain has it."

"What?! You gave it to Muerte Tormenta?!" Dylan exclaimed.

"I didn't have a choice! He made me hand it over when I was discovered on board."

"Serendipity help us, now we're all shicked! I can't believe you gave a War Dragon's egg to the most feared pirate of our time!"

"Shhh, he doesn't know what it is, and if you keep your trap shut, we might have a chance at keeping it that way. Besides, it's probably safer in the hands of a pirate who doesn't know what it is than some fool noble who does."

"I hope you're right…but if he ever discovers what it is, then you know we're all doomed."

"Shick…Who in their right mind thought it was a good idea to keep War Dragon's eggs anyway? Oh, before I forget—no one here knows my real name, I'd appreciate it if it remains that way."

"What do they call you?" Dylan asked.

"Dodger."

Dylan smiled, "That's fitting. Maybe I should come up with a new name for myself?"

"Don't bother. They'll choose one for you."

Dylan smirked, "See you soon then, Dodger."

Bastian made his way to his hammock and climbed inside. It was one of many that hung in rows from the rafters of the ship's sleeping quarters. Most were filled with sailors fast asleep, but Bastian couldn't help noticing there were a few empty that had been full before. It gave him a sinking feeling. *Am I responsible for their deaths?* he wondered. *If I hadn't taken the egg, then I might've been in the Heartland with Gwena now, and those men might still be alive.* The very thought was heart-wrenching. He'd known at the time he shouldn't have taken the egg, it was too obvious, too valuable. He recalled the strong feeling of being drawn towards it—like it was meant for him.

"Stupid," he muttered.

How could he have been so foolish? It was a stupid thing to do full stop, and now he and a slew of others were paying for it. And this was only the beginning. What if Lord Bardviss sent another ship after them? What if his blunder led to the resurrection of War Dragons?

*Stars help us all.*

# THE DIAMOND CITY

Felix and Lilliana stood behind Roy in the control room, watching the view of the approaching islands through the large front window.

"There it is!" Lilliana exclaimed, excitedly pointing out the Wendrians' island.

It was a beautiful piece of land, around thirty acres or so and lush with thick grass and groomed greenery. At its heart stood a massive red and cream stone chateau made up of towers of various sizes, each one topped with long copper spires weathered to a soft green. The architecture was timeless and elegant, comprised of two main stories that expanded out into wings on either side, featuring balconies that lined both levels.

At the front of the estate was a giant decorative fountain in the shape of a seven-pointed star. It had seven marble dragons that arched back and spit water from their mouths like jets of fire towards a large golden egg in the center. A stone pathway encircled the fountain and connected with paths leading up to the estate on one side and down through the front garden on the other, winding all the way to a long jetty protruding from the edge of the island over open sky. At the jetty's end was a tall lamppost lit with Everfire.

There were three impressive stables arcing out from the chateau's wings in a semicircle. They were the nicest stables Felix had ever seen, made of large stone blocks and huge wood beams the size of tree trunks. Above each doorway, a large decorative Everfire lantern hung from the roof on an iron hook in the shape of a dragon.

Behind the estate was a gorgeous garden with well-manicured green hedges and blooming flowers. A round glass greenhouse reflected rays of sunlight in the garden's center. Behind the garden was a fenced pasture with sheep, goats, and ducks grazing together happily. The place was beautiful, like an illustration from a fairytale.

Roy moved several cranks and dials, and the airship began to descend.

"The old girl's going to make it!" he proclaimed enthusiastically, patting the control station in front of him.

Felix and Lilliana watched as the island grew closer, and in less than a minute they were floating alongside the long wooden jetty. Roy headed straight for the companionway and then turned to Felix.

"Meet me on the upper deck, won't you, sport? We need to tie her to the bollard and get that vent opened back up to stabilize our altitude."

"On it!"

◠

When Felix got to the top of the companionway, Roy was already opening the vent to the Everfire chamber. He arrived just in time to see the huge flame leap back up through the glass cylinder that channeled its heat into the balloon above the sails.

"Can you get to the dock?" Roy asked him.

Felix looked over the side of the ship to the metal bollard on the platform next to them. The gap from the ship to the jetty was as long as he was tall. He stared apprehensively at the empty patch of blue sky between them. He'd helped dock countless ships working as a fisherman's hired hand in Westdock—leaping from boat to shore over gaps at least as wide without hesitation—but they weren't thousands of feet in the air.

Felix had been scared of heights for as long as he could remember. Despite his fear, the only thing it had ever stopped him from doing was following Bastian along the rooftops and joining him in cliff jumping. Well…except for that one time, but he was stupid drunk when he let Bastian convince him to jump buck naked off the Westdock cliffs into the ocean, and it was never going to happen again. But despite his fear, Felix had still done it. And he still scaled the wall at the back of the butcher's to get into their flat and climbed the rigging on ships when it was required. All his terror did was add an unwelcome obstacle that made anything with altitude a hundred times more challenging. And he hated it. Bastian would frequently remind him that bravery was not the absence of fear, it was facing fear and not letting it stop you. Felix reminded himself of his brother's words now before turning to Roy and saying, "Sure."

Roy nodded and turned his focus back to readying the ship. Felix took a deep breath and tried to imagine the blue sky as a calm sea. He stepped back and made a small run before leaping off the airship across the gap. He managed to make it to the center of the jetty, but his momentum carried him several steps forward and almost over the opposite side. He grabbed the light post just in time to save himself and shut his eyes tightly, taking in several deep shaky breaths while still clutching the pole. Then he slowly opened his eyes and peeked over the edge. There was nothing but blue sky as far as the eye could see. Vertigo washed over Felix and he quickly turned back around and looked up at Roy, pushing the surrounding void out of his mind.

The pilot was leaning over the railing on the top deck with the heavy line in hand.

"Ready when you are," Felix called up, and Roy threw the line down. Felix caught it and pulled the ship against the edge of the dock, securing the line to the bollard.

"Got everything you want to take in?" Roy asked him.

"Yeah. I travel light." Felix knew the joke would be lost on Roy—and it was. Roy nodded and disappeared out of sight. As far as Felix knew, Roy had no idea Lilliana kidnapped him and forced him on this journey. He wondered how the pilot thought he'd gotten there. In this world he and Lilliana could never be friends, and Felix doubted she'd even met anyone common born who wasn't a servant. If Felix were Lilliana's uncle, he'd have a lot of questions. Maybe Lilliana *had* told him of their arrangement. Either way, Roy was oddly cool about the whole thing. In truth, even if Felix did have the chance to pack for this trip, he wouldn't have known what to bring. He'd never previously traveled outside of Westdock. The only reason he knew so much about packing bags was because he lived out of one for several months when he and Bastian first left the Order. It took them a while to gain their bearings on life in the outside world, and then again to find and secure their place above the butcher's. Until they had, they'd moved from place to place finding ac-commodation wherever they could—or making do without.

Roy reappeared with Lilliana at his side, each with a large bag in hand.

"Can I toss these down to you?" he called down.

"No problem," Felix called back, and caught the bags one at a time as Roy threw them down. He placed them on the dock and watched as his travelling companions descended the rope ladder to the jetty. Roy came down first and gave Lilliana his hand to help her jump off the final rung. His assistance amused Felix—from what he'd seen of the duchess, she could most likely jump off the top of the ladder and land on the jetty in a perfect roll, while taking Roy down and trapping him in an armlock at the same time, but it was a nice gesture all the same.

Roy handed Lilliana's bag to Felix, then shouldered his own before walking towards the estate. Felix looked at the bag in his hands and then looked at Lilliana. "Something about this feels familiar."

Lilliana smirked, "That bag looks good on you."

"You know, I usually make a point of avoiding women with baggage. All this is weighing you down. I can liberate you from that, if you like?" Felix held her bag over the side of the jetty.

Fear sparked in Lilliana's eyes. "You wouldn't dare!"

Felix grinned and swung the bag over his shoulder. He started down the path whistling the tune Lilliana was singing earlier and then stopped after several paces, realizing Lilliana wasn't following him. He looked back and saw her hesitate as she gazed up at the estate. "You alright?"

"Yeah." She shook herself free of her thoughts and caught up to him.

Felix studied her. "How long has it been?"

"I was here for my uncle's funeral a couple years ago, but we didn't stay long. It's been seven years since my last real visit," she confessed, focusing on the path in front of them.

Felix held his tongue to give her time with her own thoughts. They walked side by side in silence, taking in the view of the well-groomed garden that outlined the polished stone pathway and the magnificent fountain looming ahead. Roy was waiting for them at its base.

"Seeing as this is my first time in Sky View, anything I should know?" Felix asked them.

"Don't get too close to the edge," Roy advised wryly.

Felix returned a tight smile devoid of humor.

Just then a large shadow encompassed them, accompanied by the sound of gigantic beating wings. Felix ducked instinctively, looking up just in time to see a magnificent dragon passing overhead. The majestic creature was covered with vibrant blood-red metallic scales, its underside a glossy black. Its huge expansive wings were thick and leathery, and its head was slender with horn-like protuberances swooping out behind it. The creature had a noble and wise expression, its eyes sharp with intelligence. The slender but muscular beast touched down gracefully on the path ahead of them with a woman on its back. By Lilliana's expression of anxious apprehension, Felix guessed the dragon's rider must be her cousin. The woman looked like she was in her early twenties. Felix could certainly see the resemblance between her and Lilliana. Her cousin was striking, but in a very different way. Her hair was the same rich red, only it was completely straight, tied back in a smooth knot instead of full and curly like Lilliana's. They shared the same blue and yellow eyes, but Arianna's skin was snow white, whereas Lilliana's was a warm walnut brown.

When Arianna saw Lilliana, her face lit with shocked surprise. She dismounted from the dragon like an expert gymnast, handing the reins to a waiting servant.

The dragon stretched its wings out lazily, then folded them behind its back and shook its head. It followed the servant obediently towards the stables, its long tail swinging gently from side to side. Felix watched it in awe and fascination as it walked away.

"Cousin, what a surprise!" Arianna exclaimed.

She pulled off a pair of leather riding gloves, revealing a tattoo of a dragon on her right hand, and greeted Lilliana with a kiss on the cheek.

Lilliana hugged her, "Arianna, it's been too long. I apologize for showing up unannounced."

Arianna took Lilliana's hands in hers, "Are you well? Last I heard, you disappeared from your own engagement party. Your mother's worried sick!"

"Yes, thank you. No one must know I'm here, I'll explain everything inside. In the meantime, I was hoping my guests and I might take refuge at the estate?"

"Of course!"

Lilliana's shoulders relaxed. "This is James. And you remember father's friend, Roy?"

"Oh yes, didn't you stay with us once?"

"Yes, many years ago. I'm impressed you remember. I came along for one of Drake's business trips. It's lovely to see you again, Arianna," Roy replied cordially, and kissed her on the hand.

Arianna held her hand out to Felix, "And James, is it?"

"Yes, it's a pleasure to meet you," Felix greeted, shaking her hand firmly.

Arianna's hand sat limp in his grasp and she regarded him with an odd expression. Felix realized she'd expected him to kiss it and cursed himself for making the faux pas.

"What a pleasant surprise it is to have you all here. Please, come inside. I'll have Albert prepare the east wing," Arianna announced, and led them towards the estate. As they walked she hooked her arm in Lilliana's and journeyed beside her. "I hope you can forgive my absence at your engagement celebration, cousin. With father gone, it's been exceedingly difficult to get away. Especially this time of year."

"This time of year?" Lilliana asked.

"The Sky Cup Derby."

"Of course! I completely forgot. Is it next week?"

"The day after tomorrow."

"By Kismet! I've been so consumed with the wedding I haven't given it thought. I've heard we hold the winning title?" Lilliana asked.

"Yes, we've won the last two years."

"It will be a joy to see the Derby again, especially with our dragon in the running."

"Do you have tickets?" Arianna inquired.

"No…I don't," Lilliana admitted.

"I'm afraid the Derby's all sold out. It's been selling out a year in advance for as long as I can remember. Unfortunately, I gave my complimentary passes away months ago. If I'd known you were interested, I would've saved them for you."

"Of course, I wasn't thinking. I suppose I'm so used to having father and Uncle John sort all that out—it didn't even cross my mind," Lilliana confessed.

"There are ticketless festivities in the capital, they'll be running all week. I hear they're first class, people come from all over to attend them," Arianna suggested.

Roy cleared his throat. "Sorry for the intrusion, my lady, but it might be better to avoid being in public considering the current circumstances."

"Of course, how silly of me! Roy's right—I couldn't go regardless; I'm supposed to be missing. Another year," Lilliana proposed.

"Yes, let's plan ahead to ensure it," Arianna agreed.

Felix noted Lilliana's masked disappointment. He had to admit, he was slightly disappointed himself. Seeing a dragon derby sounded like the opportunity of a lifetime—and something he wasn't keen to miss, especially when they were so close to where the event was taking place.

They reached the huge, gilded doors at the entrance of the estate and the doorman opened the door for them. Felix thanked him as he passed, and the man gave him a curt nod before closing the door and resuming the position of a human statue.

⌒

The inside of the Wendrians' Sky View estate was even grander and more elegant than the exterior. It had a light, airy feeling due to the exceptionally high ceilings and huge windows flooding the interior with natural light. The floors were made of rose-colored marble, and the entryway was open and expansive. The furniture was elegant and tasteful, arrayed in a palette of pearl whites, golds, soft pinks, greys, and royal blues. There was a grand staircase at the end of the entryway that curved upwards to a second-floor balcony. The high ceiling above it had a mural of the sky filled with flying dragons. The dragon theme was prevalent in the decor throughout the estate. On the walls were large paintings of the creatures in majestic poses. Dragons were carved into the wood of the picture frames and the staircase's white bannister. Statues of dragons supported the tables, and gold figurines of the creatures decorated their surfaces.

It was no mystery what trade belonged to this household. It reminded Felix of the time he and Bastian crashed a rich widow's house party in Westdock. She was completely obsessed with horses. There was horse memorabilia everywhere they turned, and the animals were presented in the same proud, noble fashion.

"So I take it your mother doesn't know you're here?" Arianna asked, as she led Lilliana and the others to a grand sitting room to the right of the entryway and pulled a bell cord on the wall.

"No, and it must stay that way—at least for the time being. It's of the utmost importance for her and Natasha's safety," Lilliana insisted.

The two sat down on the lounge together.

"Their safety? What's going on?" Arianna asked with concern.

Lilliana searched Arianna's eyes with uncertainty before answering. "I've suspected for some time that Lord Bardviss is marrying into our family for a sinister purpose. I don't think he has a desire to be the Duke of Westdock—I think he wants to use the position as a stepping stone for a grander scheme," she confessed.

Arianna raised her eyebrows at the accusation, "Have you told your mother this?"

Lilliana hesitated. "I've tried, but she won't listen. She thinks this matrimony is the only way to save our family from financial ruin."

"Financial ruin? Why haven't I heard about this? And what makes you so sure Lord Bardviss has ill intentions?"

Lilliana pulled out the letter from Lord Bardviss and handed it to Arianna. "This. My original plan was to stage my own kidnapping in order to buy myself some time. If I'm kidnapped, Lord Bardviss will have to stay in my mother's good favor to maintain our betrothal, leaving me free to find a solution. Only, I never anticipated this."

Arianna read over the letter and paled. "Sell you to the slavers?! Is this some sick joke?"

Lilliana shook her head. "I wish it were. He thinks he's negotiating with my kidnappers, not me."

"What do you think's his agenda?" Arianna asked.

"I've no idea. Only that it's far more sinister than I'd originally imagined. I need to find a way to stop him before he marries Natasha."

"Marry your sister?!"

"With me out of the way, we think he might be hoping to marry her in my place," Lilliana explained.

"Stars," Arianna whispered.

"I'm sorry, cousin, I had no intention of getting you involved in any of this. I'm only seeking a place of refuge while I figure out what to do."

"Of course. I'm happy you came to me, it's such a relief to see you're alright. After I received your mother's letter informing me of your disappearance, I feared the worst. Know I'm here for you and happy to help in any way I can," she assured her.

"Thank you, cousin, I can't tell you how much of a relief it is to be well received by you. It's been so long since we've talked, and considering the circumstances…I wasn't sure what to expect," Lilliana confessed.

Arianna grabbed both of Lilliana's hands and held them in hers. "My dear cousin, you and Natasha are the last blood relatives I have, no matter how much time passes between our visits together, I will always be here for you when you need me."

Lilliana smiled and hugged her cousin with tears brimming in her eyes. "I'm so sorry about Uncle John. I miss him."

"Me too. This place feels empty without his hearty laugh filling its halls."

"He was larger than life, no one can fill the space he left behind."

Arianna pulled away from Lilliana's embrace. "But I'm not the only one who lost my father that day. I'm sorry if I've let my own pain eclipse yours. I miss Uncle Drake too."

"Thank you, cousin. That's partially why we're here. It might seem silly, but Roy and I haven't completely lost hope, we think there might be a chance my father's still out there, and if there is, then we intend to find him."

Arianna returned her cousin's hopeful expression,

"It doesn't sound silly. If there's anything I can do to help, please let me know."

A tall lean man suddenly appeared in the arched entrance of the room. He was an older gentleman, with white hair neatly combed back and a well-trimmed white mustache; dressed in the traditional green and grey suit of a butler. He addressed Arianna.

"Pardon my intrusion. You rang, my lady?"

"Yes, thank you, Albert. Can you see to it the east wing is made up for Lady Lilliana and her guests? And have some refreshments brought for them as soon as possible, they've had a long journey."

"Of course, madam. How long will they be staying?"

Arianna turned to Lilliana inquiringly.

"We aren't sure, but I expect we'll see out the week," Lilliana answered.

The butler bowed his head in acknowledgment. "Very good, my lady. I'll have tea and refreshments brought shortly."

Arianna smiled. "Thank you, Albert."

The man made a slight bow to her and returned to his duties.

Arianna stood. "Now, you'll have to excuse me, I have several appointments to attend to. There's still much to do in preparation for the Derby. We'll talk again later after you've had some time to rest. Until then, let Albert know if there's anything you need. I trust you and your friends will make yourselves at home?"

"We will. Thank you again for your hospitality, cousin," Lilliana returned gratefully.

Arianna smiled and left the room.

Felix sat down in one of the plush white armchairs facing an elaborate Everfire hearth blazing with the enchanted flame and took a handful of mixed nuts from the table next to him. Roy stood with his hands in his pockets, studying one of the large paintings on the side wall, while Lilliana walked around the room restlessly.

Felix studied the painting above the hearth. The picture was a dramatic, detailed oil depicting a large War Dragon on a grassy plain scorched black and partially ablaze with red and orange fire, the sky obscured with black smoke and dark storm clouds. The gold beast was covered in armor, in a low crouch and blowing out a stream of fire while the armored knight on its back brandished a long black spear.

There was a gentle knock on the door. A maid entered with a silver tray laden with all the essentials for tea, accompanied by a silver plate stacked high with sweet biscuits. She set them down on the tea table before retiring from the room.

Felix poured a cup for each of them, before eagerly taking his own. He had his cup halfway to his lips when he noticed a small display case above the painting of the War Dragon. It was only one foot tall, tucked into a square alcove in the wall, with a rosewood interior and a glass door. Inside was a single gold egg the size of both Felix's fists put together. It was sitting upright on an ornamental stand.

*Holy shick*, Felix thought. He knew real gold when he saw it, and that egg had enough surface to buy him retirement. He immediately got the impression it was paired with the painting below it. There was something alluring about it, beyond the precious metal it was made of—like it had its own gravity.

"Is there a story to these pieces?" he inquired, nodding up towards the painting and the small display cabinet.

Lilliana followed Felix's gaze. She walked over to the painting and studied it. "It's the last male War Dragon. They were my family's trade before the world was united. When the dragons were banned, my grandfather hired the alchemists to have the egg enchanted," she said.

"Hold on, are you saying that's a real dragon's egg?"

"Yes, one of two. They were part of my father's and uncle's inheritance from my grandfather. The female one is sitting in my family's Keeping Room back in Westdock," Lilliana stated casually.

"You mean to tell me, your family has kept two War Dragon eggs that can still be hatched?!" Felix exclaimed.

"Stars, I hope we'll never need to hatch them. My grandfather was a sentimental fellow. He understood the necessity of removing War Dragons from the market to maintain peace after the war was over, but the breed is our family's legacy. It took generations to perfect it. He wasn't willing to completely destroy them. He only saved two eggs from our best stock and had them encrusted with gold and enchanted to be kept in stasis. They were created as mementos more than anything—but I think it brought him comfort knowing we have a way to bring them back if the need ever arises."

Felix looked up at the golden egg with renewed interest. War Dragons were the most devastating weapon the world had ever seen. Having an embryo for one was the equivalent to keeping a weapon of mass destruction on display in one's living room. "That's got to be incredibly illegal," he muttered.

"Pardon?"

"The egg looks incredibly regal," Felix rephrased.

"Yes, they're beautiful. When I was a child, I used to stare at my father's for hours."

"How do you know one is male and the other female?" Felix inquired.

"The male eggs are larger. My father's egg is only half that size," Lilliana explained.

There was another gentle knock at the entrance to the sitting room and the butler stepped inside.

"My lords and lady, your rooms are ready, if you'd please follow me," he announced, and picked up Roy's and Lilliana's bags before leading them out into the foyer and up the marble staircase.

The butler showed Felix to his room, and he shut himself inside. He collapsed on the massive four-poster bed richly adorned with a goose feather blanket covered in a duvet made of spider's silk. He folded his arms behind his head and sighed, looking up through the sheer blue bed canopy to a mural of stars and dragons on the ceiling. The room was fit for a king. Felix couldn't have been happier in that moment. Even though he was exhausted from his previous late night with Lilliana, he was buzzing from the high of his current situation. If someone had told him last week he'd be staying as a guest at the Wendrians' estate in Sky View, he would've said they were clinically insane. But here he was. He pinched his arm just to assure himself he wasn't dreaming. He wondered if Bastian and Gwena were doing as well. Of course they would be. They were finally together, somewhere in the Heartland making their way comfortably with Felix and Bastian's savings. He looked forward to when they would be reunited and could swap stories with one another. Then his thoughts drifted to Lilliana and their exchange earlier. He wondered if he would ever get the opportunity to be with her again. Surely she wanted to despite her trepidations? If she didn't, then Felix had completely misread her. As far as he could tell, she was as interested in him as he was in her, he was sure of it…almost.

*This bed would certainly be a lot more fun with someone to share it with,* he thought.

But his thoughts were soon interrupted by a rap at his door and Roy's voice coming in from the hallway.

"Sorry to intrude, sport. Just wondering if you're still up for a trip to the capital? We'd discussed getting you some new clothes."

"Oh, right. That would be brilliant! I'll be right out," Felix called back, and reluctantly rolled off the bed. He looked in the large oval mirror hanging above a mahogany dresser and combed his fingers through his stark black hair.

Felix was disappointed to see Roy was alone. "Is Lady Lilliana not joining us?"

"She wants to help Arianna prepare for the Derby. Besides, those two have a lot of catching up to do. Better we give them the chance to do so."

Felix smiled. "Of course. A gentlemen's outing then."

Felix and Roy passed the fountain in the front garden outside the estate and followed the path all the way to the jetty's end.

"We're not taking the airship?" Felix asked.

"Not this time. We'll take a cab. It's more trouble than it's worth to find a docking point at the capital," Roy said, and he pressed a brass button on the lamppost looming beside them. Immediately the Everfire in the lamp turned a vibrant green and a dense emerald beam shot directly upwards into the sky, penetrating the daylight as a beacon. Several minutes later a compact yellow airship with a single oval balloon pulled up in front of them at the end of the dock. It had an illuminated sign above it made of thin glass tubes filled with Everfire curving in the shapes of the words *Air Cab*.

A stout woman stuck her head out. "Need a lift?"

Felix and Roy sat behind the driver's cockpit. The air cab cut off the Everfire light in its sign and pulled away from the Wendrians' island.

Roy made small talk to the driver as Felix looked out the window in wonder. There were more airships out and about now, sailing through the airways between the Windswept Isles. Just seeing the different flying ships was a marvel. He'd seen his first one only three days before, when Lilliana forced him onto the one that took them to Sky View. The sight of Drake Wendrian's old airship had taken his breath away. But now, he could see that ship was practically an antique. The ones here were sleeker and more modern in design. Some had sails and some only had balloons of one shape or another with motorized propellers at the back. Some had wing-like contraptions on either side that moved to the best advantage for the wind. He even saw one being pulled by dragons.

Their ship took them through the smaller islands, navigating the morning traffic, and soon the capital came into view. The buzzing city was the heart of Sky View. Its island was only a quarter of the size of the six surrounding it and was completely covered with tall slender buildings, stone walkways, and meticulously manicured parks. Each building was as beautiful as it was grand. Most of them were made of white stone that sparkled in the sunlight. In their midst were two large circular glass towers filled with vibrant green plant life. Many of the roofs in the city had greenspaces with trees and hanging flower gardens that grew all the way down the buildings' sides, and some had huge suncatchers built into their spires, catching the sun's light and showering rainbows across the white polished surfaces of the surrounding buildings. Airships were crowded along the docks that fanned out along the outer edge of the island, like florets radiating from a flowerhead.

Felix rolled down his window and stuck his head out into the open air to soak it all in. The airship began to descend, sloping towards the island before descending past it and dipping underneath. The underside of the capital island was even bigger than its top surface, longer than it was wide. Its bottom half jutted downwards in jagged cliffs that were overgrown with thick green moss and lichen hanging down in wisps that waved in the wind. All the way down the rock face, long thin jetties fanned out like star rays, each one crowded with airships docked on either side of it. At the very bottom was a large circular metal grate forming a taxi rink. The cab pilot pulled up to its ledge to let them off.

Roy took out his coin purse. "Thanks for the ride, how much do we owe you?"

The woman hit a button to stop a steam-powered Nixie tube counter that had been adding up minutes since they'd left the Wendrians'. "That'll be five jolly rogers."

Felix was stunned. Jolly rogers were Equillian's third highest coin, worth ten cwips each. Back in Westdock, five jolly rogers could get him a dinner feast and a full night at a high rate cathouse with the pick of the litter. But to his surprise Roy counted out the coins without hesitation.

"Thank you," he said cordially, and handed the payment over.

The woman gave them a friendly wave. "Enjoy your time at the Diamond."

The door on Roy's side was opened by a mechanical doorman, a steam-powered android dressed in a smart bright blue uniform with gold trim and a matching pillbox hat it wore cocked to one side. "Welcome to the Diamond City," it greeted in a tinny falsetto. Felix couldn't help staring at the strange machine—he was so human-like. He had a metal face intertwined with gear work and glass animatronic eyes that stared directly at him. The most advanced steam technology Felix had come across in Westdock was Jarvis's steam-powered trawler. Now he felt naïve and vastly behind the times.

"Thanks, the Diamond City, you said?" Felix asked as he climbed out of the cab.

"Yes, sir," the droid confirmed.

Felix looked around them. "Nice."

Roy waved to their driver and the cab pulled around to pick up its next customer. Felix looked down at his feet and his face paled with vertigo. He could see straight through the metal lattice floor to the empty sky below. Roy looked at him with concern. "You alright, sport?"

"Yeah, I have a fragile relationship with heights," Felix admitted.

Roy gave a low whistle. "Bad luck. Come on, let's get you inside." He patted Felix on the shoulder and led him down the pathway towards the rock cliffside in the center. It took every inch of Felix's willpower to ignore the expansive abyss beneath them. At the end of the platform was a glass elevator that travelled through a tube disappearing into the rock above. Another mechanical doorman wearing the same smart blue uniform stood beside it. The droid tipped its hat to them as they approached. "Where to, gentlemen?" it asked in a metallic baritone.

"The Diamond Center," Roy requested courteously.

"Very good sir. Watch your step, and please enjoy your stay."

There was a small ding and the door to the elevator opened. Inside was a round glass chamber brightly lit with Everfire lamps reflecting off the floor of green and rose granite with veins of gold. Roy and Felix stepped inside, and the doorman reached in and pushed a button on a brass panel. His strange mechanical mouth smiled at them politely as the door closed.

Felix looked up to see a bell-shaped ceiling painted like a sky at twilight. Billowing clouds bathed in a soft glow of orange and pink in a sky transitioning from dark blue to purple into a lighter grey. Small painted stars dotted the ceiling in the forms of constellations. The elevator lurched and they began to rise. Felix grabbed hold of the wall. He'd never been in an elevator. He said a short internal prayer to The Watchers and focused on the glass in front of him. As they ascended they could see the dark porous stone they were passing through.

A moment later the stone was gone, and the elevator was entering a wide open shopping center built inside the core of the island.

"Whoa, I was not expecting that," Felix exclaimed in awe.

Roy smiled. "You haven't seen anything yet."

The elevator came to a gentle stop and the doors opened to reveal another mechanical doorman there to greet them.

Roy held out his arm. "After you."

Felix stepped out of the elevator onto a polished white marble floor. The walls were the bare grey porous stone the island was made of. Along its rough surface hung elegant Everfire lamps filling the space with bright warm light. The high ceiling was masterfully painted as a bright blue summer's sky with wispy white clouds, making it feel like they were outside. Between the lamps were shop after shop after shop recessed into the stone, each one beautifully presented with magnificent displays in their front windows. By the look of things, everything was made of the highest quality and no doubt expensive. There was a watch shop with a large round, ornate clockface keeping time above its door. A shoe store with polished leather footwear for men and women of every size. A hat store, a solarglasses store, one for canes and parasols, and another just for gloves. After that was a sweet shop, then a tea lounge and bakery. The place was buzzing with pedestrian traffic, all highborn aristocrats and nobles meticulously dressed in the latest fashions.

Roy rubbed his hands together. "First things first, we need a barber."

Felix lifted his hand to his chin and felt the rough stubble that had grown there over the last three days. "Indeed, I'm in desperate need of a shave."

Roy smirked. "I wasn't going to say anything. Follow me, I know just the place," he said, and led Felix through the crowd.

Soon they were entering a gentlemen's barber shop. It was clean and well-kept with three brass and black leather barber chairs in front of long decorative mirrors. Another android was there to greet them, with a perfectly combed head of hair and an equally well-groomed faux moustache. "Can I help you gentleman?"

"We both need cuts and a shave," Roy said.

"Right this way," the stylish android invited, and settled them into chairs. Felix wasn't sure how he felt about a machine approaching his throat with a razor blade, but Roy assured him they gave even better cuts than a human barber.

Half an hour later and five jolly rogers down, Felix walked out of the barber's feeling like a whole new man. They'd cut and styled his hair respectably, and his face was now as smooth as a baby's bottom.

"You hungry?" Roy asked, stepping out beside him with a fresh shave and haircut.

"I could eat."

"I'm going to take you to a friend who's a designer here. He'll help us get you outfitted. But unless he's changed, we'll be drinking. Best to line our stomachs first," Roy advised, and steered him towards the bakery.

Inside was a charming sitting area decorated with floral wallpaper. They found a small table and Felix sat down while Roy ordered at the counter. A minute later Roy joined Felix at the table.

"How come all the servers are droids? Don't they have any people working here?" Felix asked.

"A few. It's the one flaw of having a precinct populated by aristocrats. Many of them feel they're above work, and yet they're hesitant to bring in human help, scared the introduction of lower classes housed outside of private estates will incite squalor and crime. They'd rather employ programmed, predictable machines."

"I didn't know steam-tech had progressed so far."

"Only here in Sky View. The University has employed all the top engineers on Equillian and poured funding into it. It's amazing how quickly things can progress when there's ample coin, eh?"

"True," Felix agreed. He wanted to say that if they'd put half the amount of funds into the paychecks of any help they hired, they would undoubtedly receive the most exceptional service and prevent any decline into squalor or the need to turn to crime, but at that moment a mechanical waiter approached their table carrying a silver tray. "Two Dragon Roses and Storm Cloud Tea?" it asked cordially.

"Yes, thank you."

The droid placed a steaming teapot between Roy and Felix with two mugs and a small bowl of white cubes. Then it took what looked like two small bouquets of flowers wrapped in brown paper off its tray and set one before each of them. Each bundle had a group of three roses made of fried dough, each of the rose's petals shaped like dragon's scales.

"Please enjoy, gentlemen," the droid said politely, and left them to their meal.

The pastry was warm and smelled like floral sweet bread. Felix followed Roy's lead and plucked off one of the dough petals and popped it into his mouth. The warm fried dough melted away on his tongue. It was dusted in a mix of sugar and cardamom and inside was a creamed custard filling flavored with a dash of rose water. Felix's whole body stilled to relish the sensory explosion.

Roy closed his eyes to savor the flavor. "I've missed these."

Felix nodded. "So will I."

Roy smiled and gestured to the teapot, "Tea?"

"Please."

Roy filled each of their mugs.

Felix picked up one of the white cubes. "What are these?"

"Sweet cream cloud drops. They create the storm."

"The storm?" Felix asked.

"It's what makes it Storm Cloud Tea. I only take one, but you can add as many as you like to your taste," Roy explained, and dropped one of the white cubes into his mug. Instantly, milky white billows began forming in the tea like clouds churning in a storm.

Curious, Felix added one to his own cup and watched it billow and swirl. He took a cautious sip and was pleasantly surprised by the rich milky sweet flavor that masked a very strong tea.

Roy took a sip from his mug. "I can't say I like it as much as Spiced Kah, but it's the next best thing for taking the edge off a scotch breakfast."

"Can't you get Spiced Kah here?!" Felix exclaimed.

"Unfortunately, not unless you bring it in yourself. Now there's a good business opportunity," Roy declared with a lifted finger.

"Speaking of business, what's your line of work? I take it, a business of some sort?" Felix asked, plucking another petal from his Dragon Rose.

He'd been wondering what Roy did for a living. It was obvious he wasn't a noble, which meant he wasn't receiving the people's tax money to fund his lifestyle, and he certainly didn't act like he was living off a dwindling supply of family inheritance.

Roy pulled out a Spice leaf cigar from his pocket and laid it on the table in front of him. Felix picked it up. He immediately recognized it. It was the same brand of cigar Roy had shared with him on the airship when they'd first met. The cigar's dark purple exterior and the gold ribbon wrapped around it was signature to the most expensive and by far the best Spice leaf brand on the market.

"You own Zest?!" Felix exclaimed.

Roy shrugged. "It's a family business."

"Spice leaf is Westdock's largest export. Isn't ninety-five percent of that your family's product?"

Roy looked at Felix, impressed. "Indeed it is. Though it wasn't always that way. When the company got handed to my brother and me, Spice leaf was hardly sold outside Westdock. In fact, it was hardly heard of beyond our borders."

"Really?" Felix took a sip of his tea. "What changed that?"

"My brother and I couldn't spend five minutes in the same room together, and I wanted to see the world. So I convinced him to make me head of marketing. He never had to see me, and I could expand our market beyond the western border. Everybody won."

"Well played! Sounds like a fantastic career," Felix applauded.

Roy smiled. "I can't complain. Though getting the business to where it is today took hard work. I spent my youth publicizing our product to the rest of the precincts. I wasn't much older than you when I first set out. But I wouldn't trade that time for anything. It allowed me to see the world, and the adventures it's taken me on and the people it's brought me in contact with have been responsible for the best years of my life."

"If you're the one who put Spice leaf on the map, that means you're responsible for the largest success in Westdock's economy," Felix said.

"I certainly can't take all the credit. But I may've had something to do with it," Roy winked. He leaned back and sipped his tea. "You and I aren't so different, you know? My family didn't come from a line of nobility. My grandmother started our company from nothing and built it from the ground up. We weren't born into a life of opportunity; we created it for ourselves. You remind me of myself as a young man—clever, ambitious, and you don't take no for an answer. That will get you far. Times are changing, my friend—you no longer have to be highborn to reach the upper circles. Steam technology is helping to change that, it's a fruitful time for industry. There's abundant coin to be made by just about anyone with some decent business savvy. The mistake most people make is convincing themselves the life they want is unobtainable, instead of simply living it. But not you, I can tell. You're one of the rare ones who can see what he wants and grabs it without hesitation. I like that."

"Thanks, that means a lot." Felix was really beginning to take to Roy. He'd enjoyed the man's company from the start, but the more he got to know him, the more he admired him. And the more Felix learned of his story, the more interesting and intriguing Roy became. Roy and his brother were probably next in line as Westdock's most wealthy after the Wendrians. The only one wealthier in the precinct was Lord Bardviss, who owned his own merchant company with an entire merchant fleet.

For Roy to say that Felix reminded him of his younger self was incredibly flattering.

Felix picked up the cigar from the table and studied it. "You know, I could get us into the Derby if you and Lilliana want to go."

"How do you mean? Arianna said the Derby's all sold out."

Felix shrugged. "That's not really relevant. I can't remember the last time I purchased a ticket to get into anywhere."

Roy lifted an eyebrow. "Is that so?"

"It's not really that hard, all you need is the right angle—and your profession makes that conveniently easy."

Roy leaned back in his chair and sipped his tea. "I'm listening."

Felix plucked a dough petal. "I'm guessing this event is like any other, which means the only people who need tickets are spectators. Competitors and staff will have special passes that will be checked and accounted for. But there's a third category of attendees, a category that gets free ticket-less entry and slips past detection." Felix popped the dough petal into his mouth.

"Oh? And what category is that?" Roy asked.

"Promotions. People hired by companies to promote their products at these sorts of events. As long as we have something to give away, no one will question us."

Roy looked at Felix with new measure before saying, "You're exactly right, I don't know why that hadn't crossed my mind. I've promoted Zest myself in such a manner. It's been so long since I've dealt with that directly, I didn't think of it. I can apply for Zest to be added to the list this very afternoon. I think I might still even know a couple people in the Derby's advertising department that can help me hurry things along."

Felix finished his last dough petal and dusted the sugar from his hands. "We'll need some promotional merchandise. Do you have many cigars on hand?"

"Sure, I have a whole crate on the airship. I treat every trip as a business opportunity."

"Brilliant. Problem solved," Felix declared with a grin.

Roy frowned. "Not entirely. Lilliana's supposed to be missing. She can't just show up at a public event like the Sky Cup Derby and expect no one to notice."

"Easy—the Duchess of Westdock won't attend the derby."

"I can't in good conscious go without her. She'd be devastated."

"Of course not, she'll just have to go as someone else," Felix stated plainly.

"Are you suggesting some sort of disguise?"

"Why not?"

Roy rubbed his chin, "I'm just not sure we could pull it off. She would have to be completely unrecognizable."

Felix shrugged. "No problem."

"What makes you so confident?"

Felix folded his hands together on the table and leaned forward conspiratorially, "My mother used to manage the community theater in Westdock. There are techniques the actors use to transform their appearance in order to match their characters and make them more convincing. I picked up a few things. I've even played a few roles myself. My point is, transforming the appearance of one person to another doesn't take as much as you might think."

The story, of course, was grade A poppycock. Felix had never met his mother, he didn't even know who she was or if she was even alive. Nor had he ever acted in a play—the only experience he had with The Westdock Players was sneaking in to see their shows. But he wasn't about to admit he'd picked up his tricks for disguise from the working girls at the cathouses or that his acting experience came from impersonations for cons on life's stage.

"I suppose a disguise is a possible solution. As long as we don't run into anyone who knows her personally. It would have to be very convincing," Roy insisted.

"Of course," Felix agreed with a wry smile.

Roy drummed his fingers on the table. "Hmmm. The question then is whether or not the risk is worth it. If her disguise is compromised, it could ruin everything."

"It sounds to me like it's an important opportunity for acquiring intel. What better place to question the local populace about Drake and his disappearance?" Felix proposed, "but it makes no difference to me one way or the other, I'm only here to aid in any way I can."

Roy nodded in thought, "I'll have to think it over—but I think you're right, it may be well worth it. I also like the idea of using this as an opportunity to promote Zest at the same time. I wish I'd thought of it. If I'm not careful, I'll be owing you a salary," he jested.

Felix grinned. "Trade me a few cigars and I'll call us even."

"Ha! Done." Roy drained the rest of his mug. "Best keep moving. Come, let's get those clothes we came for," he said, standing from the table.

"Right," Felix agreed, and drained his own glass.

Roy led Felix around the corner of the shopping center. Both sides were lined with tailors' shops.

"Why are there so many tailors?" Felix inquired, bemused by their ability to survive with so much competition.

Roy smiled. "There are no ready-made clothes in Sky View. You don't choose a store here, you choose a designer."

He directed Felix into a place on the left that had a sign reading *Favio's Bespoke Apparel*.

There was a small bell at the top of the door that rang when they entered. The store was meticulously clean and organized, with four dark blue leather armchairs at the front, each with an accompanying side table. A beautiful black granite countertop was on the left with bolt upon bolt of high-quality fabric displayed behind it. A row of wooden dressing rooms stood at the back of the shop, alongside several stations with stepping stools encircled by tall mirrors. The walls were decorated with large portraits of men dressed in expensive, elaborate outfits. A moment after they entered, an older gentleman came to greet them. He was a couple inches shorter than Roy, with stark white hair combed to one side, half-moon glasses, and a moustache that was dyed bright blue and curled up at the ends. He was wearing a white dress shirt with the sleeves rolled up to his elbows and a yellow and grey floral vest with a long tape measure hanging around his neck.

"Welcome, gentlemen. What can I do for you this fine morning?" the man greeted with open arms. Then recognition spread across his face.

"Roy, my good fellow, what a delight to see you here!"

"Favio, it's been too long!" Roy opened his arms and pulled the man into a hug. "How are you?"

"I'm well, business has never been better! How's the cigar business?"

"Going strong." Roy turned around to have a good look at the store. "I like what you've done with the place. Looks like your reputation has finally caught up with you, my friend."

"What can I say? I do what I love, and luckily people happen to love what I do," Favio returned humbly.

"Luck has nothing to do with it. I can't tell you how happy I am to find you here. We're in desperate need of those fine skills of yours."

Favio smiled. "What is it this time? Something for pleasure or business?"

"Both. We need a whole new wardrobe."

"Excellent!" Favio looked Roy up and down. I think I still have your measurements on file. You look as though you haven't changed a bit."

"Oh, they're not for me. They'll be for my associate, this young gentleman here. James, may I introduce to you the best tailor in Sky View, Favio Fritz. Favio, this is James. He's joined me all the way from Westdock to help promote the business," Roy told him, winking at Felix.

"Westdock, eh? It's a pleasure to meet you, young man. Any friend of Roy's is a friend of mine."

"The pleasure's all mine," Felix returned, holding out his hand.

Favio looked down at Felix's offered hand and laughed lightly, then patted Felix on the shoulder. "First time to Sky View, eh?"

"Yes, undeniably so," Felix admitted, pulling his hand back awkwardly.

"That's a nice suit," Favio complimented, admiring Gwena's creation.

"Thanks."

He walked around Felix to study its make. "Who's the designer?"

"A friend of mine, actually. Her name's Gwena Stently."

"I've never heard of her. Is she a tailor in Westdock?"

"The best."

"I'll have to keep an eye out for her work, I like her style," Favio commended. Then he directed them towards the leather armchairs at the front. "Please, have a seat. We'll start with some refreshments and then the fabric," he announced, then disappeared out the back.

Felix and Roy sat down.

"So, people don't shake hands here?" Felix asked, still feeling incredibly awkward about the earlier encounter.

Roy smiled. "No. I apologize, I should've mentioned it earlier. You'll come to learn the local customs soon enough. Unfortunately, the ones we're used to are seen as…less civilized up here. Sky dwellers see the act of shaking hands as a sign of mistrust. It stems back to the custom's origin—when shaking hands was proof you were unarmed. In Sky View, they think the practice is superfluous—because they can't understand why anyone would be armed in the first place."

Felix made a mental note of the information so he wouldn't make the mistake again. In his experience, shaking hands was still used as a gesture to show you were unarmed. If not literally, then metaphorically. Either that, or as proof you didn't have extra cards up your sleeve. It was a truce, a gesture of good faith, like checking in your weapons at the door. But as he encountered again and again—the culture of the upper class came from a very different form of reality. Every time he thought he knew the ins and outs of it, he encountered something else that pointedly reminded him of his common birth.

"Any other Sky View customs I should know about?" he asked.

Roy thought for a moment and said, "Don't expect to see any meat on the menu."

"Why not? I've seen plenty of grazing animals since we've arrived."

"Dragon food," Roy stated.

"You mean to tell me, all the meat goes to the dragons and they don't save any for themselves?"

"They think eating other creatures is barbaric. To them, meat is unfit for human consumption. The act of eating it is animalistic. They wouldn't dare unless they were starving," Roy explained.

"You're joking?"

Roy shook his head with an amused expression.

"They've clearly never had a good steak or a proper roast!"

Roy smirked. "Clearly."

"Well, that settles it. I can never live in Sky View," Felix declared.

Roy chuckled.

"Gentlemen!" Favio announced, returning with two short cut-crystal glasses filled with scotch and handed one to each of them.

"Much obliged," Felix said.

Roy held up his glass to Favio, "To old friends."

"And to new ones," Favio added, smiling warmly towards Felix.

Felix lifted his glass to them both and drank.

"Now, to business!" Favio declared, rubbing his hands together. "A full wardrobe you say? Should I exclude anything, or are we talking the whole works?"

"The latter. James's luggage never made it onboard the airship. Unfortunately, it's meant that he's been stuck with what he's wearing now for the last several days," Roy told him.

"Oh, I see. Could have been worse," Favio said.

"Yes, I'm grateful I got stuck with something so fashionable, but I tell you what, I'll be even gladder to finally be out of it," Felix confessed.

Favio chuckled. "I can only imagine. When it comes to comfort, the pauper outrules the prince. Well, you've come to the right place. I'll have you feeling grateful you had to replace your wardrobe by the end. Stand up for me, lad."

Felix stood from his chair, and Favio looked him up and down.

"Can you take off the jacket, please."

"Certainly," Felix complied, and laid his jacket across the chair beside him.

Favio pulled the tape measure from around his shoulders and began taking Felix's measurements.

"Will anyone of note be wearing your pieces tomorrow?" Roy asked.

"Yes! A couple of the competitors will be showing off my latest line at the Derby."

"Fantastic! No doubt that will draw some attention," Roy commended, then he noticed they'd lost Felix in the conversation, "The Derby's as much about fashion as it is about dragon racing. It's the pinnacle of haute couture. Anyone who's anyone in the design world will have their latest ideas on display, setting fashion trends for the entire year," he explained.

"Yes, my hope is to break into the noble circles this year. One of my pieces won a fashion competition a few weeks back. As the prize, I get an audience with the Emperor himself for a private viewing of my signature pieces at the Derby," Favio said.

"Wow! Impressive, my friend. Congratulations!"

"Thank you. I'm hoping this will be the big break I've been waiting for. All I need is one royal to take a liking to my work, and the rest will be history. If it's the Emperor, I'll never have to seek out another customer again," Favio proclaimed optimistically.

Roy held up his glass to him. "That deserves a celebration! I'll have to book your services a year in advance just to see you."

"You're too kind. Unfortunately, the whole thing is falling apart. My magnum opus was going to be worn by the great jousting champion, Sasha Avery and his fiancée, only he's taken a lance to the shoulder and had to drop out. Neither of them are attending the event anymore. Now, I have no one to wear my signature pieces."

"That is a damn shame! Surely you can find a replacement?" Roy asked.

Favio frowned. "Unfortunately, it's been exceedingly difficult to find anyone this late in the game. Anyone who's attending has already secured their attire for the event."

"I haven't," Felix said.

Both the men turned to him.

"I can't say I have anything to offer as far as notoriety goes, but I still don't have an outfit for the Derby and would be glad to adorn yours if it can be of any help?"

Favio looked at Felix with a new measure. "You would wear it well. A handsome face is second best to notoriety as a fashion model. But we'd still need a woman to wear the matching piece, the two go together."

"We do have a colleague who I'm sure would be happy to help—she was just saying yesterday how she wished she had something different to wear to the event," Felix offered.

"What luck!" Favio exclaimed. "There's just one caveat, I'd need you both to attend the breakfast gala and my meeting with the Emperor at the Derby's after-party."

"Fine by me, as long as it's alright with the boss?" Felix turned inquiringly to Roy.

Roy looked at him with the gleam of one who had just seen the secret to a magic trick. "Any work of Favio's can only help sell our product," he said.

"Brilliant, you've saved my day! I can't thank you enough!" Favio announced enthusiastically.

"It'll be a joy and pleasure," Felix assured him.

"I'll give you a discount on your order today as a token of my gratitude. I'll have to take the suit in to your measurements. Sasha's a bit bigger than you are. Let me fetch it, so you can try it on—then we'll continue with the rest of your wardrobe. When do you think your lady friend will be able to come in for sizing?"

"Tomorrow morning?" Felix asked Roy.

"I think we can arrange that."

"Excellent!" Favio declared and started towards the backroom before pausing, "What's your shoe size?" he asked Felix.

"Ruby Eleven."

"Ruby Eleven." Favio repeated and disappeared out the back.

Roy turned to Felix. "I guess we're going to the Derby after all, eh?"

Felix smiled. "When the stars gift you an opportunity, it's rude not to take it."

"Ha! You've either condemned us or captured us the perfect lucky break. Only time will tell which. Regardless, it's a fine opportunity, Favio's a top-notch designer—to wear any piece from his latest line is indeed an honor."

Favio returned with a miraculously colorful suit on a hanger and a pair of blue suede shoes.

"Wow, Favio! You've outdone yourself. What a masterpiece," Roy exclaimed.

"I must admit, I'm very proud of this one, it's taken me most of the year to complete. You can change in there. Please be delicate, it's my prized piece."

"Of course," Felix assured him, gingerly taking the suit and shoes in hand and carrying them to the nearest changing room.

Felix hung up the suit on the hanger behind the door and his mouth stretched into a wide toothy grin. The suit was magnificent. It had a fitted jacket in blue-green with real gold buttons and golden thread embroidered into detailed baroque designs on the cuffed sleeves and intricate floral patterns rising up the arms. The left shoulder was laden with vibrant feathers, bright green, teal, gold, purple, and blue all fading from one to the other like the plumage of a large exotic bird. The jacket's lapel also had gold embroidery, and on the inside was a violet vest with tiny embroidered purple flowers, a lapel in teal satin, and two rows of gold buttons merging into a V down its front. The rest of the suit was just as detailed and magnificent. It was dashingly unique, different from anything Felix had ever seen. He excitedly got out of Gwena's suit and into Favio's dress pants and dark blue spider-silk shirt, before layering on the silk cravat, vest, jacket, and finally, the blue suede shoes. The suit was a bit big in parts, but wow—was it glorious!

Felix studied his reflection in the mirror and sighed with delight. He couldn't have been more thrilled to change into something that made him so handsomely debonair. Until then, Gwena's suit had been the finest piece of clothing Felix had ever worn. There was no doubt it made him into a convincing lord. But this suit was a whole other caliber, more like art than clothing. It was the kind of suit people would immediately assume belonged to someone noteworthy, even if they didn't know why or who.

Felix stepped out of the dressing room and held out his arms.

Favio clapped his hands in delight and Roy gave a low whistle.

"It's as though it was made for you. James will be the talk of the town!" Roy proclaimed.

Favio walked over to him and began pinning the suit where it needed to be taken in.

"I'm starting to be grateful Sasha is unavailable—you fit this piece even better. Leave it with me, and it will be as if it was made for no one else," he promised.

Felix felt like a million duckets. He waited patiently for Favio to pin the needed adjustments and then changed out of the suit, handing it carefully back. The designer put the suit aside and refilled their glasses with more whisky.

"Now, onto the rest of your clothes!"

Two hours later and six whiskies in, Felix stood at the counter next to Roy while Favio rung up their order. Overall, it'd been an enjoyable experience. Favio had kept their glasses full, while he and Roy chose over a dozen different fabrics they decided complemented Felix's complexion, eyes, hair, and personality, for a list two feet long with clothing items they insisted he had to have. They went through several questionnaires for style profiling, in which Roy and Favio debated fervently about which would suit Felix best—while he hardly got a word in edgeways. Then he was measured meticulously. Between the whisky and the dynamic duo Favio and Roy made together, Felix found the whole process highly entertaining. He was sure the fate of his wardrobe couldn't be in better hands. But as he watched Favio punch in the numbers for the ridiculously long list of items, Felix started feeling nervous. He never would've bought so many clothes for himself, and certainly not ones as expensive. He was beginning to wonder if he'd brought enough coin to cover the transaction. In Westdock, the amount that filled his coin pouch would last nearly eighteen months. Here, he wasn't sure if it would cover their first stop. Suddenly he was worrying whether his winnings weren't the fortune he'd thought they were. Favio finished tallying up the bill and handed it over the counter. Felix went to take it, but Roy stopped his hand. "This one's on me, champ."

"That's very generous, are you sure?"

"I insist. Consider it a business expense." Roy winked.

"Thank you," Felix returned in earnest. He was overwhelmingly relieved—especially once he saw the stack of eight duckets Roy handed over the counter.

Favio took the duckets in hand and beamed at them both. "Well, gentlemen, it's been a complete pleasure. I'll have the adjustments made this evening. Your new wardrobe will be drawn up and handed over to production straight away. Each item will be sent out to you upon completion. You should have the entire collection by the end of the week, but I'll make sure you have something fresh to put on tomorrow."

"Much obliged," Felix said.

"You're a champion, Favio. I look forward to seeing the collection."

"I must say, I'm looking forward to putting this one together. It's been a while since I've been commissioned for a complete set. And having this handsome young man showing off my work at the race, that's a gift in itself!" Favio exclaimed.

"I'm flattered. I'm honored to be representing your work, Favio. And I can't thank either of you enough. You've both spoiled me for life, now I'll never be able to go back to buying ready-made clothes again," Felix declared.

"Don't! Come back here, I'll look after you," Favio insisted as he led them to the door.

Roy left the designer with two Spice leaf cigars, and he and Felix exited Favio's shop.

"Since we're going to the race after all, we should get you a pair of solarglasses. The UV's much stronger up here. It's important to take your sun protection seriously," Roy advised.

"I'll take your word for it, sounds good. I could also use a Keeping Pouch, if there's anywhere I can pick one up here? I get the impression I'm going to need to carry a lot more coin in Sky View than what my current coin pouch can hold," Felix said.

"Ah, I know something better, and I know just the place to find It. I'll take you there after we get your glasses."

"Great." Felix followed Roy around the bend towards an eyewear shop where they found him a stylish pair of solarglasses with reflective blue lenses and a green frame.

Next, Roy took him to a little store tucked away in the back of the shopping center. Treasure Trove Antiques was dimly lit with firebeetle lanterns and a starred ceiling backlit with Everfire. Below the shining stars the high walls were covered with glass cabinets housing old antiques that looked a thousand years old. Along the center ran a long display cabinet level with Felix's waist. It was lit by tiny vials of Everfire dotting the inside edges, illuminating the ancient artefacts and trinkets inside.

Some looked like they'd been recovered from the old world deep under the ocean's surface, and others had the signature stamp of the alchemists. Each piece had a little engraved placard describing what they were. Felix was incredibly surprised to see that the majority of the objects were enchanted. There were practical ones like silver spoons that never tarnished, a china tea set that would never chip or break, a tablecloth that couldn't stain, and clocks that never had to be wound. Then there were ones with more unusual enchantments such as a glass globe necklace that displayed the weather. It currently showed a blue sky with tiny white wispy clouds moving around. There was an ornate music box that played a child to sleep. A pair of leather gloves that self-heated when it was cold. And a jewelled hair clip that changed the color of the wearer's hair.

*A store that openly sells enchanted objects,* Felix thought. He'd never seen such a thing. It would be cause for imprisonment on the mainland. But he reminded himself that the same rules didn't apply to the upper-crusters. It was becoming more and more apparent they'd continued to use enchanted objects without pause after the ban. He'd always known The Enchanted Objects Collection Agency, or E.O.C.A., used the ban as an excuse to confiscate enchanted objects from the common people to sell them under the table for a pretty price to the eastern merchants—who then sold them back to the mainland's aristocrats at black market auctions where they went to the highest bidder. But he'd always thought once the aristocrats had them, they kept them locked protectively behind display cases—to be admired but not used. When the alchemists were forced to stop production of anything other than Everfire, their creations skyrocketed in demand and value. It was the main prize Felix and Bastian sought when they crashed a party in one of the upper class households. A single enchanted object would've made them enough coin to change their stars. Only they'd been looking for something locked away, something stored as a collector's item, not something being used or worn openly. Felix now realized their mistake. He wondered if any of the seemingly everyday items they'd sold to Guido had been enchanted and they hadn't known. He had no doubt the black market trader wouldn't have told them. To see an entire shop selling them openly here, that plainly advertised their enchantments, made Felix question if they were truly ever harmful.

Roy walked straight to the back of the shop and hit an ornate bell on the counter. A high ding rang out, pulling Felix from his thoughts.

An old woman walked out through a thick black curtain hanging behind the sales counter. She stepped up onto a wooden box that lifted her to the height of the filigreed copper register there and gave them a warm smile that revealed a web of lines in her walnut face.

"Good morning, gentlemen. What can I do for you?" she asked with a sweet voice rich with age.

"It's been a long time, Rose," Roy greeted with a warm smile.

"Roy, is that you?"

The old woman put a pair of round spectacles up onto her nose, that were hanging from a pearl chain around her neck.

"It is you! Come here and give your old friend a hug," she exclaimed, stepping down from her box and coming out from behind the counter to embrace him.

Roy had to stoop down to reach her. "It's great to see you," he said.

"It is indeed! What brings you to Sky View? Are you here to sell those puffa-ma-thingies of yours?"

"Not this time. I'm here to look into the disappearance of a friend."

"Oh dear, who's that?"

"Drake Wendrian. You haven't heard anything on the grapevine have you?"

"Drake Wendrian. That was one of Scott's boys, wasn't it? Didn't he go missing a couple years ago?" she asked.

"Yes. There was a search party and investigation and all that, but nothing turned up. He was a very dear friend of mine. I've come to ensure there's nothing more that can be done—for my own peace as much as anything."

"I see. I remember now, there was a whole article about it in the local paper. Wasn't he here to care for his sick brother? As I recall, he disappeared the morning after his brother's death, is that right?"

"Yes, that's right."

"Didn't he fly into the Everstorm?"

"So they say, which is why the whole thing doesn't sit right with me. The act is completely out of character for him."

"It is very strange, I've never heard of anyone flying into the Everstorm voluntarily. If you're trying to end things, it's far easier to wander off the side of an island. I'm sorry to hear they never found him, for your and his family's sake as much as for his. I wish I could be of more help," Rose apologized.

"You've been most helpful," Roy assured her. "I'll go to the News House later today and see if I can dig up a copy of that article from their archives."

"Yes, that sounds like a good start. And is that inquiry what brought you to the Treasure Trove, or is there something else I can help you with?" Rose asked.

"I was hoping for both a visit and one of your treasures," Roy admitted.

"How wonderful! What sort of treasure are you looking for?"

"My friend here needs a coin purse. I was wondering if you happen to have any Dreg Pouches on hand?"

The woman looked at Felix as if noticing him for the first time.

"By Kismet, you know, I do. Only just came in yesterday, haven't even put it out yet. Wait here, I'll fetch it from the back." Rose disappeared behind the curtain.

"You're in luck, kid," Roy told Felix.

"Why's that?"

"Dreg Pouches are a rarity, we're lucky to find one."

"And a Dreg Pouch is…?" Felix asked.

Roy smiled. "The solution to storing your coin."

"Great." Felix had never heard of such a thing, but if it gave him a better solution for his savings than the privy's pipework on the airship, he was very interested to know what it was.

While they waited, Felix studied the lantern beside him. The thing was crawling with firebeetles. Only, they weren't the common black ones he was used to—there were several different varieties mixed together, all glowing brightly with shiny metallic exoskeletons in red, purple, gold, blue, and green. Curious, he watched them for several minutes as they crawled along the glass, until Rose returned holding a small black pouch on a long leather cord.

"Here it is!" she announced triumphantly and handed it to Felix.

Felix took the pouch and turned it over. It was a simple design, made of soft shiny leather the length of his thumb and double its width. Felix was completely confounded; the pouch was even smaller than his current coin pouch was. He couldn't see how it could be of any use at all.

"Came from a man who needed coin to cover a debt at the gambling house," Rose told them. "He said he didn't need it anymore because his debt was so great, his life would be over before he had anything to put back into it. Seems to be the way I obtain most of my merchandise these days. It's a sad state of affairs, really. Some of the people here spend their lives indulging themselves on their family's inheritance. Too proud to work, now their inheritance is drying up and they're finding they no longer have the option to work because they're unskilled and too old to be hired. They'll never admit it though—they're too proud for that too. They'd rather protect their egos and hide their growing poverty by selling their family heirlooms to me. Unfortunately, there are less and less who want to buy them."

"I find that hard to believe, with the auctions still going strong. There's nothing there that's better than what you have in your collection," Roy said.

Rose smiled. "The auctions are a social spectacle. People go to shake their tail feathers at one another like a bunch of peacocks. And the younger folk don't seem to be interested in the trinkets from days past. It's all about steam technology these days. I don't mind. As you know, I only acquired this shop because my late husband—Stars rest his soul—told me I had collected enough objects to start a bloody store and that he wouldn't permit me to buy any more unless I sold some off. Of course I thought the idea was brilliant and immediately started Treasure Trove Antiques. Stars, was he surprised. Hehe, he never expected I'd actually do it, and there wasn't a thing he could say about it because he was the one who suggested it. I've never run this place for the coin. This shop is my pride and joy. Nothing makes me happier than collecting treasures and surrounding myself with them—must have dragon's blood in me, eh?" Rose jested with a cheeky smile and a wink at Felix.

"I knew that if we were to find a Dreg Pouch anywhere, it would be here," Roy said.

"Well, as I said, it only just came in yesterday. If you had been here any sooner, you would've missed it. The Stars must have delivered it just for you, young lad," she told Felix.

"Great." He studied the pouch perplexed. "Excuse my naïvety, but what's it used for?"

Roy smiled and held his hand out for it. Felix handed it to him and Roy pulled out his own coin purse and took out a handful of coins. He funnelled them into the Dreg Pouch, and Felix was surprised to see that as soon as they fell in, it seemed as though they completely disappeared. They didn't make a single bulge in the leather—in fact, it looked like there was nothing in the pouch at all. Roy handed the pouch back to Felix. He studied it suspiciously. There was no weight to it. He pinched and rubbed the two sides together and felt only thin pieces of leather with nothing between.

He opened the pouch and looked in it—nothing but darkness. He shook it upside down over his hand. It was empty. Felix immediately felt like a proper fool. Having grown up with Gwena, he was no stranger to magic tricks. Dealing in the trade of deception himself, he felt he should've known how this one was done—but for the life of him, he didn't.

"Alright, you've had your fun. What did you do with it?"

Rose clapped her hands in delight. "Someone who can still appreciate the brilliance of the alchemists' creations!"

"It's an enchanted object?" Felix queried with renewed interest.

"Yes, one of the most useful in my opinion. The coin can only be retrieved by the person who puts it in," Rose explained.

Roy took the pouch back and turned it over into his hand, immediately all the coins fell out onto his palm. He gave the coins and the pouch to Felix.

"Try it for yourself," he invited.

Felix dropped the coins into the pouch. It still felt and looked completely empty, but when he turned it over into his hand, all the coins fell out.

"Huh, that's brilliant!" Felix exclaimed in fascination.

"Now, put the coins in once more," Roy directed, and Felix did so.

"This time, instead of tipping out the whole thing, think of the coin from the pouch you wish to retrieve."

"Alright." Felix thought of the rose wagon.

"Now, reach into the pouch."

Felix reached in and immediately he felt the rose wagon in his fingers.

"Incredible!" he laughed.

"There's more," Roy proclaimed, and put the black leather cord around Felix's neck. The pouch hung low at his chest, just under his shirt's neckline.

"It's made to hang out of view away from opportunists, and every part of its structure is indestructible."

Roy pulled out a pocketknife and tried to cut the cord. The knife had no effect.

"There's only one drawback to having a Dreg Pouch."

"What's that?" Felix asked.

"Its value added with the value it carries makes it a temptation for thieves. Dishonest men aware of their existence search for them—so keep it out of sight," Roy advised.

*I bet they do,* Felix thought. If he'd known about Dreg Pouches sooner, he would've been searching for them too.

"I recommend never using this one in the open. Use it to stock your regular coin purse with what you need before your outings, and always in private. You can assign your Dreg Pouch to one other person. They'll be the only one who'll be able to access your coin in your absence. I recommend doing this as soon as possible. Otherwise, if something happens to you, everything in there will become accessible to the first person who finds it."

"Brilliant! I'll take it," Felix declared eagerly.

"Serendipity must favor you, young man. These are such useful things, and like all enchanted objects, there's only a limited number of them. They're hardly ever seen in circulation," Rose told him.

"Serendipity happens to be a friend of mine," Felix remarked with a wink and a charming grin.

The old woman cackled, "I like this one, you must be a heartbreaker, lad—with a smile like that. If only I were sixty years younger." Then she added, "I used to be a real looker, you know."

Felix smiled, "I don't doubt it."

Rose patted him on the cheek.

"Is there anything else in particular I can do for you gentlemen?"

Felix wanted to say yes. He could've spent the rest of the day in Treasure Trove Antiques watching demonstrations of the enchanted objects' abilities. He wanted to see every one in the store. He'd been hunting for them his entire life, and here was a shop full. But before he could say anything, Roy said, "That's all for now. We best keep moving. Thank you, Rose—you and your shop are a treasure."

"Oh, you're sweet. I'll ring this up for you then."

Rose carried the pouch to the register, and Felix and Roy waited patiently as she wrote on a small card and wrapped it up carefully with the Dreg Pouch in gold tissue paper. "Where are you two heading next?"

"Up top. James has never seen the Diamond City," Roy said.

"Lovely! It's changed a lot since you were last here. I dare say it'll be a sight for you both."

"Really, how so?"

"They've put up half a dozen Sky Gardens for growing local produce. Sky View is almost completely self-sufficient now. Only specialty items are still imported."

"Fresh produce? How on Equillian are they getting the soil? There certainly isn't enough topsoil to take from any of the islands, and I can't imagine anyone here starting a business in composting," Roy remarked.

"That's just it, they don't use any soil," Rose explained.

"No soil?"

"None whatsoever. They say their system provides everything the plants need through a nutrient cold-steam solution. It's quite fascinating really—they offer tours if you're interested. I highly recommend it."

"Are they run with mechanical workers?" Roy asked.

"They don't need any workers. The whole operation is completely automated with their fancy steam technology. It's the modern age, my dear, the world is changing."

"Interesting. We'll have to have a look. Any other news I've missed?" Roy inquired.

"Let me think…Oh yes, you'll probably encounter some silly nonsense about a revolution."

"A revolution?" Roy asked in surprise.

"Yes, yes. Just some youth trying to stir things up. It's all a load of nonsense if you ask me, but they're sure making a lot of noise about it. You know how the young ones are, always wanting to rebel against the old system, thinking they can do everything better. Ha! Good luck to them, I say. Isn't it funny, the naïvety of youth makes us believe we know everything, and then when we actually live long enough to experience a thing or two we realize we hardly know anything at all. Hehe, they'll learn soon enough. I just hope for their sake they don't get what they're asking for in the meantime," Rose chuckled, and began punching numbers on the large coin register.

"That will be twenty-five duckets, my dear," she said.

"Twenty-five duck…" Felix started, and then quickly held his tongue. He completely underestimated the expense of everything in Sky View. Twenty-five duckets was more than he'd brought with him, it was more than he thought he'd need for his entire trip to Sky View, but he shouldn't have been so surprised—enchanted objects were highly valuable collectables no matter where you were. The fact he could afford one at all was a blessing in itself, and Rose was probably giving him a friendly discount. Twenty-five duckets was incredibly reasonable considering, and the Dreg Pouch was worth every cwip.

Felix took out his coin purse and poured its contents out on the table.

"Bloody Luckless, I'm ten short."

Luckless was one of the Thrixing stars. He was Lady Luck's brother and her opposite in every way, known for pleasurably foiling his sister's plans, especially when someone was celebrating a win she'd brought them. Those who were superstitious knocked on wood to keep him at bay.

"Not to worry, sport, I'll lend you the rest," Roy said, and gave another ten duckets to Rose.

"Thanks," Felix said in relief.

Rose handed over the neatly wrapped parcel to Felix. "It's all yours, darling. I've included an instruction card for its care and use. But if you have any questions, you can stop by anytime."

"Thank you," Felix returned with his charming grin.

"I'm thrilled it's found a good home." She smiled and patted his hand.

"Thanks, Rose. As always, it's been a pleasure to see you," Roy said.

"It's great to see you too, my dear. Good luck finding your friend. You two enjoy the rest of your day. And don't be strangers now, come back and visit soon!"

Felix followed Roy back through the shopping center to the elevator. They stepped inside and Roy pushed the button for the top level. The elevator jolted and within moments the glass half was displaying an open view of the Diamond City. It was breathtaking. Slim white and cream stone buildings with large glass windows towered above and around them. The building's exteriors were decorated with prismatic rays from the suncatchers in their spires and hanging gardens that hung down their sides in long strips of thriving green dotted with vibrant flowers. Amongst them were two tall round towers made completely of glass. They looked like vertical greenhouses with level upon level of lush gardens. In between the buildings were pedestrian pathways made with a light palette of polished stone and elegantly decorated with plant and water features. Marble statues of dragons were intermittently placed throughout the city in dramatic or majestic poses, each one depicting a different breed. Some were in the shapes of sleeping dragons lying on the edges of the stone pathway with benches carved into their backs. Ceramic Pet Dragons climbed up the sides of buildings or sat as gargoyles on the rooftops. Metal ones were climbing up or wrapped around the elegant Everfire lampposts. The streets were crowded with people bustling from one place to another. Some of them wore oxygen masks like the one Roy had shown Felix on the airship, though much more ornate, almost fashionable. Many people adorned live Pet Dragons perched on their shoulders like exotic birds.

"Is it always this crowded?" Felix asked as they stepped out of the elevator.

"No. A good majority of the people here will be visiting for the Derby. It's Sky View's biggest event of the year. There will be festivities all week," Roy said.

Felix followed him through the hustle and bustle down the stone pathway. It was a beautiful sunny day with a clear blue sky. There was still a chill in the air that whispered of winter, but it was nothing compared with the cold winter days in Westdock. Bakeries and teahouses lined the walkway. Mechanical waiters served richly clad clientele occupying painted baroque metal tables and chairs in front of the establishments. Soon, Felix and Roy reached the city's center. It was a large diamond-shaped plaza with a giant, extravagant water feature at its heart. The decorative fountain featured a magnificent statue of the dragon constellation, Drago. The dragon was one of the guardian constellations, known as a great protector and guide, offering strength and wisdom when needed—as well as the Time Keeper for the fifteenth hour. The statue showed Drago holding a giant seven-pointed star in his claws and rearing his head back while a jetstream of water sprayed from his gaping jaws. Next to the fountain a young man was standing on an upside-down wooden box giving an impassioned speech to a crowd of young aristocrats. Roy and Felix joined the crowd to hear what he was saying.

"…Our dragons won Lord Balthazar's war. We cleared the way for him to unite the world under his supreme leadership, and how did he repay us? By killing our dragons, the very same ones that brought him his victory! And ever since Equillian has been united, we've been paying taxes to fund the mainland. Our coin paves their streets, builds their schools, and fills the pockets of Lord Balthazar and the other nobles. Lucky for some, but what about the rest of us? Our families built the backbone of Sky View's economy and now are pouring our inheritance into a place we've never even seen. What do we get in return? Nothing! If we claim our independence, then we can breed any dragons we choose and our coin will stay here to pave our streets, to build our schools, and to better our precinct! Spark the revolution!"

"Spark the revolution!" the young mob echoed back enthusiastically.

Two officers dressed in white and gold uniforms pushed through the assemblage.

"Alright, that's enough! Move along now. Young man, you're under arrest for disturbing the peace."

The young man cooperated, stepping down from his box and allowing the officers to usher him out of the plaza. The onlookers booed the authorities as they dispersed.

"Must be the revolution Rose was talking about," Felix observed, as they moved with the throng.

Roy furrowed his brow. "I can only presume."

"I have to hand it to him, he knows how to work up a crowd."

"He's a fool. He doesn't have a clue what he's talking about, and clearly too naïve to realize the damage he can do. Everyone in Sky View agreed the ban on War Dragons was necessary. They were a ferocious breed that was difficult to control. Keeping them around after the war would've been madness. Balthazar compensated the breeders generously for every dragon lost. Everyone but The East understood the benefit in being united under one banner. And look at The East now, reduced to ashes of its former glory, filled with society's worst, ruled by thieves and cutthroats," Roy scoffed.

"Knows nothing and thinks he knows everything—the man has a promising future as a noble," Felix jested.

Roy snorted. "A dangerous combination when rallying a movement. If you're going to have a voice, you need to be careful how you use it. Guaranteed these young folk behind it all are pouring their inheritance into things other than taxes, which is the real reason behind their family's emptying coffers. This is the problem with the youth today—they feel entitled to what they haven't earned. If they were willing to work, they wouldn't need to be concerned about their dwindling allowance."

"Ah, the complications of upper-class problems," Felix muttered.

"I beg your pardon?"

"I said, shall we check out the Tower Gardens?" Felix said.

Roy looked up at the tall glass towers. "Yes, good idea. I must admit, I'm curious how they work."

Felix and Roy walked down the walkway together towards the largest garden tower they could see. On the way Felix saw several lampposts with posters on them saying *Spark the Revolution!* in large bold letters. Mechanical city workers were taking them down and washing away the evidence of their existence. Felix imagined the city would be eager for them to be gone before tomorrow's race, especially if Lord Balthazar himself was in town. Any evidence of civil unrest could be enough to disturb Equillian's hard-earned peace.

~ 124 ~

# THE WILDSINGER'S CLUB

Gwena followed Bonnie down a side alley to a shop tucked in a corner off the main street. The sign above it read *The Apothecary* in large bold print, and below those words in small, printed cursive it read *choose your poison*. The shop was closed and only dimly lit by an Everfire lamp above the door. There was a man standing outside it wearing a beige trench coat and brown fedora, smoking a puff-stick.

"Evenin', Charles," Bonnie greeted.

The man nodded to her. "Evening, Bonnie." And he opened the door to the apothecary for them.

"Thank ya kindly."

Bonnie stepped into the dark shop and Gwena followed cautiously.

"You two cats have fun," Charles called after them, and closed the door behind.

⌒

The shop was softly lit by four Everfire lamps in the corners. There was a pool of light on the floor, pouring in from the street lanterns outside the large display window. Long shadows cascaded across the polished wood floorboards from the dried herbs hanging in the window. The place was meticulously clean and organized. In the back was a long counter with shelving built into the wall behind it, stretching from the floor to the ceiling, stocked with jars and bottles filled with powders, liquids, and herbs of every hue. There were several large bulbous glass contraptions in the corner making spagyrics; these were filled with clear yellow liquid and dried flowers. And the ceiling was almost completely covered with flowers and herbs hanging upside down for drying. Though the place was empty, Gwena could hear the faint lull of music, laughter, and murmuring conversation. "Where's that coming from?" she asked.

Bonnie smiled. "Follow me."

She led Gwena down a short corridor that ended at a wall covered in shelving filled with small built-in wooden drawers, each labeled with a copperplate stating the name of a different herb. Bonnie put both hands on the shelf and pushed. The whole wall swung open like a door. Gwena gasped in surprise. Behind the secret entrance was a cocktail lounge dimly lit with firebeetle lanterns and bustling with people. Bonnie held the door open for Gwena. To her left was a long bar with a handsome bartender polishing drinking glasses to a sheen. He was wearing a white collared shirt with the sleeves rolled up, adorned with red suspenders. A woman was chatting with him, leaning seductively over the counter while twirling a long string of pearls between her fingers. Behind the bartender was a stretch of mirrored shelves stocked full with spirits of every kind, each one backlit with small colored glass vials of Everfire. To Gwena's right was a row of tables for two running along the wall. Instead of chairs, on either side of each table was a booth big enough for one, cushioned with red velvet upholstery. The small tables were dimly lit with little firebeetle lanterns made of red glass that gave off a soft ruby glow. Every table was filled with patrons in deep conversation over elaborate cocktails. At the back of the lounge was a wooden half-circle dance floor in front of a small stage. A tall dark woman in a red dress was singing entrancingly to the room.

"This place is amazing," Gwena exclaimed, as she followed Bonnie through the crowd.

"Wait tell ya see where we're goin'."

"You mean this isn't it?" Gwena asked, but her question was lost in the noise around them. Gwena weaved her way between the guests to keep up with Bonnie, and soon they came to a discreet side door. Bonnie went through it, and Gwena followed her out into a small outdoor courtyard. The square space was enclosed with a high wall of hedges and paved with cobblestones. In the center of the courtyard was a slender Everfire lamppost encircled by ornate metal fencing. A man stood casually beside it smoking a puff-stick. The man was dressed similarly to the one out the front of The Apothecary—a long grey trench coat and a grey fedora.

"Evenin', Eric," Bonnie greeted.

"Hiya, Bonnie." The man eyed Gwena suspiciously. "She with you?"

"Yes, sir. Slow night?"

"Always is on Twinsdays."

Bonnie pulled a magazine out from the inside of her jacket. "I got somethin' fer ya, might 'elp pass the time."

"Hey, *Pop Steam-Tech!*" he exclaimed, "This the latest issue?"

"Sure is."

"You're a star, Bonnie, thank you," he said gratefully, taking the magazine in hand and stepping aside as he flipped through pages showing Equillian's latest steam-powered gizmos.

Bonnie switched a latch on the ornamental fencing and a section swung open like a gate. She turned to Gwena. "Ya comin'?"

"Ye-es," Gwena answered hesitantly.

She felt rather ridiculous following Bonnie into the small space for no apparent reason, but she couldn't see much of an alternative. Bonnie closed the gate behind them and reached up towards the lamppost where there was a small metal-cast bird woven into the rest of the decorative framework. She turned it upside down and suddenly there was a jolt in the ground. Gwena grabbed hold of the lamppost in surprise as the circle of cobblestones they stood on dropped down from under their feet, descending around the pole. She let go of the post as soon as she realized it wasn't moving with them, and reached out for the metal fencing—but it was no longer there. Within moments the courtyard was gone, and they were enveloped in darkness. Gwena gasped.

"Don't worry, ya can't fall out," Bonnie assured her, and pulled out an Everfire torch—a glass ball just smaller than her fist, filled with Everfire. Bonnie hung it on a hook above them, and the small light lit the space around them. They were travelling inside a glass elevator that was plummeting downward. Gwena couldn't see anything around them but a faint glow far in the distance below.

"It's quite the surprise the first time. But ye'll get used ta it."

"Where are we going?" Gwena asked.

"'Ave ya ever 'eard o' the original alchemists, Bartleby an' 'aplo?"

"Aren't they the ones who invented enchanted objects and created The Seven Wonders of Equillian?"

"Precisely. What most people don't know is that 'aplo also created Seven Underground Wonders. Secret places known only ta a select few. Places that 'ave remained open an' active even after the ban—because they aren't even known by the E.O.C.A."

"And that's where we're going? To one of the original alchemists' secret wonders?"

"That's right. Speakin' o' which, I should probably state the disclaimer now—if ya tell anyone about this place, I'll 'ave ta kill ya," Bonnie stated candidly.

Gwena laughed nervously before realizing Bonnie was deadly serious, "Right. Got it."

Shortly after that they were surrounded by glowing light. Bonnie pocketed her Everfire torch and Gwena could see that the yellow-green glow was coming from a thick layer of phosphorescent lichen growing up steep rocky walls of a gigantic underground cavern. The elevator platform reached the rocky floor and came to a gentle halt inside an ornate metal cage. There was a handsome doorman standing outside in a gold uniform who opened the door for them.

"Good evening, Bonnie," he greeted.

"Evenin', James."

The man tipped his hat to them, "Have a good night, eh?"

"An' ya as well, mate," Bonnie returned, motioning to Gwena to follow her.

Gwena stepped out onto a gold stone path that stretched away from the elevator into the heart of the gigantic cave. The path was lit by tall filigreed Everfire lampposts outlining it as it curved to the left out of sight. Rock gardens of giant crystals lined either side. Suddenly a glowing oval the size of a tennis ball flew over Gwena's head. She ducked in surprise. "What was that?!"

"A Torch-Bat," Bonnie said.

Gwenna looked up and saw a whole group of them clustered upside down along a stalactite. Large bats with glowing bellies.

"They won't hurt ya," Bonnie assured her. "They help ta light up the place."

Gwenna nodded warily, keeping one eye on the strange creatures while continuing down the path. To their right a train track stretched away into darkness. A train was there, purring contentedly, but no steam rose from its stack. It wasn't as large as the Equillian Express, but it was just as beautiful. Painted like the night sky, with a mesmerizing mural of realistic stars and colorful birds. It looked as though it was brand-new.

Bonnie caught Gwena staring at it. "She's a beauty, ain't she? The underground line. It travels between 'ere an' Port Trinity."

"How does it run? There isn't any steam!"

"It's enchanted. The last one runnin' o' its kind."

"An enchanted train line? There are still tracks in Westdock from the one that used to run between The Seven Wonders. Does this one run between the underground Wonders?" Gwena asked.

"So it does. Come, we're goin' this way," Bonnie directed, and headed down the gold pathway.

Gwena turned from the train and followed her. As they turned the corner Gwena's eyes widened in wonder—there at the end of the walkway was a magnificent building. It towered high with wings that spread out on either side. There was a huge sign above it made of large metal letters, each lit by an outline of glass globes filled with Everfire.

"The Wildsinger's Club," Gwena read aloud, staring up at it.

Bonnie stopped beside her as Gwena soaked it in.

"Like the birds?" Gwena asked.

"Aye." Bonnie proceeded towards the building and Gwena quickly followed after.

Wildsingers were exceptionally beautiful and rare exotic birds. No two were exactly alike. They all displayed rich, vibrant colors. One was documented to have wings of bright turquoise and vibrant purple over a black body and gold circles around its eyes. Another had red, orange, and purple plumage with long bright yellow tail feathers. A woman had made it her life's work to document seven hundred of them in an illustrated book, but it was impossible to document them all—every one was different. No matter their color, however, they all shared the unique quality which gave them their name—they were called Wildsingers because when wild, their melody was the most entrancing of any bird, even more than the nightingale or the Silver Tongue. But they transformed to something common when caged. If caught, their singing ceased entirely, and they wouldn't make a single melodic sound until freed. Moreover, their impressive bright plumage lost its color. Within a week of being held in captivity, their feathers faded to shades of grey. Their beauty couldn't even be preserved after death. For when their feathers fell or the bird died, they drained of color like a withering flower. They were the beauty that could only be admired and enjoyed in the wild, never caught or preserved in any way other than photographs, paintings, illustrations, poetry, and songs. Sometimes a person was referred to as a Wildsinger—a wild spirit admired and desired by many, but one who couldn't be contained without a sort of transformation that domesticated their charm—making them lose what made them so attractive in the first place.

As they approached the entrance to the impressive building, Gwena could hear music coming from inside. It was an upbeat melody that filled her with excitement and anticipation. Two doormen opened the large double doors and welcomed Gwena and Bonnie inside with a tip of their hats. Just inside was an extravagant entryway of yellow and white marble, with a huge spotless mirror lining one wall and a grand chandelier above. There was another man dressed in the same smart gold uniform who offered to take their coats. Bonnie handed over her trench coat and Gwena gave up her travelling cloak. At the end of the entryway was another door. Beside it was a high desk with a beautiful woman standing behind it and filing her nails.

"Hiya, Bonnie," she said without looking up.

"Evenin', Carol." Bonnie stepped through the next doorway and ushered Gwena inside. Gwena stopped in awe to take it all in. The space in front of her was magnificent, a huge round room with Blush Oak floors. Beautiful polished wood pillars with gold accents surrounded the room, and long velvet drapes hung down the walls between them. There was a large stage outlined with matching velvet curtains facing an expansive dance floor. Next to it was a swanky cocktail bar, and an elaborate flight of stairs spiralled up one side to a second-story balcony that ran the room's circumference. The high domed ceiling was made of glass; beyond it was a canopy of trees bathed in glowing silver moonlight—Gwena couldn't figure out how that was possible, considering the structure was in a dark cavern, then she reminded herself the place was one of the alchemists' Wonders.

There were two woman with the longest legs Gwena had ever seen leaning over the balcony. The bottom floor was being cleaned by maids busy dusting and polishing. The place was dimly lit with Everfire lanterns made with red glass, giving the place an orangey-red glow like the ones in the speakeasy behind The Apothecary.

"Come on, I'll show ya around," Bonnie said, gently guiding Gwena forward.

"What is this place? Why is it hidden away?" Gwena asked.

"It's a club. Very exclusive. Haplo designed it as a refuge fer Wildsingers in the limelight—well-known people who need a place where they can roam free an' show their true colors away from the public eye," Bonnie expounded as she brought Gwena to the stage. "Every night there's live music and shows 'ere. We've got some o' the best talent in the 'eartland," she told her, and led Gwena to the cocktail bar.

"Ya won't find a smoother cocktail in Equillian than the ones Ramone makes. 'e'll be on later. Drinks are on the 'ouse fer employees. One o' the perks o' workin' 'ere."

Then Bonnie beckoned Gwena to follow her down a corridor that branched off from the room, "Come on, I'll introduce ya ta Madam Rouge."

Gwena followed her down the hallway. There were expansive fish tanks built into the walls on either side. Vivid colorful sea life flourished inside them. She slowed down to see a blue-ringed octopus pull an arm behind bright orange coral.

At the end of the corridor was a heavy oak door with a brass plaque engraved, *Madam Rouge—Headmistress.*

Bonnie knocked lightly.

"Who is it?" a woman's voice bellowed from the other side.

"Bonnie. I've come with a potential replacement fer Foible."

The door cracked open and a tall, solidly built woman stuck her head out. She had short red curly hair and fair skin with grey eyes.

"Thank the Stars! Where are they?" the woman demanded.

Bonnie cleared her throat. "Gwena, meet Madam Rouge—the club's Dame-mother an' overseer. Rouge, this be Gwena—she's an experienced tailor from Westdock. She's agreed ta fill the position—at least temporarily."

Madam Rouge looked down at Gwena. "Her? She's hardly left her cradle!"

"'er appearance does 'ave the benefit o' youth, but don't let that deceive ya, she's nineteen, and 'er work be well renowned. She was even commissioned ta make a prop fer Madam Pomphrey when her show passed through," Bonnie professed.

"Is that right?" the large woman asked skeptically.

Gwena nodded. "Yes, when she came to Westdock with The Travelling Curiosities."

"Quite frankly, with Pomphrey's show goin' up at the end o' next week, we're lucky ta 'ave found 'er," Bonnie said.

"Hmmm, if she's been approved by Pomphrey that *is* half the battle won. You're from Westdock, you say?"

"Yes."

The large woman looked Gwena up and down. "I can't pay you much. You can have free room and board and I'll give you a wagon a week. But don't go expecting anything more."

"Sounds perfectly reasonable—" Gwena started, but Bonnie touched her elbow lightly, and Gwena took the cue to hold her tongue.

"Come on, Rouge. Ya paid Foible three times as much fer—well, let's be honest, far less than what she'll be expected ta do. She'll take no less than two wagons with the room an' board. She's worth far more, but she'll take less as a startin' wage just fer givin' her the chance," Bonnie insisted.

Madam Rouge narrowed her eyes. "Fine. Two wagons a week," she conceded, "but keep in mind, I'm only hiring her on a trial basis. If for any reason I'm dissatisfied with her or her work, her trial will be terminated and she'll be expected to leave immediately."

"Of course," Gwena and Bonnie replied together.

"And she can't wear that. If she's working here, I want her in something respectable," Rouge demanded.

"I'll take 'er shoppin' tamarra," Bonnie promised.

Rouge crossed her arms. "Alright then. Show her to her room." She handed Bonnie a key. "And Bonnie, I'm holding you responsible for her."

Bonnie smiled curtly. "O' course, Madam."

And with that, Madam Rouge disappeared back into her room and shut the door.

Bonnie turned to Gwena, "Congratulations, ya got the job!"

"Thank you!" Gwena exclaimed enthusiastically. Two wagons a week was far more than she'd ever earned before. Still, there was one thing that did concern her, "though...I'm not really nineteen," she confessed.

Bonnie's eyes gleamed. "Course yer not. Come on, I'll show ya ta yer room."

Bonnie led Gwena back to the main stage and up the stairs to the second-floor balcony. On the opposite side of the bannister were rows and rows of colorful doors, all with a different brass symbol on them. One had a seashell and another, a flame. Another had a sailboat, another a symbol of the moon, and another a rose. On and on they went until Bonnie stopped outside one at the very end with a yellow door and a picture of a needle stuck into a spool of thread.

"Hopefully the cleaners 'ave already been through," Bonnie said, opening the door for Gwena.

She stepped inside. It was a small room, with nothing but a neatly made bed, a bedside table, a wardrobe, a humble lavatory connecting en suite and a open window with a view of the ocean and the sound of crashing waves.

"It's not much, but at least it's somethin'," Bonnie remarked.

"It's more than I need. Thank you," Gwena returned earnestly, walking to the window, her eyes widening in wonder at the view of the seashore from atop the abandoned enchanted Star Temple in Westdock. It was one of her favorite places in the whole world. She could smell the sea air and see a flock of pelicans flying overhead. It felt like she was transported straight back there, back home.

"How is this view even possible?"

Bonnie shrugged. "The place be enchanted. The view changes ta a place o' meanin' an' comfort ta whomever be lodgin' in it," she said, as if that was a perfectly logical explanation. "I'll let ya settle in. The club opens at The DreamWeavers Hour. A few o' us will be gettin' together tonight fer a monthly meetup, ya should join us."

"Alright, where is it?"

"We meet downstairs at the main stage. Come join us once yer settled in."

"Thanks, I will then. And Bonnie, thank you for everything you've done for me tonight. I don't even want to think about where I'd be without you."

Bonnie shrugged, "Then don't. I don't think it could 'ave 'appened any other way—the Stars clearly 'ad a plan in store. Besides, I think we need ya more than ya need us. See ya soon, eh?"

"Yes, see you soon!" Gwena returned, and Bonnie left to let her settle in.

Gwena closed the door and looked around the room and smiled. It might've been small, but it was all hers—and the freedom of that elated her far beyond anything a royal suite ever could. She put down her travelling bag and opened the wardrobe. Gwena gasped in surprise—beyond the wardrobe's doors was another room entirely. It was a tailor's dream. There was a sewing table with a pedal sewing machine, two adjustable sewing mannequins, magnifying lenses on extendable arms, and shelving that covered the walls from floor to ceiling with every sewing tool and material a tailor could desire.

Gwena walked down the grand stairway of The Wildsinger's Club to the main stage. There were eight people loitering around the dance floor. They all looked like they were in their early to mid-twenties. A couple chairs over from Bonnie was a tall lean woman with dark skin and impressively long legs. She was chewing pink bubblegum and blowing balloon-sized bubbles, while getting a shoulder massage from Rafael — the man Gwena had met at the pie stall earlier that evening.

There was a woman lounging on the floor next to them wearing a low-cut dress that was open at the back. She had alabaster skin that contrasted starkly against her pitch-black hair and matching lipstick. Her bare back was almost completely covered with a giant tattoo of a Wildsinger.

Standing next to her was a man with blue eyes and short blond hair neatly combed to one side. He was talking animatedly to a woman with chin-length blond curls. Another man with a kind face and dark brown hair sat off to the side with a guitar in his lap, plucking skillfully at the strings. In the corner a handsome man with caramel skin and short curly hair straddled a chair back to front watching Gwena curiously. He had an intriguing and mysterious allure that caught Gwena off guard.

"Who are you?" one of the women asked Gwena.

Gwena opened her mouth to answer the question when Bonnie stepped up beside her.

"This be our new tailor, Gwena. Gwena, this be *The Not Just a Pretty Face Club*," Bonnie announced, fanning out her arm to include everyone in the room.

"Hi," Gwena greeted, waving awkwardly.

Everyone there turned and stared at her, their eyes filled with questions, as if they didn't quite believe what Bonnie had just told them and were wondering what she was doing there. Bonnie motioned for Gwena to sit next to her. Gwena did, yet she couldn't help but feel intimidated. Everyone there was older and visually flawless and carried themselves with complete confidence. Gwena couldn't even pretend to have that kind of self-confidence.

The man with slick blond hair and blue eyes walked up onto the stage. "Shall we begin?" he asked the group.

"We're not getting any younger!" Rafael heckled.

The man on stage smiled and nodded, then spread out his arms theatrically. "Good evening my favorite Ladles and Jelly-spoons! Thank you for being here tonight for our *Not Just a Pretty Face* monthly meetup. As usual, I've made a list by drawing your names at random for the lineup. I'll leave it on a chair if anyone wants to look ahead, otherwise you can wait until your name's called. I look forward to seeing what everyone's prepared for us this time. First up, Lady Mirabella!" the man announced enthusiastically and jumped off the stage.

Gwena leaned over and whispered to Bonnie, "What kind of meetup is this?"

"It's ta encourage each other ta continue workin' on our ambitions beyond the club—an' remind one another we're more than what we do 'ere. We meet up once a month ta share what we've been workin' on, an' ta keep each other accountable fer movin' forward towards our true aspirations."

The woman with the Wildsinger tattoo walked onto the stage. Her black hair hung halfway down the open back of her dress. In her hand she carried a long thin metal sword.

"That's Mirabella, she's known as *The Black Rose* around 'ere. She sings from a hangin' moon over the stage some nights—dark, deep ballads that move the soul. But 'er true passion be sword swallowin'," Bonnie explained.

"Oh, I see," Gwena said, watching the stage with anticipation.

Mirabella looked out at the small audience with an air of mystery. She held the thin sword above her head dramatically, then threw back her head and impossibly, slowly lowered the weapon into her mouth until the hilt was resting against her lips. The room was silent—no one dared move, let alone breathe. After several nerve-racking moments, Mirabella pulled the sword back up. Gwena and the small group clapped and whistled enthusiastically. Mirabella smiled ever so slightly and walked off the stage.

"How does she ensure she doesn't slice herself open?" Gwena asked Bonnie.

"I don't think she can fully ensure that. It's what makes the feat so impressive."

Gwena gulped.

The host jumped back up onto the stage. "Well done, Mirabella! That was oddly arousing and equally intimidating," he proclaimed. "Next up is Rafael!"

Bonnie leaned towards Gwena. "The one presentin' be Fin. He hosts most o' the shows at the club, but his true passion be actin'. An' Rafael's a dancer an' piano player at the club, but he's more interested in comedy an' hat manipulation."

Rafael walked onto the stage and rolled up his sleeves. Then he took off his bowler hat and looked at it. The hat gave him an encouraging nod.

"Me and my hat have a little something we've been working on that we want to show you tonight," Rafael announced to the audience. He turned back to the hat. "You ready?" The hat nodded twice.

"Good." Rafael twiddled the hat in his fingers—spinning it up onto his head. As soon as it was there, the hat popped off out in front of him. Rafael caught it with an expression of embarrassed concern and tried again. But again the hat popped off his head. The audience laughed.

Rafael confronted the hat out of the corner of his mouth, "What are you doing? This isn't what we planned." He smiled nervously to the audience before trying once more. Again the hat popped off his head.

"Get yourself together!" Rafael demanded. He remembered his spectators and plastered on a grin, laughing uneasily as he tried to put the hat on a final time. Again, it jumped off his head. Rafael held the hat out in front of him. "Is this because of what happened last night?" he asked sternly. The hat nodded.

"I told you I was sorry. Do I have to say it again?"

The hat nodded.

"I'm sorry. Now, can we get on with the show?"

The hat nodded, satisfied.

"But honestly, I never would've sat on you if you hadn't parked yourself on my favorite chair," Rafael muttered audibly as he put the hat back on his head. Immediately the hat popped off again, and everyone laughed. The hat rolled up one of Rafael's arms and down the other as if it had a will of its own. Rafael tried to control the rogue bowler without success.

"Well, if you're going to be like that," Rafael declared, and threw his hat on the piano bench behind him and sat on it, crossing his legs and arms defiantly. He waited a moment before asking, "Are you done?" Then he took his crushed, trembling hat out from under him. "Can we do our act now?"

The hat nodded slowly—still trembling. Rafael straightened out the hat. "Good." He tossed it up into the air and caught it, brim spinning on the palm of his hand. Balancing it expertly, Rafael tossed the hat to his other hand and caught it still spinning. Then he tossed it up into the air again, and the hat flipped several times before landing perfectly on Rafael's head. Rafael and the hat took a bow.

Everyone cheered.

"That was brilliant!" Gwena exclaimed in delight, clapping enthusiastically.

Rafael smiled and jumped off the stage.

The next woman in line was the one with short blond curls. She was a contortionist named Susie who wanted to be a singer. She passionately and skillfully performed a song that was a rendition of an old classic. Then the handsome man with the guitar played a beautiful piece he'd composed himself, plucking out the notes in a way Gwena never knew could be done on the instrument. According to Bonnie, his name was Guy and he played trumpet for the band at the club, but his real passion was classical guitar.

The black woman chewing bubblegum was named Violet, an aerial acrobat for the club. She performed a beautiful dance combining ballet and her own modern style. When it was Fin's turn, he performed a dramatic monologue with such presence that everyone was on the edge of their seat.

Bonnie went up next. She had Fin spin a large wheel interspersed with glass bottles while she stood on the opposite side of the stage with her pistols drawn. From there, she proceeded to shoot every single bottle while the wheel was in motion—each one bursting in a shower of glass, sending Fin ducking for cover.

"That was explosive! Remind me never to get on Bonnie's bad side," Fin jested to the audience in good humor. "Come on, Benji, you're up next!"

The man in the corner with the alluring mysterious air called back, "I'm sitting this one out."

"Boo!" the group jeered.

"No, you're not! You know the rules—everyone who comes has to participate," Fin asserted.

Benji smirked. "Yeah? What are you going to do about it?"

"I'll drag you up here if I have to!"

Benji laughed. "I haven't prepared anything!"

"That's your problem, not ours," Susie proclaimed.

Benji held up his hands defensively. "Alright, alright," he conceded, and pushed himself off his chair, hopping up onto the stage with the air of someone completely comfortable in his own skin. He looked at the instruments around him and turned his focus to a guitar resting on its stand and a grand piano in the center of the stage. He rubbed his hands together, looking from one to the other—trying to decide which to use.

"What does he do?" Gwena asked.

"A little o' everythin'. That's Benji— 'e's a walkin' contradiction. 'e encourages everyone 'ere ta pursue their true passions outside the club an' yet 'as no aspirations beyond it 'imself—even though 'e's one o' the most talented amongst us. 'e's a real romantic, highly sought after by the club's clientele, an' yet 'e doesn't believe in love," Bonnie concluded.

"If he has no aspirations beyond the club, then what's he doing in this group?" Gwena asked.

"That's a very good question. I've no idea," Bonnie admitted.

Benji decided on the piano and sat down at the bench. He ran his hands across the keys, feeling out a lively tune before beginning to play. It was an upbeat piece intermingling shades of light and dark. After playing several bars of it, Benji looked up to the ceiling as if searching for words, and then he began to sing in a silky baritone with perfect articulation.

*Welcome to the Pleasure Wherry.*
*Why don't you step in?*
*If you're looking for thrills,*
*I'll take you for a spin.*
*We'll tumble down falls and trip on adrenaline.*
*I'll show you the stars and paint your lips with a grin.*
*Just don't drink the water or be tempted to swim.*
*It's a dangerous elixir,*
*A mind-meddling venom.*
*A chemistry concoction spiked with misconception.*
*A hallucinogen—one of the Thrixer's potions.*
*An Elysium wine labeled Love's Sweet Poison.*

*Though the high is divine,*
*positively elating,*
*the withdrawals are torturously devastating.*

*If you decide to drink it,*
*you can't blame me.*
*Every high has its fee.*

*If you decide to drink it,*
*you can't blame me.*
*Every high has its fee,*
*Every high has its fee.*
*Despite my warning,*
*You've jumped straight in.*
*You're guzzling it down—drinking the toxin.*

*Now your vision is beginning to spin,*
*The effects take hold, filling you with delusion,*
*Whirling you in and out of confusion,*
*Now you're turning to me—blaming me for its deception?*
*I tried to tell you—it would bring you to ruin.*

*What were you expecting?*
*Did you think it would be fun?*
*Did you believe all the fiction—*
*Telling you love makes someone the one?*
*Now your heart is broken in too many pieces to mend.*
*I ask you—was it worth it, my friend?*

*It must've been, because at ride's end,*
*Everyone lines up again and again.*

*If you decide to drink it,*
*you can't blame me.*
*Every high has its fee.*

*If you decide to drink it,*
*you can't blame me.*
*Every high has its fee.*
*Every high has its fee.*

Benji concluded his song by playing the melody of the chorus line a final time. There was a hushed pause, and then everyone applauded. Rafael whistled.

Benji laughed. "I'll be here all week!" he announced, jumping off the stage.

"Did he just make that up?" Gwena asked in disbelief.

Bonnie smiled and nodded, "'e's got a real knack fer the craft."

Fin, the host of the evening, jumped back up onto the stage.

"Do us all a favor, Benji, next time at least pretend you worked hard on your piece, eh? Sheesh!" he said, and everyone laughed.

"Well, looks like that's everyone. What an impr—"

"Not everyone," Benji interjected. "What about the little bird?" he said, nodding towards Gwena.

Everyone looked at her. The color drained out of Gwena's face.

"She doesn't have to go up," Fin said.

"Why not? Rules are rules, right? Everyone here has to participate—isn't that what you just said?"

"It's her first night, Benji. Let her be," Sussie called out.

Gwena turned to Bonnie.

Bonnie shrugged, "It's yer call."

Gwena thought for a moment and then she stood from her chair. "It's alright, I'll go, I don't mind. I wouldn't want you to make an exception just for me," she said.

"Alright," Fin agreed hesitantly, "well, looks like we got one more, folks. What's your name again, love?"

"Gwena. Gwena Stently."

"Give a warm welcome to Gwena Stently!" Fin proclaimed.

Everyone clapped cordially.

Gwena walked up the steps onto the stage and Fin smiled at her encouragingly before stepping down. The small audience gave her their attention. Gwena could feel her palms beginning to sweat.

"Hi, I'm Gwena. As Bonnie said, I'm your new tailor. I've really enjoyed watching your performances. You're all incredibly talented," she commended nervously.

"Wait till you see us in the bedroom!" Rafael called out, inciting laughter and whistles from the others.

Gwena blushed. "I certainly don't have the skills you all do, but I've always had a fascination with magic."

She held up her right hand and waved it fluidly, saying, "the thrill and wonderment of seeing something appear from nothing," and suddenly a card appeared in her hand as if from nowhere. She turned the card over and showed it to the audience—the ace of hearts.

"How it can transform one thing into many," she said, and closed her hands over the card. When she took her top hand away, the card was reduced to a handful of small pieces. She threw them into the air and the card pieces fluttered up like confetti and then froze there in place, suspended as if time itself had come to a standstill.

"And make the impossible possible."

The entire room fell quiet, and everyone stared at the floating card pieces in disbelief. Gwena walked over to the card fragments and plucked one out of the air and studied it. Then she collected the rest, scooping them all into her hands. She now had the room's undivided attention.

She looked into their faces and said, "And how something broken beyond repair…" she blew on her closed fist, "can be made whole again."

Gwena opened her hand and revealed the card fully intact as if it had never been torn at all. She showed the ace of hearts to the audience. They stared at it with mouths agape, not uttering a sound.

"Thank you. I too will be here all week," Gwena announced with a wry smile and a nod to Benji.

Benji nodded back to her with respect, then he began clapping loudly. The rest of the room erupted in applause.

Gwena sat around a table next to the cocktail bar having a drink with a few of the members of the meetup who stuck around.

"How did you do that?" Susie asked her.

"Do what?"

"That magic trick. How did you make the cards suspend in the air like that?"

"Come on, Susie, you know a magician never reveals their secret," Benji said.

"I've never seen anything like it."

"What I want to know, is how you got that scar?" Guy inquired with enthusiastic curiosity.

Gwena touched her scar as if she'd momentarily forgotten it was there. "A Jackal-bird, I wandered too close to its nest when I was a child."

"You poor thing! Those pests are awful!" Violet exclaimed.

Gwena shrugged. "It was only defending its nest."

"Wow. You're far more forgiving than I am."

"No offense, but I'm surprised Madam Rouge let anyone so young down here. How old are you, love?" Fin asked her.

"I'll be sixteen next week."

"Sixteen next week? She's not even a woman!" Susie exclaimed.

Rafael smiled at Gwena. "Come on, a week's nothing, she looks woman enough to me," he said with a wink.

"Every girl looks woman enough to you, Rafael," Violet stated dryly.

"Well, there's certainly no better place to celebrate your coming of age," Guy said.

Violet rolled her eyes, "Women don't celebrate their coming of age the same way you men do."

"Why is that?" Benji inquired curiously.

"What do you mean, why is that?"

"Woman can benefit from an adult education just as much as men, can't they? I think it's unfair to deprive you of that. I mean you tell me, would you birds have liked to've had a proper introduction, instead of hoping to chance your first time was with someone who knew what they were doing?" Benji asked.

"I would've, my first time was a train wreck!" Susie confessed.

"Sure, but there could never be a male version of Illumine Roses. You can't deny that any man applying for that job would surely abuse their position. It's a very vulnerable time for a woman, which is exactly why she gets to choose when and whom she spends it with," Violet stated.

"It's a vulnerable time for us all! I was terrified on my Illumine Day," Fin professed.

"Didn't it make you feel better, knowing you had an induction where you weren't expected to know anything, though?" Rafael asked him.

"Yeah, I suppose it did take the pressure off. I certainly felt a lot more relaxed about the subject after that. It took all the guesswork out of it. And man, am I grateful for my Illumine Rose, I had a lot of misconceptions about women and the whole business, which luckily she cleared up. I hate to imagine how much of a fool I would've made of myself stumbling in the dark for Stars know how long otherwise," Fin admitted.

"Precisely. It's not really fair that women can't enjoy the same benefit. Say, what if it wasn't a man?" Benji proposed.

"What wasn't a man?" Violet asked.

"What if women got their education from an Illumine Rose, same as we do."

"Women receiving their adult education from a woman?" Susie exclaimed.

"Well, why not? The night's intended to be for education—does the gender of the teacher really matter? It wouldn't be any different than Guy here having his Illumine Day celebrated with an Illumine Rose," Benji said.

Guy nodded. "True. My Sweet Sixteen knew I was as gay as a maypole, and it didn't make any difference. I'm grateful for my Illumine Day celebration. Outside of the general education, my Sweet Sixteen showed me all the tricks in her book on how to pleasure a man and gave me the opportunity to experience being with a woman without the pressure of any expectation."

Fin shrugged, "I have to admit, it makes sense. They're well versed in your anatomy as well as ours. They could take all the mystery out of it for you. Give you a full rundown on their knowledge and tricks. What to be wary of with men, as well as how to please them—and yourselves of course," he said.

Susie laughed. "Ha! I would love to see you propose that to the nobles. They wouldn't allow it in a million years!"

"True. They'd be terrified their daughters might enjoy it too much and get a taste for women. They can't risk that, now can they? It would disrupt the continuation of their perfect family lineage," Violet remarked.

Bonnie waved her hand dismissively.

"I've had women clientele seek me out at the club fer education on several occasions. They wanted ta learn ta please their partners an' themselves better. An' why not? Makes sense ta me. Why should men get a proper induction while we're left ta uncover such things on our own?" she asked.

Benji turned to Gwena. "What do you think, little bird?"

Gwena's cheeks turned bright scarlet. She hesitated before saying, "I've always wanted my first time to be with someone I love, and someone who loves me. If it's not, then I don't really see the point."

"Don't see the point?! Oh my poor innocent dove—there's a whole world you're missing out on," Susie proclaimed.

"Hey, don't tarnish the poor girl! I think it's beautiful. We all know making love with someone you adore is far greater than a night with a stranger," Fin said.

"I don't know, just because you love them doesn't mean they'll be any good," Susie rebutted.

"Love is a fallacy," Benji stated candidly.

"It's love, Benji—not an elephant," Violet returned dryly.

Benji gave her a good-humored smirk.

"I find a night with a stranger rather thrilling," Guy confessed.

"Personally, I find those who are experienced and emotionally mature make the best lovers—regardless of how well you know them. Which is why I find older men so accommodating," Violet stated.

Fin held up his hands in a gesture of truce. "I think we can all agree, the best lovers are those who're both skilled and whom you have romantic feelings for," he said.

"Maybe for the first three to six months, after that the passion fizzles out," Susie remarked.

"Speak for yourself! I was with my man for twelve years before he passed, and the passion never fizzled," Violet countered.

"Well, that's enough about that. Can't we find a different topic? Poor Gwena here looks like she wants to crawl out of her skin and disappear," Fin declared.

"It wouldn't surprise me if she did, not after that magic act of hers," Susie said.

Everyone looked at Gwena. She smiled politely with rosy cheeks.

"Actually, I am quite tired—it's been a long day. I think I'll call it a night. It's been so lovely meeting you all," she said, getting up from her stool.

"Look, we've scared the poor girl away!" Guy exclaimed.

Bonnie looked at her pocket watch. "Actually, we should all get a move on, the club opens in less than an hour," she stated, and downed what was left of her drink.

"Lovely meeting you, Gwena," Susie said.

Rafael winked. "Welcome to the crew."

"Have a good night, love," Fin said warmly.

"Night," Violet said, before rapidly draining her drink and hopping down from her barstool.

Benji raised his glass to her.

"I'll walk ya ta yer room," Bonnie offered.

"Thank you. See you all tomorrow. Have a good night," Gwena returned to the group and left with Bonnie towards the upper balcony.

"I 'ope we didn't offend ya. That lot doesn't 'ave much in the way o' filters," Bonnie apologized.

Gwena laughed awkwardly. "That's alright."

"I'll take ya ta the Central Postin' House in the mornin', and then out ta get some new clothes—though I 'ave ta say, I like the dress ya 'ave on."

"Thank you," Gwena blushed. "That would be great."

"Meet me at the bar downstairs after ya finish breakfast."

"The bar's open that early?"

Bonnie smiled, "It never closes."

Only a couple hours after Gwena had fallen asleep, she was woken by the sound of big band music floating up from downstairs. She looked at her pocket watch. It was the hour of Shick—the Star-Stirrer. He was the keeper of the midnight hour and one of the Thrixing Stars, prone to causing meddlesome mischief and stealing maidens' hearts. Gwena put on a dress, pinned up her hair, and stepped out of her room.

She looked over the balcony down into the main area of the club. It was packed full of people taking part in an extravagant party. The dance floor was filled with men and women dressed in bright, exuberant attire dancing to an upbeat band. Those not dancing were caught in lively conversations with fancy cocktails in hand. Long pieces of silk hung from each corner of the room, each occupied by an aerial acrobat twisting and turning as if the laws of gravity didn't apply.

Gwena wandered down the stairs into the crowd. People looked at her with puzzled expressions, like she was a chestnut in a box of cherries—and she felt just as out of place. Her mother's dress felt more ordinary than ever before. Not only was everyone around her beautifully dressed, they were all exceptionally beautiful people. Some of the women's attire resembled extravagant costumes. One wore a pink top hat decorated with feathers, and another, long lace gloves. Some of the dresses were long and flowing and others were shockingly short. Some of the women didn't wear dresses at all, but pants instead—Gwena saw one woman in a pair of pinstriped suspenders smoking a puff-stick from a long thin black stick. It was as if the place truly was filled with human embodiments of Wildsingers. The scenery was so grand, so glamorous and fanciful, Gwena was sure she must be in a waking dream. She spotted Benji to the side of the dance floor. He was dressed in a handsome purple suit talking warmly to a woman wearing a beaded ball gown with an open back. The woman looked at least ten years older than he was, but was absolutely stunning, with a presence that drew Gwena's attention like gravity. Benji was listening to her as if she was the only woman in the world, and she was basking in the glow of his attention. The woman whispered something in Benji's ear. He smiled, held out his elbow, and led her up the stairs towards his room.

Gwena wandered around for a couple minutes longer before her sense of being underdressed and out of place compelled her to return upstairs. But once back in her room she found it impossible to sleep. She buzzed with excitement. The club was magnificent, kindred to the alchemists' view out her window, an impossible fantasy—too extravagant and wonderful to be real, and yet somehow it was.

# CONCOCTING COCKTAILS

Bastian sat in the crow's-nest looking out at a raging storm. The sky was black with churning clouds dancing with lightning. Thunder cracked and the sea swelled, tipping the Black Mary violently from side to side. Bastian held tightly onto the metal bars of the nest as he dipped tumultuously with the ship. Out of the ocean depths rose eight gigantic, suckered limbs snaking towards the sky.

Bastian looked down at the deck. Below him at the base of the main mast was a golden egg larger than he was. Lightning struck the egg. The shell cracked. A long clawed hand broke out from within, and a golden dragon emerged. The large horned head had dagger-sized teeth and black shining eyes. It looked around curiously, then grabbed a sailor off the deck and ate him whole like a floundering fish.

"Noooooo!" Bastian yelled.

He swung himself over the nest and rushed down the rope ladder towards the beast. *Not again, not another life lost because of me,* he thought desperately.

The dragon locked its eyes on him, cocking its head curiously to the side before blowing a stream of bright red and orange flame in his direction. Bastian ducked just in time to avoid being cooked. The sails above him caught fire. Bastian jumped to the deck and rolled, then stood to face the beast. He realized it didn't matter how much he wanted to stop it—he couldn't. Even if he had a weapon, he wouldn't know how to wield it. He was completely defenseless. He screamed at the dragon in outrage.

"Take *me*, you slithering worm!" he yelled, hoping at the very least he could sate its appetite.

"Stand aside, lad!"

Bastian turned to see Falgo standing beside him with his sword drawn. There was a flash of steel and within moments the dragon's head lay lifeless on the deck. Falgo hopped up onto the ship's guardrail, holding fast to the line. He looked out at the Kraken, his coat billowing in the wind, his sword dripping with the dragon's blood. On the horizon the Kraken's limbs reached their full extension towards the cosmos and changed course, weaving towards the Black Mary. The bulbous head of the monster breached the surface, showed its cavern of jagged teeth—and screamed. Someone whispered in Bastian's ear, "...*you are the helmsman of your fate, the sovereign of your destiny.*"

Bastian woke with a start. He sat up in his hammock, covered in sweat.

"Ya alright, lad?" the sailor next to him asked.

He was an older man, with skin like tanned leather. He was sitting up in his adjacent hammock putting on his boots.

"Yeah. Just a bad dream."

"The Kraken?"

Bastian nodded.

"She's been hauntin' me dreams as well. It'll pass, it always does," the sailor assured him.

"How many krakens have you seen?" Bastian asked.

"She's not the only monster in the deep. Ya can't spend as long as I 'ave in these waters an' not encounter the thin's o' nightmares."

"How do you bear it?"

"The ocean's me mistress. It doesn't matter 'ow 'ard she be ta live with, I can't live without 'er. Ye'll understand one day," the man told him.

He nodded to Bastian and then headed out towards his duties.

Bastian wiped the sweat from his brow and winced as his fingers passed over his stitches. *Great,* now his head was throbbing. He rolled out of his hammock and headed towards the main deck.

As soon as Bastian was up top, Cricket came up behind him, "Mornin', sunshine! Ya didn't need yer wake-up call today? I 'ope yer not tryin' ta avoid this pretty face," he greeted.

"I had a nightmare. Trust me, I'd prefer your face as a wake-up call any day."

"Ha! Careful, ye'll make yer girlfriend jealous," Cricket jested, handing Bastian a mop upside down so the ropes hung down like strands of hair.

Bastian took it in hand and pushed aside its ropes as though caressing a lover's face. "Oh, how I've missed you!" he told it dramatically.

Cricket smirked. "I 'ave ta tell ya, she's been disloyal, I've seen 'er in the arms o' just about every other crewman since ye've been away."

Bastian looked at the mop accusingly, then he shrugged, "Can't say I'm surprised, she's always been a scrubber."

Cricket laughed and dropped the bucket on the boards between them.

Bastian pulled out the puff-stick he'd rolled the previous night and offered it to Cricket. "Care for a puff?"

"Before breakfast?" Cricket exclaimed.

Bastian shrugged. "Before the Black Mary, this was my breakfast."

"Go on, give us one then."

Bastian handed the puff-stick over and rolled himself another, lighting them both with his Everfire box. They took a drag, then saw Snibs come on deck—and quickly started making use of their mops.

The cool morning air was helping the throbbing in Bastian's head to subside. As he worked he watched the sun rise and the Ghost Element glisten on everything around them.

⌒

At breakfast that morning, Bastian and Cricket sat at their usual table with Stork and Rhino. Their meal was a bowl of thick gruel and a slab of fresh bread. Bastian had gruel many times in his life, but until now, he'd never had any that was palatable. As usual, Doc—the ship's cook and doctor—had worked his magic and turned something bland into a delectable delight. The oats were perfectly cooked, tender but not mushy. They were rich, creamy, and flavored with a delicious blend of spices Bastian couldn't distinguish.

"Hey, Stork, ya throwin' dice tonight?" Cricket inquired.

The tall lanky pirate looked up from his breakfast. "Who's askin'?"

"I am. I want ta take back a few o' me coins before we reach Jaxland."

"Be me guest, but as yer mate—I feel it be me duty ta warn ya, Cricket, ya should stop while yer behind, otherwise ya could be goin' ta Jaxland with empty pockets," Stork cautioned.

"Ya cocky bastard!"

Stork held up his hands in defense.

"How's yer 'ead, Dodger?" Rhino asked Bastian, clearly eager to change the subject.

Bastian shrugged, "Could be worse, could be better."

"'ave ya seen yer face this mornin?" Stork asked him.

"No. Why?"

Cricket smirked. "It's changin' color."

Bastian looked at his reflection in the back of his spoon. His cheek was the color of an eggplant. "Shick."

"Don't worry, we've all been slapped around by Snibs on one occasion er another. It practically be a term o' endearment," Cricket told him.

"Man 'as a mean back 'and," Rhino admitted.

Bastian tested the tenderness of his cheek with his fingertips. "I deserve worse," he muttered.

"What nonsense are ya talkin' about?" Stork scoffed.

"If I hadn't stowed away on the Black Mary, those galleons never would've come after you. All the men who died would still be here if it wasn't for me," Bastian said.

"Ah, come now—ya 'eard Snibs, those galleons saved our lives! If it wasn't fer 'em, it would 'ave been the Black Mary pulled down ta Davy Jones's Locker by that beast," Cricket asserted.

"If it wasn't for the battle with the galleons, maybe the Kraken never would've attacked at all," Bastian countered.

"Ya can't take credit fer the Kraken! She's been tailin' us fer years," Rhino proclaimed.

"True. Ya saw Whittler's carvin's on the old mast. She was alys goin' ta attack, it was only a matter o' time. If she 'ad attacked when we were alone, it would've been the end o' us," Stork agreed.

"That's right. Ya saw 'ow quickly she took the galleons down. If she 'adn't gone after 'em first, we never would've stood a chance," Cricket insisted.

Bastian's shoulders sunk. "I still can't help feeling like the blood of the men lost is on my hands."

Cricket pointed his spoon at Bastian. "Hey, ya can't think like that. Ya never asked fer this. Ya couldn't 'ave known it would 'appen—an' I know ya never would've wished it upon anyone. It's not yer fault. Only the Stars know the game we're playin'. We're nothin' but pawns on their cosmic chessboard, stumblin' blindly down the paths they lay out fer us—a means towards their own end game, not ta mention, Davey Jones's. We can't 'ope ta contend with that. We can only do our best with what's in our control. Ya 'ave ta let go o' the rest an' just 'ope there's some redeemable point ta it all."

Stork nodded. "Good luck, bad luck—ya never know what it's goin' ta be until the very end."

Rhino looked at them both in surprise. "Since when did ya two get so profound? I never knew ya 'ad any depth ta ya!"

"That's 'cause ya never dip yer 'ead below the surface, brother," Stork jeered.

"Oi! Just 'cause I don't share me profound thoughts with yer sorry bones, doesn't mean I don't 'ave any," Rhino protested.

Stork rolled his eyes. "Sure, brother."

Bastian laughed, starting to feel his spirits lift.

"When do yer stitches come out, Dodger?" Cricket asked him.

Bastian shrugged. "No idea."

"It'll leave a nice mark," Rhino said appreciatively.

Stork put his arm around Bastian. "Adds character."

"Scars don't bother me," Bastian admitted, thinking of Gwena and the mark she bore. He hoped he could show her his one day and tell her how it came from a real pirate adventure—just like the stories they used to make up about her scar when they were children.

"Just don't make the mistake I always do an' start pushin' yerself before yer ready. It will make yer recovery twice as long," Stork advised.

"True. Ya've 'ad ta learn that the 'ard way only about a dozen times over, 'aven't ya, Stork?" Cricket gibed.

"Don't pretend ya 'aven't either," Stork countered.

"We all 'ave—an' it's not worth doin', plain an' simple," Rhino stated.

"Well, I haven't seen today's roster, but I'm pretty sure Snibs hasn't assigned me to any hard labor," Bastian said.

"'e wouldn't, ye'd be bloody useless at it in yer condition. I reckon 'e'll 'ave ya doin' rope duty er galley work tell we reach Jaxland," Stork guessed.

"Er stuck below with the animals," Cricket suggested.

Bastian shrugged, "Could be worse."

"There's a wager fer ya, Cricket," Stork proposed, "if ya want a go at me coin—I'll bet ya two silver fish Dodger be assigned ta the galley er line duty today an' not the Green Room."

"Ya mean *my* coin? Don't get too attached ta it now—I've only been lettin' ya barrow it temporarily, so I don't 'ave ta carry it around at sea," Cricket rebuked.

Stork laughed. "Ha! Sure ya are. Ya know, if ya need coin, I'll be 'appy ta lend ya some. With interest on the return o' course," he offered.

"With interest on the return?! That's *my* coin, ya weasel!"

"*Was* yer coin. I won it fair an' square. Rules be rules," Stork corrected.

"Alright, I'll buy inta yer wager. But ya can only choose one er the other, not both," Cricket asserted.

Stork stuck out his hand, "Fine. Galley duty then," he said, and Cricket shook it.

Bastian caught sight of Falgo hunched in the corner of the mess hall and the rest of Cricket and Stork's conversation was lost to him. The sea-gypsy was sitting alone with his head in his arms, his long black hair a tangled mess cascading around them. Bastian's dream of Falgo conquering the dragon flashed back to him. The image of Falgo standing strong with his sword in hand was such a contrast to the withered figure before him now. Bastian was devastated to see him this way. As far as he was concerned, the man was a hero. Bastian could only wish he was capable of learning to fight a fraction as well. He recalled how helpless he'd felt in his dream. How helpless he'd felt the night the Kraken attacked. The rest of the men fought so bravely, and all he could do was cower in fear. He'd never been a fighter. When threatened, he'd always dodged and run. He'd been content with that—it meant no one got hurt. But on the ship there was nowhere to run to, they were fish in a barrel. Not being able to fight meant he could do nothing to defend against their foes—foes he felt responsible for. If anyone decided to come after him, he couldn't even protect himself let alone anyone else. And when he saw the way the crew fought together with relentless courage against terrible odds, it inspired him—Falgo most of all. He'd never felt so useless in all his life as when he'd helplessly looked on from the crow's-nest while the rest of the men fought an enemy he'd drawn down on them—and he hated it. He never wanted to feel that way again. Then an idea struck him—maybe he could help Falgo, and in return the pirate could teach him how to fight? It was a crazy and perilous idea, but often the best ones were. *Who better to learn from?* Bastian thought.

"Hey, ya comin?" Cricket asked him.

Bastian looked up and saw everyone else at the table was standing.

"Time ta get crackin'," Rhino declared.

"Yeah," Bastian acknowledged.

He stood and brushed the crumbs off his lap, then followed the others to the list of daily chores.

⌒

Bastian waited for his turn to look at the chore chart. Cricket and Stork were crowding in front of him, eager to see who was the winner to their bet.

Stork read Bastian's chore list first, stopping at his second assigned duty. "Assistin' Tink? I've never 'eard o' anyone being assigned ta Tink!" he exclaimed.

Cricket read on ahead. "Ya got ta be kiddin', bloody shick!"

Stork looked back at the chart and burst into hearty laughter.

Bastian found his name and read his daily duties listed for the week.

*Scrub the deck: Hour of the Dawn Breaker*
*Assist the Tinker: Serendipity's Hour*
*Line Duty: Plunger's Hour*
*Galley Duty: Kismet's Hour*

Stork held his hand out to Cricket while shaking with laughter. "Either way I went—I would've been right! That's two silver fish, thanks!"

"Tonight—double er nothin'!" Cricket snarled.

Stork laughed, "Haha! Ya may as well give me yer whole coin purse now, an' save yerself the trouble."

Cricket put up his pointer finger and turned it in a little circle. "Go shick yerself!"

"Hey now, it's not me fault yer so good at losin' coin," Stork jested.

Cricket stepped towards him threateningly. "I swear, I'm goin' ta wipe that smug smile off yer face tonight, ya slitherin'…"

"Enough!" Rhino declared, stepping between them, "We got work ta do," he growled.

Cricket fell silent and huffed off towards his duties. Stork kept laughing until he had tears in his eyes. He was taking big gulps of air between his laughter in an attempt to recover.

"Do you have any idea where I can find Tink?" Bastian asked Rhino.

"No idear, sorry. 'e 'ardly shows 'is face these days. Man's a bit o' a shadow around 'ere, only surfaces when it suits 'im."

"Great," Bastian muttered.

Rhino patted him on the shoulder. "Good luck." Then he dragged Stork away still laughing.

Bastian sighed and headed down the corridor towards Snibs's quarters. He knocked lightly on the door.

"Who is it?" Snib's voice demanded from the other side.

"Dodger. May I have a quick word?" Bastian asked.

"Come in if ya must," Snibs grumbled.

Bastian opened the door and let himself inside. Snibs was sitting at his desk writing in a ledger. "Make it quick, thief. I'm busy," he growled.

"I'm supposed to be assisting the Tinker, but I've no idea where he is, or how to find him," Bastian stated.

Snibs stopped writing and sighed, "I'll take ya. But pay attention, I'm not gonna escort ya twice."

"Of course," Bastian acknowledged, and then after a moment's thought he added, "While I'm here, there's one more thing I'd like to ask you."

Snibs looked at him wearily.

"It's regarding the prisoner in the hold," Bastian reported.

"The Navy lad?"

"Yeah. I know him. He's a Star Child, he was a year ahead of me in school at the Star Temple in Westdock," Bastian confessed.

Snibs put down his fountain pen and folded his hands on his desk.

"Ya mean ta tell me, landlubber, ya 'ad a friend on the ship ya were seeking refuge from?" he asked carefully.

"It sounds terrible when you put it that way," Bastian admitted, "I had no idea he was on the galleons or even in the Navy. I left the Order before he graduated. Besides, he's more of an acquaintance than a friend. But it's not really that surprising, anyway, if you think about it, Westdock's a small place, the odds I would know someone on the enemy's ship were quite high."

Snibs listened to his rambling with an unimpressed glare.

Bastian cleared his throat uncomfortably.

"The point is, I can vouch for him. He's a hard worker and trustworthy. I know we need extra hands to replace the ones lost, and I think he would make a valuable asset to the crew. He has no loyalty to the Navy—he joined for the coin and girls. Both things I know you can offer him more of than they ever did," Bastian advocated.

"I thought 'e was more of an acquaintance an' ya 'adn't seen 'im in years?" Snibs asked.

"I haven't. I had a chat with him last night. And we grew up together, I know his character, and I've seen his work ethic. He hasn't changed much."

Snibs looked at Bastian skeptically. "So 'e may say. But a man will say just about anythin' ta get 'is freedom when behind bars."

"He's not that sort of person," Bastian insisted.

"Everyone's that sort o' person," Snibs returned plainly.

Bastian started to reply, but Snibs held up his hand,

"I've 'eard enough, thief. I'll keep what ya say in mind. Regardless, 'is fate won't be decided until we leave Jaxland. If anyone on that island recognizes 'im from the Navy, 'e'll never make it past."

Snibs stood from his desk and held the door open for Bastian. "Now, off ta yer duties," he commanded.

Bastian ducked through the door and followed Snibs down the corridor towards the back of the ship. Before long they reached a dead end. Snibs turned to his left and knocked on the wall. "It's open," a distant voice said from the other side. Snibs nodded to Bastian. "In ya go," he directed.

"Go where?" Bastian asked, puzzled as to where in the world Snibs was referring to—there was nothing there but the wall.

Snibs put his hand on the wood planks and pushed. A door-sized piece of the wall opened inwards. Bastian's eyes's widened in surprise— the door had been completely camouflaged amongst the woodwork a moment before. "Right. Thanks," he said, and cautiously stepped through the hidden doorway.

The secret door led to a short hallway decorated like the house of an aristocrat. The walls were covered with ornate wallpaper above oak wainscoting, a fancy hall rug stretched along the floor, and an Everfire chandelier hung from the ceiling. There was a full bookshelf on the back wall and an oak door to its left. The whole place felt incredibly out of place and strange. Bastian tried the door. It was locked. He knocked on it. "Hello? Anyone there?" he asked. There was no reply but the faint click-click of gear work, and then the bookshelf behind him slowly swung open, revealing another secret passage. Bastian approached it cautiously, stepping through the hidden doorway.

As soon as Bastian was through the second door, he did a double take at the room he'd stepped into. It was so vastly different from the rest of the ship, he felt transported somewhere else entirely. The only thing similar to any other part of the Black Mary was the back wall, which was made of square glass windowpanes identical to those in the captain's quarters, framing the ocean beyond. The rest of the room felt like something that would be in the Hall of Scientific Study or The Alchemists House of Discovery, but not here. The room was spacious, much more so than even the captain's own quarters. The ceiling was high, the room brightly lit with an Everfire chandelier, and a luxurious silk throw rug covered the majority of the plank floor. The walls were lined with built-in bookshelves with glass doors, their shelves crowded with old and expensive-looking books. At the back end of the room was a large oak workbench that was a tinker's dream. It was covered with a full range of tools neatly organized—boxes of gear work, glass magnifying lenses of varying strengths on copper stands, tweezers, and other strange copper and glass instruments Bastian didn't recognize. Sitting behind the workbench was a middle-aged man with dark skin and short snow-white hair neatly combed back. He was smartly dressed in a clean white dress shirt with the sleeves rolled up and a grey wool vest. On his head, a contraption held a series of lenses in front of his eyes. He was lost in his work, his eyes alive with deep concentration.

"Sit down, if you like," the man invited, without looking up. He had a distinguished city accent. It took Bastian by surprise after days of being surrounded by nothing but thick sailor brogue. From his dialect, it sounded like he was from somewhere near the Heartland or South View—Bastian couldn't quite put his finger on it. He saw a high-backed chair with a velvet seat cushion against the wall and sat down.

"Bring it over here, lad, there's no need for us to have to shout to one another," the man directed, again without looking up from his work.

Bastian brought the chair over, setting it down in front of the desk. After a silent moment of watching the man work, he cleared his throat and asked, "Are you Tink?"

The man looked up at him for the first time, his sharp grey eyes magnified by the lenses. "That's what they call me. I hear they call you Dodger," he said.

"Yeah. It's nice to finally meet you, I keep hearing your name but haven't had a face to put it to," Bastian remarked.

Tink smiled. "The pleasure's all mine."

He took off the headpiece and placed it carefully on the desk. Without it, he looked like a pleasant, refined gentleman—which was strange, considering their surroundings. Bastian found all of it incredibly disorienting. Tink folded his hands on his desk and gave Bastian a warm smile.

"I can't tell you how happy I am to be making your acquaintance. The captain and I have been looking for someone such as yourself for a very long time," he announced.

"Such as myself?" Bastian questioned.

"Someone with the natural ability to see the Ghost Element."

"Right."

Bastian wasn't convinced the Ghost Element existed. But he couldn't figure out a reason why the tinker and the captain would be trying to convince him it did.

"Equillian's Key," Bastian said, recalling what the captain had told him.

"Precisely. Though, you might know it better as the Essence of Empyrean," Tink suggested.

*Essence of Empyrean?* Suddenly the tinker had Bastian's attention. He'd only heard whispers of the Essence of Empyrean from the senior students at the Order. It was something taught in their final years of study—and it was the only subject that made Bastian regret not completing his schooling there. He'd looked it up in the library after he and Felix had left but had never been able to find anything mentioning the topic.

"I don't understand. If the Ghost Element is the same thing as the Essence of Empyrean and it's real, then why aren't either of them recognized by the Hall of Scientific Study? From what I've read, the Hall avidly denies its existence—didn't they kick out one of their scientists because he insisted on it being real?" Bastian queried.

"Yes, they did. Do you know who that man was?" Tink asked.

"No idea."

"His name was Bartleby Foster. He founded The Alchemists House of Discovery with Haplo Tracy."

"You're telling me the same Bartleby who was kicked out of the Hall of Scientific Study was one of the original alchemists? One of the primary inventors of enchanted objects?" Bastian proclaimed.

Tink smiled. "The very same."

"Does that mean there's a connection between the Ghost Element and their objects?"

"Most definitely."

"How can you be so sure?"

"Because just like you, both Bartleby Foster and Haplo Tracy could see the Ghost Element with the natural eye. Also, because I make enchanted objects."

"You're an alchemist!?" Bastian exclaimed, leaning forward in his chair with sudden enthusiasm.

"*Was.* I suppose I still am of sorts, though my titles have all been taken from me," Tink confessed.

Bastian put the tips of his fingers together with growing anticipation. "How are enchanted objects made?" he blurted, as if the question had been burning inside him.

Tink smiled. "I only just met you, and you want me to give up my most coveted secrets?"

"I just want to understand how they work. Your objects are the only thing I've never been able to take apart," Bastian admitted.

"Ah, a bit of a tinker yourself, are you?"

Bastian shrugged. "I've found the best way to understand something is to see how it's put together."

"Very clever. However, you won't be able to accomplish that by taking an enchanted object apart," Tink informed him.

"Why not?"

"Because you can't take one apart unless you know how they're put together. And even if you could, seeing the inside wouldn't enlighten you in any way. However, knowing how regular things work will help you in using the element a great deal."

"How do you mean?"

"The Ghost Element doesn't make things—we do. If you don't know how the enchantment works, then the Element won't be able to create it," Tink explained.

"That makes no sense," Bastian objected, "the alchemists' objects do the impossible. If you already know how to make something like that work without the Element, then why do you need it in the first place?"

"Because even if you know how you want something to work, it doesn't mean it can—simply because we're working within the confines and limitations of our world's physics and natural laws. These laws are the gatekeepers as to what's possible and impossible in the first place. Equillian's Key allows you to unlock those constraints and define your own laws. As long as you're imaginative and clever enough, nothing's impossible," Tink proclaimed.

"You're telling me that if I learn how to use the Ghost Element, I can make this chair fly simply by deciding it repels gravity?" Bastian proposed skeptically.

"Exactly...that's actually not a bad idea," Tink said thoughtfully.

Bastian laughed at the ridiculousness of it, but Tink wasn't laughing at all. The tinker came out from behind his desk and leaned against the front of it casually, pulling a monocle from his chest pocket. It was an elegant piece, with a circular dark green lens bordered by bright yellow brass and a small ornate loop at its top, threaded with a thin gold chain that connected it to his pocket.

Tink squinted his left eye to hold the monocle in place and waved his hands in front of him like he was conducting an orchestra. The Ghost Element on the floor sprung to life and began to vibrate. It gravitated to Bastian's chair and disappeared inside as if being absorbed by the wood.

"What are you doing?!" Bastian asked nervously.

Tink ignored him, lost in whatever it was. Then suddenly Bastian's chair lifted off the ground and began floating upwards as if no longer bound by the laws of gravity.

Bastian was stunned. He jumped off it, landing in a roll on the floor just before the chair hit the ceiling. It stayed there bouncing around like a stray balloon.

"What the shick?!" Bastian exclaimed in shock. Tink continued to ignore him, watching the chair thoughtfully. "Hmmm, it isn't enough to simply repel gravity—or you'd end up amongst the stars. There needs to be something that allows you to control its direction and bring it equilibrium," he deduced.

Bastian looked at Tink and then up at the chair, flabbergasted. "I must be dreaming," he muttered. "Is this what you're going to teach me? How to bypass natural law using the Essence of Empyrean?" he inquired.

"Of a sort. Our main goal is to teach you how to manipulate enchanted things. Which, believe it or not, is even more difficult than enchanting them in the first place," Tink proclaimed.

He waved his hand and the chair came crashing to the floor. He picked it up and placed it in front of his desk, motioning for Bastian to have a seat.

"No thanks, I think I'd prefer to stand."

Tink smiled.

"Why is it more difficult than enchanting them in the first place?" Bastian pressed.

"Because enchanted objects are built with defenses. Once those defenses are in place, it's incredibly difficult to get past them," Tink explained.

"Is that what the captain wants me to do on Jaxland—get past an enchanted object's defenses?"

"Yes."

"And being able to see the Element allows me to do that?" Bastian questioned.

"With proper training, yes."

"Is that why the captain calls it Equillian's Key?"

"It was originally given that name by one of the Finleys—because if you can see it, the Element allows us to unlock the natural laws, yes," Tink confirmed.

"One of the Finleys? As in Rupert Finley—the optician whose death caused the ban on enchanted objects?" Bastian asked.

"Morris Finley, actually. But in the same family," Tink corrected.

"Are you saying the Finleys also believed in the Essence of Empyrean?"

"I don't think they'd ever heard of the Essence of Empyrean. They didn't know what the Ghost Element was, they only knew it existed because they developed a lens that allows it to be seen," Tink elucidated.

"No kidding? Is that what you're using now?" Bastian asked, staring at Tink's lens with itching curiosity.

"Yes."

"Then how come it's not common knowledge the Element exists?"

"Mainly because the Emperor has done his best to ensure it never is. Something as omnipotent as the Ghost Element would be catastrophically dangerous in the wrong hands. For two, the Finleys are dead and there's only two of their lenses in existence, and for someone to be able to see the Element naturally is exceedingly rare," Tink divulged.

"How come I can see it then?"

"For several unique reasons. It's a matter of not only being the right person, but also being in the right place at the right time. It's incredibly unlikely for those three things to coincide, which is what makes your ability so extraordinary."

"What makes me the right person?" Bastian asked.

"You have a variant in your physical optics."

"I assume by physical optics, you mean my eyes?"

"Yes."

"Okay, what does being in the right place have to do with anything?"

"It has to do with your primary visual cortex," Tink stated.

"Primary visual what?"

"Cortex—It's the area of the brain that processes visual information. Everything that enters the senses needs to be interpreted through our brains, and sometimes our subjective perception doesn't match the physical reality of the world. Our brains do their best to compensate for this when deemed necessary. For example, if you were to wear a pair of goggles that turned your view of the world upside down, your brain would make a correction after only a few days, making the world look right side up again. And sometimes, it's responsible for those mismatches itself. Your nose, for example—it's constantly in your field of vision, but your brain conveniently ignores it to keep it out of view. Morris Finley believed the reason most people who have the optical variant still can't see the Ghost Element is because their brain registers it as a flaw and therefore tells them it's not there. By jumping on this ship you saturated yourself in completely foreign surroundings. Without being able to predict what was around you, your brain's ability to hide the Ghost Element began to falter."

"Right…and what does time have to do with it?" Bastian asked.

"When you reach adolescence your body goes through a series of hormonal changes. For those with the optical variant, these biological chemicals increase and strengthen the eyes' ability to see the element for a small window of time. As soon as your hormones rebalance that window closes—unless, you can convince your brain to accept the element's existence, in which case the window will continue to stay open for the rest of your life," Tink expounded.

Bastian nodded. "Right person, right place, right time."

"Precisely."

"I wonder what else might exist in our world beyond our perception," Bastian remarked thoughtfully.

Tink smiled. "Indeed."

"You said you and the captain have been looking for someone with my ability. Why?"

"Because we need your help. Now, I understand that this is a lot to comprehend. I'm sure you have many more questions, but we must focus on the task at hand and make the most of every moment we have together. In order for you to succeed, it's paramount we hone your skills and have you ready by the time we reach Jaxland."

"What is it I'm going to be doing in Jaxland exactly?" Bastian queried.

"You'll be breaking into an enchanted chest. One made specifically to ensure no one ever does."

"Sounds impossible."

"Precisely. Which is why it can only be done using the Ghost Element, and it can only be done by you."

"I've seen both you and the captain use the Ghost Element—why not do it yourselves?"

"For several reasons, all of which are outside your concern," Tink asserted.

Bastian chewed on that for a moment.

"Any more questions?" Tink asked.

"Yeah, how do I do it?"

Tink smiled. "Right this way."

⁓

Bastian followed Tink to the back corner of his workroom. There was a short table there with a stool beside.

"Have a seat," Tink invited.

Bastian sat down. On the low table in front of him was a beautiful metal bowl. It displayed spectacular workmanship, made with a mix of copper and precious metals. Three constellations were imprinted around the outside. Faya—the constellation of creativity and imagination. The Star-Forger—the constellation with the ability to forge you a new destiny. And Ariya—the muse for music. The piece must have been worth a fortune.

"Look inside, tell me what you see," Tink directed.

Bastian leaned over the bowl. Inside, the bowl was empty of anything tangible—only it was coated with a thick layer of shimmering gold dust that swirled inside like early morning fog.

"The Ghost Element. Why is there so much of it?" Bastian asked.

"It's called a Humming Bowl. They're made on the Spotted Isles. It's composed of seven different types of metal—"

"Seven?" Bastian interjected. He picked up the bowl and turned it in his hands. "Gold, White Gold, Rose Gold, Silver, Rose Silver, Yellow Fanium, and Copper—this must be worth a fortune!"

"A man well versed in his precious materials," Tink commended.

Bastian shrugged. "I imagine every man on this ship is well versed in these materials, you wouldn't make very successful pirates otherwise."

Tink smiled. "I suppose you're right, though I prefer the term, *rovers*. We spend more time wandering then plundering these days."

"Rovers then," Bastian amended. "Why's it made out of these specific metals?" he asked, still inspecting the bowl.

"Because those metals attract the Ghost Element. You'll soon come to learn there are specific substances that attract the Ghost Element, and some more than others. Gold, silver, fanium, and copper attract it more than most. This will be a helpful thing for you to remember. The more condense the Ghost Element is, the easier it is to manipulate."

"The Ghost Element has expensive taste," Bastian remarked, putting the bowl back down on the table. "How do you manipulate it?"

"Watch carefully," Tink instructed, and produced a dark crystal. Its surface swirled with a full spectrum of gleaming color like an oil slick. It was the size of Bastian's fist, with all straight-edges. It had geometric protrusions jutting up in square blocks that were made of thin straight crystalline walls that spiraled inwards. Tink placed it into the center of the bowl. Immediately, glistening gold particles started seeping out of the air towards it, clinging to the crystal.

"What's that?" Bastian asked.

"Glasstanight, a rare mineral found in the caves of Everlast."

Next, the alchemist produced a wooden dowel with grey leather on one end. He touched the leather to the outside of the bowl and gently ran it in a circular motion around the bowl's outer edge. The bowl began to vibrate and hum with a low resonance that grew louder and more expansive in tone with every pass it made.

The crystal began to vibrate. Patterns formed in the gold dust around it, radiating outward in strange geometric designs. As the bowl hummed steadily, more dust gravitated towards it. Within moments the bowl was full and the crystal completely covered. Bastian's eyes widened.

"Another way to attract the element is with a range of tones and vibrational frequencies. Certain resonances will draw it towards you. Others will push it away," Tink explained.

He pulled out a pink tuning fork and hit it on the edge of the table and stuck it into the bowl. The Ghost Element retreated from it like a repelling magnet.

"There are many things that repel and attract the Ghost Element, most of which you'll learn and memorize within the week. But for now, let's see what you already know. First of all, can you see the Element clearly?" Tink inquired.

Bastian nodded absently. The gold dust was mesmerizing. It kept moving—swirling inside the bowl. Little individual eddies spun off the main mass, some curling upwards—billowing into the air and churning there like a storm cloud. He curiously reached his hand out and stuck it into the bowl. Despite the concentration of the strange stuff he couldn't feel it. To his sense of touch, it was as if the Element didn't exist at all.

"Why can't I feel it?" he asked.

"Because you haven't accepted its existence," Tink answered candidly.

"What do you mean? Are you saying, the more I believe in the Element, the more real it'll become?"

"To you—yes. The Element is already as real as anything, regardless of your thoughts on it, but the truth may as well be fiction if you're not willing to believe in it," Tink declared.

"I want to believe in it," Bastian assured him in earnest.

"Good. Only, wanting isn't enough. You must accept its actuality. Only then can you ensure it remains visible to you and learn to use it to manipulate our reality. Now, concentrate on the dust and imagine it into something."

Bastian looked at the alchemist completely befuddled. "Imagine it into something? How in the Stars am I supposed to do that?"

Tink pulled out his monocle and held it in his left eye. The dust inside the bowl began to vibrate and pull together in the middle. It rose up as if growing out of the center of the bowl, forming into the shape of a maple tree. Within moments a solid gold tree two feet high stood in the center of the bowl.

Bastian gawked at it in surprise. "How in the nine realms?" he muttered. It was just like the rod the captain had conjured in his quarters. It was impossible—and yet, there it was. Bastian reached out and felt the tree. It was solid and cool to the touch. "How did you do that?" he asked in a whisper.

"Try it for yourself," Tink invited, and he dissolved the tree back to dust with a glance.

"Right." Bastian stared into the bowl of swirling gold mist. He had no idea what Tink expected him to do. How could he hope to change something he didn't know anything about? And change it from what to what? And how? Nevertheless, he looked at the Ghost Element and tried to will it into something different. But no matter how hard he commanded it to transform in his mind, nothing happened. He scratched his head. "I don't understand what it is you want me to do here? Do I tell it to change, and expect it to obey my command?" Bastian inquired.

"No."

Bastian sat back in defeat. "I'm sorry, but I've no idea what I'm doing," he apologized.

"Of course not," Tink agreed.

"Then how can you expect me to do it?!" Bastian protested.

"I expect nothing. I'm simply gauging where to begin. It's clear now we'll have to start from the very beginning."

Bastian relaxed his shoulders. "Great, let's do that," he said in relief.

Tink walked back to his desk and gestured for Bastian to sit down in the chair in front of it. Bastian complied.

"Firstly, I want to be completely upfront about what I do and do not know," Tink told him. "I've never seen any benefit in pretending to know more than I do as a teacher. At any time you can ask me whatever question you like and I'll answer it as honestly as I can. If I don't have an answer for you, or it's sensitive information I'm not able to divulge, I'll state as much. Is that understood?"

"Yeah."

Tink nodded and continued, "In general, there's very little known about the Ghost Element. Few know of its existence and even fewer fully believe it's real. The only people I know of who've studied it scientifically are the Finleys, the original alchemists—Haplo Tracy and Bartleby Foster—the captain and me, and lastly, the nefarious Marx. I've been studying the Ghost Element and its properties for over thirty years, and still I've only just scratched the surface. That being said, I believe I have a better understanding of it than anyone else alive."

"You mean, you have a better understanding of it than the Captain and Marx," Bastian clarified.

"What do you know of Marx?!" Tink commanded with urgent intensity.

"Only that he's The East's crime lord and kingbolt for anything shady—and that he's the only one on your list besides yourself and the captain who's still alive," Bastian confessed.

Tink regained his composure. "Right, I see."

"Why's The East researching the Ghost Element anyway?" Bastian asked.

"For no good purpose, I assure you."

"Isn't that something we should be concerned about?"

"Very much so."

"How can you be so sure you know more than Marx does?"

"Because Marx doesn't have access to any of the research of those who've studied it before," Tink stated.

"And you do?"

"Yes."

"How so?" Bastian queried.

"Because I was once headmaster of The Alchemists House of Discovery," Tink confessed.

Bastian's jaw dropped. "What're you doing here?!"

Tink smiled. "That's a very long story, and one that will most definitely interfere with our lesson."

"Right."

Tink continued, "There are many applications for the Ghost Element. Because our goal is to prepare you for a particular task, I'll be focusing our lessons on how to use the Element to bypass the laws of physics and open the constructs of reality. In order to do this, we must first untrain your mind. Since your birth you've been conditioned to believe the world has boundaries that can't be crossed. That some things are simply impossible. This is only true because you believe it to be. In order to cross those boundaries, we must first free your mind of its misconstrued constraints. When was the last time you played make-believe?" Tink asked.

"Pardon?"

"Make-believe. The game of making something up and believing in it," Tink clarified.

Bastian wanted to laugh at the question, it sounded so ridiculous. But Tink's conviction was unwavering. "Uh…I don't know." Bastian thought back to the last time he could recall playing make-believe. When he was very young he used to enjoy pretending he was a dragon with Felix. And he and Gwena would often act out their own adventures. The last time he could remember playing make-believe was at Gwena's house. He and Gwena were playing pirates and imagining Gwena's bed was their ship. That was when her mother was still alive and he and Felix were still welcome in their home. It felt like a lifetime ago. How old were they? Nine, ten maybe?

"Nine or ten, I think," Bastian answered.

"Nine or ten?" Tink questioned with a sad expression.

"That's the last time I can remember," Bastian confessed.

"Certainly not as old as I'd hoped, but at least old enough to be in memory. That's workable."

"What does make-believe have to do with anything?" Bastian inquired.

"It has to do with everything. You can't make something unless you believe in it first. To believe in something before it exists takes a leap of faith. If you can't believe in it when it's nothing, it will never have the chance to become something," Tink insisted.

"I don't understand," Bastian said.

"You will," Tink assure him, and stepped away from his desk.

"For now, I recommend you stop thinking altogether and allow yourself to simply play."

Tink walked over to a school desk resting against the wall and carried it over, setting it down in front of Bastian and placing a piece of Glasstanight in its center.

"Can you see the Ghost Element on the desk in front of you?" he asked.

Bastian looked down at the desk. "Yeah." He watched the Element seep out of the air and accumulate around the crystal.

"I would like you to concentrate on it. Imagine each particle as a tiny soldier. Together, they make a large army at your command. I want you to imagine them marching," Tink directed.

Bastian stared at the dust and tried to picture each speck coming to life. But no matter how hard he tried, he just couldn't take it seriously, the whole thing felt so absurd. He scratched his head.

"Remember, the Element is affected by your intentions. You must hold what you want it to be or do in your mind and will it into existence—call it into action," Tink instructed.

"Right. I'm trying, but it's not working. To be honest, it all feels rather, well…silly. I don't understand how I can possibly change something illusive into something substantial by simply willing it. It doesn't make any sense. Don't get me wrong, I want to. Stars know, I would love to be able to make things appear from nothing as much as the next person. I just can't understand how it's feasible," Bastian protested.

"Not feasible? The universe was made from nothing," Tink declared. He snapped his fingers. "Just like that, billions of galaxies, planets, moons, and stars popped into existence like the bursting of a bubble—from seemingly nothing. And you're telling me, making one small object from nothing is unfeasible?"

"You said in order to use the Element I have to believe in it. But how can I believe in something so extraordinary? I'm not saying it can't be done, I've seen you and the captain do it. I just can't make enough sense of it to do it myself," Bastian objected.

"Don't think of it as making something from nothing then. You're making something from the Ghost Element—the basic building block of existence. In truth, *nothing* is an illusory concept that doesn't have any place in reality. Everything comes from something and eventually changes into something else—even if we don't know or understand what that *something* is," Tink declared. He pulled out his green monocle and placed it over his left eye. "In order to interact with the Element you must open your mind and expand your idea of what's possible. You'll never be able to manipulate it if you continue to think about it so literally," he asserted.

He lifted his hand and saluted the dust on the desk. Instantly the gold particles sprung to life and collected into a square formation, each one moving up and down in unison as if they were tiny soldiers marching in place. Bastian gawked at them.

"You need to stop trying to make sense of it. It isn't something you can dissect or take apart. Your brain will automatically reject it, because it acts outside the laws it thinks infallible. But they're not. Things are only impossible when you convince yourself they are. As soon as you accept that the impossible is possible, then and only then does it become so. It's as simple as that," Tink proclaimed.

Bastian scoffed. "As simple as that? If only *that* were simple."

"Most things are. People are the ones who complicate matters," Tink stated matter-of-factly.

"Right," Bastian muttered.

Tink held up his fist and the marching particles froze in place.

"Try again," he insisted, stepping back to his desk.

Bastian looked at the pile of dust disheartened. It was just sitting there now, completely lifeless. Not even moving with its usual mysterious swirling eddies and rising tendrils. He tried to imagine them again as little soldiers. Nothing happened. Bastian let out an audible sigh.

"Come back tomorrow. We'll try again then," Tink announced.

"What will that achieve? I won't have a clue of what I'm doing then either," Bastian protested.

"No, but I'll be better prepared to teach you. We'll start again in the morning," Tink asserted. He picked up a feathered quill and began writing notes. "Tomorrow, same time. In the meantime, have a look at that book and try to absorb as much of it as you can," he instructed, motioning to an old leather-bound book sitting on the corner of his desk.

"Right. See you tomorrow then," Bastian muttered, taking the book reluctantly and leaving disappointed.

Bastian left Tink's workshop and headed down the ship's hall feeling incredibly discouraged. *So, I'm some sort of freak of nature,* he thought. A lot of good it did him. Being able to see the Ghost Element didn't seem to help him manipulate it at all. Tink and the captain made it look so easy. Tink had said Bastian needed to believe in it in order to make it work. But how could he believe in something so impossible? It was as if someone was telling him every fairytale, every "magic" trick he'd ever learned was actually possible to achieve without any trick at all. It went against everything he'd known to be true. Maybe the problem wasn't his ability to believe, but that it actually was impossible—for him at least. Just because he could see the Element didn't guarantee he had the ability to do anything with it, did it? Maybe the reason he couldn't was because he was missing something necessary to make it work. Despite Tink's ability to utilize it, Bastian got the impression there was still a lot about the Element he didn't understand.

By the time Bastian reached the mess hall he was feeling depressed. If he couldn't figure out how to master the Ghost Element by the time they reached Jaxland, he would never be able to win his freedom. He decided then that wasn't an option. He would just have to find a way.

Bastian sat down at one of the empty tables and looked at the leather book in his hands. It had a faded green leather cover with an alchemy symbol on the front embossed in gold, and it was titled *Things that At-tract and Repel the Ghost Element Categorized in Seven Parts—Elements, Emotions, Colors, Tones, Stones, Human Objects, and Living Things. By Bartleby Foster and Haplo Tracy.*

Bastian recognized the original alchemists' names at once and sat up, suddenly acutely aware of the treasure he held in his hands. Instantly the drudgery of his homework assignment transformed into the tingling thrill of a rare and magnificent opportunity.

Two hours later Bastian was still sitting in the mess hall with his head buried in the alchemists' book. It consisted primarily of lists. Currently he was reading the list for living things. It was titled *Living Things that Attract the Ghost Element in Seven Parts: Sea Creatures, Land Creatures, Flying Creatures, Reptiles, Amphibians, Insects, and Plants.* And it continued to list everything from those categories in alphabetical order, such as

*Abalone*
*Coral*
*Jellyfish*
*Mermaids*
*Oysters*
*Octopi*
*Seahorses*
*Seadragons*
*Selkies*

And on the list went. Despite the entire book comprising nothing but very long lists, Bastian found them curiously interesting. There were things listed on them he hadn't thought existed at all—things like Torch-Bats and Platypus, not to mention Mermaids and Silkies. But his concept of what was possible was expanding as the day went on. Over the last several hours he'd been poring over the lists hungrily, absorbing them. There was something comforting about the information—like discovering static was an ancient language he could learn to understand. Instead of trying to ignore the Element, he suddenly felt drawn to it and wanted to drink in every detail he could with a ravenous curiosity. Bastian's favorite parts of the book were the added scribbled notes inserted here or there by Bartleby or Haplo. Little footnotes like *I've noticed the Ghost Element hangs around firebeetles more when they're glowing than asleep. I wonder if this is because the Element is attracted to the phosphorescence itself, or if it has to do with the mental or emotional activity of the beetles when they're awake.*

Bastian glanced over at the Everfire beetles beside him and watched the Ghost Element hovering and swirling around them. He stirred up some of it on the floor with his finger and watched as it spun into the air, hovering and twinkling in the sunlight that poured in through the cracks between the boards above him. He was starting to come around to the lingering presence of the Element, starting to feel grateful he could see it, instead of resentful. He wished he could've met the original alchemists. He wondered what they had been like. He'd always appreciated the inventions, but never actually thought about the people behind them. Knowing now that they shared the same strange visual trait he did made him feel connected to them in some way. It made him want to know everything about them. He wondered if Tink had any more of their books. Before Bastian knew it, he was late for line duty. He quickly stowed the book away in his locker and made his way to the top deck.

The sun was shining brightly and for the first time in weeks it was actually warm. Bastian took off his jacket and found the group of sailors sitting on upturned barrels, braiding and mending lines.

"Heya, reporting for duty," he greeted.

The half circle of three men stopped their work and looked up at him. They were an odd-looking bunch. In the center was Dagger, the half-man who acted as the ship's musician. To his left was a man who was nearly as wide as Dagger was tall. To his right was a pirate with a long thin face and a white monkey sitting on his shoulder. The monkey had a brown stripe running down its back to the tip of its tail and it was eating sunflower seeds out of a small leather satchel slung across its shoulder. It looked at Bastian curiously. Bastian recognized all of them from the crew, but they'd never been introduced.

"Dodger, is it?" Dagger asked, in a voice much deeper than Bastian was expecting.

"Yes, and you're Dagger?"

"Aye. This be Guts," Dagger told him, elbowing the man on his left with a belly like a rum barrel. The man smiled and waved. Bastian waved back.

Dagger nodded towards the man with the monkey, "An' this be Tails."

The pirate nodded to him, then scratched his monkey under the chin. "An' this be Gibber," Tails informed him.

"Nice to meet you all," Bastian greeted, sitting down on a barrel amongst them.

"Ya 'ave any experience with lines, Dodger?" Dagger asked.

"Some. I used to work as a fisherman's hand in Westdock."

Dagger nodded. "Good. Then ya need no introduction. That pile there needs stopper knots on their ends. Can ya manage?"

Bastian grabbed a rope from the pile. "Yes, sir."

Dagger laughed heartily, "Ha! Did ya 'ear that, lads? 'e called me sir! Ya sorry lot could take a tip from this one. I could get used ta that. Sir!" Dagger chuckled, then got straight back to whipping the lines. Bastian set to work tying a stopper knot on the ropes' unraveled ends. He enjoyed tying knots. He'd tracked down a book on the subject and taught himself to tie every sailor's knot in it when he and Felix first started working for Jarvis's fishing operation, hoping it would give them an edge in getting accepted into his crew. He found he had a knack for it. Since childhood he'd always needed to be doing something with his hands—rope work satisfied that wonderfully. Before long he fell into a gentle rhythm that allowed his focus to wander. He started observing the Ghost Element around him. Who and what it was attracted to, and who and what repelled it. Before he knew it, the lunch bell rang.

After lunch Bastian made his way to the galley for his final daily chore. The small kitchen was meticulously clean and organized. It was constructed with sanded polished hardwood that shined in the warm firebeetle lantern light. There were pots and pans hanging below the upper cupboards, and dried herbs hanging from the ceiling. Barrels and baskets were roped around the base of the butcher's block, holding onions, apples, and potatoes. And above the black Everfire stove was a decorative stained glass window, a depiction of a sloop with full sails made from blue, green, and yellow glass surrounded by clear textured panes. Doc and a sailor Bastian hadn't met were already inside.

Doc nodded to Bastian when he entered, then did a double take back to his face.

"What 'appened ta ya?!" he exclaimed.

Bastian put his hand to where Doc was staring and felt the tenderness of his bruise.

"Oh, right. It's nothing."

Doc looked livid. "Don't tell me that was Snibs who did that to ya?" he asked.

Bastian hesitated just long enough for Doc to have his answer.

"That slitherin' worm! 'e made me abandon all in need ta stitch ya up whole—then 'ad the gall ta give ya further injury! 'e'll be 'earin' from me, don't ya worry. I won't be standin' any such nonsense! Let me 'ave a look at ya," Doc commanded, taking Bastian's head in his two large hands and studying his stitches. "At least the stitches stayed sound. Yer 'ealin' up well. Just keep yer 'ead away from further injury," he ordered.

"I intend to, thanks. And thank you for all you did for me, I for one am incredibly grateful for it," Bastian returned in earnest.

Doc smiled at that. "All part o' the job. I wish I could've saved all 'em boys. I'm glad ya made it, lad," he said, then tossed Bastian a canvas apron. "Put that on an' wash yer 'ands."

Bastian tied on the apron and went straight to the washing basin. The other sailor was busy chopping onions and carrots and throwing them into a large pot on the stove. He was older than Bastian by a handful of years. A couple inches taller, lean and tough without an inch of fat on him.

"Dodger, Runner. Runner, Dodger," Doc introduced as he passed between them to check the ripeness of a bowl of tomatoes. Bastian and Runner nodded to one another.

"Runner, be so kind as ta tell Dodger 'ere the rules o' the galley," Doc instructed.

Runner put down his knife and began listing rules on his fingers. "Don't touch anythin' without permission. Don't touch anythin' without clean 'ands. Don't even think about eatin' anythin' until the work be done, an' then and only then if ya 'ave been granted permission. Nothin' that's in the galley, leaves the gall—."

Doc held up a hand. "That be plenty fer now. Give 'im any more an' 'e won't remember the ones that matter most. Follow the rules, an' ya get ta eat yer tea before anyone else. Break the rules, an' ya go without—savvy?"

"Perfectly," Bastian confirmed.

"Good. Then ya can start by washin' an' peelin' those potatoes," Doc ordered, motioning towards a bowl on the bench piled high with the blue vegetables.

"Right," Bastian said, and sighed inside. He hated peeling potatoes. He'd already done a lifetime of it at the Order. One of the joys of leaving the Star Temple was thinking he was being liberated from ever having to peel potatoes again. He wondered if he could use the Ghost Element to peel them for him.

Bastian finished washing his hands and set to work peeling the blue root vegetables with a short, curved knife. The glittering Ghost Element coated just about everything in the kitchen—even after washing his hands, the fine dust still lingered on his fingers. Bastian studied it curiously as he worked. After a time he turned his attention to the contents of the kitchen. On the back wall was a rack from floor to ceiling stocked with jars filled with herbs and spices. It was an impressive collection. He was interested to see that some of the jars attracted the Element more than others. He made a mental note of which ones they were. Turmeric, in particular, seemed to take the Element's fancy, and pepper warded it off. Bastian imagined Doc used the ingredients for medicine as much as cooking. He recognized several herbs and spices that were used often for medicinal purposes at the Order. The more Bastian thought about it, the more he realized how much Doc's duties as doctor and ship's cook complemented one another. Butchery was as good as any anatomy lesson, and Doc's skill with the knife in the kitchen would be just as useful in surgery, not to mention the right food was as good a remedy as most medication. Bastian discreetly catalogued Doc's full collection to his memory. As he worked, he added everything else in the kitchen to his mental log. The knives, the pots and pans, random abstract tools—metal devices used for punching holes in coconuts, metal crackers for getting through crab shells, various sizes of metal funnels, and so forth. Bastian filed it all meticulously away. It was his routine for any room with potential opportunity, and a kitchen was generally full of it. He'd been hoping he might pick up a few of Doc's cooking secrets while there, but he never had the chance. As soon as one menial task was finished, he was put straight onto the next. And there was no written recipe—Doc seasoned everything by eye and taste. Finally, when the pot on the stove was filling the galley with a mouthwatering aroma, and all the dishes were clean, their work was done.

"Runner, take Dodger down ta the cellar an' bring up a couple barrels o' grog, will ya? After all that 'ard work, the men'll be thirsty," Doc ordered, and pulled a chain from around his neck with a key on it, tossing it to Runner.

Runner caught the key and motioned for Bastian to follow him to a trapdoor in the far end of the galley floor. It had a thick metal ring on top secured shut with a chain and heavy padlock. Runner used the key to remove the chain, then hooked a rope pulley onto the ring and pulled on it, lifting the trapdoor open. Runner secured the rope on a hook on the wall, and grabbed a firebeetle lantern that was hanging there, then he descended into the cellar.

Bastian followed closely behind. As they descended a narrow flight of stairs the temperature dropped by two degrees. The steps led to a small storage room filled with crates of bottles on one side and barrels on wooden racks on the other. But the thing that caught Bastian's attention most of all was a copper spirit still at the back of the room. It had a large copper belly that tapered upward into winding pipework—and it was beautiful.

"Is that what Doc uses to make his rum?" Bastian asked.

"Yup. Finest rum on the seven seas. But don't get any idears, this place be tightly kept under lock an' key. If anyone's ever caught nickin' from Doc's stores, they're best hope be a quick death," Runner warned, pulling down one of the barrels from the racks. "Grab the other end, will ya?"

Bastian pulled his eyes from the still and helped Runner carry the barrel of grog up to the galley.

⌒

Doc let Bastian and Runner eat their tea in the small kitchen before the rest was taken out to be served. Once Bastian had been excused, he palmed an apple from one of the barrels and stowed it in his jacket pocket before heading for the mess hall to find Cricket and the twins.

⌒

Bastian sat next to Rhino, across the table from Stork and Cricket, with a full Black Jack in hand.

"Are ya still up fer throwin' dice tanight, Cricket?" Stork asked.

"O' course I am. Double er nothin'," Cricket declared.

"Alright. But when I take all ya 'ave, don't say I didn't warn ya," Stork smirked.

"What a cocky bastard ya are! Laugh it up, 'cause after tanight ya won't 'ave nothin' left ta be laughin' about," Cricket told him.

"Ooo, I'm quiverin' in me boots!" Stork jested.

Cricket stuck up his pointer finger and turned it in a little circle, "go Shick yerself, ya son o' swine," he sneered.

"Oi! leave our muther out o' it!" Rhino growled threateningly.

"I wasn't talkin' ta yew!" Cricket objected.

"No, but ya were talkin' about me muther, weren't ya?" Rhino returned evenly.

The three pirates erupted into further argument. Bastian turned his attention to Falgo, slumped in his usual corner. The man looked even worse than he had that morning. Bastian couldn't stand to see him that way. He felt compelled to help him. He knew where Doc kept his rum now. He decided then that when nightfall came, he would put his plan into motion.

Bastian sat in his hammock poring over the alchemists' book Tink had loaned him. By the time he'd finished it, the rest of the pirates were fast asleep. He tucked the book under his pillow and silently rolled out of his hammock as gracefully as a cat. He made his way down to the gun deck where Dylan was sitting slumped over his knees, asleep.

Bastian reached through the bars and shook his shoulder. Dylan's eyes flung open, then relaxed when he saw it was Bastian.

"You've got to stop creeping up on me like that, you nearly gave me a heart attack!" Dylan exclaimed.

"I brought you something," Bastian announced, and passed him the apple he'd taken from the galley.

Dylan took it hungrily, biting into the crisp fruit. "It's so fresh! How do they preserve them so well?"

"They grow them onboard. There's a whole garden on one of the decks."

"Is that even possible?!"

"This ship completely redefines what's possible," Bastian told him.

"Huh. Did you get a chance to talk to the captain about me?" Dylan asked.

"I don't have the authority to talk to the captain. But I did talk to Snibs—he's the quartermaster. He mostly runs the ship anyways."

"What did he say?"

"He said they won't release you until after we pass Jaxland."

"Jaxland, where's that?"

"An uncharted island governed by pirates. We're headed there now. Snibs said, if he let you out before, you wouldn't make it past."

Dylan thought about that for a moment. "He's right, no doubt. I've probably crossed the paths of several of them before. Protecting Equillian's trade route from piracy has been the bulk of my career with the Navy."

"Best to stay here out of harm's way then, at least until we're headed back to the mainland," Bastian advised.

"How long will that be?"

"I've no idea. A week, maybe longer," Bastian guessed.

"A week?!"

"That's not so long in the scheme of things. Just pretend you're in the Reflection Room. I'll paint a guiding star on the rafters for you," Bastian jested.

"I'm not as accustomed to the Reflection Room as you are. If only I could see the stars though, that would be enough. It's having no concept of time down here that's driving me nuts," Dylan complained.

"Hey, I have a question to ask you…" Bastian said.

"Go on then."

"You graduated from the Order, right?"

"Yeah…"

"What do you know about the Essence of Empyrean?"

"The Essence of Empyrean? That's an odd thing to ask about. What's made you curious about that?" Dylan asked.

"It's the one subject I wish I hadn't missed. I've never been able to find any information about it outside the Order."

Dylan nodded and thought for a moment, trying to recall his lessons.

"From the bits and pieces I can remember, the Sisters refer to it as the soul of the universe—the essence of everything. They said it's what connects us to the stars and everything else in existence," Dylan recalled.

Bastian absorbed that. "Is it supposed to be an element?" he asked.

"I don't know. I don't think they ever said. The whole thing sounded a bit far-fetched to me. I think it was just a bunch of Star dogma. I imagine it's more of a metaphorical idea than something intended to be taken literally."

"Right. Thanks," Bastian said, then he pulled out his pocket watch and passed it through the bars. "Here."

Dylan accepted the watch and drank in the time like water after traversing a desert.

"I'm only loaning it. Make sure you look after it—it's my favorite one. I want it back as soon as you're out," Bastian asserted.

"You just saved my sanity!" Dylan proclaimed.

"Don't be so dramatic."

"Says the free man. I literally feel like I'm losing my mind in here."

"You'll be alright. At least you're safe in there. I'll see you soon, hey?" Bastian said, standing to leave.

Dylan slumped back into the corner. "You know where to find me," he returned, with a half-hearted wave.

Bastian headed back up the companionway to the ship's lockers. He opened his and took out his homemade set of lockpicks. Then he walked silently to the mess hall. There was no one there. All was quiet except the gentle creaking of the ship. He stood there listening intently for several moments before he turned to the galley's locked door. Within seconds he had it open and slipped inside, closing the door gently and locking it behind him. He wasted no time in picking the lock to the cellar door and disappeared down the stairs with the firebeetle lantern towards Doc's distillery. Bastian collected eight bottles—six of rum and two empty ones, carefully selecting them from the back of the store where they were unlikely to be missed. Then he hurried back up to the galley. Once there, Bastian set the eight bottles out on the chopping block and grabbed a large pot that he placed on the Everfire stove. He filled the empty rum bottle with water twice over, emptying it out into the pot each time. Then he grabbed a small frying pan and tossed in a handful of barley from Doc's collection of jarred goods. When the barley was lightly toasted, he ground it into a fine powder using Doc's mortar and pestle, stopping every now and again to listen intently to make sure no one was outside. Then he poured the powdered barley inside a cheesecloth, twisted it several times, and put it in the pot of hot water to steep. He was making barley tea. Bastian had learned the hard way not to replace alcohol with water. He'd come to find that someone familiar with a spirit usually picked up on the difference in consistency and color before they even tasted it. There were several complications that came with watering down liquor—all of which Bastian was well accustomed to from his and Felix's days at the Order. Once, they stumbled upon one of the Sisters' own personal stash of Aodka—a clear ethanol-based spirit with a freezing point around −100°C. They were ecstatic at how easily they could replace the spirit with water without it appearing any different. That was, until the Sister whom it belonged to decided to share it for the winter festival and put the Aodka out in the snow for a palatable chill. When she pulled out the bottle the following day, it was solid ice. Bastian and Felix realized very quickly where they'd gone wrong. Bastian was grateful for those early lessons; he would far rather face the wrath of an angry ecclesiastic of the Stars than that of a pirate.

Bastian found a jar of brown sugar and put several pinches into the barley tea, mixing it until well combined. If he were replacing whisky, he would've left out the sugar. But most rums were derived from sugarcane, and the subtle sweetness of Doc's brew suggested it wasn't any different. Next, Bastian pulled out another pot and poured all six bottles of rum into it. He strained the tea and added half of it to the large pot, combining it with the six bottles of rum. The tea matched the color and consistency of the rum beautifully and was subtle enough in flavor not to raise any red flags. Bastian stirred it all together until he was satisfied, and then funneled his concoction back into the green bottles and replaced their stoppers. Now, instead of six bottles of rum, there were seven. Finally, he emptied the remainder of the barley tea into the last bottle. Then he took one of the kitchen knives and made an hairline etch on the bottom of each one. He quickly replaced the six he'd taken from Doc's stores at the back, as well as the bottle of barley tea, and then returned to the galley to clean up. Once he'd restored everything to its rightful place and removed the evidence of his presence, he stuffed a bottle of weakened rum in the back of his pants and slipped out of the galley, locking the door behind him.

# PUNCH DRUNK

Felix and Roy stepped out of the Sky Garden an hour after they'd entered. They'd just finished a tour given by a dashing young female engineer who'd helped to design the whole system. They'd been told they lucked out—apparently the tour was usually given by an android. The Sky Garden was like nothing Felix had ever seen or imagined. It was filled with stainless steel grow towers sprouting up through its center like a grove of trees, abundant plant life growing out of each one like branches from metal trunks. Steam-powered machines in the shape of discs with mechanical arms encircled each tower, patrolling up and down their length to plant and harvest the produce. The system was entirely automated. The compost waste from Sky View's citizens was brought to the towers and put into giant bioreactors; there it was converted into a nutrient solution to be fed back to the plants, saturating their roots in a cold steam that filled the core of each tower. The solution provided water, nutrients, and oxygen—everything the plants needed except sunlight. It baffled Felix to see this natural process harnessed in a factory. It felt so artificial and yet it made such perfect sense. Why not? People had been farming the same way for hundreds, if not thousands of years, and it was so inefficient. The amount of land and water wasted was catastrophic, as was the failure of crops due to the unpredictability of weather or pests, amongst the other various obstacles farmers contended with. And here it was all eliminated by simply growing plants in a controlled environment. Not only that, their tour guide informed them that the produce grown in the Sky Gardens grew faster and was both more flavorful and more nutritious. It made Felix wonder why the same system wasn't being used the world over.

"That was fascinating!" Felix pronounced, pulling out his silver case and lighting up a puff-stick.

"Necessity is certainly the mother of invention. Leave it to the one precinct thought impossible to farm to surpass the world in farming entirely," Roy remarked, looking down at his pocket watch. "Best we start heading back if we want to make it in time for lunch."

Felix nodded, blowing out a stream of smoke as he followed Roy through the growing crowd.

When Felix and Roy arrived back at the Wendrians' estate, the butler led them to the back garden. There was a long table set up on the lawn, adorned in white linen and laden with a grand finger-food buffet. It was a nice day to be out. The sun was shining against a stark canvas of blue, sparsely dotted with wispy white clouds. Lilliana was relaxing in a wicker chair with a giant cocktail in hand. She was wearing a wide-brimmed purple hat and a pair of yellow-framed solarglasses with rose tinted lenses. Her face was tilted towards the sun, basking in the warmth of its rays. At the sight of her, elation hit Felix like a punch to the chest. He didn't realize how eager he'd been to see her.

"You've both cleaned up well," Lilliana commented, pulling down her solarglasses to have a better look at them.

"Are you drinking without us?" Felix asked, plucking some grapes from the buffet table.

"Did I have a choice? How long does it take you two to buy new clothes and have a shave?" Lilliana returned.

"I'm sorry, my dear, have you been waiting long?" Roy asked.

"Only half the day," Lilliana replied candidly, taking a long toothpick of cherries from her glass and pulling one off with her teeth.

Felix looked around. "Where's Arianna?" he inquired, realizing no one was accompanying Lilliana besides a manservant standing at attention in the shadow of a large fig tree.

Lilliana waived her hand, "She headed into town to complete registration for the race. It appears I'll have to wait to have my conversation with her regarding the estate until the Derby's over."

"You mean you've been alone this whole time?" Felix asked.

"Not completely alone. Carl's been looking after me, haven't you, Carl?" Lilliana called to the servant.

The man gave a curt and uncomfortable smile.

"Ah well, perhaps it's for the best. Give yourself a day to enjoy being here before jumping into business," Roy suggested, sitting down in one of the wicker chairs beside Lilliana while Felix helped himself to the buffet.

Lilliana barked a laugh. "Enjoy myself? Ha! Unfortunately, the current state of my life has made that an unattainable luxury. In case you've forgotten, I'm supposed to be wed next week to a man who's paid four purses of duckets to have me sold to the slavers. If he doesn't marry me, then my sister will be next in line. No doubt, my mother's worried sick about me, yet I can do nothing to comfort her. My father's missing. I have to confront my cousin about which one of us owns her home—in order to save my own—and even though we're here, we can't attend the Derby. For the last several hours, I've been stuck here by myself with nothing to do but wallow in my own anxiety. If it wasn't for the company of this punch, I might've wandered off the island's edge," she stated, taking a long sip from the metal straw decorating her tall glass.

Roy and Felix shared a concerned glance.

"Well, at least we bear some good news. James has found us a way into the Derby," Roy announced.

Lilliana lowered her solarglasses. "How?"

"We'll be attending to promote Zest. You don't need a ticket for promotions. I don't know why I hadn't thought of it myself—I've attended similar events before to promote my product. I'll go into town this afternoon and find out who I need to talk to organize our passes," Roy reported.

"But I'm supposed to be missing. You said yourself that I shouldn't be seen in public," Lilliana argued.

"Yes, and I stand by that. We can't afford for anyone to know you're here," Roy asserted.

Lilliana frowned. "You're going to leave me behind?"

"Of course not! You're going to attend the Derby as someone else," Roy declared.

Lilliana perked up instantly. "But how? The event isn't a masquerade."

Roy looked over at Felix. "James has informed me he has theater experience with the Westdock Players. He's confident he can devise a disguise for you that will be sufficient in hiding your identity."

Lilliana turned to Felix and beamed. "Brilliant!"

"Attending the event will give us the opportunity to mingle with the local residents and acquire more information regarding your father's last visit," Roy proclaimed.

"Fantastic! Well, it sounds like you two've got it all figured out. All we need now is something to wear," Lilliana said.

"Actually, James has secured you both formal wear from a top-notch designer," Roy announced.

"Oh? How did you manage that?" Lilliana inquired.

"Favio Fritz is the one who outfitted James today. The signature piece of his new clothing line was supposed to be worn by Sasha Avery and his fiancée at the Derby."

"The jouster?" Lilliana asked.

"Yes. Unfortunately, he's taken a lance to the shoulder. Consequently, neither of them will be attending the event. James offered for you two to wear the attire in their place," Roy explained.

Lilliana looked at Felix and raised her eyebrows, "How generous of you."

"What can I say? I'm a generous guy," Felix smirked, popping a grape into his mouth.

"The only catch is that you and James will have to attend the designer's breakfast gala at the start of the Derby, and the after-party at the Opera House when the Derby's finished," Roy told Lilliana.

Lilliana smiled wryly. "Is that right? I suppose if we must, we must."

Roy chuckled. "I didn't think you'd mind. We'll have to return to Favio's in the morning to get you both fitted. I'm hoping he'll have something I can borrow as well. It will be a good opportunity to give your disguise a test-drive."

"Sounds like fun," Lilliana agreed.

"On another note, I've already started to make enquiries into your father's disappearance. I still have several contacts in the area. I'll go to the News House while I'm out and see if I can dig up the original article published in the local paper the day Drake went missing. I think that's a pretty good start for our first day, don't you?"

"Yes. Thank you, Uncle. That's a huge comfort. I don't know what I would do without you. Any ideas on our next move against my slithering fiancé?" Lilliana asked Felix.

Felix was still at the table, helping himself to a variety of stuffed olives, sweet breads and fine cheeses.

"Yes," he confirmed, "I'll compose the next letter and have it ready to send out this afternoon. I think giving Lord Bardviss assurance he has the cooperation of "The Debt Collectors" is our next best move. I'll tell him we accept his offer of employment—under certain terms, of course. And that he can rest assured he'll never have to see you again. I have every confidence your letter we sent reached your mother as intended. I'm sure by now she's shared its contents with Lord Bardviss—which means he'll have to go along with the contrived story of your kidnapping in order to keep his good standing with your mother. That will buy us some time. I imagine Lord Bardviss will be making every show of trying to recapture you and get you back. Once he's assured you're out of the picture, he'll put his energy into the song and dance for your mother and forget about us—giving you the ability to move freely," Felix reported.

"Excellent! We're much more on top of things than I'd realized—thanks to you both. While loitering here, my imagination painted a dismal picture that was incredibly depressing and counterproductive. I can't tell you how much of a relief it is to know the reality is far more optimistic," Lilliana proclaimed.

She held up her empty glass expectantly.

The servant stepped forth from the shadows and refilled her glass. Then he returned the jug to the table and resumed his position as a human statue. Felix watched the transaction curiously. He picked up the jug and poured himself a glass—there was barely enough punch left to fill it a quarter full. The pitcher contained ice and slices of citrus fruit and cherries, but no liquid. Then it dawned on him—Lilliana must have drunk the entire thing by herself. He studied her carefully. She was a little more relaxed than usual, but otherwise holding herself together surprisingly well. He took a sip of the quarter glass he'd scrounged from the dregs and coughed. It was a potent concoction of white berry rum and who knew what else. He didn't know how Lilliana managed to be coherent.

"Is everything in order for the race?" Roy asked Lilliana.

"I've no idea. Arianna won't let me near the stables. She thinks I might excite the dragons too much and insisted I spend the day resting from our journey. You two didn't miss a thing. It's been incredibly disappointing. My favorite memories of this place are from our visits for the Derby. My father and I used to help my uncle with all the preparations. Instead, I've spent the morning strolling idly through the gardens."

Felix sat down in the wicker chair next to her. "That doesn't sound half bad," he remarked.

"It was nice, for the first hour," Lilliana admitted.

"I'm sorry, my dear. If I'd known things were as they are, we would've come back sooner," Roy apologized.

"No, no. Don't indulge my self-pity, it's no one's fault. I'm just glad you're back. How was the city?" she inquired, taking another long sip of her punch.

"Quite fruitful for our purpose, wouldn't you say, champ?" Roy asked Felix.

"Indeed. Roy can finally have his nightclothes back."

"I'm glad to hear it! There's only so many nights in a row one can wear the same set of clothing and remain respectable," Lilliana declared.

"Is that so? Stars forbid, I might be considered unrespectable," Felix returned wryly, taking a sip of his potent punch.

"It was also very enlightening. Sky View's much changed from my last visit," Roy reported.

"Really? How so?" Lilliana queried.

"It's growing its own produce."

"How? Sky View hardly has any soil."

"Apparently, soil isn't needed for growing plants. They're growing it in buildings with nothing but a nutrient solution made from food scraps. The whole process is completely automated using steam technology," Roy explained.

"Produce factories, how fascinating! Who would've thought? I never would've imagined such a thing was possible," Lilliana exclaimed.

"It's the modern world, seems like just about anything's possible these days. I thought steam technology would never match the abilities of enchanted objects, but I must admit, I'm beginning to wonder. Stars only know what they'll think of next," Roy proclaimed, and he stood from his chair. "Well, if it's fine by you two, I might head out to make my inquiries. I'm eager to make the most of the afternoon. If I leave now, I can hope to be back in time for supper. You're both more than welcome to join me if you like," he invited.

"Thank you, but I think I'll stay here and prepare the letter to send out to Lord Bardviss," Felix declined.

"Very well, how about you, Everspark?"

"I think I'll stay as well. You've restored my spirit, uncle. I can finally relax enough to enjoy the afternoon," Lilliana answered.

Roy smiled warmly. "Good. I'm glad to hear it." He walked over to the table and stuck a chunk of cheese into a bread roll. "Well, you two enjoy your time. I'll see you both at dinner," he said, giving Felix a friendly nod.

Felix held up his glass to Roy and watched the pilot walk out of sight. Then he turned to Lilliana.

"I'm curious. How much have you drunk today?" he asked her.

"That's none of your business!" she scoffed indignantly and took another sip.

"I'm simply impressed. Your tolerance for rum is surprising—at least for a duchess," Felix commended.

"Your stereotype of noble women is greatly misinformed. We're exceptional drinkers. It's the result of having the finest liqueur on hand with little else to do," she informed him.

"Sounds wonderful. I would've liked to have joined you in this delightful pastime, but it appears you've drunk all the punch."

"Don't be ridiculous, it would take a small army to finish all the punch in this place," Lilliana remarked, and she held up her glass to the servant.

He immediately came and took the jug away, returning no more than three minutes later with another full decanter, which he used to refill Lilliana's glass.

"Thank you, Carl," Lilliana said.

"Would you like a top-up, sir?" the servant offered Felix.

Felix held out his glass and smiled kindly. "Yes, thank you, Carl."

Carl filled his glass to the brim and garnished it with a long toothpick of cherries, then he placed the jug on the table and receded into the background once again.

Felix turned to Lilliana. "So, what number of jug is this one?"

Lilliana ignored the question and instead held up her glass for a toast. "To the creators of this fine drink, and the salvation it brings," she announced.

"To the Disentangler, may he disentangle your Stars and fix that which is giving you strife," Felix returned.

"Wouldn't that be nice," Lilliana remarked, clinking Felix's glass and taking a drink.

Felix drained his. Then he walked over to the table and refilled his glass.

"Are you parched?" Lilliana queried.

"You've had an unfair head start, my lady. I'm simply catching up."

"If you want to make a sport of it, there's a game I know for that," she offered.

"Oh? I do enjoy games. How is it played?" Felix inquired, sitting back down beside her.

"It's called *I Have Never*. I say, *I have never* done something, and if either of us has done it, then we have to drink. Whoever hasn't, doesn't," she explained.

"Sounds straightforward enough. It also sounds like a game heavily weighed in your favor—for staying dry," Felix jested.

"Is that so? I think you'd be surprised. Besides, you're the one who said you want to catch up, and I'm well watered already," she stated.

"Alright, Duchess, you're on. Who starts?" Felix asked.

"*I have never* blackmailed anyone," Lilliana began.

Felix chuckled and took a drink. "*I have never* kidnapped anyone."

Lilliana drank. "*I have never* gone to a party I wasn't invited to," she said.

Felix drank. "*I have never* worn a dress," he said, and they both drank.

Lilliana raised an eyebrow at Felix, and he smiled back at her. She cleared her throat, "*I have never* pretended to be someone I'm not."

Felix drank while looking at Lilliana expectantly.

"What?" she asked him.

"Drink up," he instructed.

"Why should I?"

"How about the first night we met? The girl I followed to your bedroom is certainly not the same girl before me now. In fact, from what I've seen, you pretend to be someone you're not each and every day," he said.

Lilliana opened her mouth to speak—only nothing came out. She closed it and took a drink. Felix smiled satisfactorily.

"*I have never* slept in a Star Temple," Lilliana said.

Felix drank. "*I have never* slept in a castle," he countered.

Lilliana drank. "*I have never* slept with two people at once."

Felix choked on his drink. "That's a bit personal, isn't it?"

"Personal questions are what make this game interesting," she stated.

"Ah, I see how this game works now. Alright, Duchess, two can play it your way."

"Well?" Lilliana asked him.

Felix returned her gaze unabashed and took a long hard drink.

"I'm not sure I wanted to know that," Lilliana muttered.

"The danger of any question, my lady, is finding the answer," Felix told her. "It was on my Illumine Day. The cathouse I attended was having a slow day and a couple of the working girls thought it would be amusing to join in on my adult education. It was the best induction I could've hoped for. All three women were highly skilled and knowledgeable in their profession. They made excellent teachers—in fact, it was their fine tutelage that ignited my enthusiasm for the subject," he divulged.

"I'm sure it was," Lilliana remarked dryly.

"*I have never* kissed a girl," Felix said cheerily.

He took a drink while watching Lilliana carefully. She also drank.

"Really?" Felix inquired with enthusiastic interest. "How delightfully intriguing. Please, tell me more," he grinned.

"Oh shush! I was only a child. My friend and I were simply curious what the fuss of kissing was all about."

Felix smiled broadly. "Uh-huh. Please, don't spare the details," he encouraged.

Lilliana rolled her eyes. "*I have never* kissed a man," she said, and she drank while watching Felix carefully.

Felix didn't drink. "*I have*—also—*never* slept with a man—in case you're curious," he imparted.

Lilliana took a drink.

"*I have never* slept with a woman," she said.

Felix drank. "Would you like to?" he asked her.

"That's not how this game works."

Felix smiled. "*I have never—wanted* to sleep with a woman," he said, and drank without taking his eyes off Lilliana.

She returned his stare unimpressed but didn't drink. Felix's grin drooped with disappointment. Lilliana smirked and took her turn.

"*I have never* slept with someone whose name I didn't know."

Felix scratched his head uncomfortably and took a drink. "*I have never* slept with a commoner that isn't here now," he countered, and took a drink while carefully observing Lilliana.

She met his level gaze but didn't drink.

Felix smiled. "Ah, so I'm the first tarnish to your name."

Lilliana ignored him. "*I have never* slept with a duchess," she said.

Felix drank. "I have never been betrothed."

Lilliana drank. "*I have never* slept with a duchess that isn't here now," she said, eyeing him suspiciously.

"I'm not sure that's fair, you've already said you haven't slept with a duchess."

"*I have never* slept with a duchess that isn't here now," Lilliana repeated.

Felix smiled but didn't drink. He'd slept with his share of highborn, but never one quite so high as Lilliana.

"It's nice to know I'm your first *something* in that department," she muttered.

Felix smirked. He studied her thoughtfully before taking his next turn. "*I have never* had feelings for a commoner," he said carefully.

Lilliana looked at him for a moment with the level gaze of a master poker player and then said, "I think we've played enough of this game. As I recall, I owe you an arse-kicking in a round of cards. Do you still have that deck of yours?"

Felix looked at his shoes and smiled, fanning out his lucky deck in his hand as if the cards appeared from thin air.

"Good. It's getting cold out here. We can play in my room. There's a sitting area with an excellent view of the surrounding islands," Lilliana suggested, and stood from her chair.

"Lead the way," Felix invited, and drained his glass. "As fun and enlightening as that game was, you're still swimming far ahead of me, my lady," he remarked, and grabbed the jug of rum punch before following after.

⌒

Lilliana's bedroom was almost twice the size of Felix's, with an extravagant four-poster bed and a sitting area with two chairs and a table in front of a long window bordered with decorative stained glass that had an excellent view of the surrounding islands. Attached to the bedroom was a huge and luxurious en suite with green and coral marble tiles and a large circular white marble bath in the center surrounded by pillars stretching from floor to ceiling.

"Not bad," Felix remarked.

He put his glass and the jug on the table and took off his jacket, hanging it on the back of one of the chairs. Then he sat down and began shuffling his deck of cards. "What game are we playing? Shoot for the Stars, Luck Chaser, Davy Jones's Locker?" he suggested.

Lilliana took off her hat and solarglasses and threw them on the bed. "You choose. I'm going to get into something more comfortable."

Felix filled himself another glass of punch and began dealing out the cards while Lilliana changed behind her wardrobe door.

"You mind if I smoke in here?" he asked her.

"Knock yourself out."

Felix pulled out one of the puff-sticks he'd rolled earlier and lit it with his Everfire box. He took a puff as he picked up his hand of cards and began organizing it by suit. A few minutes later Lilliana sat down in the chair opposite him and picked up the cards Felix had dealt her.

Felix glanced up and then did a double take. Lilliana was wearing the small black nightdress he'd discovered amongst her things earlier that morning. The Demure silk hugged her figure perfectly, leaving little to the imagination. For the first time in his life, Felix was rendered speechless. His mouth dropped open, his puff-stick balancing precariously on his lower lip. Lilliana leaned across the table and plucked it from him, then took a graceful drag, exhaling the smoke languidly as she organized her cards. "What are we playing?" she asked.

"Ahhh…Shoot for the Stars," Felix answered, clearing his throat and using all his willpower to turn his attention back to his hand. He couldn't focus, his head was doing cartwheels. *Is this some sort of test? Or is she deliberately toying with me?* he wondered. Lilliana had said earlier that she wore the dress without occasion, but wearing it now hardly seemed appropriate. Surely it was deliberate, *but for what purpose?* he asked himself. He couldn't have been more confused. It didn't help that he was now under the hold of the rum punch.

"Perfect," Lilliana said, and took another drag from his puff-stick.

Felix cleared his throat. "I wasn't aware you puff, my lady. If I'd known, I would've offered you one."

"I hardly do. It's not considered a proper habit for a duchess," she said.

"Is that right?" Felix uttered distractedly.

Lilliana placed a Raven card on the table. Felix threw down the Jack of Shadows, then he stole a glance at Lilliana while she riffled through her cards. She placed down the Dame of Everlasting Light. Felix tossed down a Thrixing card, silently cursing himself as he realized it wasn't the card he'd intended to play. Lilliana lay down the Queen of Stars and took the pile.

*Shick.* Felix stared at the empty space where the cards had been, cursing himself for getting so distracted. "I'm sorry, but I can't concentrate with you wearing that," he confessed.

"I know. That's the point," Lilliana stated, with a mischievously seductive smile.

"I hardly think that's fair play, do you?" Felix asked her.

"My father taught me to utilize every advantage when facing an opponent," she said.

Felix studied her. "And what if I let you defeat me?"

"Then the game wouldn't be any fun."

Felix wanted to say *that's when the real fun would begin*, but he bit his tongue and instead took another drink of his punch. He wasn't drunk enough for this situation, nor was he sober enough to navigate it. It was only that morning Lilliana had told him to forget they'd ever been together. Now, she was flat-out seducing him. At least, he hoped that's what she was doing. Because if it wasn't, then it meant she was toying with him—like a cat toys with a mouse before making it her dinner.

*What's her endgame?* he wondered. *Is this some sort of trap? Does she want to be with me again, or is it just that she's drunk?*

Hooking up with Lilliana was always going to be dangerous. It was a risk Felix was happy to take as long as it was consensual—but, if something happened between them now and Lilliana decided she felt differently when she sobered, it would put him in a very fragile and compromising situation. He threw his cards on the table.

"I fold," he declared.

Lilliana raised an eyebrow. "Are you always this easy to beat at cards?"

"Almost never," he admitted.

She smiled, revealing the dimples in her cheeks and desire bloomed in Felix.

"I should go. Best prepare that letter for Lord Bardviss," he excused himself hastily, intending to stand—but finding his body unwilling to obey his command.

Lilliana walked over to his chair and sat down on his lap gracefully. Felix froze. She took the puff-stick from her mouth and placed it in his. Felix took a much needed drag. Lilliana plucked it back and took one more puff before extinguishing it on the table in front of them, then she leaned down and kissed him. Felix held himself back for all of two milliseconds before welcoming her embrace and passionately returning her kiss. *Shick have mercy,* he thought, pulling her closer to him. He was completely powerless—women were his greatest weakness, and Lilliana was the crème de la crème.

# TREASURE BOX

Gwena woke to a knock on her door. "Breakfast, mademoiselle!" a voice sang from the hallway. Gwena opened her door sleepily. There was a servant standing there with a cart and a warm smile. "Morning, miss," he said, and handed her a silver tray with a cloche-covered dish.

"Thank you," Gwena replied. She brought it to the end of her bed and uncovered the meal. It was a well-balanced breakfast, with fried fish, scrambled duck eggs, a few slices of winter melon, and a croissant. *Maybe this place isn't so bad,* she thought as she dug into her morning feast. As soon as her meal was done, she dressed and headed downstairs to meet Bonnie.

When Gwena arrived at the bar Bonnie was nowhere to be seen. The bartender was polishing glasses behind the counter, and she recognized Rafael and Benji sitting at the bar. Rafael was fishing peanuts out of a bowl full of shells, and Benji was nursing a glass of whisky.

"Good morning," the bartender greeted her cheerily as she approached.

"Good morning," Gwena returned, pulling out a stool next to Benji. "Do you mind if I sit here?"

Benji looked at her absently and shrugged. "It doesn't belong to me," he stated, taking another sip from his short glass.

"A bit early for drinking, isn't it?" she asked in good humour.

"Says the woman sitting next to me at the bar."

Gwena smiled.

The bartender nodded to her, "Can I get you anything, miss?"

"Oh, nothing for me—thanks. I'm meeting Bonnie here, she's taking me into town to run some errands," Gwena declined politely.

"You two going to see the Science Fair?" Rafael inquired.

"I hadn't thought of that. Is it worth seeing?"

"Of course! It's world class," Rafael exclaimed.

"Haven't you ever been?" the bartender asked her.

"I didn't even know it existed before yesterday," Gwena admitted.

"No kidding? I would've thought you had to be living under a rock," the bartender exclaimed.

Gwena smiled. "Almost—Westdock."

"Is that right? I've never been that far west, but I hear good things."

"Ah, Westdock—famous for its meat pies and cathouses," Rafael remarked.

"I can vouch for the meat pies, but not the cathouses—I'm more of a bird person myself," Gwena jested.

Benji smirked.

"Well, you've certainly come to the right place then," the bartender announced.

"Yeah? Why's that?" Gwena queried.

"This place's known as the birdhouse," Rafael informed her.

"Is that because it's full of Wildsingers?" Gwena guessed.

"Bingo!" The bartender affirmed.

"I'm still not sure I understand what that means exactly. I mean, the club certainly puts on quite the party and all the patrons look the part, but why keep it all a secret?" Gwena asked.

"Because most of the people who attend this place are public figures well known up top. By day their lives are in the limelight. They can't afford to have any fun without risking their reputations. They have to maintain an image of propriety, you see. But for a Wildsinger, that can be downright damaging—drains them of all their song and color," the bartender explained.

"That's why Haplo created this place. It's the opposite of a birdcage— it allows those who're caged a chance to fly free. A place where they can be themselves without fear of consequence even if only by night—keeps them from completely losing themselves while being able to maintain their lives and reputations," Rafael told her.

"Are you saying there were famous people here last night?" Gwena queried.

"Sure, they're here every night," the bartender said, polishing a glass.

"What kind of famous people?" Gwena inquired.

"Sports stars, famous actors, musicians—you name it."

"Anyone I would've heard of?"

"Most likely."

"Like who?"

"Benji was getting friendly with Scarlet Jade last night," Rafael announced with a smirk.

"Scarlet Jade?! That's the woman you were with?!" Gwena exclaimed. Scarlet Jade was an opera singer who could move a whole audience to tears by the time she was seven. Her voice was said to be like the Stars singing. She was by far the most prestigious musician on Equillian.

Benji only shrugged in reply.

"Are you two seeing each other?!" Gwena asked with enthusiastic interest.

Rafael chuckled. "You could call it that."

Benji ignored the question.

"Benji's her favorite. She requests his company every Twinsday, doesn't she, Benji?" the bartender said.

Benji took another silent swig of his whisky.

"Requests his company? What do you mean, are you some sort of escort?" Gwena inquired.

Rafael smirked, "Haha, yeah, he escorts them straight to his bedroom," he remarked wryly.

"Benji's not just some escort, he's the highest paid and most sought after escort in the Heartland," the bartender acclaimed.

"Wait, isn't Scarlet Jade married?" Gwena asked.

"Yeah, but the man's a real scumbag. She'd be a mess if it wasn't for Benji," Rafael proclaimed.

"If that's true, then why doesn't she just leave him?"

Benji snorted in his glass.

"It's a little more complicated than that," the bartender told her.

"Are you two in love?"

"No," Benji stated bluntly.

"Benji doesn't believe in love," Rafael explained, putting his arm around him.

Benji shrugged it off.

"That's right, Bonnie did mention that," Gwena recalled.

Benji scoffed. "I believe in love, I just don't believe it's the fairytale everyone tries to make it out to be."

"What is it then?" Gwena asked him.

"A drug," he declared bluntly.

"You really believe love's some sort of mind meddler?"

"That's exactly what it is," Benji asserted, sipping his whisky.

"How can you say that?" Gwena asked in disbelief.

"Have you ever taken any mind meddlers?"

"I can't say it's ever interested me," Gwena confessed.

"Well, if you had, you'd know most of them give you an incredible high. They mess with your brain chemistry—spilling out your natural supply of happy chemicals all at once. It's a real ride while it lasts, a burst of dopey joy and childlike glee—even creativity. You feel on top of the world. The problem is, afterwards your brain's vial of feel-good juice is all used up and takes a while to replenish itself, meaning that those few hours of being over the moon have cost you at least a day of misery. You'd think that would stop someone from doing it again, but it doesn't. They keep chasing that high, willing to pay any cost just to feel it again and again and again—until eventually the drug changes the brain's own chemistry to the point where the drug doesn't even get them high anymore, they start needing it just to feel normal, or at least not miserable. And people will keep up the supply because they know if they stop taking it, that's when things get really rough. To get through the withdrawals is a walk through the Nine Realms of Darkness, and people will do just about anything to avoid that. That's love. It starts you off with the greatest rush you've ever had, convincing you that you can't live without it. If you're lucky, it will be taken away from you early, before you become dependent on it. However, if you get the opportunity to drink in that person again, and again, and again, that high eventually stops being what it was—only you've become reliant on it, and you'll hang onto it desperately, because you know that the second you lose it, you'll have to walk that path of darkness," Benji concluded.

"That's super dark, man," Rafael remarked.

"That is pretty sour, friend," the bartender agreed.

Benji shrugged. "The truth normally is, once you get past the sugar coating."

"I'm sorry, but that's by far the most depressing piece of hogwash I've ever heard," Gwena declared.

"Hogwash? What do you know about love?" Benji asked her.

"Enough to know that if it's true love, then you're not falling for a feeling, you fall for a person—who they are, not what they are. A person who sees the best version of you and believes in it until you believe in it yourself. Someone who helps you battle through darkness when it's consuming you. A person who makes you laugh when you've forgotten how. Of course it isn't always easy. Love isn't supposed to be all sunshine and rainbows—it's a tempest. It ebbs and flows, changing like the tide just as much as we do. Sometimes it blows you about, and other times it holds you safely in its eye, but if the person is right, then it's worth weathering love's storm with them, because ultimately you make each other better," Gwena proclaimed.

Benji met Gwena's eyes. "That's a fine fairytale."

"I'm not surprised you think that. How can you hope to find something, if you're not willing to believe in it?" Gwena challenged.

Just then Bonnie approached the bar. "Mornin', gents. Sorry ta keep ya waitin', Gwena, ya ready ta 'ead out?" she asked her.

"Yes, yes I am," Gwena answered.

She stood up and nodded to the three men at the bar. "Have a good day, gentleman," she said, and followed Bonnie out.

Benji, Rafael, and the bartender watched her go.

"Ha! She's something else," Rafael exclaimed.

"Naïve as a newborn, that's what she is," Benji scoffed.

"I don't know, seems to me she has things figured out better than the three of us," the bartender said.

Gwena and Bonnie reached the small courtyard outside The Apothecary on the strange elevator. The same man was there as before, wearing the same trench coat and fedora.

"Hiya, Bonnie," he greeted.

"Hiya, Eric. Need anythin' while we're out?" Bonnie asked.

"Nah, thanks though."

"I'll get ya somethin' anyways," Bonnie smiled, and held the door to the speakeasy open for Gwena.

Gwena walked through. The place was empty. It looked so much smaller and dingier in the daylight. Bonnie listened at the wall that made up the next door before pushing her way into The Apothecary. There were a couple of customers inside talking to a man behind the counter. None of them even looked in their direction as Gwena and Bonnie slipped past them into the buzzing sounds of the city. Gwena noted there was no security guard outside the front of The Apothecary this time.

"I'll take ya ta the Central Posting House first," Bonnie told her, and led the way down the street.

The Central Posting House was a grand building with columns out front and tall sweeping archways. Gwena rented a small brass lockbox, one of hundreds making up the back wall. The front plate had a seven-pointed star embossed on the upper half and flowers flanking the number 73 in the middle. She was given a little brass key to open it, and the woman behind the desk assured her that anything sent to the Posting House with her name on it would be stowed safely inside. Satisfied, Gwena and Bonnie left to find some lunch. They chose a small cafe around the corner where Bonnie ordered them both fresh baguette sandwiches.

"Yum!" Gwena exclaimed through a half-masticated mouthful.

The sandwich was the best she'd ever tasted, with fresh crispy bread and thick slabs of fresh tomato, thin slices of watermelon, aged balsamic vinegar, basil, and creamy goat's cheese.

"Westdock might surpass us with their pies, but the Heartland be well known fer its other culinary wonders," Bonnie proclaimed.

"Have you always lived in the Heartland?" Gwena inquired.

"Do I sound like I'm from the Heartland?" Bonnie asked with humor.

Gwena smiled. "No. But I didn't want to presume. Where are you from?"

"I don't know. Was pulled out o' the ocean from a wreck when I was three, an' raised on the high seas," Bonnie confessed.

"How fascinating! Raised by sailors on a ship? Sounds like a real adventure! Was it?" Gwena asked.

Bonnie shrugged. "It was, until it wasn't."

"Sailing wasn't for you?"

"Sailin' be the only thin' fer me," Bonnie asserted.

"Then how come you're here instead of on a ship?"

"Because I was thrown off as soon as it became impossible fer the men ta ignore I be a woman. An' not a single ship be willin' ta take me since. Sailors be a superstitious lot—an' someone decided a woman on board brings bad luck. Doesn't matter how little sense the thin' makes, no one be willin' ta chance the so-called curse," Bonnie scoffed.

"So, what are you going to do about it?" Gwena inquired.

"I'm goin' ta buy me own sloop, an' I'm goin' ta cap'n a crew o' women so fierce that all who cross us will know the true meanin' o' bad luck," Bonnie proclaimed.

"Will you be pirates? Woman pirates—is that what you mean?" Gwena asked enthusiastically.

"I prefer the term, *dames o' fortune*," Bonnie informed her.

"Brilliant!" Gwena exclaimed. "I used to pretend I was a pirate when I was a child. It would've been nice to know there was a fierce crew of women out there."

"Ya should join us," Bonnie proposed.

Gwena laughed. "Me? Can you imagine me on a pirate ship?!"

"Why not?" Bonnie asked in earnest.

"You're serious? What would I do? I'm a tailor who dabbles in magic, what use could I possibly be?"

"Yer braver than most an' a quick thinker in the eye o' danger, I could use someone like that. An' yer skillset be quite useful on a ship—not only fer basic tailorin' needs, but also fer mendin' the sails an' stitchin' up injuries. An' we'll be needin' a flag."

"Stars, I hope to never have to stitch anyone up! If we encountered a fight, I wouldn't know the first thing to do," Gwena confessed.

"I 'ave a feelin' ye're a quick learner. Besides, a needle be nothin' but a tiny blade," Bonnie remarked, and suddenly it hit Gwena that this was a genuine proposition.

"If I did become a part of your crew, what would we do?" Gwena queried.

"We'd start by trackin' down me ship," Bonnie told her.

"Your ship? I thought you said you're going to buy a ship?"

"A ship that will command true respect, an' 'appens ta 'ave the coordinates fer somewhere I need. I was promised her by her cap'n before the crew betrayed us. I'll only be usin' the sloop ta take back what's rightfully mine, an' then we'll recover the key ta savin' the world," Bonnie declared.

"Saving the world? I didn't realize it needed saving."

"Ya will soon enough, whether ya join me er not. There's a storm brewin' on Equillian, blowin' in from The East. It 'as been fer years, but until now the danger was only fringin' on the edges like skulkin' shadows. Now it be closer than ever. An' unless we do somethin' ta stop it, it will overwhelm us all. If we're ta be successful, I'll need the best crew I can assemble, an' somethin' in me gut tells me yer a valuable asset," Bonnie told her.

Gwena hesitated. She wasn't sure whether or not to believe Bonnie. She hadn't heard of any looming world danger. "It sounds intriguing, and I'm flattered, only I'm supposed to be meeting someone here in the Heartland—that's why I need to be near the Central Posting House. I'm hoping to hear word from them any day now," she confessed.

"Is that right? What are ya plannin' on doin' in the Heartland once yer united?" Bonnie inquired.

Gwena hesitated. "I don't really know. We hadn't gotten that far," she admitted.

"Well, if ya change yer mind, let me know. I'll be leavin' Starday after next."

"Starday after next! That's so soon. Does that mean you have a ship already?" Gwena asked.

"Almost. It be waitin' fer me in Port Trinity. I only 'ave one more payment left ta make on 'er before she's mine."

"I see," Gwena said.

Bonnie pulled out her pocket watch. "The day be wanin', best get ya some clothes before we head back ta the club."

"Yes, of course," Gwena agreed.

"I'll take ya ta The Treasure Box, it's a shop o' secondhand clothes an' a true gem. I know the buyer. She collects things from estate sales and nobles who've tired o' last year's fashion. They buy it fer a fortune then discard it after it's been worn once, er sometimes before it's even been worn at all. Ya won't even be able ta buy the fabric it's made from fer a better price," Bonnie told her.

"Sounds fantastic!" Gwena exclaimed.

⌒

Soon Gwena and Bonnie were outside a quaint little shop tucked off the Main Street with a sign above it that read *The Treasure Box—Quality Pre-loved Attire*. Bonnie held the door open for Gwena, and she stepped inside. The shop was two stories high with racks and racks of clothing organized neatly in different sections for season, style, and size. Absolutely everything in the store was unique and beautiful. Gwena immediately recognized a piece by a well-known designer. She looked at the price tag and was surprised by how affordable it was. She knew the prices these sorts of pieces usually went for, and it was generally enough to cost her at least a year of her Westdock wages. Some of the pieces she found weren't her style but had exquisite fabric that was the highest caliber and could be easily altered to something of her own design. By the time Gwena and Bonnie came out of the store, Gwena had two shopping bags full and a grin that spoke of the treasures she'd found.

⌒

When Gwena returned to her room that afternoon she found a letter slipped under her door. She sat on the end of her bed and opened it. It was a list of instructions for her week's work at the club. Benji was to be measured for a new suit first thing in the morning—she was to visit his room, which was marked by a Treble Clef. *That's fitting,* she thought, recalling the musician's effortless ability with music. Second on the list was costumes for Madam Pomphrey's show. Gwena was scheduled to visit her in Theater 3 on Starday for sizing and instructions. Excitement and anticipation bubbled up inside her. She couldn't believe she would be working with the magician she'd idolized since childhood. She pulled out the clothes she'd purchased that morning and retreated to the tailor's paradise inside her wardrobe. She put her tailor's arm gauntlet on and started making alterations. By that evening she had a whole new collection of fashionable clothing she felt excited and proud to wear. She went to bed early that night, hoping to be able to explore the club when it opened.

Once again Gwena was woken by the sound of music floating into her room. She sat up with excitement and put on the dress she'd laid out for herself before going to bed and hurried out onto the balcony. She had an excellent view of everything below. Rafael played piano on the main stage while Benji sang and played guitar in a lineup of upbeat numbers for the crowded dance floor. After their set, a large metal hoop with a sparkling crescent moon lowered from the ceiling with Mirabella sitting on it wearing a sparkling black sequined leotard and a feathered headpiece. She sang a shadowy sweet ballad as she descended, and then did a series of acrobatics in the hoop. After that, Guy went on stage and performed a comedy dance act with Susie. They sang and danced in a choreographed number about a girl playing hard to get. From the first line they delivered, they had their audience in stitches. A big band took the stage after that, and the dance floor filled with lively and jubilant dancers once again.

Gwena noticed Benji retreating to his room with a woman on his arm. It wasn't Scarlet Jade this time, but another woman, younger, with vibrant red hair and a green sequined dress. Whoever she was, she was stunning and Benji was just as attentive to her as he'd been to Scarlet Jade—like he truly admired her. It made Gwena's lip curl in distaste. Last night it had seemed charming, like spotting the magic woven around two lovers. But now Gwena knew it was all just a façade. It felt like an underhanded lie or a cheap trick. No wonder he didn't believe in love. But Gwena wondered about the women and how they felt. Surely they weren't as immune to the emotion as Benji was. He was undoubtedly playing with their hearts. Gwena wondered how he did it—putting on such a convincing act with a different woman night after night and still being able to face himself in the mirror the next morning. She found she'd suddenly lost her appetite for socializing and returned to her room.

# A LESSON IN MAKE-BELIEVE

That morning when Bastian arrived at the top deck, the glow of the sun was only just cresting the horizon over a sea as still and clear as glass. The air was cool and crisp. With every exhale, his breath curled into little white wisps. The Black Mary was still anchored on the Dreg's shore. The small island's beach was outlined around its edge with the whitest sand Bastian had ever seen. Halfway up, the sand became overgrown with bushy plant life leading to the grove of Mast Trees in the center. The place was already buzzing with activity. Men were working on felling one of the huge trunks while another half dozen were on the main deck hammering and sawing, making lines, and mending sails. As the sun rose it transformed the ocean into liquid gold. A pod of Ivory Whales breached its surface, their white opalescent skin glittering in the sunlight like morning frost. They were gigantic, majestic creatures, at least half the length of the ship, with one long blue horn protruding from the front of their head. They were known as the unicorns of the sea, believed to be a good omen by sailors. A few spritzes of water shot into the air not four meters from the stern and soon more of the whales surfaced. Bastian watched them in awe as they lingered for a breath before dipping back under the water and disappearing from view.

Bastian's stomach growled. He looked up at the Guiding Star. It was almost the hour of Gumption—the Go-Getter. He was the Time Keeper of the sixth hour, which was also known as the hour for breakfast. Bastian was regretting his decision to give up his pocket watch. Normally it would be an easy thing to replace because he could walk through a crowd and come out with six lining his pockets. But he couldn't steal anything from the men on the ship without paying for it one way or another—nor did he want to. Having the pirates' trust was worth far more than anything he could take from them. As if reading his mind, the breakfast bell rang.

Bastian lagged behind in the mess hall after breakfast, waiting for everyone else to leave. Soon the only two remaining were him and Falgo. The sea-gypsy was slumped over in his usual corner. Bastian double-checked they were alone before walking over to the gypsy's table and sitting down across from him.

"I have some medicine for you," Bastian announced quietly.

Falgo groaned without lifting his head.

"It's not right, you being left to hang and dry like this. You rescued us all from the Kraken," Bastian told him, and he put the bottle against Falgo's leg under the table.

Falgo's brown eyes shot up and locked on Bastian. "What do ya want, thief?" he asked venomously.

"I want you to teach me how to fight," Bastian declared.

Falgo emitted a low chuckle. "Go shick yerself, landlubber, then rot in a corner an' die."

"Why would I do that? You're making it look so disappointing," Bastian stated.

Falgo grunted.

"Like it or not, we need one another. If I don't learn how to defend myself, I won't last out here. And if you don't have a proper drink, you'll die. I can leave you here to rot if you like, but I prefer not to. It would be a bloody waste in my opinion. Consider this bottle a gift. If you reconsider my offer, then there's more where that came from," Bastian asserted.

Falgo grabbed the bottle from Bastian's hand and wasted no time in pulling out the cork and guzzling it down. Half the bottle was gone in a matter of seconds.

"Thanks fer the gift, now piss off," Falgo hissed.

"Right," Bastian said, and left the pirate to his misery.

The fact that Falgo knocked him back didn't bother him at all. He knew the sea-gypsy would seek him out before long.

Bastian found his way back through the secret entrances to Tink's workshop. Again he was taken aback by the stark contrast between the Tinker's workroom and the rest of the ship. Tink was sitting behind his desk tinkering away on a medley of gear work. "Please, take a seat," he invited. Bastian walked over to the desk in front of his workbench and sat down. Sitting on its surface was a diary-sized notebook and a fountain pen.

"What's this for?" Bastian asked, picking up the pen.

"Your notes," Tink informed him.

"Right," Bastian sighed. He'd never enjoyed school. He liked the learning part—it was the work he found so tedious. He preferred to learn the material from a book. Having a photographic memory gave him the convenience of recalling the information on its pages much better than the words from a lecture. And with a book, he could look back at it anytime he liked without having to write one himself.

"It doesn't have to be notes from my lectures," Tink said, as if reading his mind, "though I do recommend it. I expect you to have everything I teach you committed to memory by the time we reach Jaxland. You can fill the rest with whatever thoughts or insights you like. Take it from one with years of experience, notes from your journey to discovery are invaluable. The memory is far from infallible—you'd be wise not to rely on it solely," he advised.

"Thanks for the book. Do you mind if I draw in it?" Bastian asked, opening it to a random page and beginning to doodle before he had an answer.

"It's yours. You can do with it as you please. If you fill all its pages, I'll supply you with another. Now, did you get a chance to look at the book I lent you yesterday?"

"Yeah, I finished it."

"The whole book?!" Tink exclaimed.

"Yup."

"Fantastic! It's in your best interest to commit its contents to memory. Knowing what and how things affect the Ghost Element is paramount if you hope to master it. Do you have any questions?"

"Yeah, on the list for creatures there's a note next to spiders saying they repel the Ghost Element."

"Spiders don't repel The Ghost Element—The Ghost Element repels spiders," Tink clarified.

"Why?"

"I don't know."

"What about people—why do some attract the Element more than others?" Bastian asked.

Tink put his hands in his pockets and studied Bastian. "Please elaborate."

"The Element hangs around the captain more than anyone else I've seen. Why?"

Tink studied Bastian for a beat before answering, "I don't know. The captain's an anomaly I have yet to understand. But I can tell you, part of the reason why you might see the Element collected momentarily around particular people more than others is because it's attracted to certain thoughts and emotions. Did you see those lists in the book?" Tink asked.

"Yeah. The Element is attracted to the more intense emotions, regardless of whether they're negative or positive. Like rage and passion."

Tink nodded. "The Element's attracted to truth, there's honesty in raw emotion. If you clear and quiet your mind and bring yourself present to the moment, you'll also attract the Ghost Element. However, that takes practice," he explained.

"I don't understand, how does the element even know what we're thinking or feeling in the first place?"

"It has to do with the Ciphorescent Codec."

"The what?"

"The vibrational signature of things."

"You mean—the Language of Songs?" Bastian queried.

"Precisely. The Ghost Element is attuned to it. It not only reacts to our thoughts and emotions, it also reacts to our intentions. The latter is how you can guide it to your will. By having a strong intention, you create a mold for the Element to fill. It can't help being affected by it— formed by it, if you will."

"Interesting."

"Any more questions?" Tink asked.

"Tons," Bastian admitted.

Tink smiled. "Good. Only, keep them for another time or we'll never get through our lesson," he requested. He placed the Humming Bowl on the desk in front of Bastian. "Now, try and imagine it into something."

Bastian left Tink's workshop half an hour later feeling more discouraged than ever. No matter how hard he tried to manipulate the Element, it wouldn't budge. He knew there was still a part of him filled with doubt, and he didn't know how to get rid of it.

Throughout the rest of Bastian's chores that day he paid close attention to the Ghost Element and tried to will it to obey his command. When he was on line duty, he tried to get the Element to fill in the spaces between the individual cords of the ropes to make them stronger. When he was helping Doc in the kitchen, he tried to make the Element separate into even lines so that he could use them as a cutting guide while slicing tomatoes, but nothing happened. By the time dinner arrived he was convinced he wasn't able to manipulate the Ghost Element — that he didn't have what it took, whatever that was.

☙

After dinner Bastian sat at the table in the mess hall nursing his Black Jack next to Cricket and the twins.

"I'm lookin' forward ta sleep tanight," Rhino announced.

"Why's that?" Stork asked.

"Last night I dreamt the princess o' the Spotted Isles took me ta 'er bed."

"I wish I 'ad me that dream," Cricket said.

"We all wish we 'ad that dream. Dreamin' be the closest we can come ta gettin' any tail out 'ere," Stork remarked.

"Aye, we can't reach Jaxland soon enough, I miss those girls somethin' fierce," Cricket declared.

"Those girls? Ya mean *that* girl. Don't try an' pretend ya 'aven't 'ad Jozalin on yer mind since the second ya knew we were 'eadin' fer Jaxland," Rhino proclaimed.

"I can't 'elp it with a girl like that. But a lot o' good it does me, I can't 'ave 'er," Cricket lamented.

"Course ya can, any man can!" Stork exclaimed.

Cricket looked at him pointedly, and Rhino hit Stork in the back of the head with his open palm.

"That woman fancy's ya as much as ye do 'er. I'm sure she's lookin' forward ta seein' ya, Cricket," Rhino assured him.

"It doesn't make any difference, she's a girl fer 'ire — even if she wanted ta spend 'er time with me, 'er house mistress will never allow 'er ta waste 'er time at the yearly gatherin' with an unpayin' customer," Cricket stated with sad resignation.

"Is that why ye've 'ad yer 'air in such a tizzy about coin lately?" Stork asked him.

"Course it tis! Can ya blame 'im?" Rhino interjected.

"Yeah, I can, 'e shouldn't 'ave gone gamblin' it all like a complete dunce!"

"It doesn't matter, I didn't 'ave enough ta begin with. It was the only way I could 'ope ta acquire more," Cricket confessed.

"An' where 'as it led ya? With nothin' at all ta spend at Jaxland," Stork asserted.

Cricket shrugged, "She was the only thin' worth spendin' it on."

Stork scoffed, "Awww, still me beatin' 'eart! That's so sweet I think I'm goin' ta be sick. Since when did ya become such a romantic, Cricket? Knowin' ya, I would 'ave thought any girl would be better than none."

"Not on Jaxland. She's the only one worth payin' fer. If I can't 'ave 'er, then I may as well take me chances out on the playin' field."

"Suit yerself. I on the other 'and don't share yer sentiment. 'alf the girls at the Jaxland Bawdy House will 'ave me coin in their pockets before I'm through," Stork proclaimed.

Cricket pointed his fork threateningly at Stork, "If ya even think about spendin' me coin on Jozalin, I'll ensure ya 'ave ta sit down ta piss fer the next month!"

Stork held up his hands in defense. "Besides that one, o'course!" he assured him. "I didn't realize 'ow much she meant ta ya, Cricket. I wish I could 'elp ya mate, I really do. If I 'ad enough coin fer the both o' us I'd share it in a 'eartbeat. But I've been savin' fer this trip, same as yew. An' I plan ta spend every last cwip I 'ave at Jaxland. I'll certainly shout ya some drinks, though."

"Same. Sorry, mate," Rhino apologized.

"No matter, I've already resigned meself ta me fate. I know I built me own pyre. It will be good ta see 'er face at any rate."

"Seriously though, Cricket, ya need ta do somethin' about that gamblin' 'abit o' yers. An' I say this as a friend—if ya don't stop, it's goin' ta get ya inta a lot more trouble then' bein' cwipless," Stork admonished.

"Don't ya start! Yer worse than a muther!" Cricket exclaimed.

Stork put his arm around him. "It's only because I care about ya."

Cricket pushed him away. "I'm callin' it early. I'll see ya maggots on deck tammara," he announced, and stood from the table.

"Ah, come now Cricket, don't be like that! At least let me get ya one more drink," Stork objected.

Cricket smiled thinly and gave a lazy salute to them. "Night, lads," he said, and headed for the sleeping quarters.

"I 'ate seein' 'im like this," Stork said.

Rhino looked at him aghast, "Yer a royal arse, ya know that brother?"

"Me?!"

"Yes, yew. Ya lecture Cricket about gamblin' after ye've already taken all 'is coin. Yer just as much responsible fer feedin' 'is gamblin' 'abit as 'e is! Ya let 'im do it, even when ya know 'e shouldn't."

"'e's a grown man! What am I supposed ta do? Tell 'im 'e can't do what 'e likes with 'is own coin?" Stork protested.

"The least ya could do is give it back."

"What, an' ya think 'e would do the same fer me? Cricket was out ta get me coin, that's why 'e was gamblin' in the first place! That's 'ow the game works—if ya don't know. If I start givin' people's coin back ta 'em when they lose, it will completely defeat the purpose!" Stork objected.

Rhino shook his head at him and stood with his empty plate. "Good night, Dodger. An' brother, well…I wish ya vivid night terrors," he declared, and left the table.

"Oi, I don't deserve that!" Stork called after him.

He looked over at Bastian helplessly. "Please tell me I'm not bein' insane in thinkin' I've done nothin' wrong 'ere?"

"Don't look at me, I see both sides, and I like you both too much to choose one," Bastian admitted.

"Wise words. Well, stay an' 'ave a drink with me at least, won't ya?" Stork requested.

Bastian smirked wryly, "Of course, I can't let a man drink alone."

Stork smiled and held his glass high, "Ta treasure, wenches, an' mates, may we both 'ave many fillin' our fates—hopefully on Jaxland!" he declared, and clinked Bastian's glass.

That night Bastian couldn't sleep. He sat next to one of the firebeetle lanterns sketching a portrait of Gwena. If only she were here, he thought. He had no doubt she'd be much better at using the Ghost Element than he was. She'd always believed there was real magic in the world. Something that just hadn't been uncovered yet. And she'd been right. It was as if she could sense the Ghost Element was there, even when she had no way of detecting it. And here he was, able to physically see it and still having trouble fully acknowledging its existence. When they were children, Gwena was incredible at playing make-believe. She was so imaginative and had a mind that was always open to the idea of anything being possible, no matter how ridiculous. She never made Bastian feel silly for any of his ideas when they were playing—if he said he was half dragon, half chicken, then Gwena would accept it as fact without blinking an eye and carry on as if it was the most natural thing in the world. Bastian cherished his memories of them playing together. He wished he could transport himself back to that time—when they both believed anything was possible—before life gave them a hard knock and filled them with skepticism and doubt. Even after all the challenges they'd endured, Gwena still believed in the goodness of people. That was something even Bastian lost faith in years ago. He wondered how she did it, even when everything she'd been through with her father challenged that ideology.

Bastian studied the picture he'd drawn of her face and his heart yearned more than ever to have her back in his arms. He climbed into his hammock with his notebook next to him open to Gwena's portrait and drifted off to sleep.

Bastian was dreaming of playing a make-believe game of pirates with Gwena and Felix when he was woken by a harsh whisper in his ear.

"Oi, psst!"

His eyes flung open. Falgo's face was inches from his own. Bastian jolted back in surprise.

"Easy thief, I'm not here ta hurt ya. If yer still interested in strikin' a bargain, meet me up top in five," Falgo instructed in a barely audible whisper.

Bastian nodded and Falgo left the sleeping quarters.

Bastian looked around to make sure they hadn't woken anyone else, then slipped out of his hammock and followed after.

The bitter night air cut into Bastian like a knife. It was freezing cold without a cloud in the sky. The bottoms of the freshly rolled sails fluttered in the breeze against a backdrop of brilliant stars. Bastian crossed his arms over his chest and looked up to see what constellation was below the Guiding Star. It was the Phoenix constellation—the guardian of the first hour of the new day. The constellation represented the end of one thing and the beginning of another—like a young phoenix born from the ashes of its former self. Bastian scanned the top deck but saw no one. Then Falgo stepped from the shadows into the light. He was holding the bottle of rum Bastian had given him that morning.

"Follow me," the pirate directed, and stepped back into the shadows.

Bastian followed him to the ship's gangway, then down onto the beach of the Dreg Island and up into the grove of Mast Trees looming like strange giants. He finally stopped in an open clearing and turned to Bastian, "So, ya want ta learn ta fight, thief?"

"Yes, very much," Bastian confirmed.

"Fer what purpose?" Falgo queried, taking a swig from the bottle.

Bastian searched for the words. "In the battle with the galleons and the Kraken, I was completely powerless. I never want to feel that way again. I want to be able to defend myself and the people around me. I want to be able to help in the next fray we encounter—instead of cowering in the corner without being able to contribute. And I want to better my chances at surviving long enough to reunite with the woman I love," he confessed.

Falgo studied him for a moment and then nodded. "All honorable reasons." He took another swig from his bottle before putting it down on the stump of one of the felled trees and putting up his fists. "Alright thief, show me what ye've got."

Bastian held up his open palms and stepped back defensively. "I've got nothing!—I've never thrown a punch in my life!" he exclaimed.

Falgo dropped his fists and circled around Bastian. "That's good. It means ya have no bad habits I 'ave ta break."

"Great," Bastian announced nervously, relieved the pirate had given up his attack.

"Can ya dance?" Falgo asked him.

"Can I what?"

Falgo put up his fists again. "I said, can ya dance, lad? Dancin' an' fightin' be one an' the same." He took a step towards Bastian.

Bastian backed away and Falgo lunged forward while throwing a punch.

Bastian barely dodged in time. Falgo closed the gap between them with a single step and threw another punch, and another. Bastian was forced backward, barely avoiding each blow. Falgo moved around Bastian's side and Bastian spun to face him, his heart pounding.

Falgo smiled. "See, dancin'." He relaxed his fists and walked back to his bottle, taking a casual drink.

Bastian watched him warily, beginning to wonder if training with Falgo was a bad idea.

"How are ya at fallin'?" the sea-gypsy asked.

"Falling?"

"Do I have a lisp, lad?"

"No, I'm just not sure I understand the question," Bastian admitted.

"Fallin' down be inevitable. Yer skill at it will determine whether er not ya get back up."

"Right. I'm pretty good, I guess."

Bastian cautiously watched Falgo as he put down his bottle and walked back over to him. The pirate spun around behind him so fast he didn't have time to react before he was kicked square in the back. He flew forward, stumbling several steps before diving into a roll to prevent his momentum from face-planting him in the sand. Bastian bounced back up and turned to face Falgo, preparing for another attack.

"Not bad," Falgo commended, circling around Bastian while measuring him up.

He stopped in front of him. "Alright, thief. I'll take it," he declared.

"Take what?"

"The job. Meet me here same time tomorrow mornin' an' we'll begin yer trainin'. In exchange, I want a fresh bottle brought at the start o' every lesson. Yer not ta tell anyone I be trainin' ya. If I find out ya 'ave, I'll deny it an' the deal be off. If at any point durin' yer trainin' ya become disagreeable, yer trainin' stops. Savvy?"

"Yes, thank you!" Bastian exclaimed.

Falgo nodded. "See ya in the starlight, thief."

He tossed Bastian the empty rum bottle. Bastian caught it and Falgo retreated into the shadows whistling a tune.

Bastian returned to the Black Mary. He went below deck and checked the sleeping men to ensure he was the only one awake, before silently picking his way into the galley to prepare Falgo's payment for his lessons. Now that he knew he'd be training with him, he wanted to prepare enough stock to last the week. He retrieved the seven bottles he'd doctored the previous night and poured a bit from each of the rum concoctions into the empty bottle Falgo had returned to him—increasing the amount he took away from each bottle incrementally, before replacing it with the barley tea from the last bottle. In the end he had seven full bottles of rum cocktail once again, the strength of their alcohol content decreasing by a gradual and undetectable amount each successive day. He marked them accordingly with a small etch on the bottom and restored all but one to their hiding place amongst the rest of Doc's stores. Bastian cleaned any trace of being there, then slipped back out of the galley and hid the strongest bottle of doctored rum in his locker. He returned to the sleeping quarters and climbed into his hammock, smiling to himself, *I'm actually going to learn how to fight from Falgo—the man who cut limbs from a Kraken with a single slice of his sword*, Bastian marvelled, and with that he fell asleep.

The next morning Bastian arrived at Tink's workshop ten minutes behind schedule. After his late-night training and creating liquid currency for Falgo's lessons, he didn't have much steam left. He'd spent his morning chores and breakfast in a foggy stupor.

Tink was leaning against his workbench with his arms crossed, patiently waiting for Bastian. "Good morning," he greeted.

"Morning," Bastian mumbled.

"You look like you could use a pick me up. Have you had breakfast?"

"Yeah, Just didn't get much sleep," Bastian admitted.

"Have an apple, I picked them fresh this morning. They do wonders for waking up the mind," Tink offered, motioning to a fruit bowl on a round table in the center of the room that hadn't been there the day before.

Bastian looked at the fruit bowl. It was completely empty.

"Is this some kind of joke?"

"Not at all. They're in the bowl on the table," Tink assured him, as if puzzled Bastian couldn't see them.

Bastian looked back at the empty fruit bowl. "Am I missing something?"

Tink walked over to the table and picked up an apple from the bowl—only there was no apple there. He lightly squeezed the empty space in his hand to check the fruit's ripeness and then put it back down and selected another. Satisfied, he sunk his teeth into the phantom fruit, his head jerking back slightly as he pulled a bite free and chewed.

"I like to make a habit of keeping fresh fruit on hand, one can't be productive on an empty stomach," Tink told him through a masticated mouthful.

Bastian watched him, dumbfounded.

*Could there really be a bowl of invisible apples?* he wondered. *No, that's ridiculous.* But then, so was everything else to do with the Ghost Element. He walked over to the table and reached into the fruit bowl—there was nothing there. *Of course there's nothing there.* How could he fall for something so foolish? But the way Tink had picked up the apple and taken a bite of it was so natural, so convincing, it was surprising it wasn't real.

"Very funny," Bastian remarked dryly.

"Whatever do you mean?" Tink asked.

"There are no apples."

"Ah, but if there isn't, then how can I see them? Feel them, taste them even? My stomach was empty and now I feel sated and refreshed from the apple's nourishment," Tink argued.

"Yeah? What did it taste like?" Bastian challenged.

"A little tart but mostly sweet—just the way I like it," Tink answered.

"Well...I imagine you're either lying or completely mad," Bastian proclaimed.

"You imagine? The imagination is a very powerful thing, be careful how you use it," Tink cautioned. "You can hold me in your imagination as being mad if you like, and everything I do will appear that way to you. I might even act more insane than usual, falling into the mold you've created for me regardless of what's true. A person with pox disease can be healed with nothing but a sugar pill if they imagine it's effective medicine, and I can experience the joys of eating an apple simply by imagining I'm eating one," Tink asserted.

"But you're not," Bastian insisted.

Tink regarded him with a pitying stare.

"What?" Bastian asked.

"It's a sad thing when we reserve our imagination for its worst qualities, depriving ourselves of its joy. If you were any age below ten this would be easy. Unfortunately, suspending disbelief is a child's gift that rarely survives adulthood. At least, for any topic outside our fears and insecurities, which of course we have no problem believing in whatsoever—no matter how ridiculous they are. No wonder most adults are miserable, eh?"

Tink walked over and picked up Bastian's sketchbook.

"Hey!" Bastian protested, but it was too late, Tink was already riffling through the pictures Bastian had drawn on its pages.

"You certainly don't lack creativity or artistic vision. Come back tomorrow and we'll start again," Tink announced.

"What?! Why? I've hardly walked in the door. I want to finish the lesson," Bastian asserted.

"Alright, eat an apple," Tink invited, motioning to the empty table.

Bastian walked over to the table and pretended to pick up an apple and bite into it. After a couple of chews, he dropped the act, relaxing his hand and looking up at Tink expectantly. Tink followed Bastian's imaginary apple to the floor where his hand had dropped it, and then looked at Bastian, unimpressed.

"What?" Bastian queried.

"You don't need to convince me there's an apple there, you need to convince yourself," Tink told him. "Acting out eating an apple and make-believing you're eating one are two entirely different things."

"How so?" Bastian asked.

"To act is to imitate truth. It's nothing but a magic trick, a counterfeit copy, a dead shell of the real thing. To make-believe is to believe in it yourself—even if only in the moment. There's magic in that. For when we believe, it breathes life into the imaginary and makes truth of it—no matter how ridiculous or impossible," Tink exhorted.

"I don't understand. How can I believe I'm eating something that's not there? Isn't that the definition of insanity?" Bastian queried.

"And there's where the problem lies. The apple's not there because you refuse to believe in it, and you refuse to believe in it because the apple's not there. To imagine is the only way to create something from 'nothing.' But in order to do so, you must take a leap of faith and believe in it first," Tink admonished.

He walked over to the table and pulled out his green spectacle placing it over his left eye. Then he picked up another imaginary apple from the table.

Bastian watched in fascination as gold dust started gravitating from the bowl to the alchemist's hand. It spun inside the empty space there, solidifying into a round mass that transformed into a perfect pink and yellow piece of fruit. Tink took a bite of the apple. A chunk snapped off and crunched between his teeth. Juice dribbled down his chin. He produced a handkerchief from his pocket and wiped the juice away and then threw the rest of the apple to Bastian.

Bastian caught it.

"Come back tomorrow," Tink directed, and returned to his workbench.

Bastian stared at the apple in disbelief. It was firm.

He smelled it. It smelled tart but mostly sweet—just as Tink said it would.

⌒

The rest of the day was a blur. Bastian was so tired he struggled to make it through his remaining daily chores. As soon as Doc released him from galley duty, he wolfed down his dinner and retreated to his hammock where he collapsed and fell asleep.

Bastian awoke with a start in the middle of the night, terrified he'd overslept his lesson with Falgo. He palmed the pocket watch from the sleeping sailor next to him and checked the time. It was midnight— Shick's hour. Bastian breathed out a silent sigh of relief. He returned the sailor's watch and cursed himself for giving up his own. He was going to have to figure out another way to keep track of time. Bastian slunk out of the sleeping quarters and retrieved the bottle from his locker, then made his way to the clearing where he'd trained with Falgo the night before.

Bastian sat down on a stump at the bass of one of the Mast Trees. He pulled out a puff-stick and lit it with his Everfire box. The clearing was covered in a shroud of mist illuminated in pale moonlight. Bastian huddled with shaking hands as he waited in the cold for Falgo. Just as the Phoenix constellation moved under the Guiding Star, the swordsman stepped into the clearing.

"Ye 'ave me payment, landlubber?" he asked.

Bastian pulled the bottle of barley tea and rum from his jacket and handed it to Falgo, who snatched it from him and pulled out the cork, knocking it back greedily. He drank a full quarter before stopping for air. Bastian put out his puff-stick on the stump and tucked it away. He stood and buried his hands deep into his pockets, waiting patiently for Falgo's instruction.

The pirate wiped his chin and put the cork back in the bottle, stowing it in the belt of his pants. "Ten laps around the clearin'," he ordered.

"Laps?"

"Run!"

"Right," Bastian acknowledged, and began to run around the clearing.

When he'd finished circling it ten times Falgo led him through a series of stretches that Bastian had never done before.

"Last night ya proved ya can fall, but there are many more ways than one," Falgo told him, and proceeded to demonstrate sideways rolls in both directions, backward rolls, and a practiced collapse that allowed him to rock onto his back and immediately get back up again. He took Bastian through the movements of each one and had him practice each of them half a dozen times.

"Good, good. It be a start. Don't expect ta master 'em in a night," Falgo said. "Now, onta footwork! Without it, everythin' else be useless. Stand tall," he commanded.

Bastian stood tall.

"Keep yer knees bent at all times when facin' an opponent. Put yer feet shoulder width apart an' one foot in front o' the other like so," Falgo instructed, demonstrating the position.

"This stance creates a good center o' balance, givin' ya a better chance at stayin' on yer feet."

Bastian placed his feet in a wide stance and put his left foot forward. Falgo kicked them into the correct position. "Tuck yer pelvis under, relax yer shoulders, engage yer stomach muscles" he instructed, pushing on Bastian's stomach to make sure it was tensed and correcting the rest of his posture.

"Ta move forward, lift the toes o' yer front foot an' push yerself forward with yer back. Like so," Falgo said, moving forward with the ease of a master fencer.

"Ta move backward, shift yer weight ta yer front foot, an' lift yer back—pushin' yerself with yer front foot like so," Falgo demonstrated.

Bastian clumsily mimicked his movements. "Where do I put my arms?" he asked.

Falgo picked up Bastian's left hand and rolled his fingers into a fist, placing it out in front of him. Then he picked up Bastian's right hand and did the same, placing it at the base of Bastian's jaw.

"'old yer arms thus fer the time bein'. Elbows in. Shoulders down," Falgo directed, again correcting Bastian's stance. Bastian felt completely awkward in the position, but he did his best to follow Falgo's instruction.

"Walk twenty passes from this tree ta the one on the other side. Ten forward an' ten passes back. Begin!" Falgo commanded, relaxing against a Mast Tree and taking another swig of rum.

Bastian began practicing the steps, up and down the length of the clearing. The footwork felt awkward and slow. He couldn't imagine how it was an effective means for moving anywhere, especially in fighting. But he practiced it all the same, making small adjustments here and there according to Falgo's instructions.

"Good. Now fer some dodgin' practice," Falgo announced, finally, and came at Bastian swinging punches and kicks.

Bastian dodged each attack, barely missing the blows. Falgo swept under his leg and knocked him to the ground. Bastian groaned, laying in the sand.

"Ya gonna give up? Er ya gonna get back up?" Falgo asked him.

Bastian kicked himself back to his feet and faced Falgo once more. Falgo came at him, and Bastian dodged each blow until he felt like he was moving in slow motion, his body refusing to continue following his commands. Finally Falgo announced, "That's enough fer tonight."

Two hours had already passed, and Bastian was dripping sweat despite the night's chill.

"Forty sit-ups an' push-ups," Falgo ordered.

Bastian groaned inside but he complied, pushing through his exhaustion. After his last push-up he collapsed on the sand and rolled over to look up at the sky.

"Well done, thief. See ya in the starlight on the morrow," Falgo said, looking down at him. Then the pirate walked back towards the ship whistling a tune.

Bastian watched him go, then he closed his eyes for several moments, mustering the energy to get up. He finally forced himself to move and made his way back to the Black Mary.

# SOAKED

Felix woke to find himself in Lilliana's bed for the second time that day. He looked over and saw her fast asleep beside him and panic bloomed. He rolled off the bed silently searching for his pocket watch. He found it in the pocket of his trousers on the floor. "Thank the Watchers," he whispered. It was only just the thirteenth hour. He couldn't have been asleep for more than a couple of minutes. The thirteenth hour was the hour of Lady Luck. If she was kind to him, nothing unsavory would happen on her watch. He thanked her for that. He got dressed and collected his deck of cards, his drinking glass, and what was left of the jug of rum—doing his best to remove any evidence he'd been there. Then he quietly cracked the door open and scouted the hallway before slipping out. Felix made a beeline for his bedroom down the hall, shutting himself inside and leaning his head back against the hard oak door. He looked up at the star mural on the ceiling.

"Stars, what've I gotten myself into?" he whispered.

He walked into the room and put the glass and jug on the dresser and met his reflection in the looking glass above it. "You fool, you're playing with fire. Like a moth drawn to a flame, and it will end you," he told himself.

He wondered if Roy had returned. Surely not—it had only been a couple hours since he'd left. Felix walked over to the window and looked out anxiously over the front garden to the long jetty stretching away from the island. The airship was docked there, its sloop design almost invisible with its mirrored surface reflecting the hot air balloon above its sails. Not that it told him anything. He was almost certain Roy took an air cab to run his errands. It seemed to be the smartest way to travel in Sky View. Felix imagined the cab fare would be cheaper than a valet docking service or the trouble of self-docking around the city. He desperately hoped he was right and that Roy's intended business would indeed keep him out until dinner as he'd anticipated. Felix needed to finish the reply to Lord Bardviss before he did. Otherwise, he would have to be incredibly creative in devising an excuse for what had been capitalizing his time, and to do that, he needed to be sober. Felix looked into the adjoining en suite with its huge tub and smiled.



Felix lay in the large round bathtub with his eyes closed and his face turned towards the skylight above him, bathing in its golden glow. The bathroom wasn't as large as Lilliana's en suite, but it was just as grand. It was a round room decorated with rich blue and metallic gold glazed tiles. They gleamed in the light of five long glass and copper Everfire lanterns mounted on sconces on the wall. There were black dimmer bags hanging by chains above them that disappeared into the wall behind. There would be a switch somewhere to lower the bags over the lanterns in order to soften their light. He'd seen similar setups before in other wealthy households.

Felix sunk underneath the steaming water, letting the heat soak into his bones. He stayed there for a moment before coming up and relaxing his head against the back of the tub. He couldn't remember the last time he'd had a hot bath. It would've been at the Order. Ever since leaving the Star Temple, he'd bathed only in water that was tepid at best. Thinking of his and Bastian's old place led his thoughts to Bastian. He missed his brother. He could use his advice now more than ever.

Felix ran his hands over his face. *What's happening to me?* he wondered.

He'd always thought of himself as an expert when it came to women, but his current predicament was way over his head. He'd no idea how Lilliana truly felt about him or what her intentions with him were. She'd implied that morning that their first interaction together was nothing but a one-time fling, then she completely contradicted that directly after lunch. The game, the personal and topical questions, and that dress… but then, she had been drunk… *Oh Stars, don't tell me I took advantage of a duchess!* he lamented mournfully.

*Stupid! Why didn't I stop myself? Why couldn't I have played the gentleman and talked her through it or turned her away? This isn't what I'm here for! I'm supposed to be securing the means to change mine and Bastian's stars, maybe make a few rich connections and help Lilliana cut Lord Bardviss a slice of what he deserves along the way. If I continue sleeping with her, it can only lead to one thing—disaster!*

Felix sunk deeper into the water.

*I should pack my things and leave now. I can catch an air cab to the city and charter a ride on an airship back to the mainland. With the coin*

*I have I can surely make it back and still have some left over. I no longer have any obligations to Lilliana, according to our contract. The smart thing to do is to take my winnings and disappear. It will be better for everyone. Lilliana will most likely banish me herself the second she sobers anyway, and even if she doesn't, she doesn't need her life to be any more complicated—she has enough on her plate as it is.*

Felix stopped his internal monologue, suddenly realizing his thoughts held no conviction. It didn't matter how logical they were, it wasn't what he wanted. He was enjoying his time in Sky View, and he was glad Lilliana welcomed him back into her bed, very glad. In fact, he was very much hoping it would happen again.

Before now, Felix had never had romantic feelings for the women he'd slept with, or for anyone. He loved women for everything they were, for their company and conversation as much as their beauty and shared physical pleasure. There were women whose company he liked more than others and ones he had a great deal of respect for, but he'd always felt the very idea of declaring ownership over another person's affections was silly—he was a firm believer that people weren't meant to possess one another. He realized then that was because he'd never met anyone like Lilliana. He'd never had to wrestle with the obsessive longing to capitalize another's attention. The need to be near them. The potent desire to dissolve an afternoon entangled in their embrace—soul kissing until the break of dawn just to be as close to them as physically possible—regardless of whether or not it led to a sexual climax. Those were the feelings Felix wrestled with now, feelings completely foreign to him. They ensnared him, and he was powerless against them. He found Lilliana intoxicating. She made him feel like an addict, hungry for his next fix—and he wasn't entirely sure he liked it. In fact, it terrified him. He liked being in control, being able to weigh things logically, being able to cleanly walk away. All things he was quickly losing grasp of.

*Where's Bastian when I need him?* Felix thought. His Star-brother had only ever been in love. Felix had never seen him more than mildly interested in any woman besides Gwena. He longed for Bastian's advice, for his steady and level-headed reasoning. Felix needed someone to guide him out of the giddy, foggy stupor blinding him and help to make sense of it all. He needed someone he trusted to give him sound direction—because for the first time, Felix felt his own compass couldn't be trusted. He was only too aware that if he and Lilliana continued as they were, it would just be a matter of time before their little affair was discovered.

Roy already knew Felix was a commoner. The upper and lower classes were not encouraged to mingle. Felix had seen what the blue bloods did to people who were caught crossing that line, and it wasn't pretty. He knew the smart thing was to take his winnings and disappear. It would be better for both of them. But logic and reason were in direct conflict with the burning desire in his heart, and right then, desire was diminishing his logic to a whisper.

"Shick," he muttered.

*This is your doing, Star Stirrer. This has your name all over it!* he thought to Shick accusingly. And yet, even if it was, Felix knew there was nothing he could do about it.

⤐

Felix stood in a towel looking at the suit Gwena had made. He wished he'd had something clean and different to put on. It had felt so good to be in something else for a moment at Favio's. The man's work was incredible. The fine three-piece number Gwena had made for Lord Bardviss with its blue jacket, matching pants, and purple and grey checkered vest was masterfully beautiful. But there were only so many days he could wear the same thing and still admire its charm. This was the fourth day in a row Felix had worn the outfit, and he was eager to receive his new wardrobe. Felix put on just the pants and white undershirt. Then he dried his short black hair and sat down at the writing desk to occupy his mind with the next letter to Lord Bardviss.

⤐

After ten minutes of staring at the blank parchment in front of him, Felix realized he was still too drunk to be productive. He recalled seeing a bottle of Spiced Kah in Roy's stash on the airship. Spiced Kah was the perfect cure for a hangover. If you drank it soon enough, you could prevent the misery altogether. It could be taken either cold or warm and had the rejuvenating properties equivalent to a fifteen-minute sleep, making it a nice alternative to tea. It was expensive stuff—a luxury for the wealthy. With Spiced Kah on hand, people could drink as much alcohol as they liked without ever having to suffer repercussions. It was another perfect example of the elite evading the undesirable consequences of their actions. But Felix was far more interested in finding ways to share that privilege than brooding on the injustice.

He stood decidedly and threw on his white dress shirt, then paused, remembering the Dreg Pouch. He found his jacket and pulled out the neatly wrapped paper bundle from Treasure Trove Antiques.

Felix made his way through the front garden and down along the jetty to the airship. He avoided looking over the edge of the landing stage as he grabbed the ladder on the side of the ship and climbed onto the main deck. Then he went straight below to the galley and opened one of the upper cupboards where the liquor was stored. Inside were half a dozen bottles of various types of booze. He was thrilled to see Spiced Kah amongst them. He grabbed a bottle and pulled out the cork, eagerly guzzling down several large gulps. He leaned against the wall and sighed as the drink started to take effect. Then he went into Roy's quarters, locking the door behind him. He recovered the four purses of duckets he'd stowed behind the toilet earlier that morning and dumped them out on the bed before organizing them into piles. When he finished, there were eighteen piles of ten duckets and one of five. He added the fifteen duckets he'd spent that morning and gave a low whistle. Lord Bardviss had given him two hundred duckets—the equivalent of one hundred thousand cwips. Felix chuckled with giddy delight. Duckets were the highest coin on Equillian. In Westdock, he could eat out every meal and only spend nine or ten cwips in a day, twelve if he included drinks. A single ducket would cover almost two months of his living expenses.

*Stuff working for Jarvis's fishing operation,* he thought. With this much coin, Felix could buy his own steam trawler and he and Bastian could be the captains of their very own fishing crew. Felix grinned. Then he remembered he'd already spent twenty-five duckets on the Dreg Pouch. He recalled the stack of duckets Roy spent on his new wardrobe and suddenly, his small mountain of coin didn't feel as exorbitant. If he was going to have enough to get him through his time in Sky View, with enough left over to set him and Bastian up, then he'd need to inspire an even bigger sum from Lord Bardviss. He pulled out the Dreg Pouch, still in the bundle of tissue paper. Inside was the black leather bag on its long leather cord and a paper card with written instructions in fine calligraphy.

"Right," Felix muttered.

He put the card down and took out his own plain leather coin pouch. He put thirty-five duckets into his pouch for spending—including the ten duckets he owed Roy. Then he funnelled the rest of the coin into the Dreg Pouch.

Felix marvelled at how the coins disappeared as they fell into the bag—as if the pouch was a portal to somewhere else entirely. He grinned. Now that he had the enchanted coin purse, the problem of storing his fortune wasn't a problem at all. Which meant he had no limitations on the next sum he could request from Lord Bardviss. If he played his cards right, he could inspire enough to not only see out his time in Sky View, but also to take his life in any direction he pleased.

Felix went to the writing desk in the corner of the chamber and scribbled Bastian's name on a scrap of parchment, then dropped it into the Dreg Pouch.

Nothing happened.

Felix had no idea if something was supposed to. He could only hope that whatever was, did. He put the Dreg Pouch around his neck and tucked it underneath his shirt. The pouch was light and felt cool and smooth against his skin. It felt good—like it'd always belonged there. Felix tucked his old coin purse into his coat pocket, cleaned up the evidence of his presence, then unlocked the door and made his way through the main cabin, picking up the bottle of Spiced Kah from the table as he passed. He continued towards the companionway and then paused, retracing his steps to the liquor cabinet. He opened it and selected a bottle of Black Currant wine—Black Currant Wine was more of a liquor than a vintage, with enough alcohol content to start a fire. Its sweet and tart flavor mixed with the taste of oak from the barrels it was aged in made it a fine drop, an expensive brew that went down dangerously easy considering its potent kick. After a moment's thought, he grabbed one more. He tucked the bottles under his arm and made his way off the ship and back towards the estate.

Felix sat at the small writing desk in his room, staring at a blank piece of parchment with a feathered quill in hand, contemplating the best way to construct his letter to Lord Bardviss.

*What's his endgame?* he wondered.

It was clear Bardviss was using the Wendrians for their position, but to what purpose?

*Could he really be so disillusioned as to think becoming the Duke of Westdock will be a stepping-stone to becoming the next emperor of Equillian—as Lilliana suggested?*

Felix couldn't see how that could work. There'd never been a supreme leader besides Lord Emperor Balthazar. He'd taken Equillian by winning approval, clever negotiations, and by only using brute force when absolutely necessary. The man was brilliant. He'd united the world when he was only nineteen and he'd united most of it with minimal bloodshed. People were happy to have him rule the world because he was good at it. Equillian was better for it. Felix wasn't so sure the precincts would be as accommodating to someone who hadn't earned their place. Lord Balthazar didn't have an heir. Once he'd lived out his time, no one knew who would take over. Felix didn't think any of the precincts would allow someone to take his place if they killed him. The precincts were too stubborn to follow a leader they didn't respect. Balthazar had been incredibly clever in ensuring no one tried to take the throne by force. Along with War Dragons, he'd disbanded all of the armies outside his personal guard the moment he gained supreme power. The nobles only complied because they trusted him—and trusted he wouldn't abuse that power. It was true that Lord Bardviss owned and commanded an impressive naval merchant fleet that was already armed as war galleons, but they wouldn't be any good on land. Controlling the oceans wouldn't be enough to gain control of Equillian. Besides, the oceans were infested with pirates. And Felix imagined pirates wouldn't take kindly to anyone trying to take their territory. So, what was it that Lord Bardviss was trying to achieve? If he was simply trying to elevate his status, he wouldn't have a reason to get rid of Lilliana. There were people who would've killed to marry her. She was a duchess who was not only young and beautiful, but also courageous and smart. It was a winning—and rare—combination. Felix imagined Lord Bardviss would be the envy of every other noble if he had her by his side. So why did he want to get rid of her? Because she was courageous, smart, and…difficult. If he had bigger, more sinister plans in play than simply gaining the status of duke, then Lilliana would be an unwelcome obstacle and liability. She was already on to him. And she was clever and stubborn enough to royally stir up his plans. Felix had the impression that Lilliana's younger sister, Natasha, was far more malleable. It made sense Lord Bardviss would prefer her as a bride. But Felix still couldn't figure out what he could possibly be trying to achieve. The one thing he was certain of was that Lord Bardviss deserved to be milked for all he was worth.

*Dear Lord Henry Bardviss,*

*Thank you for your generous donation. You have posed a tempting and interesting proposition. I must admit, we were surprised by your lack of concern over the well-being of your intended. Most men would send a legion to recoup such a bride. Instead, you have offered good coin to ensure you never do. Which poses an interesting question—what do you have to gain by her disappearance? It appears the dirt under your name, Henry, is even blacker than we'd realized. Luckily for you, one thing you mentioned has spiked our interest more than the details of your affairs: "name your price." If you really wish to hire us for our services and to take the unsavory action of abandoning our current employer to dispose of your betrothed, we will need sufficient compensation. Send us another eight hundred duckets, and you can consider your little "problem" dealt with. You will never hear from us again, our employer, or the Duchess of Westdock. However, send anything less and we'll foil this little boiling-pitch plan of yours and show the world just how twisted you truly are.*

*The Debt Collectors*

Felix put down his quill and smiled to himself. There was something incredibly satisfying about toying with people like Lord Bardviss. He only hoped he was playing his cards right. He knew he was walking a fine line—if he didn't ask for more coin, or if he asked for too little, Lord Bardviss wouldn't take The Debt Collectors seriously. However, if Felix asked for too much, or pushed Lord Bardviss too far, he would no longer be willing to cooperate.

Felix stood and paced the floorboards for several minutes waiting for the ink to dry. Then he folded the letter neatly and slipped it into his jacket pocket. He looked at his timepiece. It was the fourteenth hour, the hour of Karmithos—the Karma Keeper. Karmithos was not only one of the Time Keeper constellations, he was also an Overseer. It was his responsibility to keep people accountable for their actions. If you did something with ill intent and didn't get a timely consequence for it, you could expect to receive a reprimand from Karmithos—usually something similar to what was done to attract his attention in the first place, inspiring the phrase *what goes around comes around*. Felix had always done his best to stay on Karmithos's good side by choosing his targets from the Keeper's own hit list—people long overdue for a little justice, people like Lord Bardviss.

Felix wondered if Lilliana would be awake. No doubt she would be suffering from a hangover if she was. He wondered what she'd say to him now her inhibitions were restored. Would she pretend it hadn't happened, as she had before? Would she tell him to get lost? Or would she pull out her knife and dispose of his body off the side of the island? All felt like plausible possibilities.

*Well, I may as well hear it now and get it over and done with. If she wants me gone, better to find out before Roy returns,* Felix decided.

Using the letter in his pocket as an excuse, he grabbed the bottle of Spiced Kah and headed for her bedroom.

# FAERIE STAR–MOTHER

Felix took a deep breath and knocked softly on Lilliana's bedroom door. "Who is it?" she answered.

"Your faerie star-mother, I come bearing gifts," Felix announced.

"Well in that case, come right in," Lilliana invited.

Felix stepped inside cautiously, leaving the door open behind him. He'd already learned the hard way how formidable Lilliana could be when crossed, the memory of her pistol aimed at his back and her dagger against his throat was still clear in his mind.

The duchess was sitting up in her bed looking surprisingly fresh for being newly sober. By the looks of it, she'd also had a bath. She was wearing a casual green dress with her hair tied up in a loose knot and was looking at a copy of the *Words of the Watchers*.

"Brushing up on your Star Wisdom?" Felix asked.

He was surprised to see her with the thick book. Besides his and Bastian's copy, he'd never seen the written collection of the Night-Watchers' wisdom outside the Order.

Lilliana looked up at him and smiled. "*Someone* convinced me to leave all my books on the airship. So, I went browsing in the estate's library and this sort of jumped out at me. Have you read it?"

"Once or twice," Felix admitted, though in truth it was more like a hundred times. He had most of the book committed to memory. Every child at the Order was given one and made to study it. He'd read over his more times than he could count. The book made him think of Bastian—his Star-brother kept his copy by his bedside and thumbed through it often.

Lilliana looked back at the collection of articles. "I've never even heard of it."

Felix came over and sat down beside her. He reached out for the book and Lilliana handed it to him. "It's sacred to the Order, they gift one to every Star-child," he told her.

"You don't say? I have no idea how it got here. I can't imagine it belongs to Arianna, and I'm sure it's not my uncle's or my father's. I wonder if it was my aunt's," Lilliana pondered.

"Arianna's mother?" Felix asked.

"No, I doubt it would've been hers either. I'm talking about my father's sister."

"I thought he only had a brother?"

"He had a sister too. She was the youngest of the three of them, but he rarely talks about her. She passed away quite young, before I was born. I think she was in her early twenties," Lilliana divulged.

"Shame. How'd she die?" Felix inquired.

"I don't know, it was some accident I think, Father never talks about it."

Lilliana passed her hand over the pages of the book lovingly. "However it's gotten here, it's wonderful, I adore every piece I've read so far," she confessed.

Felix read the passage on the open page. "Ah yes, article 27— *'You cannot flee from the fate for which you came.'*"

"Do you believe we're all destined for a purpose?" Lilliana asked him.

"Yes. Now, what that purpose is, is another thing entirely. It could be as simple as gifting a child a smile on a bad day or to be dragon food—sustaining the creature for another night. As the sisters would say, 'a purpose destined by the Stars is not about an individual's life accomplishments, but often a single deed that affects or leads to something that affects the whole world. No deed is too small to turn the cogs of Empyrean's machine'," he quoted, mimicking the high falsetto of one of the Order's sisters.

Lilliana laughed at the impression.

"If someone's purpose is only a single deed, then what about the rest of their life? What's a person supposed to do if they've already fulfilled their purpose?"

"Ah, that's the beauty of it, you get to create your own purpose. It's when we don't that we fall victim to someone else using us to fulfill theirs."

"Hmmm, that's an interesting way of looking at it. And what's your chosen purpose then?" Lilliana asked.

Felix turned the question over before answering. "I don't know. Up until now all I've ever wanted was to create a life of happiness and comfort for my brother and me. I'm the only family he has, and he deserves it more than anyone else I know. But now, I'm not entirely sure," Felix admitted. "How about you, what's your chosen purpose?"

Lilliana frowned. "I've never really felt like I've had a choice, it's always been to fulfill my duties as a duchess and to look after my family—no matter the sacrifice," she confessed.

"If you did have a choice, what would it be?" Felix asked.

Lilliana thought about that for a moment. "I don't know," she admitted.

Felix smiled warmly. "You know, I'm incredibly impressed by how well you've freshened up. If I didn't know you've recently drunk enough to knock out a well-seasoned sailor, I'd never have guessed."

Lilliana laughed. "I told you, you've greatly underestimated a noble's tolerance for drinking."

"Clearly. Then you mustn't need this," Felix announced, holding up the bottle he'd brought with him.

"Spiced Kah! Where did you find it?" Lilliana exclaimed.

"It was on the airship, thought it would be a good chaser for the haunts of the rum punch—but clearly you don't need it."

"Give it here!" Lilliana demanded, and grabbed it from his hands. She pulled out the cork and took a long swig directly from the bottle. "That's exactly what I needed. You make an excellent Faerie Star-mother," she commended, and handed the bottle back to him.

Felix studied her curiously. This was a side of Lilliana he hadn't seen. She was suspiciously upbeat. Such a sunny disposition was the last thing he'd been expecting—he found it oddly confusing and entirely disarming.

*Maybe she's still drunk?* he wondered.

Felix held the bottle up to her and then took a swig, welcoming the familiar taste of Westdock's spice palette before passing it back. As Lilliana took another drink, Felix tried to decipher her. "How *are* you feeling?" he inquired.

"Great, all things considered."

"All things considered?" Felix asked carefully.

"Well, as you said—we did consume a lot of punch."

"Yes, that we did. Do you remember…anything else?" Felix queried.

Lilliana looked at him as if he wasn't well in the head and laughed. "Of course."

"And—you're fine with that?" Felix asked.

"As I recall, I was the one who took advantage of you, not the other way around," Lilliana stated.

Felix breathed out a silent sigh of relief. "So…we're good then? You don't want to toss me off the island or send me back to the mainland on the next airship?"

"Of course not!" Lilliana laughed.

Now Felix was utterly bemused. He opened his mouth to say something and then thought better of it.

"What's that sticking out of your back pocket?" Lilliana inquired.

Felix felt his pocket and found the letter for Lord Bardviss. "I finished our next installment. I thought you might want to see it before I send it out," he said, and gave it to her.

"I certainly do!" she confirmed, taking the letter in hand.

Felix drank the Spiced Kah in silence while she read it over.

"Eight hundred more duckets?!" Lilliana exclaimed.

"I know it sounds like a lot, but the amount's been carefully calculated," he assured her.

Lilliana cocked an eyebrow.

"If we don't ask for more coin, Lord Bardviss won't believe the false identity we've conjured up and won't take The Debt Collectors seriously. You have to remember, we're supposed to be a powerful and formidable group—only a complete novice would be gawked into silence over four purses of duckets. It was a clever move on his part, if we'd been bluffing amateurs we would've taken the coin and fled, not wanting to push our luck any further. But if we are professionals—which of course we are— then Lord Bardviss has given us just enough coin to show he's serious about trumping our current employer. If you recall he said, 'Name your price,' that's an invitation to tell him how much our service is worth, which requires a careful response. First, we are a high-class service, our employment isn't cheap. Second, what Lord Bardviss is asking us to do requires significant compensation. Not only is he asking us to abandon our current contract—which will tarnish our reputation—he's also asking us to make a royal 'disappear.' Getting rid of a noble isn't the same as getting rid of a commoner. You can't just dump their body in the ocean somewhere and think no one will come looking for it. People always come looking for nobles, and when they're found, they start looking for who put them there—and all the miserable ways they can make an example out of them to ensure it never happens again. Taking all that into consideration, I think the amount I've requested is quite reasonable," Felix expounded.

Lilliana stared at him and blinked. "I'm hesitant to ask why or how you know all this. You've considered details I never would've imagined."

Felix opened his mouth to reply, but Lilliana held up a hand. "Don't tell me. I don't want to know. I'm grateful for your knowledge and experience on this topic—wherever it's come from. I would've completely failed at carrying out this plan without you. I thought I had it all figured out. I now realize just how naïve I've been. Having you here feels too lucky to be merely coincidence," she confessed.

Felix met her eyes, "Maybe it's not."

He suddenly had the strong urge to kiss her, finding himself greatly regretting his decision to not close the door. Lilliana held his gaze, and Felix wondered if she was thinking the same thing.

"Five hundred thousand cwips, what will you do with all that coin?" she inquired.

Felix took a sip from the bottle of Kah. "Fulfill my purpose," he answered.

Lilliana took the bottle from him and held it up. "A worthy cause. Wring him for all he's worth," she declared, and drank.

Felix looked at her for a beat and then walked to the door and closed it gently.

Lilliana raised a questioning eyebrow.

Felix scratched his chin. "You know…normally I'm really good at this 'let's pretend it never happened' thing," he said, "only I find myself in new territory here, and for my own personal sanity and preservation I need to know what it is I'm getting myself into."

"What in the stars are you talking about?" Lilliana asked.

"No, don't do that. You know exactly what I'm talking about. This morning you pretended our night together never happened. Then this afternoon…happened. Which was incredible, by the way, but it completely contradicted what you'd said earlier and has quite honestly left me completely bemused—delighted, but utterly bemused. I just need to know, is it something I should never hope to have happen again, is this just a bit of fun, or is it something…more? Because considering our current circumstances, I think it's important we're both on the same page," Felix asserted.

Lilliana looked at him quizzically and then sighed. "I can't give you the answer you're looking for," she conceded.

"Why not?"

"Because I don't have it! This is also unknown territory for me. I didn't ask for this, you know? I've never cared about boys, not really. They care about me and I find it mildly amusing. I've always found courting a time-wasting bore. I think the very notion of romantic love is ridiculous, only I can't stop thinking about you, and the feeling in my chest every time I see you is irritatingly overwhelming. My head and my heart are in complete conflict with one another. My head keeps telling me how foolish this is, and my heart longs for more. The timing and circumstances couldn't be worse. It's an all-around and total inconvenience!" Lilliana exclaimed.

"I'm sorry for being such an inconvenience!" Felix blurted. "You might recall, you're the one who kidnapped me, not the other way around. An…" Lilliana stopped him with a finger to his lips.

"The truth is, I don't care, because whatever this is, it's completely wonderful," she confessed and smiled at him.

That smile hit Felix like an arrow to the heart.

Lilliana continued with a soft and earnest tone, "I've lived my whole life according to what's expected of me, by my family and as a duchess. Three days ago I finally stepped in a direction of my choosing, and for the first time I feel like I can breathe—I also have no idea where I'm going or what I'm doing. Quite frankly, it's both frightening and incredibly liberating. And whatever this is between us, I can't explain it, I know how dangerous and irresponsible it is. I know I should tell you to never hope for it to happen again. Only I don't want to. Just for once, I want to be able to do what I like without having to worry about how it will affect my position or my reputation. The only true answer I can give you is that whatever this is, no matter the consequences, I don't want it to end," she professed.

Felix smiled. "That's enough."

He pulled Lilliana into his arms and kissed her. She sank into his embrace. Then she interlaced her fingers with his and smiled. "Come, I want to show you something," she said, and led him out the door.

⌒

Lilliana led Felix out of the manor house and past the front courtyard towards the giant stables arcing down the left side of the estate.

"Where are you taking me?" Felix asked.

"You'll see," Lilliana said, and pulled him to the giant double doors of one of the stables.

"I thought Arianna told you not to disturb the dragons?"

"Oh posh! That's nonsense. Besides, none of the ones in here are Racing Dragons," Lilliana said, and pushed the stable door open. The large iron hinges creaked and Felix followed Lilliana inside. It felt like he was stepping into a Star Temple—the ceiling lofted high above their heads, held up by large wooden beams the size of entire trees stretching across the length of the structure. Inside was warm and humid and filled with the song of snuffling, grunting dragons shifting their huge weight against piles of rocks.

There were six stalls in the stable, three lining either side. Each stall had a dragon behind a heavy metal gate. They were lying on beds of large steaming rocks, resting contentedly.

"What are they laying on?" Felix asked.

"Beds of iron ore. The raw ore is heated by Everfire from underneath. Dragons are cold-blooded creatures. In the wild they collect anything with metal content for their beds and heat it up with their fire to stay warm."

"Doesn't that cook them? It sounds like sleeping on a barbecue," Felix remarked.

"It would if they were any other creature, but dragons' scales and skin are impervious to fire and unaffected by heat. Sometimes they purposely get their beds so hot the metal liquifies and welds onto their scales, giving them extra plating on their underside," Lilliana explained.

"They're all asleep, are they nocturnal?" Felix asked.

"Dragons don't have regular sleeping hours; they sleep whenever it suits them. With a hot bed and plenty of food, they'll happily spend most of their time asleep," Lilliana informed him.

"Fascinating," Felix remarked, staring apprehensively at the gigantic creatures with their horned heads and vibrant metallic scales.

"Here's who I'm looking for," Lilliana announced, stopping outside the last stall on the left. There was a large blue and purple dragon behind the gate curled up on its rock bed, sleeping peacefully with wisps of smoke trailing from its nostrils.

"His name's Twillos. I was here when he was born and he was my favorite, so my uncle let me name him. He's the runt of the litter, came out just after the sun went down—on the start of the Twillos hour."

"A fitting name. He certainly doesn't look like a runt," Felix observed.

"I know, he's grown so much! He's not a racer, but he'll always be my favorite," Lilliana told him, looking in at the dragon lovingly.

"Did you spend much of your childhood here?" Felix inquired.

"We came for the Derby almost every year when I was young. Occasionally we would make it for other visits, but those occasions were few and far between. Regardless, I still feel like this place is a second home," she shared.

"Would've been a nice place to grow up around," Felix remarked.

"Yes, yes it was. I only wish I could've spent more time here. It suits me more than Westdock ever has," she confessed, and then she walked up to the bars of the dragon's enclosure.

"Twillos, Twillos wake up. It's me," she called to the dragon.

"Shouldn't we let him sleep?" Felix asked.

"Course not, I don't know when I'll get another chance to see him. Twillos!" Lilliana called again.

The dragon opened a giant slitted eye and peered at them. As soon as he saw Lilliana, he lifted his head enthusiastically and walked over to the gate, putting his large nose against the bars. Lilliana held out her hand to be sniffed and the dragon made a low purring sound.

"It's good to see you too," Lilliana laughed delightedly. "Would you like to go for a flight?"

Twillos nodded his huge horned head.

"He understands you," Felix remarked in surprise.

"Of course, dragons are highly intelligent. More so than most humans, if you ask me."

Lilliana grabbed a harness from off a hook beside the stall and unlocked the gate.

"Are you sure that's a good idea?" Felix asked.

"Of course!" Lilliana laughed.

She stepped inside the stall with the gigantic beast, and he lowered his head so she could put on the harness, then she beckoned to Felix. "Come in so I can introduce you."

"I'm good, I'll wait out here," he said.

"He won't hurt you."

"How can you be sure of that?"

"Because, I've known him his whole life, and he's the biggest sweetheart there is," Lilliana asserted, "Isn't that right, Twillos?" she asked the dragon.

Twillos purred.

Felix swollowed. "Let's just hope my Star purpose isn't being his dinner," he muttered.

Lilliana laughed.

Felix stepped cautiously inside the gate, giving the dragon a wide berth.

"Twillos, this is James, he's a friend—so be nice. James, this is Twillos," Lilliana introduced.

The dragon slanted his eyes at Felix accusingly as if he knew James wasn't his real name.

"Hi, Twillos," Felix greeted nervously.

The dragon snuffed disapprovingly.

"Don't be rude!" Lilliana scolded the dragon.

"Hold out your hand so he can smell you," she directed.

Felix held out his open palm and the dragon sniffed his hand suspiciously before lifting his head to gaze into Felix's eyes. Felix stared back at the amazing large blue irises with black slits for pupils and, like looking into the eyes of a Sendsong, felt the dragon was undressing his very soul.

*Yes, James isn't my real name. I'll tell Lilliana when the time's right. So please, don't screw this up for me. I promise I've only good intentions and care about her at least as much as you do, he thought.*

The dragon seemed to understand him perfectly. He studied Felix as if considering, then he nodded slightly and turned his attention back to Lilliana.

"See, I knew you two would take to one another," Lilliana smiled, stroking the top of Twillos's nose.

Felix breathed a quiet sigh of relief and Lilliana led the dragon out of the stall, stopping just outside where a saddle hung on the wall.

"Can you help me get this saddle on his back?" she asked.

"I'll certainly try," he said, and assisted Lilliana in lifting the saddle onto the dragon's back just behind its muscular shoulders and wings. Once the saddle was in place, Lilliana went to work buckling the hanging straps around Twillos's ginormous belly.

"Can't pack a bag, but you can expertly saddle a dragon," Felix remarked.

"Saddling dragons and horses has been the only ticket to the small amount of freedom I've had in my life. A skill I was eager to obtain," Lilliana admitted.

"I can imagine. Did your father teach you how to ride?"

"Yes, he started my sister and me as soon as we could walk. He was so fond of it himself, having grown up here."

"I imagine it's thrilling to soar through the clouds on the back of a dragon," Felix remarked.

"It's beyond anything imaginable, but I don't need to tell you that, soon you'll see for yourself," she told him, leading Twillos out of the stable.

"Oh, no thank you. I'm sure it's quite the experience, but it's not for me. You fill your boots—I'll stay here and hold the fort," Felix said, following her out of the stable into the sunlight.

Lilliana stopped and turned to him with a half-annoyed, half-puzzled expression. "You'll do no such thing! There's something I want to show you and we have to fly to get there," she asserted.

Felix scratched the back of his head. "Right, that *is* a problem. Can't we just take an air cab?"

Lilliana stared at him incredulously. "I thought you would've been eager, this is the chance of a lifetime! When will you ever get the opportunity to ride a dragon again?"

Felix returned her stare apologetically. "Look, it's not that I don't want to, it's just…I'm terrified of heights," he confessed.

Lilliana blinked. "Oh, that's not a problem. You'll just have to get over it," she declared, and continued towards the side of the island.

"Get over it?! I don't think you understand, it's not a choice I can simply choose to abandon. It's a visceral reaction that's completely involuntary and totally debilitating. It takes any sort of thrill that might come from these sorts of things and turns it into petrifying terror," Felix protested, tromping after her.

Lilliana stopped at the edge of the island and turned to him, while Twillos sat down and stretched his wings.

"Then close your eyes. I'll blindfold you if you like, whatever you need—but you're getting on this dragon. Because if you don't, I'll never let you touch me again," she asserted.

Felix opened his mouth and then closed it. "Right. Looks like I'm getting on the dragon."

Lilliana smiled. "Excellent choice."

She climbed onto Twillos and held out her hand to Felix. He took it gingerly and climbed into the saddle behind her. *Stars help me,* he thought.

"You won't regret this," Lilliana told him.

"I already do," Felix muttered.

"Hold on!" she called back and flicked the reins. The huge blue dragon lurched upwards, leaping into the sky. Felix's stomach stayed on the island behind them as they soared off its edge. He wrapped his arms tightly around Lilliana's waist and closed his eyes as vertigo overwhelmed him. They soared up into the billowing clouds and Lilliana laughed in delight.

"Isn't it beautiful?!" she called back over the wind.

"I'll take your word for it," he returned with his eyes tightly shut.

"Open your eyes or I'm doing a loop-the-loop!" Lilliana threatened.

"What happened to *whatever you need*?!"

"You're not missing this. I won't let you!"

"Keep in mind, if I vomit it's going straight in your hair."

"You wouldn't!!"

"Don't try me." Felix opened one eye and then the other. They were gliding through a heavy blanket of clouds. He held out his hand, dragging it through the cool moist air, creating a little trail in the billow beside them. A moment later they came out of the cloud into the clear blue sky with a blanket of clouds beneath them. Felix stopped fighting his terror and tried to embrace it, relaxing into it until it transformed into an exhilarating rush, making him feel potently present and alive. He laughed. It was beautiful. Twillos was impressively graceful for his size, his powerful wings beating silently every so often before returning to a steady glide. They flew beyond the larger islands into the cerulean abyss, until there was hardly anything left in sight. There was nothing but sky for a handful of minutes before they came to a group of scattered fragment islands. There must have been at least fourteen of them. They were all too small to live on, some only big enough to hold one or two trees.

"I thought there were only twenty-one islands in the Windswept Isles?" Felix queried.

"None of these islands are charted. They're too small to document and no one owns them. I've never seen anyone else here. I used to come this way when I wanted to be alone," Lilliana told him.

She led Twillos through the field of floating rocks to one a little larger than the others. It had a small cluster of trees and was covered in green grass dappled with blooming winter wildflowers. The dragon set down gracefully and bowed down for them to dismount.

Felix jumped down first, eager to have his feet on solid ground. Then he held his hand up to Lilliana. She ignored it and jumped down after him. Felix smiled. Twillos walked straight to the center of the island and rolled over onto his back into the long grass.

Lilliana laughed, "You're like an overgrown puppy dog, Twillos! You clearly need to be taken out more often."

Twillos grunted in agreement.

"This place is magnificent," Felix proclaimed, looking around them.

Lilliana smiled. "Isn't it? You should feel very privileged, I've never taken anyone here."

"Not even your sister?" Felix asked.

"Not even my sister."

"Then I do," Felix smiled. He observed how happy Lilliana looked in that moment. She was positively glowing. "You really love this place, don't you?"

"Of course, how could I not?" she said, turning her head into the gentle wind and welcoming its embrace.

"Are you sure you're willing to give it up?—sell the full estate to Arianna, I mean."

Lilliana enjoyed the wind tousling her hair for a moment before answering. "No, I'm not. This place means so much to me. It holds so many memories, especially of my father. The moment it's no longer part mine, I fear I'll lose it entirely. My mother never comes here, and with Uncle and Father gone, and Arianna and I being so estranged…everything's different now. I just wish things could be how they used to," she confessed.

"Maybe you don't have to give up your half. Surely there's another way," Felix proposed.

Lilliana turned to him. "I wish there was. It's the only place I feel I can escape from everything. Even if just for a moment. Sometimes, I wonder what it would be like to keep going, flying into the horizon, I mean. What I might find if I did. I used to fantasize about finding a new island that's populated but has never had any contact with Sky View or the mainland and disappearing on it, being able to completely reinvent myself."

"Maybe that's what your father was thinking the day he went missing," Felix suggested.

Lilliana laughed dryly. "Not likely."

"Why not?"

"Because my father isn't an emotional person. He's always acted with calculated purpose. I'd say he's made of clockwork if I didn't know better. Everything he's ever done, he's done strategically. Even marrying my mother. Like a move on a chessboard. He's never done anything with my sister and me that didn't have some greater motivation. Sometimes I wondered if we were all simply game pieces to him, only valuable because we're a means to some end. I only wish he'd clued me in on what that end is," Lilliana replied thoughtfully.

"If that's true, then why do you want to find him so badly? No offense, but he sounds like terrible company."

Lilliana smiled. "He can be, but he's my dad. And luckily, whatever his plan is, raising us well has been part of it. It just felt calculated sometimes — instead of organic. More than sometimes, actually. I think that's what's left me wanting. One of the foibles of being human, I suppose." Lilliana gazed out at the ocean of sky. "At any rate, that's why I know my father didn't have any fantasies of flying off into the sunset. He'd only do that if there was a logical reason with some advantage."

Felix studied her. "You miss him a lot, don't you?"

"Yes I do. I miss him because he's order in a world full of chaos. He always knows what to do and has a solution for everything. As much as I resent his strict conduct and rules — and I hate how much he underestimates me — I still love him. And I need him to put our family back together. He's the glue that binds us. Without him, everything's falling apart."

"Have you ever tried to send him a letter via Sendsong?" Felix asked.

The mechanical birds were supposed to be able to find anyone anywhere. Surely if the duke was still alive, a letter would reach him.

"More times than I can count. I tried at least once every day for over a year before my mother made me stop. She gave up long before I ever could," Lilliana confessed.

"What happened? Did they get delivered anywhere?"

"No. When I place the letter in the Sendsong and give it my father's name, it starts to move like it's going to take off to deliver it, then it stops and sort of wanders around lost — then its chest pops open for me to take the letter back."

"What's that supposed to mean?"

"I don't know. No one does. I inquired into it extensively, no one's ever seen or heard of anything like it."

"What happens if you try to send a letter to someone who isn't alive?" Felix inquired.

"The Sendsongs won't take it, their compartment won't even shut. They just stand there waiting for you to take it back."

"Well, that's gotta be a good sign, right? I mean, it sounds like it would be pretty clear if your father was dead," Felix reasoned.

"That's what I think too. I just have no idea what it means. If he's alive, why won't the Sendsong deliver the letter to him? And if he's not, then why would the Sendsong act like it's going to, even for a moment?"

"That's a very good question. Maybe he's halfway between—stuck in a coma, for example," Felix suggested.

Lilliana frowned. "Stars, I hope not."

"Well, even that's better than him being gone completely."

"I suppose."

Felix walked over to Lilliana and wrapped his arms around her shoulders, hugging her from behind while resting his chin on her shoulder. He followed her gaze out to the surrounding fragment islands and said, "I hope you do find your father. But not because you need him—you don't. You're every bit as capable of solving the world's problems as he is—maybe even more so. You just have to believe it. That's where your father went wrong, he solved things for you, instead of empowering you to solve them for yourself. That's why things are falling apart in his absence. Not because he's the only person capable of keeping it all together, it's because he never showed you and your sister how—or let you believe you could. But look at you now. Despite that, you're tackling mountains."

Lilliana smiled. "Thank you. That means a lot." She leaned back into his embrace, "though I feel like the mountains are tackling me," she confessed.

"Of course you do, if you didn't they wouldn't be mountains. Just keep putting one foot in front of the other and you'll conquer your way to the top," Felix assured her.

Lilliana squeezed his arm, then frowned at the horizon. "We better head back, those clouds look like they're bringing rain."

Felix followed her gaze to a large clump of heavy grey clouds in the distance moving towards them. "Oh, yes. I imagine flying isn't much fun in bad weather."

"Twillos, time to go!" Lilliana called.

The dragon looked at her and she pointed to the clouds. He sniffed the air and sat up, looking out at the oncoming storm, suddenly anxious to get moving. Felix and Lilliana mounted the huge beast and he leapt into the air.

Felix and Lilliana arrived at the Wendrians' island just as the rain began to pelt down. They dismounted Twillos and led him hurriedly to the stable through the heavy downpour. By the time they closed themselves inside they were drenched.

"At least it's warm in here," Felix laughed.

Lilliana squeezed out the excess water from her dress into a bucket. "I'm soaked through!" she exclaimed.

Twillos nudged her with his nose.

"I know, I know, I'd be eager to get back to my hot bed too. Just give me a moment, I don't repel water the way you do," she told the dragon.

Lilliana led Twillos back to his stall and Felix helped her take off the reins and saddle. As soon as they did, the dragon hurried to his rock bed and used his nose to push the ore into a pleasing pile, then plopped down on top. Steam rose from his scales with a gentle hiss.

"I'll take you for another ride when I can," Lilliana promised, resting her forehead against his. Twillos closed his eyes and gave a low, gentle purr. Lilliana touched the side of his face lovingly and then left his stall, locking the iron gate behind her.

There was a steady thrum of rain on the roof above them.

"Should we brave the weather and head back to the house, or wait it out?" Felix asked.

"There's no way I'm going out in that, do you have any idea how long it takes to dry this hair?"

Felix smirked. "No, I can't say I've ever thought about it."

"There's a secret entrance to the old hatchery in here. My grandfather built it during the war when my family was producing War Dragons. It's been abandoned for years. Come on, hopefully there's still the old handling suits down there, it will give us something dry to put on," Lilliana proposed, and led Felix to a supply closet along the back wall. She walked into it and gestured for Felix to follow. He joined her inside, looking around at the riding equipment and the tools for cleaning the dragons and maintaining the stables, all of which were clean and well organized. Lilliana went to the back wall, stomped on the ground several times in a rhythmic pattern, and stepped aside. There was the sound of gear work before a trapdoor opened from the floor. Satisfied, Lilliana beckoned Felix to go inside.

Felix looked down at the steps leading into darkness and said, "please, ladies first."

"You don't trust me?" Lilliana asked.

"With all due respect, my lady, the last time I followed you down a secret passageway you kidnapped me and threatened to kill me," Felix stated.

Lilliana smirked, "If I'd wanted to get rid of you, I would've had Twillos finish you off at the secluded island."

Felix considered that. "Makes sense, a lot less cleanup that way."

Lilliana shrugged and nodded. "Far more practical," she agreed.

"Still, I try to make a habit of not repeating my mistakes if I can help it. Please, after you," Felix insisted.

Lilliana smiled and headed into the darkness. As soon as her foot hit the top step the board sank with a *click,* and instantly bags were mechanically drawn from Everfire lanterns lining the passage, filling it with light. Felix followed cautiously behind. The stairs descended through a narrow sloping corridor with steep stone walls on either side.

"Is this taking us underground?" he asked.

"Yes, my grandfather wanted it completely hidden so no one could steal any of the hatchlings or any of our family's research. He had the dragons sterilized before selling them off, which made it impossible to reproduce them anywhere else. Before he built this place there were several attempts to steal our hatchlings. After the war was over, there was no more need for it. My sister, Arianna, and I used to play down here when we were children," Lilliana told him.

They navigated their way down the flight of steps to a small room that had a wood bench against the wall, with boots neatly paired underneath and jumpsuits hanging from hooks above.

"Yes! They're still here!" Lilliana exclaimed enthusiastically, handing one of the jumpsuits to Felix, and taking down one for herself.

The jumpsuit looked like it had been washed recently. It hardly gave the impression of something sitting idle for years. Lilliana looked at Felix expectantly.

"What?" he queried.

"Turn around."

"Really? After everything we've been through, you're feigning modesty?"

"I'm not feigning anything, now turn around!" she commanded.

Felix smirked. "Alright, I'm turning around," he yielded, and turned his back to her, pulling off his own clothes unabashedly and replacing them with the jumpsuit. "Can I look yet?" he asked.

"Almost. Alright, I'm ready," Lilliana announced.

Felix turned around. The blue cotton jumpsuit fit her surprisingly well—too well, making his thoughts wander into fantasy.

"Come on, I'll show you around," Lilliana announced, and pushed through a door on their right.

Felix followed Lilliana into a brightly lit room and found her standing there paralyzed. He followed her staring gaze into the large open space. It was similar to the underground bunker at the Wendrians' castle in Westdock, except it was filled with row upon row of glass and metal incubators on sturdy iron pushcarts, all with steam rising from them. In the center of the room was a long metal table covered in glass vials, beakers, and neatly organized paperwork. The room was warm and alive with the gentle chatter of baby dragons.

"I thought you said this hatchery was retired," Felix said.

"It was," Lilliana replied, still staring. She walked over to the closest incubator and looked inside. "What are these?"

"What do you mean, aren't they dragons?" Felix asked, coming to stand beside her. Inside the incubator was a sleeping baby creature that looked like some sort of dragon. It was stout compared with the ones Felix had seen previously, with thick muscular legs and wings that looked too small to carry their bodies.

"They're dragons, but this is a breed I'm unfamiliar with. They have the general characteristics of Pack Dragons, but they're clearly some sort of hybrid. Look at their wings—the size is all wrong. They'll never be able to fly with those."

Felix looked down at the baby dragon in the incubator. It was smiling up at him as if expecting something. "Pack Dragons? I don't think I've heard of those," he said.

"Hardly anyone uses them anymore. They're for hauling cargo, mostly. It's one of the two breeds allowed to be shipped to the mainland," Lilliana explained.

"I thought the mainland was only allowed Pet Dragons?" Felix queried. They were the only dragons he'd seen in Westdock.

Lilliana shook her head. "Pet Dragons and Pack Dragons are both legal outside Sky View, as long as they're fixed—to prevent them from being bred on the mainland. Pack Dragons were used frequently after the Last War to rebuild and renovate the cities. After the war ended, Lord Balthazar set the mainland to improving infrastructure and Sky View to providing the Pack Dragons for it. It was a way to stimulate the economy and give Sky View a commodity to replace War Dragons. It united the precincts under a common goal and got them to work together in building a better world and future for us all. But I haven't heard of anyone using or producing Pack Dragons for years. They're a restless breed when left idle—people struggle to figure out what to do with them once their work is done. Now, steam technology has replaced the need for them. I can't imagine why anyone would want one these days. And this is a large order, there are twenty-one dragons here. That's three whole litters. I wonder who they're for and why? And why Arianna is hatching them down here instead of in the regular nursery," she questioned. She walked over to the table in the center of the room and began riffling through the paperwork.

Felix held out his open palm towards the baby dragon. It sniffed his hand eagerly and then blew out a small gust of fire as if intending to roast his fingers for a meal. Felix pulled back his hand in surprise.

"This doesn't make any sense," Lilliana exclaimed. "These are a Pack Dragon and Bermese mix."

"Bermese?" Felix asked.

"They're classified as a Pet Dragon, but only because of their size. No one in their right mind would keep one as a pet—they're far too aggressive. They used to be bred for making armor. Their colors are spectacular and the strength of their hide and scales is superior to any other breed. The practice was banned for being inhumane when they realized how intelligent the creatures are—and how many had to be used for a single set of armor," she expounded.

"How do they breed a Pet Dragon with a Pack Dragon? Isn't that… physically impossible?" Felix inquired.

"Not with artificial insemination," Lilliana stated.

Felix looked back down at the dragon. "I guess that explains why the wings are so small."

Lilliana walked over to look at the hybrid in the incubator. "I can't imagine why Arianna would do this. Mixing Pack Dragons with Bermese will make them more aggressive. It's a terrible combination. Imagine a dragon intelligent, restless, and aggressive. Who would want that?" Lilliana asked.

"I can think of someone," Felix admitted.

"Who?"

Felix shrugged, "The East, of course. Who else on the mainland would be interested in something this shady? I've heard they fight dragons in pits for sport. This breed sounds like a perfect candidate for that. Think about it, even the small wings have an advantage, they wouldn't have to cut them off or chain them down to keep them from escaping," Felix proposed.

"What a horrid thought, that would be completely unethical and illegal!" Lilliana exclaimed aghast.

Felix smiled at her innocence. "Since when has that ever stopped The East from doing anything? They capitalize on everything illegal and shady, thrive on it, in fact. It's what runs their economy, if you hadn't noticed."

Lilliana squinted her eyes at him. "Your knowledge on this topic is starting to concern me. How do you know all this?"

Felix laughed before realizing she was serious. "How do you not know this? I thought everyone knew that."

Lilliana stiffened her lower lip. "There's no way Arianna would conduct business of this nature. Especially with The East, my uncle despised them!" she asserted.

"Are you sure? I mean, how much do you really know about your cousin?" Felix asked.

Lilliana turned back to the paperwork. "There must be a perfectly logical explanation to all of this," she declared, riffling through several stacks of papers before coming across an old book—she paused and then opened it tentatively as if it might burn her. As she skimmed through its pages her eyes widened in horror. "By the Watchers," she whispered.

"What is it?" Felix inquired, coming to stand beside her.

She handed him the book with shaking hands. Felix turned it over—it was old and leather bound with a gold dragon engraved on the front. Inside was a neatly kept account of breeding experimentation in blue ink with fine penmanship. Accompanying it were graphite notes made all over the pages in a less meticulous hand.

"My grandfather's log book. It's what he used to document his work when he created War Dragons. I thought my father and uncle had destroyed it. These notes around his accounts, they're Arianna's...I think she's trying to find a way to reproduce the breed within legal guidelines," she confessed in horror.

"And why would she want to do a silly thing like that?" Felix asked.

"I don't have the slightest—"

"Hey! Who gave you permission to be down here?!"

Felix and Lilliana turned to see a servant standing in the doorway.

Lilliana drew herself up to her full height. "Excuse me? I'm Lilliana Wendrian—niece of John Wendrian and heir to this estate, I don't need permission to be here. Who are you?" she demanded hotly.

The young man hesitated and then bowed his head. "I'm sorry, my lady, I didn't know who you were, please forgive my mistake. Lady Arianna's given strict orders for no unauthorized persons to be down here."

"I see, and why did she do that?" Lilliana queried.

The man hesitated again, looking exceedingly uncomfortable, "I'm only following orders, my lady."

"Since you seem to be good at that, I'll give you another. You're to say nothing of us being down here to Arianna or anyone else. In return—I'll say nothing about you seeing us down here, understood?" Lilliana asked.

"Yes, perfectly, my lady," the man complied obediently, and bowed his head again.

"Come on, James, I think the rain's stopped," Lilliana announced, leading Felix out of the hatchery.

Felix sat on the end of Lilliana's bed watching her pace her room anxiously,

"I don't understand, why would Arianna do this? War Dragons are a monstrosity! Everyone knows that. It's exactly why Lord Balthazar had them put down after the war," she proclaimed.

"Yeah, but he loved having them during the war, didn't he? There's never been a more effective weapon," Felix pointed out.

"Nor one as inhumane!" Lilliana argued.

"War itself is inhumane. And yet, even after 'The War to End All Wars' it clearly still persists. What I don't understand is—if Arianna wants War Dragons back so badly, why doesn't she just hatch the eggs your grandfather had enchanted?" Felix asked.

"Because she would never get away with it. Don't you see? Pet Dragons and Pack Dragons are allowed anywhere on Equillian—she's creating a weaponized breed that's technically legal. Besides, she'd need both of the enchanted eggs together in order to bring back War Dragons. It was the fail-safe my grandfather incorporated into them. It's why he gave one to each of his sons instead of both eggs to one. They would've had to have agreed they were needed in order to bring them back. Arianna knows my mother and I will never support resurrecting War Dragons," Lilliana asserted.

"I wonder if this new breed has any connection to Sky View's brewing 'revolution,'" Felix proposed.

"Brewing revolution?" Lilliana questioned.

Felix nodded. "Roy and I saw a soapbox speech in the city center this morning. Something about Lord Balthazar taking away their dragons after they won him the war and then robbing them with taxes. They were stirring up a crowd, calling for Sky View's independence. There were posters for it being torn down by officials all around the city."

Lilliana scoffed. "That's an incredibly narrow-sighted perspective that hardly coincides with reality."

"You don't have to tell me. The people up here don't know the meaning of injustice. They certainly won't be inspiring my sympathy," Felix assured her.

"This dwarfs everything. If there's unrest brewing in Sky View, then we need to warn The Emperor before it turns into another war!" Lilliana exclaimed.

"And how do you suppose we do that? The Emperor's so unreachable he may as well be one of the constellations."

"Actually, he's my cousin—well, second cousin anyway," Lilliana admitted.

Felix's jaw dropped, "You're joking?"

"On my mother's side, they're cousins. They're not close—I've never actually met him, but we're still family," she explained.

Felix laughed. "Of course you are, I don't know why that surprises me. Well, if it's any help, he'll be at the Derby."

"Emperor Balthazar?"

"Is there another?"

"How do you know he'll be there?" Lilliana asked.

"Because we're supposed to be modelling Favio's latest collection to him at the after-party. Favio was the winner of some design competition."

Lilliana's face lit with optimism, "That's perfect! This solves everything. Once I'm in front of him, I can request an audience. He has to grant me one—after my mother I'm the main representative of Westdock. It's my duty to notify him of any matter affecting the peace of Equillian," she declared.

"Only you're supposed to be missing," Felix reminded her.

"The fact that I'm missing won't matter if I can get an audience with him, don't you see? If I can get in front of the Lord Emperor without anyone else finding out I'm here, then I can show him Lord Bardviss's letter—proving he offered coin to have me removed. That's all the justification I need for my disappearance. Having someone like Lord Bardviss as duke doesn't only affect me, it sullies the entire web of nobility and the foundation of The Emperor's bureaucratic system. Lord Balthazar's someone who'll actually listen and do something about it. And if I'm right about Arianna's intention to create a legal strain of War Dragons, then me being here and seeking out The Emperor will play a crucial part in preserving our world peace. It'll make my decision to stage my own kidnapping look practically heroic. I'll be able to come out of hiding and return home regardless of whether or not we find my father. Maybe Lord Balthazar will even reopen the investigation into my father's disappearance!" Lilliana proclaimed.

"Whoa, slow down. What about Arianna? You know if you accuse her of creating a weaponized breed, she'll be sentenced for life. Are you prepared to subject your cousin to that?"

Lilliana hesitated. "She makes her own choices. If she's truly chosen to act against the wellbeing of Equillian then she's condemned herself," she declared resolutely.

"You two still share a family name, your reputation is tightly linked to hers. This could ruin it—along with your family's business, no doubt. And there will be those who'll never trust you because you betrayed your own blood," Felix cautioned.

"What other choice do I have? Stay silent and allow her to re-create the greatest weapon of mass destruction the world's ever known? Killing Stars knows how many innocent people and ripping apart the peace we've worked so hard for? That's not an option!" Lilliana asserted passionately.

"And what if she's innocent? She might be sentenced anyway. And if she's proven innocent, your relationship will be broken beyond repair and the blame will fall on your shoulders," Felix pointed out.

"Innocent?!" Lilliana exclaimed hotly, "There's no way to explain what she's doing that's innocent!"

Felix held up his open palms and spoke his next words gently, "I'm only trying to help you think this through. There's a lot of information we still don't have. I don't want you to rush into anything without knowing what you're in for and then regret it."

"Then what would you recommend I do? Because from my perspective I can't see a single avenue that'll leave me without regrets—but it's not about me or my relationship to my cousin. It's about what's right for the greater good of Equillian," Lilliana returned passionately.

"You could try talking to her. Give her a chance to explain herself. Maybe it's not what it looks like, maybe there's an angle we just don't understand. And if there isn't, then you could try and sway her to stop whatever it is she's doing. Maybe even find a way to turn it around," Felix suggested.

Lilliana let out a huff of frustration. "You say that like it's easy! I've tried talking to her. She's avoided me at every opportunity," she protested.

"Give it more time, we've hardly been here. We still have all of tomorrow before the Derby. Surely there'll be a window of opportunity. And don't misunderstand me, I never for a moment presumed it would be easy. If it were easy to talk and listen to one another, the human race might actually have a real shot at harmony. Unfortunately, that's not the world we live in. But that doesn't mean we shouldn't try. You'd be surprised at how much can be changed or cleared up with a simple conversation. At the very least, talking to her will give you information. Right now we have very little. If you're going to be ruining your cousin's life, don't you want to be sure it's justified and you're doing it for the right reasons?" Felix admonished.

"Yes," Lilliana admitted, collapsing onto the bed beside him, "but what if there isn't a good explanation? What if she's doing exactly what we fear the most, and by talking to her I put our lives in danger? No one knows we're here. If she wants to get rid of us, she could get away with it."

"Do you really think your own cousin's capable of such a thing?"

"I don't know. I'm finding that I know very little about who Arianna truly is these days," she admitted.

"So, don't give her a reason to feel threatened. Don't accuse her or confront her about what she's doing. Just ask questions and listen," Felix advised.

Lilliana sighed. "You're right. I need to find a way to talk to her—why is that so hard? I'd rather face an unknown opponent out for my blood than have a conversation with someone I love. Does that make me a terrible person?"

"Ha! No, it makes you human. It's only terrifying because you care about her. You don't care about an unknown opponent, and their attack would justify your actions against them. There's a lot at stake when having a conversation with someone you love. Which is also precisely why it's so important to have it. Silence is a far more potent killer than a bad argument. Just remember, bravery's not the lack of fear—it's facing your fear and not letting it stop you," Felix imparted, quoting the phrase he recited to himself every time he climbed a ship's rigging.

Lilliana nodded. "You're right. Stars bring me courage."

# TREBLE CLEF

Gwena finished her breakfast in her room and prepared herself for Benji's measurements. Part of her wished it was anyone but the cynical philanderer, but it was her first assigned task as the club's tailor, and she was determined to do it well. Even he couldn't destroy the elated optimism she felt. It was only her second day in the Heartland and she'd already crossed everything off her to-do list. She had a well-paying job, accommodation, a postal box set up at the Central Posting House, and a whole wardrobe of new clothes. Now all she had to do was bide her time until she heard from Bastian or Felix. She pocketed her measuring tape and left the room, walking down the hallway in search of the door with the treble clef. She found it halfway down the corridor on a green door. She straightened her dress and knocked lightly.

"It's open," Benji called from inside.

Gwena let herself in and closed the door behind her. Benji was nowhere to be seen. The room was surprisingly larger than she'd expected. In fact, it was more of a studio apartment than a room. It was extravagant in design, with a high arching ceiling over an open-plan living space that included a kitchen with a marble island bench top, a dining and lounge area, and a bedroom with the biggest bed Gwena had ever seen—adorned with silk blankets and cushions, and a large bay window beside with an expansive view of a tropical rainforest. Gwena walked to the window and stared out it in wonderment. Benji walked in from an adjoining en suite behind her wearing nothing but boxer briefs, with a toothbrush in his mouth. "Morning," he greeted.

Gwena turned around and blushed, quickly covering her eyes with her hand in embarrassment. "Oh! I'm so sorry!" she exclaimed, "I can come back later, if there's a better time?"

Benji cocked his head curiously, then he smiled with amusement. "I just assumed this is how you'd want me. Our last tailor wouldn't take measurements any other way."

"Oh! Of course," Gwena blurted, laughing nervously, "that's fine, I just wasn't expecting, I don't normally—never mind. However you're most comfortable," she stammered. She realized she was still covering her eyes and quickly put her hand down, smiling awkwardly.

Benji stared at her like she was some strange new creature, and Gwena wished she could crawl under his ridiculously large bed.

"One sec, let me get rid of this," he said, gesturing to his toothbrush.

"Of course!"

He disappeared into the en suite, and Gwena bit her fist in overwhelming mortification. Benji returned a moment later with empty hands.

"How do you want me?" he asked her.

Gwena's cheeks turned deep scarlet. "Pardon?"

"Should I stand anyway in particular?" he rephrased.

"Oh, right. Just there's fine. You can stand as you are, it will only take a few minutes," she informed him, and tried to ignore his bare golden brown skin and well-toned figure as she began measuring his arms.

"If you don't mind me asking, how'd a little bird from Westdock land a job here?" Benji inquired.

"I ran into Bonnie, and she mentioned the club was in need of a tailor. I was in need of work and accommodation—so it suited us both perfectly," she answered, writing down his measurements on a small notepad.

"Is that right? I'm surprised Rouge hired someone so young. But then, we were desperate. I just hope your tailor skills are less wet behind the ears than you are," Benji remarked.

Gwena's cheeks flushed. "My tailor skills were sought after by lords and ladies in Westdock, I'll have you know," she returned indignantly.

Benji smiled. "Good, because I need an exceptional suit."

"What's the occasion?"

"Mine are falling behind in fashion and I like to maintain a high standard. I can't expect my clients to pay top coin for my company if I don't come in fancy packaging."

"I see, Scarlet Jade doesn't keep company with you for your personality?" Gwena jested.

Benji smiled. "No."

"Or the woman you were with last night—what's her name? I honestly don't know how you keep track," she jeered.

"Simone Simmons," Benji told her.

"Simone Simmons? As in the author?!" Gwena exclaimed.

"You know her work?"

"Of course, it's magnificent! Especially *Changing Tides*, the prose is like poetry—" Gwena stopped herself, noticing the amused expression on Benji's face. "Have you not read it?" she asked him.

"I can't say it interests me, I'm more of a detective-novel guy," he admitted.

"That must be incredibly embarrassing for you—I hope she's never asked you about her work?"

"My clients generally come here to get away from their work," Benji stated.

"Well, you should read it, it's a beautiful piece that would be a shame to miss."

Gwena wrote down her last measurement and began rolling up her measuring tape. "You're all done, I have what I need. Will this suit be for business or pleasure?" she asked.

Benji smirked. "My business is pleasure."

Gwena blushed and tightened her lips. "Of course it is. Do you have any idea what you want the suit to look like?"

"I do. I'll draw up some sketches now and bring them around."

"Alright. I'll make up a basic template and figure out how much fabric we need."

"Great," Benji agreed with a curt smile, and he opened the door for her.

Gwena found his unwavering self-confidence infuriating. She collected her things and stepped out.

By the time Gwena had mapped out the new outfit there was a knock at her door. She opened it to find Benji fully dressed on the other side.

"The sketches, as promised," he announced, handing her two sheets of paper.

Gwena took them in hand and looked over his designs. They were handsome pieces with a modern twist Gwena had seen worn by several patrons visiting the club. She picked up a pencil from her desk. "Can I make a suggestion?"

"Go right ahead," Benji invited.

"I've found that if you wish to stand out, it's far better being ahead of the curve than trying to chase it," Gwena told him, and made several alterations to his design.

Benji cocked his head. "I've never seen anything like it."

"That's the point," Gwena emphasized.

Benji smiled. "I like it."

"Alright. I'll start on it as soon as I have the fabric. I'll have to speak to Madam Rouge about our budget."

"As little as possible—generally. But don't cut expenses on her behalf, I'll cover whatever she doesn't."

"Fine by me. What kind of fabric do you want?" Gwena asked.

"I don't know yet. I was going to pick some out now. How much should I buy?"

"That depends, the type of fabric will change the amount. If you want spider silk we'll need extra."

"Why don't you come with me to eliminate any chance of error," Benji suggested.

"Me, go shopping with you?" Gwena asked.

"Do you have other plans?"

Gwena hesitated. "No, I suppose not," she admitted. She grabbed her bag. "Alright then."

Gwena and Benji travelled together up top in the elevator and out into the busy streets of the Heartland in silence. Benji led her to a small upmarket fabric store. The place was well stocked with every variety of fabric Gwena had ever seen or heard of—and some she hadn't. Each one was available in countless colors and designs, displayed on shelves that covered every inch of the walls, stretching from the floor to the ceiling. She looked at the price tags of the medium range and gasped. "These prices are preposterous!" she whispered to Benji.

"Do you have an alternative?" he asked.

"Actually, I do," she admitted, and led Benji out of the store.

He followed her down the street and through several back alleys.

"Where're you taking me?"

"You'll see soon enough, here it is!" Gwena announced, leading Benji to the door of The Treasure Box.

"*Pre-loved quality attire*," Benji read skeptically.

"Keep an open mind. Come on," Gwena encurouged, leading him inside.

Benji stepped in and looked around, "I don't get it. How am I supposed to get ahead of the curve with something second hand?"

"Just find a suit with the fabric you like, and I'll alter it. Everything here is made by top designers. The quality's top-notch, and once I've made a few changes you won't even recognize where it came from," Gwena promised.

"Alright. I do like the quality," Benji admitted.

He tried on half a dozen before finally choosing three. He purchased them and he and Gwena left the store, stepping back out onto the street.

"How'd you know about this place?" Benji inquired.

"Bonnie showed it to me."

"Is that right? I've lived here most my life and I've never even heard of it. Who would've thought one could get such high-quality wear secondhand," he remarked.

By the time they got back to the main street it was crowded with people.

"Is it always this busy?" Gwena asked.

"Only when the Science Fair is on. Did Bonnie take you yesterday?"

"No. We didn't get the opportunity," Gwena admitted.

Benji stopped dead in the street. "Didn't get the opportunity?!" he exclaimed, "Criminal." He grabbed her hand and wove her through the pedestrian traffic.

⌒

Benji led Gwena to the grandest, strangest building she'd ever seen, labelled with an aureate sign that read, The Hall of Scientific Study. It looked like two buildings put together—as if one was the upside-down reflection of the other. It reminded Gwena of a house she'd seen built on a lake. Outside of this strangeness, the style of the architecture resembled a large stately museum combined with a castle. It had four tall, impressive stone pillars at the front that spanned both levels. And towers at each corner that also spanned the entire length of the building, ending in the same way they'd begun—with battlements at both the tops and bottoms. The whole building was decorated with intermittent, large sweeping archways and huge windows, the grandest of which outlined a magnificent entrance featuring large double doors made of carved Blush Oak decorated with artistic ironwork. The double doors were open, and there was a swarm of people streaming in and out.

Benji led Gwena through the crowd inside. As soon as they were through the doors Gwena looked up in wonderment. The ceiling was seven stories high with a magnificent mural depicting famous milestones in the history of science throughout the ages. The entryway was a wide open space with a polished granite floor inlaid with a mosaic of the cosmos and the elements. In the center was a giant grand orrery modelling Equillian's solar system and the movements of its planets. Seven balconies encircled the foyer, ascending above them. Gwena could see the next story up, a huge library with large armchairs and ornate globes of Equillian. The foyer was swarming with human activity. Temporary tables had been erected around it, each one holding the latest scientific wonders on display. There were steam machines billowing clouds of water vapor into the air on almost every one. The first one to catch Gwena's eye was a set of leather wings powered by steam technology that were said to give a person the ability of flight.

"I'll believe it when I see it," Benji remarked.

"There's a demonstration on at Lady Luck's Hour," the woman behind the table informed politely.

"Hmm, thanks," Benji said, and they walked on.

Some of Gwena's favorite inventions were ones that did simple everyday tasks in unexpected ways, like a top hat that had a working clock built into it and could also make a cup of tea, and a ridiculously large machine for polishing shoes, and on and on it went. Gwena took her time going to each table and delighting in the inventions. *Bastian would love this*, she thought. And then her heart sank as soon as she thought it—if only he could've been there. The fact that he wasn't felt so unjust, so unfair, like the Stars had made a mistake, robbing her of the perfect future that was meant to be.

The Science Fair was a huge event. Besides the inventions on display, there were lectures being given on the hour by various scientists at the top of their fields. Gwena would have loved to spend the whole day delighting in it all, but by the time she and Benji had seen everything on the floor, it was well past lunch. As they stepped out of the Hall of Scientific Study the demonstration for the wings was taking place. A man was flying high above them with a ring of spectators staring up in awe from below.

"Wow, can you believe it? It really works!" Gwena exclaimed.

"Will ya look at that. Steam tech has come a long way, who knows what they'll think of next," Benji remarked.

They weaved their way through the crowd back to the main street and then down a quiet laneway. After a time Gwena said, "That was magnificent, thank you."

"Of course. You can't be in the Heartland during the fair and not see it."

Then Benji's expression turned introspective, and he added, "It can be easy to forget about the world up here when you're at the club. If you do, it will pass you by. Don't forget that."

"Alright, I won't"

They walked together in silence for a time after that. The sky had cleared of clouds and despite the cool temperature the sun was shining brightly.

"It's a beautiful day," Gwena observed, reaching for some gateway into conversation.

"Ha!" Benji laughed.

"What's so funny?"

"People only talk about the weather when they've nothing else to say."

"Well, at least I'm trying to engage in some sort of discourse," she replied defensively.

"Frivolous conversation is worse than no conversation at all. You may as well be making noise," Benji declared.

"What would you like to talk about then?"

"How about that necklace of yours. What's the story behind it?"

"My necklace?" Gwena asked in surprise, suddenly realizing she was twirling the pearl between her fingers. "What makes you think there's a story behind it?"

"It's a Dewdrop pearl. They're incredibly rare. And it's clearly an item of comfort for you—you touch it whenever you're lost in thought or discomfited," Benji remarked.

"I was given it by someone very dear to me."

"A family heirloom?"

"If you must know, it was a birthday present from my best friend," Gwena confessed.

"Are you in love with them?"

Gwena blushed. "What makes you ask that?"

"It's written all over your face."

"Don't presume you know anything about me!" Gwena rebuked.

"I wouldn't dare, that's why I'm asking the question—are you going to answer it?"

Gwena glowered at him before saying, "More than anything in this world."

"Ah, that's why you defend true love so passionately!" Benji proclaimed.

"I don't need to defend it! It's strong enough on its own. If you don't wish to believe in it, that's your loss, no one else's. Well, except for the poor women you lead on with false adoration," Gwena accused.

"False adoration?!" Benji asked indignantly.

"I've seen the way you look at them. Like you really care about them. That plays with a woman's heart, you know. How do you think they'd feel if they knew what you really think about love?" Gwena posed.

"They know exactly what I think about love. Besides, it's not what they come to me for. They come to me for a service, and I provide it, end of story."

"And does that stop them from forming feelings for you?" Gwena asked.

"You can't possibly be blaming me for their feelings?!" Benji scoffed.

"What, you think you play no part in them? That women just emote without provocation?"

"Not that it's any of your business, but I look at them the way I do because I do genuinely care about them, and I give them something worth far more than love," Benji asserted.

"What's that?" Gwena queried skeptically.

"Respect. Love is a fickle thing that comes and goes without rhyme or reason. Respect is something solid, something that sticks, something that's actually worth something. I have great respect for each and every one of the women who hire my company, not for what they've accomplished, but for who they are. The same can't be said of their partners— who've lost sight of the incredible women by their sides. They treat them like garbage and yet, they still stick around. You know why?" Benji asked.

"Why?"

"Because of love. It shackles them like a ball and chain," Benji declared.

"If they still love their partners, then why are they coming to see you?" Gwenna argued.

"It's complicated, you're far too young to understand."

"I don't see how it could be complicated! They're either in love with their partners or they're not. Once they've decided which one it is, the rest should be reasonably straightforward," Gwena asserted.

"Perhaps we should've stuck to the weather," Benji said.

Gwena barked a laugh, "Ha! It's far too late for that now."

Benji looked at her, seething with frustration, then he huffed a gust of air out his nostrils. "The world isn't black and white—and the older you get, the more grey it becomes," he told her.

"That's not an answer. By the sounds of it, your clients' partners are the real victims—not the other way around. It's their wives who're jumping into your bed. It's not love that's the villain here, it's lust!" Gwena declared.

Benji prickled at her accusation, his body visibly tensing. "This topic is beyond your years. There are some things you can't possibly understand."

"If you think me so naïve, then enlighten me!" Gwena pressed.

"Alright, imagine being with someone who no longer desires or values you. You've built a life together; you might even still love them. You can't go out and seek the attention of someone else, or you'll lose everything. So instead, you resign yourself to your fate. You might find it fine for a while, distracting yourself with other things—until you find your confidence diminishing, and you start to actually believe you're undesirable, worthless even. Then before you know it, you've withered away to a shadow of what you once were, your true potential discarded as a silly and impossible dream. Meanwhile, your partner has all the confidence in the world because they're flirting with people in the office or off at the local cathouse. Think of it as you will, but for some, a night with me is simply self-preservation."

"Self-preservation? Surely there's other things they can turn to, to bolster their confidence!" Gwena scoffed.

Benji turned on her in irritation. "Like it or not, little bird, humans need intimacy. It's not some vile vice, it's a real visceral necessity. Without it, we're left wanting. My clients don't come to me for love, or because I get them off. They come to me because I make them feel like they're worth something. I make them feel wanted and desired. I provide a safe place for them to be vulnerable, a place where they know they can be themselves without judgment. And they walk out of the club feeling like a million duckets. You can judge and scoff at it all you want, but you can't tell me what I do isn't a valuable and beneficial service!" he proclaimed passionately.

"And you can't tell me love isn't valuable! Just as the world isn't black and white, love isn't either. It isn't one side of a spectrum, it's a whole spectrum in and of itself. You can't honestly believe there isn't a good side?" Gwena countered stubbornly.

Benji sneered. "Oh, sure. I've seen the so-called good side. When two people are so drunk on one another they throw everything away for love. Sure, they might be happy for a time, but they've given up everything else. Even their own dreams and aspirations. If their love doesn't last, then what do they have left?" he asked her.

"I think you'll find your accomplishments very lonely without love," Gwena admonished.

"I've never minded my own company," Benji stated, and started walking again.

Gwena hurried to keep pace. "You speak of love like it's some sort of curse. If you really believe that, then you mustn't really know it. Not the way I do!" she proclaimed.

Benji stopped in his tracks and turned on her venomously. "You think I don't know it?! People come to me broken from love and it's my job to put them back together. No one knows the damage it does more intimately than I do. If there's a love like the one you described back at the bar, I've never seen it. The love I know brings great people to their knees, shackling them to a life of misery. Holding them back from their own ambitions and deeming them powerless to defend themselves against it, because they're so convinced they need it—even when it's tearing them apart! If you've found a love that doesn't do that, then hold onto it. Because as far as I'm aware, love like that is nothing but a fairytale."

Gwena clenched her fists, holding back the tears welling in her eyes. "One day you'll see. It'll find you, and it'll be the greatest thing you've ever known, and you'll know I'm right," she declared trembling.

"Yeah? If it's so great, and your best friend's so in love with you, then where is he now?" Benji asked.

His words pierced Gwena like a knife to the heart, and in an instant all her strength drained out. She stood feeling powerless to move as Benji walked ahead without her.

～

Gwena found herself shaking and had to sit down on the side of the road. She clutched at her necklace as tears fell from her eyes. Her heart ached so much she could hardly bear it. If only Bastian were there. Their love was true, she knew it was. So why was she so adamant on trying to convince Benji of it? Why did it matter what he thought? Maybe because the love she had for her father felt like the love Benji had described. Even after everything he'd done to hurt her, she still cared about what he thought, wanted him to be proud of her, craved his affection. And for what? All he'd done since her mother died was make her feel less than she was and keep her from living the life she wanted. Maybe there *was* a dark side to love after all. Maybe it could be a weakness and a blindness. But the love she shared with Bastian was different entirely. It gave her strength when she was weak, it lifted her up when she was down and carried her as if on wings. It gave her hope in darkness and made her better. How could two things that were so opposite from each other share the same name? How was it that one was able to transform into the other? And what was it that turned such a magnificent elixir into a poison? Gwena realized then she was so determined to argue with Benji because she was terrified he might be right. Maybe true love was a fleeting thing that couldn't last—except by those like Raemeo and Julietta, whose lives ended before their love could, preserving it for eternity. Maybe love was a living thing, like a rose blossom, and would always wither with time—in the same way a sweet fruit turned rotten if given the chance to over-ripen. If that were true and Benji was right, then even if Gwena was reunited with Bastian, their happily-ever-after would never stand a chance. And the happiness she so longed for really would be nothing but a fairytale.

# POWDERED GLASS

Bastian stood in the Order's backyard with his longbow drawn. He was staring down the length of his arrow towards a target at the end of a field. There were three classmates on either side of him, each standing tall with their own bows drawn. It was their archery lesson—though the sisters made it abundantly clear the class was not to teach them how to shoot a weapon, but how to focus their minds.

"In order to succeed in any endeavor, one must learn the skill of relaxed concentration," Sister Avery called out to the class. She was a tall slender woman with jet black hair and dark brown eyes. She had an amazing presence that commanded attention. As she gave her lecture, she patrolled behind them like a drill sergeant.

"You might think the two states contradictory and wonder how one could possibly go with the other? The answer is—harmoniously. Relaxation and concentration together form the perfect balance needed to achieve the right focus for anything. If you relax too much, you'll miss the details, your work will be sloppy, your shot inaccurate. If you concentrate too hard, you'll become rigid, your awareness too narrow—you might see the details on a single point, but you'll miss the ones surrounding it that form the bigger picture. It's when these two opposites come together and meet in the middle that you find the right mindset to succeed," she told them.

Bastian wished she'd stop talking so he could shoot his bow. It was a hot summer day, the sun beating down relentlessly. His forehead was beading with sweat. He wanted the opportunity to wipe it away before it started dripping into his eyes.

"Repeat after me: I am nothing, I am everything," Sister Avery instructed.

"I am nothing, I am everything," Bastian chorused with his classmates, his arms beginning to shake.

"Now allow your sense of self to melt away. Your busy thoughts, your emotions, your physical discomforts, your fear and self-doubt. None of it exists in this moment because in this moment, *you* don't exist. Instead of being your singular self—you are now *everything*. The wind, the bow and arrow you hold in your hands, the target across from you. You are all of it," Sister Avery said.

Bastian could see her doing something to his classmates in his peripheral vision, but he wasn't sure what it was until she was behind him tying a black cloth over his eyes. Panic leapt in his chest as he was blinded, how in the nine realms was he supposed to relax or concentrate now? he wondered.

"Say it again, *I am nothing, I am everything,*" Sister Avery instructed the class.

The class repeated the phrase, only this time with more purpose. Bastian took a deep breath and turned his full attention to the exercise. He silenced his thoughts, relaxed his mind and opened his focus to everything around him. His panic subsided, the fatigue in his arms and the discomfort from the heat melted away. He felt the wind in his hair, and he also was the wind. He was the bow and arrow in his hands, and the target across from him. Though he couldn't see it, instinctually he knew precisely where it was. He adjusted his aim.

"Release your arrows!" Sister Avery called.

Bastian took a deep breath in and released his bowstring as he exhaled. His arrow soared through the air, and he felt he was soaring through the air. He was also the target waiting patiently on the other side. *Thunk.* Bastian took off his blindfold. His arrow was lodged in the center of the target's bull's-eye. He smiled in triumph, and then there was a tapping on his cheek. He put his hand to his face, "What the...?"

⸎

"Rise an' shine, princess!" Cricket sang, tapping Bastian's cheek repeatedly until his eyes opened.

Bastian groaned and swatted Cricket's hand away. "Shick, Cricket! Could you think of a more irritating way to wake me?"

"O' course! Would ya like me to?" the pirate asked cheerily.

Bastian gave him a hard glare.

Cricket smiled. "Hurry now, yer girlfriend's waitin' up top," he announced, and left to scrub the deck.

Bastian ran his hands over his face trying to clear his head from his dream. It was another one of the boxed-up memories in the attic of his mind. A replay from his days at the Order. He wondered why his past was coming back to haunt him now. Normally, his dreams were mashups of his life mixed with strange fiction—not recollections.

He rolled out of his hammock and headed after Cricket.

Bastian's whole body felt stiff and sore. He swabbed the deck that morning in a fog of exhaustion.

"Didn't sleep well?" Cricket asked him.

"Just not enough," Bastian admitted.

"I couldn't sleep much either." Cricket nodded towards the large round moon that still hung in the morning's sky. "I never seem ta be able ta sleep when she's full."

Bastian nodded and lit two puff-sticks, handing one to Cricket. "Have you emptied Stork's pockets yet?" he asked him.

Cricket's demeanor darkened and Bastian instantly regretted the question.

"No," Cricket answered bluntly, and that was the end of their conversation.

When Bastian arrived at Tink's workshop that morning the tinker was waiting for him patiently, leaning against the front of his desk with his hands in his pockets.

"Morning," Bastian mumbled.

"It is indeed. I hope yours finds you well?" Tink inquired.

Bastian shrugged, lacking the energy for pleasantries.

"Have a seat," Tink directed.

Bastian walked to the desk in the center of the room and sat down.

"For today's exercise we'll be working on your visualization. Your imagination off paper is clearly out of practice, so we'll start from the beginning—with recollection. Memory's a perfect gateway, because it's often embellished with the imagination as much as any piece of fiction, but you think of it as substantial truth, and because it's based off your own experiences it's easier to visualize," Tink explained. "To begin you must close your eyes."

Bastian closed his eyes.

"I want you to choose a memory from your childhood. Something easy to recall."

Bastian thought back to his days at the Order. It didn't take him long to stumble across a memory he'd forgotten was there.

"Got it," he announced.

"Good. Now take a few minutes to relive that moment."

Bastian let the memory play.

Bastian was nine. He was sitting on the stone wall that bordered the edge of the Order's expansive backyard, launching acorns with his slingshot. He was supposed to be in Sacred Geometry. He ditched the class because Geoffrey Tormino had been bullying him all morning, and when Bastian finally stood up to him, he was the one who got in trouble. He'd had enough of the Order. He was tired of always getting blamed, even when he wasn't doing anything wrong. The sisters had it in for him—they'd decided who he was without ever taking the time to get to know him. He was dubbed "The Trouble Maker" and was treated as such regardless of what he did. He figured if he was going to get in trouble anyway, he may as well not even try.

"Let me guess, Geoff the Tormentor again?" Felix's voice came from behind him.

Bastian turned to see his brother approaching. "What are you doing out here?" he asked. He hadn't seen Felix since breakfast. They didn't have any classes together anymore. The sisters had separated them in an attempt to keep them out of trouble.

"I saw you out the window and got a toilet pass," Felix told him, waving the red piece of paper and then coming to sit down on the wall beside him.

Bastian huffed and stowed his slingshot in his back pocket. "He's such a conniving arse—he knows the sisters will blame me, and they do! He gets away with it every time!" he exclaimed.

Felix flipped his feet over the wall and jumped down the other side. "Where are you going?"

"I'm going to turn your frown upside-down," Felix proclaimed.

"You know we're not supposed to be over that side of the wall."

Felix grinned. "We're not supposed to be out of class either."

He walked several paces and then turned back. "You coming?"

Bastian jumped down from the wall, and Felix led them through the woods to a narrow gravel pathway that connected to the road winding towards the harbor. They walked until they came to a sweets vendor by the roadside. Felix and Bastian drooled over the array of colorful sugar sculptures on sticks. They were all made out of heated sugar, masterfully crafted in different colors to look like glass birds, fish, spiral swirls, stars, roses, and more. They were made so well they could've easily been mistaken for hand-blown glass art. There was a little sign hanging from the stall that said *Sugar Sticks, 1 Cwip.*

The vendor was restocking sugar tall ships while talking to a sailor about the storm that passed through two days before. Felix waited until the serving man was midsentence and then he held out his hand to him expectantly. The man handed him one of the sugar ships without looking away from the sailor he was talking to, then he picked up another—his attention still absorbed in his conversation. Felix held out his hand again, and the man handed him that ship too. Felix put a cwip in the man's hand in exchange, and the man put it into his coin box without looking at it. Felix handed one of the ships to Bastian and then waited patiently and expectantly by the stall. After a moment the vendor noticed he was waiting.

"Can I help you with something else, lad?" he queried.

"I just need my change," Felix announced politely.

"Oh." The man scratched his head and opened his coin box. "What did you give me?"

"A silver fish. I just need three cwips back, thanks."

The man pulled out three cwips and handed them to Felix.

"Thanks. Your Sugar Sticks are the best in Westdock. Honestly, if they weren't so delicious I'd say they belong in a gallery," Felix praised with genuine enthusiasm.

"Thank you, young man! That made my day. You and your friend enjoy your afternoon," he replied with a grateful smile, beaming with pride as he returned to his conversation. As Bastian and Felix walked away they heard the vendor say, "What an upstanding young man, if only all the youth were as well mannered these days."

Felix led Bastian to a rocky outcrop overlooking the ocean and they both sat and enjoyed their sugar tall ships. Felix noticed Bastian's subtle frown and asked, "What's wrong?"

"Do you think we're bad people?" Bastian asked.

"What do you mean?"

"Sister Felicity looks at me with such disappointment, like I'm all that's wrong with the world."

"Ignore her! You're the best person I know. Sister Felicity wouldn't know a good person if they collided into her. Look at Geoffrey—he's a terror and she thinks he's born amongst the Stars. Besides, the world isn't black and white, there aren't really bad and good people, we're all just people. It's just that people sometimes do bad things, and some do worse things, and some more often than others," Felix asserted.

"Like us taking the sugar ships?" Bastian asked.

"No, not like us taking the sugar ships! Like Geoffrey Tormino intentionally bullying you just because he knows he'll get away with it."

"He *is* a royal arse," Bastian agreed, "but what makes us better? We lie and steal."

"We're better because we don't hurt people. Something's only bad or wrong when someone gets hurt. Geoff hurt you, which is what makes him the worst kind of royal arse. We haven't hurt anyone. In fact, we've done the opposite. Did you see the way that man looked when we left?"

"Yeah, he was practically glowing," Bastian admitted.

"Precisely. I wasn't lying when I said these are the best Sugar Sticks in Westdock. Anyone can put sugar on a stick and charge a cwip, but these are masterpieces. They're not only cooked to perfection, neither burnt nor coarse—they're art. He's good at what he does, and he obviously puts a lot of time and care into these things. But what's the point if no one appreciates it? He was glowing because there was honesty in my words, and having someone recognize and value his hard work is worth far more than a few cwips," Felix insisted, and bit off the top sail of his sugar ship. "Do you know what brings me joy?" he asked after a moment.

"What?" Bastian inquired.

"Generosity. Even if it's only sharing the gift of a smile. Because life is generally rubbish and unfair, and if I can bring even a little bit of joy into it, then I feel like I've done something worthwhile. I've given a lot today, you know?" Felix claimed.

Bastian smiled wryly, "Yeah, like what?"

"I gave that vendor reason to keep doing what he loves, I gave you a sugar ship to sail your blues away, and I gave us two cwips to put towards changing our Stars. I also gave Geoffrey Tormino the finger and told him to go shick himself. And that's far more generous than what he deserves," Felix declared.

Bastian laughed, "You're the best person I know, Felix. No matter what the sisters say about us, I never want us to be any different."

Felix grinned. "There's the brother I know and love." He held his sugar ship up to Bastian and declared, "More charming, cunning, and able than the best. Never apologize for being better than the rest!" They tapped their sugar ships together and both took a bite. Then Felix put his arm around Bastian. "You and me, brother, together—we're going to take on the world."

⌒

Bastian opened his eyes. Taking in Tink's quarters he was immediately reminded of just how far away from Felix he was. He felt an ache in his chest, and suddenly he missed his brother more than ever. *Why did I have to choose that memory?* he thought.

"What's wrong?" Tink asked.

"Nothing," Bastian told him, and closed his eyes again.

"Now, I want you to freeze all the people in your memory, as if time is standing still," Tink instructed.

Bastian retreated back to the rock outcropping overlooking the ocean.

"Where are you?" Tink inquired.

"Westdock."

"What can you see?"

Bastian recalled the place in detail. It wasn't hard, he'd been there hundreds of times. "I see the ocean under a blue sky. I see the stone path along the cliffside leading down to the harbor, with green seagrass on either side of it."

"Good. Give me more. I want you to transport yourself there completely and look around. What does it smell like? What does it sound like? What does it feel like?"

Bastian honed into the surroundings in his memory. "I hear the seagulls and the ship bells from the harbor. I smell the salt from the sea. I feel the cool ocean breeze coming over the rocks."

"Excellent! Now, I want you to reach down and feel the ground at your feet. What's there? What does it feel like?"

Bastian bent down in his mind's eye and touched the seagrass and the sandy dirt below it. "The grass is thick and coarse. The stones are smooth and cool, and the dirt's mostly fine moist sand that crumbles easily between my fingers."

"Very good! You can come back now," Tink said.

Bastian opened his eyes.

"Now, I want you to look into the Humming Bowl," the tinker directed, setting it down on the desk in front of him.

Bastian stared into the Humming Bowl. It was filled with the glittering, swirling Ghost Element.

"This time, I don't want you to try to change the element. I want you to discover what it feels like."

"But I can't feel it," Bastian objected.

"Shhh, you must suspend all disbelief. You *can* feel it, if you only allow yourself to."

Bastian looked back at the bowl and attempted to open his mind. He watched the swirling, billowing gold mist for several moments and then he stuck his hand into it. He felt nothing. His mind kept shouting it was an illusion that didn't exist. He closed his eyes and recalled his dream of his archery lesson at the Order.

*I am nothing, I am everything,* he chanted in his mind. Then he opened his eyes and looked at the dust again. The particles were so fine, they were almost like smoke.

*Maybe that's why I can't feel it?* he wondered, *but then, I shouldn't be able to pick it up,* he thought. He scooped up a fistful of the Ghost Element and let it fall through the gap in the bottom of his hand in a steady stream — like fine sand draining from an hourglass. But as it fell it twirled and billowed, sparkling in the light. Bastian wondered whether the Ghost Element might feel like fine sand — no sooner had he thought it, he could almost feel sand passing through his fingers. *Or maybe it's slightly sticky like old dust,* he thought. Bastian closed his eyes again and tried to home in on his sense of touch — *perhaps it's sharp like finely ground glass.* Bastian tried to imagine what ground glass would feel like. "Gah!" he gasped as a sharp pain sliced through his fingers. He looked down to see blood pooling from his finger tips. He put them to his mouth and then quickly pulled them away as they cut his lip. He looked closely at his hand. There was a thin layer of glistening powder, not the Ghost Element, something different, something…more substantial.

Tink noticed he was bleeding and rushed over to him. "What happened?"

"I don't know, I was trying to imagine what the Element feels like — just like you said."

"And what did you imagine?"

"I thought maybe it might feel like powdered glass. It looks like it," Bastian confessed.

Tink ran his own finger over Bastian's hand picking up the dust particles and rolling them between his fingers, little beads of blood bloomed on the tips of his thumb and pointer. "Well, it certainly is now," he said.

"The Ghost Element did this?" Bastian asked.

"No. you did this with the Ghost Element."

"Does that mean I figured out what it feels like?"

"No. It only feels like powdered glass because that's what you imagined it into. Congratulations, you've managed to successfully transform the Ghost Element," Tink commended, studying his bleeding hand.

"I made it into this?!" Bastian exclaimed in bewilderment.

"Yes. Now go and wash your hands before you injure yourself further."

Bastian laughed with delight and triumph as he looked at his bleeding fingers. He went to Tink's basin and poured water from the pitcher over his hands and watched in fascination as the powdered glass washed away into the porcelain bowl.

"Can I try again? Can I imagine it into something else?" Bastian asked eagerly.

"Of course. Only this time make it something you can't hurt yourself with," Tink advised, washing his own hands.

Bastian sat back down at the desk and looked into the Humming Bowl. The Ghost Element was transformed—it was brighter somehow, more vibrant. There was a new richness to its shadows that gave it more dimension. And when Bastian put his hands into the swirling mist, he felt something. What was it? It felt cool and soft like fine snow flecks on a winter's morning. He picked up a pinch of the dust and it smudged between his fingers in a way it never had before, soft and silky like icing sugar stored in an icebox. The skin on his hand was covered in shimmering gold residue—it reminded him of the powdered mica paint pigments they used in art classes at the Order. Bastian laughed out loud. Suddenly for the first time, the Element felt and looked completely, undeniably real.

He dipped his hands into the swirling dust and closed his eyes. He recalled a memory of holding a rose wagon—the second highest coin on Equillian, worth a hundred cwips. He'd only ever held one once, but he could still remember the way the coin felt in his hand. He recalled every detail, its thickness, its dense weight, the embossed floral pattern encircling its face, and the circular hole in the coin's center. Bastian recalled the coolness of the metal against his skin and suddenly, he didn't need to imagine it anymore—he could feel the coin in his hand. Bastian opened his eyes. He was holding a rose wagon. He grinned with astonished glee as he turned the coin over, inspecting the flawless detail.

Tink came over to see what he'd created. "Very imaginative," he stated dryly.

"Can I keep it?" Bastian asked.

"It won't last."

"What do you mean, why not? It's right here, as real as any coin I've ever seen."

"True. But the second you're not holding it in your mind as a rose wagon, it will be nothing but dust," Tink told him.

"You're kidding? Surely there's a way to do it. What about enchanted objects and the Seven Wonders?" Bastian argued.

"Enchanted objects are exactly as their name suggests—objects that are enchanted. The objects themselves have been crafted in the traditional fashion, by the hands of the alchemists. The Ghost Element is only used to make the enchantments. When the enchantment is housed in a physical part of this world, then and only then can it last forever," Tink explained.

"Right. So you're saying, if I want to make coins that will last, I need to make a physical form for them first? Like wooden coins—for example, then I could enchant them to look and feel like real ones?"

Tink put his hand to his temple. "I give you the ability to conjure up anything in the world, and you want to make coin?" he asked flatly.

Bastian shrugged. "You have to admit, it would be useful."

"I gave you more credit than that. I suppose I shouldn't have—leave it to the thief to have a one-track mind on his coin pouch," Tink remarked.

"Sorry," Bastian apologized, and discreetly slipped the rose wagon into his pocket.

"Using your gift for such base and meaningless trivialities will only waste it, and bring you nothing but trouble. Chase your life goals, and coin will follow—chase coin, and you'll never achieve your life goals," Tink lectured.

"Right," Bastian muttered. Though, he was pretty certain more coin would help him achieve his life goals.

"I'm very happy with today's progress—now that you're beginning to grasp how to manipulate the Ghost Element, we can begin on how to use it to enchant an object," Tink announced.

"Brilliant!" Bastian exclaimed.

"I want you to come up with an object to enchant—including its ability. It must be something functional that can't be used for personal gain or capable of inflicting harm. Have your plan drawn up and ready by tomorrow morning."

"Done," Bastian declared eagerly, instantly perking up.

"And for Stars' sake, make it something unrelated to coin," Tink asserted.

"No problem."

Bastian stood, sensing the class had come to a conclusion. Then he hesitated.

"Something on your mind?" Tink inquired.

"Do you have any more books by the original alchemists?" Bastian asked.

Tink raised a questioning eyebrow.

"I really enjoyed the last one—even though it's only lists. It's just nice reading something from someone else who can see the Element. It makes me feel less…alone, if that makes any sense?"

Tink smiled warmly. "I'll have a look and see what I can find."

"Thanks."

Tink cleared his throat. "One more thing before you go. Now that you know how to manipulate the Ghost Element, you must be very careful how you use it. It's imperative no one else knows about your ability."

Bastian nodded in acknowledgment and left the room.

⌒

As Bastian walked down the corridor of the ship towards the mess hall he felt an ascending optimism. *Me, making an enchanted object?!* He and Felix had been searching for objects with abilities most of their lives, hoping to find one in the houses of aristocrats. Just one would've been enough to set them up for the future they wanted. He'd become convinced they could only dream of ever acquiring one. And now, he was going to be taught how to make them. Him! Bastian William Sanders—a Star-brat from Westdock with nothing to his name—was going to be taught the secrets of the alchemists. Just one enchanted thing could give him enough coin to go anywhere in the world. He, Gwena, and Felix would never have to worry about coin ever again. If he could make enchanted objects they would be set for the rest of their lives.

Bastian reached into his pocket to pull out the rose wagon he'd conjured up earlier. It wasn't there. He pulled his pocket inside out. Gold dust billowed into the air.

*Ah well, coin might as well be dust once it's spent anyway,* he thought with a grin.

# BREAKING BREAD

Felix and Lilliana were sitting in the estate's eastern sitting room playing cards as they waited for Roy and Arianna to return for dinner.
Large windows encircled the room, bathing it in the waning light of late
afternoon. They were playing Thrixer, a gambling game named after the
Thrixing Stars—the cosmic cluster of mischievous meddlers. The object
of the game was to swindle high cards from an opponent, and to thwart
them from obtaining high cards for their own hand. Felix and Lilliana
were using a variety of mixed nuts as currency. Lilliana's pile was higher
than Felix's—primarily because he kept eating his. He was popping a
cashew into his mouth when Roy walked into the sitting room.

"I'm glad to see you two've found a way to keep yourselves occupied," the pilot announced, taking off his coat and handing it to a waiting servant.

"She's a better card player than you," Felix told him.

"Ha! That doesn't surprise me. Her father's the best card player I
know," Roy remarked, sitting down beside them.

"How was your outing?" Lilliana inquired.

"Informative."

Roy motioned to one of the waiting staff to bring them tea.

"Did you find the original article?" Lilliana queried.

"I did. After hours of digging through the News House's archives
I managed to procure the article regarding your father's disappearance.
But it didn't tell me anything useful. Everything in it is information we
already have. He was discovered missing the morning after your uncle's
passing. There were eyewitness accounts of his airship flying directly into
the Everstorm and parts of his ship were found floating in the ocean
below, but there was no sign or evidence of your father. Luckily, the trip
wasn't an entire waste of time. As it so turns out, one of the witnesses is
an old friend of mine. Her name is Katarina. She has a small estate on
the very edge of one of the border islands—in direct view of the Everstorm. She's a retired scientist who's made a personal hobby of studying
the tempest. She knows everything that's known about the natural phe-

nomenon. I paid her a visit this afternoon and discovered some very interesting information."

Lilliana leaned forward. "Do tell."

"Katarina told me she saw your father's ship pass into the Everstorm the morning after your uncle passed. She's always been an early riser, and luckily she happened to be looking out her window when your father's ship went by. She said she immediately grabbed her telescope for a closer view, and she'll never forget what she saw, because she thought it was so peculiar a ship was flying directly into the Everstorm—with no one on it," Roy reported.

"Unmanned?!"

"Yes, she said there was no one at the control station or visible anywhere else on the ship. At first, she thought it must be a research expedition sending an unmanned ship into the storm for collecting data and wondered why she'd never thought to do the same. But then something came behind the ship—as if in pursuit."

"There was something following father's ship into the Everstorm? What was it?" Lilliana asked.

"A dragon. Furthermore, a dragon bearing a rider."

"Someone flew into the storm on a dragon?!" Lilliana exclaimed.

Roy nodded.

"And I thought flying an airship into that monstrosity was madness," Felix remarked.

"Katarina said she reported it immediately, and the authorities took note of the information—but besides Drake's ship entering the Everstorm, none of the rest of her report made it into any of the published articles. No one even followed up with her during the investigation. She made a few inquiries, but they never led to anything. No one else saw the dragon or noticed that the craft was unmanned, and no one seemed to take her account seriously. She finally gave it up—realizing that further pushing of the matter would begin to affect her reputation. She said if she'd known earlier that Drake and I were friends, she would've passed the information onto me directly at the time," Roy expounded.

"Why would Father's ship be flying into the Everstorm unmanned?" Lilliana queried.

"Why and how? It certainly wouldn't be able to do that on its own without some tampering."

"Maybe your father's the one who sent the ship into the storm as a decoy, to stage his own disappearance?" Felix suggested.

"If that's the case, then why haven't we heard from him, and why would someone follow after the airship?" Lilliana argued.

Felix leaned forward in thought. "Could it have been one of the staff members here trying to save your father, thinking he was on the ship?"

"No. We would've heard if one of the staff members went missing from the estate."

"That's a good point," Roy agreed. "Do we know if there were any other missing persons reported anywhere in Sky View after the event? Maybe it was someone going out for a morning ride who saw the ship and was trying to be a hero?"

"I've no idea," Lilliana admitted.

Roy scratched his chin. "Hmmm. I'll inquire into it after the Derby."

Lilliana furrowed her brow. "None of this makes any sense. If there was someone else reported missing with a dragon, and your friend made a report that matched, then surely there would've already been an inquiry into it already."

"Unless someone didn't do their due diligence and file the report," Roy pointed out.

"Or if someone was purposely trying to hide the information," Felix proposed.

"Yes, I'm afraid this news has created more questions than it's answered. But it's also restored my hope. Knowing Drake wasn't on his ship when it flew into the Everstorm is a huge relief. It was the discarded pieces of his craft that led the authorities to believe he was gone for good," Roy said.

Just then the servant returned with a tray of the accoutrements for tea, placing it in front of them on the low table. Roy thanked him, and the servant nodded politely and left.

"The official report says the duke flew into the storm in grief after the death of his brother, is that right?" Felix asked.

Roy poured a cup of tea for each of them. "Yes, that's the current conclusion. But I know damn well Drake didn't fly into that storm to commit suicide. It's completely out of character. He loves his wife and his girls more than anything—he never would've abandoned them willingly," he asserted.

"It's true. I know my father, and it's not even the last thing he'd do. He just wouldn't do it. The only way my father would go into that storm is if he had an exceptionally good reason for it," Lilliana agreed.

"So, either he didn't go into the Everstorm at all, or he went in on a dragon chasing his unstaffed airship. Either way, there's clearly more to the story than what everyone's been led to believe," Felix remarked.

Roy nodded. "Yes, we've uncovered nothing but more questions. I believe there's more we can learn from Katarina, I think she might be able to give us some of the answers we're looking for. She's invited us to have dinner with her tomorrow."

"You told her I'm here?!" Lilliana asked in surprise.

"I told her I'm travelling with my niece and a friend. We can trust her. She keeps mostly to herself these days and detests gossip and politics," Roy assured her.

Lilliana nodded. "It's good to know there's someone here we can trust."

"Yes. I think our next best step is to find out what happened during your father's last visit, especially everything leading up to his disappearance. Do you think you can talk to Arianna about the details surrounding the time of your uncle's death?" Roy asked.

"It's a sensitive subject, but I'm certainly going to try. Surprisingly, Arianna's been far more accommodating than expected. I was hoping to broach the subject today, but it seems I won't be able to get anything out of her until after the Derby."

"Well, that's not far away. Any news on your end?" Roy asked them.

Lilliana glanced at Felix before saying, "Yes, James and I stumbled upon something very unsettling."

"What's that?" Roy inquired, taking a sip of his tea.

"There's a secret underground hatchery my grandfather used for producing War Dragons during The Last War. It's been retired for years, only—now it's filled with live hatchlings, and it's a breed I've never seen before..." she hesitated, searching for her next words. "I think Arianna's trying to recreate War Dragons," she divulged in a whisper.

Roy sat silently aghast for several moments before saying, "Stars help us all."

Just then the butler appeared at the entrance to the sitting room, "Excuse the intrusion, dinner will be served shortly. Lady Arianna has requested your presence in the dining room," he announced.

"Thank you, Albert. We'll be there shortly," Lilliana assured him.

"Very well, my lady," he acknowledged, and retreated down the hall.

Lilliana and Roy shared a concerned glance.

"We'll speak more on the matter later," Lilliana asserted.

Felix followed Roy and Lilliana into the dining room. Down the center ran a long table, its glass top supported by a marble dragon's outstretched wings. It was set with deep emerald placemats set with fine black and gold porcelain plates and polished rose silverware. The rose silver's warm golden-pink hue contrasted tastefully with the black dishes with their gold rims. Tall gold candles burned in the middle, flickering with real fire. Seeing real fire anywhere was a novelty these days. Felix felt drawn to it—he had to stifle the urge to pass his fingers through their flames.

Arianna was seated at the head of the table, dressed in a high-necked, long-sleeved black dress that looked more appropriate for a funeral than dinner. Her straight dark red hair was pulled back tightly in a knot that sat on top of her head like a dinner roll.

Felix pulled out one of the tall-backed white aspen chairs and sat down. The butler pulled out the seat adjacent to his for Lilliana, and Roy sat down next to her.

"Good evening, cousin. I hope your errands were successful?" Lilliana inquired.

"Yes, thank you. It was a very productive afternoon. I'm sorry we haven't been able to spend more time together. After the Derby you'll have my full attention—I promise."

"No need to apologize, we showed up completely unexpected right before a very important event. I only wish there was some way I could contribute," Lilliana said.

Arianna smiled politely. "Thank you, as much as I appreciate the sentiment, really the best help you can give me is to excuse my duties as a host until the Derby's over. I'm so used to preparing for it on my own, it's easier if I stick to my routine."

"I understand. If there's anything I can do, please don't hesitate to ask. I have such fond memories of helping Uncle John prepare for the Sky Cup."

"I'll keep that in mind. How was your afternoon? I hope you found a pleasant way to pass the time?" Arianna asked.

"Yes, thank you. It's a joy to be back here. It's been wonderful to have the opportunity to recall old memories," Lilliana told her.

Arianna smiled warmly. "I'm pleased to hear it."

Felix was surprised by how well the two hid their true feelings for each other. They exchanged pleasantries like a ball in a professional tennis match. A man in waiting filled the crystal flute in front of Felix with a bright pink liquid from a chilled metal decanter. Felix had never seen a drink that color. He picked up his glass curiously and took a sip. The pink liquid was ice cold and had the consistency of syrup, with a slightly floral, slightly fruity flavor. It was so different from anything he'd had previously, he couldn't decide whether or not he liked it. "What an interesting beverage, what is it?" he queried.

"Luscious wine. It's made from the jelly pulp of juvenile Luscious Trees. They grow wild on the fringes of the larger islands," Arianna informed him.

Felix took another sip. "It's quite a unique flavor."

Lilliana smirked. "It's an acquired taste. It will grow on you," she assured him.

Two more waiting staff entered the room carrying four small plates, setting one down in front of each of them. The plate in front of Felix was beautifully presented but proportioned for a small child. It was a piece of roasted eggplant garnished with winding threads of white and green sauce, topped with a red nasturtium. Felix looked at the array of rose silverware that stretched out on either side of his place setting, trying to differentiate between the four forks on the left side of his plate. He couldn't remember which one was appropriate for the current course. He had once educated himself thoroughly on the topic, but it had been a while since he'd put the information into practice. The majority of upper-class events he'd attended were parties with finger food, rather than formal dinners. He unfolded his cloth napkin and laid it across his lap to buy himself some time while he waited for his company to pick up their utensils first. Arianna led the way and he followed immediately with no sign of hesitation. He could've finished the ensemble on his plate in a single bite, but he cut the appetizer in half with perfect etiquette before taking his first mouthful. It was wonderful. The flesh of the eggplant was warm, creamy, and bursting with flavor. He couldn't remember ever having a vegetable with such a complex, delightful flavor palette. "My compliments to the chef, this is beautiful. Is the eggplant from the Sky Gardens?" Felix inquired.

"Why yes," Arianna replied in surprise. "Rose, our head cook, visits them for the best pickings every morning. Are you familiar with the gardens?" she asked.

"Roy and I had a tour of one this morning, they're incredible."

"Aren't they? I'm so glad you got the opportunity to see one. They've been a fabulous addition to the city. Because of the low soil content on the Windswept Isles, we've never been able to farm here. The new technology has allowed us to begin working towards better self-sufficiency and sustainability. We hope to have at least one Sky Garden on every major island within the next five years."

"Fantastic!" Felix commended.

"There's no comparison to fresh local produce," Roy proclaimed.

The waiting staff cleared their plates away the second they were finished, and within moments they were replaced with a bowl of pureed cold soup composed of three bright colors carefully ladled in place to prevent mixing the vivid palette. One part was vibrant orange, another was light green, and the third was pink. The center was topped with an herb garnish and a winding drizzle of white cream. Felix watched Lilliana pick up her soup spoon and delicately swirl it in her bowl, mixing the three colors together before taking a mouthful. Felix did the same and was pleasantly surprised by another burst of flavor.

"Everything ready for the race, cousin?" Lilliana inquired.

Arianna picked up the fine cut-crystal flute in front of her and took a sip of her pink Luscious wine. "Almost. I still have several things to do tomorrow, but all's on schedule. Regardless, I can't shake the feeling I've forgotten something. I get the same feeling every year."

"I'm sure you're not," Lilliana assured her.

"I think that's a good sign, isn't it? Generally, it's when you don't have that feeling you have to worry," Felix remarked.

"True. Guaranteed, the year you convince yourself you've got it all together will be the year you forget something," Roy concurred.

Arianna smiled. "I'm sure you're right."

If Felix had been in different company, he might've remarked that Madam Irony or Jinx would've made sure of that. And if not them, then one of their Thrixing brethren. The Thrixing Stars were always waiting for someone to be too certain or too confident in one thing or another, just so they could amuse themselves by publicly humbling them. Felix had always made sure to maintain a dash of humility with his pride, for fear he might tempt one of the Thrixing Stars to prove how human he truly was. But the majority of the aristocrats didn't believe in the Watchers. They might use their names as figures of speech from time to time, but they didn't believe the Stars had any influence over them. From what

Felix had seen, they tended to favor the opinion that the reccurring co-incidences in life were random acts of happenstance.

"How many events is our house competing in tomorrow?" Lilliana asked.

"Three. We have a dragon in the One Circle Dash, the Pre Race, and The Grand Final," Arianna told her.

"We aren't competing in the jousting tournament this year?"

"No. Not since Father died. I haven't found a knight for hire decent enough to replace him. Anyone taking up the sport who's any good competes for their own households."

"I miss seeing him out there. Watching Uncle John joust was always a highlight for me," Lilliana lamented.

"As for me. It's a shame Natasha isn't here, I know how much she favors the Beauty and Brawn events—they're more interesting now than ever," Arianna proclaimed.

"Really? How so?" Lilliana asked, taking a drink from her flute.

"Some of the breeders have been playing with gene splicing. They've not only managed to create colors I've never seen before in dragons, they've also managed to add phosphorescence to their scales by mixing their DNA with various bioluminescent sea life."

"How fascinating!" Lilliana exclaimed.

"What an amazing age we live in. What will they think of next?" Roy remarked.

"Yes. The Sky Cup Derby seems to get greater every year. It breaks my heart I have to miss it," Lilliana confessed.

"It's true, I've never seen a year that didn't eclipse the last. Which means you have plenty to look forward to. Next year will come around before you know it and be even better. I'll reserve you tickets. Do you think you'll be able to attend?" Arianna queried.

"Yes! Please do. I'll look forward to it," Lilliana said.

The waiting staff reappeared and whisked away their soup bowls, replacing them with the main course. The medley on the plate in front of Felix was something completely foreign to him. He was used to having the main course feature meat of some sort, accompanied by something in the starch family, with a side of some variety of vegetable. There was no meat whatsoever in front of him now. Instead, there was a large yellow mushroom that was almost the size of his dinner plate. Its cap was upside down—being used like a bowl. The edges naturally ruffled like sea coral. The mushroom was filled with something that looked like a mixture of seaweed and dried dates. Felix feigned delight to mask his disappointment. He'd been avoiding mushrooms for the last five years. The last time he'd eaten one was when he and Bastian experimented with Prophet mushrooms—a small rich purple fungi that prophets used for divination. They'd come across them exploring the forest behind the Star Temple during their lunch recess, and their curiosity got the best of them. Immediately after eating one they both regretted it. The mushrooms gave them visions that lasted through the rest of their afternoon lessons. Along with the vivid hallucinations came a paranoia that made getting through the rest of the day a living nightmare. The moment their classes were finished they escaped to their quarters to sleep off the effects, and Felix had avoided mushrooms of any kind ever since. He looked down at his dinner plate and suddenly found he'd lost his appetite.

"Which of the dragons will be competing tomorrow?" Lilliana inquired.

"Midnight Revelry, Duke's Dasher, and Charred-I'm-Sure," Arianna listed.

Felix smiled. "Excellent names. Did you come up with them yourself?"

"All but Duke's Dasher, who was named by my uncle—Lilliana's father."

"I didn't know Father named one of the racing dragons?!" Lilliana exclaimed in surprise.

"Oh yes, he was born on one of your father's visits, he was visiting alone that time—I think he was here on duke's business. At any rate, Dasher has qualified for one of the pre-races. He's a large and stubborn green. He's very good when he wants to be, but lacks discipline. The crowd likes him because he's a wild card. Somehow, he tends to know when the bets are weighed against him—if the expectations are too high he puts in minimal effort, but the second they're not weighed in his favor, he becomes a rocket at the last minute and steals the race."

Roy chuckled. "Sounds like a real showstopper."

"And who's Midnight Revelry?" Lilliana asked.

"She's a juvenile Blue. This is the first year she's qualified for the Derby. She's incredibly fast and agile, but doesn't have much stamina. She's racing in the One Circle Dash. I don't have high hopes of her placing this year, but I think she'll be a great racer in the future."

"Which means that Charred-I'm-Sure must be our champion," Lilliana deduced.

"Yes, two years in the running. We call him Charr for short. He's the Red I was riding this morning. He comes from great stock. Both his mother and father were excellent racers. He's not only incredibly fast, he has excellent stamina and loves the sport. I have to take him out for three flights a day just to keep him sated."

"And who'll be riding him tomorrow?" Lilliana inquired.

"I will," Arianna declared.

Lilliana's bottom jaw dropped. "You'll be racing the standing champion dragon in the Grand Final?"

"I have been for the last two years. Why's that such a surprise?"

"I just can't believe no one told me! I can't believe we haven't been here to support you. I never even knew you were interested in being an active participant in the races."

"There's much we don't know of one another. The important thing is you're here now. Perhaps after the Derby we can get to know each other a little better and make up for lost time," Arianna proposed with a warm smile.

"Yes. I would like that very much," Lilliana agreed, returning her smile.

"Will you be riding for all three events?" Roy asked.

"No. Gerald Manswald will be riding Midnight Revelry and Duke's Dasher. He's been our family's jockey for over a decade."

"Well, I wish you both all the luck," Roy said, holding up his glass.

Felix held up his as well. "Yes, here's to you and all three dragons, may Charr be champion for another year," he toasted.

"Here, here!" both Lilliana and Roy called in unison and they all drank.

Arianna laughed delightedly. "Thank you. Now, enough about that. What did you think of the Diamond City?" she asked Felix.

"It's a magnificent wonder. Our visit this morning was very pleasant. I look forward to exploring it further. I hear there are festivities taking place in the capital all week?"

"Yes. People come from all over just to partake in the side events. I've never had the opportunity to attend them myself, but I hear they're top-notch," Arianna confirmed.

"Fantastic! I think I'll explore them tomorrow."

"Earlier, you mentioned Sky View's growing independence. Is independence something Sky View's striving for?" Roy queried.

"It's more about being less reliant on the mainland. If our supply chain had been interrupted before the Sky Gardens were in place, we would've been stuck without food. Becoming self-sustaining is the most viable option for insuring that never happens," Arianna asserted.

"I only ask because James and I encountered a young man giving a public talk on the subject this morning," Roy told her.

"Oh?" Arianna queried.

"He was quite the speaker, really knew how to work up a crowd," Felix remarked.

"Yes, he was calling for a revolution. I was wondering if you could tell us anything about it?" Roy asked.

Arianna's spoon paused on its trajectory to her mouth. "There are some who talk of independence," she confessed.

"Independence from the mainland?" Lilliana asked in surprise.

"Yes…"

"Why is that?" Roy inquired.

Arianna hesitated. "Some believe our alliance with the mainland takes more than it gives."

"I see, and what's your opinion on the matter?" Roy queried, taking a mouthful of his mushroom.

Felix noted the sudden rigidity in Arianna's posture before she answered.

"I understand their perspective," she admitted. "We live so far from the mainland, most of the younger generation has never even seen it. We're becoming more self-reliant as each year passes, and yet we continue to pay the highest taxes of all the precincts. I must confess, part of me does wonder if it's in our best interest to remain tied."

"Sky View pays the highest taxes because its residents earn the highest coin. Eighty-five percent of the wealthiest families on Equillian live in Sky View. Lord Balthazar is a just man. He takes the most from those who can afford it—in order to benefit us all!" Lilliana argued.

"Does it though? I've never seen any evidence of your tax coin benefiting Sky View. Yet, our coin certainly benefits you," Arianna disputed.

"The fact the Windswept Isles are thriving is evidence in itself that being united has benefited Sky View as much as the rest of Equillian," Lilliana countered.

Roy nodded. "It's true. If you have any doubts, you only need talk to those who were around before the war. They'll tell you how becoming unified has led to the entire world prospering more than ever."

"Is that so? There's one precinct that would avidly disagree with that statement," Arianna asserted.

Roy looked taken aback. "Who? Surely you aren't talking about The East?"

"It can't be denied that Eastgate was thriving before the war."

"Only because they were inflating the prices on metal so no one else could use it to build anything!" Lilliana exclaimed.

"That's because they were the only ones who'd figured out a way to mine metals from the old world. The alchemists didn't create the mining spheres until after Equillian was united. Mining was an incredibly risky business before then. The East wanted the bulk of their hauls to be used for the progress of their own precinct. Can you really blame them for that? And that wasn't all they had going for them. They had a well-established form of government with the Scillion Seven. They had a booming internal economy, an excellent education system. They excelled in architecture, engineering, and innovation. They had the largest army on Equillian, one that was highly trained with their very own fighting technique, and they even had their own breed of dragon. This was all in a time when except for the alchemists, the rest of the precincts were too busy quarrelling with one another to accomplish anything useful. Would you want to join with the rest of the world if you were in their shoes?" Arianna challenged.

Lilliana was too taken aback to speak.

Roy cleared his throat. "Their circumstances are unfortunate, but it's a result of their own stubbornness. There was no other choice but to take them by force. If we hadn't inspired them, we never would've been able to successfully unify the world," he proclaimed.

"Inspire them? Is that what you call publicly executing the Scillion royal family? If it wasn't for the princess's escape, they would've slaughtered them all. And we all know, if she hasn't been killed already, then she will be the second she shows her face. The other precincts never had any desire to offer fair negotiations to The East—they wanted to force King Andrew and Queen Saraphina Scillion to kneel down from the start. And many of them were hoping they wouldn't cooperate, they wanted war. Emperor Balthazar's greatest mistake was misjudging the jealousy and bitterness of the other precincts. They resented The East for their success. Divided they feared the precinct, but as soon as they were united, they hungered to defeat it—to bring it down to their level. And it took all the other precincts combined with War Dragons to do so," Arianna asserted ardently.

"That may be true. But none of that changes the fact that Equillian's better off being united. Now, six precincts are thriving instead of one. We must focus on the present and the well-being of our future, not the past," Lilliana insisted.

"It's true, we can't undo what's been done. We must look forward. And unfortunately, everything about The East that was once worth defending, is gone," Roy agreed.

"I don't understand you, cousin. Since when have you become so sympathetic with The East? Uncle John despised them!" Lilliana asked, staring at Arianna like she was some sort of imposter.

Arianna blinked, as if suddenly realizing who she was talking to. "I simply understand there's more than one side to every story, and the importance of looking at each with equal value," she stated, brushing some crumbs off her dress.

"Forgive me if I'm wrong, Arianna, but do you think there's a comparison between Sky View and The East?" Roy asked her.

"I won't deny I see certain similarities. Can you blame me for having concern when Equillian's version of making things equal is pulling those at the top down?" Arianna asked.

"No. No, I can't. I understand your perspective perfectly, and it has validity. However, it's only a small piece of the bigger picture. I think it's easy to lose sight when we become too focused on a single problem. It's important to take a step back every now and again in order to see things from a broader view," Roy imparted.

"Broader view?" Arianna queried.

"For example, you might be self-sufficient in your basic food source, but I imagine you won't want to part with the vast selection of wines and spirits from the mainland? How about the spices that flavor your cuisine, or the fine fabric from the fashion precinct that make up your clothing? What about the metals from the miners guild needed to make the Sky Gardens? If you separates from the mainland, you'll need to establish an agreement with Lord Balthazar if you want to maintain free trade with the other precincts and keep your supply chain from being interrupted," Roy explained.

"I imagine losing trade with the mainland would affect Sky View quite drastically, don't you, cousin? I mean—besides your produce, just about everything you have is imported—and what would we be losing? Pet and Pack Dragons?" Lilliana proposed.

Arianna frowned.

"Most importantly, if you claim independence, you'll destroy the peace The Emperor and your forefathers worked so hard for. The moment Sky View removes itself from the mainland is the moment it removes itself from its protection. You no longer have a trained military or War Dragons. How do you expect to fend off anyone interested in taking the Windswept Isles for themselves?" Roy inquired.

Arianna's expression looked like she'd eaten a sour lemon. She quickly composed herself. "Those are all good points, but you must admit—it's hardly fair to penalize citizens for success. I'm sure you can relate to the fact that creating a profitable business is no small feat. Those of us who've been successful have worked incredibly hard for it. Not only that, we're creating supply where there's demand—for the entire world. What incentive does it give people to provide such a service when a quarter of their earnings are being taken with nothing given back in return?" she asked.

"I understand your point, please know I heartily do. I used to feel the same way, until I explored Equillian and was enlightened by the truth of our economic machine. This is not a dog-eat-dog world as you might presume. Everything you put into Equillian comes back around. In truth, the better off everyone is, the better off our businesses are and the more we all profit. For example, you might be spending good coin every year to fund schools on the mainland—schools that even if you have children they most likely will never attend. That might feel unfair, but you must think of the larger picture. A good education creates a skilled worker who can be a valuable cog in the workforce and community. It gives people the tools to come up with and create new inventions that can enhance our businesses, or advance science, medicine, and technology in ways that ultimately improve life for us all. And if they create their own businesses, they will not only be helping to create supply in another area where there's demand in the world, but it also gives them enough coin to put back into the market—for example, to buy their own dragons. The more coin individuals have to spend, the more they'll purchase our products. They flourish, we all flourish. It's about spreading the wealth to ensure everyone on Equillian has the opportunity for a high quality of life," Roy advocated.

Arianna snorted. "Spreading the wealth to ensure everyone on Equillian has the opportunity for a high quality of life? What about The East? Aren't they part of Equillian?"

Felix rolled his eyes but held his tongue. From what he'd learned on the street, The East's self-proclaimed crime lord was richer than The

Emperor himself. He'd risen up from the underworld of Eastgate after the royals fell, and everything that had happened to the precinct since its downfall only helped to further fill his pockets—and none of The East's commoners ever saw any of it. If you were unlucky enough to be born in Eastgate, then the only way to make enough coin to feed your family was to turn to crime yourself. Most of the time that meant joining one of the assassins' guilds, human trafficking for the illegal slave trade, or working in the Haze fields—a mind-numbing drug that led to a nasty dependency, one which most of the harvesters inevitably acquired. The East's crime organization poisoned the rest of the precincts with the illegal goods and services they peddled—and they profited grossly from it. They had nothing left to elicit sympathy from anyone. Yet, they clearly were, and by the sounds of it, doing a very good job of it too. It was apparent they'd gotten their claws into Arianna. It wouldn't surprise Felix in the slightest if the order of "Pack Dragons" was getting shipped straight to their shores.

"The East doesn't receive any tax coin because they don't pay any taxes. An arrangement made at their own request. It's the only way Eastgate would cooperate with Lord Balthazar's rule. Do you have any idea how things can be done differently? The East's a problem all of us are eager to solve," Roy proclaimed.

"I wish I did. Unfortunately, I think the damage done to The East runs far too deep to repair," Arianna confessed.

"What other choice did we have? If any of the precincts were left out it would've created room for further conflict. Balthazar didn't want The East to fall, he wanted them to join us. It was The War to End All Wars. With Equillian united, there's no other side to fight, we can finally work together and all be on the same team—fighting for the greater good of humanity as a whole instead of for a single precinct," Lilliana argued.

"What good is it being united when it's not by choice? As long as The East remembers the injustice they've faced, their loyalty will remain divided. Wouldn't yours?" Arianna asked.

"No. I would think of what's best for my children and all the future generations of Equillian. Our children shouldn't be made to inherit our hate or have to pay for our mistakes. A tongue for a tongue does nothing but make the whole world dumb! A future with Equillian united and working together—no matter how we got here—is brighter and better for us all," Lilliana asserted passionately.

"Here, here!" Roy agreed.

"Easy for you to say, you and your family aren't victims of the injustice," Arianna rebuked.

"Neither are you, cousin! And we're from the same family or have you forgotten? Which brings me to question—why are you so bothered with the fate of The East?"

Arianna stiffened her lower lip in silence.

"I agree with Lilliana. We can't change what's already passed. If we're to progress, we must look to the future," Roy said.

Lilliana smiled. "Thank you, Uncle."

"Unfortunately, that outlook is rare to come by. Do you think there's enough backing for this 'revolution' that Sky View might act on it?" Roy asked Arianna.

"There's more support for it every day. As I said, the majority of the youth here have never been to the mainland. Most of them live idle, relying on their inheritance for support. If you think my perspective is limited, I'm sure you can imagine the extent of theirs. With their inheritance waning and little else to do, they have taken up the cause with impassioned purpose."

"Hmmm, I can't completely fault them for that. It's clear there's a disconnect between Sky View and the mainland. If we can't find a way to bring the two together and repair the fissure, I fear they'll break apart entirely. I'm surprised the nobles haven't already intervened. Surely they don't back this revolution?" Roy inquired.

"I don't think they take it seriously. They themselves are removed from the common happenings and goings-on in the city. I'm sure whoever reports to them is downplaying the whole situation. They see the youth leading the charge as harmless children, not realizing how strong and influential their voices have become. There's unrest in Sky View. The wealth of many of the families is dwindling, and they want someone besides themselves to blame for it," Arianna told them.

"I see. I'm glad we've come. Already this trip has been enlightening. With every passing year Equillian seems to spin faster. I forget how quickly the world can change," Roy remarked.

"Yes. Well, speaking of time—it's time I retire. Please excuse me, I still have much to do in preparation for the Derby. If I'm to be at the top of my game on Thrixday, I must get my rest," Arianna announced.

"Yes, of course! I do hope this conversation has brought no offense. I appreciate you taking the time for it, Cousin. These discussions are incredibly important. Especially when we have contrasting opinions.

Above all else, if we are to progress as a society we must continue to listen and hear one another, despite our differences," Lilliana insisted, meeting her eyes.

"Yes, I agree. In turn, I hope I've not offended, I tend to get quite passionate around these subjects," Arianna admitted.

"As you should! If only everyone took such an impassioned interest in the state of the world," Roy commended.

Arianna smiled politely and stood from the table. Roy and Felix immediately followed suit.

Arianna inclined her head to them. "Good night to you all. I'll be occupied for most of the day tomorrow, but I'll look forward to seeing you at breakfast."

"As will we—good night," Roy returned.

"Good night, cousin," Lilliana said.

Felix gave her a respectful nod and Arianna left the table. As soon as she was clear of the dining room Lilliana glanced at Roy and Felix. "That dinner was exquisite, shall we retreat to the conservatory for a nightcap?" she asked lightly, but her eyes held the clear message *We need to talk.*

⌒

The conservatory was at the base of the East Wing. It was made up of seven tall stained glass windows stretching from the floor to the high ceiling, each depicting a scene with a different young dragon playing in the mountains of Sky View. The room was warmly lit with an Everfire crystal chandelier and abounded with potted plants—lemon and lime trees, basil, kaffir lime, rosemary, lavender, thyme, and a slew of other herbs and edible flowers. set on a beautiful white marble floor with a floral tile mosaic in the center. There were stone benches against the walls and a polished wooden table in the center inlaid with a wood and marble chessboard. Four wood chairs sat around it. Felix and Lilliana sat down at the table while Roy closed the glass doors behind them. He joined them and lit two purple Zest cigars, handing one to Felix. The two sat silently for a moment enjoying the aromatic Spice leaf while Lilliana sipped port from a long-stemmed sipper glass.

"This 'revolution' concerns me," Roy announced.

"My cousin concerns me! Did you hear how sympathetic she is with The East? I was hoping to gain some proof she couldn't possibly be working with them, but now I'm more concerned than ever. If her father knew, his star would become a supernova! The way these pieces are falling into place reveals a frightening picture," she exclaimed.

Roy nodded. "Her view of The East is certainly concerning. More so, because I fear she isn't the only one who thinks that way. I wonder how many of the residents here would agree with her. I never imagined Sky View and The East as allies. But the more I think about it, the more it makes sense. As Arianna brought to light, they're both separate from the mainland and both have reason to resent it. Furthermore, no one's a bigger customer for what The East is peddling than Sky View. They rely on its services, and both precincts benefit from doing business with each other. It seems that relationship has spawned sympathy for them. It's frightening to think what might happen if they join forces."

"Especially if Arianna successfully brings back War Dragons. Even the thought is madness. How I wish Father and Uncle John were here! This would never happen on their watch. They always found ways to bring Sky View and the mainland together. I think we might be the last influential family that's split between the two. It surprises me that Arianna's in favor of the divide. I hadn't realized how estranged our families had become. I guess our fathers were the only ones holding us together," she remarked.

"These youth spreading the propaganda are too naïve to realize the damage they can do. They're taking for granted everything our forefathers worked so hard for. If they're successful in dividing Sky View from the mainland, we'll all have bigger problems than coin to worry about," Roy proclaimed.

"I don't think the youth up here like peace," Felix commented absently.

Roy looked over at him in surprise. "What do you mean?"

"It leaves them with nothing to fight for," Felix explained.

"And what's fighting ever achieved?" Lilliana queried.

"It doesn't have to achieve anything—it gives them purpose."

"You're young. Do you feel the need to fight in order to have purpose?" Roy asked.

"Stars no! But then, I've had to fight for one thing or another just about every day of my life. The youth up here haven't had to struggle to survive. They don't have problems because they've all been taken away from them. Their families have looked after their every need from the day they were born. They get the best education in professional fields they'll never work in—and why would they? They have no need to work at all. They don't have to do anything but refrain from tarnishing their family's reputation and one day produce an heir. I think for some that's grand, they take up a few hobbies and are perfectly sated. For others, not being financially independent and not being needed for anything makes them feel powerless, useless—insignificant even. It's no surprise they're looking for something to give their lives meaning. And what's more significant than fighting for a noble cause?" Felix proposed.

"This is not a noble cause," Lilliana asserted.

"They don't know that though, do they? You have to put yourselves in their shoes. They've never been to the mainland. None of their friends or family are from there. They don't actually know how things work. All they see is their family's coin going out with nothing coming back. From their perspective, it's robbery. I imagine they see being united with the mainland as comparable to being united with a giant leech," Felix stated.

"That's very insightful for one outside their station," Roy remarked.

Felix shrugged. "Some things can be seen more clearly from an outside perspective."

Lilliana took a sip of her port, thinking aloud, "If that's true, then what the youth of Sky View really need is someone to help guide their enthusiasm in a different direction. Someone who can make them feel valued and provide a new cause for them to rally behind—preferably something that's actually productive."

"And who up here can do that?" Roy inquired.

"I don't know, I'm not on familiar terms with the nobles here. Father always made his business trips to Sky View alone," she admitted.

"I wish he hadn't. One of your father's faults was underestimating you girls. He should've included you and your mother in his duties as duke from the very beginning. Then things wouldn't have fallen apart in his absence," Roy remarked.

"I wish I didn't have to be missing, I wouldn't mind seeking out Sky View's nobles on my own—if I could only talk to them, I might be able to make use of my position here."

"Hmmm yes, I believe it would make a real difference if you could intervene. If you can bring the attention of the local nobles to the situation, they can end the whole thing before it becomes anything substantial," Roy agreed.

Lilliana brightened with sudden optimism. "Maybe I can. James said Emperor Balthazar's attending the Derby tomorrow."

"Yes—Favio did mention that. He's got a private viewing with The Emperor to show off his latest line—the prize for some fashion competition. Won't you two be modelling his work?" Roy asked.

"Yes, and I think it allows us the perfect solution! Balthazar's the one noble I can reveal my identity to without compromising everything, and he's the one person who can truly fix this. If I can inspire an audience with him at the fashion showing, I can warn him of the unrest here, and he can nip this nonsense in the bud before it blooms into another war," she proclaimed.

"Good point—why talk to other nobles when you can go straight to the true source of power," Roy agreed.

"Precisely!"

"It could work. Though I'm hesitant to interfere with Favio's show. He's worked very hard to get that private viewing. If we hijack it I'll never forgive myself," Roy admitted.

"Of course, I'll make sure it doesn't interfere," Lilliana assured him.

"Maybe it's best if you prepare a letter stating everything you want to say to The Emperor. That way you can hand it to him if you don't get the opportunity to talk to him during our window. It should be enough to entice a proper meeting if nothing else," Felix suggested.

"Great idea! I'll prepare one tonight," Lilliana said, then she added, "and I'll try and find a time to talk to Arianna tomorrow to extract any information I can regarding the dragons."

"Good plan. We'll go to Favio's to finalize things directly after breakfast," Roy declared.

"Though probably best not to clue Favio in on it. I think it's safest if he doesn't know Lilliana's true identity," Felix advised.

Roy nodded. "I agree."

"There is one more thing," Felix added. "I've been wondering, has anyone talked to the staff about the duke's disappearance?"

"They were questioned by the authorities after my father went missing. They all swore they didn't know anything," Lilliana said.

"Typical. Also a load of hogwash," Felix remarked.

"Why do you say that?"

"Think about it. The household staff should know more than anyone. They're a network of eyes and ears that have been here the whole time. They would've been waiting on your father while he was here—even if they noticed nothing but his disposition, that's still useful information. Was the duke anxious or depressed before he disappeared? Did he meet with anyone suspicious? Any of those observations could be necessary pieces to helping us solve the puzzle. And believe me, if Arianna has been meeting with The East at this estate, or if she's been breeding dragons for them, the staff will know. Someone needs to help run things and wait on visiting guests," Felix reasoned.

Both Lilliana and Roy looked at him like what he was saying was a complete revelation. As if they'd never thought of the hired help as intelligent human beings.

"Then why didn't they report anything to the officials during the investigation? After Uncle John, my father would've been the lord of this household," Lilliana queried.

"Yeah, but he wasn't here, was he? The staff have to look out for themselves. And generally, if they stick their neck out for a noble who can't protect them, it gets chopped off. They have a duty to protect their jobs and their families, and part of that means feigning naïvety and staying out of the business and affairs of their employers. You can hardly blame them. It's self preservation," Felix stated.

"If that's true, then what makes you think they'll talk to us?" Roy asked.

"Oh, they won't talk to either of you. But they'll talk to me," Felix asserted casually.

"Why's that?" Lilliana inquired.

"Because I'm one of them. I'm a common outsider who poses no threat. If it ever comes back on them, they'll simply deny it. Why should anyone believe an outside commoner over their loyal, trusted household staff?" Felix proposed.

Roy nodded in thought. "It certainly can't hurt to try. I say we should explore every avenue possible to get as much information as we can. If the staff are willing to share their experience on these matters, I would be very interested to hear it."

"I agree. I would be grateful for their knowledge. If you're happy to talk to them, please do," Lilliana said.

"I will then. I have to admit, I'm curious myself," Felix confessed.

Lilliana nodded and gave Felix a grateful smile.

Roy pulled out his pocket watch. "Well, if that's everything, we should all get some rest. Sounds like a busy day ahead."

Lilliana yawned. "Yes, I'm fading, I think I'll be out the second my head hits the pillow," she agreed and stood. "Oh, I almost forgot," she announced and turned to Roy, "James has the next letter for Lord Bardviss. I've already looked it over. Could you please help him send it off tonight?"

Roy nodded. "Of course, consider it done."

"Thank you, Uncle. Good night." Lilliana rested her hand on Roy's shoulder and kissed the top of his head.

Roy patted her hand.

Lilliana turned to Felix and smiled. "Good night, James."

"Good night, my lady," he returned, with a warm glint in his eye.

Lilliana left the conservatory.

The second she was gone, Felix pulled out his black pouch and turned to Roy. "Before I forget, here's the coin I owe you for covering me this morning," he told him, handing over ten duckets.

Roy took them with a smile. "You may as well keep them. No doubt they'll be yours after our next round of cards."

"That may be true, but the game won't be any fun if we don't at least pretend you have half a chance," Felix jested wryly.

Roy chuckled and pocketed the duckets. Then he took several thoughtful puffs on his cigar. "I'm curious to know, how did you and Lilliana come to meet one another?" he asked.

Felix's blood ran cold. *shick*. It was the question he was hoping he'd never have to face, sure it would be directed to Lilliana if it ever arose. He cleared his throat. "She hasn't told you?"

"No, she hasn't."

Felix casually took a puff of his cigar to buy himself some time. He and Lilliana never worked out the narrative of his story. He didn't know how much she wanted Roy to know. But Felix liked the man, and he'd found that when caught in a corner, sometimes the truth was the best way out. "I may have crashed one of the castle's parties…" he alluded.

Roy chuckled. "Is that so?"

"Your class has much better hors d'oeuvres than ours does," Felix admitted.

Roy grinned. "And you were discovered?"

"The duchess was the only one who saw through me. When she found out about my skillset—she thought we could mutually benefit one another."

"You pose as her kidnapper and in return you get to keep the ransom," Roy concluded.

"Bingo."

"Then haven't you accomplished what you set out for?" Roy asked.

Felix studied the stained glass window behind Roy for a beat. "Four purses of duckets is hardly reasonable compensation for disappearing a duchess, don't you think?"

Roy smiled. "Ah. You have a good sense for business. And you're right, that man deserves no concessions. But that's not really why you're still here, is it?"

Felix tensed. "What do you mean?"

"You like her, don't you?"

The smoke from Felix's cigar caught in his throat. "Who?" he coughed.

"Lilliana," Roy stated with a smile.

"Sure, she's a nice girl once you get past her thorns," Felix admitted.

"Ha! I wasn't born yesterday, kid. There's a saying in the Heartland— disguising love is as useless as hiding a dragon behind a flagpole."

Felix frowned. "Love is a very strong word," he remarked weakly, feeling the blood drain from his face. *This is it—the end. It's all over now, and I was enjoying myself so much,* he thought. His whole body suddenly tightened, ready to spring like a hare cornered by a predator.

"Relax. I'm not going to do anything about it. Stars know, I couldn't even if I wanted to. And I don't. It's not my place to tell Lilliana what she can and can't do with her life. She's a grown woman—she's free to make her own choices," Roy told him.

"So…you're not going to lynch me or throw me off the side of the island?" Felix asked.

Roy laughed. "How can I blame a man for the whims of his heart?"

"Many do."

"True. But they're fools and hypocrites. Being common born doesn't make you any less human. My father taught me that a man's worth should be determined by his character, not his coin purse. We can't choose the life we're born into, only what we make of it. If you ask me, I think it's refreshing. The stiffs Lilliana's normally around lack character, but it doesn't really matter what I think. I'm not her father, and Lilliana's always done what she likes regardless of anyone else's opinion. When it comes to her, the only thing I've come to expect is the unexpected."

Felix's shoulders relaxed. "Thank you, for being so—understanding," he said, feeling overwhelmingly relieved.

"Never thank a man for giving you liberties you have a natural right to. It's your right to live freely and be treated with respect, and it's not anyone else's to take that away. Don't forget that," Roy asserted, taking another puff of his cigar. "I must warn you though, if we're successful in finding Lilliana's father, either make sure he never finds out or get ready to run. He doesn't share my sentiments—especially when it comes to his daughters."

Felix swallowed. "Right. Thanks for the tip."

Roy stood and patted Felix on the shoulder. Then he handed him the slender gold whistle used for calling his Sendsong. "I'm heading to bed. Be sure to return it in the morning," he told him, and left the conservatory.

Felix watched him go before drawing in a deep breath and letting it out slowly.

"Shick," he muttered, and sucked down what was left of his cigar.

Felix stepped outside the manor house into the clear night air and followed the path to the back garden. Underneath the large fig tree was a wooden bench carved like a stretching dragon. Felix sat down and listened to the gentle wind rustling through the leaves for a moment, before pulling out Roy's slender gold whistle. He blew gently on the instrument, hoping it was working even though it made no sound. He knew not to expect one this time—the whistle's tune was a frequency undetectable by human ears. While he waited for Roy's Sendsong to arrive, he looked out at the encompassing view of the night sky. It was blanketed in a cloudy glow of stars, with constellations dotting the forefront like cut diamonds. He found Serendipity and stared up at her.

"If you're truly a champion of star-crossed lovers, please give me your sympathy now. Trust my heart to choose a woman so far out of my reach. I've no idea what I'm doing. I feel my ship's heading towards rocky shores obscured by darkness, and yet, I'm reluctant to change my course. My fate's in your hands, fair maiden. Have mercy," he prayed to the constellation.

The sound of heavy beating wings passed over Felix's head and Roy's white porcelain Sendsong landed gracefully on the bench beside him.

"Hello," Felix greeted.

The mechanical bird nodded slightly to him and then cocked its head and looked into his eyes inquisitively with its piercing violet stare. Felix was surprised by what he saw reflected back. Unlike the clear dishonesty mirrored to him the last time he'd faced the bird, the Sendsong's gaze revealed something more obscure, like a secret passage in a garden labyrinth, clouded by dense mist. Felix couldn't put his finger on what it was, but it felt like a deeper part of himself. Something only freshly uncovered. *Interesting,* he thought, and he mused that the Sendsong appeared to be thinking the same thing.

"Don't look at me for answers. I'm just as bemused as you are," he told the bird, smiling back at its probing stare.

The bird blinked and then looked away, turning its attention to preening its feathers. There was a click-click-click and the gold box in its chest popped open. Felix took his letter for Lord Bardviss out of his pocket and placed it into the bird's chest, then pronounced, "Lord Henry Bardviss." The compartment immediately snapped shut and the bird leapt into the sky.

Felix went back inside the Wendrians' manor house and took the long way towards the stairs so he could pass by the kitchen. He listened intently as he went and was happy to hear the gentle hum of voices coming from behind its closed doors. It was exactly what he'd been hoping for. There were generally at least a few household staff who met up for a drink after they knocked off. It was their one moment to socialize freely on a working day, and the kitchen was their domain. It was also the one moment Felix could hope to talk to them with their guard down. He smiled to himself—after days in the company of the upper class he was beginning to miss the less dignified. Not to mention he was in desperate need of a stiff drink. This was an errand he was eager to undertake.

He made his way up to his bedroom and grabbed the two bottles of Black Currant Wine. He paused as he passed by the looking glass and gave his reflection a once-over. He unbuttoned the cuffs on his sleeves and pushed them up to his elbows, and then he unbuttoned the front of his shirt so it hung open over the white singlet he wore underneath. He ruffled his neatly combed hair and smiled with satisfaction before leaving the room.

Felix walked quietly down the marble staircase and passed the entryway. All the Everfire lamps were adorned with dimmer bags for the evening, casting the interior of the mansion in a dim gold glow. The place was immaculate and almost completely silent except for the faint murmur of laughter and conversation trailing from the kitchen. Felix followed the noise to the swinging wood door outside. He waited for a pause in their conversation and then pushed his way in.

There were four household staff sharing a flagon of beer around a folding card table in the middle of the kitchen: an older thin gentleman with grey hair combed back and a well-groomed grey moustache, a young man no older than twenty with a clean-shaven face, and two women—a middle-aged plump one with bright rosy cheeks and a young woman only a year or two older than Felix. The four serving staff stared at him in surprise.

"Can we help you, my lord?" the plump woman asked, starting to stand.

"Please, don't get up. And for Stars sake, don't call me lord. I'm taking a night off from all that nonsense. I'll wager, I'm the most common born here," he declared, pulling over a spare chair from the corner and sitting down amongst them. "Black Currant Wine, anyone?" he asked, placing the two bottles in the center of the table.

Black Currant Wine was just nice enough to be inaccessible on a servant's pay. The four staff members looked at one another, bemused.

"If you're not a lord, then what are you doing with that? And what are you doing in the company of the duchess?" the younger man asked suspiciously.

Felix could see he was thinking it was some sort of trap. "I was hired for the journey as their star navigator. James Turner, at your service," Felix introduced, with a hand flourish and a bow of his head. "The wine admittedly doesn't belong to me. But I promise, it's not from this household and it won't be missed," he assured them, pulling the cork out of the first bottle with a loud *pop*.

"No offense, but how did you get the job as star navigator if you're not highborn? I mean, don't they have upper-class people for that kind of thing?" the young woman queried.

"No offense taken. Fortunately for me, my skill outweighs my status. No one knows the stars better than I do," Felix proclaimed, and he folded his left ear forward to reveal his seven-pointed star tattoo.

"You're a Star Child!" the plump woman exclaimed.

"Guilty as charged."

"I'm from the Spotted Isles—the Star Temple in our village cured my father from the Red Weeping. He was abandoned by all other physicians. No one would go near him but the Order. They saved his life. Any child of theirs is a friend of mine."

Felix silently thanked his lucky stars. The Red Weeping was a terrible disease, it made the infected sweat out their own blood. Most physicians believed it was horribly contagious and abandoned the inflicted, a fallacy that had cost many lives. Because of the Order's dedication to medical research, they ignored such common misconceptions made by the other medical factions and helped those cast aside.

"I'm pleased to hear the Order could be of service to you and your father. The Red Weeping is a terrible thing. I'm glad he found his way to them in time. The temple I grew up in could cure the illness in three days if caught early—with nothing but an ice bath and a simple ointment. I hear the common practice for treating the disease amongst the physicians willing to risk exposure these day is to bleed their patients. An odd remedy for someone already perspiring their own vitality, if you ask me. Let us toast to your father's good health and to the health of us all," Felix announced, and he held up a bottle of wine.

"Hear, hear!" the rest of the group returned in unison, and Felix filled their glasses.

"I'm Rose," the plump woman introduced, and motioned to the young woman next to her, "and this is Kareen."

Kareen waved awkwardly.

Felix smiled at her and she blushed.

"And this is Harold and Ivan," Rose said, pointing first to the older man and then the younger.

"Pleasure to meet you all. I can't tell you what a relief it is to find you here. As pleasant as it's been getting a taste of the bluebloods' luxury, it's hard work continually maintaining a posture of starched arrogance. I really don't know how they do it. I certainly enjoy their wine though," he confessed, holding up his glass.

His companions chuckled, and Harold held up his glass in return. "Aye, I don't care about being in their circles, just give me the milk and honey, I say!" he declared full-heartedly.

"I'll drink to that," Felix proclaimed and clinked Harold's glass before drinking. "Now, have any of you heard of the game Old Mother Shicker?"

The staff looked at one another blankly.

"None of you? Well then, tonight's your lucky night!" Felix proclaimed, pulling out his deck of cards with a wry grin.

An hour after Felix entered the kitchen, he was sitting around the card table with a nice buzz and a burning puff-stick in hand. The rest of his surrounding company was thoroughly lubricated. They were paused halfway through a round of Old Mother Shicker, Kareen taking in large gulps of air in an attempt to catch her breath from a five-minute fit of laughter. It must have been contagious, because it had quickly spread around the table and stopped the entire game. Felix and Bastian had invented the drinking game years before. They devised it around a tongue twister they'd picked up from local sailors in Westdock:

*Old Mother Dicker had a rough-cut punt.*
*A rough-cut punt had she.*
*Not a punt cut rough,*
*but a rough-cut punt.*
*With a pole at the stern and a flag at the front.*

The verse was easily botched if not well practiced. When it was botched, it turned a very clean rhyme into something gloriously inappropriate, and as a result, the offender had to drink. The trick was that no one was ever well practiced at the verse besides Felix and Bastian. Anyone who played the game got sloshed before they could master the words, and by the time they did, it was too late—they were already too drunk to have any chance at being able to say them properly. Within an hour the players became completely inebriated, while Felix and Bastian remained sober—or at least, as sober as they wanted to be.

As soon as the laughing stopped, Felix swooped in.

"Arianna seems a bit tightly wound," he remarked casually, taking a drag on his puff-stick.

"Ha! That's a polite way of putting it. Can I bum one of those?" Ivan asked.

"Of course." Felix lit another puff-stick and handed it over to him.

Ivan took a drag. "Thanks."

"Is she always like that, or is it just because of the Derby?" Felix inquired.

"Always," Rose, Kareen, and Ivan all answered at once.

"Shame, it's not her fault. Even before her father died, her life's been all work and no pleasure. She's consumed with the family business is all. Been carrying the bulk of the work for the last five years," Rose explained.

"She has no friends or suitors?" Felix queried.

"Nope," Ivan stated.

"Surely, she's had one in the past? A girl with her looks and such fine prospects."

"Not a one. Never has as far as we know. I remember when Lord John used to invite all the young men around to his parties, hoping she'd find one she fancied. But she never showed a hint of interest. She's never seemed to care about anything outside of work and dragon riding," Ivan remarked.

"I miss those days. Lord John threw the best parties," Kareen sighed dreamily.

Ivan nodded. "Yeah, me too."

"Those parties were running this place into the ground. They cost a fortune—and one Lord John couldn't afford," Harold asserted.

"And yet, they got bigger every year," Ivan remarked.

"It's why no one knew he was bankrupt, not even Arianna," Kareen said.

"Oh, I knew. Lord John was always borrowing from his mates. I was the one who had to make up excuses and turn the poor sods away when they came to collect," Harold declared.

"Poor Arianna had such a shock when she saw the books, didn't she? I remember how cross she was at Lord John when she first took over running their finances," Rose recounted.

Kareen nodded. "I remember, they were arguing for weeks."

"Course! I would've been outraged. I can only imagine how much in the hole they were. I thought for sure we'd all get sacked," Ivan exclaimed.

"It's no wonder Lord John did his best to hide the truth from her for as long as he could," Kareen said.

"He was only trying to protect her. He didn't want her to have to worry," Rose asserted.

Ivan tapped the ash from his puff-stick into a bowl on the table. "But it made it worse in the end, didn't it? I don't think Arianna's ever forgiven him for that."

Rose tightened her lips. "Shame, I think everything he did was for her. He loved his little girl more than anything."

"I do think he thought he could turn things around. Remember all those inventions he came up with?" Ivan chuckled.

"The machine that cleaned your shoes!" Kareen exclaimed.

Harold laughed. "It nearly took his foot off!"

"And the nutcracker that also worked as a cigar lighter," Rose recalled with a twinkle in her eye.

"I remember that! He used original fire and it nearly burned the house down!" Ivan cackled, and the others joined in.

Rose put her hand to her heart. "I think he really did want to do things right. He just didn't know how."

"I miss him, he really brightened up this place. Put a bounce in everyone's step. Arianna couldn't be more different, could she? I don't know how the apple fell so far from the tree," Ivan remarked.

"She certainly turned things around, though. It's a good thing she took over the business when she did. Place is making a roaring trade these days. She has her fingers in every pie in Sky View. The lead con-tractor for the Sky Garden project was here having a meeting with her last week. I overheard him thanking her for generously funding eighty percent of the project," Harold announced.

"I still wonder how she's done it. It would've taken a lot of coin to pull the estate out of its debts. All those months Lady Arianna spent in her office, sending out letters every other day while Lord John was cooped up in bed. I imagine she must've struck up a business deal with some so-and-so on the mainland because we started breeding a lot of Pack Dragons after that. No one uses Pack Dragons here anymore. Still, Pack Dragons aren't worth the amount of coin she's been raking in, and as expensive as Racing Dragons are, we don't sell more than a few every year," Ivan deduced.

"The estate makes most of its coin from breeding the cup champion, not from selling dragons. Do you know how much a single mount from Charred-I'm-Sure rakes in? Even if he doesn't get the mare pregnant, just the opportunity to try costs a fortune!" Kareen proclaimed.

"Yeah, but that still doesn't account for it all," Ivan asserted.

"Lady Arianna also gets a lot of coin from being the Sky Cup cham-pion. She's paid to be at just about every event she attends," Kareen pointed out.

Harold shook his head. "Ivan's right. The races aren't what brought Arianna out of debt. They've only just started to carry the estate's expenses this year."

"It has to be the Pack Dragons, right?" Ivan queried.

"Those aren't Pack Dragons," Harold stated, staring into his wine glass.

"What are they then?"

"It's a mix. The dragons we've been breeding are Bermese mixed with Pack Dragon. I used to work in a Bermese armory before they were outlawed. I'd recognize the species anywhere no matter how watered down it is," Harold declared.

"Do you think someone wants to make armor out of them?"

Harold snorted. "Unlikely. I recognize the cargo ship that comes to collect the stock. It's highly unlikely they're looking to produce armor."

"Where've you seen the ship before?" Ivan queried.

"Supplying enchanted artefacts to the auctions."

"Are you suggesting Arianna's doing business with The East?!" Kareen asked conspiratorially.

"I'm not suggesting anything, I'm only stating what I saw."

"Why would The East want a Pack Dragon-Bermese mix?" Ivan inquired.

Harold shrugged. "Maybe they want to sell them as fancy guard dogs. No doubt there'd be a market for them on the mainland."

"A specialized breed like that would be quite popular, I imagine. Especially considering it's technically legal. They're probably selling them on the shadow market for a fortune," Kareen proposed.

"I suppose that makes sense. But we've been breeding a lot. Do you think there could be such high demand?" Ivan asked.

"You know how the wealthy are. Once one person has one, they all have to have it," Kareen remarked.

"It would fill in a lot of blanks. I didn't think anyone in Sky View's game enough to do business with The East—besides acquiring enchanted artefacts or hiring them to do their dirty work. But it would explain how Arianna climbed her way out of debt. If they offered her good coin—she was desperate enough to take it," Ivan admitted. He finished the wine in his glass, and Felix refilled it for him with the remainder of the second bottle.

"There's plenty who'd take their business up here these days. It seems like in the last five years bankruptcy has been passing through Sky View like a plague. Everyone seems to be drying up all at once, though no one's willing to admit it, or change their exorbitant lifestyles. I wonder how many are doing business with The East now," Harold expounded.

"Especially if they know Arianna's had success with them," Kareen emphasized.

Felix wondered if the eastern leader had anything to do with the aristocrats' bankruptcies. It wouldn't surprise him—it all seemed too coincidental and convenient that the families here were in need of coin right when The East was in need of their employment. Eastgate was like a shadow on the rest of Equillian. The nobles believed it was harmless, because it didn't have a noble leading the precinct—that it was reduced to squalor and made up of the lowest of unmentionables incapable of achieving anything beyond killing and petty crime. It made them turn a blind eye, which of course created the perfect opportunity for Eastgate's crime lord. He leeched off the greed, arrogance, and spiteful nature of the upper class, and then used their coin and dark secrets as puppet strings to control them, having far more power over Equillian than anyone dared to realize. Felix wouldn't be surprised if The East was also behind the revolution—influencing the people with whispered words here and there, stirring up discord and bending Sky View to their will with no one being the wiser—and then stepping forward to help, as if they were their liberators. Felix had to hand it to them, it was a crafty plan. If The East was successful in an alliance with Sky View, they might actually have a chance at taking over the rest of the world—and that was terrifying, Felix thought with a shudder. He'd never cared about politics or who was in power. But if the East was in control, it would drastically affect everything. He'd no longer be able to hope for a bright future, because there wouldn't be one for anyone.

"Surely, Arianna wouldn't do dealings with The East! Lord John would've rather let this whole place sink to the bottom of the ocean than have anyone in his family take coin from them," Rose exclaimed.

"Yes, but Arianna isn't him, is she?" Ivan pointed out.

Rose's cheeks flushed, "I don't believe it! That poor girl has poured her life into rescuing this place. We still have jobs thanks to her, and you're trying to sully her triumph with this nonsense!"

"We're not trying to do any such thing, Rose. We're only calling things how they are. Just because the coin paying our wages isn't clean, doesn't make me any less grateful to have it. We all do what we must to survive in this world. But I'm not going to bury my head in the sand. We can't deny the facts," Harold asserted.

Rose crossed her arms and huffed.

"I tell you what, I preferred it when Lord John was running things, even if he was running the place into the ground. At least things were fun around here," Ivan confessed, taking a drag from his puff-stick.

"Come now, I'm sure Arianna would be different if she hadn't had such a hard run. You wouldn't be happy either if both your parents were gone and you had all that responsibility on your shoulders," Rose retorted.

"Don't kid yourself, Rose, she wouldn't be happy even if things were different—it's not in her nature. You and I both knew her when she was young, and she hardly smiled then either," Harold stated.

"That's because Lord John kept her cooped up here her whole childhood. He was so terrified of anything happening to her after her mother died, he hid her from the world. I don't think she's ever had a friend outside of Draya."

"At least Draya brings out her smile," Kareen said.

"Who's Draya?" Felix asked.

"Her handmaiden. Lord John brought her on to keep Arianna company when she was a child. The two hardly left each other's side when they were younger," Rose explained.

Ivan snorted. "They still hardly leave each other's side."

"Where's she now?" Felix inquired.

"Oh, she's around. Off running some errand for Arianna at the moment—in preparation for the Derby no doubt. But she'll be back," Harold said.

"She's more like Arianna's personal page than a handmaiden these days. She's always running errands for Arianna and speaking on her behalf. Since Lord John passed, she even occasionally eats at the table beside her. It's not proper if you ask me. The girl's forgotten her place!" Kareen scoffed.

"O posh! Don't be like that. I think it's lovely those two are such great friends. Draya's the closest thing she has to family up here," Rose said.

Felix took a drag on his puff-stick. "Arianna sounds more like the descriptions I've heard of her uncle than her father," he remarked.

Ivan nodded. "That's a good point. You're exactly right, now I think about it. That makes Arianna make a lot more sense."

"Yes, Arianna and Duke Drake do have a lot in common," Rose agreed.

"Were the two close?" Felix inquired, knocking the ash from his puffer.

"Not really. Duke Drake's family only came here for the Derby once a year, and he would come out on his own once or twice a year beyond that but never stayed for long," Rose said.

"I never saw him much with Arianna. His trips were always more for business than pleasure," Ivan affirmed.

"True. I think the fact that he and Arianna have anything in common is due to genetics rather than any influence from her uncle," Harold stated.

"Yeah, he's the silent type. Only said something when he needed to and didn't like frivolous conversation much. I got the impression he thought socializing for the sake of it was a waste of time," Rose commented.

Ivan snorted, "Certainly does sound like Arianna."

"I never had much interaction with him. Even when he was here visiting Lord John at the end, he was either occupied at his side or off running some errand. Then, he disappeared," Kareen said.

"Yeah. What happened there? I've only heard bits and pieces of that story and none of it seems to add up," Felix inquired.

"Don't get us started on that subject, or we'll be here all night!" Ivan exclaimed.

"I'll be the first to tell you, there's something fishy about that whole situation," Rose disclosed conspiratorially.

Harold rolled his eyes. "Oh boy, here we go."

Felix leaned forward. "Do tell."

Rose lowered her voice, "If you ask me, there's no way the duke committed suicide. He had several meetings planned the week after he'd gone missing. We had enquiries from their staff when he didn't attend. And Lady Arianna and the duke had a heated argument that night. I was pacing the halls in the wee hours when it happened—I couldn't sleep. I couldn't make out what they were saying, but it sounded like there was some dispute over the will. Arianna was accusing Lord Drake of manipulating her father to change it somehow. That's not even the strangest thing. I heard a noise later that night and looked out the window and saw someone lurking around the duke's airship on the dock. When I opened the window and stuck my head out to have a closer look, the figure was gone. Early the next morning, I woke to shouting. Lord John was dead and the duke and his airship were missing. The strangest part is that the officials acted like they weren't even interested in solving the case. Even Arianna adopted the suicide story far too quickly and easily if you ask me. And everyone seems to ignore the fact that the very same morning, one of the estate's dragons also disappeared," Rose expounded dramatically.

"Really, one of the dragons went missing?" Felix queried.

Harold cleared his throat. "I think that's enough for one night. Let's get you to bed, before you say something you'll regret in the morning," he told Rose, giving her a hard stare.

"Don't you shush me! I'm only saying—the whole situation's odd. I just wish we knew what really happened, is all. I can't put it together so it makes sense. You said it yourself, Harold, we can't bury our heads in the sand," she asserted.

Harold put a gentle hand on her forearm. "Okay, it's clear we've all had a bit too much to drink. I hardly think this gentleman's interested in our conspiracy theories. Let's call it a night, shall we?"

Rose pulled her lips into a thin line, but said nothing.

Ivan looked at his pocket watch. "By the Time-Thief, it's already the Dream Weaver's hour! Better get to bed if we still want jobs in the morning."

He and Harold stood and collected the glasses from the table.

Kareen yawned. "I don't even want to think about tomorrow." She smiled at Felix dreamily. "I enjoyed that game, 'Old Mother Shicker' was it? You'll have to join us for another round during your stay, it was fun."

"I assure you, the pleasure was all mine," Felix returned charmingly.

He helped clean up the remaining evidence of their gathering. Ivan, Rose, and Harold said good night and filed out of the kitchen, leaving Felix and Kareen behind. Felix was getting ready to leave when he caught Kareen's eyes undressing him. She was leaning against the wall in the kitchen with a seductive smile.

"I have a nice cherry port tucked away in my room if you want to share it with me?" she invited. Any sign of her bashful nature, which had been so evident before, was now washed away with the Black Currant Wine. Felix studied her. In the past, he would've eagerly accepted her invitation, but Lilliana had completely monopolized his libido—something he wasn't accustomed to.

"That's a very generous offer, but I'm afraid I can't. I'm supposed to do some work for the duchess. If I don't get to it, I could be out of a job myself," he told her.

"Maybe another time then," Kareen suggested.

She bent down to pick something up off the floor in front of him, purposely showing off her well-formed figure. She straightened up and gave him an inviting smile before leaving him alone in the kitchen.

Felix shook his head. *Who am I, and what have I done with Felix?* he asked himself, and then left for his room.

Felix sat up in his bed, his thoughts plagued with Lilliana and their encounter earlier that morning. He desperately wanted to sneak into her bedroom and spend the night with her in his arms. *If only her room wasn't right next to Roy's*, he lamented. He looked at his pocket watch—it was only half past the Dream Weaver's hour. He thought it best to wait until Shick's hour before he attended his next point of business. He wanted to make sure the household was well and truly asleep. He turned his mind to the conversation in the kitchen and mentally catalogued all he'd learned. The staff's story of the estate's missing dragon aligned with Roy's friend's story of a dragon pursuing the duke's airship. But if that was the case, then why wasn't the missing dragon ever reported? *That's more suspicious than anything,* Felix thought. Especially the way Harold silenced Rose the second she mentioned it. Did that mean Arianna had something to do with the duke's disappearance? Why else wouldn't she report the missing dragon? Felix wondered.

If Arianna really was working with The East and had some dispute with the duke over the will, then maybe she had The East disappear Lilliana's father. It wasn't that far-fetched; The East was known for their skilled assassins for hire. If you wanted someone gone, for the right price they'd make it happen. But then again, if it had been organized crime, it would have been cleaner, a well-thought-out plan that spread a logical explanation for the duke's death that wouldn't inspire questions. That's what they did, and they were good at it. That didn't coincide with Drake pursuing his ship into the Everstorm on a dragon. There were still pieces of the puzzle missing. From what Felix had gathered from the staff, Arianna was funding projects to help support the independence of Sky View. And she was clearly sympathetic with The East. The question was, if her father wasn't a fan of Eastgate, then what inspired her sympathy? Taking their coin was one thing, joining them and sympathizing with their cause was another.

Felix didn't believe for a second that Arianna never had a suitor. If she wasn't interested in anyone at her father's parties, then perhaps her attention was already occupied with someone else. And, if no one knew of it, then it meant she'd made an effort to hide it. He wondered if it could be someone from Eastgate. It was clear that Black Market traders frequented Sky View, supplying them with enchanted objects obtained from the mainland to be sold in their auctions. And every Black Market trader came from Eastgate. It's something Felix had taken note of a long time ago. There was no hiding their high cheekbones, gold-brown eyes, and thick eastern accents. They were the only ones who were able to get away with collecting illegal artefacts from the mainland. They had every top official from The E.O.C.A. on retainer to ensure they were the only traders who would be overlooked, giving them a monopoly on the trade. The E.O.C.A. confiscated any enchanted object it found in the possession of common people and sold them under the table to the Black Market traders, who then peddled them to the aristocracy. For the wealthy it was a perfect arrangement. They got exclusive access to enchanted objects, without ever having to get their hands dirty. The E.O.C.A got filthy rich, and Eastgate even richer—resting assured their stock was being sold to the highest bidders possible.

It seemed highly likely that Arianna could've fallen for one of their merchants. It would explain her sympathy for them and her reason for hiding the relationship. Felix had so many questions, for every new piece of information that surfaced he gained ten more. But questions were strings that led to answers—he simply needed to detangle them and follow them to their ends.

Felix realized just how drunk he was the moment he started to descend the stairs. Luckily, they were wide enough he caught his misstep without tumbling down them. He cursed The Star Stirrer as he grabbed the bannister and proceeded more carefully, listening intently every step of the way. The place was eerily quiet, especially for how large it was. He walked silently to the main floor and past the front entryway, before turning right at a corridor he'd never been down. It led him to a hallway stretching along the back of the dwelling, with rooms on either side. Most of the rooms didn't have doors, just arched entrances leading into different spaces. There was an extravagant ballroom, a billiard room, an indoor heated pool made of blue and gold tiles that shimmered in the Everfire lantern light under crystal clear water. Felix found himself wishing he'd known it was there when he and Lilliana were alone earlier that morning. Soon he stumbled upon a cocktail lounge with glass cabinets stocked to the hilt with the finest liquor. He could imagine the extravagant parties that the staff had mentioned—the mansion felt like it was made for it. *What a shame Arianna isn't more like her father,* he mused.

He walked farther down the hall towards the back corner of the house and came to a room with a door. It was the only room that had one, except for a small storage closet he'd wandered into. He looked down the passageway to ensure he was alone and then tried the handle. It was locked. Felix sighed silently. He wasn't good at getting through locked doors he couldn't talk his way through. Bastian was the locksmith; he could pick his way into anything. Felix had never bothered to master the skill, mostly because his brother had always been there to unlock doors for him. He cursed himself for that now. But he didn't lose hope—outside of Keeping Rooms, interior doors usually had a layman's way of opening from the outside. Felix didn't even bother with the keyhole. Instead, he ran his finger over the surface of the brass plate under the door handle and was relieved to find a small hole directly below it.

*Thank you, Lady Luck.*

Felix felt inside his pockets for something he could use. Finding nothing that suited his purpose, he looked around the hall. There was a decorative marble table behind him with a bronze statue of a knight riding a War Dragon. The knight was carrying a long thin spear, pointing it forward ready for combat.

Felix studied it more closely and was pleased to find the spear wasn't secured. He wiggled it out of the statue's grasp and stuck the end into the tiny hole and pushed. There was slight resistance before it gave way with a quiet *click*. Felix tried the handle again and the door opened. He silently thanked Serendipity as he slipped inside and locked the door securely behind him.

Felix found himself in a well-lit study with dark green walls. There was a robust oak writing desk to the left, clean and well organized with a large map of Equillian framed on the wall above it. The other side of the room had a floor-to-ceiling built-in bookcase. Two open letters lay on the desk. Felix picked up one and looked it over.

*Dear Arianna,*

*I write this with a heavy heart. Liliana is missing. She disappeared from her engagement party last night and no one has any idea what happened to her. I wanted you to hear it from me before seeing it in the papers. Please keep an ear out and let me know if you hear anything.*

*Warmly,*

*Aunt Everitt*

Felix put down the letter and picked up the other one on the desk.



Felix put down the letter with trembling hands.

*Oh shick.* Marx was a name well known in the dodgy parts of West-dock. The man wasn't just an Eastgate trader, he was Eastgate's crime lord, the kingbolt himself. And Felix could only presume that by "Henry," Marx meant Lord Henry Bardviss. If Marx was connected to Lord Bardviss, then Felix was stepping into boiling water, and this little holiday wouldn't be a game anymore. And if Marx was the one who Arianna was doing business with, then this whole thing was far worse than Felix ever could have imagined. Marx was the last person to cross. The man had a bad reputation for animating the stuff of nightmares.

"Shick! Felix muttered, suddenly greatly regretting the letter he'd just sent to Lord Bardviss.

*Why would Arianna be working with Marx? And what arrangement could she have with him and Lord Bardviss that involved Lilliana's betroth-al?* he wondered.

Felix put the letters down and began rifling through the desk drawers. He came across carefully filed papers recording business transactions and correspondence with clients from the last several years. There was a divider labeled with Marx's name. Felix dove into it, pulling out a stack of papers. The first one was a long list of orders for Pack Dragons, all being sent to The East, all signed by Marx. A bad feeling sank in Felix's belly. If the Pack Dragons being sent were the hybrid cocktail being concocted in the underground hatchery, then that was a serious problem. Felix couldn't think of anyone worse to have control over War Dragons—or any version thereof.

*What's Marx planning to do with them? Are they simply moneymakers for the dragon pits, or something more sinister?* he wondered. He thumbed through the rest of the paperwork and came across a series of letters. He pulled out the stack and started reading them.

*Hello Miss Wendrian,*

*I must say, I am delighted to hear from you! I've sent several inquiries to your father over the years, but never received a reply.*

*We are very much still interested in doing business with you and your family.*

*As stated in my letters to your father, we are willing to pay top coin for a litter of your best Pack Dragons. If all goes well, we plan to be ordering many more.*

*I dearly hope you will consider our offer and this can be the beginning of a lasting and fruitful business relationship.*

*Kind regards,*

*Marx*

Felix put the letter down and picked up the next one.

*Miss Wendrian,*

*We are so happy with the stock we purchased, we would like to order more.*

*There are a few specific dragons with physical and character attributes that are particularly exceptional for our need. We would like to use those dragons to father the next generation in the hope that we can perfect a breed for our purpose. I will send sperm samples to be used for artificial insemination. Of course, we will pay you whatever you require for this specialized service.*

*Kind regards,*

*Marx*

Felix placed the letter carefully on the last and picked up the next.

And the next…



And the last…



Felix's blood ran cold. Suddenly Lord Bardviss's behavior made so much more sense. Felix wasn't dealing with a pompous lord, he was dealing with a professional criminal.

*Shick, shick, shick!*

Marx said a friendship between Lord Bardviss and Lilliana's mother—Lady Everitt—would be mutually beneficial. Did that mean Marx was behind Lilliana's engagement? But why? What did he have to gain by having Lord Bardviss marry Lilliana?

Felix looked up at the map of Equillian on the wall and suddenly it clicked. He put the letters down on the desk and walked over to the map, running his hand along the illustrated landscape. Westdock and Eastgate were on opposite sides of Equillian. The eastern and western tips of the mainland stretched in a long line between them. Eastgate's borders were closely watched, and Westdock was a small precinct generally overlooked by everyone but merchants. If Lord Bardviss was in power there, it would open up a major mainland port to The East free of checkpoints. Lord Bardviss's merchant fleet would be able to move anything to and from Westdock without it being checked or questioned. He could bring crates of Haze and spread the poison throughout the mainland, or worse.

*Stars—he could bring a whole army...or a shipment of War Dragons and no one would be the wiser,* Felix realized in horror.

Once there, Marx could attack Equillian's mainland from both sides, crippling it before anyone knew what was hitting them. *Stars.* And if the East was allied with Sky View, there would be no one left to defend the mainland. There wasn't even enough people in Everlast or the Spotted Isles to save them.

"We're shicked!" Felix muttered.

Lilliana was right. Her betrothal to Lord Bardviss wasn't simply condemning her to a miserable marriage, or even Westdock to a useless and self-riotous duke. It was condemning the world to tyranny and destruction. And if that was the case, then why was Arianna helping them? In the letters, Marx sounded refined and cordial. If that was all she knew of him, she might actually believe he had good intentions and be blind to how he was using her.

*Could she really be so naïve?* he wondered. Then again, even Lilliana was surprised by Felix's knowledge of the underworld, knowledge he thought was commonplace, but maybe that sort of information didn't make its way to the upper class in their sunny bubbles of luxury. Even so, it surprised Felix that Arianna would do business with The East at all. They had a bad reputation most of the aristocracy steered clear of. Unless of course, they were doing something dodgy themselves—like hiring an assassin, purchasing a slave, or buying enchanted objects on the Black

Market, in which case they never did business with them in the open. For Arianna to take them on as a documented client was incredibly risky. It did, however, confirm how she managed to pull her family's business out of debt. By the sound of things, she'd been limited on options. However, she wasn't limited anymore. The business was clearly making a roaring trade these days. Which meant she was either choosing to continue working with them or she'd gotten herself into a position where she no longer had a choice. It would justify her decision to keep their business transactions on record. If things went sour, then an investigator could trace back to who it was. Whatever was going on, Felix needed to find out as much as he could if he and Lilliana were to have any hope of stopping it.

Felix searched through the rest of the drawers and found nothing else of interest—just more business records of scattered racing dragon sales and profits from breeding Charred-I'm-Sure, as the staff had suggested there would be.

Felix sat back on his heels with both desk drawers open on either side of him, thinking. Then he noticed something odd. The file folders in the right drawer were raised higher than the ones in the left. He pulled out a file from each and held them side by side. They were the same size…and so were the drawers. He pulled out all of the filed paperwork from the drawer on the right and knocked on the bottom of the drawer. It made a hollow sound. Felix inspected it for a false bottom. There was a small niche at the very back, just big enough for his little finger. He pulled up the thin wood base, revealing a secret compartment. Sitting inside was a large brown paper envelope with fine calligraphy on the front: *The Will of John Westoff Wendrian.* Felix picked the envelope up carefully, making sure not to mark the paper in any way, and opened it.

THE WILL OF JOHN WESTOFF WENDRIAN

I, JOHN WESTOFF WENDRIAN, LEAVE 90% OF MY HALF SHARE OF THE SKY VIEW ISLAND, FAMILY ESTATE, BUSINESS, AND ALL CONTENT THEREIN, INCLUDING BUT NOT LIMITED TO LIVESTOCK, FAMILY ARTEFACTS, BUSINESS WARES, AND HOUSE FURNISHINGS TO MY BROTHER, DRAKE DEVON WENDRIAN. I LEAVE THE REMAINING 10% OF MY PORTION OF THE FAMILY ESTATE AND BUSINESS TO MY DAUGHTER, ARIANNA OLIVIA WENDRIAN. ALL OF MY PERSONAL ITEMS ARE TO BE LEFT SOLELY TO MY DAUGHTER, ARIANNA OLIVIA WENDRIAN.

Felix stared at the will in puzzlement. *Why would Arianna's father only leave her ten percent of his half of the estate and business?* he wondered.

Wouldn't he want to leave his daughter and sole heir his entire half? Especially considering Arianna was the primary caretaker of the estate and business and his brother already owned the other half. Felix recalled Rose saying she overheard Arianna and the duke having an argument over the will the night he disappeared, and Lilliana saying that Arianna never responded to her letters regarding the topic of the will after her father's death. Felix could now understand why. He could imagine himself having the same argument in Arianna's position. This place was her home. Not to mention she'd been running the business on her own for years and even saved it from near ruin…it might have been through the dodgy means of doing business with the most notorious and dangerous mob boss on Equillian—who he doubted had anything but ill intentions with whatever she was selling him—but still, surely she deserved more than ten percent.

Unless her father knew she was dealing with The East. Marx said in his initial letter to Arianna that he'd been trying to strike up a business relationship with her father for years. And Lilliana said her uncle detested The East. If he'd found out what Arianna was doing and that she'd been conducting business with them behind his back—maybe he cut her mostly out of the will to get the business out of her hands? Could that have given Arianna incentive to have something to do with Drake's disappearance? It would explain why she hadn't shown the will to Lilliana.

Felix looked at his pocket watch. It was already half past the hour. He was eager to leave the study. The more he learned of the Wendrians' whole predicament, the less he wanted to be a part of it. It was like Lilliana came with lit sticks of dynamite in her pockets. He feared at any minute one might blow up in his face, and yet, he still believed she was worth it and couldn't convince himself otherwise. At any rate, she needed to see the will, and he couldn't simply take it—if Arianna discovered it missing, it would cause a right mess. He looked around the room at what was available on hand. Next to the leather armchair was a small round glass side table. Its base was a marble dragon statue. Arianna had several different types of parchment and ink pots organized neatly in the upper compartments of her writing desk, and he'd recalled seeing a full collection of pen nibs in one of her drawers. There wasn't any paper that matched the will perfectly—even if there was, the original would have a watermark that would be near impossible to replicate with what he had on hand, but one of the paper types was close enough that if everything else was perfect, it might be overlooked. He could work with that. Felix took a piece of paper and a piece of graphite and made a quick sketch of Arianna's desk and its contents, marking out where everything was. Then he carefully cleared the desk. Next he chose a piece of the whitest paper in Arianna's collection and laid it down in the center of the desk. He borrowed eight encyclopedia volumes from the bookshelves behind him and stacked two around each side of the paper, framing it nicely. He took his Everfire box out of his pocket and opened it to expose the enchanted flame inside, and placed it on the center of the white paper. Then he carefully picked up the glass from the side table and laid it gently over the frame of books. Felix placed the will on the glass. He studied the lettering; it was written in black ink with a flat nib. He scanned Arianna's stationery collection and chose a black ink pot and the appropriate quill. Then he layered a thin piece of blotting paper over the will. Next, he carefully selected a piece of parchment that closely resembled the will and placed it on top of the blotting paper. He made sure all three of the layers were meticulously aligned. Feeling satisfied, he walked over to the wall and flipped a switch near the door. There was a click-clicking sound as the dimmer bags lowered themselves over the Everfire lanterns. Felix was incredibly grateful the estate had spent to have dimmers in each room. If he was in a commoner's house, he could never hope to find that feature. He was pleased to see that his improvised light table worked efficiently. The white paper underneath his Everfire box reflected the light upwards to the small stack of papers above it, making the lettering on the will clearly visible through both layers. Felix set all of his writing tools in place and took off his dress shirt, placing it over the back of the chair. Then, carefully preparing his pen, he set to work tracing the legal document.

Thirty minutes later at the turn of the Lover's hour, Felix held an almost perfect copy of the will in front of him. He let the ink dry fully before placing the replica into the brown paper envelope and returning it to the secret compartment in the drawer. Then he set to work putting everything in the room back to its rightful order, using his prepared sketch to ensure it was restored the exact way he'd found it. Just as Felix finished buttoning his dress shirt, he heard someone in the hallway outside the door. He quickly tucked the real will in the back of his pants underneath his shirt and looked for a place to hide. Being limited on options, he squeezed himself into the small space between the wall and an armchair in the corner. No sooner had he crouched down, the door to the study opened and in stepped Arianna accompanied by a woman Felix had never seen. The woman was tall and slender with long dark brown hair pulled back in a tight plait that emphasized her high cheekbones and golden-brown eyes. She wore simple travelling clothes—the kind Felix would expect to see on a servant or the page of a wealthy noble.

Arianna closed the door and turned to the woman. "Thank the Stars you're back, what took you so long?"

"I got held up, there were some…complications. What's your cousin doing here? I thought she was supposed to be missing?" the woman asked, pulling off a pair of riding gloves.

"I'm as surprised as you are to see her here. She showed up out of the blue this morning. With everything I've needed to do for the Derby, I haven't had the opportunity to have a proper one-on-one conversation with her," Arianna confessed.

"Do you think she's here to see the will? This is what happens when you ignore a problem—it festers! If you'd only responded to her letters from the start, it never would've come to this," the woman accused in frustration.

Arianna put her hand to her temple. "She hasn't mentioned anything about the will. There's no reason to jump to conclusions. I'm going to figure this out, I just need time. As soon as the Derby's over I'll be able to think more clearly," she asserted.

"Did she say anything about why she's come?"

"She said she's here to look into the disappearance of my uncle. She believes he may still be alive," Arianna admitted, leaning back against the desk.

The woman sat down in the armchair in front of Felix. "Wouldn't that be terrible luck? Actually, I take that back—it could be great luck. Maybe she'll go looking for him in the Everstorm and disappear too!" she exclaimed optimistically.

"Watch your tongue, that's my cousin you're talking about!" Arianna rebuked.

"Sorry. I thought you detested her?" the woman apologized flippantly.

"She's family. I don't have much of them left. And she's different this time, less…entitled."

"That's good to hear. So, what's the plan then?"

"I don't have a plan. I'll carve out some time to talk to her. I need to get a better understanding of what's going on…she mentioned something about Lord Bardviss having a sinister purpose," Arianna said.

"A sinister purpose? What, fathering her children?" the woman jested.

Arianna ignored the comment. "She showed me a letter signed by his hand. It implied he wanted her sold to the slavers."

"Ha! That would certainly humble her, wouldn't it?" the woman scoffed.

Arianna turned on her incredulously. "Has Lilliana done something to offend you?"

"I don't like her. She's always acted like a pompous princess and treated me like I'm below her," the woman admitted.

"You are below her! She's a duchess and you're still my handmaiden—or have you forgotten?" Arianna reminded her pointedly.

Felix cocked his head. Arianna's handmaiden. This must be Draya, the woman the staff were talking about, he realized.

"Of course. Forgive me, sometimes I forget that swallowing disrespect comes with my job description," Draya remarked.

"Don't be like that! You only have trouble with it because I've always treated you as my equal. Don't take that for granted," Arianna cautioned.

"You're right. I'm sorry. I'm only tired from my trip. You should talk to her sooner than later, though. If you don't give her answers, she'll uncover the ones you don't want her to find," Draya warned.

Arianna rubbed her temple again. "I know."

"And you should change the will, just in case she does ask. If Lilliana sees it the way it is, everything we've worked for will be ruined," Draya insisted.

Arianna nodded without conviction.

"I don't understand why you hesitate! It's what you're entitled to. Give it to me, I know just the person for the job. I'll have a new one written up for you by tomorrow afternoon."

Arianna thought about it for a moment. She reached for the drawer Felix had only just put back together a few minutes before, then hesitated and pulled her hand away. "No. That won't be necessary," she asserted.

"Why not?"

"There are things you don't understand. I'll look after it."

"You're right, I don't understand. I wish you'd tell me so I could," Draya pressed.

Arianna glared at her, a look that said she was crossing a line.

"I don't mean to pry—I just want what's best for you. Please, at least consider changing it?" Draya implored, walking over to Arianna and gently touching her arm.

"I'll consider it," Arianna conceded.

"Thank you. Now, enough about all that. Let's not let any of this spoil our night. I've missed you," Draya announced, taking her hand.

Arianna's anxiety melted away and she looked at Draya warmly. "I've missed you too," she confessed, and Draya leaned in and kissed her— Arianna welcomed her embrace as though it was something they'd done a thousand times.

Felix tensed. *Oh shick.*

He was suddenly acutely aware that what he was witnessing was potent enough to cost his life. So it was true—Arianna did have a secret suitor, and good reason to keep it hidden. There was a deep trench between the upper class and their help, one that ran even deeper than the one between them and the common born. Even addressing their help conversationally was highly frowned upon. It could ruin the reputation of any highborn, and in the world of aristocrats your reputation was everything. It all boiled down to the fact that they couldn't afford for their help to get the idea they might be equal to those they work for. If they did, then the aristocrats would have to pay fair wages and accommodate a smaller workload. Since that wasn't in their favor, it was easier to simply declass whoever "stooped" to their level. If it were to get out that Arianna was involved romantically with her handmaiden, then she would be shunned from the higher social circles—and by the sound of things, she'd worked very hard to earn their respect. Felix's familiarity and knowledge of the inner workings of the upper class social system allowed him to exploit it and make a profit for the last four years. He knew the exact weight of the situation, and he had no doubt Arianna would be willing to do dark things to keep her secret hidden. From his conversation with the household staff, they were none the wiser, which meant she'd already gone to great lengths to keep it that way. And there was no telling what she might be willing to do to further preserve her secret. Felix sat as still as stone, slowing his breathing, fearful his racing heartbeat might give him away.

"Come, let's to bed," Draya cooed, gently pulling Arianna towards the door. Felix let out a silent sigh of relief as they left the room. He waited until he could no longer hear their footsteps in the hall before leaving the study himself and cautiously making his way back up the stairs.

Felix stood outside Lilliana's door, debating whether or not to go inside. He dared not knock for fear of waking Roy in the neighboring room. He cracked open her door decidedly and slipped inside.

Lilliana was laying in her bed fast asleep, her cherry curls fanned out on the pillow. She looked so peaceful and serene. He sat down on the bed next to her and put his hand gently on her arm. "Lilliana," he whispered. She groaned and turned away from him.

"Lilliana," Felix whispered more urgently, this time shaking her lightly. Lilliana woke with a start. Before Felix could blink she'd pulled her dagger out from under her pillow and had it pointed at his throat. Felix held up his hands in defense.

"James?" she gasped in surprise.

He smiled weakly. "Your Faerie Star Mother."

Lilliana lowered her blade. "What are you doing here? You can't just come into my room whenever you please! You really need to learn some proper etiquette," he scolded.

"We need to talk," Felix asserted gravely.

"Can't it wait until morning?"

"I'm afraid not."

Lilliana sat up in bed while Felix paced her room. "Arianna's working for Marx. That's who the hybrid Pack Dragons are for," he announced, running his hands through his hair anxiously.

"Who?" Lilliana asked with a yawn.

"Marx," Felix repeated.

Lilliana stared at him blankly. "Does he have a surname?"

"Does he have a sur—no! Marx—the ruler of Eastgate and king-bolt of every organized crime syndicate on Equillian," Felix exclaimed in exasperation.

"Eastgate doesn't have a ruler," Lilliana stated blankly.

Felix laughed dryly. "Oh, yes it does."

"No, it doesn't. That was one of the arrangements they made with Emperor Balthazar. He tried to appoint several dukes and duchesses there in the early days and every one was driven away. They refused to be ruled by anyone," she proclaimed.

"No, they refused to be ruled by an outside noble, and they didn't have any of their own nobles left. Lord Emperor Balthazar made an arrangement with The East—yes. It was an arrangement with Marx. He agreed not to appoint a noble to the precinct and to turn a blind eye to Marx's business, in exchange for Marx keeping the precinct under control, and from 'corrupting' or infiltrating the rest of Equillian," Felix corrected.

"How come you know about this and I don't?"

"That's a very good question," Felix remarked, then he paused in thought before adding, "I suppose that sort of information might be more commonplace on the streets. It's certainly not something you'll discover in history books or the paper."

"I suppose it would pay to leave my castle every now and again," she admitted.

Felix grunted.

"So, who is this man—besides being the mob boss of Eastgate?" Lilliana inquired.

"He's a monster. He has more blood on his hands than an execution-er. A complete psychopath who preys on people's weaknesses to manip-ulate them for his own purpose. He runs the slave market, he produces Haze—purposely targeting children to get them addicted to the stuff as young as possible. And I've heard he even has a lab in Eastgate dedicated to experimenting on humans," Felix reported with a shudder.

"Surely that can't be true! Otherwise, Emperor Balthazar would've intervened," Lilliana insisted.

"It's not that simple. Since the Scillion royal family fell, Marx is the only one who's been able to control The East. And the world is supposed to be united. If The Emperor storms into Eastgate it would ruin his hard-earned peace. And anyone who sympathizes with them—as Ari-anna does—would see the Emperor as a tyrant for doing so. Besides, it wouldn't be that easy. Marx is smart. Of course he can't have an army if he wants The Emperor to continue turning a blind eye, so instead, he's set up assassins' guilds throughout Eastgate. He makes sure they get plenty of work and are paid well to incentivize his protection. The only way to earn a decent wage in Eastgate is to work for Marx. I've heard it's really the only way to survive there, and it's no secret the mainland doesn't welcome them anywhere else," Felix explained.

"Disturbing. What business does my cousin have with him?" Lilli-ana queried.

"She supplies him with dragons."

"You have proof that the dragons we found in the hatchery are for him?" Lilliana asked.

"I've seen letters between them stating as much and order ledgers signed by his own hand," Felix affirmed.

Lilliana put her fingers to her temple.

"Lilliana, you need to forget everything I said before. Do not talk to Arianna about this, she can't know that we know what she's doing. You were right, there could be deadly consequences. Especially if she tells Marx," Felix admonished.

Lilliana nodded somberly. "I can't believe Arianna would work with someone like that, she's putting our entire family on the line. It doesn't make any sense."

"I don't think she had a lot of options," Felix stated.

"What do you mean?"

"I spoke with the staff tonight. They said your uncle was running the business into the ground before Arianna took it over. I think doing business with Marx was the only way she could find to pull it out."

"What? That's not possible, Uncle John had more wealth than he knew what to do with. You should've seen the parties he used to throw," Lilliana proclaimed.

"Apparently it was all a front. Those parties were thrown on borrowed coin."

"Why didn't he tell us? Why wouldn't he ask my father for help?" Lilliana questioned, mortified.

"Pride—I imagine."

"Stars. Just like my mother," she remarked absently.

"That's not even the worst of it," Felix announced.

"What could be worse?"

"The first night we met, you told me you were saving us all from having to suffer Lord Bardviss as duke, that once he's in power he'll cast your family aside and do whatever he pleases. You were right. He's a friend of Marx's. Arianna was the one who set up the initial introduction between Lord Bardviss and your mother. I think Marx has been the one behind your engagement all along. With a friend and ally in power in Westdock, it's almost as good as him having conquered the place for himself. He'll be able to get anything he wants through Westdock's port without having to worry about checkpoints," Felix revealed.

"Even War Dragons," Lilliana concluded. Felix nodded and Lilliana paled. "We have to tell Emperor Balthazar!" she exclaimed.

"Yeah," Felix agreed, "and it's more important now than ever that until we do, no one discovers you're here. Arianna might've informed

Marx that you're here already. We can't let her know we're going to the Derby. Marx will no doubt have agents there. We need to make sure your disguise is impeccable," Felix asserted.

"Are you confident we can do that?" Lilliana asked.

"Yeah…pretty confident."

"Stars help us," Lilliana muttered.

Felix paced in thought. "Everything makes so much more sense now. The way Lord Bardviss replied to us in his letter—I knew something was off. He didn't act like a noble responding to blackmail; he was too cool and confident. He must've assumed The Debt Collectors were linked to Marx—most criminals are. Of course an organized group like The Debt Collectors would be. I thought that would work to our advantage— usually dodgy nobles cower if they think they're getting threatened by anyone connected to organized crime. Especially if they're dodgy enough to have used its services. But Lord Bardviss must have been relieved to receive our letter—as if we're working on the same side. By kidnapping you, we were helping him," Felix elucidated.

Lilliana went white. "How could Arianna and my mother allow that?" she asked in horror.

"You can't blame them. I'm sure they had no idea. I hear that Marx can be very manipulative. I read the letters between him and Arianna— he came across completely respectable."

"My mother always has been a sucker for a perfect gentleman," Lilliana remarked with distaste. "I knew Lord Bardviss was hiding something! This is one instance where I wish I wasn't right. The thing that doesn't make any sense is why my father flew into the Everstorm."

"I think I might have a lead on that too," Felix told her, and pulled out the will from beneath his shirt.

⌒

Felix sat on the bed next to Lilliana while she looked over the will. He tried to figure out what she was thinking, but she remained expressionless.

"Why wouldn't my uncle leave his half of the estate and business to Arianna? It doesn't make any sense," Lilliana remarked.

"I thought the same thing initially. But what if her father knew what she was up to and wanted to separate her from the business? The estate and business go hand in hand. By leaving her ten percent, he's ensuring she has enough to gain profit, but not enough to have any sway or control. What if your father and uncle were making plans for your father to take over the business?" Felix proposed.

"That would make sense. Do you think Arianna knew of it?"

"One of the staff said they heard your father and Arianna arguing over the will the night your uncle died. They also said there was a missing dragon from the stables that was ignored during the investigation."

"Stars. Do you think Arianna could be responsible for my father's disappearance?"

"I don't know. She does have a motive—that being said, she had the chance to alter the will and didn't take it, she seemed hesitant to change it. She said she wants to talk to you," Felix reported.

"She said that to you?" Lilliana asked in surprise.

"No...I overheard a conversation she was having with her hand-maiden," Felix admitted.

"Draya?"

"I presume so. High cheekbones, long dark brown hair, gold-brown eyes."

"That's her. I've never liked her. My cousin gives her way too much slack, she's completely forgotten her place. She talks to Arianna like they're equals and whispers poisonous influence into her ear."

Felix smirked. "Funny, she doesn't like you either."

"Did she say that?!" Lilliana exclaimed.

Felix answered with a telling expression.

"The nerve! My uncle rescued her from the slave market when she was a child, you know? He employed her as Arianna's handmaiden to provide company for my cousin after my aunt died," Lilliana divulged.

"She's certainly doing that," Felix remarked.

Lilliana narrowed her eyes. "What's that supposed to mean?"

"I saw them...kissing."

Lilliana gasped. "No!"

Felix nodded. "I got the impression they're in love."

"Nonsense! Arianna wouldn't dare stoop so low!"

Felix cocked an eyebrow. "Like you stooped to me?"

Lilliana opened her mouth and then closed it again. "I didn't mean it like that. I'm sorry. I keep forgetting that..."

"We're not equals?" Felix offered.

"I keep forgetting, because in my mind we are," she asserted.

Felix smirked. "Nice recovery. Maybe Arianna keeps forgetting too?" he proposed.

Lilliana pursed her lips. "The difference is, even if Draya were highborn I would still see her as below my cousin, because she's a terrible person."

"Really? How well do you know her?" Felix asked.

"Well enough. I'm an excellent judge of character," Lilliana proclaimed.

Felix smiled. "Ha! You're a terrible judge of character."

"What makes you say that?" Lilliana asked indignantly.

Felix took a step towards her. "Because you're keeping company with me," he said, then he leaned down and kissed her.

# THE BLUE FAERIE

Gwena sighed, the pain of Benji's words finally subsiding. She sat on the side of the road where he'd left her, watching the world go by. She watched people in conversations with one another, some in intellectual discussions or animated arguments, and others filled with love and joy. She watched the carriages roll past carrying nobles in high fashion and the poor children in dirty rags running behind them, rolling hoops down the street with laughter. Somehow it brought her peace, reminding her how small her problems were in the grand scheme of things. It was such a beautiful world she lived in, and she felt overwhelmingly lucky to be a part of it. Not just for the clean and tidy bits, but for all of it. All of the sorrow and pain and hardship, the diversity that gave it color—all of it made the joys and pleasures that much sweeter. Despite the doubt Benji sowed, her love for Bastian was still there warming her heart, and she treasured it. She thought about him and no longer cared what the future brought for them, as long as they were together. If only they could have the opportunity to become bored with each other, that would be wonderful.

"Please Stars, please bring him back to me," Gwena whispered to the Watchers.

Then she stood and dusted herself off and made her way back towards The Wildsinger's Club.

When Gwena reached the club, she couldn't even think about working on Benji's suit. He'd walked off with the ones he'd purchased for her to alter anyway. So instead, she found her way to the cocktail bar and pulled up a stool. The bartender from the day before was there cleaning glasses.

"Hey, little lady, how was the city? Did you see the Science Fair?" he inquired.

"I did, it was brilliant!"

"See, I told you it's first class."

Gwena smiled. "You were right."

"What can I get for you?" he asked.

"I'm not sure, I've only really had ales and ciders. Is there something you can recommend?"

"Only had ales and ciders?! My dear, you've been drinking all wrong," the bartender proclaimed.

Gwena laughed. "Is that right?"

"Do you prefer sweet or sour?" he asked her.

"Hmm, is it possible to have a little of both?"

"Why of course! How about a Gypsy Kiss? It's slightly sour, slightly sweet, with a nutty finish. It's very nice."

Gwena smiled. "Sounds perfect."

She watched as the bartender began adding ingredients into a metal shaker with expert precision. He shook life into the concoction and poured it into a frosted glass, dusting the foamy egg white with nutmeg and topping it with a cherry. She took a sip and was delighted by the flavor. "It's delicious!" she exclaimed in pleasant surprise. "I never knew alcohol could taste so good."

The bartender laughed. "In my opinion, if it doesn't taste good it isn't worth drinking."

"I've been converted," Gwena proclaimed and took another sip of her Gypsy Kiss.

"If you're going to be a part of the club then you must know your cocktails. Come see me once a day and I'll serve you something new. Consider it job training," he said with a wink.

"Well, I do take my work very seriously," Gwena returned wryly.

"Ha! Name's Ramone, by the way. I'm the bar manager. I work here most days," he said, and offered her his hand.

Gwena shook it. "Gwena Stently. Pleasure to meet you."

"I hear you do magic?" Ramone asked.

"I dabble," Gwena admitted.

"Know any card tricks?"

"A few."

Ramone put a deck of cards on the bar in front of her. "I'll give you ten cwips if you can show me a trick that I don't know."

Gwena smiled and picked up the deck of cards, shuffling it with one hand.

Half an hour later, Gwena was on her third cocktail and Ramone was staring at the card in his hand in disbelief. "How'd you do it?" he asked her in wonderment.

"With magic of course," she told him with a twinkle in her eye.

"I almost believe it. I've never seen any card tricks so good, they're going to keep me up at night," he declared in earnest, and put a stack of ten cwips on the bar.

Gwena smiled. "Can I ask you a question, Ramone?"

"Sure, go right ahead."

"Do you believe in love?"

Ramone looked at her with concern. "Benji get in your head, did he?"

Gwena held up her pointer and thumb with an inch between them.

Ramone sighed. "I think love's a complicated thing. Even poets haven't solved its mystery. But of course I believe in it. My wife passed on years ago and my love for her still burns true. Now it's just our daughter Macy and me. And I tell you what, the love I have for that girl is like no other. I don't think you really know what love is until you have a child. That love burns fierce and it never dies," he said.

Gwena smiled. "She sounds nice."

"She's the best. That girl brings sunshine everywhere she goes."

"She's very lucky to have a father like you," Gwena remarked.

"Ah, I'm sure she could have better. But lucky for me, I'm the one she's got," Ramone said, then took her empty glass away and wiped the counter under it. He put his cloth down and looked at Gwena. "Don't let Benji's pessimism get to you. He's only the way he is because his heart's all broken up inside."

"What do you mean?"

"No one else knows this, but Benji was engaged to a girl before he worked at the club. He thought she was the love of his life—until he caught her in bed with his brother. It broke him up good. I think part of the reason he works down here is to try and escape love altogether," Ramone told her.

Gwena digested that. "Thanks, Ramone. For everything. I'll be coming back tomorrow for my job training," she promised with a warm and grateful smile, and stood to leave.

"Don't forget your cwips," Ramone reminded her, gesturing to the small stack on the bar.

"Consider it a tip for your excellent hospitality."

Ramone smiled. "Have a good night, little lady."

"You too," Gwena returned, and headed for her room.

When Gwena reached her door, she found a card and a bouquet of yellow tulips sitting outside it. She picked them up and read the card.

*I'm sorry for being a complete twat.*

*— Benji*

Gwena smiled. *Perhaps Benji has some redeemable qualities,* she thought. Right after she'd arranged the bouquet on her bedside table, there was a knock at her door. She answered it and found Benji on the other side.

"You alright?" he asked her.

She was surprised to see him genuinely concerned.

"I'm getting there, thank you for asking. And thank you for the flowers, they're beautiful."

Benji nodded somberly. "I really am sorry, I was a complete arse back there, you didn't deserve that. I want to make it up to you. It's my night off. Let me take you out tonight."

"Oh, that's really not necessary. But thank you."

"Yes, it is. You've been in the Heartland a couple days now and you've hardly seen it. It's a whole different place at night. That's when it really comes alive. And if you don't let me, we'll both spend the evening stewing on what a terrible person I am," Benji insisted.

Gwena smiled. "I'm not sure that's exactly true, but I would like to see the city at night. Alright, I'll come out, thank you."

"Great," Benji said, "I'll pick you up at the Thrixing Hour. Oh, and wear something nice," he added.

Gwena watched him go in complete bewilderment.

Gwena stood looking in her mirror ten minutes before the Thrixing Hour. She was wearing one of her new dresses from the Treasure Box. It was an original by a well-known designer from Water-Town, the fashion district of Equillian. She never thought she'd be able to own something from her line. Brand new, the dress would've cost her three years of her

Westdock wages. But the Treasure Box was practically giving it away. She imagined the original owner to be an aristocrat who wore it to a single dinner party and then gave it up as old hat. *Her loss,* Gwena thought. The dress was a beautiful seafoam green, almost an exact match of Gwena's eyes. It fit her snugly on top, had short sleeves, and fanned out at the waist in a wide skirt that ended at her calves, with stiff white lace underneath. It was a style she'd never seen in Westdock, and one she liked very much. The bright green belt around her waist fastened with two gold metal circles. She wore her hair up in an intricate knot held together by a long decorative pin and finished off the outfit with cream white shoes. She smiled at her reflection. For the first time, she actually felt like a woman rather than a girl. She couldn't believe her coming of age was only a week away—it felt like she'd hardly had a childhood and now it was almost over. If only Bastian could be there to celebrate her birthday with her. She instinctively touched the pearl around her neck and then there was a knock on her door. Gwena grabbed her handbag and answered it. Benji was standing there dressed in a handsome navy blue suit.

"Nice dress," he remarked.

"Thanks. I like your suit," she returned.

"Cheers. Shall we?"

Gwena cleared her throat. "I just want to clarify one thing. This isn't intended as a date, is it?"

Benji chuckled. "Of course not," he answered with an amused smile.

When they reached the small courtyard outside The Apothecary's speakeasy, it was raining lightly. Benji produced an umbrella from his jacket just large enough to protect them both. He held it over Gwena's head and guided her to the door.

The speakeasy was hopping. They had to squeeze through the crowd. There was a swing band playing lively music and the dance floor was filled with people jiving, flipping, throwing, and dipping their partners around the floor. Smoke hung in the air like tendrils of fog. By the time they got outside to the main street the rain was coming down hard. The cobblestones glistened with the light from the Everfire streetlights. Gwena had to stay close to Benji to keep from getting drenched.

"You hungry?" he asked her.

"Yes, I suppose I am."

"Good," Benji said, and led them down a few laneways until they came to a door with a beautifully ornate entrance. It had brass embellishments around it like a fancy picture frame, and the sign above it read *The Deluge* in looping cursive.

Benji opened the door for her, and Gwena stepped inside. The dimly lit entryway led to a dark hallway with a ceiling lit with tiny points of light that looked like stars. Benji guided her through to the restaurant, and Gwena gasped. It was domed with a high dark ceiling lit like the night sky. The floor seemed to be a lake, its dark water dotted with lit floating candles. In the center, a classical ensemble played soft music on a wooden raft. Surrounding that were twelve little islands, each one covered in lush grass and only big enough for a ring walkway around the single table and chairs that adorned them. The tables were lit with real candles in their centers. Several gondoliers ferried guests to and from their tables on the islands. A gondola pulled up to where Gwena and Benji stood.

"Good evening, monsieur Moon. Welcome back to the Deluge. Your reservation is ready for you," the gondolier announced.

"Thank you," Benji replied.

"Right this way," the man said, offering his hand to Gwena to help her inside the gondola.

Gwena stepped inside and sat down on one of the velvet benches. Benji sat across from her, and the gondolier pushed them off from the shore.

Gwena looked out in wonder as he rowed them to one of the islands.

"Can I get you anything to drink?" he asked.

"Please. The lady will have your Enchanted Rose cocktail and I'll have the Smoking Gun. Also, some sparkling water for the table. Thanks," Benji ordered.

"Very good, sir," the gondolier said.

Benji pulled out Gwena's seat for her, then sat down across from her.

"This place is amazing," Gwena exclaimed in awe.

"It's one of my favorites, I reserve a table once a month," Benji told her.

"Oh, I hope I'm not taking anyone's place?"

"Not at all, I generally come alone."

"Oh, I see. Are there menus?" Gwena asked.

"No. It's chef's choice, the meals change every night. It's always exquisite. But if you have any dietary restrictions, they're able to accommodate."

"Only rare and endangered species, oh, and I tend to steer away from humans and house pets," Gwena stated candidly.

Benji chuckled. "I'd be worried otherwise."

Gwena shrugged, "One woman's house pet is another woman's delicacy."

"As revolting as that is, I'm sure you're right."

"You eat fish, don't you?" Gwena asked.

"Only the ones that haven't been named," Benji returned with an amused smile, then he asked, "So tell me, what do they do for fun in Westdock?"

"You mean, besides visiting the renowned cathouses?" Gwena jested.

Benji smirked. "Yes, besides that."

"I wouldn't know, my father always said work was too important for me to waste my time in other ways—especially partaking in such frivolous pastimes as having fun. Didn't stop him though, he was off at the pub every night," Gwena remarked.

"And your mother?" Benji asked.

"She died when I was twelve," Gwena replied somberly.

Benji frowned. "I'm sorry. I have some taste of what that's like—my mother died when I was seven."

"I'm sorry to hear that, it's a terrible thing to lose a mother."

"Yes, and even worse to have to go through life without one," Benji stated.

"Yes, true," Gwena agreed.

"If your father had such a tight grip on you, how'd you end up here?" Benji queried.

"My friends' acquired a pair of train tickets to the Heartland. We were going to escape Westdock together—unfortunately, circumstances didn't allow them to join me."

"Why not?"

"It's a bit of a long story, and one you might find hard to believe."

"Now you've got my attention. I enjoy a good story, and we have plenty of time to fill," Benji said.

Just then the gondolier returned. He pulled the boat alongside the island and tethered it to a wooden stake. He lifted one of the velvet seats in the gondola to reveal a hidden compartment and pulled out a tray with sparkling water and a silver cloche, which he lifted to reveal their cocktails. He served Gwena first. Her drink was presented in a glass rose with a chilled red drink in the decorative bud. The rose glass was covered with a clear bell jar filled with smoke. The waiter lifted the bell jar and the white vapor wafted out with the smell of lavender. The fragrant fog was still pooled in the bud of the glass when Gwena lifted it to her lips.

Benji's glass was almost as impressive, a tall thin glass filled with a dark brown drink that was smoking with the smell of mahogany.

"Your Smoking Gun, sir. Please enjoy," the waiter announced, and then left them alone.

"This is quite magnificent. I've completely forgotten what we were talking about," Gwena laughed.

"You were about to tell me why you came to the Heartland alone," Benji reminded her, taking a sip from his cocktail.

"Right. Have you heard about the Duchess of Westdock's disappearance?" Gwena asked.

"I recall reading something about it in the paper."

"Well, my friends were at her castle the night she went missing. And somehow they got mixed up in all of it. One went missing with the duchess, and the other was targeted as a suspect and pursued by the castle's guard. He barely escaped on a ship that was leaving port. Now that ship is being pursued by Lord Bardviss's galleons with the intention to sink it, and I don't know if I'll ever see him again," Gwena confessed, clasping her pearl necklace.

"The man who gave you that necklace is the one on the ship?" Benji queried.

Gwena nodded.

"Wow, that's a much more intriguing story than I expected...and makes me feel even more like a royal arse than I already did. I'm sorry for what I said this morning—about your friend not being here. That wasn't fair," Benji apologized.

"No, it wasn't. Thank you...I suppose I also owe you an apology. I judged you unfairly. I can't blame you for your clients' choices, nor presume to know or understand their situations. And whatever you think of love, it's none of my business. You can think of it however you like. I shouldn't have tried to convince you otherwise."

"Thank you, and I you. Just because my cold heart has given up on love, doesn't mean I need to ruin it for everyone else," he admitted.

"I really do hope you find it, or at least it finds you."

Pain and discomfort flashed in Benji's eyes. "As much as I appreciate the sentiment, please don't. Every love I have ever had in my life has brought me nothing but misery."

Gwena smiled sadly. "Well, currently it seems both of us are destined to live without it, regardless. So, here's to happiness without love," she toasted, holding up her glass.

Benji smiled and clinked her glass with his. "To happiness without love."

By the end of dinner the rain had stopped. Benji led Gwena through the Heartlands's network of laneways to a boutique cocktail bar that made unique concoctions to fit your taste. Their server asked them to recall their favorite smell. Gwena's was a spring garden in bloom after a thunderstorm. She was given a sunny cocktail consisting of gin, sparkling water, and simple syrup flavored with elderflower, rose water, cucumber, and lemon. It was lightly sweet, very refreshing, and positively delightful. After that, Benji took her to a glassed-in rooftop lounge overlooking the whole city—the expanse of lights from the roads and buildings reflected the night sky. Next, they went to see a live band playing in the Heartland's botanical gardens. They were walking back towards the club several drinks past tipsy, when Gwena heard music pouring out of a little hole-in-the-wall joint. She walked towards it curiously.

"Oh no, don't go in there," Benji warned.

"Why not, what is it?" Gwena asked.

"It's where music goes to die," Benji proclaimed.

Gwena ignored him and popped her head inside. "It's a Lyrebird bar!" she exclaimed enthusiastically.

"Exactly," Benji stated dryly.

"Come on!" Gwena urged, pulling Benji inside.

"Please no, I'd rather listen to a bag of screeching cockatoos."

"Oh shush! People like me need Lyrebird bars. For those of us who don't have your talent, it's our only opportunity to sing on stage," Gwena insisted.

"Anyone can sing well with proper training. Singing without it is as bad as screeching an untuned violin. And just as cruel to everyone in earshot," Benji remarked.

"Go on back to the club then. I'm not leaving until I've sung at least one song," Gwena asserted stubbornly.

Benji sighed. "I can't let you wander these streets alone. If anything happened to you, Bonnie would kill me—and I mean that literally, not figuratively."

"Well then, I guess you'll just have to stay and listen to me screech my untuned strings," Gwena declared.

Benji groaned and followed her inside. It was a small place with a three-piece band playing the background melody for the woman singing onstage. She was belting out an old classic. Benji put his head in his hands. Gwena walked up to a woman who was taking down names and added hers to the list. Then she sat down on a bench at the back beside Benji.

"What song are you going to sing?" Benji asked her.

"None of your beeswax."

"Please tell me you're not far down the line?"

"There's two ahead of me. You should sing something, it'll give these poor people's ears some respite," Gwena suggested.

Benji laughed. "Nice try, little bird."

"Well, why not?"

"Sing your heart out all you like, just leave me out of it," he asserted.

"Clearly you need another drink, my round!" Gwena declared, and stood resolutely, walking off to find the bar. She returned several minutes later with two shot glasses and handed one over. They clinked them together and threw them back.

"What was that?!" Benji exclaimed with a ghastly expression.

"I'm not sure. I asked the bar woman for two shots of liquid courage, and this is what she gave me. She called it the Blue Faerie."

Benji's eyes shot wide, "The Blue Faerie?! Please tell me you're joking?"

"No, why?"

"Haha, shick. Well, little bird, you said you've never tried mind meddlers—I suppose tonight's your opportunity," Benji laughed.

"What are you talking about?"

"The Blue Faerie's a liquid hallucinogen…amongst other things. It was concocted in a lab by some apothecary trying to cure depression using a cocktail of various endorphin-inducing chemicals and the essence of a toxic blue mushroom from the eastern marshes. It was discarded as legitimate medicine, but taken up eagerly by those looking for a little extra kick to their social evening," Benji explained.

"Extra kick? As in a drug?!" Gwena exclaimed in panic. "Oh, Stars! I think I'm going to be sick."

"Relax, you'll be fine. The trick is not to fight it. Just imagine you're in a boat on a rogue wave and ride it out."

Gwena took several deep breaths in an attempt to calm her panic and tried to relax. It didn't take long before she could feel the effects of the Blue Faerie kicking in. It was a rush of overwhelming euphoria. She gave herself over to it and felt as giddy as a schoolgirl, a fit of giggles bubbled out of her.

Benji smiled. Then Gwena heard her name being called from the stage and her face drained of color. "Oh, Stars, what do I do?!"

"Don't worry, there's no way you could be any worse than those two," Benji comforted.

"That's not what I'm concerned about!" Gwena exclaimed in panic.

Benji laughed, "Come on, what's the worst that could happen? You'll be fine, just enjoy it."

Gwena straightened her dress and walked up onto the stage, her inhibitions melting away with every step. The band began to play her song. She looked out at the small audience and felt delightfully joyful. The colors in the room were richer and more vibrant. She saw details she hadn't noticed before—the Everfire chandelier lighting the room had crystals shaped like stars, the carpet was an underwater scene with fish and coral. The fish seemed to be swimming, as if they were coming to life. It was all so strange and oddly mesmerizing. She found herself completely present in the moment. She began to sing, and it was as if she could feel her breath vibrating her vocal chords and see it floating out her mouth and resonating into the room.

*Lips of cherry, hair of soot, skin of ivory.*
*your love rides the wind,*
*never changing with the tides,*
*no matter how far,*
*it always finds me.*

*Without it, I'd be lost at sea.*
*The battering gales would've long ruined me.*
*But in everything, I find your love's serenity.*
*It's the light in the stars that guide me,*
*Leading me back home to your sweet melody...*

Gwena sang sweetly, her voice spellbinding the whole room into silence. Once she finished, the audience clapped enthusiastically. Gwena smiled drunkenly and walked off the stage back to Benji.

"Wow, I'm impressed, little bird, you've got a nice set of pipes," Benji remarked.

"Thank you," Gwena returned with a slight curtsy. "That was quite the experience. Everything feels so…so…visceral. It's like I can see and feel absolutely everything!"

"Yup. I think we better get you back to the club, hey?" Benji advised, and started to stand.

Gwena pulled him back down. "Not until you sing a song, mister!" she asserted stubbornly.

"We're here for you, not me, remember?"

"Alright then, if you're going to be like that." Gwena pulled a deck of cards from her handbag and fanned them out. "Pick a card, any card."

"What are you doing? Is this a magic trick?"

"Just pick a card."

Benji chose a card and looked at it without letting Gwena see it was the three of clubs. Gwena cut the deck in two. "Put it here," she instructed, and Benji placed his card in the center of the deck face down. Gwena put the two halves back together and started drawing cards from the top of the deck and placing them face up on the table in front of Benji one at a time. One after the other she laid them out in a snake-like pattern so that all the cards could be seen. About three quarters of the way through the deck Gwena stopped, she held onto the next card at the top of the deck and said, "I'll bet you the next card I flip over will be your card."

Benji looked down and saw the three of clubs amongst the cards that had already been laid on the table. "Alright."

"If I win, you have to sing a song. If you win, we can leave right now," Gwena proposed.

Benji smiled. "Sounds good to me."

Gwena held out her hand and Benji shook it, then she leaned forward and flipped over the three of clubs. Benji's smile dropped.

"What song are you going to choose?" Gwena asked cheerily.

"You completely played me!" Benji protested indignantly.

"True. Surely you realize 'trick' is the word following *magic*. You stated as much yourself," Gwena remarked frankly.

"You're really going to make me do this?"

"Don't be such a sourpuss. Who knows, you might actually enjoy it."

"Ha! Alright, little bird, I know just the song to sing," Benji proclaimed, and went to put his name on the list.

When Benji's turn came, he stepped up onto the stage and said a few words to the band. They began to play and he gave them a little gesture to pick up the tempo before he began to sing,

*You played me, honey.*
*You set a trap to catch me,*
*And I wandered right inside.*
*I wandered right inside.*
*But don't you misjudge me,*
*I let you have me,*
*And came along for the ride,*
*I came along for the ride.*

*Don't think I don't see*
*Those aces up your sleeve.*
*That look in your eye*
*As you saunter up to me.*
*Don't mistake me, honey,*
*I'm far from easy,*
*I just like what I see,*
*I just like what I see.*

*So come here, baby,*
*Let's dance tell we're dizzy,*
*Come waste the night with me.*
*Come waste the night with me!*

Benji performed the upbeat piece with vigor. Gwena laughed in delight, and the room erupted in a roaring cheer at the song's end, Gwena whistling loudest of all. Benji smiled and shook hands with the band, complimenting them on their performance and they complimented him profusely in return, handing him a business card with the hope he might be interested in singing some gigs with them in the future. Benji pocketed the card and came back down to join Gwena.

"That was brilliant!" Gwena exclaimed.

Benji put his hands in his pockets. "Can we go now?"

"Certainly!" Gwena grinned, happy to see that despite his trepidations, Benji was clearly enjoying himself. Together they walked out, stepping into the Everfire lamplit streets wet and glistening from the falling rain. It felt like a waking dream. Everything was so still and so alive. Benji pulled out his umbrella and held it over Gwena. She stepped out from its protection and tipped her face towards the rain with her eyes closed and smiled, welcoming the water's embrace. She laughed and held both her arms out, spinning amongst the falling drops that reflected the lamplight like sparkling diamonds. "I have to say, this feeling is extraordinary!"

Benji pulled a silver case from his pocket and lit up a puff-stick, "Sure, there's a reason people chase it."

"You don't seem to be enjoying it," Gwena remarked.

"It's great. I just know what's on the other side."

"Have you ever heard the saying—don't let fear of the approaching dawn keep you from enjoying the stars?" Gwena asked.

"I can't say I have," Benji admitted.

"If you don't enjoy the moment while it's good, then the payment for it will feel like robbery," Gwena cautioned.

The night air was filled with instrumental music from a couple of buskers playing a fiddle and a guitar under the awning of a closed shopfront. Benji dropped a few coins in the guitar case as they passed. "Alright, little bird. How shall we make the most of it then?" he asked her.

"Put down that grumpy face and just—what is it you said? Ride the wave?" Gwena smiled, making a little wave with her hand.

Benji laughed. "Alright." He put out his puff-stick and closed his umbrella, tucking it away. Then he held out his hand to Gwena. She took it and he twirled her into his arms and led her through a dance, spinning her this way and that in perfect time to the buskers' music beneath the falling rain. Gwena smiled and laughed at the song's end.

"I know what we should do next!" Gwena announced enthusiastically.

Benji raised a questioning eyebrow.

"Come on!" Gwena grabbed Benji's hand, pulling him towards a little vendor selling roasted chestnuts and hot chocolate. She bought a hot chocolate for each of them and then took a long drink. "Have you ever tasted anything so wonderful?"

"Never in my life," Benji smiled, cradling the warm paper cup in his hands.

"Speaking of enjoying the stars, is there anywhere we can see them around here?" Gwena inquired, looking up at the cloud-covered sky. "It's what I miss most from home," she confessed.

"Not really, the city creates too much light pollution," Benji said, then paused in thought. "Actually, there is one place."

"Really?! Where?"

"We'll have to break a few laws to get there," Benji told her.

Gwena grinned. "Sounds brilliant!"

Benji laughed, "Follow me then," and led her in a new direction.

Gwena followed Benji through several winding back streets until they came to the Hall of Scientific Study. It looked even more grand in the evening. There were small Everfire spotlights encircling it on the ground, directing their beams up at the building, casting long shadows between the streams of light. The whole grounds was closed off with a locked gate.

Benji led her around the back and helped her climb over the fence before jumping over himself. Normally, Gwena would've had reservations about performing such a task in the dress she was wearing, but with her inhibitions washed away and awareness heightened by the Blue Faerie, she scaled the fence expertly without a care in the world. Benji led her to an entrance tucked in the back wall. It was locked of course, but he seemed to have anticipated that and stepped into the back garden purposefully, searching under a statue of Pansophy—the Time Keeper of the nineteenth hour and the constellation of universal knowledge—and produced a small key. He walked back to her and used the key to unlock the door, holding it open for her.

"I used to work for the groundskeeper here when I was a kid, looks like his habits haven't changed," Benji explained.

"Is that right?" Gwena said, stepping cautiously inside the building.

The place felt even more expansive and grand without the people in it. Their footsteps echoed throughout the hall. The grand orrery looming above them in the center moved in perfect time with the rotation of the stars and planets. Gwena walked up to it and gazed at it in awe before Benji grabbed her shoulders and gently guided her away.

"Come on, there's a guard who keeps watch at night. We need to stay out of view. Follow me," he whispered, leading her up a flight of stairs.

Gwena followed Benji up three stories before he took her through a discreet side door that led them to a narrow staircase spiralling upwards. Gwena followed Benji, running her hand along the stone wall as she climbed. All of her senses were enhanced, every bump and divot her hand passed over felt so interesting and wonderful. The staircase led them to a round open room. The walls and ceiling were a glass dome—making it feel as though there were no walls or ceiling at all. In the center of the room was a huge telescope on a raised platform. Gwena realized they must be in one of the building's towers. She walked to the glass wall and gaped at the view of the city and the stars—they both shone brilliantly, as if one was a reflection of the other. "Wow," she whispered.

"You haven't seen anything yet," Benji proclaimed, and guided her to the telescope.

Gwena stepped up onto the viewing platform and looked through the eyepiece. Benji helped her adjust the focus until the view became clear. Gwena gasped. She could see not only the stars, but also the clouds of purple and gold dust that encircled them. When Benji guided the telescope to the moon, she could see the craters on its surface. "It's incredible!" she exclaimed.

"I don't think you can get a better view of the stars than this," he remarked.

"It's beyond anything I could've imagined. Do you want to have a turn?" Gwena pulled away from the eyepiece and found herself inches from Benji's face. She froze, her nose almost touching his. They both stood there paralyzed, gazing into each other's eyes. She felt his breath on her lips, and it sent a tingling current of electricity down her body all the way to her toes. She felt a warm magnetic pull in his direction—but she didn't dare move. Benji was just as still, gazing into her eyes with the look of someone battling the same feelings she was. He turned away.

"That's alright, I've seen it many times. I used to sneak up here often when I was a boy," he told her, stepping down from the viewing platform and walking to the glass to look out at the view of the city.

"What made you stop coming?" Gwena inquired.

Benji didn't reply for several moments. "Some things are better left unknown, little bird. Probably best we head back, hey? It's getting late," he announced, and started back down the stair pathway. Gwena took one more look at the view before following after.

Gwena and Benji spent the rest of the journey back to The Apothecary in silence. Once they were in the elevator on their way down to the club, Gwena finally spoke. "Thank you for bringing me out tonight. I had a really lovely time."

"Yeah, me too. It was fun."

"It was, wasn't it? You really are an incredible singer, you know? I saw the band hand you their card. Have you ever thought about leaving the club and singing full time?" Gwena asked him.

"No. I like things the way they are. Life at the club's less…complicated. I need that right now."

"How long have you worked there?"

"Three years."

Gwena and Benji came out of the lift and rounded the corner on the path to The Wildsinger's Club.

"Do you get every Thrixday off?" Gwena asked.

"Yeah, currently."

"Well, next Thrixday happens to be my birthday. It seems serendipitous. Maybe we could get a few of us together, make a small night of it on the town?" Gwena proposed.

Benji scratched the back of his neck uncomfortably. "Sure, sounds good," he said, but Gwena got the impression he didn't think it sounded good at all.

By the time Gwena and Benji got back to the club, the party there was in full swing. Benji showed Gwena a back way up to their rooms so they didn't have to pass through the nightly carouse at the club. He brought her to her door and said goodnight, and Gwena closed herself behind it. She leaned her back against the door and clutched at her pearl necklace. The world was still swimming in the state of some strange waking dream. "Shick have mercy, what are you playing at? I'm too fragile for your games, leave me and my aching heart in peace," she told the Star-meddling spirit. Then she readied herself for bed and fell into a sleep riddled with troubled dreams of her and Benji's night together combined with horrifying images of Bastian on a ship being attacked by Lord Bardviss's galleons.

# SPINNING DICE

As Bastian sat repairing lines that afternoon, he thought about what his enchanted object would be for his following lesson with Tink. He wished his head wasn't so fogged with exhaustion. Using it would be so much easier if he could only catch up on some sleep. His nightly lessons with Falgo were tiring enough, but the worst part was having to stay up for them—for fear if he fell asleep, he wouldn't wake on time, or at all. He paused in his work and massaged the back of his neck, then suddenly had the answer. *That's it! That's what my enchanted object will be. A personal alarm. Something to notify me at a desired time, so that I can sleep without having to worry about missing my lessons with Falgo,* he thought. *It will have to be something I can wear on my person, something small that can be disguised as something common...*

Bastian looked around at Guts, Dagger, and Tails. They all wore some sort of jewelry or other. Dagger wore a gold hoop earring and rings on his fingers. Guts had both his ears pierced with gold. And Tails wore several leather bracelets and a gold ring. The rest of the crew were similarly adorned. Jewelry was common fashion amongst the pirates. If Bastian made his object into something similar, it would only help him blend into his surroundings better. But what would it be? It would have to be something he could fashion out of the materials he had on hand. If Bastian were back in Westdock, he could've used the blacksmith's forge. The blacksmith he'd worked for on Thrixing days made everything from jewelry to horseshoes to armor. His skill ranged from beating bars of iron as if they were butter to intricately twisting precious metals into fine jewelry like a spider weaving its silk. Bastian had learned a lot from him. He only wished he could have access to his workshop now. Since that wasn't an option, he began running through the materials he had available to him. The kitchen had metal, he could palm a spoon or a fork—surely Doc wouldn't miss it. There was plenty of wood and canvas from tattered sails and the like in the pile of discarded debris on the shore. But if he was going to be wearing the piece all the time, he'd want it to be something flexible and comfortable, as well as durable and strong. Bastian looked down at the line he'd been mending and almost laughed out loud.

*Of course!* It had been right there staring him in the face the whole time.

On galley duty that evening Bastian was given the task of cutting carrots. Now that he was finally able to use the Ghost Element, he tried creating cutting lines along the purple vegetable, just as he'd tried on the tomatoes the day before.

This time the Ghost Element separated itself into twenty fine vertical lines evenly spaced across the carrots length. Bastian used them as a guide. While he chopped he grinned in delight. And Doc commented that he'd never seen more even cuts in all his life. After that Bastian began looking for ways he could use the Element with everything he did. The more he used it, the easier and more intuitive it became.

At dinner, Rhino and Stork were talking about all the things they hoped to spend their coin on in Jaxland—girls, daggers, a new pair of boots. Cricket, however, wasn't joining he conversation. He was sitting next to Bastian on the opposite side, eating his food in miserable silence. Bastian listened absently to the men talk, stirring up the Ghost Element under the table, turning it into a rose wagon in the palm of his hand and then disintegrating it back to dust again.

*Why doesn't Tink want me to make an enchanted object that can create coin?* he wondered.

He would've thought it would be the first thing an alchemist would create on a pirate ship. Having the ability, it seemed silly not to. It would solve so many problems. Bastian would never have to worry about coin again. He could pay back Cricket for the clothes he'd lent him, providing his friend with the means to spend time with the woman he loved. He hated seeing Cricket so miserable. He had such a carefree disposition most of the time, and to see him so down was downright depressing. Then Bastian was struck with an idea.

"Hey, Stork. Are you throwing dice tonight?" he inquired.

Stork stopped talking to Rhino in midsentence. "I plan ta. Why? Ya interested in tryin' yer luck?"

Cricket looked up with concern.

"Don't *yew* start now, Dodger!" Rhino exclaimed.

"Take it from me, mate, if ya 'ave any coin, it be best ta keep it," Cricket admonished.

"Hey! Dodger be a grown man, 'e can do what 'e likes," Stork objected. "Are ya seriously interested?" he asked Bastian.

Bastian shrugged. "Sure. I'll try my luck," he said, and placed the rose wagon on the table.

All three of the pirates eyes widened and Cricket quickly threw a handkerchief over the coin and looked around to make sure no one was looking in their direction. "Are ya stupid? Don't go flashin' coin like that 'ere!"

"Where'd ya get a rose wagon?" Stork asked evenly.

"I've been saving it for a rainy day," Bastian proclaimed, placing the coin back into his pocket.

"Do ya 'ave anythin' lower?"

"Nope. That's it."

"The men won't gamble anythin' that high. The farthest they'll go be bettin' jolly rogers. An' good luck findin' someone ta break it," Stork said.

A rose wagon was worth ten jolly rogers. And it was true, they tended to be hard to break. Vendors didn't like accepting them if they had to give you much back, because it emptied the change reserve they needed for other customers. And unless you were in one of the ritzier parts of Equillian, few things were priced that high.

"Actually, I was hoping you'd break it for me—temporarily, mind you. If you give me ten jolly rogers, you can hold onto the rose wagon as security on the loan. I'll trade you back when the night's done, and even let you keep one jolly roger to compensate you for the trouble," Bastian proposed.

Stork laughed. "An' what if ya lose it all?"

Bastian shrugged. "Then you keep the rose wagon."

Stork thought about that for a moment. "Alright. I can't find much fault in that. Besides, I'm lookin' forward ta 'avin' ya spin with us," he declared, clapping Bastian on the shoulder.

Stork counted out ten jolly rogers from his coin pouch and handed them to Bastian under the table, and Bastian handed him the rose wagon in exchange.

Stork bit into the coin to make sure it was real. Satisfied, he dropped it into his coin purse. "Meet us up top at the start o' Twillos," he said.

Bastian nodded. Cricket and Rhino looked at each other with concern.

After dinner, Bastian found his way to the top deck and joined the group of sailors huddled around a barrel on the poop deck. On top of the barrel was a Moon Die half the size of Bastian's fist. The die was made of white polished whale bone. It had four square sides that tapered to a point on the bottom, and a thin straight handle coming out of its crown used for spinning it like a top. Each of the four sides had a moon phase on it—a full moon, depicted by a painted dark blue outline of a circle, a new moon, represented by a circle completely filled in, a Half Moon, illustrated by a half-filled outline of a circle, and lastly, a crescent moon, represented by a circle completely filled in, except for a thin crescent along one side. At the start of the game everyone playing anted up the agreed denomination of coin into a pot in the center. Then the men took turns spinning the die in clockwise order. If a player spun the die and it landed on the full moon, it meant the player took the whole pot. A new moon meant nothing happened. A half moon meant the player took half the pot, and a crescent moon meant the player had to put a coin into it. Four pirates would play at a time, while those watching bet on who they thought would be the winner. A round of the game was finished when the pot was emptied—at which point the players could choose whether they wanted to play again or step out of the game.

Stork held up his hands to get the men's attention, and they all fell quiet.

"Alright everyone, listen up!" he announced, "Tanight we're startin' a round with jolly rogers. Ye'll need at least five in pocket ta play. Who's game?"

By the men's hesitation, Bastian could see it was a higher bet than they were used to. Bastian raised his hand to volunteer. "I'm game."

"The Dodger o' Death 'as come ta try 'is luck!" Stork declared. "We need three more ta play. Who else wants ta dance with chance?"

Another pirate with a gruff black beard raised his hand.

"Growly, good man! Who else?"

There was mumbling throughout the group. "Come now, don't all raise yer 'ands at once…remember, a bigger risk reaps a higher reward," Stork enticed.

One more pirate raised his hand.

"That's-a-boy, Mumbles! We only need one more," Stork announced.

No one else stepped forward. "Alright ya cheapskates, I'll play. But that means someone 'as ta step in fer me as overseer," Stork declared. "Rhino, ya take over fer me this round," he told his brother.

"Any bets placed on the players are placed with me," Rhino announced loudly.

The four players stepped in close to the barrel and everyone else stepped back a pace. Cricket stood amongst the watching men, silently observing with a somber expression. The pirates around him started calling out bets to Rhino and handing him coin.

"Alright, all bets are placed. Ante up, boys!" Rhino announced and held a small copper pot out to all the players. Bastian dropped one of his jolly rogers inside.

"Yer up first, Dodger," Stork declared, and handed him the die.

Bastian spun it on top of the barrel. He left his chances up to the Stars and watched as the die twirled in a tight circle and then fell on the new moon—nothing. Stork spun the die and it landed on a half moon. There were cheers and jeers behind them as Stork counted out half the pot and added it to his pile. The pirate called Growly was next. He spun the die and it landed on the new moon—nothing. Mumbles went last, he spun the die in a tight circle and it landed on the crescent moon. He scowled as he added another jolly roger to the pot. Next, it was Bastian's turn again.

*Well, Stars, I gave you your chance. Now, it's time for me to take the helm,* he thought.

He pictured Gwena and felt the warmth in his heart reserved only for her. The Ghost Element began gravitating towards him from all directions, landing on him as if the particles were curious creatures coming to explore some allurement. Bastian held out his open hand nonchalantly and let it fill up with the shimmering stuff. Then he picked up the die and took his turn. The top spun for several long moments. Bastian sent out little tendrils of the Ghost Element towards it making it stay upright as he willed it to spin faster and faster. Then he envisioned the full moon in his mind and let the die fall. The die teetered on its edge for several wavering seconds as the crowd held their breath all around, and then it fell, landing on the crescent moon.

*What?! Why didn't that work?*

"Add one in mate," Stork prompted.

Bastian shook himself free of his shocked surprise and added another jolly roger to the pot. Stork took up the die and spun his turn. Bastian sent out the Ghost Element once more and willed the die to fall on the new moon. Once again the die teetered, wavering as if caught in a conflict of indecision before finally falling on the full moon. Bastian stared at the die in disbelief, as Stork emptied the pot with a grin. "Sorry lads, better luck next time," he said.

Again there were cheers and jeers and grumbling from the men around them.

Bastian looked up at Cricket, and the pirate returned a sad, helpless shrug.

"Anyone up fer another round?" Stork asked.

The men surrounding the barrel shook their heads and stepped back.

"Alright. Let's 'ave a round o' silver fish then," Stork declared.

Immediately there was a slew of volunteers. Bastian stepped away from the gambling circle feeling utterly bemused. He'd lost. How had he lost? *Why didn't the Ghost Element work?* He wondered. He couldn't help feeling incredibly disappointed. Cricket stepped up beside him. "Can ya roll me one o' those thing-a-ma-jiggys?" he asked.

"Sure," Bastian replied absently. He pulled out the puff-pouch and rolled a couple puff-sticks for them, handing one over to Cricket.

"Walk with me," Cricket requested, leading him away from the gambling circuit. "Don't let Stork's win get ya down—'e always wins," he told him.

"Always?" Bastian queried.

Cricket nodded. "'e might lose a round 'ere er there, but 'e always wins in the end. Whether it be by the player 'e bets on er 'avin' himself in the game. 'e's in bed with Lady Luck I tell ya."

"No one's that lucky," Bastian asserted.

Cricket shrugged. "I used ta think the same thin', but the die isn't weighted. I've given it a good check over dozens o' times. The trouble is, the more ya start ta lose ta Stork, the more ya become determined ta beat 'im. Trust me, I know the feelin', an' I can see it in yer eyes now. But don't fall inta that trap, mate, er ye'll just end up as broke an' miserable as I am. If ya be smart, ye'll save the coin ya 'ave."

Bastian took a drag on his puff-stick, blowing out the smoke in a steady stream. "It would be nice to beat him though, wouldn't it?"

Cricket smirked, "Mate, it would make me year."

Bastian nodded and took another drag. He was certain something was blocking him from using the Ghost Element on Stork's die, and he was determined to find out precisely what it was.

❧

That night Bastian stayed up after the rest of the men had gone to sleep. He sat in a corner of the mess hall under one of the firebeetle lanterns with his notebook in hand. He was drawing a concept sketch for his enchanted bracelet, deciding to use a carrick bend knot for the weave. He'd taken two long pieces of thin rope cord from the offcuts at line duty and tucked them away. His drawing had three seashells woven into the bracelet. He was hoping to be able to enchant them like buttons to activate the abilities. One for setting the time, one to engage the alarm, and one to stop it. The last thing he still needed to figure out was how the bracelet was going to wake him. He couldn't have it make a sound without waking the other sailors. He needed it to wake him silently, but how in the Stars could it do that? *Could it be possible for it to play a noise in the head of the person wearing the bracelet, something no one else could hear?* Bastian wondered. He thought about Cricket waking him that morning with a repeated tap to his face. He couldn't imagine anything more irritating. But, potentially it would be less irritating if it were on his wrist instead—maybe he could get the bracelet to tap it somehow? The very thought seemed ridiculous. Bastian continued to work on his design until it was almost time to meet Falgo for his lesson. He tucked his notebook away in his locker and fetched Falgo's payment before making his way to their meeting ground.

❧

Bastian wiped the sweat from his brow and looked up at the large moon. He'd been practicing his steps for the last half hour, forward and back, up and down the sandy clearing on the Dreg Island while Falgo watched on. The sea rover corrected his every micro-movement and Bastian strived unsuccessfully to stream them all together. He panted in exhaustion, paying for his lack of sleep with waning stamina.

"Alright, alright, that's enough. Time ta dodge, Dodger," Falgo declared, and came at Bastian with a fresh sequence of attacks. Bastian struggled to avoid them for the next twenty minutes until Falgo finally stopped his pursuit.

"Forty push-ups an' sit-ups, an' we can call it a night," he said.

"Am I getting any better?" Bastian asked.

"O' course. But ya still 'ave a long way ta go."

Bastian sat down on the sand and started his conditioning. As soon as he finished, he collapsed on the ground in exhaustion.

"See ya in the starlight on the marrow," Falgo said, waving with the back of his hand as he headed back down the beach towards the ship.

Bastian watched him go and then waited for his heartbeat to level out before he pulled the pieces of thin rope from his pocket. He walked to the shoreline and began to scan the sand for shells. The bright moonlight lit up the white beach, and the gentle waves lapped the shore in a steady rhythm. Before long Bastian had a piece of red coral, a flat turquoise shell that spiralled inward on one side, and one as black as ebony with a streak of pearl. What made Bastian choose those in particular were the holes in them that he could pass the cord through. The coral had natural empty spaces, but the others Bastian knew had been made by moon snails. He was incredibly grateful for them in that moment. Their barbed tongues bore through sea shells to eat the creatures inside, leaving flawless round punctures perfect for Bastian's purpose.

Bastian sat down on the sand and pulled the lines from his pocket and set to work.

Once Bastian finished his weave, he looked it over. He was very pleased with it—the bracelet turned out better than he'd hoped. The two cords were woven together tightly and incorporated the coral and the two shells. Now, all that was left was the enchantment and figuring out how it would wake him. Bastian sat with the bracelet in hand and looked out across the ocean towards the horizon. His thoughts hardly had a moment to breathe before being disturbed by something shivering underneath him. Something…alive.

"What the—?" Bastian jumped up and looked down at the sand. A crab the size of a saucer was rising to the surface. It wasn't using its claws to climb—it was sitting in place, vibrating. The motion was loosening the sand around the crab, making it easier for him to climb out. Bastian smiled. "Huh. Brilliant."

# PAINTED FACE

Felix woke in his bed to a gentle knock on the door. "Yes?" he croaked. "Breakfast will be served in fifteen minutes," Alfred announced from the hall.

"Thank you. I'll be down shortly."

"I also have a package for you, it arrived early this morning. Would you like me to leave it outside the door?"

"A package? Yes, that would be great, thank you."

"Very good sir."

Felix threw on his pants and shirt and cracked the door open. On the floor outside was a brown paper package tied with some decorative green twine and a fancy card tucked in the top with *Favio's Bespoke Apparel* written in an ornate font. Felix's face lit up. He grabbed the parcel and pulled it inside, closed the door and opened the package on the bed. Inside was a pair of tailored slacks and a handsome fitted blue button-up shirt with a detailed embroidered dragon on the left breast. He eagerly changed into the new clothes. The ensemble fit his measurements perfectly and completed his disguise as a well-to-do aristocrat. And, he had to admit—he looked damn good in it. He smiled at his reflection before heading for the dining room.

Felix entered the dining hall to find he was the last one there. He groaned to himself. The rest of the household was already enjoying tea while they waited for breakfast to be served. Lilliana looked stunning as always, her deep red curls piled on top of her head in an intricate set of knots held in place with a large decorative pin. Remembering what Roy had said about how obvious his feelings were for her, Felix used every ounce of his willpower to ignore her. Arianna was seated at the head of the table, wearing a green silk blouse with her hair tied back tightly in a bun. She looked exhausted. Felix wondered if she'd gotten any sleep at all. Roy was seated next to Lilliana. They were all staring at Felix.

"Good morning. I hope I'm not holding you all up?" he asked.

"Don't be silly, we've only just sat down ourselves," Lilliana said, grinning widely at him.

"Looking good champ!" Roy exclaimed, admiring his attire.

"Cheers. It's all thanks to you. I can't tell you how good it feels to have something fresh to put on."

Roy smiled. "I can only imagine. Come, join us. Tea?"

"Please," Felix said, sitting down across from him.

Roy motioned to one of the servants and they brought Felix a cup of tea. A moment later breakfast was served. It was a lavish spread of fresh fruit, scones with jam and cream, duck egg omelets, and several different kinds of freshly squeezed juices.

*I could get used to this,* Felix thought.

One of the serving staff offered Felix a warm towel for washing his hands. He took one graciously off her tray before noticing the woman was Kareen—the serving girl who'd invited him to her room the night before. She smirked at him wryly before moving on to serve Roy.

Felix cleared his throat and turned his attention down the table to where Arianna was staring absently at her empty plate.

"Aren't you hungry, cousin?" Lilliana asked her.

Arianna looked up as if coming out of a daze. "Pardon?"

"I asked if you're hungry."

"Oh, no. I have a strict diet the week before a race."

"You mean, you aren't going to eat anything?" Lilliana queried with concern.

"I'll eat something at lunch. It's important I stay as light as possible, even one extra stone slows down our pace," Arianna explained.

"Oh, I see. What a sacrifice. I admire your strength. I could never skip a meal, my concentration goes out the window if I so much as miss brunch or afternoon tea," Lilliana remarked.

Arianna smiled politely, but didn't say a word.

"Do you have much more to do in preparation for the race?" Lilliana inquired.

"Just a few last-minute things. I'll take care of them after I take Charr out for his morning flight."

"Do you think you'll have any time today for us to talk together? I'd like to catch up before the Derby if we can," Lilliana asked.

"Yes, of course, I was going to request the same thing. How about after lunch? I should be able to spare an hour," Arianna proposed.

"Yes, thank you. I would like that very much. I'll look forward to sitting down together this afternoon then."

"Splendid. I've informed the staff to provide you with anything you need while I'm out."

"Thank you, cousin. Much obliged. I can't tell you how grateful we are for your hospitality," Lilliana said.

"It's the least I can do. I'm afraid with the distraction of the Derby, I've greatly neglected my duties as a host."

"You've neglected nothing. I'm only grateful you've taken us in unannounced and hope our presence doesn't distract you too much from your preparations," Lilliana returned.

"Don't be silly. You're always welcome here—I'm glad you've come. Now, if you'll excuse me—I have a dragon who's waiting for his morning exercise," Arianna announced, and stood from the table.

Lilliana stood with her. "Of course. Until this afternoon then, cousin," she said warmly.

Arianna smiled tersely and then turned to Roy and Felix. "Gentlemen," she said with a curt nod, and then left the dining room.

Roy turned to Felix and Lilliana. "Best we get started on that disguise. We need to meet Favio while it's still morning. Especially if we're to be back by lunch."

Felix turned to Lilliana, "I'm ready when you are."

Roy pulled out his pocket watch. "Do you think you can be finished in an hour?"

"That's more than enough time. I'll prepare what's needed. Do you have a makeup case, my lady?"

"Of course, what woman doesn't?" Lilliana proclaimed.

"Do you mind if we use your quarters? I think it will be the most discreet," Felix suggested.

Lilliana smiled. "Certainly. I'll show you up now."

"I might come join you after I've gotten myself ready. I must admit, I'm curious about the process," Roy announced.

"Certainly. After you, my lady," Felix offered Lilliana politely. He followed behind her, stopping Kareen on the way out.

"Yes, my lord?" the serving woman asked, with a warm spark in her eyes.

"I'm in need of a hot iron, would you be so kind as to prepare one and have it brought to Lady Lilliana's quarters?" Felix requested.

"If you have any ironing to do, I'd be more than happy to do it for you, my lord."

"That's very kind, but I prefer to do it myself, thank you."

"Very well, I'll have it brought up straight away."

"You're a star. Oh, and could I also trouble you for some shoe polish and a few spears of aloe vera? If I'm not mistaken, I saw some growing in the back garden," Felix said.

"Yes, my lord. What color would you like the shoe polish to be?"

"Black, thank you."

"Right away, my lord." Kareen gave Felix a small flirtatious smirk.

"Much obliged," Felix returned before continuing with Lilliana towards the stairs.

"Are you always so charming with the help?" Lilliana asked him.

Felix smiled. "It pays to be charming, especially to those doing you favors."

They reached Lilliana's room and she let him in. Felix pretended it was the first time he was seeing it, making loud comments about the view just in case Roy was anywhere in earshot. Lilliana found her makeup case in her bag and handed it to Felix. He put it on her dresser and opened it. The ornate silver chest was the size of a bread box. Inside were three tiers of high-quality makeup, and two more that fanned out to the sides.

Felix rubbed his hands together, "Fantastic!" he exclaimed.

"I'm impressed you know what any of that is," Lilliana remarked, looking over his shoulder.

"Everyone wears makeup on stage," Felix stated.

"Too much, if you ask me. Is it really true, everything you said this morning about your mother and the Westdock theater?"

"Not a word," Felix confessed.

"I knew it! So you've no experience in acting then?"

"Well, I've never taken part in the work of thespians, if that's what you mean? Don't get me wrong—the plays are wonderful, but I find the actors' performances too dramatic. I prefer the subtleties of mimicking the complexity of true human nature. It's far more gratifying," he told her.

"So, how did you learn how to navigate your way around a makeup case then?" Lilliana inquired.

"I don't think that's a question you really want me to answer," Felix said.

Lilliana thought about that for a moment. "You're right, don't tell me."

Felix smirked as he unbuttoned his sleeves and pushed them up to his elbows. He certainly wasn't eager to admit he'd picked up his skills in disguise from the girls at the cathouse. The working girls would completely transform their faces and hair to what they thought was desirable for their clients, often hiding their most interesting features. Felix thought they looked far better with no makeup at all, but he'd been fascinated by how transformative their techniques were and convinced them to teach him their craft. He'd used the techniques more times than he could count since. They proved to be incredibly useful for disguise.

"I'll need a towel," Felix announced.

"You'll find one in the bathroom," Lilliana told him.

"Perfect."

Felix hunted one down and returned to Lilliana's bedroom.

"You may as well get comfortable," he advised, and Lilliana sat down at the dresser in front of the tall oval mirror. Felix riffled through Lilliana's makeup collection. He pulled out a glass jar of lotion and applied it lightly all over her face. Then he took a dark bronze powder and a fine brush and carefully painted two straight lines down the bridge of Lilliana's nose, and a V shape on the tip. He chose a larger brush and dusted over the lines lightly with a powder that matched Lilliana's walnut complexion. He used a similar technique to change the contour of her cheekbones, her chin, and the arches of her eyebrows. Next, he used a dark liner and a rich brown eyeshadow to change her eyes' shape. Last, he went over her lips with a fine brush, using Lilliana's lipstick as if it were paint. He covered the edges of her lips that were outside his lines with a base cream the color of her skin—making them look thinner than they were. Once he'd finished, her face was completely transformed.

Lilliana stared in the mirror transfixed. Felix had painted her face so skillfully and light-handed that the changes looked completely natural. Her nose looked narrower, her chin pointed, her cheeks gaunt, and her eyes slanted in a way that made her look part sea gypsy.

"How did you do that?" Lilliana queried, touching her face like it was somebody else's.

"It's not much different from painting a canvas. Shapes are nothing but shadow and light. If you change the shadows, the shape is transformed," Felix explained.

"I've had painting lessons most of my life, but I've never thought to apply the same techniques to my face."

"And why would you? Altering perfection is nothing short of criminal."

Lilliana smirked, "What does that make you then?"

"A true villain," Felix declared.

Lilliana laughed. "What are we going to do about my hair? I suppose I could wear a hat—" she proposed, but was interrupted by a knock on the door.

"Perfect timing," Felix said and answered it.

Kareen was on the other side holding a tray with a hot metal iron, a tin of black boot polish and a plate with several long plump aloe vera spears.

"Thank you kindly," he said, gifting her a wink before closing the door and carrying the tray inside.

"What are you going to do with those?" Lilliana asked.

"Iron out your curls."

Lilliana's eyes widened in horror. "You'll do no such thing!"

"Don't worry, it'll bounce back to its natural spring the second you wash it," Felix promised.

"How can you be certain?"

"I've seen it done many times."

"You mean to tell me, you've never done this yourself?" Lilliana exclaimed.

"I've always wanted to iron out my curls, unfortunately they've never grown in," Felix jested.

Lilliana looked at him dubiously.

Felix smirked in good humor. "It'll be very difficult for me to disguise you, my lady, if you won't let me change your most notable feature. People read faces the same way they read the pages of a book, top down and left to right. Your hair is the first thing that'll give you away. I tell you what, I'll only do one section—just to demonstrate. And wait to do the whole thing when I've had your approval," he proposed.

Lilliana sighed. "Alright. What do I do?"

Felix laid the towel out on the bed. "Stand, if you'd please."

Lilliana stood, and Felix took her chair and backed it up against the side of the bed. Its back only came halfway up the high mattress and luxurious feather-filled blanket behind it.

"Please, have a seat my lady," he requested, motioning with his hand like a true gentleman.

Lilliana sat down in the chair rigidly.

"Now tilt your head back," Felix directed.

Lilliana did so, and Felix took her beautiful bundle of long cherry curls and laid them out across the towel on the bed behind her. Next, he took the aloe vera pieces and broke them open, scooping out all of the clear jellied flesh from inside. He squished it between his fingers and spread it throughout Lilliana's hair like gel.

"What's that you're doing?" Lilliana asked anxiously.

"Moisturizing your hair, it'll help protect it from being damaged by the heat," he explained, then he picked up the iron and began ironing her hair. After ten minutes her whole head of locks was completely straight.

"Alright, you can sit up and have a look," Felix invited.

Lilliana sat up and immediately went to the mirror. She stared at her reflection in utter surprise,

"It's straight!" she exclaimed.

"And you doubted me."

"You said you were only going to do a small section," she accused.

"Did I?" Felix asked innocently.

She narrowed her eyes at him. "I would've snuffed you out if anything had happened to my hair."

"You do know it grows back, right?"

Lilliana ignored him and ran her fingers through the long straight strands. "It's so real."

"Exchanging it for fake hair would've been much more impressive," Felix jested.

Lilliana smacked him in the arm, "You know what I mean! It looks like my hair's naturally straight. I never knew I could do this."

"The things you learn at a cathouse," Felix muttered.

"Pardon?"

"Your hair's as soft as a mouse's," Felix pronounced.

"A mouse's? That's an odd thing to say."

"They have very soft fur. It's just a pity their coats are too small to be used for anything useful," Felix told her.

There was a gentle knock on the door.

"It's me. Can I join you?" Roy's voice came from the hallway.

"Of course, Uncle, come right in!" Lilliana invited.

Roy stepped inside, closing the door behind him. "How's it all going in here? he inquired, finding a seat at the table in front of the window.

Lilliana turned to face him. "You tell us."

Roy's eyes widened in surprise. "My dear, you're completely transformed!"

"All that's left to do is change her hair color," Felix announced.

"How are you going to do that?" Lilliana asked.

"With this." Felix held up the tin of shoe polish.

"Blacking?!"

"It's only temporary. It will wash out with the rest of it," Felix assured her.

Lilliana wrinkled her nose in distaste. "Isn't there any other way?"

"Not unless you want to change it permanently."

"Fine. Just get it over with then."

Felix opened the tin and put a generous amount of polish in Lilliana's hair and brushed it through.

"Ugh! It feels horrid," Lilliana exclaimed, "and now I smell like shoes."

"A small price to pay considering the circumstances. Wouldn't you say, my dear?" Roy asked.

"Don't worry, the smell is easily covered," Felix assured her.

He finished converting her hair from dark red to a shiny black. Then he brushed it back and doused it with Lilliana's perfume.

He handed the brush to Lilliana, and she used it to style her hair into a decorative knot. As soon as she'd finished Felix used the towel to wipe off the polish that had gotten onto her skin.

"All done, my lady," he announced.

"Stupendous!" Roy declared, clapping his hands together. He stood up and walked over to Lilliana to inspect her disguise. "I never would've thought so much could be done with so little. I imagined you were going to add some sort of mask or prosthetic, but clearly there's no need. She's completely changed!"

"I suppose it's worth putting up with a bit of polish in my hair for a day. I can't imagine anyone will recognize me—I hardly recognize myself," Lilliana admitted.

"Well done, champ! I must say, I was a bit apprehensive, but you've far exceeded my expectations," Roy commended, clasping Felix on the shoulder and looking down at his pocket watch, "and all in less than an hour! Shall we proceed to the city?"

"There's one more thing," Felix announced. "If Lilliana isn't the Duchess of Westdock, then who is she?"

"That's a good point. We'll need to come up with a new identity for you," Roy proclaimed.

"Brilliant, who shall I be?" she asked excitedly.

"It's probably best if you're a newly attained acquaintance rather than a contact from Westdock," Felix suggested.

"That's a good point, we don't want anything connecting you to your true identity," Roy agreed.

Felix stroked his chin in thought. "How about—you and I met last night at one of the clubs in the Diamond City. You're not a noble, but you come from a well-to-do family. You've come from out of town with a friend for the event. Let's say you're from…"

"Everlast!" Lilliana declared.

"Everlast? You've been there?"

"Yes, my family has a holiday chateau between the Silver Falls and the Evergold Forest," she told him.

"Of course, they do," Felix muttered. "Good. You and your friend came up from Everlast. You couldn't get tickets to the Derby, but you decided to come anyway to enjoy the side events," he improvised. He tapped his chin and then pointed to the ceiling in revelation, "Only, your friend met someone your first night here, leaving you all alone. Feeling frustrated you went out by yourself to a club," he proposed.

"Yes! You saw me there by myself and came over to talk to me," Lilliana added.

"That's right. We hit it off, and when I found out you didn't have a way into the Derby I offered to get you in with us as part of Zest's promotion gig. You accepted, eager to attend," Felix concluded.

Lilliana clapped her hands excitedly and Felix rubbed his together.

"I think it's best if we don't know much about each other. It will give us room to improvise on the fly. I reckon I would've had to convince Roy to let you onto our team," Felix proclaimed. "You were hesitant to accept at first, worried she would distract me from our work," he told Roy.

"Sounds reasonable," Roy agreed.

Felix smiled. "But I convinced you it would be better for the business to have a woman representing the product as part of our promotional team."

Roy chuckled. "That's a hard angle to argue with."

"I introduced you two this morning. We all had breakfast at one of the tea houses in town. And now, we're taking Lilliana with us to Favio's because she needs a last-minute outfit for the event. I think that will be just enough to cover us, what do you think?" Felix asked.

"It's brilliant!" Lilliana exclaimed.

"I think you should've been a playwright," Roy declared.

Felix smirked. "You'll have to be willing to do some role-playing, my lady. A disguise and backstory alone won't be enough. We need a personality that fits. Maybe you're a real social butterfly—a gal who can talk a million miles an hour who likes to captivate an audience. Someone independent and courageous, one who doesn't take life too seriously. Think you can play the part?"

"Who, me? I can play anything. Watch out, or I'll play you like a set of ivory keys," Lilliana jested in a sassy tone.

Felix grinned. "That'll do."

Roy laughed. "I think you missed your calling, my dear."

Lilliana smiled. "Is it terrible I'm looking forward to this?"

"Of course not," Roy asserted. "It reminds me of a game I used to play in my Manford days. We'd sneak into the faculty events at the university and pretend to be professors of completely fictional subjects. The winner was the one who could hold the longest conversation with a real professor without their falsehood being detected. I used to team up with a friend of mine named Charles, we'd pretend to be professors of something called Integrative Abstract Expressionism—a highly evolved way to express emotion through abstract movements. Mainly it was outbursts of silly gestures and poses that were to be taken very seriously. We found we were more successful when we played off one another," he recounted with a reminiscent chuckle.

"Ha! I wish I could've seen that," Felix exclaimed.

Roy smiled. "I miss those simple days."

Felix smirked wryly. "Well, hopefully today can be just as fun. Now, all we need is a name."

<hr>

Felix stood at the end of the Wendrians' jetty with Roy and Lilliana. He was warming his hands while they waited for an air cab.

"We'll be hard pressed to find a cab that will fit more than two people. We might have to split up," Roy said.

"You and Lilliana go ahead. I don't mind waiting for the next one, it will give you both a chance to get your attire sorted. I'm only trying mine on," Felix said.

Roy nodded just as a small orange airship pulled up beside them. It was fully enclosed with metal the color of a tangerine, and two portholes on either side. Just as Roy had predicted, there was only enough room for two passengers. Lilliana gave Felix a look that told him she was sorry they weren't going together, before disappearing into the cab.

"You sure you'll be alright, champ?" Roy asked him.

"Of course. I'll see you there shortly."

Roy patted him on the shoulder and stepped into the airship after Lilliana. Felix waved to them as they pulled away. Then he pressed the button on the lamppost to hail another cab and lit himself a puff-stick while he waited. It was a crisp morning. Despite the clear bright blue sky there was a chill in the air. Felix blew out a succession of smoke rings and watched them float out into the empty airspace. It was only a few minutes before another air cab arrived. It was a small red ship, sleek in design like a fish with fin-like wings on the sides and a single high, skinny sail on top. The sail looked like it was rigged to be dropped and lifted by gear work controlled from the inside. Felix hadn't seen another ship like it. A boy who couldn't be older than thirteen stuck his head out of the control station window.

He was wearing a green newsboy cap that covered thick, messy, brown hair, and he had a lollisucker sticking out of his mouth—its white stem protruding like a puff-stick.

"Need a lift?" the boy asked.

"Yeah," Felix said, and opened the side door of the air cab and climbed in. The interior was surprisingly roomy. It was well-lit with vials of Everfire in the corners and decked out with two plush cushioned seats with drink holders on their sides. There was a wall behind the control station dividing the back seats from the cockpit, with a glass viewing window cut into it. Felix could only see the top of the driver's back and upward. The boy had a falcon sitting on his shoulder. The bird was looking out the front window as if studying the morning's traffic.

"Where are you headed?" the boy asked.

"The Diamond City."

"No problem." The boy hit the Nixie tube counter on his dash and pulled the ship away from the jetty.

"Welcome to Cabby's Express! There's refreshments in the compartment next to you. Help yourself," the boy offered, looking at Felix through a mirror above him that reflected the rear view.

"Thanks."

Felix searched the back and found a compartment that opened to reveal several glass bottles of some sort of fizzy drink and a bowl of pistachios. He helped himself to a handful of nuts. "Cabby. Is that your name?"

"Sure is," the boy replied.

"Is that what your mother calls you?"

"Never you mind what my mother calls me, that's what my friends call me," Cabby proclaimed.

Felix smiled, "Thanks for the refreshments, Cabby."

"You're welcome."

"That's a pretty cool bird you got there."

"You bet she is. She looks real, right?"

"She's not?"

"She's an enchanted object. Runs off clockwork."

"No kidding! Is it a Sendsong?" Felix queried.

"Better. It was my grandfather's. He was a spy in the last war. There were only fourteen of the birds made by the alchemists, they were issued to an elite intel group to be used for secret communication between the forces. The alchemists made them look real so they wouldn't be detected. Instead of needing a whistle to call them, they follow a calling card that can be drawn on anything. It's a symbol that's unique to each bird. I use it to get repeat customers. Here," Cabby pushed open the dividing window that separated them and flicked through a coin.

Felix caught it. The copper coin was the size of a ducket, and on its face was a complex geometric symbol. On the back of the coin it said *Need a lift? Trace and toss and I'll be there—Cabby's Express.*

"Just trace the symbol with your finger and then toss the coin in the air when you need a lift, and I'll come pick you up," Cabby told him.

"Nice," Felix remarked, and rolled the coin over his knuckles before storing it in his coat pocket.

"You from around here?" Cabby asked.

"No. Westdock."

"No way! I hear you guys have great spiced pies."

"The best."

"What brings you to Sky View?" Cabby inquired.

"I'm here for the Derby."

"You're going to the Derby?! How'd you manage that? You usually got to know a guy who knows a guy."

"I'm going for work, we're promoting a new product," Felix told him.

"Is that right? What's the product?"

"Zest cigars," Felix said, and held one out to the boy.

"Oh, no thanks, I can't stand the stuff."

Felix shrugged and pocketed the cigar.

"Is that a good line of work—I mean, do you enjoy it?" Cabby asked.

"What's not to like? I get paid to go to exclusive events and hand out top candy to some of the greatest names of our time."

"That does sound pretty sweet. Does the job pay well?"

"Better than most."

"I'm clearly in the wrong business," Cabby remarked.

"Driving a cab up here seems alright. You enjoy it?"

"It depends what day you ask me. Sometimes it's the best, and sometimes it's the absolute worst," Cabby admitted.

"What makes it the best?" Felix inquired.

"Meeting new people and getting a window into their lives. I've met a lot of really interesting characters and acquired some great stories. The job's given me a better understanding of the world. It's like I get to read people instead of books. Though, I do plan to write a book about it one day, *The Tales of Cabby's Express.*"

"Nice. Sounds like a book I'd like to read. So, what makes the job the worst?" Felix queried.

"Cleaning vomit off my seats from drunk imbeciles."

"Yeah, I can see how that would make it the worst," Felix remarked.

"This job's only temporary. I'm saving up to become a diver on one of the mining vessels. I'd be there already if my parents would only let me. As soon as I'm sixteen, I'm outta here."

"Really? I hear that's a hard gig. What makes you want to do that?" Felix asked.

"It's not so hard these days. The mining vessels have mining orbs from the original alchemists. All they have to do is drop one into the ocean and it clears the water out in a three-mile radius. The device makes it possible to properly explore the ruins of the old world—and the miners are the only ones who have them. The divers get paid top coin to be the first ones to scout new sites for mining operations. They don't even get wet. I'd give my left arm just to see what they see. That's why I really want to do it. I couldn't give two cwips about mining—but imagine actually being able to see the remnants of the civilization sunken beneath us, uncovered in an instant. I hear the ancients were even more advanced than we are. They say that before the oceans rose, Equillian was thirty percent land, and the ancients inhabited every part of it. Imagine how much is down there just waiting to be uncovered. Word is, the divers get to keep any treasure they find on their scouts. The mining vessels only care about pulling up ore. A single artefact from the old world is worth a fortune, and that's the cherry on top of an already exorbitant wage," Cabby expounded.

"Wow, I never knew that's how the miners did it. That does sound pretty incredible. What do you plan to do with the coin?" Felix queried.

"Bail my family out of poverty. They'll never admit it, but any wealth my family once had is long gone now. And Sky View's expensive! We all have to work despite what my dad tells the neighbors—'We make our dear boy drive a cab because it builds character.' Shick that! I'm so sick of the hypocrisy in this place. I can't get out soon enough," Cabby exclaimed.

"Really? You're the first person I've heard in Sky View say they want anything to do with the mainland. It seems independence is the favored topic up here."

"Ah yes, independence. Seems to be all anyone wants to talk about these days. 'We're being robbed with taxes!' 'Bring back the good old days!' 'If I was in charge, I would've divided from the mainland years ago!'" Cabby mimicked in a variety of adult voices.

Felix laughed. "I've heard a similar narrative. Saw a compelling soapbox speech on the topic just yesterday."

"That doesn't surprise me. I hear it all the time."

"Why does Sky View want to divide from the mainland so badly, aren't they worried about starting another war?" Felix inquired.

"Are you kidding?! That's exactly what they want. Most of the families up here profit from war. In fact, they're struggling without it. After War Dragons were banned, a lot of the breeders never recovered. The smart ones turned to other things to keep their businesses going. But most of them could no longer turn a profit and retired altogether. They were all grossly rich from The Last War, but with their spending habits, their funds are dwindling. Most people here want a reason to bring War Dragons back."

"Is that even possible?" Felix queried.

"Don't know. I've heard rumors there's a way."

Felix thought of the egg sitting in the Wendrians estate and the secret hatchery filled with Arianna's strange hybrid. He wondered how many other breeders in Sky View were doing the same thing. No doubt, Marx had reached out to more than Arianna. If the families were suffering financially, they might be as eager to take his business as Arianna was. Felix wondered how many War Dragon knockoffs Marx had stockpiled in Eastgate and what he was planning on doing with them. Whatever it was, Felix knew it couldn't be good.

⌒

Fifteen minutes later Felix stepped out of the air cab onto the taxi rink beneath the capital. He paid Cabby his fare and waved to him as he flew off. Then Felix headed for the elevator. The door droid tipped his hat to him as the doors closed and the elevator lurched upwards. Felix marveled at the lift—there wasn't anything like it in Westdock. He never realized how behind his hometown truly was until stepping outside it. It felt like stepping forward in time.

The shopping mall was even more crowded than it was the day before. People in finery bustled about from shop to shop, raising their voices to be heard over one another. Felix wove his way to Favio's boutique. When he reached it, there was a closed sign on the door. Felix looked through the display window and could see Roy talking to Favio inside. He knocked on the glass. Favio looked up from his conversation and waved to Felix. He waved back. Favio said another few words to Roy, then made his way to the door and welcomed Felix inside.

"Good morning," he greeted, then he looked Felix up and down. "Looking sharp! How do you like the new outfit?"

"Fantastic! I can't tell you how grateful I was to receive it. Stepping into this getup is a breath of fresh air," Felix exclaimed.

Favio smiled. "I'm thrilled to hear it! Come join us," he invited, and led Felix to the back where Roy was. There was no sign of Lilliana.

"Glad to see you made it," Roy said.

"Nice suit," Felix remarked, admiring the tailored plum suit Roy wore.

"You like it? I've never had anything this color, but it's growing on me."

"It suits you, no pun intended," Felix smirked.

"Ha! Did you have any trouble catching an air cab?" Roy asked.

"Not at all. I had a nice chat with the driver on the way over. Where's Liza?"

"She's getting changed. Favio's given her the matching piece to yours to try on," Roy told him.

Favio turned to Felix. "Your suit is hanging in Room 1 waiting for you. If you'd be so kind as to try it on, we can see if it needs any further adjustments."

"Certainly," Felix said, and headed for the changing room.

Felix looked in the mirror. The suit fit him perfectly. He wanted to laugh with delight. It was far more showy than anything he'd wear outside the event, but damn was it fine, and man, did it look damn fine on him. He'd been doing everything in his power to successfully blend in with the cream on top ever since he and Bastian had left the Order, just for a taste of life with privilege and opportunity. And for the first time in his life, it felt like he didn't have to pretend, that he was actually one of the aristocrats. Felix only wished Bastian was there to share it with him. He stepped out of the changing room and Roy whistled.

"Glorious! Yes, yes, yes!" Favio exclaimed and circled him to inspect the whole outfit.

"It couldn't be more perfect! You do this piece far better justice than Sasha. It's meant to be!"

"Looking good, champ," Roy commended.

Felix grinned.

"Now go take it off before anything happens to it!" Favio insisted, ushering Felix back towards the changing room. Felix laughed and did as he was told.

When Felix came back out Lilliana was standing with her back to him in front of Roy and Favio. His heart skipped a beat. She was wearing a blue-green dress that matched the color of his suit. It was fitted on top with a ribbed corset beaded with thousands of tiny black pearls and had long sleeves made of elegant navy blue lace. The skirt of the dress was made of vibrant feathers that ran out in a long train behind her, and two patches of matching feathers rested atop either of her shoulders like small wings. The piece was extravagant, but what really made it was the way it fit Lilliana, accentuating her figure perfectly.

"Spectacular!" Favio was saying, pinning the dress in a couple of places for some minor adjustments.

"That dress looks stunning on you, my dear," Roy remarked.

Lilliana turned to Felix and held her arms out, presenting herself to him. "What do you think?"

Felix smiled broadly. "I think it's perfect," he said, his eyes burning with love and desire.

"I'm so glad you approve," Lilliana smiled, reflecting his warmth in her own eyes.

"You and that dress belong together. This is all turning out so well!" Favio exclaimed. "I'm so excited for tomorrow, I can hardly bear it. Now, everyone change back into your daywear and we'll have a drink to celebrate!"

⁓

Two hours later Felix was pulling up to the Wendrians' island jetty in an air cab with Lilliana and Roy by his side. After several celebratory drinks with Favio they'd managed to find a cab that could fit all three of them for the trip back. Felix and Lilliana stepped out onto the landing platform first, and then Roy stopped halfway out the cab's door behind them. "Oh damn!"

"What is it?" Lilliana asked.

"I forgot to pick up the promotion passes for the Derby. I'll have to zip back into town."

"Oh shame, do you want to go now?"

"I'd better. You two go ahead, I'm not sure if I'll be able to make it back before lunch," Roy said.

"No problem. I'll let Arianna know you had some business to attend to," Lilliana assured him.

Roy nodded and turned to the driver. "Can you take me back to the capital?"

"Sure thing," the woman said, and Roy waved to them as the air cab pulled away.

Felix turned to Lilliana, "We better get you out of your disguise before Arianna returns."

Lilliana smiled, "Of course! I almost forgot. Can you imagine? I wonder if she'd recognize me."

"It's best not to find out," Felix advised, and they made their way to the estate.

⁓

Felix lay on Lilliana's bed rolling his Lady Luck charm across his knuckles while Lilliana had a bath.

"Do you think you can help me get this polish out of my hair?" Lilliana called to him from the en suite.

"Sure," Felix called back, and rolled off the bed, pocketing his coin. He found Lilliana lying in the large circular tub almost completely obscured by a cloud of bubbles. Felix grinned. "Have enough soap there?"

"I can't get the polish out. It's so greasy," she complained.

"Right, let me have a go at it." Felix unbuttoned his sleeves and rolled them up to his elbows. Then he knelt down behind the bath and Lilliana leaned her head back towards him. Felix took a large dollop of shampoo into his hands and began working it into her hair. It was certainly a lot harder to get the polish out of Lilliana's curls than his own short locks. But after a couple of washes she was finally free of the stuff, and Lilliana's bath had turned an unpleasant dark grey.

"I think I need a bath from my bath," she proclaimed, stepping out with a wrinkled nose. Felix was waiting for her with an open towel that he put around her. "Not much point. You'll have to do it all again tomorrow," he said.

"Hopefully for the last time. I don't mind the rest of it, but that shoe polish is just awful!"

Felix wrapped his arms around Lilliana. "How're you feeling?" he asked her.

"In regards to what?"

"In regards to your pending talk with Arianna."

Lilliana thought about the question before answering. "Apprehensive, nervous, and incredibly anxious to get it over and done with," she admitted.

"Do you want to talk about it? I find it helpful to go over my key points before entering into these sorts of conversations. Otherwise, it's easy to become derailed once they start."

Lilliana grabbed a second towel and used it to dry her hair. "That's sound advice. There are so many things I want and need to talk to her about, but I suppose the only thing I really have to cover before the Derby is whether or not she's actually trying to re-create War Dragons. And if so, why," she said, walking into her room and heading to her wardrobe.

"And how are you going to approach that?" Felix inquired, sitting at the foot of her bed.

Lilliana frowned, "I'm not sure."

"Just remember to use *I* instead of *you* statements. You don't want to accuse her of anything, that will only make her defensive and either shut down or lash out. I recommend compliments, questions, and listening. Compliments will help her feel you're on her side, which will allow her to feel comfortable opening up and sharing information, questions will give her the opportunity to hand you the information you're looking for on her own accord, and listening shows her you care and value her and her side of the story—which will inspire her to share further. Just make sure when you ask a question, you're not coming across as if you're interrogating her, but rather are genuinely interested in her answers without judgement," Felix advised.

Lilliana narrowed her eyes. "Your grasp on how to manipulate the human psyche is worrying."

"I'm not talking about manipulation, I'm talking about good successful communication," Felix asserted.

"You do realize I'm trained in diplomacy?"

"Right. Course you are. Great, you've got this covered then," Felix said with a tight smile, and anxiously ran his hand through his hair.

Lilliana laughed. "I think you're more nervous than I am."

Felix knew she was probably right. Now that he knew Lilliana's situation was connected to Marx, his fun and games had come to a screeching halt. The stakes were now so high, he found himself nervously sweating.

"In truth, I'm not nearly as prepared as I'd like to be," Lilliana admitted. "Maybe I can compliment her on how she's been handling the business and inquire into what's made it so successful?"

"Hmmm, you could try that, but I don't know if it will be enough. Her winning streak in dragon racing has done a lot to bring in coin. She could use that as an explanation for all of it."

"Well, I don't know! What would you recommend?" Lilliana huffed in exasperation.

"You could try asking her if the business is breeding many dragons these days, and if so what types. Tell her she's been doing a great job running the business on her own, but that she doesn't have to do it alone anymore—that you want to be here for her and do what you can to help. Show genuine interest," Felix suggested.

Lilliana rubbed her temple. "It's too late for all of this, I'll never be able to retain any preparation at this point. We'll be having lunch in less than half an hour. I'll just have to jump in and do the best I can—thank you, I do appreciate your advice and I know it's sound, but she's my cousin, not some foreign diplomat. I just need to talk to her honestly and not overthink it too much," she asserted.

"You're right. I'm sorry, I don't mean to be adding to your burden. You're going to do great," Felix smiled reassuringly.

"Thank you," Lilliana returned in earnest. "Now get out, so I can get dressed!"

"Really? I just saw you naked moments ago."

"Go!" Lilliana commanded.

Felix held up his hands in defense and smirked. "Alright, alright, I'm going. See you at lunch."

Roy didn't make it back in time to join them for lunch. Felix had a quiet meal in the back garden with Lilliana and Arianna, leading a frivolous conversation about the weather for over twenty minutes in a poor attempt to ease the tension that was so solid he could've stood on it. He breathed a sigh of relief when the two girls got up to walk through the garden together for their conversation. Felix wished he could be a fly on Lilliana's shoulder, he was almost certain he was more anxious about the whole thing than she was. He wasn't sure Lilliana quite understood the weight of the predicament they were in. If Arianna decided to tell Marx they were here, only the Emperor or the Stars could save them.

Felix went inside and paced the hallway a couple of times before deciding he had to know what the girls were saying. He collected *The Words of the Watchers* from Lilliana's room and retreated to one of the small circular balconies overlooking the back gardens. He buried his head in the book and tuned his ears into the girls' conversation taking place below him. To his relief, he could just make out Lilliana's and Arianna's words as they meandered through the flowering hedges.

"Are you nervous?" Lilliana asked Arianna.

"Of course, but I'm also anxious for it to come. There's nothing I love more than racing," Arianna declared.

"I'm devastated I have to miss it. I'm devastated I've missed all your races!"

"Hopefully, there'll be plenty more ahead."

"I've no doubt. Even though you don't need it, I'll be keeping my fingers and toes crossed for you."

Arianna smiled. "Thank you, I'm grateful for your support."

"Uncle John must've been very proud," Lilliana said.

Arianna was silent for a moment before saying, "My father never knew I was in the grand finale."

"But you've won the last two years. Surely he knew the first year?"

"Father was already bedridden and near the end. He didn't want me to race. He always said it was too dangerous. I did it anyway, winning every qualifying race and then the grand finale in my first year, but I never told him," Arianna confessed.

"He really never knew?" Lilliana exclaimed. "Surely he would've forgiven you and rejoiced if he'd known you won, how could he not? He loved the races, and racing dragons is what our house is known for. Your achievements honor and elevate our family name!" Lilliana declared ardently.

"I wish he'd seen it that way. There's a lot you don't know about my father—if I'd been born a boy I think things would've been different. He could never stop seeing me as his precious baby girl. Only, what he thought was protecting me was actually stifling me. His fear and over-protection taught me to fear the world and made me lose confidence in my own ability to do or accomplish anything myself. I was never allowed to take chances on anything. Draya was the only one who believed in me, she convinced me to enroll in my first race. I didn't even believe I could win—but I yearned to try, the longing burned in my veins—and winning that first race changed everything. It empowered me. You've no idea how much I wanted to share that with my father, how much it hurt me not to. But I knew if I did and he reprimanded me for it—or worse, made me promise I wouldn't do it again—I'd lose the one thing that gives me strength and purpose. I miss him more than anything, and yet, his death has liberated me. I struggle every day with the conflict that's created inside me. On one hand, it's complete relief—which rarely comes without guilt—and on the other, it's a deep mourning for the loss of him and the fact that I'll never be able to share my victories with him or have him see how far I've come. With him or without him I'm caught in torment. Regardless, whether his star likes it or not, I race and win for him," Arianna expounded.

"I never knew. I'm so sorry. You should be incredibly proud of yourself, Arianna. You've accomplished so much—and all on your own. It must've been very difficult at times. Especially having to take over the responsibilities of the family business with no support."

A shadow passed over Arianna's face. "It has been difficult," she admitted, "but I've managed. The business is doing exceedingly well now, far better than it ever had in my father's care."

"Yes, I can see that. And of course we're all grateful for it. Unfortunately, with my father missing, our family hasn't been able to receive the dividends. It's one of the things I've wanted to discuss with you. If he were confirmed deceased then his portion would pass to mother, Natasha, and me, but with him missing, we have no way of accessing it," Lilliana told her.

Arianna stopped walking and turned to her. "Is your family in need of coin?"

"Very much so, I'm afraid. Our Keeper ran off with the majority of our family's fortune after my father went missing. With father gone, we've been struggling to recover. It's why my mother agreed to my betrothal with Lord Bardviss, she doesn't see any other way of preventing our financial ruin."

"Why didn't your mother tell me? I would've been happy to help if I'd known."

"I think she didn't want to burden you. After we didn't hear back from the letters I sent you, my mother went looking for other alternatives."

"I had no idea you actually needed my help, I thought…I'm sorry. I should've written back. Is that why you ran away from your betrothal and came here, to ask for support so you don't have to marry Lord Bardviss?" Arianna asked.

"Partially."

"Is he really that bad?"

"He's awful. But that's beside the point. I'm prepared to do my duty to protect the future of our family and Westdock. I've always understood that would include a politically favorable marriage. Only I'd be neglecting that very duty if I let this betrothal go forward, Lord Bardviss is completely corrupt. If he becomes duke, it could be detrimental for all of Equillian. I can't let that happen. And the only way I can see our way out of it, is to either acquire enough coin to prevent the need to have to marry him or to find my father."

Arianna processed the information with a subtle frown. "What makes you so sure Bardviss is corrupt? The letter you showed me is disturbing, but you said that came after you left Westdock. What made you so sure before that?"

"He wants the Lord Emperor's seat. I overheard him discussing it with one of his merchants. He's never shown any compassion or care for our family. He's been giving orders to our guards and hardly paying us mind since the moment the betrothal was arranged. The small fortune he paid to ensure I never return to Westdock is proof of the corruption

I already suspected. And I've since discovered he's a close friend of East-gate's tyrant leader," Lilliana divulged.

"Eastgate's tyrant leader? Eastgate doesn't have a leader. They still follow the laws of their precinct that were established by the Scillion Seven. Anyone who breaks the law is judged by their court and punished accordingly. The economy is driven by business. Everyone is equal there. It's one of the things I admire most about their precinct."

"Is that so? Have you traveled to The East, cousin?" Lilliana queried.

Arianna blinked. "No. But my top client's from Eastgate. Since taking over the business I've worked closely with them—they aren't the villains everyone would have us believe them to be."

"That's very brave of you to do business with them. Your father's star would implode if he knew," Lilliana remarked coolly.

"Unlike my father, I don't judge people by where they come from. If it wasn't for The East, our family's business would've gone bankrupt years ago!" Arianna exclaimed indignantly.

"Really? What sort of business do we do with The East that brings in so much revenue?" Lilliana inquired.

Arianna hesitated. "Why do you care all of a sudden? As long as your family's receiving your dividend, you've never cared about where it comes from," she scoffed.

"Of course I care! I don't know what story you've been told about me and my family, but we very much care about the world beyond ourselves. Arianna, I know we've been absent from each other's lives for far too long, and you've done an exceptional job of running everything on your own, but you shouldn't have to anymore. From this day forward I want to help you carry that burden. This business belongs to all of us, and we should carry the weight of it together," Lilliana asserted.

"It's no burden. At least, not anymore. I could've used your support before, when the business was on the brink of bankruptcy and I was left to shoulder it alone. But I don't need it now. I've worked hard to get it to where it is, and I've successfully turned things around without any help from the rest of the family. Thanks to me, the business is now thriving. Any help from you now would be a disservice!" Arianna reproached.

"I admire your strength and everything you've done. I really do. But like it or not, this business doesn't belong to you, it belongs to *us*. And I have every right to know what business we're conducting with The East. Despite your experience with them, you must admit, they have a terrible reputation. You can hardly blame me for having trepidations."

"I don't know what you're concerned about, I'm only selling them dragons."

"What type of dragons?" Lilliana asked carefully.

"I'm not doing anything illegal if that's what you're implying? You know the mainland can only have Pack Dragons and Pet Dragons," Arianna replied defensively.

"Is that how you're justifying this to yourself?! You think you're being clever by putting both species together—because technically it can't be classified as illegal?!" Lilliana exclaimed.

Arianna stopped short and stared at her. Felix tensed behind his book. *So much for not accusing her,* he thought.

"What are you talking about? Put what two together?" Arianna inquired evenly.

"I saw the monstrosities you're creating in the old War Dragon hatchery. They may as well be War Dragons themselves! I'm curious, what has your client told you he's planning on doing with them?" Lilliana asked.

"How dare you! You have no right, I told you not to enter the stables!"

Lilliana rose to her full height. "No right? You seem to be forgetting that this is a family business, not your own personal experiment project. What are the dragons for, Arianna?" she demanded.

Arianna raised her chin. "It's not my job to question my clients' intentions with the merchandise I sell them, only to provide it."

"It should be part of your job! If you're going to create a violent breed then you should know and care how they're going to be used. That's your ethical responsibility to the world. The people of Equillian should come before your pocket book!" Lilliana asserted ardently.

"I know how they're being used. It's nothing like you think."

"What then? Enlighten me."

Arianna hesitated. "The East fights dragons in pits for sport. It's a popular pastime in their culture—and a lucrative business. They wanted an aggressive breed that's intelligent enough to make the fights interesting, but can't fly away," she confessed.

"And you're ok with that?! Creating dragons you know will be mistreated and forced to kill one another?" Lilliana asked aghast.

"What other choice did I have?! When I took over the business from my father we were exorbitantly in debt. Selling racing dragons in Sky View wasn't enough. I did everything I could to get business from every dragon seller there is on the mainland, but no one's interested in Pack Dragons anymore. The East are the only ones who responded to me.

They're the ones who rescued our family from ruin, they're the ones to thank for our estate and business still being here. Not you or my father, or even your father for that matter. We couldn't have made it without The East. They're the ones who were there for me when no one else was. I don't care what they do with those dragons, or what people say about them, I'm grateful for their business!"

"Arianna, you need to care. What if the East is using them to build an army to move against the rest of Equillian?"

"That's ridiculous!" Arianna scoffed.

"Is it? You said yourself they have reason to resent the mainland and want independence. What if they're the ones stirring up things here and implanting the ideas for this revolution? Sowing discord and chaos to crack the foundation of our unity and split the world apart? What if it's all part of a master plan to take control of Equillian for themselves?"

"For what purpose? Marx has no reason to do that. He's a businessman, not a conqueror."

"He's a friend of Lord Bardviss, is he not?" Lilliana asked.

"How do you know that?"

Lilliana balked the question. "Don't you think it's a coincidence that a merchant who's a friend of a powerful man from The East is trying to secure himself as the Duke of Westdock? If he succeeds, then this Marx character will be able to ship anything from one side of Equillian to the other using Lord Bardviss's merchant fleet to avoid checkpoints. The Eastern border is closely watched. But what if they come in through the West? What if Lord Bardviss has them conveniently overlooked? Don't you think there's a reason why Marx has targeted you and our family personally? Our family was not only the prime supplier of War Dragons in the Last War, a betrothal to me secures them passage through the back door of Equillian. Arianna, your dragons and my position could be the key to The East executing their revenge and destroying the rest of the precincts!"

Arianna straightened her back defiantly. "Do you have any proof of these outlandish accusations? Or is this something you've concocted out of boredom from all that spare time you have—spinning these schemes from the shadows and fears of your mind?" she accused venomously.

"Shadows and fear?! Arianna, just connect the dots! This is too important to ignore. At the very least, look into your client, see if I'm right. I've heard the man who runs the slave market and the assassins guilds in Eastgate bears the same name as your client—Marx," Lilliana asserted.

"Don't you think I've already done that? I had Draya look into him extensively before I took him on as a client. He's a well-respected businessman, nothing more."

"Draya?! How do you know you can trust her? She's originally from The East, they're her people!" Lilliana exclaimed.

"I trust Draya more than anyone. And through all of my dealings with Marx, he's been nothing but generous, polite, and professional. I'm not going to dishonor him by poking into his past and personal business anymore, especially after he's done so much for us! These are huge claims you're making, Lilliana, and from nothing but hypotheticals. Be careful—if you start accusing people of such things you'll get yourself into a lot of trouble. I think you should go back home, apologize to your mother—who's worried sick about you by the way—and move on with the betrothal. It's a good alliance. Having a connection to The East isn't such a bad thing, you know? It could be the bridge that can help heal the divide between us," Arianna admonished.

Lilliana stared at her in outrage. "How can you even suggest such a thing?! He paid to have me disappeared and sold into slavery!"

Arianna shrugged. "Maybe if you weren't so difficult, he'd feel differently."

Lilliana's jaw dropped. "How dare you! You *want* me to marry him, don't you? That would be so convenient for you. Then you wouldn't have to own responsibility for being the one who introduced Lord Bardviss to my mother, getting us into this whole mess!"

"You got yourselves into this mess! I was giving you a way out of it. You should be grateful. Lord Bardviss is more than you deserve. But you're clearly too spoiled to recognize that," Arianna reviled coolly.

Lilliana shook with anger. "It was a mistake coming here. I should've known you wouldn't help us. You've never cared what happens to us, only yourself and what's best for business!"

"You're incredibly naïve if you think that. Everything I do with the business is for the family. Go if you want to, I won't stop you. Your presence has been nothing but a distraction from my work. I'm already behind schedule, thanks to you!"

"Fine!"

"Fine."

Lilliana bunched her hands into fists and stormed back towards the estate, shaking with anger.

"Shick," Felix muttered, "that couldn't have gone much worse." They'd be lucky now if Arianna didn't relay everything she'd just heard from Lilliana directly to Marx and Lord Bardviss. At the very least, he didn't think Arianna would continue harboring them. They'd have to go into hiding somewhere else, but they couldn't leave Sky View, not until they'd had their audience with The Emperor. What would they do now? Felix wondered. He looked down at the book in his hands and realized he'd been flipping through the pages absently while listening to the girls' conversation. The book lay open on his lap on the final page. There was an inscription scribed on it in a well-drawn hand:

*For A.S.,*

*A string to your boy, Copperweather.*
*I hope with all my being the Stars allow you to be with him again. Until then, I thought it might bring you comfort to read this book knowing he might also be reading it somewhere in the world.*

*Love, Sisi*

A chill ran up Felix's spine. He sat paralyzed, staring at the book with trembling fingers. *Copperweather.* That was his name, and he'd never known anyone else to have it. Surely it was a coincidence. Just because he hadn't heard of other Copperweathers didn't mean there weren't any. Every child was given a new name when they were received by the Order. Whomever brought them had the option to choose it themselves, or to let the Order choose one on their behalf. Felix never knew whether his name was chosen by whoever bestowed him to the Star Temple's doorstep or by the sisters. Maybe it was more of a common name than he'd realized. Just because *The Words of the Watchers* was the book every Star Child received at the Order didn't mean the Copperweather mentioned in the inscription had any connection to the Order. *The book could've been bought by anyone who wanted it*, Felix thought. But his internal ramblings simmered to silence because in his gut he already knew the truth. He sat staring at the page for several drawn-out moments, captive to the haunting knowledge that the book he held in his hands had once belonged to his mother.

# HANGOVER CURE

Gwena woke at noon with a sunken, hollow feeling far worse than any hangover she'd ever experienced. By the time she surfaced, the meal under the silver cloche waiting outside her door was well and truly cold. She couldn't stomach the thought of eating anything anyway. She felt rotten and knew it must've been the haunts of the Blue Faerie, no doubt worsened by the countless drinks she'd consumed on her night out with Benji. A night of drinking had never made her feel like this. She guessed it was most likely the combination, mixed with her vivid dreams of Bastian in trouble, that had left her feeling so utterly sorry for herself. She could only remember the previous night clearly up to seeing the band in the botanical gardens, and then everything was bits and pieces after that. Instead of eating, she had a bath and then wandered down to the bar. When she arrived there, Ramone was having an animated discussion with one of the serving girls. He threw up his hands in frustration as she walked away. Gwena climbed gingerly onto one of the barstools.

"Everything alright?" she asked him.

Ramone huffed in frustration and began taking it out on the glasses with his polishing rag. "If I'm honest, no," he admitted. "One of the serving girls who's supposed to be working tonight has reported in sick. If it's like the other times, she'll show up here tomorrow in perfect health. This is the fourth time she's done it to me this month. I wouldn't be so frustrated if it weren't for the fact she's left me in the lurch with no time to replace her, on a day that's particularly busy. I'm this close to taking her job away," Ramone asserted, holding up his thumb and pointer with an inch between them.

"What does she do?" Gwena asked.

"She's one of the roving waitresses—she carries trays of drinks and passes them out on the floor."

"Sounds like a job anyone can do. Surely there's someone at the club who can step in?"

"Not just anyone. It needs to be someone who's good with people and not already working tonight, preferably a female," Ramone said, then he looked at Gwena and his eyes widened with hope. "You're not working tonight, are you?"

"Me?!"

"Please. You would be saving my arse," Ramone implored.

"As much as I'd like to help, I don't think I'll be any use to anyone today. I went out last night and drank more than I should've. My head's in an awful state," Lilliana said.

A smile spread across Ramone's face. "I can help you with that!" he proclaimed, and reached for a bottle off the top shelf. "This stuff is very expensive, but it will fix you right up. It's not supposed to be included as one of the complimentary drinks for staff, but I'll make an exception for you—if you'll make an exception for me," he proposed.

"It'll cure my hangover?" Gwena queried skeptically.

"I guarantee it," Ramone asserted, and poured her a glass of the dark drink.

Gwena picked up the glass and sniffed—it smelled like Westdock's spice palette, like home. The visceral reminder of the place gave her a pang of homesickness that only added to her growing despondency. It was just the morning of her fourth day in the Heartland, and already she felt she'd been away a lifetime.

"What is this?" she asked Ramone, looking into the glass.

"The antidote to alcohol's poison. It's called Spiced Kah. It's a spiced liquor that not only cures a hangover, but also rejuvenates the mind equivalent to a quarter-hour's sleep," he said.

"Sounds too good to be true."

"Only for those who can't afford it," Ramone said.

Now that Gwena thought about it, she recalled hearing Bastian and Felix mention something about Spiced Kah. From what she remem-bered, they'd discovered it crashing an aristocrat's party and said it was the best treasure in their stores.

Gwena drank. Almost immediately her headache began to ease. "Wow, it's helping already!" she exclaimed.

"It only takes one glass. It'll take about half an hour for it to have the full effect. But if it doesn't set you right, come back and see me. So, do we have a deal?"

Gwena eagerly downed what was left of the glass. Then she thought of Benji. From the bits and pieces she could remember, she knew she was at least partially responsible for the misery they no doubt were sharing.

She couldn't in good conscience grab a lifeboat while leaving him to drown. "Give me one more glass and we have a deal," she countered.

"Whatever for?" Then realization dawned on Remone's face. "You're not the only one hurting today, are you? I'm sorry, but I can't offer any more—this stuff is incredibly precious."

Gwena shrugged. "Alright, I'm not too keen on working tonight anyway."

Ramone's expression melted into anxiety. "Hold on a moment, alright, alright. I'll give you one more glass, if and only if you take the shift."

"Done!" Gwena agreed, and she held out her hand.

Ramone shook it and poured her another glass. "Pays to be friends with you, eh? I hope that whoever they are, they're grateful," he remarked, pushing the glass over to her.

Gwena smiled. "Thanks, Ramone. Do I need to prepare anything for tonight?"

"Just wear something nice and be here at least fifteen minutes before the Dream Weaver's hour. I'll have some dinner ready for you."

"Thanks, I'll be here," she promised.

Gwena knocked lightly on Benji's door. He answered it wearing a pair of long pyjama pants and nothing else, looking just as wrecked as she did.

"Good morning!" Gwena greeted cheerily.

Benji groaned.

"Since that headache you're no doubt feeling is partially my fault, I've come to make amends. Here," she announced, and handed him the glass of Spiced Kah.

Benji smelled the drink suspiciously. "Spiced Kah! Who'd you have to jump in bed with to get this?"

Gwena grinned. "How dare you insult my honor! I'm covering a shift tonight for one of the girls, Ramone gave it to me as bribery."

"And you're giving it to me?" Benji asked skeptically.

"I've already had one, that one's for you."

"Ramone gave you two glasses of Spiced Kah?"

Gwena shrugged. "I negotiated."

Benji smiled and drained the glass, "Thanks. Usually Ramone keeps this stuff under lock and key. He doesn't even let us buy it because he's so concerned about having enough on hand for the club's clientele. I've tried to source some myself, but it's surprisingly difficult to acquire."

"I suppose that's not that surprising. No doubt a cure for a hangover in this business is on high demand," Gwena remarked.

Benji smirked. "True."

"I only wish there was something as effective in curing the effects of the Blue Faerie, I feel positively hopeless," Gwena admitted. The Spiced Kah had done a good job of curing her hangover from the alcohol, but not the drugs lingering depression.

"I do have a tea for that. It's not an antidote, but it'll help. Come in, I'll make you some," Benji invited, and walked back into his room.

Gwena stepped inside the apartment and closed the door behind her. She walked to the island bar in the small kitchen and pulled up a stool. Benji pulled a shirt over his head while putting on the kettle for tea. "Have you eaten?" he asked her.

"No, my stomach hasn't been in the mood."

"The Spiced Kah will fix that up, you should regain your appetite shortly. I'll make us something," Benji said, and began busying about the kitchen. "Whose shift are you covering tonight?"

"One of the serving girls who works the floor, I'm not sure what her name is," Gwena admitted.

"Those girls work hard, the job's not as easy as it looks. Especially on Phendays—this place gets packed out," Benji told her while chopping tomatoes.

"Hopefully it'll be alright. Ramone sounded pretty desperate for the help."

Benji smiled. "Clearly, otherwise he wouldn't have given out the Spiced Kah."

"Are you performing tonight?" Gwena asked.

"Yeah, I'll play a couple sets."

Benji placed a cup of tea in front of Gwena before squeezing half a lemon into it.

"Thanks," she said, wrapping her hands around the warm mug. "And who's the lucky lady this evening?"

"Morgan Brontē."

"I don't know that name, who's she?"

"The Emperor's niece."

"Holy shick!" Gwena exclaimed, nearly spitting out her tea.

"You're telling me? It's terrifying. Don't tell anyone—she comes here under an alias. I think she sneaks down as some sort of rebellion against her family. If The Emperor ever finds out, I'll probably be cooked."

"Surely he can't hold you accountable? She's the one hiring your service, what are you supposed to do? It's your job!"

"Ha! Try telling that to her uncle," Benji laughed. "Luckily, he's out of town in Sky View at the moment." Benji put a plate in front of Gwena with a thick slab of sourdough toast topped with diced tomatoes, avocado, shredded basil, and marinated goat cheese—all garnished with a splash of aged balsamic.

"Yum!" Gwena remarked and dug in. "I read something about that in the paper. Isn't he there for some sort of derby?" she asked.

"Yeah, the Sky Cup. It's a big hoo-ha for the well-to-do. A lot of bigwigs will be up there for it. It's Sky View's annual dragon tournament—dragon racing, dragon jousting, dragon polo—you name it. It's also a big deal for the fashion industry. Designers spend the entire year constructing outfits for it. They're practically wearable art."

"Sounds incredible!" Gwena exclaimed through a mouthful of bruschetta.

"Yeah, too bad you have to be famous, a noble, or ridiculously wealthy to attend. Sky View isn't fond of us 'bottom dwellers,'" Benji remarked, creating quotation marks with his fingers.

"Is that what they call people from outside Sky View?"

"So I've heard," Benji said, biting into his breakfast.

"I imagine those steam-powered wings will be a game changer. They'll have trouble keeping us out once we can fly up there without an airship," Gwena professed.

Benji laughed. "I'd pay to see the look on their faces."

"Speaking of the news, I need to check my postbox today. I better head up soon before the crowds get too congested."

Benji looked at his pocket watch. "Actually, at this point you're better off waiting another half hour or so, otherwise you'll get stuck in the lunch-hour congestion."

"Alright, thanks."

Gwena finished her breakfast and walked over to Benji's window. She rested her arms on the sill and looked out at the beautiful rainforest beyond. "Bonnie told me the view from our windows changes for whoever's staying there, that it's supposed to be somewhere meaningful to us."

"That's right," Benji said, watching Gwena as she gazed out his window.

"Where is this?" she asked.

"Everlast. It's where I was born, my father moved us here a couple years after my mother died. He grew up in the Heartland."

"It's beautiful. Do you miss it?"

"Very much."

"What do you miss most about it?" Gwena asked.

Benji blew out a breath. "Everything," he confessed. He walked over to stand beside her, looking out at the view. "It's completely different there. Before I came to the club I desperately missed the sounds of the birds. There's so many different varieties in Everlast, I would wake up to their songs every morning. But now I get to hear them here—thanks to the alchemists."

"I can hear them now, they're wonderful! And are those starflits?" Gwena queried, pointing to small points of light that blinked in and out amongst the trees, coming from small flying beetles—a small fly-like cousin to the firebeetle.

"Yup."

"It looks so magical there."

"It is," Benji said, as if he were far away.

"What else do you miss about it?" she inquired.

"It's slower there, and much more alive. There's literally plant and animal life everywhere. Very different from the city."

"Is that where your mother's from?"

"Born and raised. My parents met when my father was holidaying there."

"You must really miss her," Gwena said.

Benji stared out at the view in silence for a moment. "Yeah." Then he turned his back on the window and headed back to the kitchen.

Gwena immediately regretted bringing it up. "I'm sorry, I didn't mean…"

"Don't worry about it. I keep thinking I'm over it until the topic comes up—it's generally one I try to avoid," Benji told her. "To be honest, I wouldn't have chosen this view if I'd had the choice. It was the view from my bedroom window when I was a kid, and it makes it very difficult to forget."

Gwena's heart ached with Benji's pain. She could relate to him perfectly. Her eyes filled with compassion, and she spoke softly, "It's okay to never be over it. I don't think I'll ever stop missing my mother…and even though it hurts, I think it's better not to forget."

"Yeah." Benji scratched the back of his neck uncomfortably. "Look…I hate to have to kick you out, but I got a few things I need to do before my shift tonight."

"Right, of course! I'll get out of your hair. Thank you for breakfast and the tea. I'm starting to feel human again," she proclaimed.

"No problem, thanks for the Spiced Kah—that was beyond generous. Good luck with the shift tonight, eh? Maybe I'll see you out there."

"Yes, I look forward to hearing your set! Oh, and I almost forgot, I'll take those suits from you now too. I'll get started on them when I get back, it'll give me something to put my mind to before my shift."

"Great. They're just by the door," Benji told her, and walked to the entrance, picking up the paper bag from The Treasure Box.

"Thanks." Gwena reached for the bag and her fingers brushed lightly against his. Benji's touch sent an electric pulse tingling through her. The moment between them in the observatory tower flashed back to Gwena, and suddenly she became exceedingly self-conscious.

Benji opened the door for her. "I look forward to seeing what you do with them."

"With what? Oh, the suits! No pressure," she jested and laughed awkwardly, her cheeks flushing crimson.

Benji smiled. "None whatsoever. See ya."

Gwena waved and left the apartment, walking briskly back to her room down the hall. As soon as she was inside she collapsed onto her bed and put her head in her hands. "What was that? Stars help me."

# ENCHANTED

"**R**ise an' shine!" Cricket chimed, shaking Bastian awake. Bastian opened his eyes and sat up in his hammock with bright enthusiasm. "Thanks, Cricket! I was deep under," he exclaimed, and hopped down onto his feet.

Cricket looked at him with concern. "Are ya alright?"

"Yeah, why?"

"Yer just a lot more chipper than usual, I thought maybe somethin' 'appened ta yer 'ead injury while ya were sleepin'."

Bastian thought about that and realized he *was* more chipper. He shrugged. "It's going to be a good day, I can feel it." He patted Cricket on the shoulder and headed towards the top deck. Cricket watched him go in utter bewilderment.

Bastian came into Tink's workshop that day feeling invigorated. Despite his lack of sleep and his exhaustion from that morning's training with Falgo, he was alert and filled with energy.

"Morning!" he greeted Tink, his notebook tucked under one arm.

"Good morning," Tink returned, surprised by Bastian's sudden enthusiasm. "You seem to be in good spirits."

"I came up with the object I want to enchant," Bastian announced, laying his notebook open on the desk. Tink walked over to look at his design.

Bastian produced his bracelet from his pocket and laid it down next to the notebook. Tink picked it up. "Nice weave, did you make this yourself?"

"Yeah."

"Very nice. And what's the enchantment you intend to give it?" Tink queried, pulling his half-moon glasses out of his pocket and putting them on to inspect Bastian's drawn plans.

"It's a device to alert me at a designated time," Bastian said.

"What do you want that for?"

"To wake me up in the morning—and to keep me on schedule for my chores."

Tink raised his eyebrows. "That's actually not a bad idea."

Bastian smirked. "I do have them on occasion."

Tink ran his finger over the three colorful sea beads woven into the bracelet. "What are these shells for?"

"I'm hoping to enchant them as buttons to activate the functions on the device. This one sets the time I want to be alerted. The turquoise one activates it once the time's set, and this red one is to stop the alert and turn off the alarm," Bastian explained.

"And what will the alert be?" Tink queried.

"Oscillations."

"Oscillations?"

"Yeah, I want to make the rope cord vibrate."

"Huh, what an interesting idea. And how will you set the time with only one button?" Tink asked.

"I was hoping I could use intention. I push the shell and think of the time I want to be notified."

"That will be sufficient. Well done. I must say, I'm pleasantly surprised by your design. What you've come up with is straightforward, practical, and completely harmless. To be honest, I wasn't expecting much—it couldn't be more perfect for your first object with ability," Tink commended.

"Great! How do we begin?" Bastian asked enthusiastically.

Tink walked back to his desk. "At The Alchemists House of Discovery we use a special device called the Empyreanmagniscope to enchant objects. It was created by the original alchemists specifically for that purpose. Anyone with proper training can use it, even without being able to see the Element or know it's there. Unfortunately, it's only used for one thing these days. The Alchemists House of Discovery has been reduced to a factory for Everfire. Most of the people there who dare to call themselves alchemists these days can't create anything enchanted outside the eternal flame. It's a sad state of affairs if you ask me, but I digress. Luckily, with your ability you don't need that specific device. However, you do still need a device similar in nature in order to enchant an object. This here's my own creation. I've modelled it after the one at The House, but it's much simpler in design because it's made for someone who can see and manipulate the Ghost Element," Tink explained, and motioned to a strange contraption on his desk. It was a tall odd-looking thing held up by a retort stand. The top looked like a copper funnel with a glass tube running straight down from its base to three round lenses, one layered on top of the other. One was yellow, one was blue, and one was clear. Below them was a chunk of clear crystal, and below that was a gold plate resting at the base. The glass tube expanded outward, encompassing the lenses and the crystal, and then formed a glass box that housed the gold plate at the bottom. It looked like a glass python strung up after it swallowed an apple and a shoebox.

A bright light was coming from inside the funnel and shining down through the glass tube, passing through the lenses where it was concentrated into a dense green beam that passed through the crystal and fell onto the gold plate.

"I thought being able to see the Element is what allows you to use it for enchantments? If a device is needed, then how did the alchemists enchant the Seven Wonders?" Bastian inquired.

"Very good question, and one I'm afraid I don't have an answer for. It's true, the original alchemists were able to enchant anything without using a device. I'm not sure how they accomplished that. They clearly knew something we don't. Unfortunately, they never trusted anyone beyond themselves with their most valuable secrets."

"But what about this ship? It's clearly enchanted. This room undoubtedly is especially."

"Yes. I've created an enchanted device for that, one that allows me to alter the ship in ways that bypass natural law. The captain has a better natural knack at it than I do. But his ability is unique as far as I can tell. I don't think it coincides with the techniques of the original alchemists. It's less…tamed. Now, shall we begin?"

Bastian nodded. "Yes, of course." Tink's answer to his question had inspired a dozen more, but his curiosity was far outweighed by his eagerness for the day's lesson.

Tink opened a sliding door on the side of the glass box at the base of the Empyreanmagniscope and placed a small piece of glasstanight onto the gold plate.

Instantly the Ghost Element in the tube was drawn to it, creating a layer of dust on the crystal and the plate around it. Bastian stepped up to the device to have a closer look and saw that in the beam of light was a concentrated stream of the Ghost Element passing freely through the lenses as if they weren't there at all.

"How can the Element pass through solid objects?" Bastian queried.

"The Ghost Element travels with light, like a hitchhiker on a train. It can pass through anything light can pass through — as long as the light is passing through with it. Without light, the Ghost Element can't move at all," he explained.

"Interesting." Bastian studied Tink's setup. "How does the device work?"

"The top is made of copper; it attracts the Ghost Element in through the funnel's mouth where it collects in a pool. Inside the funnel is an Everfire globe." Tink reached his hand into the funnel and pulled out a glass ball with Everfire inside. Everfire globes were used as a portable light source, like a small torch. After showing it to Bastian, he placed the globe back into the funnel and continued.

"The glass on the outside of the device is a Finley Light Wall Lens. Even though it's clear, the lens prevents any light from passing through it. With nowhere else to go, the light's directed down through the tube — acting as a conduit for the Element. The Ghost Element is carried downward as if by the current of a stream, drawn towards the glasstanight at the bottom. On its way there the Element passes through the lenses and the crystal, where its properties are filtered and magnified. The device works as a siphon — once the stream's been initiated, it continues to pull the Element down even after the glasstanight's been removed. The object you wish to enchant is then put in its place on the gold plate, with the green beam focused on it. With nowhere else to go, the Element is forced into the object — and with a very clear intention, it can be used to imbue the object with an ability," Tink expounded.

"Can I see a demonstration?" Bastian asked.

"No. Seeing me manipulate the Ghost Element won't enlighten you in any way. You won't be able to see how it's done because it's all done up here," Tink asserted, tapping the side of his head. "The best I can do is help guide you through the dark until you strike a light."

Bastian rubbed his hands together eagerly. "Right. When can we start then?"

Tink smiled and walked over to the wall where he flipped a switch. There was the familiar click-clicking of gears as a black bag was lowered over the room's chandelier. The only light now was coming from the top of the device where the Everfire Globe shined out of the mouth of the funnel.

Tink walked over and placed a cover over the top, trapping the light inside. Instantly the room went dark. The strange tubular lens was brightly lit, but just as Tink had said, none of that light escaped outside the glass. It was strange seeing such a bright light that didn't illuminate anything else beyond it. Bastian put his hand up against the tube. He could see the form of his hand contrasted starkly against it, but it was nothing but a black silhouette, as if his hand was made entirely of shadow.

He leaned in towards the tube to have a closer look. The light was saturated with the Ghost Element, making it appear like glittering liquid gold as it flowed downwards towards the glasstanight.

Tink removed the piece of glasstanight from the box. "Put your object inside here, on the plate," he instructed.

Bastian reached into the box and laid his bracelet on the gold disk.

"If there's more than one core enchantment for your object, then you have to enchant it in layers, focusing on one aspect at a time. Let's start with enchanting the rope to vibrate," Tink suggested.

"Sounds good," Bastian agreed.

"I recommend flipping the bracelet over to begin with, so the shells are out of the way."

Bastian flipped the bracelet facedown. The green light fell on its center. Tink closed the box, securing the bracelet inside.

"Good. Now have a seat," Tink directed.

Bastian felt in the dark for the seat behind him and sat down.

"Now the Ghost Element has nowhere to escape. As you can see, it's trapped in the beam of light looking for someplace to go. And we will give it one, by guiding it into your bracelet using intention," Tink announced.

"Alright. How do I do that?" Bastian asked.

"Clear your mind."

Bastian closed his eyes and took a deep breath. *I am nothing,* he thought, and his thoughts and self-conscious sense of self fell away, *I am everything.* Suddenly Bastian was the darkness all around him, he was the instrument before him, and the light within it, he was the bracelet and even the glittering Ghost Element.

"Now, make your intention clear. You must create a mold for the Ghost Element to fill. Don't speak it, visualize it—just as you recalled your memories yesterday, imagine your object with its enchantment as if it exists already," Tink guided.

Bastian pulled up the image of his bracelet in his mind. He recalled playing the violin at the Order, the way the strings vibrated when bowed. He imagined each strand of the weave in his bracelet oscillating like the strings of his violin. Holding the image clearly in his mind, Bastian opened his eyes and stared at his bracelet, projecting the image from his imagination onto the physical object in front of him. He imagined the bracelet was vibrating before him—and then *it was*.

For a moment Bastian wasn't sure if the bracelet was actually moving or if it was still just his imagination.

Tink grasped Bastian's shoulders. "You've done it!"

"It worked?" Bastian asked in surprise.

"It worked!" Tink exclaimed enthusiastically. "Now, onto the rest!"

Bastian opened the box and flipped his bracelet over—he could feel the cord shivering in his hand. Disbelieving joy and excitement invigorated him. He closed the box and proceeded to enchant the red coral as the off button, ensuring the beam of green light stayed on the coral while the whole bracelet vibrated. Then he pushed the coral and the vibrating stopped. Bastian laughed out loud in delight. Feeling more confident now, he enchanted the black shell to set the time for the alarm using the intention of the wearer, and then finally he enchanted the green shell to activate the alarm.

Once it was done Tink raised the bag from the Everfire chandelier, restoring light to the room.

"Can I take it out?" Bastian asked, looking at his bracelet through the glass box, itching to inspect it.

"Not yet. The enchantment still needs to be secured with the three standard Safety Enchantments," Tink said.

"How do I do that?"

"You don't. You're not quite ready for that. Please, step aside."

Bastian gave up his chair reluctantly, and Tink sat down with his green monocle up to his eye. He took the bracelet out of the glass box and laid it on the desk in front of him, then he pushed up his sleeves and held up his pointer finger as if it were a brush. Then he proceeded to move his finger in a series of strokes in the air, quickly and nimbly as if he was painting a picture he'd painted a thousand times before. With every stroke a line was drawn in glittering gold. They hung suspended in midair—as if the Ghost Element were paint or ink. Within less than a minute there was a complex geometric symbol hovering in front of Tink.

Tink moved his hands together and the symbol shrunk down in size. He guided it downwards over the bracelet where it glowed for a moment like hot iron—branding itself into the object, and then it dissolved into the rope's cords until it was gone completely, with no sign of it ever having been there at all.

"What was that?" Bastian queried.

"The next phase of your training."

Tink walked over to his bookshelf and pulled out a large brown leather book that had a strange symbol on the front embossed in gold with the title *The Alchemists Book of Symbology*. He motioned for Bastian to have a seat at the desk in front of his work table and placed the book in front of him.

"This book was created by the original alchemists as a companion to the Empyreanmagniscope. It includes symbols for complex enchantments that can't be created with intention and the Ghost Element alone. The symbols are incorporated into the device and can be selected as filters when being applied to an object. Using the symbols is necessary to ensure none of the objects created by The House can ever do harm or be harmed. They're also useful for creating extra security features for certain specialized objects. This book acts as a sort of key or instruction guide for those using the Empyreanmagniscope, guiding them to the symbols needing to be applied. Luckily for us, since we're able to see the Ghost Element, we have the ability to create the symbols and apply them to objects ourselves, without needing a device," Tink expounded, and opened the book to a chapter titled "Safety Enchantments."

"The Anti-Tampering enchantment I just applied is one of three standard symbol safety enchantments placed on every object made," Tink informed him, and turned the page to a symbol titled *Protection Enchantment*. It was a circle with a line down the center that overlapped the top and bottom.

"The Protection symbol is used to protect the object from harm," Tink explained.

He turned the page to another symbol that looked like a sideways figure eight.

"The Everlasting symbol is used to protect the object from aging and decay."

On the page adjacent was a more complex geometric symbol that intertwined hexagons and triangles within a circle.

"And finally, the Anti-Tampering symbol—used to prevent anyone from being able to take apart or alter the enchantment."

"Take apart or alter the enchantment—is that even possible?" Bastian queried curiously.

"Of course. Without the Anti-Tampering Enchantment any knowledgeable tinker could scrap an enchanted object for parts and build their
own monstrosities."

"Really?" Bastian asked—with a little too much interest and
enthusiasm.

Tink looked at him with concern. "As creators of enchanted objects,
it's our duty to ensure we protect the world from what they have the
potential to become," he said.

"Of course. And…what's that?" Bastian asked.

"Objects of great power used for destruction or harm."

"Right, of course."

"I want you to draw each of these symbols on paper seven times. The
more symmetrical the symbol, the stronger it will be," Tink instructed.

"Do I have to draw them freehand?" The first two were fairly simple
designs, but the Anti-Tampering Enchantment was the sort of geometry
Bastian was accustomed to using a ruler and compass for. He'd studied
both mathematical and sacred geometry at the Order, and constructing
geometric forms was something he rather enjoyed doing, granted he had
the right tools to work with.

"The Ciphorescent Codec is the only tool you'll need. It will guide
you on how to form the shapes," Tink assured him.

"How?"

"Relax your mind and tune into the Codec by using the Ghost Element as your conduit. Once you are connected to the Language of Songs
it will guide your hand as if by instinct or intuition. Trust it, and your
forms will be perfectly accurate." Tink instructed.

Bastian took a deep breath. *I am nothing, I am everything,* he thought,
and brought his mind into a state of relaxed concentration. The state was
becoming easier and easier to fall into the more he did it—the man-
tra from the Order helped with that a great deal. He was grateful for
the dream that rekindled the memory. It had been a long time since
he'd consciously exercised his schooling from the Order, and for the first
time, he was beginning to appreciate it.

Bastian drew the Ghost Element into his hands and used intention
to tune into the Language of Songs, and then began to draw the symbol
for protection using the illustration from the book as a reference. When
tuned into the Language of Songs—or Ciphorescent Codec, as Tink
called it—it felt like he had a sense he'd never had before. A sense that
allowed him to know things he had no way of knowing—like being able

to see in the dark. Bastian related it to his intuition, but the Ciphorescent Codec was much stronger and clearer without a doubt or hesitation as to whether it was right, because it undoubtedly was. Somehow, when tuned into it he just knew where to put his pen to draw each line in the symbol. His hand was perfectly steady because he had complete confidence in each stroke. He could intuit where to start and where to stop and how to move his pen to form each circle and line with perfect proportion. Using the Ciphorescent Codec made such a monumental difference he immediately wondered how he'd ever done anything without it—it felt like a sense he was always supposed to have—and now that he'd experienced it, the thought of being without it felt as profound as being blind.

Once Bastian finished drawing the protection symbol, he looked at it in surprise—the circle was perfect. The line centered exactly and as straight as if it had been measured and guided by a ruler. Bastian smiled in delight and drew the symbol again. Each time he drew it the Ciphorescent Codec felt easier and easier to access, and he could draw it quicker than the time before. He was so delighted by the ease in which he could construct perfect geometry, he breezed through the rest of his practice for each of the three symbols.

Tink came over when he was done to look them over and nodded with satisfaction. "Good. Now you can finish enchanting your object."

Bastian sat down at Tink's desk with his bracelet in front of him.

"This time, instead of drawing the symbol on paper, you're going to draw it in the air in front of you, as if your finger is the pen and the Ghost Element the ink," Tink instructed.

Bastian collected some of the Ghost Element into his hand and used it to draw the Protection symbol in the air in front of him. It hung there suspended in glittering gold, just as it had when Tink had drawn the Anti-Tampering Enchantment.

"Well done. Now move the symbol into your object with the intention of what you're using the symbol for," Tink directed.

Bastian guided the symbol down over the bracelet and then into it, just as he'd seen Tink do, holding his intention for protecting his bracelet clearly in his mind.

Just as before, the symbol glowed red and then was absorbed into the bracelet and disappeared. Tink instructed Bastian to do the same thing with the Everlasting Enchantment. Bastian finished the last one with ease, and finally his object was complete. Tink picked up the bracelet and handed it to Bastian. He accepted it gingerly.

"Congratulations on completing your first enchanted object. If you were an apprentice of The House, you would now be able to call yourself an alchemist," Tink announced.

Bastian stared at the bracelet in complete wonder, beaming from ear to ear.

"Now, for your homework I want you to memorize the seven foundation symbols most commonly used in enchanted objects. It's imperative you're able to recognize them and their abilities for our lesson tomorrow," Tink asserted, handing Bastian a thin book titled *The Foundation Symbology for Alchemy*.

Bastian accepted the book gratefully. "Thanks, see you tomorrow," he said.

"Aren't you going to try out your new object?" Tink inquired.

"Right! Of course." Bastian put the bracelet on his left wrist, wavering for a moment before pushing the small black and pearl seashell. *Five seconds,* he thought clearly in his mind. Then he pushed the turquoise shell to activate the alarm. Bastian counted down in his head, hoping with every part of his being the enchantment worked. 4, 3, 2, 1, the whole bracelet began silently oscillating. Bastian grinned. It was exactly how he'd imagined it. He was astonished he'd actually done it! He'd manifested something completely impossible into reality simply by imagining it. The little boy inside him was jumping up and down in glee saying, *I told you so, I told you real magic exists! And you didn't believe me. And now you need me more than ever, because without me, you lack the ability to believe in wisps of fancy, and without that, you can't conjure anything at all.* Bastian had forgotten that little boy was there.

"Oh, before you go—I do have one more thing for you," Tink announced.

He walked over to his bookshelf and pulled out two old books, one bound in blue leather and another with green. He blew off a cloud of dust from them and handed them over to Bastian.

"What's this?"

"You asked for more books from the original alchemists. These are Bartleby Foster's and Haplo Tracy's personal journals. It's more about them than alchemy, but I thought you might find them an interesting read," Tink told him.

"Great, thanks! See you tomorrow," Bastian exclaimed, and left Tink's quarters.

For the remainder of the morning Bastian felt like he was on top of a cloud. He'd made an enchanted object! Not just that, he was now able to make enchanted objects. It was completely ridiculous and completely wonderful. Now he knew how to use the Ghost Element, enchanting something—which had always felt impossibly out of reach, now felt so simple.

*Oh, the possibilities!* he thought, admiring his bracelet proudly.



"Where'd ya get that?" Cricket asked Bastian at lunch.

Bastian looked down at his bracelet. "I made it."

"A souvenir from the Dreg Island, is it?" Rhino asked.

"Yeah, something like that."

"It's a nice weave. Did Dagger show ya how ta do that?" Stork inquired.

"No. I taught myself. I used to have a book on sailors' knots. It gave me something to do on the fishing trawler in Westdock when we weren't working," Bastian said.

"Huh. Ye'll 'ave ta show me how it's done. Wouldn't mind makin' a souvenir fer meself," Cricket remarked.

"I'd be happy to," Bastian returned cheerily.

"Ya goin' ta spin the die with us again tonight, Dodger?" Stork asked.

"Not tonight. I have a few things I need to catch up on for my work with Tink."

"How's all that goin' anyways?" Rhino inquired.

Bastian shrugged. "We're making progress."

"Makin' progress on what, exactly?" Stork queried.

Cricket snorted. "Like 'e can tell ya. 'es workin' with Tink—doesn't that say enough?"

"No, it doesn't. That be why I'm askin' instead o' jumpin' ta conclusions like a dunce," Stork remarked irritably.

All three pirates looked at Bastian expectantly.

"There's not much to tell. Tink's preparing me for the task to test my loyalty on Jaxland," he replied frankly.

Stork narrowed his eyes. "No one's ever been assigned ta work so closely with Tink. 'e 'ardly makes time fer anyone but the cap'n. I can't even imagine what the two o' ya might be up ta."

"Best not ta. If the cap'n wants us ta know about it, we will," Rhino cautioned.

Stork eyed Bastian suspiciously. "Right. Well, won't be much longer now. We should be done with repairs by the end o' tomorrow. Probably be headin' Jaxland way in the next day er two."

"Can't come soon enough. I'm lookin' forward ta puttin' me feet up fer a few days," Rhino declared.

"Puttin' yer feet up?! Me feet are gonna 'ave ta wait fer that. No way am I wastin' me time at Jaxland on 'em. There be far too much ta do, an' far too little time already," Stork proclaimed.

"True! Our feet can rest when we're dead," Cricket agreed.

Rhino sighed. "I suppose."

Stork held up his glass. "Ta us all 'avin' too much fun ta rest at Jaxland," he announced, and the other pirates hit their steins against his.

# THE FALLEN STAR

Felix paced outside Lilliana's room for several moments before decidedly opening her door and stepping inside. Lilliana turned in surprise. She had her bag open on her bed with several belongings stuffed into it.

"By the Stars! You can't keep barging into my room without invitation!" she exclaimed.

"Sorry, I just have a quick question. Your aunt you were telling me about, what was her name?"

"What in the world are you talking about?!"

Felix held up *The Words of the Watchers*. "You said you thought this book had belonged to your aunt."

"What?!" Lilliana shook her head as if shaking off a pestilent fly and grabbed a pair of shoes to stuff into her bag.

"Did her name start with an A by any chance?" Felix inquired.

"No! My aunt's name was Rosalyn." Lilliana grabbed her hat and added it to her growing pile of things.

"What about your father's sister, the one you said died when she was still young?"

"Silvia? Why on Equillian do you want to know about her?"

"Silvia, Silvia—did anyone call her Sisi by chance?"

"Now that you mention it, I think they did. How do you know that?" Lilliana asked.

Felix breathed out a quiet sigh of relief. Sisi was the name of the person who'd gifted the book, not the one to whom it had belonged. If he and Lilliana had been related it would've felt like a sick cosmic joke. He could just see Shick and the other Thrixing Stars rolling with laughter along with Lady Irony.

"How about the initials A.S.? Do they mean anything to you?"

"Nothing whatsoever," Lilliana stated, jamming her makeup case into her bag.

"Do you know if she knew someone who gave up a child to the Order?"

"I have no idea; I hardly know anything about her!" Lilliana exclaimed in exasperation. She stopped packing and turned to him. "What's all this about?"

"Hmm? Nothing," Felix said distractedly.

"Good. Then go pack your bag and meet me on the airship. We're leaving!" Lilliana declared, taking the book from Felix and placing it in her bag.

Felix looked up at her as if only just remembering the current circumstances. "The conversation didn't go well?"

"You think?! No, it didn't go well! Now, if you could please collect your things. I don't want to stay here another minute longer than we have to," Lilliana asserted.

"Right. You alright?"

"No, but I will be as soon as we're on the airship out of here."

Felix nodded and gave her an encouraging smile before leaving her room. He made his way down the hall, stopping a maid who was dusting the paintings in the corridor.

"Would you mind packing Roy's things and having them brought to the airship? We have urgent business elsewhere and will be departing shortly," he requested.

She nodded. "No trouble at all, my lord. I'll have his things brought down straight away."

"Thank you." Felix walked to his room thinking, *Lord,* I'm going to miss that.

⁂

Felix looked around at the few belongings he had. Besides Gwena's suit, he could fit everything he owned in his pockets. He was wearing the only outfit that had arrived from his order with Favio, the rest weren't due until the end of the week. He grabbed one of the pillows on the bed and dumped it out of its casing, and then used the casing as a makeshift bag and stuffed Gwena's suit inside. He took a couple sheets of parchment and a pen from the writing desk and dropped them in as well, and then left the room and made his way towards the airship. It was a pity they had to leave so soon, he'd highly enjoyed his time at the Wendrians' Sky View estate. He was going to miss the luxurious bed and the five-star cuisine.

*Oh well. It was good while it lasted,* he thought as he walked down the jetty. He was just reaching the end when Roy pulled up in an air cab.

"Good timing," Felix remarked, as Roy stepped out onto the landing platform beside him.

"Hi, champ, what are you doing out here?"

"We're leaving. Lilliana's talk with Arianna didn't go well. She's packing up," Felix informed him.

"You're joking?"

"I wish I was."

"What happened?"

Felix shrugged. "You'll have to ask her."

Roy frowned. "I see. I suppose I better go and fetch my things then."

"Don't bother, I've already requested your belongings be brought down."

As if on cue, a servant came down the jetty carrying Roy's bag. "The luggage you requested, my lord."

Roy took the bag. "Thanks, we'll take it from here."

"Very well, sir. Safe travels," the man said, and headed back towards the estate.

"I hope you don't mind. I didn't know when you'd return," Felix said.

"Not at all. Saves me the trouble. I suppose we better load them onboard and prepare for departure. Where's Lilliana?" Roy asked.

Felix nodded to the path leading up the front garden. Lilliana was marching towards them with her overstuffed bag in hand. "Thank the Stars you're here, Uncle! We're leaving," she announced.

"Yes, I can see that. What did I miss?"

"I'll fill you in onboard. But first, let's away, I'm eager to depart. Do you think your friend will mind us coming over a little early?"

"Katarina? I can't imagine she will."

"Good. Off we go then!" Lilliana commanded and climbed the ladder towards the ship.

Felix and Roy looked at one another.

Felix shrugged. "Off we go then," he said, and climbed up the ladder after her.

⌒

The airship was locked in autopilot gliding east towards the precinct's outskirts. Felix and Roy sat in the leather armchairs in the common room while Lilliana paced the length of the floor in front of them.

"I thought Arianna had changed. She was so welcoming when we first arrived and now it's all fallen apart! Maybe I should've waited until after the Derby to talk to her. She's clearly stressed and overworked. It could've completely changed the outcome," Lilliana lamented.

"Probably. But that wasn't an option, was it? Tomorrow's your one chance to report everything to The Emperor. You needed to know what her intentions are with the dragons," Felix affirmed.

"I'm still not clear on her intentions!"

"It sounds to me like they're more innocent than we feared. I think Arianna's no more guilty than an arms dealer selling pistols to an underground circus. Even if her client is the leader of Eastgate's crime syndicate, she's not breaking any laws—and as far as she knows the dragons are being used for nothing but entertainment. I think you can tell The Emperor, The East has been buying a good number of hybrid dragons with violent tendencies and leave her out of it. Guaranteed he'll look into what they're using them for—besides, there's no telling how many other breeders up here are providing the same service. The main thing is informing him of the unrest in Sky View and ensuring Lord Bardviss doesn't end up as the next duke of Westdock," Roy proposed.

"Yes. Yes, you're right," Lilliana agreed.

"After the Derby's over, maybe you'll get the opportunity to patch things up with your cousin," Felix suggested.

"I hope so. She's been through so much—as cruel as she was, I still hope one day we really can be friends," Lilliana confessed, sitting down at the table.

"I don't see why not. You'll be forever connected whether she likes it or not. With your father gone, you own ninety-five percent of the estate and business. And of course, you two are family. There's no escaping that," Roy told her.

"On the bright side, it's better for your disguise this way. Now we don't have to excuse ourselves from dinner or worry about the staff discovering we're getting ready for the Derby tomorrow. The event is the last place Arianna will expect us to be. She probably thinks we're leaving Sky View right now," Felix said.

"Yes, James is right. It might turn out to be good luck in the end," Roy agreed.

"Wouldn't that be nice," Lilliana remarked, completely dry of optimism.

"Has there been any word from the mainland?" Felix asked, getting up to put on the teakettle.

"None. With my Sendsong tied up, we'll have to miss out on the report for a few days," Roy said.

"Doesn't Sky View have a local paper?"

"They do, but there's nothing in it regarding the mainland. I had a look at it this morning at Favio's."

"Really? There's no mention of the missing duchess?" Felix queried in surprise. Considering Sky View was populated with nobles and aristocrats, he would've thought surely they'd be interested in knowing one of their own was missing.

"None. The entire thing's filled with write-ups on the derby. The majority features the big names attending tomorrow and what designer they'll be wearing."

Felix smirked. "A clear insight into Sky View's priorities. Is there anywhere we can get a copy of the *Equillian Times?*"

"Sure, but it'll be at least three days behind. It takes a day and a half for a Sendsong to fly round trip, and six days for an airship. The news agencies get their papers delivered by the merchant ships. We won't be able to see today's paper until at least three days from now."

"That's unfortunate. I imagine there aren't many people up here who read it, then," Felix remarked.

"Mostly those still connected to the mainland somehow. Now that you mention it, it's probably part of the reason there's so much disconnect. Sky View and the mainland don't report much on each other, and there's little incentive for people to read the other's paper. The news would be a good place to start bringing the two together," Roy reflected.

Felix nodded. "True. I can't say I've thought much about Sky View before coming here. It's so far out of reach, it may as well be another planet. I think the majority of the people on the mainland wouldn't blink an eye if they broke off and became independent. It's blocked off to most of them anyway, it wouldn't feel like they were losing anything."

"Except Sky View's taxes do prop up the mainland quite a lot. The changes would be noticed by everyone, even if they don't know where they're stemming from. Things people take for granted would be taken away or downgraded. It's not an ideal situation for anyone," Lilliana proclaimed.

Roy stroked his chin. "Yes, you're exactly right. I think the precincts need a reminder of what they have to offer one another. Then maybe they won't resent each other so much."

Felix turned to Lilliana, "At least without you being showcased in the local paper, there's less worry of you being recognized tomorrow."

Roy nodded. "Except the noble households here make an effort to stay up to date with the mainland. We still need to be cautious."

"Yes, and I've met several of them. Bumping into one will be the day's greatest danger," Lilliana agreed.

"Well, if that happens, just don't drop your cover for a moment. Your disguise will carry you. As long as you don't hesitate in your conviction they won't be certain it's you even if they have suspicions," Felix counseled.

Lilliana smiled weakly. "And there you have it. It's as easy as that."

"You're going to be great," Felix assured her.

Roy looked out the porthole. "We're approaching the Everstorm, I better go pilot this bird. We'll be at Katarina's soon, best if you two get ready to disembark," he told them, and disappeared into the cockpit.

"You sure you're ok?" Felix asked Lilliana, placing a cup of tea in front of her.

Lilliana wrapped her hands around the warm mug and gazed into it for a moment before answering. "No, I'm not. Arianna's words linger in me like a poisoned arrow bedded in my heart. Family have a way of slipping past my defenses. But my feelings on the matter will have to wait. I know too well such venom only becomes harmful if I believe in it. I can't afford that. We've got too much work to do," she asserted. She took a sip of her tea, then put the cup down and walked to her quarters.

Felix watched her go and sighed. He looked out the porthole. The Everstorm was close now—the size and force of it was overwhelming. Its sound was like the roar of a mountain waterfall dumping an entire ocean. He tried to picture the duke flying into it on the back of a dragon and couldn't see any plausible way he could've survived. They were approaching a small, isolated island on the outskirts of Sky View. It was the only one near the Everstorm. Felix couldn't imagine why anyone would want to live so close to the enormous tempest. The island was only a quarter of the size of the Wendrians'. Despite being so close to the storm, it looked calm and tranquil. It had a huge metal chain stretching straight down from its base that disappeared into the sky below it. Felix wondered if it was to keep it from being sucked into the storm.

On the island was a quaint two-story house painted purple and blue as well as a beautifully manicured garden. There was a large shed out back, and two ancient trees that twisted on either side, their branches stretching towards the storm as if they'd grown being pulled by it. A swing chair sat underneath one of them, facing out towards the giant hurricane. The island's surface was covered in lush green grass. Two jetties protruded out from the island. One had nothing but the Everfire lamppost for calling air cabs at its end. The other jetty had two airships docked on either side, a smaller one the size of an air cab and another long, slim one that looked more like a red torpedo with an inbuilt balloon on the top and bottom of the vehicle.

Roy brought the ship down towards the unoccupied jetty. Felix went to the control room and poked his head inside. "Need a hand docking?" he asked.

"Yes. Thanks, champ, I'll bring her as close as I can."

Felix nodded and headed towards the upper deck.

⌒

A light wind had picked up ruffling the sails of the airship. Felix turned the crank to close the Everfire box and made ready to jump to the jetty beside them. This time, Roy had pulled the ship directly alongside, leaving a gap no wider than Felix's foot—he was grateful for that. He held onto the ship's line and stepped nimbly onto the platform beside them, tying the line to the bollard, and waited for the others to disembark.

He felt eyes on him and looked up the sloping lawn towards the house. A tall dark woman with long hair made up entirely of tiny braids was looking down at them. She was wearing a full-length, loose blue dress that fluttered in the wind as she shielded her eyes to see who they were.

Roy waved to her from the deck of the airship and she waved back. A moment later Roy and Lilliana joined Felix on the jetty and the woman walked down to greet them.

"You're early," she announced, in a voice as smooth as satin.

"Yes. I hope it's no inconvenience?" Roy asked.

"None at all," the woman replied with a warm smile, revealing a row of sparkling white teeth. She hugged Roy and turned to Felix and Lilliana. Roy immediately took the cue for introductions.

"This is Katarina. Katarina, this is James—he's helping us in our search for the duke. And this is—"

"Lady Lilliana Wendrian, the Duchess of Westdock," Katarina declared, holding out her arms to embrace Lilliana.

Lilliana looked at Roy accusingly. "I thought you hadn't told her?"

"He didn't. Your face has been all over the *Equillian Times*, my dear. And your enquiring about your father—it's not hard to put one and one together."

"At least there's someone up here who still reads the paper," Roy remarked.

"Your discretion would be much appreciated. If anyone finds out I'm here, everything we're trying to accomplish will be compromised," Lilliana implored.

Katarina smiled warmly, "Don't worry child, your secret's safe with me." She turned to Felix. "And James, is it?"

"Yes," Felix confirmed, stifling his urge to offer her his hand.

"Welcome, it's a pleasure to have you. Now, I imagine you must all be hungry. Since you're here, we may as well have an early supper. That way we can have time to savor the evening."

Katarina led them up the path to the house. Inside, the place had a much more modern feel than the exterior suggested. The walls were clean and bright. It was an open plan with high lofted ceilings and large bay windows that looked out towards the Everstorm. A large brass telescope stood by the windows, near a chalkboard on a stand. The chalkboard was covered with advanced equations. From the ceiling hung a rotating model of the solar system that moved with a gentle hum. A large Ever-fire hearth stretched along one wall with built-in bookcases all around it stocked with leather-bound books. Next to the open kitchen was a round wooden dining table already set for five. It appeared that Katarina lived alone, with no servants or household staff. It was surprising and also refreshing to see an aristocrat willing to do their own household chores, Felix mused.

"Please, have a seat," Katarina welcomed, gesturing to the table.

Felix pulled out a chair for Lilliana and sat down next to her. Roy sat across from them on the other side. Katarina hummed to herself as she busied about in the kitchen for a few minutes before bringing out a fresh loaf of honey rye bread and a pot of hearty stew. She set them down in the center of the table and then fetched a tray of baked salmon and a steaming bowl of rice mixed with a medley of vegetables. "Please help yourselves," she invited, and then filled everyone's glasses with water from a tall thin pitcher and sat down.

"Smells delicious! Thank you, Katarina," Roy said with a warmth in his eyes that spoke of deep familiarity.

Katarina returned his smile and patted his hand.

"Yes, that fish is a sight for sore eyes. I didn't think anyone in Sky View ate meat," Felix remarked.

"I'm not originally from Sky View, and old habits die hard," Katarina returned with a mischievous smile.

"Where do you get it from?" Roy asked, piling a large portion onto his plate.

"I catch the fish myself. I drop down pots and traps every morning. Occasionally I'll pull up a few crobs and lobtors—unfortunately I didn't get lucky today."

"There's no meat better than fresh seafood," Felix proclaimed, helping himself to the tantalizing meal.

Lilliana followed suit shortly after, with a much more polite and humble portion. "This is indeed a treat, thank you."

Katarina smiled warmly. "The pleasure's all mine, I assure you. It's a joy to have company to cook for. Food always tastes better when you have someone to share it with."

After the meal the four sat around the table in a purr of pleasant conversation. Katarina cleared the table with Roy's help and brought out a pot of tea with homemade almond biscuits.

"Roy says you're a scientist?" Lilliana asked her, while picking up her cup of tea.

"I was, once upon a time. I was the meteorology professor at Lachlan University for fifteen years. My husband and I worked extensively in the university's research program, deciphering Equillian's weather patterns."

"Impressive. What makes you less of a scientist now?" Felix inquired.

"Ha! Good question. Not being paid, I suppose," Katarina admitted with a smile.

"I'm surprised no one's willing to fund your research on the storm," Roy remarked.

"There's plenty who are curious. But no one sees the financial benefit of understanding it. I can't blame them. I don't know if there is one. I only know that my curiosity and passion to explore it and discover its secrets is relentless. The Everstorm is what inspired me to become a meteorologist in the first place. And that passionate curiosity is what drew my husband and me together. As soon as we had the means we moved up here to study the phenomenon and we never looked back. There's nothing I'd rather be doing or anywhere I'd rather be," Katarina confessed.

Felix walked over to one of the large windows and looked out at the storm. "There is something alluring about it, isn't there?"

"There is indeed," Katarina agreed with a knowing smile.

"Where's your husband now?" Lilliana asked.

"He passed away five years ago."

"Oh, I'm so sorry to hear that."

"Thank you. We always thought the storm would be the end of us, but he fell ill and it was the storm inside him that got him in the end."

"Was he also a meteorologist?" Lilliana inquired.

"No. My husband was an instrument engineer. He made all of our instruments for studying the Everstorm."

"The ship that's docked outside, the red one. Is that for studying the storm?" Felix queried.

Katarina nodded. "It was our pride and joy. Charles finished it a few days before he passed. It was going to take us inside."

"Inside the storm?"

Katarina smiled. "Of course."

"Why would you want to do that?"

"Have you ever heard of the story of Tuatakan?"

"Tuatakan. No, I haven't," Felix admitted.

"I know that one. It's one of the stories my father used to tell my sister and me when we were children. I'd completely forgotten about it. It's a legend about a lost city in the center of the Everstorm. A sort of time capsule—a place protected from time," Lilliana recalled.

"Is that even possible?" Felix asked.

Katarina shrugged. "Every mature storm has an eye at its core. The Everstorm is as mature as they come, it's been raging in the same place for at least as long as we've been recording history. Its eye spans over eighty miles—a place with calm weather inside a ring of towering thunderstorms and deathly high winds. That's a lot of space that's been isolated and protected from the outside world. It's entirely possible that if there's any land there, the storm's preserved it. There could be flora and fauna that's gone extinct everywhere else in the world. Living creatures that exist nowhere else."

"It could also be nothing but open sky," Roy pointed out.

"True. But we'll never know unless we explore it," Katarina asserted.

"Was that your and your husband's plan, to break through the storm to explore the eye?" Lilliana inquired.

Katarina nodded. "That was our life aspiration, the dream that held us together."

"But if you were successful, how would you get back out? It sounds like a one-way ticket," Felix remarked.

Katarina shrugged. "There's a good chance it might be. We've always been willing to take that risk. But that doesn't mean we haven't done everything in our power to prevent it. Our work would accomplish nothing beyond satisfying our own curiosity if we weren't able to share it with the world. The ship is designed to survive the storm, at least in theory—we won't know for sure until she's tested. None of that matters now at any rate. After Charles passed and I saw the duke's airship heading into the tempest with no crew it changed everything. I've been working on automating our ship to pilot itself ever since. It's taken quite some time to complete without Charles, but luckily he'd created an autopilot program that's been instrumental in the endeavor. The ship's just about ready now. If I can send her in on her own with our instruments, I'll be able to retrieve the data once she's found her way out. If I can prove there's anything but sky inside there, then it will be enough to get the funding for a proper expedition."

"If my father entered the storm, do you think it's possible he could still be alive?" Lilliana asked.

"I like to refrain from saying anything's impossible," Katarina answered.

"How long before your craft is operational?" Roy inquired.

"Oh, it's about a month out, I suppose. The system's finished, but there's still several tests I need to run. One simple failure could compromise everything. If the launch isn't successful, then I may never get the opportunity to try again."

"I see. Once the Derby's over, perhaps we can stay awhile, and I can help you finish the final adjustments?" Roy proposed.

"I'd be delighted to have your help and company," Katarina returned with a warm smile.

"Would we be able to stay the night tonight and use your place to prepare for the Derby? I'm afraid our accommodation with my cousin has run its course," Lilliana asked.

"Of course, child! My home is your home. You're welcome to stay as long as you like. it's been too long since I've had company."

That night Felix had trouble sleeping. He lay on a cotton mattress on the floor with a soft pillow and a thick blanket. It was comfortable enough, but the problem wasn't the bedding, it was the storm. He was lying near a huge window overlooking the raging cyclone, and the double-glazed window was being pommelled with heavy rain. It felt like sleeping next to a war zone. Besides the constant rumble of thunder and the flickering light show inside the billowing swirl of clouds, there was a sort of electricity in the air all around it. A strange excitable energy that buzzed outward and through Felix like ripples in a pond. He lay there awake, staring at it, tormented by the feeling it might envelop them at any moment, and yet he also felt compelled by it—in the same manner the voice of a siren lured men to the ocean's depths. The feeling sent a shiver down Felix's spine.

He reached into his pocket and pulled out a torn piece of paper. It was the last page from the copy of *The Words of the Watchers* that Lilliana had discovered at the Wendrians' estate. He looked at the inscription written there.

*For A.S.,*

*A string to your boy, Copperweather.*

*I hope with all my being the Stars allow you to be with him again. Until then, I thought it might bring you comfort to read this book knowing he might also be reading it somewhere in the world.*

*Love, Sisi*

He read over the inscription several times. The words *your boy, Copperweather* struck a strong chord in his chest.

*So, I have a mother after all. I guess I wasn't hatched from an egg in a faerie's nest*—such as some of the Star-brats at the Order liked to jest about their heritage. *Shame that, it's a much more interesting story,* he mused.

He'd never given much thought to who his mother might be. He'd never had any romantic notion of her wanting to see him again or even caring who he was, or vice versa. He liked to think of himself in the singular sense, as if he really had sprouted into existence independent of anyone else. The Order taught that being a Star Child was a fresh beginning liberating children to fulfill their own destiny and path. And Felix had embraced that wholeheartedly, glad to be free to steer his life in the direction of his choosing. In the minimal thought he'd given the topic, he'd figured that for whatever reason, his path had been chosen for him and had been a clean cut for all parties concerned. Only the inscription before him suggested otherwise. It suggested that his mother *was* hoping to see him again. That he was abandoned out of necessity rather than by choice. And if that was the case, then ignoring her existence was going to be a lot harder.

*Who are you?* he wondered. The initials A.S. meant nothing to him. More curious was the question of her connection to the Wendrians. It was clear she'd been familiar with Lilliana's aunt. A friend? A lover, per-haps? But then, who would be the father? Whatever it was, the connec-tion most likely meant his mother was highborn. Maybe an aristocrat who had a child out of wedlock and was forced by her family to give him up? That would fit the bill. It wouldn't be the first time such cir-cumstances had led to a baby being left on the doorstep of the Order. In that case, she would probably be married off by now and have a whole new batch of brats considered socially acceptable. He doubted she'd still have any sentiment for him—if he ever found her, she would most likely deny their connection.

The idea of having blood siblings somewhere in the world didn't bring Felix excitement or warmth. Instead, it made him feel exceedingly uncomfortable. Less unique somehow. Like there were copies of himself living privileged lives while he was discarded as a reject. He shook the feeling from himself and was about to crumple the paper to discard it when he noticed something. There was very small writing in graphite in the bottom corner of the page. Felix held it up to the window light.

*The Phoenix Wing, 1484 Shifter Street, Plum Row, Eastgate — Thrixing Day at the Seventh hour. Ask for Sven — Tell him you're the Fallen Star.*

*The Fallen Star, what does that mean? And Eastgate? What business did my mother have with The East?* he wondered. Then he yawned, feeling sleep finally knocking at his door. He folded the piece of paper into a small tight square and dropped it into his Dreg Pouch. Then he fell into a troubled sleep riddled with dreams of flying into the Everstorm in search of his mother and being torn apart by vicious winds.

# MURDERING MAGIC

The Heartland was still bustling with crowds of people by the time Gwena surfaced to the main streets. She was glad she'd taken Benji's advice and waited for the lunch rush to clear—even past it, the streets were still congested with pedestrian traffic. She fell in with the slipstream and followed it to the Central Posting House. She went to her box eagerly and used her little key to open its ornate door. The box was empty. Her shoulders deflated in disappointment. She knew she shouldn't have expected to receive any news from Bastian or Felix on her first Phenday in the Heartland, but she couldn't help hoping all the same. She left the Posting House and found a newsie selling papers on the street. She bought one from him for three cwips and reminisced on how two cwips for a paper in Westdock used to sound expensive. Then she tucked it under one arm and returned to the club.

Gwena sat on the end of her bed and thumbed through the newspaper. There was nothing new on the disappearance of Lady Lilliana or anything concerning Bastian and Felix. It was mostly articles about the Science Fair and The Emperor's visit to Sky View, featuring the steam-tech wings Gwena and Benji had seen being demonstrated the day before, and a writeup on the Sky Cup Derby. It left Gwena feeling overwhelmingly disappointed. She sighed and added the paper to her growing recycling pile. Then she turned her attention to Benji's suits. She pulled out her sketchbook and the drawings he'd come up with and began designing. An hour later she was busy at the sewing machine making alterations to the suits Benji had chosen from The Treasure Box. She'd redesigned each one to be unique and was altering them to his measurements. By evening they were lacking only the final touches. It felt good to put her mind to work. Tailoring was something with order and predictability, something familiar, something to bring her comfort when nothing else in her life made any sense. She set her work aside and looked at her pocket watch. It was an hour before she needed to report to Ramone for her fill-in shift, which gave her just enough time to figure out what she was going to wear. She was so pleased with her newly altered items from The Treasure Box, it was exciting to have an opportunity to wear them. This time she chose a red dress and a pair of black heels. The dress was a similar style to the one she'd worn the night before. She tied her long blond hair back into a clean smart knot and headed down to the bar twenty minutes before the Dream Weaver hour. When she arrived, Ramone had dinner waiting for her.

"Thanks," she said, sitting down at the bar to enjoy her meal.

"Dang, you clean up well, nice outfit!" Ramone exclaimed.

Gwena laughed. "Thank you."

"How's your head feeling?"

"Much better, thanks. That Spiced Kah is a starsend!"

"It is indeed. Worth its weight in gold."

"So, what am I supposed to do tonight?" Gwena asked, tearing off a chunk of bread roll with her teeth.

"Just grab one of these trays and pass out the drinks to anyone who wants them. Sometimes people will ask for specific orders. Jot it down on this notepad if you can't remember and come get the drinks from me. If anyone gives you any lip or trouble, don't serve them—and be sure to tell me about it. There's a waiting list for this place a mile long, if they're going to be arseholes we don't need or want their business, Ramone asserted.

"Right. Sounds straightforward enough, I can do that. What time do you want me to start?"

"As soon as you see a customer."

An hour later the club was packed like a can of sardines, with patrons clustered in every corner. Gwena weaved her way amongst them with a tray full of drinks in hand. She had to use all her concentration to keep the drinks from tipping off her tray. Luckily, they were never on it long. Ramone told her to stop taking orders and just send anyone who wanted custom drinks to the bar. There was no way she'd be able to find them again in that crowd. The hours passed by in a blur and before Gwena knew it, it was the hour of Faya. Only one hour before the club closed and the sun surfaced. Equillian's night hours were longer than the day hours—each one doubled in duration, making the seven hours of the night equal to the fourteen hours of the day. Gwena was exhausted. She'd hardly stopped since her shift began, and she'd only had a moment of seeing anything but a sea of people all night. That moment was when she'd spotted Benji amongst the crowd. He was standing next to an extraordinary-looking woman with dark skin and prize-winning cheekbones. Gwena guessed she was The Emperor's niece. She looked to be around Benji's age. They were talking to another couple. The Emperor's niece was laughing and holding onto his arm. But Benji looked distracted, like his mind was somewhere else. He must have felt Gwena looking at him, because he turned and stared directly at her. They locked eyes. Gwena smiled and gave a small wave; he smiled back and held her gaze for what felt like a suspended moment—as if time had frozen just for them. Then Benji looked away, directing his attention back to his current company, and the moment was gone. Gwena blinked, then turned her attention back to the sea of patrons swarming around her.

By the time the night was winding to an end, Gwena's feet ached. She couldn't remember the last time she'd stayed up so late. The club had finally thinned out, though a singer and pianist still haunted the stage. The singer was a woman in a low-cut dress sitting casually on the piano wielding a long puff-stick holder with a smoking puff-stick on its end. Its smoke curled above her as she serenaded the small clusters of patrons still hanging around in quiet conversation. As Gwena was doing her rounds she noticed a young man performing amateur magic tricks to a couple of women watching with waning interest. The young man had the look of a classic blue blood—blond hair, blue eyes, and skin so fair it looked like it had never seen the sun. He was fumbling over a deck of cards, his movements clearly underpracticed. Of course it didn't help that his audience was doing nothing to hide how underwhelmed they were. Gwena couldn't help but feel sorry for him.

"Choose a card, any card," the young man requested.

One of the women drew a card from the fanned-out collection in front of her, while the other yawned.

"Now put it to your head and visualize the card," the man directed, cutting the deck into seven piles.

The woman put her card to her head unenthusiastically.

"Good. Now put it on top of any one of these piles," the man instructed.

The woman chose the middle one, and the young man started fumbling through a poor attempt at a story while he combined the seven piles back into a single deck. He offered the deck to the woman to be shuffled and knocked her drink right out of her hands while simultaneously sending the cards cascading across the floor. The woman gasped in outrage, and the man apologized profusely.

Gwena came over and helped him collect the cards. Then she handed him a fresh flute of iced sparkling wine from her tray. He looked at her confused.

"For the lady," she whispered with a wink.

"Oh right, thanks." He handed the glass to the woman. The woman took it without thanks and drank from it, and then she stopped, frozen in surprise. "How did you do that?!" she exclaimed.

He and the other woman looked back at her in puzzlement.

"What on Equillian are you talking about, Mildrid?" her friend asked.

"Look. My card, the four of hearts—it's in the ice in my drink!"

Her friend and the man leaned in to see. Sure enough, the four of hearts was folded up and frozen in one of the ice cubes in her glass.

The man looked over his shoulder at Gwena, but she was already gone.

At the end of the night Gwena returned her tray to Ramone in exchange for a small bag of coins as her payment. She said goodnight, ready to make her way to her room, when the man performing amateur card tricks tracked her down.

"Hi," he greeted.

"Hi."

"The name's Richard," he said, sticking out his hand.

Gwena shook it. "Gwena."

"I just wanted to thank you for what you did earlier. You really saved my reputation."

Gwena smiled kindly. "It was nothing."

"Nothing?! That was certainly more than nothing! I can't even imagine how you did it. How did you do it—if you don't mind me asking?"

"You should know a magician never reveals their secret," Gwena replied conspiratorially.

"Right. Of course! There must be something I can do to repay you?"

"Oh, no. Please, don't even mention it. Seeing a fellow magician in need, I couldn't help myself."

"Was it a Jackal bird?" Richard asked, staring at Gwena's face.

"What?"

"Your scar," Richard said, tracing a line down his own face to mirror hers.

Gwena put her hand to her face. "Yes, how did you know?"

"My grandmother had one just like it. Except it started at the base of her chin and ran down her neck. My father has made it a personal vendetta to take revenge on the whole species. Any time one flies onto our land he fires at it with his pistols."

Gwena laughed at the thought of such a thing. "I can't really hold it against them. They're only trying to protect their young."

"I suppose. That's a very optimistic way of looking at it. Say, have you ever seen Madam Pomphrey perform?" Richard asked.

"Have I ever?! I saw her in Westdock with the Travelling Curiosities. It was a masterful show! She's always been one of my inspirations."

"Mine as well! I'm actually her assistant in her upcoming show, we run rehearsals most nights in Theater 3. She's the one who taught me the tricks I was murdering back there. You should come by sometime," Richard invited.

"I'd love to! I didn't realize that was allowed."

"It usually isn't," Richard admitted.

"You don't think she'll mind?" Gwena asked.

"Not at all. I'll let her know I've invited you. You should come by this afternoon; I'll introduce you two."

"Alright, actually now that I think about it, I'm already scheduled to meet with her today to go over her costumes. I'm the club's new tailor. I was only covering a shift tonight as a favor," Gwena explained.

"Is that right? How serendipitous. I look forward to seeing you later then," Richard said with a charming smile and left.

Gwena glanced at him curiously before heading to her room.

# GEOMETRY

Bastian excused himself directly after dinner that night—he was eager to look at the books Tink had loaned him in their lesson that morning. He went up to the top deck and found a place all the way at the stern near one of the back lanterns, where he could read in peace. It was a warm night, a moment of respite from the cold chill of winter. The stars were as bright as ever, and there was a light warm breeze that danced playfully through his hair.

Bastian got himself comfortable on the boards of the deck and looked at his bracelet proudly. He was still buzzing from the fact that he'd enchanted it. He pushed the black shell and set the alarm for fifteen minutes before the Phoenix hour and pushed the turquoise shell to engage it. Then he set his attention to the books, brushing off the remaining dust from the front of the journals.

*Better get through my assigned work first,* he thought, putting the journals aside and opening the book on foundation symbology. The book comprised seven illustrated symbols, each labeled with a title overhead and a description underneath stating what it was used for. The first three were the ones Bastian had learned that morning. He was relieved about that, and it left only four more for him to memorize. The remaining symbols were all similar combinations of different shapes layered together to form geometric patterns, each one with a different ability. They reminded Bastian of the geometric shapes he used to have to construct in his Sacred Geometry class at the Order. His favorite was Empyrean's Cube, a form that held every shape in the known universe. Now that he knew how to use the Ciphorescent Codec, it made forming complex symbols a breeze. There was something fulfilling and satisfying about it. He drew each of the four new symbols seven times in his notebook and memorized the ability for each one. Half an hour later he was finished and finally free to look inside the alchemists' journals.

Bastian looked at both of them side by side and settled on starting with Bartleby's. He hardly knew anything about either of the original alchemists, but Bartleby he'd at least heard of. He ran his hand over the blue leather cover and opened it to a random page.

*7/2/1668*

*Tonight I made an extraordinary observation. I was working late at the Hall of Scientific Study when one of my colleagues from the astronomy department invited me to look through the observatory's telescope to see a large comet passing through Equillian's atmosphere. I accepted his offer thinking nothing significant of it, but when I saw the comet magnified through the telescope's lens, I was completely taken aback. There was a vast quantity of luminous dust around the comet; it was so saturated with the stuff, it streamed from it, creating a long tail in its wake. It immediately struck me that it was the Ghost Element. When I asked my colleague—in a discreet fashion—if he could see the dust, he answered no, confirming my instinct. What was even more extraordinary was that when I turned the lens towards other stars, they were also saturated with the Ghost Element, every single one. This discovery is so profound because it means that the Element is not something bound to our world, but a by-product of the universe itself.*

*14/2/1668*

*I've been staying back at the Hall of Scientific Study to observe the stars through the Hall's telescope for the last week. Last night was a full moon. I thought the moon's light would obscure the visibility of the stars, but on the contrary, the dust seemed somehow magni-fied. It was falling down from all the stars as if they were leaking. It streamed down from the cosmos to Equillian's surface in great glittering bands forming an aurora. I can't help but wonder if this is the answer to where the dust originates. Perhaps the Ghost Element is indeed residue from the stars.*

*10/3/1668*

*I've been expelled from the Hall of Scientific Study. I foolishly shared my findings with my colleague. Fearful for my mental well-being, they reported me to Glenda, the Hall's director. When I confessed my findings, she asked if I had any evidence. I told her I was working on it, and she gave me two weeks to come up with something. When after the two weeks I still had nothing but theories to offer her, she asked that I drop the subject entirely and requested I see a doctor. When I refused, I was immediately dismissed and discredited as a scientist. Now, I am completely ruined. I can't even get any funding to further my research independently because of it. I have pursued chemistry my entire life, it's all I've ever known. With experience in nothing else, who will hire me?*

*3/5/1668*

*I've been hopeless for weeks, surviving on my last cwips. But tonight, for the first time since I was removed from the Hall, I have had hope restored. At the tavern where I was taking my dinner I saw a young man—younger than I by a handful of years—who was sitting alone. His glass was transforming in his hand, changing shape without rhyme or reason. No one else seemed to take notice. More so, there was a great deal of the Ghost Element lingering around him. And every time his glass changed, the Element was absorbed into it. I immediately approached him and asked if I could join him at his table. He obliged me and I asked him how he was able to change his glass. He was surprised that I'd even noticed, and told me that I wouldn't believe him if he told me. I asked him if it had something to do with the gold dust. He replied, "You can see the dust?" with quite some surprise. When I said I could, he told me that he'd thought he was the only one. I said that I'd thought the same, and introduced myself. We stayed there lost in conversation until closing hours, when the tavern finally kicked us out. I told him about my discovery with the stars, and he told me how he used the Element to manipulate things using visualization and intention. His name is Haplo Tracy, and it turns out that he comes from a very wealthy family who'd all died in a tragic accident when he was quite young, leaving him with a very substantial inheritance. He's been spending the last several years living a roving bachelor's life with no real purpose. He was very interested when I told him that I was a scientist who had been studying the phantom element, and he wanted to know everything I'd discovered. When I told him I'd lost my job because of it, he immediately invited me to share his apartment in the city, suggesting that we carry on my research together. I normally wouldn't have accepted such an invitation from someone I knew so little, but considering the circumstances I was eager to accept. And it was strange, but as Haplo also said that night, sharing the gift of sight somehow made us feel more connected to each other than to any family we'd ever had.*

*5/7/1668*

*Haplo and I have decided to open up a research center dedicated to the Ghost Element. We're calling it The Alchemists House of Discovery. With my scientific knowledge and background and Haplo's gift of transmutation using the Element—and of course his generous gift of funding—I am incredibly optimistic and excited about what we might discover and achieve together. I can't even begin to explain what joy and relief it gives me to be able to devote my life to my true interest and passion so openly. Meeting Haplo has indeed been a starsend.*

*7/2/1670*

*The House has finally come to completion and both Haplo and I have taken up residence there. We spend most of our waking hours studying the element together. It feels like a dream. We've already made great progress. Haplo has taught me how to do some basic transmutation, and I've been educating him on the scientific method and practices I've been implementing. Both of us bring a different perspective to our research. I couldn't have imagined a better work partner.*

*17/2/1671*

*Haplo and I have figured out how to enchant objects! Having failed at getting our own transmutations to last, we've been working on trying to house enchantments in existing objects, imbuing them with abilities that will last forever. And it works!*

*4/7/1671*

*Haplo's fortune is waning. We've been ignoring the financial side of things for too long and admittedly living beyond our needs. But luckily, I had a meeting with an investor this morning who is very interested in our enchanted objects. Haplo and I have discussed it, and we've decided that if we secure a legal patent on our products, then we'll never have to disclose our secrets and can openly sell our objects to the public.*

*18/1/1672*

*Our patent has been secured for some time now and we're making a good profit selling enchanted objects, in fact, it's been far more* successful than we ever imagined. So much so that simply keeping up with demands has capitalized most of our time. As successful as we've become, Haplo seems to be down these days and unsatisfied. I must admit, I share some of the same sentiment. With our capital success, we've lost most of our freedom, bound to fulfilling orders rather than continuing with the research we started it all for. The situation troubles me. In order to continue our research and keep operating we need funding, and in order to gain funding we need to appease our buyers, which then leaves us with no time for what it's all supposed to be for in the first place. A conundrum I'm eager to solve.

5/3/1672
A representative from the Hall of Scientific Study came by today and offered me a prime position and package to return to their employment. Ha! I of course politely turned them down, and boy, did it feel glorious.

22/11/1672
We've solved it! Haplo and I have designed a machine that allows a layman to enchant basic objects—within reason, of course. We would be irresponsible to give away our full power, or any without installing proper safety precautions. The good news is that this development means that Haplo and I are finally free once again to continue with our own research!

2/5/1679
We've completed the Seven Wonders, a true accomplishment!

12/11/1679
I've met a woman, her name's Sarah. I must admit, she has stolen all of my drive and attention along with my heart. I find it difficult now to see the same importance in things I once did. The idea of a family is suddenly more tantalizing to me than discovering the secrets of the universe. I find myself making excuses to slip away from The House early so that I might pass my time with her. She's the sun of my world.

*4/9/1680*

*I'm worried about Haplo. He's been talking to me less and spending more time at the taverns and bawdy houses. I fear that my time with Sarah's upset him. Admittedly, I have been distracted and less eager for our own research, I just wish he could be happy for me. To make matters worse, neither he nor Sarah like one another. Sarah finds him too outspoken and Haplo finds her a bore. If only he could find a partner of his own to settle down and have a family with. Sarah and I are expecting a baby any day now, I fear the baby will demand even more of my time, leaving very little for I and Haplo.*

Bastian turned the page to find the rest of the journal empty. *Perhaps the baby demanded even more of his time than expected?* he wondered, and eagerly picked up Haplo's journal. He blew the dust from the green leather cover and opened it to the first page. Written in fine calligraphy were the words *Property of Haplo Tracy.* On the next page was the start of an autobiography as dry as one of his old history lessons, far from the person suggested in Bartleby's descriptions.

Bastian put his hand on the page to turn it and froze. As soon as his skin touched the paper it pulsed beneath his fingertips, the ink rippled outward in several expanding rings—and suddenly the words on the page were completely transformed.

A chill crept up Bastian's spine. He began reading from the top of the page once again.

*3/01/1672*

*Where do I begin? I've forgotten how to do this. I remember jotting down accounts of childhood discoveries and leisurely days in a journal as a boy. Now it seems I've forgotten how to talk to anyone—even the empty pages of a book. This journal was a gift from Bartleby. Nice, isn't it? Bartleby's always had the irritating knack of knowing exactly what I need—even before I do. He's been trying to get me to keep a journal for years— "one day people will look back at us as important totems in history, they'll value our accounts and insight. It's worth jotting them down," he'd say. I'm not sure if there's any value to my accounts or insight, but I must admit, it's nice to be able to speak my mind freely—even if no one's listening. In truth, I don't know why I rejected it for so long. I'm currently sitting in the library of The House's west wing, hiding from the guests we've invited for the celebration of The Alchemists House of Discovery's 2nd anniversary. I've done as much shmoozing as I can take for one night. Bartleby's always been much better at that than I. It's never been a part of the job I've been fond of. Probably something to do with how much I despise people. No, that's not fair. I don't mind people so much, as long as they're the right ones. Unfortunately, these days I mostly find myself surrounded by people with whom I have nothing in common. I find the small talk we share laborious and irritating and, quite frankly, a waste of time. Too many people speak of things they know nothing about and are too proud to discuss it when challenged. Sometimes I wonder if they actually care about what they're saying, or merely care about the praise they think it will inspire.*

*They clearly don't realize the only things they're inspiring are fools and looking like one.*

*If you ask me, there's no such thing as common sense. Sense and common just don't go together. What's common is the vast naïvety of humanity and the lack of courage to admit it, even to ourselves. O the things I wish I could say to people. To see their faces when their true nature is unveiled to the ones they're trying so very hard to impress. And if not that, then I at least wish I could steer the topic of conversation to something with substance—like how we hide ourselves in a manufactured reality that's less interesting than the one outside our door. Confining ourselves to boxes, and then trying so very hard to convince ourselves we're free despite the instinctual feeling of being trapped.*

*How we deny ourselves many of the pleasures of being human and shame those who don't. How we fill ourselves and each other with so many lies we can no longer recognize the truth—even when it's staring us directly in the face. How as a pastime, we engage ourselves in frivolous conversation that's even less significant than we are. I can't stand it. I don't want to waste another moment amongst such absurdity! People seem so content with their lies, I don't think they even want to know the truth. I can't understand it. I thirst for truth. The truth behind the secrets of our world, the truth behind us and what and who we are, the true history of the ancient world sunk beneath our oceans, the truth behind the stars and the vast universe they occupy, and the truth about the ghostly shimmer that has haunted me since I was sixteen.*

*If it were up to me, I would happily spend all my working hours
at The House investigating, discovering, and uncovering the truth
rather than attending these silly social events. Life's too short to waste
such precious time. But unfortunately, in order to do so Bartleby and
I need funding, and people are much more interested in funding
gizmos with intriguing and enchanted abilities than uncovering the
truth. Even worse than having to attend these events is having to tolerate the guest list and stay on my best behavior—which is why I'm
here in the library, hiding amongst books while I talk to one.
O look, here comes Bartleby now. I suppose my hiding place wasn't as
good as I'd hoped...*

*4/01/1672*
*I want to start this entry by apologizing for my opening rant. I was
in a particularly somber mood. I don't retract anything I said, it was
all honest. I only apologize because you had to read it. Here I was
talking about people wasting my time with senseless chatter, and I
was wasting yours. In truth, I'm no better than they are. Since you're
still reading, I'll reward you for your patience. If I've ever had anything of value to offer, here it is: In my opinion, there are four things
one should do with their life while they have it:
1. Unapologetically and fullheartedly indulge in as many mortal
pleasures as humanly possible (As long as it doesn't involve hurting
anyone—including yourself.).
2. Discover as much as one can about the world—even if only on a
single topic.
3. Gift that knowledge to following generations.
4. And finally—either create or help to create something of value
that you love and that will outlive you.
If you do nothing else, you'll have lived a full, rich, and meaningful
life. This book is my gift to any poor fool patient enough to read it.
In truth, I hope not many do. My discoveries are not intended for
everyone. But I can't let the knowledge I've obtained die with me, it's
far too valuable and besides, it would turn me into the worst kind
of hypocrite. I don't keep work logs the way Bartleby does, so this is
it. I hope this book finds its way into the hands of the right person at
precisely the right time—I've never been a religious person, but in my
experience the universe has an odd way of doing exactly that.
To that person I say: First, keep your mind, eyes, ears, and heart*

open. If you wish to experience the best this world has to offer and uncover its secrets, then you have to be receptive when they are presented to you. Otherwise, you'll miss them entirely.

Don't be afraid to walk a path never walked before. That's where you'll find the hidden gems that haven't already been uncovered or plundered.

Now, I'm going to present to you the greatest thing I've discovered. However, it's not my responsibility to convince you of it, I'm simply documenting what I've learned. Whether or not you're receptive to it is completely up to you. The Ghost Element is real. Yes, there is an element that saturates our world, so potent that it powers the imagination like steam to an engine—making it come to life. How do I know this? Because I can see it. Bartleby can too. It's the one thing that binds us together regardless of how different we are, like blood binding two brothers—because as far as we know, we're the only ones in the world who can.

Now, you have a choice to make. You can either decide I'm mentally unwell and ditch this book entirely—shutting the door to what I'm telling you—and go on your merry way continuing to believe in the boundaries you've been so convincingly told define what is and is not possible. Or, you can suspend disbelief for a moment and be receptive to the notion that what you've been told your entire life is a lie, opening the door to infinite possibility. The decision is yours.


*21/11/1672*

It's the hour of Faya and I've not yet been to sleep. Bartleby and I have been working on a machine to enchant objects. The demand for our products has become far too great for us to continue fulfilling orders on our own—that's the problem with being tied to investors, we've enslaved ourselves to their agendas, no longer having time to pursue our own. But that's all about to change. The machine we've made will allow people without our ability to enchant objects. We must be careful because in the wrong hands such power could break the world. To prevent any such thing we've enchanted the device with several safety features. No one can use it to make an object with intention to harm or gain power, nor can the device be moved from The Alchemists House of Discovery—it's been enchanted in place. We'll begin recruiting apprentices tomorrow. We'll make sure they have loyalty to The House and ensure they adopt our philosophy, and

*then we'll train them to use the device to create enchanted objects
for the public. In time, they can take over that side of the business
entirely—freeing up Bartleby and me to put our full focus into our
own endeavors, and also to fund those endeavors with our own coin.
I look forward to that, more than you can possibly know. But for
now, sleep.*

*15/4/1676*

*It's been a while since my last entry, I'm not very good at this. The
House has been operating smoothly for several years now. The public loves us. With over two hundred alchemists employed we've been
able to release more enchanted objects than ever. The apprentices
and senior alchemists have come up with all kinds of things I never
would've thought of, I'm very proud of their work. Their objects have
revolutionized the world far beyond what I'd imagined, creating
objects that have not only advanced technology but have saved lives.
It still baffles me that the public doesn't question how we're able to
do it. When what we can do is housed within an object that provides
people with convenient abilities, they don't seem concerned about
how it's done. They're simply thrilled to have it, though I can't say
that's true of everyone. There have been a few curious noses from
high places poking into our business, trying to uncover our secrets for
themselves or buy us or our employees out. But luckily we give our
people enough incentive not to be bought. I do fear one day they'll
succeed, which is why it's so paramount that no one, not even our
employed alchemists, ever discover the true nature of Bartleby's and
my work.*

*2/5/1679*

*We've done it! Bartleby and I have created the Seven Wonders—sev-
en enchanted monuments around the world. It's such a feat because
never before have we found a way to enchant whole buildings. They
are a spectacle for the architecture alone, but with the enchantments
housed within the structures they're each a magnificent wonder. And
the greatest feat of all is that we've ensured they'll last forever. After
years of experimentation and trial and error, we've finally done it,
we've cracked the code! We now know how to make objects truly
invincible and immortal. Not just protected with charms that can be
hacked by those with proper vision and instruction, but true invinci-*

bility on a core level. We've reserved this for only the most significant objects, because in order to accomplish such a feat, the objects must be turned into living things. No one knows this, but every one of the Wonders is a living entity. Not as a creature is living, but rather more comparable to a tree. Because of the dangers of this information getting out, I will not document how it can be accomplished. Part of me hopes no one will ever discover what we have. But I am beyond ecstatic to announce it can be done!

## 10/12/1689

You must excuse me, I'm drunk. Along with my pen I'm holding a bottle of mulberry wine that's near empty. Bartleby and I have had a falling out. Ever since he got married we've grown more and more distant with one another. His wife Sarah doesn't like me, never has. And now that they have children, Bartleby's family has completely capitalized his attention. Everything that used to be important to us is no longer important to him. I was hoping that at least one of his five brats would be born with the gift of sight like we have, in hopes I might be able to continue our work with them as an uncle of sorts. But none of them were. I suppose there's still time. I didn't start seeing the Ghost until I came of age. But I'm not welcome with their family these days regardless, so no point in hoping.

Bartleby and I were supposed to be brothers, we were going to use our discoveries to obtain the impossible together, making it possible to uncover all Equillian's secrets—and maybe even the secrets of the universe. We used to agree that humankind could accomplish so much more if only we had more time. Now we're gaining real understanding of the world, we are already running out of time, past our prime and declining into old age. Just as we begin to figure things out! We were going to change all of that together. But now Bartleby's lost all interest. He doesn't want to risk the potential consequences now he has a family, nor does he have any desire to live beyond his family. And I find myself too cowardly to do it alone. Forever's a long time when you have no one to share it with. I never thought there would be an end to our friendship, I was so sure that together we could accomplish everything we wanted—and that we would. But I was wrong. Now that I've lost him and have few obligations at The House these days, I've found myself spending most of my time in ale houses and brothels. I think Bartleby has always hoped I'd find a

*partner to settle down with like he has. But I've never desired that, I
don't even like the thought of it. I like to be alone when it suits me,
and I like being able to choose a partner depending on the mood I'm
in—when I'm in the mood, that is. And I hate the weight of expectation or the feeling of others' disappointment when I don't turn out
to be who they think I am. I find more comfort in strangers these
days than the people I know. I once heard it said that the only perfect
people are strangers, and I agree with that fullheartedly. Rather than
suffering the disappointment of others' undesirable imperfections—or
their disappointment in mine—I prefer to keep company with people
only long enough that we might maintain our glossy mystery and
be enriched by each other's imagination. But apparently, that's not
fashionable. Bartleby keeps telling me I have a reputation to consider.
Not just for myself, but also for Bartleby and The Alchemists House
of Discovery. I say bah humbug to that. This is my life, everyone else
can go shick themselves!*

*7/6/1691*

*I've met someone. A man. And he's like no person I've ever met
before. He's wild and intelligent and daring and absolutely thrilling.
And he doesn't give a cwip what anyone thinks of him. It's damn refreshing. His name's Kieren. He has a tattoo of a Wildsinger over his
heart, I think that describes him perfectly. He's inspired me with an
idea that's reinvigorated me and filled me with new purpose. I'm going to make a new Seven Wonders, all secret places underground for
people like us. Places where Wildsingers can come together and thrive
outside the judging eye of society. And I have no plan to tell Bartleby.*

*15/8/1694*

*Again, it's been years since my last entry. The Seven Underground
Wonders have been completed. Kieren and I have become inseparab-
ble, our friendship reaches far beyond what mine and Bartleby's ever
did. Though Kieren and I are lovers when it suits us, we're not bound
to one another—at least not romantically. We're like two halves of the
same person, and we've grown attached to each other as such—free
to do as we like but forever connected. I couldn't have dreamed of a
more favorable partner. I can't imagine the bond we have will ever
sever. Not this time. And there's no one I'd rather spend forever with.
He doesn't have the scientific knowledge Bartleby does, nor does he*

*have the sight. Admittedly, there are times when I miss Bartleby's scientific skillset and intellect. But Kieren has passion and vision far beyond what Bartleby ever did. I wish I could introduce them to one another. What the three of us could accomplish together! But I fear the wedge between Bartleby and I has grown too thick to mend. We hardly talk these days, except when we need to for business. The only personal thing Bartleby's told me in years is that none of his five children have inherited the ability to see the Ghost Element, even after reaching adolescence—much to his disappointment. It makes me wonder how we acquired the ability ourselves. In the early days Bartleby and I compared our lives trying to find anything we had in common that might have brought on the sight outside genetics. But our lives have been so different. It makes me wonder if I ever have children if it will be the same. It's entirely possible I have illegitimate children out there already. Stars, isn't that a frightening thought.*

*23/9/1706*
*Kieren is dead. It turns out immortality doesn't make us invincible. I've thought about following him into the afterlife, but I don't have the courage, and there's still so much to do—once I find the strength to do it, that is. I've decided to go away. I'm going to end this journal now. I've put a lot of thought into what I want to do with it. It's not something I want to take with me where I'm going, nor do I have the heart to destroy it, and it's not something I want to be left to be discovered by just anyone. Instead, I've decided to enchant it. I'm leaving it at The Alchemists House of Discovery with the headmaster—but what people will see when they open this book is going to be very different to what you're reading now. Some pleasant fiction about a boring life that will be more palatable for the public eye. I can't risk the information in this book falling into the wrong hands. If you're reading this now then you meet four very specific require-ments.*

*1. You have the gift of sight.*
*2. You have no maniacal disorder or ill intention upon the world.*
*3. You have enough attention span and interest on this topic to've gotten this far in my journal.*
*4. And finally, you have enough of the right blood running through your veins to make you my bastard heir...*

Bastian stopped, then read the fourth requirement again. Shivers ran down his spine. He began reading again eagerly.

*...I apologize for the latter. I'm sorry if you've had to pay for my absence, I dare say you're not the only one. But since you are the one who's stumbled upon this book and fits the requirements, I will at least leave you with the greatest inheritance I can. The secret to unlocking everything.*

Bastian leaned his head back and took a deep breath, glaring at the Stars accusingly. He made himself a puff-stick and took a long drag before reading on.

*There's one main component beyond the gift of sight to accomplishing the things I have. Geometry. Not the sort of geometry you might have studied in your mathematics class at school, no, I'm talking about the geometry that forms the underpinnings of our universe. The DNA, so to speak, architecture and blueprint of absolutely everything—and the avenue to understanding it. And not just the universe, but everything inside it. You see, geometry acts like a genetic code of sorts that not only identifies, but also defines properties and limitations. More so, one can learn to read it. And once you come to understand the fundamental geometric code of our universe, then you can use the Ghost Element to rewrite it. I'm sure you can imagine the kind of doors and possibilities that might open.*
*Bartleby and I spent years studying and documenting the code. It works in patterns that with proper observation one can come to recognize. I first stumbled across it when Bartleby and I were documenting things that attract the Ghost Element. We were working on our list of sea creatures and I happened to be observing a sand-grain seahorse in a water-filled petri dish under a high-powered microscope. While studying the creature, I observed patterns forming on the water's surface when I was speaking to Bartleby, complicated geometric forms that seemed to change with every word. This was such an interesting phenomenon, that Bartleby and I spent the next several weeks studying it. We soon came to the conclusion that there's a vibrational frequency that's created from our words when we speak—not just from the sound, but from the meanings, emotions, thoughts, and intentions behind them. One that affects the surface of liquids and who knows what else. This discovery was the key to figuring out why*

*things transmuted using intention and the Ghost Element alone don't last. Because it's the intention being carried by the Codec which gives the object form—as soon as the intention is no longer being projected, it fades away. We realized that what we needed to do was somehow freeze the vibrational patterns, locking them in place. We first tried holding an intention in a compound comprised of water and the Ghost Element, while freezing it with dry ice. The experiment was a success, the object held the enchantment until the ice melted, then the enchantment faded with it. We next tried the same technique with a molten metal compound and a liquid glass compound, holding the intention until the materials cooled and hardened. They were also a success. This is how we began making our first enchanted objects. We found we could use the same technique for imbuing glaze for porcelain objects and varnish for wood. It wasn't until sometime after that we realized we could study and learn the patterns of each intention, that each form had meaning like a sort of language or writing. And that we could then create those forms ourselves and use them to imbue any object we wanted, without having to actively hold the intention until it set. And that's when we were able to create the safety enchantments. It wasn't until later that I discovered that seers have already discovered how to read these vibrations, it's what they use to read fortunes. They have some sort of liquid in their crystal balls that amplifies the patterns, making them far easier to see. I stumbled upon this by chance. I was frustrated that though we'd discovered how to enchant objects, we still were unsuccessful at being able to create something solely from the Ghost Element and have it last independently of a pre-existing object. At a loss of where to turn for answers I went searching for guidance from a Seer. She used a crystal ball to read vibrational patterns forming in the liquid from the questions I asked, vibrations that I immediately recognized from our own research—vibrational patterns that occur whether they can be seen or not. Which led me to think there are likely many things in the world beyond our perception—just like the Ghost Element is to others. It made me wonder if perhaps the reason we couldn't create things that lasted independently was because we were missing something fundamental about the true structure of things, something that was perhaps also beyond our perception. The Seer confirmed as much, so I spent the next six months figuring out how to create an enchanted pair of glasses that might reveal it to me. The lenses were*

*made of clear crystal with no magnification or special properties.
Seers and crystal merchants sell them for strengthening your eyes
while reading. The perfect blank canvas for adding an ability. I then
calibrated them to show me the internal coding—or rather, natural
blueprint—of things. And they revealed to me geometry. Beautiful,
intricate, and complex geometry in absolutely everything. I later
came to realize that what I was actually looking at was the physical
form of the Ciphorescent Codec—otherwise known as the Language
of Songs. This discovery changed everything. Bartleby and I found
that once we could see the Geometric Code, then we could alter it
using the Ghost Element. As soon as we could properly recognize and
understand the internal coding of nature and even man-made objects, there was nothing we couldn't construct, deconstruct, or change.
We've made countless mistakes along the way. We got things wrong
many times before we got them right. Early on there were horrific ep-
isodes when we tried to alter things in positive ways and got negative
outcomes. Especially when we tried to alter certain aspects of small
living things. Science isn't always pretty. But every mistake we made
brought us progress.*

*The discoveries Bartleby and I have uncovered through our research
have opened up a power so omnipotent, we dare not share it with the
rest of the world. I have been in conflict with myself over documenting this here. But out of principle, I've always felt it's my obligation
to ensure my discoveries don't end with me. Therefore, I've included
in the following pages much of what I've come to understand about
the Codec, as well as the instructions for creating a pair of glasses that
will allow you to see it. Next, I will cast this book out like a message
in a bottle thrown into the sea. The odds of someone who can read
it coming across it are so low, that I feel if they actually do, then it's
a necessary part of the universal equation. Therefore, if you can read
the true nature of this book, it belongs entirely to you. Good luck.
Who knows, maybe one day our paths will cross.*

*Your wanting father,*

*Haplo Tracy*


Bastian put the book down with trembling hands.

*Could it actually be possible? Could I really be the bastard heir of Hap-
lo Tracy? Or is this some twisted joke Tink is pulling for a laugh?* Bastian
wondered.

Haplo would be over a hundred by now, Bastian wasn't even sure it was possible he could have conceived him. And it was hard to believe Tink had no idea what the book was when he'd loaned it to him. The odds of the whole thing being chance seemed too ridiculous. But he recalled the way the ink had rippled on the page when he'd touched it, revealing the hidden text. And Haplo's obscure remarks about having found the cure for mortality, and suddenly, Bastian wasn't so sure.

*What if it is part of some universal equation?* Bastian wondered.

He finished his puff-stick while gazing up at the stars, wondering what it was they had in store for him.

# SKY CUP DERBY

Felix woke early to the smell of something sweet wafting from the kitchen. He hardly felt refreshed. To top off his night of poor sleep, he had a pounding headache. Outside the window was a carpet of grey clouds. Light rain showered the large window.

*Great,* he thought, *weather to fit my mood.* But once he'd sat down for breakfast to a plate of freshly made crepes and filled his stomach, his excitement for the Derby sunk in and energized him. "Does anyone know if it's forecasted to be like this all day?" he asked.

"I've seen the weather report. It's the only piece of useful information in the local paper this morning. These clouds will dry out in a couple hours, and we can expect clear skies for the rest of the day," Roy announced.

"I'm relieved to hear it. Bad weather would certainly put a damper on things," Felix remarked.

Lilliana smirked. "Quite literally."

"Have you finished the letter for the Emperor?" Roy asked her.

"Yes, I finished putting it together last night. I think it'll be sufficient in getting his attention."

"Good. Best we get you in disguise as soon as possible. It'll take us a while to reach the capital from this far out, especially with the event's traffic."

"Certainly," Lilliana agreed. She turned to Felix, "I'm ready when you are."

Felix nodded and drained what was left of his tea. "Let's get to it then."

❧

Felix stood behind Lilliana in a cozy yet elegant bedroom. Lilliana was sitting at a dressing room table running her fingers through her straightened hair as she studied her reflection in the mirror. A metal iron was standing on end, steaming on the table next to them.

"I used to wonder what I would look like with straight hair," Lilliana remarked absently.

"Well, wonder no more. Do you like it?" Felix asked.

"I don't know, it's different. Do you like it?"

"I don't think it really matters what you do with your hair, you could chop it all off and you'd still be exquisite."

"Ha! I'm sure you say that to all the girls."

Felix smiled wryly. "Maybe, but in your case it's actually true."

He pulled out the round tin of shoe polish they'd acquired from the Wendrians' estate the day before—luckily, Lilliana had the sense to pack it. He scooped up a large dollop and globbed it onto the top of her head.

Lilliana wrinkled her nose in distaste. "Is this part really necessary?"

"Completely," Felix assured her, and brushed the black polish through her hair. Once it covered Lilliana's cherry red tresses, he helped her pin it up with her jewelled hair pins. Then Felix riffled through Lilliana's make-up case on the dresser and began applying her disguise. When he was done, he sat back on the bed behind Lilliana looking at her through the mirror. She was staring at her reflection like it was a stranger, someone disconnected from her actual self.

"Have you ever wondered what it might feel like to be someone else?" she inquired.

"What makes you ask that?"

Lilliana hesitated before saying, "Everywhere I go people know who I am. Well, my name and face anyway, and how the media portrays me to be. Which actually prevents anyone from ever really knowing me at all—because they've already got some preconceived notion of who I'm supposed to be. When people hold such a strong image in their minds of who they think you are, it's difficult not to fall into it. I hate that. I hate the mold they've created for me. I hate how easily I conform to it. It's not who I really am or who I want to be. I've fantasized about what it might be like to be someone no one recognizes, the simple pleasure of getting lost in a crowd and having the freedom to change. The freedom to reinvent myself every time I meet someone new. Today, I might be able to experience that, thanks to you."

Felix smirked. "I'm so glad I can help you experience the joys of being insignificant and ordinary," he jested.

Lilliana laughed. "That's more of a gift than you realize!" she exclaimed in earnest, then she bit her lip with uncertainty and looked down.

"What's wrong?"

"I'm just a bit nervous."

"You have nothing to worry about, you're going to be magnificent."

"It's not that. I'm accustomed to playing someone else. It's just that I've only played the one character for so long. I don't know if I can be anything else, even myself," she confessed.

"You have to think of it as a game. Have you ever played make-believe?"

Lilliana was taken aback by the sheer oddness of the question. "Of course," she laughed, "though not for a very long time."

"It's no different. This other person you're playing, it's just some old costume you pulled out of a box that you're trying on for a day. It doesn't really matter how you play her, because as long as you're wearing the costume, you *are* her. If you fully embrace that and have fun with it, you can't go wrong," Felix asserted.

"And you'll be with me the whole time, right?"

"I wouldn't dream of being anywhere else."

Lilliana nodded.

"Shall we go get lost in a crowd then?" Felix proposed, offering her his hand.

Lilliana smiled and placed her hand in his.

⌒

Felix, Roy, and Lilliana walked down the jetty with the lamppost at its end and hit the green button for hailing an air cab. Immediately the Everfire in the lamp turned a bright green.

"I'm not sure how hard it's going to be to hail a cab from this far out. You two take the first one, I'll come along after," Roy suggested.

"Maybe we can catch one at the same time," Felix proposed.

He pulled out the coin Cabby had given him the day before and traced the strange symbol on its face with his finger. Then he threw it into the air and caught it again.

Roy watched him curiously. "What's that?"

"A sort of calling card. The cab driver I rode with yesterday gave it to me. He said I can use it to call him from anywhere."

"Is that right? Can I have a look?"

Felix handed the coin over to Roy.

"Hmm, I've never heard of or seen anything like it," Roy proclaimed, and handed it back.

"Well, we'll soon find out if it works." Felix pocketed the coin and looked out into the dense morning mist. At least the rain had cleared. But the heavy fog still made the air feel damp. Felix rubbed his hands together to warm them. After fifteen minutes or so two cabs pulled up alongside the jetty. One, Felix immediately recognized as Cabby's Express, the other was a small green ship with three propellers at the back.

"Will you look at that," Roy uttered in wonder and waved to the drivers.

"I'll see you both at Favio's then," he said, and stepped into the green cab.

"See you there," Felix returned and opened the door to Cabby's airship for Lilliana. She climbed inside and he followed.

"Hey! The man from Westdock," Cabby announced as they settled in.

He was wearing the same hat as the day before and was chewing on a wad of chewing gum, with his mechanical bird perched comfortably on his shoulder.

"Good morning, the calling card worked! I'm surprised I was able to catch you this far out," Felix remarked.

"You're lucky, I always hang around the outskirts during the big events. Less competition and better fares. Never been out this far though, didn't even know anyone lived this close to the Everstorm. What brings you guys out this way?" Cabby asked as he hit the Nixie tube counter and pulled the cab away from the jetty.

"We're staying with a friend. She's a meteorologist, she studies the storm," Felix explained.

"Neat. Where you two headed, you going straight to the Derby?"

"The Diamond Center," Felix requested.

"You sure you want to go there? All the shops will be closed today for the event."

"It's where we're meeting our designer."

"Oh yeah, I was going to say you two look a little underdressed. Which designer is it?"

"Favio Fritz."

"Cool name. Never heard of him. Not that that's saying anything—I don't even know why I asked. I don't pay much attention to that stuff. There's only a few names I'd recognize and only because it's all they talk about in the paper a week before the event. You going to introduce me to your company?" Cabby asked, adjusting his rearview mirror to focus on Lilliana.

"Of course, where are my manners? This is Silvy, we met at a club last night. She's going to help me with promotions at the Derby. Silvy, this is Cabby, cab driver extraordinaire," Felix announced.

"Good day, Miss," Cabby said with a tip of his hat.

"It's a pleasure to meet you," Lilliana returned.

"Pleasure's all mine. Westdock's a lucky guy, you from there too?"

"No. Everlast," Lilliana said.

"Everlast, really? I hear that's a beautiful place."

"It is."

"Is it true you grow your houses there?"

"Yes, the island's so fruitful just about everything grows there. You'll see fence posts sprouting into trees," Lilliana told him.

"Whoa. So how does that work? Do you plant trees in the ground for your houses or something?"

"There's a whole ceremony for making a house. The community comes together for it. We plant special posts in the shape we want our house to be, and within weeks the posts take root and begin to grow. In a year all the trunks form together making solid walls and are taller than two of the tallest men stacked on top of one another. It's quite fascinating. Every building there is alive," Lilliana expounded.

"It sounds incredible!" Cabby exclaimed.

"I'd like to see that," Felix said, smiling at Lilliana with dazzling warmth in his eyes.

"Help yourselves to refreshments, it'll be a while till we reach the capital," Cabby told them.

"Thanks." Felix opened the side compartment under his drink tray to reveal a selection of chocolates and mixed nuts. He offered a chocolate to Lilliana and then put his arm around her. She leaned into him as she enjoyed the treat. Felix was elated to finally be able to be alone with her. He had to watch his every move when they were around Roy. Even though Roy knew his feelings for her, Felix was still very conscious of having boundaries. Having him gone meant he could finally relax a little, and having Lilliana playing someone other than a duchess, meant he could relax even more.

"This is the perfect opportunity for us to get into character," he whispered into Lilliana's ear, "That was quite the club last night. You're a fantastic dancer, Silvy," he declared audibly.

Lilliana smiled. "You weren't so bad yourself."

"Do you have places like that on Everlast?" he asked her.

"Better. The clubs in Everlast are all open to the sky. At night, you can dance under the stars. The whole place is decorated with flowers growing on everything."

Felix smiled. "Sounds like a dream."

"It's like nowhere else. You'll have to come see it one day," she said.

"I'd like that." Felix admired the joy in Lilliana's eyes. He'd never been so enamored of anyone. He met her gaze and then leaned across the seat and kissed her. Lilliana welcomed his embrace and kissed him back passionately.

Cabby saw them in the rearview and whistled.

Lilliana pulled away from Felix laughing.

"Isn't there some sort of privacy curtain back here?" Felix asked.

"Are you kidding?! I'd miss out on all the action!"

Felix chuckled. "You little perv."

"Hey, there aren't a lot of perks to this job. I gotta take what I can get."

Felix turned to Lilliana and pointed at Cabby with his thumb, "I think he's asking for a show."

"Absolutely not! We shouldn't encourage him, he's only a child!"

"Cabby, a child? Look at this kid, he has his own air cab. I'm sure kissing is something he's well accustomed to."

"True," Cabby confirmed from the front.

"That's not the point! I'm not making an exhibitionist of myself!" Lilliana asserted indignantly.

"Look what you've done, Cabby, now you've gone and ruined everyone's fun."

"It's not my fault the broad's a stiff," Cabby protested.

Lilliana's jaw dropped.

"And you're calling him a child?" Felix asked Lilliana with a wry smirk. He took off his jacket and hung it up in front of the window between them and the cockpit.

"Hey!" Cabby objected.

"Better?" Felix asked Lilliana.

She smiled, "Much."

And Felix kissed her again.

⚬

As soon as the capital was in view, the sky was filled with traffic. There were airships of every size and color flying flags with regal family crests. Dragons glided between them, scales shining in the morning sun as their riders steered them towards the Diamond City.

Lilliana was looking out the window beside Felix with eyes filled with wonder. "Isn't it magnificent?"

"Beyond words," Felix marveled.

Cabby called to them from the cockpit, "Hold onto your seats, I'm going to get us out of this congestion."

Felix pulled his jacket down from the opening. "Pardon? What was that you said?"

"I said, hold on!"

The airship jolted forward. Felix put his arm across Lilliana and braced his other hand against the roof as the ship tipped into a nosedive. "Bloody shick! Are you trying to kill us?!" he shouted.

"Just one sec, we're almost through," Cabby called back, maneuvering the levers and switches with expert precision.

They dipped down below the traffic into clear airspace and Cabby righted the ship again.

"You should be thanking me, I just saved you fifteen minutes on your fare," he announced.

"I'm surprised your ship's still in one piece with you flying like that!" Felix exclaimed.

Cabby straightened his hat. "Relax, I was runner up in the R.A.R. I would've been the champion if I had enough coin to upgrade this old girl. Gave Jeffrey Faulters a good run for his coin though, and his airship's one of the latest models with *all* the fancy upgrades."

"What's the R.A.R?" Lilliana inquired.

"The Royal Aviation Rally. It's like the Derby, except for airships and with a lot less recognition."

"I've never heard of it."

"As I said, less recognition. It's a local thing," Cabby asserted. He pulled the airship abruptly into the docking station that fanned out below the capital island. "Here we are," he announced cheerily, and pushed the button on top of his Nixie tube counter to stop the clock. "That'll be three duckets, thanks."

"Three duckets?! Do you also specialize in highway robbery?" Felix exclaimed.

Lilliana put her hand gently on Felix's knee, and fished three duckets from her coin purse, handing them to the driver. "I've added an extra wagon for your trouble—put it towards upgrading your ship," she told him.

Cabby tipped his hat. "I guess you're not such a stiff after all—Thanks, lady!"

A droid in a smart uniform opened the cab door for Lilliana, and she stepped out onto the platform.

"Thanks for the lift, Cabby. Your ride's anything but dull, I'll give you that," Felix told him.

Cabby smirked. "I take that as a compliment."

Felix smiled and climbed out of the air cab. He made a point not to look down at the open sky as he hurried Lilliana towards the elevator at the opposite end of the platform. He only relaxed once they were behind the elevator's gold doors.

There were three other people in it with them, all dressed to the hilt in over-the-top gaudy fashion. They gave Lilliana and Felix a single quick glance and then turned up their noses. Felix was relieved he and Lilliana were the only ones getting out on the shopping level. Just as Cabby had said, all the shops were closed. The doors were locked and the Everfire lamps inside were covered with dimmer bags.

Felix led Lilliana past them towards the tailors' row, and soon they were standing in front of Favio's Bespoke Apparel. His shop was the only one with any lights on. Seeing them through the front window, Favio came to the door to greet them. "Morning! It's good to see you both again. Come in, come in, you're just on time," he announced, ushering them inside. "Where's Roy?"

"The cab could only fit two of us. He shouldn't be far behind. He left the same time we did," Felix explained.

"Ah, very well. Would you like some tea?" Favio offered.

"Yes thanks, much obliged."

Lilliana smiled. "Thank you, Favio."

Favio gestured to the armchairs, "Sit down and make yourselves comfortable. Won't be a moment. I have your outfits hanging up in the changing rooms for you, but wait until after tea, we'll go over the day while we drink," he told them, and disappeared out the back.

Felix sat down in one of the big leather armchairs next to Lilliana and squeezed her hand encouragingly. A moment later Favio returned with a tray bearing a hand-painted porcelain tea set that he placed down in front of them.

"So, we've a big day ahead. I can't tell you both how excited I am to have you representing my work. You only need to attend the before and after events. Besides that, you'll be free to roam where you like amongst the spectators for the rest of the day. We'll start with the Designers Breakfast Gala. It's a special event for the who's who of the fashion world. All the top designers will be there accompanied by one or two models representing their new line. All you'll have to do is stand around and look pretty, while I rub shoulders with the attending fashionistas."

"Sounds good to me," Felix said.

Lilliana nodded enthusiastically. "Yes, I look forward to it."

"Great! The after-party for the competitors and VIPs will be held at the Diamond Opera House. That's where we'll have our audience with The Emperor. Make sure you head there as soon as the Derby's over. There's a private room that's been prepared for us to present my work at the hour of the Dream Weaver. It's imperative we're on time. I want you there an hour early to be prepped in hair and wardrobe. I'll give you your passes now, don't lose them," Favio asserted, and handed them each a small gold badge with a purple ribbon attached to the bottom.

"Pin this onto your attire somewhere out of sight until you need it," he instructed.

Felix and Lilliana accepted the badges.

"Any questions?"

"So, we'll accompany you to the Gala this morning, and then we'll split ways until the after-party?" Felix confirmed.

"Precisely," Favio nodded.

"Where shall we meet you at the Opera House?" Lilliana inquired.

"Great question. There's a large statue in the foyer. Let's meet there at the hour of Pansophy and I'll show you where to go."

"Large statue in the foyer at Pansophy's hour. Got it," Felix acknowledged.

There was knocking on the glass. All three of them looked up to see Roy looking at them through the front display window. Favio got up to let him in. "Welcome, my friend. Now, we can begin!"

An hour later, Felix, Lilliana, Roy, and Favio stepped off the gold elevator into the Diamond City, dressed in the dazzling display of the designer's masterpieces. The white buildings with their dragon accents and long windows towered all around them. The place was densely crowded with aristocrats dressed to the hilt in finery, wearing brightly colored suits and dresses, lace parasols, and ornate hats that looked more like art pieces than headwear. One woman's hat had a detailed wooden tall ship the size of a bread box floating in an ocean of swirling folds of blue fabric. A man wore a top hat featuring a castle with a dragon curled around it. And the men's beards were just as spectacular, either dyed with colors and patterns that made them look more like printed fabric than hair or styled into shapes or pictures. One man's facial hair was molded into the shape of a miniature dragon-drawn carriage. Another was spiked out in all directions as if it didn't adhere to the laws of gravity. Felix saw one decorated densely with real flowers, and another styled into an elaborate scene of an airship flying through billowing clouds. Many of the aristocrats had fine ornate tattoos on their arms or hands in baroque or floral patterns. Some even delicately adorned their necks or outlined a section of their face.

Felix had never seen so many upper class. In Westdock, blue bloods were the minority, the privileged few. They gathered in small- to medium-sized groups at fancy house parties and private events. Here, the titled were the commoners. In fact, there was no one else. Felix couldn't see anyone who looked less than genteel amongst the crowd. And they were all flowing towards the front entrance of the Derby.

Favio, Roy, Lilliana, and Felix were swept into the sea of pedestrian traffic and carried forward by the current. At the edge of the city loomed a grand archway made completely of colorful flowers. As they drew nearer Felix could see at the front two huge sculptures of dragons rearing on their hind legs, made with a stunning variety of bright, perfect blossoms. Jets of fire shot up into the air from their mouths every few minutes. On either side stretched a tall wall blocking off the event from the rest of the city. The wall was densely covered with flowers as far as the eye could see and outlined with ornate lampposts that stretched high above them with dragon sculptures curling up their poles, which were also adorned with garlands and hanging baskets of more flowers.

Felix couldn't help but wonder where all those flowers had come from. Did they buy and import every living thing on Equillian, or did they grow them themselves, dedicating an entire island for the decorations of the event? Maybe both, Felix mused.

Soon they were at the entrance. There were two guards posted out front, and doormen dressed in fine gold uniforms greeting attendants and taking tickets at the door. When it was their turn, Favio produced a shiny green pass embossed with a gold dragon on it. And Roy presented the promotion passes for the rest of them. The doorman waved them through.

"Where should we meet you after the Gala?" Lilliana asked Roy once they were inside the entrance.

"I think it's best if we separate and meet back at Katarina's tonight when the event's concluded. You're less likely to be recognized if we're not seen together. Everyone knows your father and I are fast friends," Roy suggested.

"What are you going to do?" she asked.

"Mix amongst the nobles and get as much intel as I can on your father's disappearance. If you run into any trouble or need to get in touch with me before then, leave a message at the whisky tent. I'll check there around lunchtime."

"Alright, we'll see you back at Katarina's tonight then," Lilliana agreed.

"See you tonight. And hey, Everspark—don't forget to have some fun," Roy told her with a wink.

"Thanks, you too," Lilliana beamed in return, and they watched Roy disappear into the crowd, before following Favio towards the Gala. As they weaved through the pedestrian traffic, Felix slipped his hand into Lilliana's. She started to pull away anxiously and then seemed to remember she was disguised and smiled, squeezing his hand. Felix held onto her tightly as they followed Favio. As soon as they were through the initial jam surrounding the entrance, the crowd poured towards the cushioned stadium seating encircling the outer edge of the island, and the congestion around them cleared a little. Felix finally relaxed his instinct to protect the contents of his pockets. Though he doubted any of the patrons here would do anything as base as pocket thievery, it was a hard habit to shake in a crowd.

Favio led them to a stone tower that shot up well above the rest of the spectators. At the tower's base was a guard checking passes. Favio flashed his and the guard welcomed them inside, gesturing towards an elevator. They stepped into it and Favio pushed a button with an arrow pointing up. The elevator jolted upwards.

"I've always wondered what's in this tower," Lilliana told Felix, "does this lead to the designers' gala?" she asked Favio.

"Yes. It's a exclusive event for special ticket holders. Anyone who's anyone in the design world will be here. As well as their signature pieces and fashionistas eager to see the latest trends," Favio informed them.

A moment later the elevator came to a stop and the doors opened to a large circular room surrounded by glass windows that stretched from floor to ceiling. The polished oak floor and lavish cocktail bar in the center spoke of tasteful elegance. As they stepped inside, they were welcomed by a pretty woman in a gold suit who handed them each a chilled peach Bellini in a long-stemmed flute.

Felix smiled at Lilliana as they followed Favio. The place was buzzing with the hum of conversation. A group of fifty or so people filled the open space. They stood about mingling in small groups while they sipped lavish cocktails. Everyone was dressed to the hilt in the highest fashion, their decadent attire sparing no expense on materials. Some were beaded with precious stones, others incorporated fine embossed and dyed leather, and some were made with spider silk and richly printed fabrics. Felix took it all in, elated. Crashing exclusive events was his second favorite pastime. He could immediately identify who was who amongst the crowd of meticulously manicured guests. The fashion models were in a variety of sizes and colors with perfectly painted makeup and flawless skin. They looked more like dolls than people. Each one dressed in garb that made a statement—created for visual effect rather than practicality. They stood silently in fashionable poses next to their designers—as if a fashion accessory themselves. The designers had far more imperfections than their creations—most wore extravagant garb that would seem gaudy anywhere else. The special ticket holders, or fashionistas, as Favio called them, were a mixed bunch. They could only be labeled by one defining characteristic—the way they looked at the models as if they were merchandise rather than people.

"Come this way my pretties, I must introduce you!" Favio exclaimed excitedly. He grabbed an hors d'oeuvre from a wandering waiter and steered Felix and Lilliana towards a cluster of five people standing in a tight circle talking loudly to one another. A woman in a long green sequined dress held up her arms when she saw them approaching. "Favio, my darling! Come here, I'm so pleased to see you!"

Favio kissed the woman on both cheeks. "Rhianna, my dear. The pleasure's all mine. I hope I haven't missed anything?"

"Nothing at all. Are these your pieces?" she inquired, running her eyes up and down Felix and Lilliana.

"Yes, this is James and Silvy. They're representing my new line. I have others that will be displayed on some of the Derby competitors this evening."

"How positively delightful! They're gorgeous!! Absolutely stunning! You have outdone yourself, my dear fellow."

"You're too kind. Is this yours?" Favio asked, nodding towards a delicate young woman next to Rhianna who was wearing a dress that looked like a tapestry. It was cream colored with an opalescent quality, and in the center of the bodice was a painted picture of a wooded glen. It was so detailed, it looked like you could step inside the fabric and be transported to another place.

"What a wonderfully interesting idea. It's a masterpiece," Favio commended.

"Oh, you're too kind. It's part of my fairytale collection. I'm sure you'll recognize my other piece wandering around here somewhere," she said, looking about and pointing to another delicate model whose dress looked like it was pages from a book, its skirt covered in fine calligraphy.

"Splendid!" Favio exclaimed.

Felix tuned out for the rest of the conversation. He was disappointed to find they were never invited into it. It seemed they were expected to be nothing more than animated manikins. Lilliana was sated all the same, either enjoying simply being an observer of the event or doing a splendid job of at least pretending to be. Felix busied himself with some of the passing hors d'oeuvres and another glass of peach Bellini.

After an hour of mind-numbing introductions and four Bellinis down, Favio finally said, "You two are free to wander for the rest of the day. Just be sure to come straight to the Opera House as soon as the closing ceremony's over."

"We'll be there," Felix promised.

"Spectacular! I look forward to seeing you both then. You have your badges?"

Felix showed Favio his pinned on the inside of his jacket, and Lilliana showed him hers.

"Excellent! You can stay up here as long as you like, it's a superb view of the Derby," Favio proclaimed, as he brushed a crumb off Felix's jacket. "And please be sure to look after the apparel, I want it spotless this evening."

"Of course," Felix assured him.

"Thank you, Favio. It's an honor to be representing your work," Lilliana smiled charmingly.

"Aren't you a doll. It's an honor to have someone so charming wearing it! Now, go have some fun, you two!" he insisted, and turned to the man next to him to spark up a conversation.

"Come, the Derby's starting!" Lilliana exclaimed excitedly, leading Felix to the edge of the glass window. The Gala building had an excellent 360-degree view of the racetrack encircling the capital. The track was nothing but open sky between the islands, outlined with a railing covered in flowers that ran along the island's edge.

"I'm going to grab another drink, you want anything?" Felix asked.

Lilliana shook her head. She'd found them a couple of seats in front of the central window and was glued to it as the trumpets sounded for the opening ceremony.

Felix walked up to the long bar that stretched along the middle of the round room. There was an android behind it cleaning glasses, wearing a collared shirt with rolled-up sleeves and an apron. His faux moustache was styled so that it stuck straight out on either side of his face like cat's whiskers.

"Can I get you something, sir?" the android asked.

"Yeah. You got any Ash Whiskey?"

"Certainly. How would you like it?"

"On the rocks," Felix requested.

"Fine choice, sir. Coming right up."

Felix noticed a stack of programs sitting on the bar beside him, "Can I have one of these?"

"Help yourself. They're there for the taking," the mechanical bartender answered, and put a solid ball of ice in a short glass and then filled it with the top-shelf whiskey.

"Thanks," Felix said, taking the drink. Ash Whiskey was the most expensive whiskey on the market. Felix didn't know when he'd get another opportunity to enjoy it, and he intended to make the most of this one. He tucked a program under his arm and stopped by the buffet table to fill up a small plate with gourmet finger food before returning to Lilliana's side.

"Did I miss anything?" he asked her, offering Lilliana the plate of hors d'oeuvres. She popped an olive into her mouth. "Not yet. The duke's opening speech is about to begin."

"Which one?" Felix inquired.

"The Duke of Sky View."

"Well, of course," Felix remarked, settling into his seat beside her.

A man with stark white hair and a fine floral suit stepped onto a podium on the stage erected at the forefront of the event.

"Ladies and gentlemen, welcome to the sixtieth anniversary of the Sky Cup Derby!" he announced, and the audience cheered loudly.

"I've had the absolute pleasure to see this event grow from its very beginning. What was once a simple celebration of dragon racing has now bloomed into a celebration of excellence across the board. Not only in the varied dragon sports, but also in art, fashion, music, and the magnificent scientific advances that our precinct has made with breeding. I look forward to this event every year because every year I'm surprised and delighted by the vast talent that resides within our precinct. I couldn't be more proud of what we've achieved together, and I couldn't be more proud to be able to share it with everyone visiting!"

The crowd cheered again until the duke held up a hand to silence them. Their voices dimmed.

"Now, before we begin, I have an announcement to make. This will be the last year I'll be running the Derby."

Murmurs ran through the crowd.

"It's been a wild ride, one I've enjoyed thoroughly, but it's a young man's game, and I'm getting old and tired—and I wish to devote more of my energy to the governing obligations of Sky View. So, I'm handing the responsibility down to my son, Frederick—the marquess of our fine precinct. I have no doubt he'll prove to be an exciting improvement and make a far better leader of the event than I. I very much hope you'll all give him the same magnificent support and respect you've shown me all these years, and I look forward to joining you as a participant next year!" he announced.

The crowd cheered with enthusiasm.

"Thank you. Now, I'll hand the stage over to Fredric so that he can say a few words," the Duke concluded and stepped down from the podium. A well-built handsome man with blue eyes and thick blond hair stepped onto the stage. He looked to be aged twenty-two or twenty-three, to Felix's best guess.

"Is *that* Frederick Remington?" Lilliana queried.

"Do you know him?" Felix asked.

"We met once when I was a child, but he was very spindly then."

"I suppose he's been eating his duck eggs," Felix remarked, taking a sip of his whiskey.

The marquess smiled broadly with perfect white teeth and waved to the crowd. "May I just say, you people are looking sensational!"

The crowd went wild with applause. Felix rolled his eyes. *Great—another egotistical, cocksure, douchebag noble,* he thought dryly.

"I'm honored that my father has decided to pass the reins of this event to me. Since I can first remember, the Derby's been something I've looked forward to every year with eager anticipation—"

At that point Felix tuned out of the grandiloquent speech and looked down at the program. The Derby had quite the lineup, beginning with a parade of the competitors and their dragons. Then jousting and the pre-races, before a game of dragon polo. Then a halftime dragon air show and music number. Then a beauty and brawn event, and a fire-breathing competition, followed by the final race, then a firework and glow dragon spectacle—whatever that was. For the most part, it sounded quite entertaining. When Felix looked up, he was disappointed to see Frederick was still talking.

"Now, if you'll excuse me, I have to go prepare for the parade! Thank you and enjoy the show!" the marquess announced, finally leaving the podium.

"Thank the Stars," Felix muttered as the crowd cheered.

"Why is he in the parade?" Lilliana queried.

"To sate the appetite of his obese ego?" Felix suggested.

Lilliana hit his arm with the back of her hand. "The duke and his family have never been in the parade, it's only for participants in the events," she said.

Felix shrugged.

"Is that the program?" Lilliana asked.

Felix handed it to her and took a generous sip of his Ash Whiskey.

Lilliana flipped through the booklet. "He's a competitor in the jousting tournament!" she exclaimed.

"Well, that certainly explains his growth spurt."

"I'm surprised the duke is letting his son compete. It's such a violent sport, normally the royals refrain from jousting, leaving it to the lesser households. Especially when they only have one heir, like Frederick."

"If my son was Frederick, I'd let him joust too," Felix remarked.

Lilliana laughed. "He's not that bad! I've heard he's quite compassionate towards the common people. I would've thought that was something you'd admire?"

"What common people? There aren't any common people in Sky View. Unless you're referring to the slightly less elevated toffs in the bleachers?" Felix asked.

The trumpets broke through the crowd's applause and the parade began, pulling their attention. Dragons with scales like sparkling gemstones flew in a line along the track below them with riders on their backs. Some were clad in armor, others in jockey or polo gear, and others in dazzling leotards.

"Now, this is the perfect opportunity to get a first glance at the racing dragons. You can often determine who'll be the winner by their behavior in the parade," she explained excitedly, leaning in towards the glass.

Felix perked up suddenly. "Really? How can you tell?" he asked, watching her and the parade with renewed interest.

Lilliana pointed to a large yellow dragon with two black stripes along its back that looked like it was ready to bolt. "Do you see how that one is overly excited?"

"Yeah…"

"It's too eager. It'll use up all its energy at the start and lack stamina to place," Lilliana explained, and flipped through the program. "What's his number?" she asked.

Felix read the white number painted on the dragon's saddle. "Eleven."

"His name's Eat-My-Stinger. He's a Yellow-Wasp dragon. Do you have a pencil?"

"Hmmm…" Felix patted down his pockets, "Look at that, you're in luck," he announced, pulling a small graphite pencil from inside his breast pocket.

Lilliana took it in hand and started jotting down notes next to Eat-My-Stinger's name in the program. She pointed to a slender purple dragon whose rider was struggling to keep it from eating the flowers on the fencing. "And you see that one there?"

"You mean the one more interested in the adornments than the track?"

"Precisely. I would avoid betting on that one entirely; it clearly has no drive or ambition."

"So, how do you know which dragons will place?" Felix inquired.

"We're looking for dragons that are well balanced, energetic without being overexcited. It's also important to take the dragon's physique into consideration. You can tell the dragon's health by the shine in its scales and the clarity of its eyes. A healthy dragon with good muscle definition is more likely to perform well. On the other hand, being too big and muscular can slow it down," she explained.

"You know a lot about this," Felix remarked.

"My uncle taught me most of it, the rest I figured out on my own during our time here. My father used to bring us out here every year. The majority of people choose their bets by the dragon's name or the numbers representing them. But dragon racing isn't like spinning dice—there are sure tell-tale signs to choosing a winner."

"Have you chosen the winner often?" Felix queried with genuine interest.

Lilliana smirked. "My father used to call me his little luck charm."

"Did he? It looks to me like luck had little to do with it, nor that it was his. Let me guess, he was the one placing the bets and collecting the spoils too?"

"Of course, I was only a child! He would buy me a stick of fairy cotton when we won," Lilliana told him.

"How generous," Felix stated dryly. "Well, you're not a child anymore. It's time you placed your own bets. When do the races start?"

"Right after the jousting. The jousting used to be my favorite event."

"Used to?"

"When my uncle was around. He'd compete in the tournament every year. He brought so much joy to everything he did. He loved the sport for what it was, It didn't matter if he won or lost, his enthusiasm was contagious. He made such a show of it—it made watching him joyous. I'm not sure if the event will be the same without him," she admitted.

Just then Arianna rode into view on Charred-I'm-Sure, taking up the tail of the parade. The audience cheered spiritedly as she passed them by. Lilliana's enthusiasm fell with the sight of her. She clapped politely, but Felix noted the animosity in her expression.


"First up in our jousting tournament this year is Lord Dufton Berkenshaw from South View, and from Everlast, Sir Melton Bowbrick!" the presenter announced.

A roar of loud cheering passed through the crowd like a wave.

"Look at that, Melton Bowbrick—your home representative. I hope they win," Felix said with a wry grin.

Lilliana smiled. "That's as good a reason to root for him as any, I suppose. I haven't been keeping up with the jousting competitors."

Two armored dragons raced along the track from opposite directions with armored knights on their backs. Each rider carried a long lance that they held erect, decorated with colored ribbons that trailed behind them.

One knight was adorned all in yellow, and the other all in purple. Their ribbons and lances colored to match—with painted lines spiraling up the weapons.

The yellow knight rode his dragon past the audience that hugged the track's outer edge, pumping his lance into the air. The crowd in the cushioned tiered seating cheered in response. The purple knight did the same along the adjacent side of the track, and the audience there cheered enthusiastically in turn—doing their best to be louder than the fans of the other jouster.

"Which is the one from Everlast?" Felix inquired.

"Melton Bowbrick's the yellow knight; he's Everlast's champion," Lilliana informed him, and Felix was glad to see her enthusiasm restored.

The knights readied themselves at either end of the jousting strip. A flag in the center was raised and a trumpet sounded. The knights plowed forward head on, the sun reflecting brightly off their dragons' scales.

As soon as they got within range of one another, the dragons pulled their wings in tightly by their sides and shot past one another like torpedoes. Each knight's lance hit and splintered against the other's shield in a shower of wooden shards as they swooped past. The crowd cheered.

"How does this game work exactly?" Felix inquired.

"There are three rounds. A hit to the body is worth one point. A hit to the body that breaks a lance is worth three, and a knock off a dragon is worth five. The winner is the competitor with the most points after all three rounds," Lilliana explained.

"Right. So, does that mean no one gets a point because the lances hit the shields?" Felix asked.

Lilliana nodded. "That's right. No points this round."

The knights resumed their starting positions and readied their dragons for the next bout. Squires on smaller dragons wearing their knight's colors flew up from the sidelines and handed their knights new lances before hurrying back off the track.

The knights aimed their weapons at one another and charged. Steam from the dragons' hot breath billowed up from their nostrils as they sped forward. The yellow knight's dragon blew a gust of fire. The purple knight deflected the flames with his shield, but it cost him his visibility.

He pointed his lance abstractly at his opponent and missed. The yellow knight struck him in the chest with his lance as he passed.

The point keeper raised a yellow flag high in the air and stuck it into a flag holder for the yellow side. The fans of the Everlast champion cheered wildly, while the other fans booed.

"This is fun," Felix remarked, clapping with the crowd.

Lilliana smiled broadly. "I knew you'd like it."

The knights turned their dragons and readied themselves once more for their final pass. The flag in the center was raised and they sped forward. The dragons pulled in their wings as they reached the center, shooting past one another. The purple knight stood up in his stirrups and rammed his lance towards the yellow knight as he passed. The yellow knight put up his shield while thrusting his own lance forward. Both lances passed the other's defenses and hit their opponents, knocking them back in their saddles. Both a purple and a yellow flag went up. The whole audience cheered loudly. Then a large yellow flag was raised, declaring the winner.

The knights held their lances high and flew the length of the events track as they were cheered by their spectators. They nodded to one another respectfully and then cleared the jousting stage for the next competitors.

"I quite enjoyed that. Well done, Everlast! You must be proud to have your home champion declared winner," Felix said.

Lilliana smiled. "Very."

"So, what's the verdict? Is jousting still your favorite event despite the absence of your uncle?" Felix asked.

"Yes," Lilliana confessed with a grin.

"For our next round, we'll be welcoming back Sir Gerald Westoff from the Harvest Lands. And we're very pleased and honored to be introducing a new competitor—Lady Emily Swift from the Southern Isles," the presenter announced.

Murmurs ran through the crowd.

"Lady Emily Swift—a woman?!" Lilliana exclaimed in surprise.

"Well, why not?" Felix asked.

"It just isn't—well, hasn't been done."

"I think it's refreshing," Felix said.

Lilliana opened the program and scanned the pages. She gasped and began to read aloud.

"Lady Emily Swift, a relative of the Swift nobles on the Southern Isles, won three separate qualifying matches disguised as a man. When her true identity was revealed, it became impossible to deny that women are indeed capable of the sport. After much debate amongst the Royal Jousting Association, the Duke himself invited Lady Swift to take the place she had rightfully earned and compete in the Sky Cup Derby!" Lilliana read. "This is incredible! How have I not heard of this—or her?"

"Well, you've been very busy. Weddings don't plan themselves," Felix remarked.

A red knight and a green knight flew onto the track. Felix squinted towards the riders and could see that the breastplate on the green knight was indeed built for a woman. The red knight was twice her size and looked as solid as his muscular orange dragon. He stopped in front of the audience and held his lance up into the air, his dragon beating its wings and rearing up while blowing a large stream of fire above the audience's heads. The crowd erupted in cheers of approval.

The green knight mounted on a large purple dragon was like a twig in comparison. She stood up in her stirrups and held her lance up over her head, pumping it towards the sky as her dragon carried her past the audience on the capital side.

Most of the crowd cheered hesitantly. Lilliana whooped and cheered as loud as she could, spurring stares from the fashionistas surrounding them.

"I don't think she can hear you," Felix told her with a grin.

Lilliana ignored him.

"Having these two paired makes me nervous. Woman or not, those two are obviously unevenly matched. Look at the size of him, he looks like he might eat her for breakfast," Felix exclaimed.

"Competitors are paired for their skill level, not their size. It might appear to be an unfair match, but they've qualified to compete against each other—which means they each probably have strengths that are the other's weakness. For example, the red knight has brawn where the green knight might have agility. The contrast in their skillsets creates a more interesting bout," Lilliana explained.

"But if the green knight gets hit, it will be devastating."

"Yes…that is the trade off," Lilliana admitted with concern.

Felix looked down at the competitors and found himself feeling anxious for Lady Swift. After the two knights finished their introduction, they flew their dragons to opposite ends of the track. They lowered the visors on their helmets and pointed their lances towards each other. Trumpets lit the air and the starting flag was lifted. The two dragons were off, racing towards each other. As they approached their opponent the dragons pulled their wings in, but instead of shooting past each other as the last competitors had done, the purple dragon spun upside down, maneuvering beneath the orange dragon.

The green knight came back up alongside the red knight's right flank and planted her lance into his armpit, pushing him up and over with the upward momentum of her dragon's motion. The red knight hardly had time to blink before he realized what was happening. He instinctively put up his arm to shield himself, but his actual shield was in the opposite hand on the other side. The blow knocked him clean off his dragon.

The crowd gasped as the red knight fell. Lilliana stood up against the glass window to get a closer view.

Felix stepped up beside her. "Whoa!"

The red knight was caught with a jerk by a harness around his waist connected him to his saddle. He dangled for a few moments over the empty sky while his dragon beat its wings heavily in an attempt to stay upright while its rider pulled himself up onto its back.

A green flag went up to show that Lady Swift had won the first round. The crowd was stunned in silence.

"Did you see that! Did you see what she did?! That was incredible! I've never seen anyone pull a move like that; the red knight didn't even have a chance!" Lilliana exclaimed.

"Is that even allowed?" Felix asked.

Lilliana laughed in delight. "Apparently. I don't know why anyone hasn't thought to move that way before!"

"Indeed. She's made the event five times more thrilling," Felix agreed.

Lady Swift stood up in her stirrups and pumped her lance to the sky inspiring hoots and cheers as her dragon glided back to their starting place. Now, everyone in the audience was watching. The red knight flew back to his end and the two readied themselves for another round.

Trumpets sounded and the two knights rushed towards each other again, their visors lowered and lances pointed at one another with ribbons streaming behind.

As the two competitors approached each other, the orange dragon lowered its head and sprayed a wall of fire underneath it. The purple dragon turned on its side barely avoiding the flames, and Lady Swift aimed her lance at the chest of the red knight as she came past. Only this time, the red knight was ready for her. He turned his torso to dodge the attack and planted his own lance into her shoulder.

The lance broke apart in a shower of splinters as Lady Swift was thrown back. Her lance flew out of her hand over the chasm below, catching on the cord attached to her wrist. She barely managed to stay on her dragon, holding on by her legs. The crowd gasped. Everyone held their breath as she lay back against her dragon, motionless. Several seconds passed before Lady Swift stirred. She grabbed her lance and slowly pulled herself up. There was an eerie stillness cast across the crowd as she flew her dragon back to the starting position and readied herself for the last round.

Lady Swift's shoulder was injured badly—she could hardly lift her lance. Felix could only imagine the amount of pain she must be in. But she clearly wasn't ready to give in. She unfastened her shield and dropped it into the open sky below her, and then used the reins to lash her lance to her arm so she didn't have to hold onto it. Then she dropped her visor down and aimed her lance towards the red knight with both arms. Everyone watched with bated breath.

The trumpet sounded and the flag was raised.

Lady Swift and the red knight sped forward towards one another. Swift held her lance aimed directly at his chest.

As the dragons pulled in their wings and launched inches past one another, Swift's lance didn't waver.

The red knight thrust his lance towards her chest and Lady Swift subtly turned her body to the side and the lance barely brushed her, only missing her by a fraction. For a moment Felix thought she'd been speared through the center—but she hadn't. Before the red knight could register whether he'd hit her or not, Lady Swift's lance shattered against his chest in a shower of wood splinters.

"By shick," Felix muttered in amazement.

The crowd stared in surprise as their minds caught up to what had just happened, and then they erupted into a roar of cheering. Lilliana hooted and hugged Felix.

"Did you see that?! Did you see it? She won! A woman jouster, and she won!" Lilliana exclaimed enthusiastically.

"She was incredible," Felix agreed.

"You don't understand the magnitude of this. When I was a child, I used to imagine I was a jouster, but I always did so imagining I was a man—because I never thought it could be possible any other way. Lady

Swift just proved to every girl out there that it is possible!" she declared passionately.

A shadow dimmed Felix's enthusiasm. "Every *noble* girl, you mean."

Lilliana opened her mouth and then closed it again.

"You're forgetting that if anyone from my class tried to register for the event—male or female, we'd be laughed at and turned away—all because we weren't born with a silver spoon. It's certainly a step forward, but Equillian's still a far stretch from reaching equality, my lady."

"You're right, of course. Forgive my shortsightedness. I suppose the problem's more widespread than I'd considered," she confessed.

Felix smiled. "That being said, there's no denying we witnessed history today. Male or female, I'm pretty sure Lady Swift just revolutionized the sport of jousting."

"Yes, she did, didn't she?! I would love to hear her story, it must be fascinating!" Lilliana exclaimed.

"Maybe she'll be at the after-party tonight and you can ask her."

"Yes! I hope she is, wouldn't that be wonderful?"

"Indeed," Felix agreed with a smile, enjoying how happy Lilliana was. "I'm going to get another drink, you want one?" he asked.

"Can you get me a blushberry wine?"

"You can have anything you want, and you're asking for a blushberry wine? I thought drinking was a hobby of yours."

"One of us has to stay at least mildly sober," Lilliana stated.

Felix shrugged, "I'm glad it's not me."

When Felix returned with their drinks the presenter was halfway through introducing the next bout. "—and last, but certainly not least, please welcome Sir Patrick Gildenstien from Northbank and our very own Sky View marquess—Frederick Remington!" he announced.

The crowd cheered.

Frederick, the Sky View marquess, wearing pink, rode out on a silver dragon standing up in his saddle's stirrups and pumping his lance to the sky. His opponent, Sir Patrick Gildenstien, adorned in navy blue, rode out on a black dragon. He was a large man who held his lance high without any superfluous display.

The two jousters faced each other seated, with their lances aimed forward, eagerly awaiting the signal to charge. The flag was raised and they bolted towards one another.

Lilliana leaned forward in her seat. Frederick's lance hit the blue knight in the chest and it broke apart. The large man jolted back from the force of the blow.

A pink flag was raised, and three points were marked for Frederick. The crowd cheered. The competitors readied themselves for another round and Frederick's squire replaced his lance. The flag was lifted and again the knights charged.

This time both the men's lances glanced off each other's shields as they passed.

"I have to say, none of the other competitors have been nearly as exciting as Lady Swift," Felix remarked.

Lilliana laughed. "I know, I think she's ruined jousting for me!"

"You watch, next year it'll be a completely different sport," Felix asserted.

The blue and pink knights sped towards each other for the final round. Frederick planted his lance into the blue knight's chest and knocked him clean off his dragon.

The blue knight flew back as if hit by a cannonball, dangling over the clouds in the sky—held only by the rope connecting him to his dragon. The dragon beat its wings frantically to keep itself upright while the large man climbed back to his saddle. The pink flag went up and the crowd cheered loudly.

"Well, there you have it. He can knock a man off his dragon—I'll give him that," Felix said.

"It was a good bout. But disappointing compared with the last one. I don't know why no one else has thought of moving laterally the way Lady Swift did," Lilliana commented.

"Tradition. People follow it blindly, constrained by some fictional fallacy that new and different things aren't allowed, simply because they haven't been done before. That fallacy condemns us all to our predecessors' lack of insight and imagination. Sometimes it just takes someone from the outside to stir things up."

"Yes. Though, a lot of people don't like change. There's no doubt she'll encounter resistance," Lilliana returned with a subtle frown.

"True. But in the end she'll win. She has to; her way is far more entertaining. And let's face it, the spectators have more sway than the Royal Jousting Association."

"I hope you're right."

As they talked, the award ceremony commenced. When it was Lady Swift's turn to claim her prize the audience cheered the loudest.

"What's next?" Felix asked, feeling overwhelmingly glad they'd made it to the Derby.

Lilliana looked down at the program. "I think it's the pre-races, isn't it? Yes, it's the One Circle Dash. Come on, we need to get closer to the track so we can see the competing dragons on the parade lap. Each competitor does a round before their race, it will give us an even better insight into who will be the winner," she declared, standing and pulling Felix by one hand while he downed what was left of his drink with the other.

⁓

As soon as the elevator reached the ground floor and the doors opened, Lilliana pulled Felix through the crowd to the railing of the track. It was fragrant from its sleeve of flowers. Felix looked down into the empty sky and felt a wash of vertigo.

He took a step back, standing slightly behind Lilliana as she leaned over the edge in anticipation. The view wasn't nearly as good from the ground level, but it felt wonderful to be lost in the crowd. Now, they could blend in amongst the sea of handsomely clad spectators instead of feeling like they were stuck in a fishbowl. Felix slipped an arm around Lilliana, and she smiled up at him.

"Look, here come the dragons for the Dash!" Lilliana announced, pointing at a parade of seven dragons flying towards them.

They were smaller and slimmer than the jousting dragons. Their metallic scales shimmered in the morning's light.

"Do you have your pencil handy?" Lilliana asked.

Felix pulled his small pencil out of his pocket.

"Get ready to take notes," she directed.

Felix flicked through the pages of the program until he came to the list for the One Circle Dash.

"These names are incredible. Sound Breaker, Rogues Revenge, Don't-Blink-or-You'll-Miss-Me, See-You-Next-Twinsday. Ha! Who comes up with these?" he inquired.

"It's customary to entice bets with a good name. The more people like the name, the more likely they are to place coin on the dragon," Lilliana explained.

"Clever. So, we're looking for a dragon that's energetic without being impatient. Muscular but not stiff. With all the signs of good health as in—shiny scales and clear eyes?"

Lilliana grinned. "You're a quick learner."

"How about that one?" Felix asked, pointing to a green dragon that looked like it fit the description.

"Hmmm, I would bet on him to place, but not to come first," she said.

"Can you bet on them to place?" Felix queried.

"Yes. You don't get as much of a return, but it still counts as a win if they come in first, second, or third place that way. That dragon does have the qualities we're after, but it doesn't have as much spirit as that one," Lilliana said, pointing to a dark blue dragon that looked eager to fly but still in control. "What's that one's name?" she asked.

Felix matched its number to the list in the program, "Catchfire."

"And the other one?"

"Rogues Revenge."

"I would bet on Catchfire to come first, and Rogues Revenge to come second. That one there looks good too, but she's a gamble. Why don't we bet on her to place. What's her name?"

"Ride-My-Wake. You're not going to bet on your cousin's dragon— Midnight Revelry?" Felix queried.

"Midnight Revelry won't place. My guess is she'll be fourth," Lilliana said.

"How can you be so sure?"

"She's too eager. She'll bolt at the start and run out of stamina before the end."

"I'll take your word for it. Where do we place our bets?" Felix asked.

"Oh, I don't need to put any real coin down. I just like guessing for fun," Lilliana said.

Felix's face fell. "You just like guessing for fun? Don't be ridiculous! Of course we're putting real coin down."

"No. I really don't see the point," Lilliana asserted.

"Don't see the point?! Lill—my lady, you clearly have a gift. You would be insulting the Stars not to use it. Besides—it makes it a lot more fun, trust me," Felix persuaded, scanning the fairgrounds for the Betting House.

"Ah, there it is, I can see it. Come on, right this way," Felix insisted, grasping Lilliana's hand and guiding her through the crowd towards the building.

Felix stood beside Lilliana in the round Betting House. There was a man behind the counter wearing a pinstriped shirt rolled up to his elbows and a green vest over the top.

"Can I help you?" he asked them.

"Yes, we'd like to place a bet," Felix announced.

"Certainly, what bet would you like to place?"

Felix turned to Lilliana, "I have no idea what I'm doing, feel free to take the reins," he said.

The man looked at them expectantly and Lilliana cleared her throat, "We would like to place three bets on the One Circle Dash. One on Catchfire for finishing first, Rogues Revenge for finishing second, and Ride-My-Wake to place." she concluded.

"Excellent, how much would you like to put down?"

"Two duckets on each," Felix said.

"Make that ten duckets on each," Lilliana interjected.

Felix looked at her in surprise. "Ten duckets?! What happened to Miss I Just Bet For Fun?"

Lilliana shrugged. "If you're going to put down coin, then you may as well make it worth it—go big or go home, isn't that what they say?"

"If you put down coin like that, you'll soon have no choice but to go home," Felix remarked.

Lilliana smiled. "I tell you what, if we lose I'll cover the losses, and if we win, I'll split it with you fifty-fifty," she proposed.

Felix smirked. "Alright, deal."

But he couldn't help thinking that for someone worried about their financial future, Lilliana certainly didn't have a problem spending coin. Even with her guarantee, gambling that much made Felix nervous. He looked at the man behind the counter. "Alright, ten duckets on each," he declared.

"Very good sir," the man said, and Felix pulled thirty duckets out of his Dreg Pouch and reluctantly handed them over. The man took the stack of coins and handed Felix three tickets, which Felix carefully stored in his pouch.

Felix and Lilliana managed to find a couple of seats in the tiered seating. As they waited for the race to begin, Felix found himself feeling incredibly anxious. The amount of coin Lilliana convinced him to put down was too much to simply make the race fun—it made it positively nerve-racking.

*Serendipity be kind,* he thought, unconsciously rubbing the number seven tattoo on his hand.

A fog horn blared and the dragons shot forward. Felix and Lilliana stood in their seats to see. All seven of the dragons raced past them so quickly it was nothing but a colored blur.

"Maybe we should go back up into the Sky Dome?" Felix suggested.

"The race will be over before we make it," Lilliana said.

Sweat began to bead on Felix's brow as they patiently waited for the dragons to traverse the other side of the isle. The One Circle Dash was only a single lap around the track encircling the capital island. Felix found himself wishing they were up in the dome where they could see what was going on. After several excruciating seconds, the dragons came back into view. Felix saw most of the spectators had small ornate binoculars they were using to see and wished he'd had the same. He squinted towards the oncoming dragons, but they were moving so fast he couldn't discern one from the other.

"Midnight Revelry's holding first place, with See-You-Next-Twinsday hot on her tail. Catchfire's in third, with Rogues Revenge close behind and Ride-My-Wake in fifth..." the commentator's voice rang through the amplifier.

"Shick," Felix cursed.

Lilliana gripped his arm as she watched with anticipation. The dragons raced forward at breakneck speed, their huge wings pumping up and down a couple of times every few moments before they pulled them into their sides and shot through the air like rockets.

"Catchfire just passed See-You-Next-Twinsday, putting her in second, and is now hot on Midnight Revelry's heels. With Rogues Revenge holding her place in fourth, and Ride-My-Wake close behind ..." the commentator called.

"Come on Catchfire!" Lilliana cheered enthusiastically. Felix was too anxious to mutter a word.

"Rogues Revenge just passed See-You-Next-Twinsday—stealing third place, Midnight Revelry still holds the lead with Catchfire close behind..." the commentator blared through the loudspeaker.

The rest of the dragons were only inches behind as they sped towards the finish line. Felix held his breath.

"Come on Catchfire!" Felix yelled.

"Go Catchfire!" Lilliana hollered.

The rest of the crowd was cheering for their chosen dragons. The racing dragons pumped their wings for the final stretch and shot forward.

"It's clear Midnight Revelry's losing stamina as they near the finish line, she's fallen behind as Catchfire takes the lead, and Rogues Revenge steals second. But the race isn't over yet, folks…would you look at that! Ride-My-Wake makes a startling recovery, passing both See-You-Next-Twinsday and Midnight Revelry, taking third only moments away from the finish!"

The dragons flashed past the finish line and the race was over.

"And the winner is Catchfire! With Rogues Revenge in second place, and Ride-My-Wake coming close behind in third," the commentator announced through the amplifier.

Felix stood stunned. He couldn't believe it. The dragons all placed exactly as Lilliana said they would.

"We won!" Lilliana exclaimed in delight.

Felix laughed in astonishment. "Holy shick, we won!" He lifted Lilliana up in exultation and spun her around with disbelieving joy.

⌒

After all three of the pre-races, Felix and Lilliana stood inside the Betting House watching the man behind the counter count out one hundred twenty duckets for them. Felix halved the fortune and pushed one half towards Lilliana. Lilliana pushed it back, "My payment for your services as per our agreement," she asserted. Felix had entirely forgotten she'd agreed to give him sixty duckets when she'd initially hired him as her kidnapper. With the way everything had gone, he didn't feel like she owed him anything.

"You don't need to do that," he told her.

"I pride myself in being a woman of my word. Besides, I want to," she smiled.

"If that's truly what you want."

"It is," she insisted.

Felix emptied the entire fortune into his Dreg Pouch, then tucked it back under his shirt. Then he offered Lilliana his arm, and together they stepped out into the high noon light.

"That's an incredible talent you have. I think you've earned some fairy cotton," Felix declared with a wry grin, and steered Lilliana towards a stall selling colored spun sugar, a pink cloud on a stick.

"I haven't had fairy cotton in years!" Lilliana exclaimed delightedly.

Felix bought one for each of them, and the vendor handed over two sticks generously laden with the fluffy stuff. Lilliana took hers with childlike enthusiasm, and they walked side by side enjoying the delicacy of sweet cottoned sugar dissolving in their mouth with every bite.

*What a gift Lilliana has,* Felix thought. *Even if the duchess was penniless, with her by my side, we'd never have to worry about coin again.*

He'd had his luck in the Westdock gambling circuit spinning dice and playing cards, but this had far better odds. It was less of a game of chance when you had insight like Lilliana's. It was like having the ability to see through the back of playing cards. If only she wasn't a noble, they could disappear together to some far-off corner of Equillian with an airship of their own and fly up to Sky View to attend the races every year for their annual income. They would only have to work that one day a year and then they could spend the rest of it doing whatever they pleased. Felix couldn't think of anything better.

Soon they found themselves near the stables for the competing dragons. There weren't many other patrons around. They passed by an inconspicuous shed and Felix stopped outside its door.

"What are you doing?" Lilliana asked.

Felix pulled back the sliding door just enough to slip inside and held it open for Lilliana. "Come on, just for a minute," he enticed.

"We're not supposed to go in there!" she protested in a high whisper.

"Live a little, you're not a royal today, you're Silvy the adventure seeker!" Felix proclaimed with a wry grin.

"Fine. But I think Silvy would be even less inclined to follow you in there considering how long we've known each other," she asserted.

"Are you kidding, who wouldn't trust this charming face?"

Lilliana laughed and slipped inside the shed. Felix slipped in after her and closed the door behind them. As soon as the door was shut the temperature dropped several degrees. The interior of the shed was dimly lit by a single Everfire lamp by the door covered with a dimmer bag.

"Alright, are you going to tell me what we're doing in here?" Lilliana queried.

Felix wrapped his arms around her waist and gently pulled her towards him. "I just needed a moment to do this," he confessed and leaned down to kiss her.

Lilliana laughed, sinking into his embrace. Then she gasped and pulled away from him, staring up at the ceiling in horror. Felix looked up. Sheep carcasses hung from hooks in the rafters, all neatly gutted and skinned.

"Dragon food," he stated. "This must be the storeroom. No wonder it's so cold."

"It's awful!" Lilliana exclaimed, putting her hand over her mouth in disgust.

Felix shrugged. "Where do you think meat comes from? It certainly doesn't grow on trees."

"Of course not! But I've never seen it like this. It's so…heartless, as if their lives had no value other than the flesh grown on their bones."

"It's exactly like that. At least, from our perspective. Hopefully for them their lives were full of value and meaning. I'm sure this one pursued the world record in grass eating. And this ram was a hopeless romantic who fell in love with every sheep in the flock—which was all fun and games until the sheep started finding out about one another and banding together to form their revenge, at which point I'm sure the ram was begging to be put out of his misery," Felix jested.

Lilliana laughed and Felix pulled her back into his arms. "To stay alive, we must consume life. It's an unfortunate fact. The people of Sky View might think they're all high and mighty for not eating meat, but plants are still living things—and who's to say the life of a plant has any less value? Everything alive on Equillian is devouring others in one way or another," Felix remarked.

"It's quite disturbing when you put it that way."

"I suppose. But I'm not willing to give it up. Are you?" he asked.

"I suppose not. Though I do refuse to eat rabbit," Lilliana confessed.

"Had one as a pet, did you?"

"My father got one for my sister and me when we were young. Admittedly, I've never been able to eat them since. It was the only pet I've ever had—besides our horses, of course."

"And I'm guessing you haven't had the opportunity to turn down roasted horse?" Felix inquired.

"Course not!" Lilliana exclaimed.

"You're not missing anything, they're a bit gamy in my opinion."

Lilliana looked at him, horrified. "Surely, you've never eaten a horse?!"

"Well, not the whole thing—they're bigger than I am."

Lilliana stared at Felix in shock.

"What? It wasn't one of yours."

Lilliana's jaw dropped, and Felix burst into laughter.

"You should see your face! Come on, where would I get the opportunity to eat horse? They're far too expensive and valuable. Now rats on the other hand…"

"Oh stop it!" Lilliana exclaimed, hitting him in the shoulder. Then she shivered and wrapped her arms around herself.

Felix took off his jacket and draped it around her shoulders. "Come on, let's get you out of here before you catch a chill. Just one more for the road?" he asked her, then leaned in and stole a kiss before she had the opportunity to answer.

Felix and Lilliana stepped out of the shed, shielding their faces against the harsh sunlight. "Where to next?" Felix asked.

Lilliana pulled out the program. "Dragon Polo's up next."

"Sounds invigorating," Felix remarked ironically.

"It's probably already started, come on!" Lilliana exclaimed and grabbed his hand, pulling him back towards the stadium.

# SHOW BIZ

It was Starday. Gwena had finished working her shift on the nightclub floor early that morning. She'd spent only the last four hours asleep, waking in a panic when she remembered her meeting with Madam Pomphrey. Gwena barely poked at her breakfast before heading off for the appointment. She was both eager and nervous to be working with the magician. Madam Pomphrey had been an idol of hers for so long, it was surreal to think of her as a regular person.

Gwena followed the copper signs along the corridor of the club looking for Theater 3. She finally found the double doors labeled with the brass number. There was a poster on the wall outside advertising Madam Pomphrey's upcoming show. Underneath the magician's name in bold print it announced a guest-starring woman escapologist.

Gwena pushed her way through the double doors into the large dimly lit theater. Rows upon rows of tiered seating led down to a magnificent stage. Madam Pomphrey stood in the center, draped in a spotlight. She looked much older than Gwena remembered, but still resplendent—tall and slim, with long strawberry blond hair curled into ringlets. She was wearing layers of silk cinched at the waist with a belt and stood in a dramatic pose in front of a large glass water tank, holding a piece of paper out in front of her. Gwena recognized Richard sitting in the front row. She got the impression he'd already been there a while and wondered if he'd gotten any sleep at all. A young man with slicked-back hair stood beside him holding a clipboard.

"Pimpernella, Pimpernella! Where is that girl?" Madam Pomphrey demanded.

The man with the clipboard cleared his throat. "You fired her yesterday."

Madam Pomphrey raised her eyebrows in surprise. "Did I?"

The man looked down at his clipboard. "I believe your exact words were, 'I don't know why you refuse to be a mermaid, you're already a talentless fish—being a mermaid would be a vast improvement,' and then she said, 'My feats are superior to any of your deceitful drivel, I'll do my act my way or not at all,' then you said, 'There's the door, ensure you never come back through it," the man concluded, and looked up at Madam Pomphrey indifferently.

"Why don't I remember any of this?" she asked.

"Because you were blind drunk," the man stated.

"Oh posh, that hardly counts!"

"What are we going to do? Tickets have sold out largely because people are expecting to see a woman escapologist," Richard interjected.

"Largely? A trained monkey could do what she does. She's nothing but a glorified lockpick with the lungs of a bullfrog! The only thrill in watching her act is the anticipation of seeing her die," Madam Pomphrey scoffed.

"Her act is what got us our funding. The producers could drop the show," Richard argued with concern.

"Oh, stop being so dramatic! Just hire her back if you must, tell her it was all a misunderstanding," Madam Pomphrey dismissed with a wave of her hand.

"I already tried, she told me we couldn't pay her enough to work with you again, in this life or the next—she said she'd rather have her eyes eaten out by moonworms," the man with the clipboard declared.

Madam Pomphrey rubbed her temples. "I get the picture, Raverly, thank you, that's more than enough. Be a doll and fetch me a Spiced Kah, won't you? And then, maybe you can do something useful for once and try your job a little harder. You clearly weren't offering her enough—everyone has their price."

"Actually, this is no longer my problem. I accepted a job as stage manager at the Mon Lorriet this morning, I only came in as a courtesy. Good luck with the show, Madam Pomphrey. I quit," Raverly announced, and placed his clipboard on the stage before walking out.

Madam Pomphrey threw up her arms. "Good riddance!" she called after him. "Why is it so hard to find decent help these days?" she scoffed and began pacing the stage.

Richard sighed and put his head in his hands. "Well, what now? The producers are coming to watch the rehearsal tomorrow morning."

"I suppose we'll just have to find a replacement for Pimpernella."

"And where on Equillian will we find someone for that? I've never heard of another woman escapologist."

"Somewhere, or Stars help me, I'll climb in that tank myself!" Madam Pomphrey declared.

Just then Richard noticed Gwena standing in the aisle. "You came!" he exclaimed enthusiastically.

"Is this a bad time? I can come back later," Gwena asked awkwardly.

"Nonsense! Come down so I can introduce you."

"Who's this?" Madam Pomphrey asked.

"This is Gwena—the girl I was telling you about, the one who rescued my magic act last night."

"Oh right, the mysterious magician! Come here, child," Pomphrey requested, beckoning to Gwena.

Gwena walked to the base of the stage. Madam Pomphrey squinted at her. "Have we met before? You look familiar," she proclaimed.

"Yes, I saw your show in Westdock when you came through with the Travelling Curiosities years ago. I made you a magician's bag," Gwena confessed.

"So you did! I remember now. I recognize your scar. I remember thinking what a pity it was that foul bird ruined such a pretty face. I still use that bag, you know. It's the finest craftsmanship any seamstress has ever done for me," she remarked. "What is it that's brought you here?"

"I've been hired as the club's new tailor."

"You have?! Why hasn't anyone told me? I've been desperate for a tailor for days!"

"I have a scheduled meeting with you today to go over your costumes," Gwena told her.

"Fantastic! Let's start now," Madam Pomphrey declared, guiding Gwena up onto the stage.

Richard cleared his throat. "Actually, I invited Gwena here to watch the rehearsal. She's a real fan, I'm sure she'd love to see it. Can't you look at costumes after we finish the run-through?"

"Well, I don't see why not. What do you say, child? Would you like to sit in on our rehearsal?" Madam Pomphrey asked.

"I'd be delighted!—only if I'm not intruding?"

"Of course not, my dear!" Madam Pomphrey assured her.

Richard motioned for Gwena to sit in the front row, and she did.

"From the top!" Madam Pomphrey called out into the empty theater. The lights onstage immediately changed to purples and blues, and a backdrop of the night sky lowered into place. The glass water tank moved sideways across the stage as if by magic, disappearing into the wings.

"There was supposed to be an escapologist in that tank. She was going to dress like a mermaid and free herself from chains while under water. Madam Pomphrey had a beautiful story composed for the piece," Richard told Gwena.

"What happened to her?" Gwena asked.

"Madam Pomphrey and her had a falling out. The escapologist didn't like the mermaid idea, and Madam Pomphrey wasn't willing to compromise her vision for the show."

"I see. So who will perform the act now?"

"I've no idea. I wanted to volunteer, but I'm already in the show. Besides, there's no male mermaids—any boy birthed by a mermaid turns into a man with gills and no tail. Only the females become proper mermaids," Richard told her.

Gwena laughed lightly. "Surely you don't actually believe in mermaids?"

"Sure, why wouldn't I?" Richard asked.

"Because they're from fairytales, they don't actually exist," Gwena said.

"What makes you say that?"

"Because, well, that's just how it is. I've certainly never seen one, have you?"

"Of course not, they avoid humans. But I've also never seen a dragon or a platypus, and until this morning I'd never seen you. Does that mean I shouldn't believe in any of them either?" Richard asked.

"I suppose not," Gwena admitted.

"My father's seen several mermaids and that's good enough for me. He worked on one of the naval ships in the Last War," Richard asserted.

"I see. Does the escapologist have to be a mermaid?" Gwena inquired.

"Of course. The story goes—Madam Pomphrey found one caught in a fishing net on the shore and rescued her. The mermaid was so terrified of being trapped after that, she became determined to face her fear by dedicating her life to escapology—so that she could not only conquer her greatest trepidation, but also ensure she was never trapped again," Richard recounted dramatically.

"That is a beautiful story, only...well, never mind," Gwena said.

"No, tell me. What is it?"

"It's just—well, mermaids can breathe underwater, won't that dramatically lower the stakes? And if the escapologist can't really breathe underwater—don't you want the audience to know that so the feat's more impressive?" Gwena asked.

Richard furrowed his brow, and then nodded. "You're exactly right. I don't know why we hadn't thought of that. I'll suggest it to Madam Pomphrey."

"Oh, please don't! It's her show, I wouldn't dare suggest a thing," Gwena exclaimed.

"Don't worry, I'll tell her it was my idea. I'm one of the few she'll listen to."

"Oh, why's that? Are you her son or something?" Gwena inquired.

Richard coughed. "Stars no," he asserted uncomfortably.

Then Madam Pomphrey came out onto the stage in a sequined dress with a low-cut front, "Richard, be a dear won't you and help zip me up?" she requested from the stage.

"Certainly!" Richard returned obediently and hopped up onto the boards to do up the back of her dress.

"Thank you, my dear," Madam Pomphrey cooed, placing her hand on his cheek and kissing him fondly on the lips.

"Pleasure," Richard said, clearing his throat and jumping off the stage.

Gwena blushed, instantly regretting her earlier assumption. "I'm so sorry! I didn't realize you two were an item. I meant no offense—I shouldn't have presumed," she stammered.

"Don't mention it. You're not the first person to make that assumption. I'm well aware there's a fairly substantial age gap between us. I used to watch her shows as a boy. I've always been fond of her. Being able to be with her now is the fulfilment of a childhood dream."

"I see. That's lovely! Really. I think it's wonderful when two people can be happy together, no matter their differences."

"Thanks," Richard said with a curt smile. "Now if you'll excuse me, I need to get ready for the run-through."

"Of course! I look forward to seeing you in the show," Gwena said.

Richard smiled and headed backstage. Gwena felt so embarrassed she wanted to shrink into her seat, but soon the lights in the audience seating went black, and the show began.

Gwena watched spellbound as Madam Pomphrey levitated a rose, making it wither and revive before it combusted into flame. The magician, with Richard as her assistant, ran through a whole series of tricks using play of light, dramatic smoke, and carefully planted mirrors. They hung things from invisible wires and used props that were built for deception. And around each act Madam Pomphrey wove an enchanting story that brought the trick to life and inspired chills on the back of Gwena's neck. But despite the grandeur of each piece, and the excellence of their execution, Gwena couldn't help but find them wanting. The stories were magnificent, and the tricks were wonderful—they would've dazzled her years before—but now, she could identify how each and every one was done. She'd been hoping to rekindle that feeling of wonder she'd had as a child when she'd first seen Madam Pomphrey's show in Westdock, the feeling that magic could actually be real and that anything was possible. Gwena longed to feel that again. It almost made her regret her pursuit in magic. If it wasn't real, she thought she'd rather be deceived than live in a world without it. She'd thought surely if anyone could still surprise and dazzle her, it would've been Madam Pomphrey. But the show didn't even impress her as a magician. None of the tricks used any sleight of hand or even required much skill—everything Madam Pomphrey did relied heavily on the props she was utilizing, making them doable by anyone. It seemed the only real skill Madam Pomphrey was exercising was her stories and dramatic gestures. But when the grand finale came, a glimmer of hope leapt inside Gwena—and for a single moment her disbelief was suspended as she watched Madam Pomphrey weave her magic in bemused wonderment. The magician had her two hands placed together and when she pulled them apart, there was a flowerpot between them. It looked as old as time. Madam Pomphrey gave a dramatic speech about how she'd bought it off a merchant who pulled it up from the depths of the ocean—a relic from the old world. She placed a seed into the pot and put it down on the stage. Immediately the seed grew, becoming a silver tree that twisted upward, branches springing from it in all directions. Then the branches sprouted gold leaves and blossomed bright yellow flowers that turned into gold and silver fruit, all in a matter of seconds—as if time had sped up to reveal the process of nature in a series of mere moments. Madam Pomphrey picked each of the fruit into a basket, and then cast them into the air over Gwena's head, where they transformed into a flock of white doves that glided over the tiered seating.

Gwena clapped enthusiastically. Madam Pomphrey smiled widely and took a deep bow.

"Bravo!" Gwena cheered, getting to her feet for a standing ovation.

Madam Pomphrey held her arm out to Richard and he bowed with a beaming smile brightened by Gwena's applause. Then the lights dimmed, and Madam Pomphrey's smile faded, proving to be as genuine as the acts in her show. She put a hand to her temple and furrowed her brow.

"Richard darling, fetch me a Spiced Kah won't you? That bottle of Aodka I had last night has left me with a horrible headache," she announced, handing Richard a bag of coin.

"Certainly," Richard complied, and hopped down from the stage to fulfill her request.

"Now, come here, my dear child, and I'll show you around back," Madam Pomphrey beckoned to Gwena, plastering on her dazzling smile.

Gwena joined Madam Pomphrey on the stage.

"Reset the show!" the magician called out to the open theater, giving the command with a wave of her hand.

Immediately the birds flew back to Madam Pomphrey, and from up close Gwena could see they were mechanical. They folded in on themselves returning to the shapes of fruit, and Madam Pomphrey hung each one from the branch she'd originally plucked it from. The gold tree started retracting in on itself. Gwena watched it in fascination. Its trunk was open at the back, revealing thousands of tiny gears. Gwena watched mesmerized as the tree went through a reverse cycle of how it emerged.

"Fascinating, isn't it?" Madam Pomphrey asked.

"It's incredible!" Gwena exclaimed, leaning in to study the mechanics of the machine.

"The contraption was designed by my Imagineer Mallini, he's an artist in truth. He designs and creates the majority of the props for my show," Madam Pomphrey told her.

"You don't come up with them yourself?" Gwena queried.

"Stars no! I could never do what Mallini does. My specialty is the stories, you see. These tricks are only spellbinding because of the stories behind them. Stories can take something completely mundane and ordinary and turn them into something extraordinary. That's the real magic," Madam Pomphrey divulged with a wink, and led Gwena backstage.

The dusky room they stepped into was the last thing Gwena had been expecting. It was filled with mechanical contraptions, levers, buttons, and pulleys. In the corner, bending over a workbench was an older gentleman with a pair of magnifying goggles over his eyes. He was working on a mechanical hand.

"Hi Mallini, this is Gwena. She's the club's new tailor, she'll be helping us with the costumes," Madam Pomphrey introduced.

The mechanical hand waved to Gwena, and Gwena waved back.

"Pleasure to meet you," she said.

"Humph. How'd the show go?" Mallini asked, ignoring Gwena and turning his attention to Madam Pomphrey.

"Don't mind him, he doesn't have much in the way of social skills. Fine—all your pieces moved like clockwork," she said.

"Good. So, what's the problem?"

"You know me too well, Mallini—we no longer have an escapologist," she confessed.

"Why not?"

"She quit."

"When?"

"Last night."

"Humph."

"The producers are coming to watch the show in the morning. If we don't find someone to replace her before then, I'm afraid we're through. You know how things are, Wildsinger is the launching ground. If we can't make the show a success here, we'll lose our best clientele. We'll be lucky to perform in a peanut gallery after that," Madam Pomphrey proclaimed.

Just then Richard returned with a tall mug of warm Spiced Kah and gave it to Lady Pomphrey. She eagerly welcomed the mug with both hands. "Thank you my dear, you're a lifesaver!" she exclaimed, taking a long hard drink.

"Are we talking about the show?" Richard asked.

Madam Pomphrey nodded. "I just told Mallini about our escapologist scenario."

"Right. About that, I was thinking—maybe it's worth rethinking the mermaid idea. Won't it detract from the thrill of it all if the escapologist can breathe under water?"

Madam Pomphrey cocked her head to one side and blinked, "I hadn't thought of that."

"Humph," Mallini said.

"No, you're right. That's a hole in the story, it will ruin the entire effect. I'm glad someone has the intellect and courage around here to catch such things. I only wish you'd done it sooner," Madame Pomphrey remarked.

"Actually, it was Gwena who caught it. I only adopted the idea because her fine sense of propriety didn't want to intrude or offend, but credit should be given where it's due," Richard announced.

Madam Pomphrey turned to Gwena, "Did you now?"

Gwena shrunk.

"Well, thanks to you, now I need to come up with a whole new story as well as an escapologist."

"Not necessarily," Gwena proposed.

The two men looked at her in surprise—and Gwena instantly got the impression Madam Pomphrey wasn't used to being spoken to so candidly. The magician lifted an eyebrow at her, and Gwena cleared her throat uncomfortably before continuing,

"You could make a point of putting a choker on the mermaid to block her gills. It could be her way of facing her ultimate fear—being trapped underwater like she was trapped in the net, but this time she can't breathe," Gwena suggested.

Everyone paused waiting for Madam Pomphrey's response.

"I love it! Ha! What an interesting and clever specimen you are," she exclaimed. "What did you say your name was again?"

"Gwena, Gwena Stently."

"Gwena, that's right. And did you say you have an interest in magic?"

"Yes, it's been a hobby of mine since I was a child," Gwena confessed.

Madam Pomphrey looked her up and down with new measure. "I think you'll do perfectly, yes. You'll be our escapologist!" she declared.

"Me?!" Gwena asked in surprise.

"Yes. You're absolutely perfect! Your fair skin and long hair will create a splendid effect, and your scar will add to your mystery and intrigue—it will be from an injury you acquired when you were captured by the fisherman," Madam Pomphrey announced, already weaving her story around her.

"But I have no knowledge or experience in escapology," Gwena objected.

Madam Pomphrey waved her hand dismissively, "You don't need any of that! Mallini will create the locks himself. They'll be completely failproof—opening at the touch of a button, won't they, Mallini?"

The man shrugged, "It can be done."

"Perfect!" Madam Pomphrey exclaimed, clapping her hands together.

"I'm not so sure I'm up for that. I've never been comfortable underwater for any lengthened period of time," Gwena protested.

"Would you be willing to at least try it? We can run through it today—and if it works out, it would only need to be for one performance tomorrow morning—just to keep the producers at bay, so we at least have the opportunity to look for someone else," Richard implored.

"Please, you'll be saving the show," Madam Pomphrey pleaded.

Gwena hesitated. "Alright. Just the one show. But you'll have to walk me through everything I'm supposed to be doing."

Madam Pomphrey squealed in delight. "You're a real star! Come, forget about the costumes for today. We need to make you into a mermaid escapologist!"

For the rest of the day Gwena stayed in Theater 3 with Madam Pomphrey, Richard, Mallini, and the rest of the crew. They had food delivered, and everyone brainstormed and workshopped Gwena's act.

Gwena was to wear a mermaid's tail that had been constructed by specialists using real scales. It glittered in the light with silver and gold, highlighted with ultramarine and pastel violet. It was so real, it almost convinced Gwena it was actually taken from a real mermaid. With some minor alterations, it fit her snugly. She was to wear the tail and sit on a swing that would be lowered down just above the tank. There, Madam Pomphrey and Richard would wrap her in chains secured with two locks, and an added locked choker that went around her neck, covering the bit below her ears where a mermaid's gills were said to be. Gwena was meant to drop into the tank before a lid was shut over the top and locked in place. She would escape by pulling a long ornate pin from her hair and make a show of using it to pick the locks on her wrists and around her arms, before trying to unlock the one around her neck. Failing to unlock the choker, she would make a desperate attempt at unlocking the lid to the tank. Succeeding, she'd pull herself out just in time to save her life with a breath of air. After recovering herself, she would then unlock the choker successfully, and dive back into the water to seal the story. If everything went well, the audience would be on the edge of their seats, thinking she'd brushed death that day, when in fact, she would never actually be in danger at all.

Mallini designed each of the locks to have a discreet latch on the side that Gwena could push to open them, and a backup mechanism on the bottom as a failsafe. It took the rest of the day to plan, rehearse, and finalize everything. But by the end, they were all feeling optimistic about the following day. And Gwena couldn't have been happier to fall into her bed that night and drift off into a deep and dreamless sleep.

Gwena woke the next morning filled with anticipation. She could hardly eat her breakfast due to her nerves. She went to Theater 3 directly after her meager meal and met Madam Pomphrey, Richard, and Mallini to prepare for their run-through. The producers were scheduled to arrive at the Knight's Hour. Which gave them exactly two hours to ready themselves.

Gwena got into her costume—a seashell corset and the glimmering tail that she wore over a swimsuit bottom. She held one of the locks in her hand backstage, repeatedly locking it and releasing it with the switch nervously. She could hear Madam Pomphrey and Richard greet the producers at the front of the stage and show them to their seats. There were three of them—two men and one woman, sitting right in the center of the front row. The rehearsal began, and before Gwena knew it the show reached her act and she was being cued onto her swing. She felt cold and yet her palms were sweating. She climbed onto the perch and breathed out slowly as the swing was raised. Then the curtain opened, and the swing began to lower into the spotlight.

Gwena saw the three producers, all smartly dressed and sitting with an air of importance and absolutely no expression. She thought her heart might leap out of her chest, but she ignored it. Instead, she focused on the task at hand and retreated into her imagination, imagining that she was indeed the mermaid Madam Pomphrey had envisioned her to be. Richard wrapped the chains around her and locked them in place, while Madam Pomphrey spun her story to the producers. The choker was put onto Gwena's neck and locked, and then her cue given. Gwena took a large breath as she moved her weight forward and plunged into the warm water below. With the weight of the chains, she sunk like an anchor. She had to wriggle to keep herself upright, which luckily added to the effect of her struggle. She moved her hands and arms against the chains binding them together, until they loosened enough for her to reach up and pull a long decorative pin from her hair. She stuck it into the lock binding her wrists and fumbled with it for several seconds before releasing the lock by the switch. She fumbled with the next lock binding her arms very briefly, before opening it and clawing at her choker in desperation. After her attempts to free herself from it failed, she turned her attention to the lock on the tank's lid, releasing the vault and pushing it open in triumph. She popped her head to the surface and took in a large gulp of air. After catching her breath, she made a show of pick locking the choker, and once free of it, she dived under water again as if eager to breathe it in. She spun around in the tank gracefully and smiled at the producers with tiny bubbles releasing from her mouth, and then the curtains closed.

Immediately Gwena took off the tail and was helped out of the tank by Richard who was waiting for her with a towel robe. Gwena accepted it gratefully, and the two of them hurried backstage.

"That was brilliant! You're a complete natural!" Richard exclaimed.

"Thanks," Gwena blushed, overwhelmed by the rush of it all.

At the end of the show Gwena and Richard stood behind the curtain trying to listen in on the feedback the producers were giving to Madam Pomphrey. But as much as they tried, they couldn't hear a thing. Once the producers left, Madam Pomphrey had the curtains opened and drew them both out. She addressed them with a somber expression and then a broad smile spread across her face. "They loved it! What stars you both were! I couldn't have dreamed of that going any more fabulously. Gwena, my dear, you're a complete natural! Your first time and you already make a better escapologist than that glorified blowfish ever did!" she exclaimed.

"It's your story that made the act, I only played the part," Gwena returned humbly.

"And played it swimmingly! If I didn't know any better, I would've been completely convinced you're a real mermaid. In fact, the producers were! The majority of their excitement came from the fact that we have a real mermaid. They wouldn't stop asking questions about you. They even requested that we change the poster from woman escapologist to mermaid escapologist!" Madam Pomphrey declared.

"Really?!" Gwena asked in disbelief.

"Indeed! You simply must be our escapologist for the show. No one else will do!" Madam Pomphrey implored.

"It wouldn't be the same without you, you really did bring the story to life," Richard asserted.

Gwena was so enraptured by their praise that before she could stop herself, she'd agreed.

That evening, Gwena stayed back at the theater with Richard and Madam Pomphrey to celebrate. Madam Pomphrey popped open a bottle of champagne and entertained them late into the evening with stories of her fascinating and often humorous experiences as a travelling magician. At moments Richard would jump in and add details that Madam Pomphrey had forgotten, often sending them both into fits of laughter. Gwena couldn't remember the last time she'd laughed so much or felt so at home. That night when she fell into bed she forgot all about Benji and the Wildsinger's club—sleeping straight through the club's nightly carouse and dreaming of being back at the theater again.

# OBSTACLES

Bastian woke with a start to something vibrating on his wrist. He looked down at his enchanted bracelet and relaxed, pushing the red coral to make it stop. He rubbed his face before realizing he was still outside on the top deck of the Black Mary. He quickly gathered that he must have fallen asleep looking at Haplo's journal. He looked down in panic and was relieved to see the book still in his lap.

*Lucky. And lucky it's a warm night,* he thought.

If it had been any colder, he might've never woken up. The temperature was already beginning to drop considerably. Bastian looked up towards the Guiding Star, and saw the Phoenix constellation on her way underneath it.

*Shick.*

He hurried below deck and stowed the books away in his locker, trading them out for another bottle of Falgo's watered-down rum, before going out to meet him.

Bastian was only in the clearing for a few minutes before Falgo joined him. He wondered how the pirate managed to always be so punctual.

"Morning," Bastian greeted, blowing warm air into his hands and shaking his legs in an attempt to warm them.

"So it is," Falgo agreed.

Bastian was looking forward to summer. In the warmer seasons, this time of morning might actually be pleasant. He looked up and saw Falgo looking at him expectantly.

"Oh, right." Bastian pulled the bottle of rum tea from his coat, and handed it over. The pirate took it eagerly and skulled down his dose of medicine. Bastian was happy to wait. Falgo was always more pleasant after he'd had his drink.

"Do yer warm up then. Round ya go," Falgo instructed, and Bastian began to run around the clearing. As soon as he'd finished, Falgo wasted no time in calling out his next order, "Side steps up an' down the length, an' then ten passes front an' back with jabs an' 'its."

Bastian assumed the stance he'd been practicing religiously for the last four days. Left foot forward, left hand jab. Right foot turn and push—while throwing a right punch.

Falgo watched him traverse the sand, calling out instructions while he reclined against a mast tree. "Chin down. Relax yer shoulders. Pelvis tucked under. Follow through with yer punch. Remember, yer target be beyond yer opponent. Ya don't punch at 'em, ya punch through 'em! The power comes up from yer legs, not from yer shoulders!"

After five passes Bastian stopped. "How much longer do I have to keep this up? I've been practicing the same steps all week."

"Ye'll keep it up until I'm satisfied ya 'ave it down," the pirate asserted.

"But we'll be at Jaxland in a matter of days, and I still haven't even touched a weapon. Can't you at least teach me the basics with a dagger or something?"

"A dagger? Ya think yer ready fer a dagger?"

Bastian shrugged. "I thought it might be a good place to start."

"I'm goin' ta tell ya somethin'—so listen carefully. Pullin' a weapon on the men in Jaxland be nothin' but an invitation fer them ta kill ya. If yer goin' ta pull a blade then ya best be prepared ta use it—are ya prepared ta take another man's life, thief?"

Bastian hesitated.

"Didn't think so. Only stupid men pull daggers out ta scare their opponents, normally as an attempt ta hide how small their manhood be. But yer not one o' those men, are ya, thief?" Falgo asked.

Bastian shook his head.

"No, yer not. A smart man doesn't boast strength he doesn't have, he hides the strength he does. If a man approaches ya lookin' fer a fight, feign fear an' weakness. He'll let 'is guard down, think ya be easy prey. Let 'im think so. Take advantage o' 'im thinkin' so. Take advantage o' every opportunity ya 'ave—if ya crap yer pants, grab a handful an' shove it in yer opponent's eyes. Honor an' pride 'as no place in a battle with thieves an' cutthroats. The only weapons ya can fully rely on be the ones ya already have," Falgo declared and rolled Bastian's hand into a fist. "Yer body can't be taken away an' used against ya. Ya can take it wherever ya go without detection, an' ye'll never 'ave ta cover it up er worry about leavin' it behind. Once ya master yer own body, ye'll be able ta wield any weapon as if it were an extension o' yerself. An' if yer goal truly be ta survive, then ferget about masterin' any one weapon. Instead, start ta see how everythin' around ya can be turned inta one," he advised.

Bastian chewed on that.

"Now, never underestimate the power o' footwork. Most do, which is why they'll end up on their arse, an' ye'll still be standin'. Again!" Falgo commanded.

Bastian sighed and resumed his passes for the rest of the lesson.

By the time Bastian returned to his hammock that morning, he was exhausted. He set the alarm on his bracelet for sunrise and was swallowed by sleep.

Bastian was woken by his enchanted bracelet at the exact time he'd set it for. He rubbed his eyes and looked around at the sleeping men in the hammocks around him and smiled. This was the first morning since he'd boarded the Black Mary that he'd woken for his daily chores before Cricket's wake up call. He lay back down with his eyes closed, feigning sleep. He listened intently, waiting for the sound of Cricket's boots on the boards. He didn't move a muscle until he could feel Cricket's presence right next to him, then he flung open his eyes and hollered, "Boo!"

Cricket jumped back in surprise. "Shick! Ya nearly scared the starlight out o' me, Dodger!"

Bastian laughed so hard he thought he might pee his pants.

Cricket stared at him, unimpressed. "Very funny mate, yer a real wag. Come on, the decks aren't gonna scrub themselves," he said, and headed out without waiting for Bastian.

Bastian grinned and followed behind.

When Bastian arrived at Tink's quarters that day, the alchemist was absorbed in his work, tinkering with a clockwork beetle on his desk while sipping from a steaming cup of tea.

"People think the rise of steam technology is eliminating the need for enchanted objects. But in truth, the rise in steam technology is *because* of enchanted objects. Their machines would be completely inefficient without Everfire. Steam needs a heat source, and without an enchantment, fire has an insatiable appetite," Tink remarked absently, not even looking up to acknowledge Bastian was there. He put his cup down on the workbench and tightened a screw on the beetle, and then sat it over the top of his teacup. The beetle's gears began to spin, and its legs moved from side to side as if running in the air.

"They take for granted what they have, because they've no concept of what life would be like without it. Never stopping to acknowledge how a single enchantment has revolutionized the world. If only given the opportunity, the alchemists' work could benefit modern technology in so many ways beyond Everfire. Young people are bedazzled by modern invention, they think we've come so far. But to know where we could've been, makes where we are now so…disappointing. We've been robbed of the future we could've had, all because of greed and the spiteful nature of humankind—think of where we'd be today if our progress had never been obstructed by these inherent flaws. Without them, we could advance so much further…but alas, no one misses what they've never known they could've had," Tink proclaimed, throwing up a hand as if to say *what can one do?*

Bastian listened patiently without any idea as to what Tink was talking about. He cleared his throat awkwardly, just in case Tink hadn't realized he was there. Tink looked up at him as if coming out of a daze. "How'd your bracelet go?" he inquired.

"Brilliant! I can finally sleep in peace."

"Good. I'm thrilled to hear it. Hopefully it will ensure you're punctual here. You have no excuse now," Tink smiled.

Bastian shrugged, "A small trade-off," he said with a wry smirk.

Tink laughed, "did you get a chance to look it over?" he asked, gesturing to the copy of *The Alchemists Book of Symbology* in Bastian's hand.

"Yeah. I've memorized all the symbols," Bastian reported, handing the book back to him.

Tink nodded. "Good."

"I thought I might keep the journals you loaned me a while longer, if you don't mind? I haven't had the chance to finish them yet."

"Not at all. I'm glad you're getting something out of them. There's rumors of Haplo being a promiscuous drunkard. But he seemed to be a pretty straight fellow from his accounts. It's a shame the alchemists didn't write more about their work with alchemy though. Still, it's an interesting insight into their lives," Tink remarked.

"Yes, very interesting," Bastian agreed, though he was certain now that the version of Haplo's journal he'd read was very different to the one Tink had.

"What is it we're working on today?" Bastian asked, eager to divert the subject.

Tink picked up the metal beetle from the top of his cup and carried it over to the smaller desk and placed it down.

"Now you've learned how to enchant an object, we can begin working on unenchanting one. A feat much more challenging."

Bastian picked up the beetle and turned it over curiously. It was the size of his hand, its exoskeleton a glossed metallic green that changed to shades of blue when turned in the light and its underside comprised of intricate layers of different-sized gears.

"First things first, in order to know what you're dealing with you must discover the nature of each enchantment," Tink instructed.

"How do I do that?"

"You're going to read them using the Ghost Element. All enchantments are applied to an object in layers—just like how you enchanted your bracelet yesterday. You must tackle them one at a time," Tink explained.

"You're going to talk me through that, right?"

"Have a seat." Tink gestured to the chair at the desk, and Bastian sat down. Tink took the Humming Bowl from his table and put it on the desk in front of Bastian, then he plucked the beetle out of Bastian's hands and placed it next to the bowl. He hit the side of the Humming Bowl with the wood and leather dowel and the bowl began to hum, drawing in the Ghost Element from every direction.

"Close your eyes," Tink guided.

Bastian closed his eyes.

"I want you to take the Ghost Element and send it into the object in front of you like a blind man using his sense of touch to feel his way through the dark."

Keeping his eyes closed Bastian scooped two handfuls of the Ghost Element out of the bowl. He could feel its cool softness so clearly now, like icing sugar stored in an icebox. He opened his palms and imagined the Element curling upwards, snaking towards the beetle and going inside it.

"Be careful not to turn the Element into anything. You want to use it like a sense, which means you mustn't visualize the Element as anything other than it is. Instead, you want to guide it to your purpose using intention. Make it clear in your mind what you're using the Element for and what you want it to do," Tink directed.

Bastian took a deep breath, *I am nothing, I am everything.* His mind cleared as if stepping out of fog into a crystalline starlit night. *Find the enchantment.* He held onto that one commanding thought and opened his mind to perceive what the Ghost Element was perceiving. The beetle was made of metal and glazed porcelain. It had over a hundred moving parts, all powered by a hot-air engine fueled by Everfire.

Bastian began to probe further and came across what felt like an iron wall he immediately recognized as the Anti-Tampering Enchantment. Behind that was the Everlasting and Protection Symbol. There were no more symbols attached to the object, but he could sense something else, something complex and illusive, like…consciousness. The machine was a beetle, only at the same time it wasn't, and yet it was undeniably alive. Somehow Bastian knew this to be true, but he didn't understand what it meant.

"Does the core enchantment make the clockwork beetle mimic life?" he asked.

Tink smiled. "Very good. Only it doesn't mimic life, it is alive in every sense of the word except—it has no waste, never ages or dies, is made of metal clockwork, and can be put to sleep at the touch of a button. It was made as a child's educational toy. To be used in classrooms in order to study the behavior of beetles."

"How can an object be alive?" Bastian queried.

"I don't know. The original alchemists were the only ones who could do it. Unfortunately, they never passed that knowledge down to anyone else," Tink admitted. He picked up the beetle from the desk and pushed a button on its underside. Immediately it came to life and scurried up his arm and onto his shoulder, scanning Tink's shirt with its wire antennas.

"How did I do that?" Bastian asked.

"Do what?"

"As soon as the Ghost Element was connecting me to the object, I had this instinctual feeling of what it was. Somehow, I just knew without anything telling me."

"The Ciphorescent Codec told you. It's the language of truth. You tuned into it using the Ghost Element and it revealed the object's true nature," Tink explained.

"I didn't realize that's what I was doing. Does that mean that I can use it the same way to access the truth of anything?" Bastian inquired.

"Theoretically speaking. What other enchantments are bound to the beetle?" Tink pressed, redirecting Bastian to the task at hand.

"The three standard symbol safety enchantments—Anti-Tampering, Protection, and the Everlasting enchantment. After that it's just the single core enchantment," Bastian answered.

"Good. Now, you must unmake it. But in order to do that, you'll have to get through the safety symbols first. This is not an easy task—every one of them has been put into the object to prevent the very thing you're trying to accomplish," Tink proclaimed.

"Wait, won't deconstructing the core enchantment be like…killing the beetle?" Bastian queried.

"That's a philosophical question I don't have the answer to."

"Isn't there something else I can unmake, something less—alive?" Bastian asked. He didn't know how all this enchantment stuff worked, and he got the impression Tink didn't fully understand it either. But metal or not, if the beetle was alive in any way, Bastian didn't want to end its spark for a simple exercise.

Tink studied him and smiled. "Sure," he said, and walked over to his desk. He scanned the items there and picked up a gold feathered quill. It looked just like the one Bastian had taken from the Wendrians' castle, and made him wonder whether the one he'd stashed below the floor boards on the gun deck was also enchanted.

Tink laid the quill on the desk in front of Bastian. "Far more useful, but less *alive*. Now, what's its core enchantment?"

Bastian closed his eyes and cleared his mind. Gold dust billowed up from his palms and curved towards the quill—like smoke being drawn in by a fan. The quill had the same three safety enchantments as the beetle. Bastian let his perception pass them as he searched for the core enchantment. A moment later he opened his eyes.

"It never runs out of ink," he declared.

"That's one of its core enchantments, it has four. It also never blots, its ink dries instantly, and it can be written with upside-down—without being impeded by gravity," Tink told him, picking up the quill and examining it. "The core enchantments are in layers; you'll have to unmake them one at a time."

"Right. How do I get past the safety enchantments?" Bastian asked.

Tink put the quill back on the table. "First, you must feel their form in your mind's eye. The symbol's abilities will keep you from unmaking them, so you must find a way to bypass them instead. The most important thing is truly believing that it can be done and that you are the one to do it. Remember, nothing's impossible. The first challenge is overcoming the doubt in your mind. Second, you must take advantage of the greatest tool you have to lead you through the fog—the Ciphorescent Codec. You must use it to find the way through the enchantments. Hone into your inner senses and let the Codec guide you."

"Right." Bastian took a breath and closed his eyes.

*I am nothing, I am everything.*

He tapped into the Ciphorescent Codec using the Ghost Element and sought out the Anti-Tampering enchantment. It rose before him like an impenetrable iron wall. Even without being able to see it, its looming presence was undeniable. Bastian probed for its weakness, looking for a way in—but it was like a vault door.

He opened his eyes. "How the shick am I meant to do anything with the Anti-Tampering enchantment? The shape's made specifically so it can't be tampered with."

"And yet, it can be. Remember, nothing's impossible. The enchantment's only impenetrable because you believe it is. Your own belief in its defenses are reinforcing them. You must trust there's a way in order to find it—even what we think of as the solidest of objects are made of individual atoms that can be forced apart," Tink insisted.

Bastian closed his eyes and focused his mind on the Anti-Tampering symbol again. He felt truly like he was a blind man in the dark. He tried to alter the symbol's shape, but every time he tried he couldn't even concentrate—like something was blocking his mind. He tried to imagine the symbol dissolving away, to no effect. He tried to picture a door in it that he was able to open and go through—still, nothing. Bastian tried asking the Codec if there was any way through the enchantment. It told him there wasn't. So, that was it—wasn't it? *The Codec is truth, if it says there isn't a way through, then there isn't a way through—right?*

"Even the Codec's telling me there's no way through the enchantment," Bastian announced.

"That's because there's not," Tink admitted.

"But you just said…how in the nine levels am I supposed to—"

Tink held up a hand to silence Bastian. "If you can't go through it as it is, what else might you try?"

Bastian breathed out a slow and steady stream of air and focused on the enchantment again. If he couldn't go through it, could he go around it? he wondered.

"How do I unmake the core enchantments?" Bastian asked.

"To unmake the core enchantments you only need to know what they are, and then you can unmake them using visualization and intention in much the same process you used to create them. Except this time, instead of constructing, you'll be deconstructing the ability," Tink explained.

"Sounds fairly straight forward. So the only real obstacle is the safety enchantments?" Bastian queried.

"Yes."

Bastian ran his hands over his face. He stared at the gold quill on the desk and closed his eyes again. He reached out and sensed the forms of the core enchantments. They were in four layers as Tink had said, the first layer was the enchantment that kept the quill from blotting, the second was the one that made the ink dry instantly, the third was the enchantment that made the ink everlasting, and the fourth was the Anti-Gravity enchantment. He had a clear feeling of exactly what their purpose was and how they fulfilled that purpose. He couldn't visualize them, but he had a clear sense all the same—in a similar way to how he could feel someone's stare burning in the back of his head.

Bastian held the first core enchantment clearly in his mind and tried to imagine it disappearing. Immediately he was blocked by the Anti-Tampering Enchantment once more.

"Gahhh!" Bastian growled in frustration.

"That's enough for today. Don't be too hard on yourself, it takes most apprentice alchemists at least a year to accomplish what you've done in less than a week. Come back tomorrow and we'll try again," Tink instructed.

"Tomorrow? We're running out of time! I have to be able to do this before we reach Jaxland!" Bastian protested.

"Yes. But impatience will only make it take longer. When you're in a hurry, you must take your time. Trying to jump ahead before you're ready will only result in a fall that will waste what precious time we have. In order to reach the end, you must start at the beginning and keep putting one foot in front of the other," Tink advised.

"Right. I'll see you tomorrow then," Bastian said curtly, and he stormed out of Tink's quarters in aggravation.

Why couldn't he get it? He'd been doing so well, he'd finally been making progress. And now it felt like he was back at the beginning all over again.

# COMPLICATIONS

Felix and Lilliana clapped and cheered with the rest of the crowd as the closing ceremony for the Derby came to an end. The whole lineup had been spectacular. After the polo game was a dragon air show with death-defying stunts done by fearless riders on the backs of dragons. The display was accompanied by the local symphony playing dramatic compositions to add to the effect. The Beauty and Brawn event showcased dragons with bright stripes of fluorescent blues, greens, and purples. There were muscled dragons with horns trained into artistic designs. Dragons with colorful patterns on their wings like butterflies, and others that were phosphorescent. Even the sunset that evening was dramatic, painting the sky in a breathtaking array of fiery reds, oranges, and yellows that saturated the clouds surrounding the capital. After the sun went down, there was a golden glow on everything for one magical hour—just before the Watchers took over the sky. With night as backdrop, the fire-breathing competition began. It far exceeded Felix's expectations, with seemingly impossible targets being reached with jets of bright fire shooting through the sky like flaming arrows released from the gaping jaws of dragons. It featured color-changing effects from chemical powders added to the flames, and even impressive fire-breathing from the dragons' riders while they flew on the dragons' backs. Arianna and Charred-I'm-Sure won the grand final by a hair. And the Firework and Glow Dragon Spectacle topped it all off spectacularly with fireworks being lit and thrown into the air from the backs of glowing dragons.

As it came to an end, Felix felt like he'd been spoiled for life. He couldn't imagine anything on Equillian being able to top it. He and Lilliana sat in their seats basking in the grand joy of it all, until they noticed the crowd clearing around them.

"That was incredible," Felix exclaimed.

Lilliana nodded, beaming from ear to ear.

"It's the greatest I've seen yet. This has been the best day of my life," she declared ardently, and she turned to Felix glowing with joy.

He smiled radiantly back at her. "And it's not even over yet. Shall we make our way to the opera house?"

"Yes, let's! I'm in desperate need of the ladies' room," she confessed.

"Ah, let's not linger then. I believe the opera house is this way," Felix announced, standing and offering Lilliana his hand.

Sky View's Diamond Opera House was beyond decadent, made to look like two outspread dragon's wings. Its white stone shimmered in the light of the Everfire streetlamps. There was a long deep purple carpet that led up the steps to the entrance, where Felix and Lilliana were greeted by two large bodyguards who checked their passes before letting them through the double doors. Inside was decorated with a lavish ornate cornice gilded with gold. The high vaulted ceiling was decorated with a mural of dragons flying in a cloudy sky, and thick velvet champagne-colored drapes hung from every corner. The floor was polished black marble with gold veins that glittered in the Everfire's light. A marble statue stood in the center that depicted a naked muscular man, his hand resting on the flank of a towering dragon standing next to him. The place was swarming with the stars of the Derby and well-known aristocrats. Felix couldn't help but think how abundant it was with opportunity. But he reminded himself that wasn't why they were there. Felix helped Lilliana find the restroom and waited for her outside. Just as he pulled out one of Roy's Zest cigars he noticed Frederick—the Sky View marquess—tumbling by drunkenly with an arm around a busty woman in a low-cut dress.

"Don't you dare go anywhere, I'll be right back!" the woman giggled flirtatiously and headed for the toilets.

Frederick came to stand beside Felix, wafting the potent stench of top-shelf liquor and expensive cologne. "Nice suit!" he said, giving Felix the once-over.

"Thanks. It's part of Favio Fritz's new collection," Felix told him, offering him one of Favio's business cards.

Frederick took it, and Felix noticed a slender tattoo of a lance on his right hand. The marquess looked at the designer's card before stowing it clumsily in his pocket. "Thanks. I haven't heard of him, but I like his style," he said, then his attention quickly diverted to Felix's cigar. "Is that a Zest?"

"Yes, it is," Felix confirmed, lighting the end with his Everfire box and taking a puff.

"A man with fine taste. I don't suppose you have another you'd be willing to share?"

"Certainly."

Felix pulled out another cigar and handed it over. "Need a light?"

"No, thank you. I should have one somewhere."

Frederick patted down his pockets then pulled out a fancy Everfire globe decorated with intricate solid gold metalwork. Its chain caught on something in his pocket, and the globe slipped through Frederick's fingers, sending the rest of his pocket's contents to the floor with it.

"Shick," Frederick mumbled, and scrambled to recover his lost property.

Felix bent down to help him. He picked up Frederick's Everfire globe and slipped it discreetly into his own pocket before picking up the marquess's gold pocket watch. The watch had come open with the fall, revealing a picture on the interior of the cover. Felix froze—it was a portrait of Lilliana.

Frederick stood up, brushing himself off and held his hand out for his pocket watch. Felix closed the lid and handed it over to him.

"Thank you," Frederick said, "you must think me a fool. I don't usually drink so much."

"If I ever judged a man a fool for having too much to drink, I'd be a hypocrite," Felix declared.

The marquess smiled. "Name's Frederick," he said, holding out his hand.

Felix shook it. "I didn't think there was anyone in Sky View who did handshakes."

"I recognized your accent. I've spent a lot of time on the mainland. I like your customs, I find them intriguing," he admitted.

"I saw you in the tournament. You're quite the jouster," Felix commended.

Frederick smiled humbly. "Thank you. I love the sport. My father doesn't approve, but I need to do something to keep myself occupied. I think that's the real reason he's handing the Derby over to me. He believes I'll give up competing if I'm running the show," Frederick confessed, and started searching his pockets for his Everfire globe again.

Felix offered him his Everfire box, "here."

"You're too kind." Frederick used the Everfire box to light his cigar. "It's been a long time since I've had one of these. There aren't many who puff up here," he remarked, blowing out a cloud of smoke.

"I couldn't help but notice the portrait of Westdock's duchess in your pocket watch. Is she a relative of yours?" Felix queried.

Frederick was surprised by the question. "No," he said, then quickly added, "We were supposed to be betrothed. Right after the marriage was arranged her father went missing. He never had the chance to make it official."

"Does she know that?" Felix asked.

Frederick hesitated. "I'm not actually sure."

"You never thought to approach her directly, after her father disappeared, I mean?"

Frederick laughed. "Of course not! That's not how things are done. After it became clear her father wasn't returning, my father and I tried to contact her mother, but we never got a response. We gave up in the end, thinking maybe her daughter didn't want to be married. But now, Lady Wendrian is betrothed to someone else. I still don't know what happened. Without her, the idea of marriage sounds like the Nine Realms of Darkness," he confessed.

"Do you know her well?" Felix queried.

"Hardly, I only met her once when we were children," Frederick admitted.

"She seems to have made quite an impression on you."

"Yes—I know it sounds foolish, but she's never left my mind. I was elated when our fathers arranged the marriage. I guess a part of me keeps hoping things might still work out. Any of the other potential prospects my father is considering for me are all mind-numbingly dull…I don't know why I'm telling you all this. Sorry. My tongue runs away from me when I've been drinking," Frederick apologized, laughing awkwardly.

"I'm guessing the woman you're waiting for isn't one of those prospects?"

"Stars, no!" The marquess laughed with a snort.

Felix smiled. "It's a touching story. I hope it has a happy ending." *For me,* he thought.

"Thank you. You're a good man, what's your name?"

Just then, the woman Frederick was waiting for stumbled back from the restrooms. Frederick wrapped his arm around her shoulders.

"Did you miss me?" she asked him.

"Of course," the marquess replied. He looked back at Felix and winked, "I hope to see you again, friend. Have a good evening."

"And you," Felix returned, and the lord stumbled off with the woman giggling by his side.

Felix waited until they were out of sight before taking Frederick's watch out of his pocket. He opened it to look at Lilliana's portrait.

*So, Lilliana's father intended her to be betrothed to Frederick, not Lord Bardviss. Then why didn't Lilliana's mother respond to the inquiries sent?* Felix wondered.

It would've been the perfect solution to all her family's problems. They'd no longer have to worry about financial ruin, Lord Bardviss would be out of the picture, and their betrothal would help to strengthen ties between Sky View and the mainland—preventing the revolution and possibly even war. It was a perfect match—one Lilliana might even be happy with. She could ride dragons to her heart's content and spend her days planning the next Derby with Frederick Remington. *Perfect for everyone but me,* Felix thought.

"Sorry for the wait. Maneuvering around this dress was an absolute nightmare!" Lilliana exclaimed, returning from the lavatory. Then her smile fell when she noticed Felix's expression. "You look like you've just eaten sour grapes. What's wrong?"

"Nothing. Let's go find Favio, shall we?" Felix suggested, offering her his arm and a smile that didn't extend to his eyes.

Felix and Lilliana waited for Favio at the base of the statue in the foyer.

"Are you sure you're alright?" Lilliana asked.

"Of course, why wouldn't I be?"

She looked at him skeptically. "I don't know. Ever since I came out of the restroom a change has come over you, you're…distant."

"Am I? I must be sobering up, that's easily remedied. Surely there's somewhere we can get a drink around here," Felix proclaimed, gazing around them. He spotted a wandering mechanical waiter with a tray full of long flutes of vibrantly gradient cocktails and held up his hand to get his attention. The well-dressed android came over and offered them a drink. "Thank you," Felix said, taking one for each of them. Lilliana accepted the drink with a searching expression. Felix held up his glass, "To us. May the night be at least as fruitful and delightful as the day," he toasted.

"I'll drink to that!" Lilliana declared and clinked his glass.

"This party's full of VIPs. Have you noticed how many of the competitors are here?" Felix asked.

"Yes! It's wonderful, isn't it? I'm used to being in a room full of big names, but usually none of them have accomplished anything interesting, whereas everyone here has real talent. I find it positively thrilling! I'd love to talk to just about everyone, I so hope Lady Swift makes an appearance."

"Are you worried about running into your cousin?"

"Stars no! She never comes to these sorts of things; she hates crowds and being the center of attent—" Lilliana trailed off midsentence as they were passed by a clump of people swarming excitedly around Arianna.

Felix turned to her. "You were saying?"

"Shick!" Lilliana cursed, ducking to the other side of the statue.

Felix stepped casually beside her. "Smooth, very discreet. Hiding is the perfect way to avoid drawing attention to yourself," he jested.

"What are we going to do?! We can't let her see me!" Lilliana whispered in panic.

"Relax. You're forgetting your disguise. Right now, you're Silvy—remember? Arianna doesn't know you. She'll never expect to see Lilliana here. As long as you play it cool and stop acting like you're smuggling something, you'll have nothing to worry about. The important thing is not to draw attention to ourselves," Felix advised.

"My beauties! What a delight and relief it is to find you here!" Favio announced loudly, coming up to meet them.

"Oh Stars," Lilliana muttered.

"Bottoms up," Felix said with an encouraging grin and knocked his drink back. Lilliana followed suit.

"Favio! I'm glad you were able to find us," Felix greeted.

"Me too, believe me. I don't think I've ever been so nervous in all my life!" Favio exclaimed, grabbing a cocktail from a passing waiter and throwing it back.

"You've nothing to be nervous about. Your work speaks for itself. I couldn't even keep count of the amount of compliments we've gotten today," Felix reassured, clapping Favio on the shoulder.

"Really?"

"Look here, out of the business cards you gave me, this is all that's left," Felix told him, handing over two cards.

Favio took them and smiled broadly. "I must have given you at least fifty!"

"I know."

Favio took a self-soothing breath. "That's wonderful! I knew you were the right man for the job," he proclaimed enthusiastically. "I'm so grateful for you two. You're right, I just need to let the work speak for itself. Are you both ready?"

Felix looked at Lilliana. She returned his gaze with a desperate expression.

"I think we're as ready as we'll ever be," he said.

"Good, good. The others are waiting for us down the hall. We better get you to the wardrobe department to freshen up. The Emperor has requested we move the showing forward—he's expecting us in half an hour. No time to waste!" Favio declared.

"After you," Felix smiled encouragingly.

# PICKING LOCKS

Bastian paced up and down the sleeping quarters in frustration. He'd worked so hard this last week and where had it gotten him? No matter how hard he trained, he was still getting his arse kicked by Falgo, and he still didn't have any real grasp of the Ghost Element. It didn't matter that he could manipulate it or make enchanted objects—if he couldn't unmake or bypass enchantments by the time they reached Jaxland, he'd have no chance of succeeding in the task to win his freedom.

In Bastian's agitation he misstepped and tripped on a raised floorboard. He fell forward between two rows of hammocks, only just managing to grab one and catch himself before his face collided with the floor. Bastian sat down and took a deep breath to steady his nerves.

*How ironic,* he thought, as Tink's words echoed back to him — *Trying to jump ahead before you're ready will only result in a fall that will waste what precious time we have.*

Sister Strata's followed after, like a lecturing ghost haunting his mind— *Mastering anything only takes five things: Patience, Persistence, and Practice, Practice, Practice.*

Bastian sighed. *Feeling sorry for myself isn't going to accomplish anything. I just need to pull my head out and start putting one foot in front of the other,* he thought decidedly.

He retrieved Haplo's journal from his locker and flipped through its pages until he'd found where he'd left off. Haplo had said understanding the Geometric Code made anything possible. That it was a sort of language that could be learned and used to change things. Which meant the answer had to be in his book. The Anti-Tampering enchantment was nothing but geometry after all.

*A Guide to Deciphering Alchemical Geometry*

*In alchemy, geometry isn't just the foundation of our world and universe—it's a code. One you can learn to understand. If you take the time to do so then there's no need to memorize pre-existing core enchantments, you can decipher them for yourself and manipulate them specifically for your purpose. Learn the meaning of each of the principle shapes and there'll be no bounds to what you can do.*

Bastian turned the page. On the next page was an illustration of a curved line, like a large C, with a straight line beside it.

*Everything in the world—even the most complex designs—are comprised of only two shapes: straight lines and curved lines. And every shape, even the most basic, has meaning.*

Bastian traced his finger over the straight and curved lines, pondering how Haplo had drawn them himself on this very page. Underneath the straight line was written a very long list of attributes: *Clarity, Dependability, Entirety, Logic, Mechanical Motion, Order, Solid, Strength,* and so on. And under the curved line was written *Creativity, Divergent, Divergence, Diverging, Emotion, Flexibility, Grace, Ingenuity, Organic Motion, Liquid, Vapor,* and on it went.

Bastian turned the next page to a picture of a perfect circle. Underneath the illustration were the words *Birth, Celestial Body, Closed, Community, Connection, Continuation, Cyclic, Ego, Identifier, Life, Reliability, Safety, Selection, Self, Trust, Unbreaking, Unchanging, Whole…*

And so it continued. Bastian flipped through the next few pages until he came to an illustration of the infinity symbol used as the Everlasting enchantment.

*The Everlasting enchantment is one of the easier protection enchantments to master and a good example of how the foundation shapes are used to construct the symbols we use in alchemy. As you can see, the Everlasting enchantment is two circles joined together with intersecting curved lines. The circles individually are used for their Reliability, Unbreaking, and Continuation aspects as well as for identifying what is being enchanted. The curved lines connecting them give the symbol organic motion structured in a repeated pattern designed to go on and on forever. This calibrates the object to remain preserved as it is indefinitely. Both the benefit and downfall of this symbol is that it makes the object incapable of any change…*

Bastian thumbed through pages and pages defining ellipses, hyperbolas, triangular prisms, quadrilateral pyramids, dodecahedrons, icosahedrons, and more. Haplo listed every form of polygon, solid, circle and angle there was. The book held far more content than its size suggested, with a whole series of chapters dedicated to various combinations of shapes and angles.

When Bastian got to the very back of the journal, his heart leapt. On the page were instructions for creating a pair of glasses to see the Geometric Code. Bastian dog-eared the page and drank it in eagerly, before at last reaching the journal's final passage.

*There is more to learn than is documented here, but this book will give you the fundamentals and the tools for discovering more on your own. The Ghost Element is the glue that binds the Geometric Code and gives it life. The two go hand in hand and are both essential ingredients to mastering alchemy. Use the glasses to see the Geometric Code like it's the guts of a pocket watch and study every gear. When you learn the patterns around you, you learn the workings of the world. And when you know how something works, you can build it from the ground up, take it apart, fix it, and put it back together.*

*H.T.*

After that was nothing but several blank pages for notes. Bastian retrieved his pencil and drew the Anti-Tampering symbol on the first blank page. Then he started to dissect it, drawing each of its component shapes separately—circles, triangles, hexagons, and straight lines.

Next he flipped back through Haplo's journal and looked up the properties for each of those shapes and their angles, studying their individual attributes meticulously—making notes of which specific ones were most likely to be the ones used for the Anti-Tampering enchantment. The triangle was a triad of strength, the circle used for unbreaking and protection, and so on, until the pages were saturated with scrawled notes surrounding each component of the symbols' forms. Once Bastian had everything drawn and written out, he sat back and studied it.

*Great, I understand the symbol. Now, how in the Nine Levels of Darkness does that help me get past it?* he wondered.

He ran his hands over his face feeling lost and overwhelmed and then he froze, struck with the spark of epiphany. He took his hands away and looked at the symbol and its individual components again, and suddenly it all became clear. He'd been looking at it all wrong. He'd been struggling to grasp Tink's instructions because he'd been trying to do things Tink's way instead of his own. It had kept him from properly observing what was right in front of him. But now that he was looking at the symbol with a clear perspective, it finally made sense. The symbol enchantments were locks—the symbol the keyway, and its individual shapes the wards within. The Ciphorescent Codec was just like an L-shaped feeler—the thin metal rod from Bastian's personal collection of picking tools crafted for feeling out the inside of a lock. It allowed him to find where the wards were and what they were shaped like. He was using the Ciphorescent Codec in the same way—to feel out the wards of the enchantment. A lock was something Bastian knew, something he could wrap his head around. All he had to do now was pick it.

Bastian took a deep breath and looked again at the individual foundational shapes the symbol was made of. He analyzed the meaning of each one and why it was being used more closely. The symbol comprised primarily triangles and hexagons, the two strongest shapes woven together, each line of them clearly being chosen for their property of strength. He wondered if maybe he could bypass the enchantment by altering its properties. He knew he couldn't change the shapes themselves—the symbol itself prevented him from doing so—but each shape being used had at least a dozen different properties, with only one or two being utilized for the enchantment—cherry-picked by the enchanter and locked into place using intention. What if he used intention to select a different property from the shape's own list of attributes? He could change all the straight lines standing for strength to instead stand for clarity or logic. And instead of the circles standing for unbreaking, he could change them to stand for safety or trust. If he was simply shifting the shape's properties from one of its natural attributes to another without changing its form—then the enchantment might not detect his changes as something obtrusive, it might not detect his changes at all—like a skeleton key passing smoothly through the wards of a lock.

Bastian looked at the lists of properties for the foundational shapes in front of him, and one by one he selected a new one for each. Then he took off his bracelet and laid it on the floor in front of him. Crouching over it he cleared his mind and drew the Ghost Element into the palms of his hands. Using the Ciphorescent Codec he located the Anti-Tampering enchantment in his bracelet and focused on changing the attributes of the foundational shapes in the symbol. He cleared his mind of any preconception of what the enchantment was, and instead focused completely on the new identity he was giving it—as if it was and always had been that way—and then suddenly, it was. Almost instantly he was able to bypass the enchantment. Bastian reached out with the Codec to see what he'd done. The symbol was completely transformed. He was now able to alter it easily and even unmake it by simply imagining it dissolving away.

Bastian laughed out loud with sheer exhilaration and relief. He remade the Anti-Tampering enchantment on his bracelet and then got rid of it several times, running through the process again and again until he felt satisfied it was reliably repeatable. Then he remade the enchantment a final time—restoring its protection to his bracelet—and headed to the top deck for line duty.

That afternoon Bastian was lost in thoughts about the symbology of Haplo's journal while he chopped potatoes on galley duty. Then he became distracted by how sharp Doc kept his knives and his thoughts turned to what Falgo had said to him at their last lesson—how if he wanted to survive he needed to forget about mastering a single weapon and instead figure out how the things around him could be turned into one.

Bastian looked around the galley with that in mind. The knives, of course, were an obvious weapon choice.

*Maybe I could practice throwing them?* he wondered.

Then he recalled Falgo's warning about knives and decided that the obvious choice might not be the best one. He thought about how close he'd been to throwing a knife at Spitz when they were playing Spitting Daggers. He knew then he was capable of it, and he would've done it too if it wasn't for Snibs stopping his hand. He was grateful to the quartermaster for that. The very idea of what would've happened if he hadn't, sent a chill up Bastian's spine.

He looked around at what else he could use in the kitchen as a weapon. The cast iron pots and pans would knock a heavy hit or could be used as an efficient shield. The meat tenderizer could do some serious damage, and even the forks would be something to contend with. The apples and onions could work as effective projectiles. The metal steins could clobber someone over the head. The hand towels could wrap around someone's face from behind…Bastian stopped. It gave him goosebumps as the realization dawned on him that there wasn't anything in the galley that couldn't be turned into a weapon. All it took was a little imagination. Even the spices would be debilitating if rubbed in someone's eyes. To look at the objects around him in that way gave Bastian an unsettling feeling. He realized then that the only thing distinguishing the galley as a place of nourishment from an arsenal was perspective.

At dinner that night, Cricket was in a sea of misery.

"What's up with you?" Bastian inquired, sitting down beside him.

"Nuthin'," Cricket stated bluntly and took a long drink from his black leather stein.

"I find yer relentless determination inspirin', Cricket. No matter how many times ya lose, ya never give up hope," Stork laughed.

Cricket didn't even look up from his Black Jack, his spirit defeated.

"You're gambling again?" Bastian asked him.

Cricket just shrugged and took another drink.

"Ya let 'im gamble more coin?!" Rhino exclaimed, hitting his brother with an open palm on the back of the head.

"Oi! I didn't make 'im play!" Stork protested.

"But ya didn't stop 'im neither, did ya, brother?"

Stork answered with silence.

"Come on, Stork, cheating your own friend? I thought you were better than that," Bastian accused.

"Cheatin'?! I never! Don't ya start on that rubbish too! Ya can't blame a man just fer havin' a bit o' luck," Stork objected defensively.

"No one's that lucky," Bastian asserted.

"Oh, come on! Not that nonsense. If ya want ta check me die, ya only need ask," Stork declared, and pulled his die from his pocket, spinning it on the table.

Bastian caught it and weighed it in his hand, and then he spun it himself. He used the Ghost Element to try and steer it to his will as before, and yet again his attempts had no effect. He reached out to it again, but this time he used the Codec to inspect the die and find out why his influence wasn't working. He was met immediately by an invisible solid wall. *The Anti-Tampering symbol.* He recognized the enchantment immediately. Bastian sat up straighter. "Stork, where'd you get this die?"

"Found it on a dead man in the Southern Isles. An' it's been bringin' me luck ever since," Stork said.

"Funny that, somethin' on a dead man bein' lucky," Rhino remarked.

Bastian both was and wasn't surprised to find the die was enchanted. He'd expected as much, it was the only way to explain the relentless luck Stork had been having—only the alchemists weren't supposed to make anything for personal gain. According to Tink, it was a hard and fast rule—a rule this object shamelessly shattered.

Bastian picked up the die and turned it over in his hand. The whalebone was masterfully carved, it was beautiful workmanship. Bastian used the Codec to explore it further. It had two symbol enchantments. The Anti-Tampering enchantment and one more that had been in the book of foundation symbology that Tink had given him to memorize. It was an Identity-Set enchantment. It bound the object to the owner, making at least one of its core abilities only work for them. It set the owner of the object by either having it given to them as a gift from the owner or by being bought from the owner. And if the owner died without the object being passed on, then it reset itself to the first person who found it.

If Stork had found the die on a dead man, it would make sense that the identity lock was set to him. Bastian searched past the symbols to the core enchantment. It was simple and straightforward. The die favored whomever it belonged to, bringing luck to the bearer with enough variety to not be obvious. That explained Stork's winning streak and Cricket's inability to beat him. Bastian found it odd that the object was missing the Protection and the Everlasting symbol enchantments. According to Tink, they were standard safeguards put on every object made by the alchemists—yet another indication that the object was most likely made by someone else. Even the symbols being used were a bit different from the versions Bastian had been taught. They felt almost like twins to the originals, yet different—like a counterfeit copy or knock-off of the real thing. He wished he could borrow the die to fully translate the forms of the symbols using Haplo's journal. The question that burned inside him was *If the alchemists didn't make this object, then who did?* If there was someone making enchanted objects outside The Alchemists House of Discover, it meant one of two things—either they had a lens like the one Tink used, or they had the gift of sight.

"Alright, Stork, count me in. I'll spin your die tonight," Bastian declared.

"Ha! Yer as stubborn as 'e is. I'll be happy ta 'ave ya, Dodger, but if yer goin' ta spin then understand ya do so at yer own risk. I don't want ya blamin' me when yer pockets turn up empty," Stork warned.

"I understand perfectly."

After dinner that night Bastian waited until Dagger was playing his music and the men were distracted before slipping down to the gun deck with a partially filled stein. He was relieved to find Dylan asleep in the hold. He slipped past him and made his way to the locked door of the armory. The master gunner spent the majority of his time in there, using it as his own personal workshop for concocting explosives and creative fireworks, but Bastian knew that Boom wasn't in there now—he'd seen him in the galley minutes before, enjoying himself as he swayed along to Dagger's song. Bastian put his Black Jack on the floor and effortlessly picked his way inside the armory using his own handmade picks. Then he took up his stein and slipped inside, closing the door silently behind him. He tapped one of the firebeetle lanterns to awaken the creatures inside and assessed the room. It was a jumble of organized chaos. Boom's long worktable stretched across the center, littered with tools and colorful materials of his trade. Large spiky sea mines sat idle on the floor. Bastian stepped around them carefully as he made his way to the table. He was relieved to find what he was looking for: a large, strong magnifying glass on an extendable, moveable arm. Bastian wasted no time. He put his stein down on the table and moved the magnifying glass over the top of it. The Black Jack was only a quarter of the way full of grog, which was plenty for his purpose. He pulled Haplo's journal out from the back of his belt beneath his jacket and laid it on the table beside his stein. He flipped through the pages until he found the one he'd dog-eared with the Identity-Set enchantment. He knew that if he was going to have any chance of beating Stork with his own die that night, he needed to figure out a way to reset the Identity-Set enchantment to himself. The problem was, even if he found a way to do that, he still needed the geometric symbol representing the code for his own identity. Without Haplo's special glasses, he couldn't see what that form was. But he figured that if the Geometric Code really was the physical form of the Language of Songs, then theoretically he should be able to see it in any liquid that could be affected by its vibrations. *Here's hoping*, he thought. He looked through the magnifying glass into the grog below it and said his name. As the sound hit the water and rum concoction, fine ripples cascaded outward—but they were too light and fine for him to discern. He recalled a chemistry lesson at the Order where they were playing around with surface tension, and how water could be changed by adding different compounds. One of the first experiments they did was to darken the water with ink to show how much more reflective it made it. Bastian looked around Boom's workbench and found a jar of black powder. He poured a substantial amount into his Black Jack and gave it a good stir. The once clear liquid was now a dark black. Bastian looked into its reflective surface through the magnifying glass and spoke his name again. This time a clear and complex geometric form bloomed outward. Bastian almost laughed out loud. He pulled out his pencil and repeated his name once more, this time copying the form down in the back pages of Haplo's journal.

That night was cooler than the one before, but still pleasant. Pirates were crowded around the gambling barrel with Stork's die at its center.

"We're starting a round with silver fish, who's in?" Stork announced.

A slew of sailors raised their hands, but this time Bastian kept his down. Stork picked four players and the rest of the onlookers called bets around them. Bastian placed a bet himself, choosing a random sailor he didn't know amongst the four players and putting down one of his remaining jolly rogers from the night before. Once the bets were laid, the players anted up and the game began. Bastian watched the gamblers spin in turn, keeping his eyes fixed on the die. As the game progressed he silently reached out with the Ghost Element and began unlocking the Anti-Tampering enchantment. As soon as the properties were changed the enchantment let him through without protest, and the die didn't even skip a beat in its spin. Bastian didn't bother messing with the core enchantment. Instead, he concentrated on the Identity-Set enchantment. He held its symbol in his mind's eye while using his tongue to draw his own identity symbol on the roof of his mouth, then using intention he projected his symbol onto Stork's die, recalibrating it to be set to himself. The die was spinning when the change was made. It stopped midspin, standing upright and balancing there for a single instant, it wavered once and then fell to the side in favor of the man Bastian had bet his coin on. Bastian collected his winnings without drawing any attention to himself and then bet on someone else for the next round. Again, the man that Bastian had bet on won, and this time he hadn't had to interfere in any way. Now that the die was set to him, all he had to do was sit back and allow the enchantment to do its work.

"Yer 'avin' far better luck tanight," Rhino observed.

Bastian shrugged. "Must be my lucky night."

Stork declared the next round would be played with jolly rogers and Bastian volunteered to play. He stood around the barrel with three other men he didn't know. They all anted up, and the first player spun the die. It landed on the crescent moon. The sailor cursed and threw another coin into the pot, and the next sailor took his turn. This time the die landed on the new moon, then was passed to the next sailor. His spin landed on the crescent moon as well, and the pirate added a coin to the pot.

It was Bastian's turn next. He picked up the die with an anticipatory thrill and spun it. As the die pirouetted he reached out with the Ghost Element and imagined it spinning faster. The die sped up, twirling in a blur and then Bastian let it go without instructing it which way to fall. The die teetered on a point and then fell onto its side, landing on the full moon.

Bastian smiled in triumph and the small crowd lit with a mix of cheers and jeers behind him. He chose to take his winnings and stay in the game, finding it a lot more enjoyable now the odds were in his favor.

❧

Ten minutes later, Bastian's pile of winnings had grown substantially, and all the surrounding sailors leaned forward around the barrel watching the die spin with renewed interest, Stork most of all. Finally, after Bastian took the pot for the fourth time, Stork decided to join the game. Instantly the circle of spectators grew, and an anticipatory buzz sparked amongst the men. Many fresh bets were called, and Bastian knew the pirates were putting coin on either Stork or himself, with the odds leaning in the former's favor. He feigned concern that the gambling shark was entering the game, and the round started with the pirate to Bastian's right. The die spun and then fell on the crescent moon. The sailor cursed and added an additional coin to the pot. Bastian took his turn and the die also landed on the crescent moon. He cursed, contradicting his internal delight as he tossed a jolly roger into the pot. He was thoroughly enjoying himself now.

The sailor to Bastian's left spun the die and it landed on the new moon. Next, it was Stork's turn. He spun the die and Bastian directed it to land on the half moon. Stork smiled with satisfaction and took half the pot. The next pirate spun a crescent moon for a second time and cursed even louder than before.

Bastian took his turn and steered the die to land on the new moon. The pirate to his left got a crescent moon, throwing another jolly roger into the pot. Stork also got a crescent moon and added a jolly roger to the growing store. Bastian ensured that Stork got the crescent moon for the next two rounds, almost completely filling the pot. After Stork's third time in a row adding a jolly roger, he was beginning to look concerned.

Bastian glanced up to see Cricket grinning amongst the huddled crowd around them. Nothing could've encouraged and delighted Bastian more. And the next time he looked up, their audience had grown. The next player spun the die and it landed on the new moon. Bastian took his turn and steered his die to the crescent moon once more, adding another jolly roger to the pot. The next sailor also spun a crescent, and Stork did as well. When Stork placed his coin into the pot, the men around them cheered the loudest of all. And Bastian knew then that Cricket wasn't the only one eager to see Stork lose. Stork rolled his eyes in good humor, but Bastian could see his underlying uncertainty. It was Bastian's turn next. The pot was full now, and the men around him were silent with anticipation, their attention hanging on Bastian's every move. Bastian spun the die, holding it up and encouraging it to spin longer for dramatic effect. He could almost feel the men holding their breath around him. Then the die fell on the full moon. There was a moment of disbelieving silence and then immense cheers rose up all around as Bastian took the full pot. He knew the cheers were because Stork was beaten, and not for him, but he basked in the triumph all the same. Stork stood staring at the die in stunned, disbelieving silence, and Cricket stood amongst the crowd grinning wider than Bastian had ever seen him.

"Well, I've always believed in stopping while I'm ahead," Bastian declared with the winnings in hand.

Stork looked at him in shock, and Bastian winked at him with a grin. Stork's expression instantly transformed into one of suspicion, but Bastian had already graciously bowed out of the game. Men he'd never been introduced to were patting his shoulders enthusiastically. Bastian smiled as he stepped away from the ring, leaving the rest of the night's gambling in the capable hands of Lady Luck.

Bastian walked to the poop deck to have a puff, and shortly found Cricket by his side. He handed the puff-stick he was rolling over to him, and rolled himself another, lighting them both with his Everfire box.

"Ya rascal, ya did it, ya bloody beat the bastard!" Cricket exclaimed, clapping him on the shoulder.

Bastian grinned.

"Ya must tell me how," Cricket insisted.

"What do you mean how? It's a game of chance."

Cricket narrowed his eyes. "Right. Just like it's chance that Stork hasn't lost a game until now?"

"Precisely. Exactly the same," Bastian proclaimed.

Cricket smirked. "Alright, don't tell me. I'm just glad ya beat 'im. Don't get me wrong, I love the man, but 'e needed ta be brought back down ta the ground."

"True. I don't believe it's healthy for anyone to win continuously for such a prolonged period of time," Bastian remarked.

"How much did ya haul in?" Cricket asked.

"Three rogers," Bastian answered plainly.

"Come on, don't be like that! I saw how big the pot was when ya collected."

"I only won three jolly rogers, because outside the ten I owe Stork and three for myself, the rest belongs to you."

"What nonsense are ya talkin' about?!" Cricket scoffed.

Bastian counted out thirteen jolly rogers, and then handed the rest of the full purse to Cricket. "For compensation for the clothes you gave me, and a small token of my gratitude for saving my life. I owe you far more."

Cricket pushed the purse away. "Don't be stupid! Ya owe me nothin'!"

"Take it, Cricket. I won it for you. I know what it's like to be away from the person you love. Helping you be reunited with yours brings me more joy than anything I could buy with this coin," Bastian asserted.

Cricket looked at him, ready to argue, then his expression softened, and he took the purse. "Yer a true friend, Dodger."

Bastian shrugged, "I can't say it was all selfless, I wanted to see the look on Stork's face when his luck ran out. It was worth it just for that," he smirked.

Cricket grinned. "Absolutely."

⌒

Bastian headed back towards the main deck and saw Stork alone clearing away the evidence of the gambling circuit. He walked over to him, and Stork clasped his arm in greeting.

"Ya played well tanight," he commended, "if it wasn't me own die, I'd question yer luck."

"But it *was* your own die," Bastian replied with a wry smile.

"Aye, so it was…," Stork trailed off in thought.

"I hope there's no hard feelings?" Bastian asked.

"Course not! What kind o' 'ypocrite would I be? Besides, I think it was ta me benefit ta lose a game. I've been 'opin' fer it, if I'm honest. 'alf the men 'ere 'ave been 'oldin' a grudge. It's good ta take the pressure off an' let out some o' that steam before Jaxland," Stork admitted, then added, "though I did lose more than I was expectin' tanight. I'd feel a lot better if ya buy me a drink er two on Jaxland."

"Ha! Consider it done. And as promised, the ten jolly rogers I owe you for loaning me the rose wagon," Bastian declared, holding out the coin.

Stork took the coin in hand and smiled. "I've never met a more honest thief than ya, Dodger."

"Thieves and pirates aren't really that different, are they?"

"I suppose not," Stork admitted, dropping the coins into his coin purse and riffling through it. His brow furrowed with concern. "It's not here."

"What's not?"

"The rose wagon, I swear I haven't touched it since the day ya gave it ta me."

Bastian had completely forgotten Stork was supposed to give him the rose wagon in return — the rose wagon that would be nothing but dust by now. *Shick.* He held out his hand to Stork. "Let me see."

Stork handed him his purse.

"It's right here, ya git!" Bastian exclaimed, reaching into the small leather bag and pulling out a rose wagon. Stork looked overwhelmingly relieved.

"You probably just need a bit of rest," Bastian told him, dropping the coin into his pocket and clasping Stork on the shoulder.

Stork scratched his head. "Aye, yer probably right."

Bastian quietly sighed in relief as they both headed below deck, and the coin in his pocket dissolved to dust.

<hr>

"Alright, yer finally lookin' half decent, thief. It's time ta dance," Falgo declared after he'd drained his usual quarter of a bottle of diluted rum. It was becoming more and more watered down by the day, but luckily it had been gradual enough that Falgo hadn't noticed. Bastian wondered when or if he would.

"At the ready," the pirate ordered, and drew his long, razor-sharp cutlass from its scabbard, assuming a perfect fighting stance.

"Are you sure I'm ready for this?" Bastian queried uneasily, assuming the stance Falgo had taught him.

"Unless ya want ta continue practicin' yer steps?" Falgo offered.

"No, no, I think I'd rather take the chance of being sliced open, thank you," Bastian asserted quickly.

Falgo smiled and began circling Bastian. He kept his eyes on the pirate, turning to stay facing him. "Isn't this a little unfair? I mean, I'm unarmed and you have a lethal weapon," Bastian pointed out.

"Yer armed," Falgo argued, nodding to Bastian's arms.

"Oh right, great. Very funny. I might not be soon if you don't give me anything to defend myself with."

"This still be dodgin' practice, Dodger. Somethin' ya'll want ta ensure yer good at with yer title," Falgo smirked. "Besides, any weapon ya wield will only slow ya down," he insisted.

"Right," Bastian remarked dryly.

"Sheath yer fear, lad, I can smell it from here. Fear be a mind killer. It does nothin' but blind ya—yew must banish it from yer thoughts. Dodgin' a blade be no different from dodgin' a blow."

"Except it'll kill me if it hits its mark," Bastian stated.

"I have no intention o' killin' ya. Who would bring me my drink then?" Falgo asked wryly.

"Ha! Very comforting."

"Now, concentrate. Clear yer mind," Falgo instructed.

*I am nothing, I am everything.*

Bastian took a deep breath and tried to calm his nerves. Falgo sliced his sword through the air towards Bastian's head at half speed. Bastian avoided it with a wide berth to the side. Before he could even blink, Falgo's leg swept under his, dropping him to the ground. Bastian landed on his back in the sand with a thud.

"Yer first choice should never be ta dodge ta the side, it's too predictable. Anyone with decent trainin' will be thinkin' two steps ahead an' expect as much. Ta have the advantage ya must go where yer opponent least expects."

"And where's that?" Bastian inquired, standing up and dusting the sand off his pants.

"Towards the danger," Falgo declared. He turned his sword around and handed the hilt to Bastian. "It's me turn."

Bastian took the sword hesitantly. "Are you sure this is such a good idea? I mean, you have been drinking."

Falgo smirked. "Give me yer best shot, thief. No holdin' back."

"Alright. Don't blame me if I kill you," Bastian muttered. And he began circling Falgo with the blade held high. The sword was lighter than he'd imagined it would be, and perfectly balanced. He raised it back above his head and sliced downwards towards the pirate with speed. Falgo didn't move. Bastian's chest blossomed with panic just before he realized that somehow, he'd still completely missed him. Falgo was now only inches from Bastian's face. The pirate smiled and Bastian could smell the rum on his breath. While his brain was trying to decipher what in the nine realms just happened, Falgo pushed up Bastian's chin with the open palm of his hand and grabbed the sword while simultaneously sweeping Bastian's legs out from under him and pushing his weight forward. Bastian lost grip of the sword and tumbled into the sand.

"Shick. What was that?" Bastian exclaimed, completely bemused as he returned to his feet and dusted himself off.

"Subtlety is an art. By dodgin' with the unexpected, ya confuse the mind," Falgo explained.

"Okay, so you're going to walk me through that, right?"

Falgo turned his sword around handing the hilt back to Bastian. "Again. Only slower," he commanded.

Bastian brought the sword down as if in slow motion, and Falgo moved likewise. As the sword neared the pirate's head, he stepped forward. The subtle shift of his positioning meant he missed the blade by no more than several centimeters. Because the blade was so close and Falgo's movement so subtle, it made it appear as though it passed right through him. But by the time the mind caught up with the fact that it hadn't, it was too late. Falgo was too close to avoid.

"Once yer here, ya be spoiled fer choice on the ways ya can thwart yer opponent. Ya can keep 'is momentum goin'," Falgo pulled Bastian's sword arm forward, causing him to stumble several paces before having to dive into a roll.

Bastian got back up and returned to his starting position with the sword in hand.

"Ya can trip him." Falgo swept Bastian's feet out from under him, knocking him to the ground.

Bastian stood back up.

"Ya can wind him." Falgo punched him in the solar plexus, causing Bastian to double over in pain. Bastian came back to his starting position more reluctantly this time, while giving the pirate an accusing stare.

"Ya can knee him in the groin."

Bastian's hands flew up in defense, "I get it! No need to demonstrate."

Falgo shrugged. "Ya can knock him out." He brought his elbow down in a slow arc coming to touch Bastian lightly on the temple. "Here or here," he said, also lightly touching his elbow to Bastian's chin, "or alternatively, ya can cut his throat." Falgo motioned a cut across Bastian's neck with his sheathed dagger.

"Killin' be a last resort. The most important thin' ya gain by learning ta fight be the ability ta stay in control when ya feel threatened. Being in control gives ya options ya don't otherwise have. If ya feel ya aren't in control, yer mind floods with fear—and that's when someone dies. Take me word fer it, thief—just as much as ya don't want ta die, ya don't want ta take a man's life either, er it will haunt yew fer the rest o' yers," Falgo admonished, taking the sword.

"Now, it's yer turn," he said, and pointed his blade at Bastian.

Bastian puffed out a breath of air and faced Falgo's raised sword. The pirate brought it down in slow motion with a trajectory aimed at slicing Bastian in two. Bastian stepped forward towards the sword and closed his eyes, feeling the blade slice the air only a couple centimeters from his ear.

"Well done," Falgo commended, "only this time, keep yer eyes open fer stars sake! The act be simple—the true obstacle isn't the blade, it's yer own mind. Again!"

# SOUL INSTRUMENT

Felix stood behind Lilliana in a lineup of extravagantly dressed models. She was looking more herself again. She'd removed her disguise except for the black polish in her hair and replaced the cosmetic illusion with her usual makeup.

They were standing outside the door to where Favio was giving The Emperor his presentation. They could hear him delivering his introduction. All of the models buzzed with anticipation. It didn't matter how well seasoned they were, it was a privilege and honor to be seen by The Emperor, and every one of them was beside themselves. Lilliana gripped tightly onto Felix's hand.

"How're you doing?" he asked her in a whisper.

"Good. To be honest, I'm eager to get it over and done with," she whispered back.

"After this, maybe you and I can sneak off somewhere to celebrate?"

"I don't even want to suggest we'll have anything to celebrate until I know it doesn't turn out to be a total disaster."

"It won't," Felix assured her, and squeezed her hand.

The door to the back room opened and they were all invited inside. Felix and Lilliana waited patiently for everyone to file through before taking up the tail.

The room was just as ornate as the rest of the opera house, only it was almost completely empty, set up as a place for performers and dancers to rehearse between shows, with a polished wood floor and a mirror that stretched along one side.

At the far end of the room was a dais with a throne-like chair atop it. The Emperor sat in the chair casually with a half circle of guards and attendants fanning out behind him. He was a tall man, built like he was the offspring of boulders, with skin as dark as night. His presence commanded attention. Felix had met plenty of high-class aristocrats with high opinions of themselves, their egos inflated far beyond their worth.

The Emperor was not one of those people. He didn't exude an air of arrogance. He exuded the cool confidence of a god.

Emperor Balthazar watched expressionless as the parade of men's and women's fashion pranced by, stopping to bow to him and do a slow turn to show off their attire before exiting the room. Finally, it was Felix and Lilliana's turn. They came to the front and stopped before the Lord Emperor to perform the proper formalities. When Felix came up from his low bow their eyes met, and Lord Balthazar stared into him, a question hovering in his gaze. Felix quickly looked at the floor, desperately hoping he hadn't committed some sort of social faux pas. He'd never learned the proper etiquette for meeting the ruler of the world. He completed his slow turn to show off his attire—as instructed by Favio, and when he was back facing the front, the Emperor was smiling warmly at Lilliana.

"Lady Lilliana Wendrian, it appears you're not missing after all," he declared, his voice a deep and smooth rumble.

"No, my Lord. But I assure you, I've convinced the world otherwise for good reason. I've come here today with the hope that I might be granted an audience?" she requested.

Favio gasped behind them. "Lady Wendrian, the Jewel of Westdock?!" he muttered in surprise.

"Favio! Thank you for your presentation," The Emperor announced loudly, "it's clear why you won the competition. These last few years I've found the fashion world a bore. Everyone seems to be copying their neighbors or recycling old styles. But your work is tastefully unique. I find it refreshing. I would like to book a full session with you while I'm here and commission you for several pieces. If I'm pleased with the result, you'll find me a loyal customer."

"Th-thank you, your highness! Serving you will be the honor of a lifetime. I am beside myself with gratitude," Favio stammered with a low bow.

"The honor's all mine. My attendant, Amelia, will organize a time with you and give you the first installment for my order," The Emperor said, and made a small motion with his hand.

A woman from The Emperor's entourage stepped down off the platform and walked Favio out of the room. Felix wondered if he should be leaving also, but he ignored the social cue, not wanting to leave Lilliana's side if he didn't have to. As soon as the door closed The Emperor turned his attention to them. "I have ten minutes before my next engagement. I'll give you five."

Lilliana inclined her head. "Thank you, my lord. I'll get straight to the point then. I believe my betrothal to Lord Bardviss is the first part of a scheme to overthrow you," she proclaimed.

Lord Balthazar raised his eyebrows. "That's quite the accusation."

Felix was surprised to see The Emperor's attendants remain completely stone-faced at the news, as if they couldn't hear the conversation.

"I've had suspicions of Lord Bardviss's ill intentions from the very beginning of our betrothal, but having no solid evidence, I staged my own kidnapping to buy more time. I know my actions may seem drastic, but I believe they were necessary for securing the safety of my family and the people of Westdock. To make things convincing I left a ransom letter on the night of my disappearance. For whatever reason, the letter never surfaced to my mother or the press. Which meant that instead of my kidnapping being reported, it was said I had disappeared. To confirm our suspicions that Lord Bardviss had intentionally disposed of the letter, we sent another ransom note directly to Lord Bardviss. This was his reply," Lilliana handed The Emperor the letter from Lord Bardviss.

The Emperor read it in silence.

After a moment Lilliana continued. "I believe Lord Bardviss wants me removed because he's worried I might disrupt whatever he's planning. I've discovered he was introduced to my mother by my cousin as a favor for a client of hers—a client whose name I've been told is very prominent in The East."

"And what name is that?" Emperor Balthazar inquired, his eyes still on the letter.

"Marx, Your Highness."

Emperor Balthazar looked up, suddenly seeming a lot more interested. "Marx is a client of your cousin?"

"Yes. My uncle left our family business in debt when he died. My cousin was desperate to find new clients, and Marx was looking for a breeder. I fear she might not be the only one with whom he contracted at the time. There's unrest in Sky View. Many of the old breeding families' wealth from The Last War is waning. Sky View's independence is hot on everyone's tongue. The young people are pushing for a revolution. And The East seems to be taking full advantage of this, even encouraging it. They're forming a bond with the prominent families. I worry the unrest here might even be contrived by The East to divide Sky View from the mainland," Lilliana concluded.

Emperor Balthazar listened without expression. "What type of dragon is your cousin producing for The East?"

"A large and aggressive breed."

"You do realize the accusation you're making puts your cousin in a very compromising position."

"That's just it, she's not breaking any laws. The dragons are a hybrid comprising regular pack dragons and a type of pet dragon. As you know, both are legal on the mainland, and no one's ever said they aren't allowed to be mixed together. The problem is, the particular type of pet dragon my cousin is using has violent tendencies. The combination produces a large, aggressive breed. After talking with her, I'm convinced she's completely naive as to what they're being used for. Her real crime is catering to her client without asking questions, even when she knows the danger of what she's making. I don't know what their intentions for the dragons are, but I think the potential threat warrants an investigation," Lilliana reported.

"And what does this have to do with your betrothal to Lord Bardviss?" The Emperor queried.

"I believe Marx is planting Lord Bardviss in Westdock to gain access to Westdock's port. With Lord Bardviss appointed Duke, The East will have open access into the mainland from the West."

"Anything else?" The Emperor asked.

"No, Your Highness."

"Do you have any proof of Lord Bardviss's ill intent besides this letter?"

"No, Your Highness. For the sake of us all, I dearly hope I'm wrong—but if I'm not, the consequences are too dire to be ignored."

"Hmm. I must admit, I'm very impressed with your courage, Lady Wendrian. It was a daring move coming here to deliver this report. You've discovered all this on your own since your disappearance was announced?" he asked.

"Well, not entirely on my own," Lilliana admitted, and looked at Felix with a grateful smile.

The Emperor followed her gaze. "Ah, and who is this?"

"This is James Turner. He's been essential to the discoveries I've made."

"James Turner. Have we met before?"

"No, Your Highness. I'm certain I would've remembered that."

The Emperor smiled. "Your face looks familiar; I can't quite put my finger on it. What house are you from?"

"He's a Star Child, your highness," Lilliana answered.

Lord Balthazar looked at Felix with new interest. "Is that right?"

"Yes, I was raised by the Order of the Stars in Westdock."

"Very interesting. I find both your stories and how they came to intersect intriguing. Unfortunately, we're all out of time. Thank you for your report, Lady Wendrian. Your loyalty and bravery will be remembered. In times like these such daring acts are essential to preserving Equillian's peace. To the peace of Equillian," The Lord Emperor announced.

"To the peace of Equillian," Lilliana returned with a bow, and Felix bowed as well. The Emperor nodded and dismissed them. As Felix and Lilliana walked to the door, Emperor Balthazar called out, "How's your mother?"

A lump caught in Felix's throat—for a second he thought The Emperor might be talking to him.

"Hanging in there," Lilliana answered.

"Good. I was sorry to hear about your father, he was an excellent duke. You remind me of him. No doubt he would be very proud," The Emperor commended.

"Thank you, Your Highness," Lilliana replied with a grateful curtsy.

⌘

"Thank the Stars that's over!" Lilliana exclaimed, pushing her way through the greenroom doors. All evidence of the other models and Favio were gone. Lilliana sat down in front of one of the large mirrors and pulled a travel-sized makeup case out of her handbag. She gave it to Felix, and he began reapplying her disguise.

"How do you think it went?" he asked her.

"I have no idea. Part of me feels like a fool. I was so convinced of everything I told him until it came out. Now I'm not sure about any of it. What if none of it's true and I've allowed my fears to run away with me?"

"Well, if none of it's true, then we'll all be better for it. And if it is, and you just told The Emperor something he doesn't know, then you might have just prevented another war. I think that makes it worth it, don't you?" Felix asked.

Lilliana nodded absently. "Yes, I suppose you're right. Thank you, that is encouraging."

But Felix could tell she wasn't convinced. He finished applying her disguise and then sat on the desk in front of her. "At least it's done now. You've played your part. Now you can rest easy and have some fun."

"I don't even want to go out there anymore. I'm too terrified I'll run into Arianna or someone else I know."

"Don't then. I bet this place has all kinds of interesting hidey-holes to explore."

"Like where?" Lilliana inquired.

"Well, this is the greenroom after all, it's used for getting ready for performances. One of these doors must open into the theater," Felix proclaimed, hopping down from the table and searching the outer wall. He found a door at the back and opened it. "Bingo!"

"What is it?" Lilliana queried.

"Come, have a look for yourself."

Lilliana got up and followed Felix into the dim light beyond. The door led backstage in the main performance hall. Felix found his way into the side wings hung with thick velvet drapes and looked out upon the skeletal structure of an orchestra—a large, beautiful stage littered with instruments and empty chairs. A grand piano stood at the forefront and empty tiered seating fanned out on the floor below the stage for the audience. Felix had never seen a performance hall so grand.

Lilliana walked past him and sat down at the piano, "Do you think anyone will be able to hear us?"

"Not a chance. These places are acoustically sound. You wouldn't be able to hear a symphony from the other side of the doors. And I'll bet ten cwips all the other entrances to this place are locked," Felix said, sitting down on the piano bench beside her. "Do you play?" he asked.

"No. My mother was adamant I learn the harp. Do you play an instrument?"

"Of course, I'm a Star Child. It's mandatory at the Order. The sisters say music is the language of the soul."

"Do they? What instrument do you play?" Lilliana inquired.

Felix smiled. "Guess."

"Guess? Alright, hmmm. Does everyone learn the same instrument?"

"No. At the Order, we don't choose an instrument, it chooses us."

"How do you mean?"

"It has to do with the Language of Songs. Every person has a soul instrument, like a soulmate of sorts. You can play any instrument you like, but there will be one in particular that will come to you more natu-rally and act as your voice '*for that which cannot be translated into words,*'" Felix said, quoting the line spoken by the sisters of the Order.

"But how do you know which instrument is your soul instrument?" Lilliana queried.

"You have to try each one. When you find the right one, you'll know it."

"I like that. I wonder what my soul instrument is," Lilliana remarked thoughtfully, looking out at the instruments.

"It's not the harp?" Felix asked.

"I doubt it. Learning it has been a chore."

"Hmmm, can you show me?"

Felix walked over to a large object covered with a heavy cloth amongst the orchestra seating. He pulled off the drape to reveal a magnificent harp and pushed it to center stage. He placed a chair next to it and motioned to it with a bow. "My lady."

Lilliana laughed. "If I must." She sat down in the chair and pulled the harp towards her, resting it against her shoulder. She thought for a moment, and then her fingers began to dance expertly across the strings. It was a beautiful, entrancing melody. Felix sat down on the piano bench and listened attentively. He recognized the piece. It was a well-known number by a famous composer called Manuel Wayward. When Lilliana finished, Felix clapped.

"Absolutely superb. But you're right, it's not your soul instrument," he agreed.

"How can you be so sure?"

"Because your playing was perfect. The truth is never perfect—it's raw and often messy. It's the imperfections that expose our humanity, you see—it's in our nature. To be human is to be imperfect—which is why we can't achieve perfection and remain honest. The two just don't go together. That doesn't stop us from trying of course, but in doing so, we sand away all the bits that make us interesting, hiding our greatest features behind an inferior mask—all because we're terrified of exposing our true nature."

"Are you saying my playing wasn't interesting?" Lilliana queried.

"Oh, don't get me wrong, your playing was flawless. It just had no reflection of you in it. Anyone else just as practiced could play the same piece and make it sound exactly the same. You could create a steam machine to play it perfectly and it would sound no different. But when you play from the heart, no one can replicate that. And I'm far more interested in hearing your soul sing than a perfect copycat of even the greatest composer."

"Hmmm. Alright, It's your turn. Where's this 'soul instrument' of yours?" Lilliana asked him. She stood from the piano bench and walked to the instruments at the back of the stage. "The saxophone?"

"No. A very cool instrument, but not mine," Felix replied with a smirk.

"Hmm, the drums?"

"Not even close."

"The violin?"

"Nope. That's my brother's instrument."

"That's right, you have a brother. Is he as handsome as you are?" Lilliana inquired.

Felix smiled. "Almost."

"I would like to meet him."

"I hope you will one day," Felix replied in earnest.

"Ah, I know!" Lilliana exclaimed, picking up an accordion decorated with abalone shell and moving it in and out dramatically.

Felix laughed. "You're getting warmer."

Lilliana scanned the instruments on the stage again. She looked at Felix and studied him. Then she smiled. "You're sitting at it, aren't you?"

Felix grinned wryly. "I thought you'd never guess."

"I should've known. Will you play me something?" Lilliana asked, coming to sit on the piano bench beside him.

"I suppose it's only fair." Felix stood up, took off his coat and laid it on the bench, then rolled up his sleeves. "But you have to play with me," he said.

"I don't know how!" Lilliana objected.

"Of course you do. It's not that different from the harp. Just let your instincts guide you." Felix stood behind Lilliana and gently placed her left hand on the keys and reached his right hand around her right shoulder and began to play. He started with only a few notes that Lilliana mimicked on the bottom of the scale. He played a little more and she followed. Then he waited for her to play something. Lilliana felt out a combination of pleasant notes. Felix played a joining tune that complimented hers. Lilliana laughed with delight and began to play again. Getting braver, she moved her fingers gracefully across the keys. Soon, the two were improvising an uplifting and playful duet that reflected the bubbling joy Felix felt in Lilliana's company, finishing it with a crescendo.

"I think we found your soul instrument," Felix declared.

"You really think so?" Lilliana asked.

"You tell me, how did it feel?"

"Positively thrilling! Like I finally have a voice. I think I could play all night and never tire. The harp's never felt like that," she confessed.

"That's because it's not your soul instrument."

"Will you play for me? On your own I mean. I would really love to hear you play," Lilliana implored.

Felix smiled and sat down, and Lilliana slid across the bench to the end.

Felix's hands hovered above the keys for a moment and then he began to play. He expressed the strength he saw in Lilliana, her fiery passion, her raw unguarded presence when they made love, and her delicate and exquisite beauty when she was sad. He played the overwhelming feeling of his love for her. His deep sorrow that their worlds were held apart, and his fear that he would lose her. He played it all, exposing the inner fibers of his heart. When he finished he looked up at Lilliana—she had tears in her eyes.

"That was beautiful," she whispered.

Felix smiled and met her gaze. "It was beautiful because it was about you."

Lilliana leaned over and kissed him. Felix drew her closer and relished her kiss, meeting her with untamed passion, savoring every moment, then he rested his forehead against hers and whispered, "Run away with me."

"Pardon?"

"Run away with me. You've told The Emperor everything, now he can look after the rest. The world already thinks you're missing. Tonight, we can disappear and make every day an adventure like this one," Felix proclaimed. The words tumbled out involuntarily before he had the chance to stop himself.

"Oh, James! How I wish I could. But I can't abandon my family. They need me."

Hearing Lilliana use his false name was a harsh reminder that their relationship was a pleasant fiction that never really had any basis in reality. Felix wanted to change that. He wanted desperately for her to know his true name, to know everything about him, and he wanted her to love him for the man he was. *And why not?* She showed the world a false face as much as he did. He wondered if anyone had seen her true self as much as he had in the last few days. He felt like he knew her better than anyone. Then an idea struck.

"What if your sister were to marry the Sky View marquess?" he proposed.

"Frederick?!"

"Why not? It would solve all your family's problems and unite Sky View with the mainland, ending this silly revolution."

Lilliana put her hand to her chin. "That's not a bad idea, but I've no idea if the Duke of Sky View would even consider such a thing."

"Oh, I think he would…"

"What makes you say that?"

"I ran into Frederick while you were in the ladies' room. He told me that before your father disappeared, he arranged a marriage between you and Frederick."

"A betrothal for me and Frederick Remington?!" Lilliana queried in surprise.

"Yes, only your father disappeared before they could finalize things. The Duke of Sky View is still in favor of uniting with your family. With you missing, your mother could arrange for your sister to marry him instead. It would be a good match; one your sister will probably be in favor of. It would solve everything, including your freedom—giving you the chance to live the life you choose," Felix proclaimed ardently.

Lilliana stood up and began pacing the stage. "That makes perfect sense! That's exactly what my father would've done. If he was in the middle of finalizing the marriage before he went missing, that proves he never intended to disappear! He was planning a future! I knew he wouldn't have left us to ruin. James, this is a huge development. But why didn't the Duke of Sky View contact my mother after my father went missing?"

"Frederick told me they tried, but your mother never responded to any of their letters."

"Why wouldn't she respond? It would've been the perfect solution… oh, the Receiver!" Lilliana declared with realization.

"The Receiver?"

"After Father disappeared, our family's financial Keeper told my mother that the rest of our family could be in danger. He told her about a powdered poison that's sometimes put in letters to target one's enemies. He convinced her to employ a Receiver—a man who opens all her mail to ensure it's safe before it's given to her. Our Keeper betrayed us shortly after, disappearing with the majority of our family's fortune. My mother didn't want to report it. I could never understand why—it's the reason we're on the verge of financial ruin. But she's kept on our Receiver because we didn't think the two had any connection. Do you think he could be responsible for keeping the letters from reaching her?"

"Sounds incredibly likely," Felix admitted.

"That means even if my father's tried to contact us, we never would've gotten his letters. I have to tell my mother!"

"Hold on, you're supposed to be kidnapped, remember?"

"Oh shoot! What are we going to do?" Lilliana exclaimed, sitting down on the bench beside Felix.

Felix opened his mouth to speak, but Lilliana cut him off.

"I know! We'll talk to the Duke and enlist his help. If he still wants our families to join, then surely he'll make a trip down to my mother in person once he knows she hasn't been receiving his letters. And when my mother discovers the betrothal was arranged by my father before her arrangement with Lord Bardviss, she'll break off our engagement!" Lilliana declared in triumph.

"But if they know you're not missing, then the Duke and your mother will want to maintain the original betrothal agreement—marrying you to Frederick..."

Lilliana looked at Felix apologetically, "I have to help my family."

Felix's heart sank as realization dawned on him. "Of course, how could I be so stupid? You *want* to marry Frederick—he's a marquess with a pretty face who's a champion in your favorite sport, I can't believe I let myself be so blind!" he exclaimed, aghast.

"James, it's nothing like that. I'm a duchess, I have responsibilities. I can't just run away. If I did, I would be as selfish as you accused me of being the first night we met. This will give me the chance to not only help my family, but as you said, heal the divide between Sky View and the mainland—possibly preventing another war. It's a sacrifice for the benefit of us all!"

"A sacrifice?! Living in a castle in the richest precinct on Equillian, second only to The Emperor's palace, sure, that's a big sacrifice," Felix scoffed sarcastically.

"That's completely unfair! I've never liked living in a castle. They're big and cold and empty. The only thing having that much space around you is good for is reminding you how alone you are."

"If that's true, then why do it? Doesn't your happiness matter? You don't have to do this, your sister—"

"It can't be my sister! I love her dearly, but she's useless when it comes to politics. I was groomed for this—while she was spoiled with whatever she wanted. James, I know I can actually make a difference, it has to be me."

Felix looked at her, forlorn. "You know, for a moment there, I actually believed you could love me."

Lilliana returned his gaze with deep sorrow. "I told you when we first met, my life doesn't allow me the luxury of love."

"Right. Thank you for clarifying that. I wish you'd done it a little sooner, before I allowed myself to fall head over heels for you. I don't do that, you know? Fall for people. Thank you for elucidating why," Felix remarked coldly and grabbed his jacket, heading off the stage.

"James! Come back, please! You don't understand, this is bigger than us! I still need you, please!" Lilliana called after him.

Felix turned back. "Yeah? What exactly is it you need me for?"

Lilliana opened her mouth and then shut it again.

"Good luck with it all, Duchess. I hope you make time for your own happiness once in a while, amongst all that responsibility," Felix remarked, and walked off. His insides were awhirl with a raging storm of emotion he didn't understand. All he knew was that he had to run—either that or he was going to break something. He found an emergency exit and pushed his way outside into the clear, crisp night.

⌒

Felix walked briskly for several blocks before stopping to take a deep breath of fresh air. He looked up at the stars and attempted to tame his temper. Then his conscience came knocking, Lilliana was all alone. He couldn't just leave her there by herself. "Shick!" He kicked a loose stone across the street. A few passersby stared at him. Felix gave them a terse smile and walked back down the street towards the opera house with his hands buried deep in his pockets.

*How did I get myself into this mess? Oh that's right, I didn't. Lilliana pulled me into it! She forced me into her life and wriggled her way into my heart and now is dumping me like garbage at the first mention of a way out of her predicament. Has she been using me this whole time? Is that what she does? Jumps from man to man, choosing them according to how useful they are for her purpose? Maybe she's more like her father than I realized,* Felix thought. *What did I expect? She's a noble. This was never going to end well,* he told himself.

"Shick!" Felix blurted as he stormed up the street.

The emergency exit Felix had come through only minutes before was locked from the outside. He cursed and made his way to the front entrance. The crowd of VIPs at the door had grown exorbitantly. He carefully weaved his way through an ocean of finely dressed elite and flashed his badge at the entrance. As soon as he was inside he hurried back to the greenroom and into the theater. But it was too late. Lilliana was already gone.

Felix ran back out through the emergency exit and onto the street, looking for Lilliana in every direction. The streets were crowded now. He pushed his way through the pedestrian traffic looking for her this way and that. Then his heart sank as he realized she was probably back inside the opera house. Even if she wasn't, there was no way he was going to find her amongst the sea of pedestrians.

"Shick!" Felix tried to piece together the most logical place she would've gone. If she hadn't gone after him, then he hoped she was catching an air cab back to Katarina's island. *Maybe she went in search of Frederick?* he thought. The very idea made his blood boil. *Who am I kidding? There was never going to be a future for me and Lilliana. How could I be so stupid?! What did I expect? She would choose me and unite the common people with the royals? More like commit social suicide and leave her family to destitution. Even if Lilliana's family wasn't on the verge of financial ruin, in what world could a commoner like me ever end up with Lilliana Wendrian? This was never going to be anything but a bit of fun, a bit of upper class rebellion before Lilliana ties herself down. I set out to give her a night to savor through her matrimony, and now she has had a whole week. I should be grateful I got that,* he thought. So why did his chest ache and jealousy run hot through his veins? Jealousy was Felix's least favorite emotion. He hated when it came knocking, reminding him of all the things he could never have. And always for the same reason—the station he was born into. Only, until this moment, he'd never felt jealousy over a woman. He'd always thought that was ridiculous. But then, he also thought claiming ownership over a woman was too. Now he understood. He yearned to be able to call Lilliana his, to be able to tell the world they could never have her—wanting to continuously bask in her undivided attention. It was ridiculous, of course. No healthy relationship capitalized one's full attention. People needed freedom and independence, or they withered.

But it didn't stop Felix from wanting it all the same. He couldn't help it. Lilliana's light was intoxicating, and he'd earned it, she'd chosen *him*. Where people like Frederick got everything they wanted handed to them without ever having to earn any of it. It didn't make any difference what he and Lilliana wanted, even if Felix was a better man than Frederick in every way, the marquess would still get Lilliana in the end. The game of life was rigged in his favor. Felix might be allowed to play for a time, but he'd never be allowed to win. The injustice was palatable. If only he'd never run into Frederick. If only he hadn't mentioned it to Lilliana. If he hadn't, he and Lilliana could've had the perfect end to a perfect day.

Felix stepped out onto the cobblestone street and made his way towards the city's edge. There were people everywhere, mostly drunkards stumbling and hollering down the streets in jovial spirits. Felix wished he was one of them. He wished he was feeling anything but the torture that twisted inside him. *Is this love?* he wondered. *If so, Shick can keep it! Nothing's worth such torment,* he thought bitterly.

The worst thing was how it kept him from thinking clearly and made him act completely irrationally. How was it that the same emotion could make him feel invincible one moment, and then weak and powerless the next? It was like some potent drug that gave the greatest high one could dream of and then with the slightest threat of being taken away pierced the heart with a gruesome comedown. The torment was so potent it made Felix feel desperate to do anything just to be lifted up by it again. He felt sure he couldn't live without it—even though he had done so perfectly before it had come.

*I need a drink,* he thought.

Felix stepped out onto the cobblestone street in search of the nearest pub. After a few moments he came across a fancy-looking establishment, The Thirsty Dragon. It was overflowing with patrons. He squeezed his way inside and waited patiently at the crowded bar to be served a long glass of a very stiff drink. He found a small space in the corner and nursed his glass in thought.

*How could I have been so stupid as to think Lilliana would rather run away with me than marry the Sky View marquess?* he wondered. In truth, Frederick and Lilliana were the perfect match, as far as noble matches went at any rate.

*Why did I allow myself to lose my head?* he wondered. *I have no ownership over Lilliana. She owes me nothing. I always knew there couldn't be a future for us. My mistake was forgetting that, allowing my heart to hijack my intellect and carry it away from reality. She's right. As duchess, she has duties. Her position gives her the ability to make a difference in the world. It's wonderful she wants to. It's more than I've seen or come to expect from any other noble. Who am I to take her away from all that? And for what? To do nothing in some backwater corner of Equillian, making a living from gambling and cons? She's far too good for that. What was I thinking?!*

"If anyone's being selfish, it's me," Felix declared aloud.

The person on his left looked at him. "Pardon?"

"Nothing," Felix muttered.

*Let's hope I can still salvage things before it's too late,* he thought, and left the pub.

# SCARRED

Gwena's last several days at the club had passed in a blur. She'd spent the majority of her time at Theater 3, with Madam Pomphrey, Richard, and Mallini. The three of them treated her like she was one of them. Madam Pomphrey took Gwena under her wing and taught her tricks she didn't know and how to embellish ones she did. The magician shared tips on how to entrance an audience with a good story, and she kept Gwena and Richard laughing with her lively sense of humor, even when something wasn't going quite right. Gwena loved every moment of it. She felt like she was finally where she belonged.

It turned out that Richard was the son of a well-to-do family from the Harvestlands. They'd sent him to the city to study medicine at one of the major universities, only Richard had no interest in becoming a doctor—he'd always had a passion for magic and the stage. One night a friend brought him to the club as their guest, and he ran into Madam Pomphrey. He'd idolized her since he was a boy. They hit it off and she invited him to be a part of the show. For Richard, it was a dream come true. He never returned to university; he hardly ever even left the club. And Mallini wasn't the grouch he originally appeared to be—once Gwena got to know him she found he had a big soft center. He gave her a book on escapology, and she studied it religiously, throwing herself into learning the craft with vigor. The book had sections on how to pick locks and loosen chains when bound and others on how to improve one's lung capacity to maximize your available time underwater. The whole thing was filled with detailed black and white illustrations. Gwena used it to do everything she could to improve her act—prolonging her lung capacity through daily breathing exercises and practicing how to pick locks, even though she knew she wouldn't actually need the skill. Once she put her mind to a craft, she wanted to master it and know everything about it. Besides, working on untangling the inner workings of locks reminded her of Bastian. The craft felt like it connected her to him somehow and brought them closer together. Bastian had always had a knack for picking—he wasn't only good at it, he genuinely enjoyed it. Gwena asked to borrow a real lock from Mallini and worked ceaselessly at bypassing its defenses until she'd managed to open it. Encouraged by her feat, she practiced even more until she could unlock it quickly and easily. Afterwards, she exchanged it for a new one from Mallini's collection and soon, she was borrowing a new lock to conquer every day. When Gwena wasn't preparing for her own act, she was making costumes for the show. Elaborate dresses that transformed from one to the other without having to be taken off, and cloaks with secret pockets and folds. She'd become so consumed with the project, she almost entirely forgot the outside world. If only Bastian could see her now, she thought. Her, performing her very own act in a real magic show! How proud he'd be. She only wished he *could* see it. Gwena treasured watching the show come together, and being a part of it felt like a dream. She would sit in the front row and clap with delight as each act was finalized and polished. And Gwena enjoyed just as much being backstage to watch Mallini work. She would sew while he worked on his magic machines and soon they were both making suggestions for each other's work. Again, his work reminded her of Bastian, who would've loved to have seen Mallini's inventions. Watching how it was all put together gave her more confidence than ever before that she and Bastian really could make a successful magic act together—if they ever had the opportunity, that was. Between his tinkering ability and her knowledge and practice of magic, she was sure they could make a magic spectacle beyond what anyone had seen before. Gwena felt so inspired, her head was full of ideas. Before long her notebook was full of sketches and notes for magic acts rather than clothing designs. It wasn't until the following Weensday that Gwena realized she hadn't been checking the paper for the last several days. She took the morning off and made her way to the city's surface. It was almost strange coming back up to the city after a time of absence, like it and the club were two different worlds entirely. Gwena recalled Benji's words on how easy it was to get caught up in the club and forget about the outside world. Thinking of Benji, she remembered his suits and realized she'd been neglecting them entirely. She bought a newspaper and quickly perused the pages, seeing no mention of anything related to Bastian or Felix, she tucked the paper under her arm and headed back towards the club.

As Gwena reached the courtyard outside the apothecary, she saw Bonnie just closing herself behind the short metal gate that led to the secret elevator.

"Wait! Can I ride with you?" Gwena called after her.

Bonnie looked up. "O' course! I've been wonderin' what became o' ya. I 'ear ya've joined Madam Pomphrey's magic show?" Bonnie inquired as Gwena stepped in beside her.

"Yes! I'm playing a mermaid escapologist."

"Is that right? Congratulations," Bonnie said, shifting the metal bird upside down to cue their descent. The ground beneath their feet began descending into the glass tube, carrying them into the underground cavern.

"Thank you," Gwena beamed. "How are you? Any news about your ship?"

"Aye, she's been bought an' paid fer. I'm leavin' the club this Starday night ta collect her in Port Trinity."

"I'm so happy for you! How wonderful it'll be to have your very own ship and be reunited with the sea," Gwena exclaimed.

"Aye. An' I can see that ya 'ave found yer element, yer positively glowin'!"

"I must admit, this week has been wonderful."

"Ya must've really charmed Madam Pomphrey," Bonnie said.

"What makes you say that?"

"She doesn't usually take ta women so well, she's the jealous type. Tends ta see other females as threats an' competition. Usually, she's kickin' 'em ta the curb after a few days," Bonnie told her.

"Oh, I see," Gwena returned with a subtle frown, thinking of the last escapologist. "I think it must be because we're so alike, there's not much we disagree on."

"No, yer nothin' alike—that can't be it. It must be yer scar," Bonnie remarked.

Bonnie's words stung Gwena. She put her hand to the line across her face. These last few days she'd almost forgotten it was there.

"What do you mean?" she asked, feeling hurt that Bonnie would even suggest such a thing.

"Sometimes beauty can be more o' a curse than a blessin'. Don't mistake me, yer more beautiful than most, but that mark o' yers protects ya from those too shallow ta see past it, an' from those envious souls that feel the need ta punish a pretty face with bitter malice. If I were ya, I would be grateful fer it. It's that one imperfection that keeps Madam Pomphrey from seein' ya as a threat. Without it, there's no way she'd be lettin' ya inta the show, no way at all—fer one simple reason," Bonnie asserted.

"What's that?"

"Because yer far better than she is, don't ferget that."

Gwena didn't know what to say, she had so much respect and admiration for Madam Pomphrey. She, Richard, and Mallini had done nothing but embrace her into the troupe and treat her like one of their own. She couldn't even imagine Madam Pomphrey being so spiteful. But before she could find the words to say as much, the door to the elevator opened, and Bonnie stepped out.

"Good luck with the show. I won't be around fer yer birthday—I 'ave some business ta attend ta, but I look forward ta seein' ya on openin' night—I already 'ave me ticket," she announced with a warm smile, and headed towards the enchanted train.

Gwena watched her go before taking the path in the opposite direction towards the club.

Gwena got into her room and closed the door, still haunted by what Bonnie had told her. She didn't know why it had bothered her so much, but she couldn't shake the negative feeling it brought her. Instead of rushing to get back to the theater—as she had been the last several days—she decided to take her time finishing off Benji's suits. She still had a few hours before their rehearsal was scheduled to begin, and she felt terrible she hadn't finished them off already. She'd become so distracted with the show, everything else seemed to disappear from her mind. She found a rhythm in her work, and by the time she'd finished, two and a half hours had drifted past. Gwena folded each of the suits neatly, placed them back in the brown paper bag they'd come in originally, and left them outside Benji's door with a little note, apologizing for it having taken so long. Then she made her way to Theater 3.

That afternoon Gwena sat in the front row as usual, watching the rehearsal. The show had come so far from the previous week when Gwena had first seen it. Madam Pomphrey had enthusiastically taken many of her suggestions on board, and with all four of them putting their minds together, it was now better than ever. Gwena felt like they were finally ready for opening night. It was only three days away now. The time had gone so quickly. And because the show was so polished, Gwena felt an overwhelming excitement instead of the fear and nerves she'd anticipated. What a big week it was. She couldn't believe it—the following day was her birthday, her coming of age. She'd officially be a woman after that. And for the first time she actually felt ready for it, proud to be an independent adult and eager to step into the next chapter of her life to see what its pages might hold.

After the rehearsal had finished, Madam Pomphrey was going over some notes with Mallini in his workshop, and Gwena was changing out of her costume in the dressing room backstage. As soon as she'd finished hanging everything up, there was a gentle knock at the door.

"Yes?"

Richard poked his head in. "Mind if I come in?"

"Not at all, what is it?"

Richard stepped inside the room with his hand held behind his back. "I have something for you," he announced.

"For me?" Gwena queried in surprise.

"Yes, it's an early birthday present."

"Oh, you didn't have to do that!"

"I know, I wanted to," he said, and he produced a small box wrapped in pink paper with a bow.

"Thank you, but you shouldn't have. Would you like me to open it now?" Gwena asked.

"Please."

Gwena untied the bow and pulled the lid off the box. Inside was a beautiful necklace made of silver—a mermaid holding a gold pearl. "Oh, Richard, it's beautiful!" Gwena exclaimed.

"It belonged to my grandmother."

"The one with the scar?" Gwena inquired, taking the necklace delicately from its box.

"Yes, she commissioned the alchemists to make it."

"Are you saying it's an enchanted object?" Gwena queried in surprise.

"The only one of its kind."

"Oh, Richard! I can't possibly take this; it must be worth a fortune!"

"I want you to have it. Please, try it on," he insisted.

Gwena took off her dewdrop pearl necklace from Bastian, and carefully placed it in her pocket. Then she opened the clasp of Richard's gift and allowed him to help her put it around her neck. As soon as the necklace was in place, Richard gaped at her in surprise and then looked at her hungrily—like she was an exquisite delicacy he was eager to devour.

"What is it?" Gwena asked uneasily.

Richard directed her to the mirror in the change room. She walked over to it and looked at her reflection. She gasped. Her scar was gone!

She put her hand to her face and felt nothing but smooth skin. She stared at her reflection, disbelieving and completely mesmerized. She couldn't count the times she'd imagined what she'd look like without her scar, how her life might be different if she'd never had it. And there she was, a perfect version of herself staring back at her, as if from some alternate reality. Before Gwena could say anything, Richard planted his lips on hers. Gwena froze. She was too shocked to move as he kissed her. Then she was shaken from her paralysis by a piercing scream. Gwena pushed Richard away and whipped around to see Madam Pomphrey standing in the doorway. She was glaring at them both, her face contorted in outrage. Gwena and Richard drained of color.

"You little slut! I embrace you with open arms and this is how you repay me?!" Madam Pomphrey screeched.

"No! It's not what it looks like, I never wanted this!" Gwena protested, while Richard just stood there in stunned silence.

Madam Pomphrey paused, noticing Gwena's scar was gone, she looked down at the necklace around her neck and realization dawned on her face.

"You think now you don't have that blemish you're better than I am, is that it? That you can replace me and take what's mine?!" Madam Pomphrey bellowed in fury.

"No, of course not! Please believe me, I never meant for this to happen. I don't want it!" Gwena asserted pleadingly. She tore off the necklace and fumbled it back into the box, shoving it into Richard's hands. Her scar instantly reappeared. "Please, Madam Pomphrey. I have so much respect for you. I'd never do anything to hurt or betray you!" she cried imploringly.

Madam Pomphrey stared down at her with fire in her eyes. "There's nothing you could've done to hurt or betray me more."

Gwena collapsed to her knees in tears.

"Leave!" Madam Pomphrey commanded, pointing at the door, and Gwena fled.

Tears fell from Gwena like rain. She felt so weak, so helpless, so utterly lost. How had this happened? How had things gone so terribly wrong? Was it her? Just when she thought she was finally obtaining the happiness she longed for, it all shattered around her. She wanted desperately to take it back, to be able to go back in time and have another chance to make things right. Everything had been going so well, and now that happiness was crumbling, falling between her fingers like sand. The pain in her heart felt like stabbing shards of glass. She stumbled down the hallway gulping for air. It was only after she was already there that she realized she was outside Benji's door. She sunk down the banister across from it with her knees against her chest shaking with uncontrollable waves of misery. Was she destined to find pain wherever she went? She felt so alone and found herself missing Bastian more than ever. Having him come back into her life only to be taken away was worse than if he'd never come back at all—at least then she would've stopped hoping, stopped thinking life had something better to offer. She had almost resigned herself to that. Almost made peace with it, and then he came and opened her heart again, made her believe again, and where had it gotten her? Lost and utterly alone, far away from anyone and anywhere she knew, with her heart exposed to the injustice of the world once again.

Benji's door cracked open. "Little bird?"

He walked over and knelt in front of her, taking in her miserable state. He gently brushed the hair out of her face and tucked it behind her ear. "You alright?"

Gwena shook her head. Benji scooped her up into his arms and pulled her close to him.

"Yes, you are," he whispered into her ear, "you're with me now."

His compassion filled Gwena with a new wave of sorrow, and she felt another bout of tears overtake her. She buried her face into his chest and wept uncontrollably. Benji carried her into his room and shut the door behind them. He walked over to his leather armchair and sat down with her in his lap, hugging her tightly as she sobbed.

"Let it all out, little bird. That kind of sorrow doesn't belong in a heart like yours," he told her.

It took Gwena several minutes before her tears subsided enough that she felt like she could breathe again. Her eyes ached and her heart felt numb. She looked up at Benji to see the same look in his eyes that she'd seen from Bastian. "There's only one other person besides my mother who's ever looked at me the way you do," she remarked.

"What way is that?"

"Like I'm actually beautiful and worth something exactly how I am. Even with this," she said, motioning to her scar as fresh tears sprang to her eyes. Benji smiled at her and gently traced his finger across her scar.

"This is not who you are, little bird. It's just a small part of the story of what's made you into who you are. Everyone's scarred in one way or another. Most women try to hide them and pretend they don't exist, others are embarrassed by them—silently and wordlessly apologizing for not being perfect. You do neither. You wear yours like a badge of honor, as if saying to the world *yes, I've been through the Nine Realms of Darkness and back again and I'm still here, I dare you to survive the same.* And that is incredibly attractive. I don't think you have a clue just how beautiful you truly are. You have to understand, most people who judge you are only doing so because your strength shines a light on their own inadequacies—or because they're shallow jackasses who simply don't know you nor deserve to," Benji proclaimed.

The corners of Gwena's mouth lifted, and she laughed gently through her tears. The joy brought pain to her chest—as if it were pulling open a door tightly bound by the sinews of her broken heart. "I'm not as strong as I appear to be, I have other scars. Scars created by my own father—I was too weak to stand up to him, instead I ran away like a coward. I couldn't even face him to say good-bye," she confessed with a fresh sob.

Benji lifted her chin gently and looked into her eyes. "That isn't fair. When we love someone, it can make us feel powerless against them—they are our weakness. That doesn't mean we're weak. The very fact that you left and removed yourself from a bad situation is a sign of your strength. That takes incredible courage, especially when it means walking away from someone you love."

Gwena smirked. "I understand now why you're so sought after by the ladies," she remarked with a half laugh, half sob, wiping her dripping nose with the back of her hand.

"Ha! Women don't often come to me for conversation," Benji admitted, offering her a tissue. Gwena accepted it gratefully. "Maybe they should," she said. Benji smiled.

"Can I stay for a bit? I just don't want to be alone right now," Gwena asked.

Benji hesitated briefly before saying, "Sure, I have no plans until the club opens."

He carried her to his bed and placed her gently on the mountain of lavish pillows.

"Do you want to talk about it?"

Gwena shook her head. "Can you just hug me, please? You don't have to if you don't want to, I could just really use a hug right now," she implored through ragged breaths between sobs.

"Of course," Benji said softly. He kicked off his shoes and climbed up onto the bed beside her, pulling her into his arms. Gwena closed her eyes and relaxed into his embrace, and all of the sorrow she'd been holding onto—the abuse from her father, leaving him the way she did, losing Bastian when they were so close to starting a life together, everything that had happened that night with Richard and Madam Pomphrey, and missing her mother more than ever—all of it poured from her like water bursting through a dam. Benji just held her silently as it all came out, until eventually Gwena fell asleep in his arms.

# BREAKING BOUNDS

Bastian, Cricket, Stork, and Rhino sat at the table in the mess eating their breakfast. It was the morning after Bastian beat Stork at dice, and he found himself suddenly on everyone's radar. Many of the other crew members around the mess were looking at him and talking quietly amongst themselves. When he returned their stares, they nodded to him respectfully. Attention was not something Bastian had been hoping to acquire, nor something he'd even considered when challenging Stork at his game. Yet somehow, ever since he'd come on board the Black Mary he kept attracting more of it. He shrunk down in his seat in a feeble attempt at being less visible.

"Ye've been 'oldin' out on us, Dodger. Yer a real gamblin' shark," Rhino proclaimed.

Bastian laughed. "I've spun dice a few times in my life, but I'm no shark. Not by a long shot."

"Ha! Right, sure yer not," Stork remarked.

"Takes a shark ta know a shark. Don't it, Stork?" Cricket asked him.

Stork waved Cricket's comment away. "Whether a shark er just damn lucky, makes no difference ta me. Either way, I'm not fool enough ta spin a die with Dodger again."

"Are you sure? Because I was thinking about coming back to try my luck tonight. I thought surely you'd want a chance to win your coin back?" Bastian offered.

Stork smirked. "No thanks, Dodger, that's very kind o' ya, but I like ya better when yer stayin' clear o' me gamblin' circuit."

Bastian shrugged. "Fine by me," he said, and grinned wryly.

Rhino patting Stork on the shoulder. "I'm sure ye'll make it up from everyone else's pockets regardless, won't ya, brother?"

Stork grunted but remained in good spirits, and the conversation soon turned to Jaxland. The pirates talked merrily about how they were going to spend their time there, and Bastian basked in the joy of seeing his friends united once more.

When Bastian arrived at Tink's quarters that morning, the tinker was behind his workbench looking over papers. Next to his desk there was a large blackboard on a rolling wood frame half-covered with equations. The feathered quill Bastian had been trying to disenchant the day before was lying on the desk waiting for him. Tink looked up. "Ready to try again?"

"Yeah," Bastian answered, and walked over to the desk.

"I'll be right with you. I apologize—I was hoping to have this finished before our lesson. Won't be a moment," Tink told him, and turned his attention back to his papers.

Bastian filled his hands with the Ghost Element and sent it into the quill. Within moments he bypassed the Anti-Tampering enchantment the same way he'd done with his bracelet and Stork's die the day before. Then he altered the Everlasting and Protection enchantments. Next Bastian focused on the core enchantments and imagined them dissolving away. As he did, gold dust seeped out of the quill like a departing soul. Bastian frowned. He suddenly had the sinking feeling he'd lost something of value—like losing an ancient relic in the sea. "It's done," he announced.

Tink looked up from his papers, "Pardon?"

"I disenchanted the object, it's done."

"Ha! Very funny. Just give me one more minute," Tink said.

Bastian sat down and waited patiently for Tink to finish what he was doing. After a couple of minutes, the tinker put the paperwork down and came over to Bastian.

"Right. Thank you for your patience. Today we're going to try a different tactic."

"It's already done," Bastian declared.

Tink looked at him blankly and blinked.

"Have a look for yourself," Bastian offered, gesturing to the quill on the desk.

Tink studied him for a moment before realizing Bastian was being completely serious. He pulled his green monocle out of his chest pocket and put it up to one eye to examine the quill. He turned to Bastian in shock. "What did you do?"

"I bypassed the safety enchantments and dissolved the core abilities. Isn't that what I was supposed to do?"

"Yes, yes of course. But how in the Stars did you do it?" Tink pressed.

"I changed the properties of the enchantments."

"You changed the properties of the Anti-Tampering enchantment?" Tink asked slowly.

"Yeah…"

"Just like that?"

Bastian shrugged. "It seemed the most practical way through."

"But the enchantment itself keeps you from tampering with it. Altering it in any way is impossible," Tink objected.

"You said nothing's impossible."

Tink raised his eyebrows, "So I did." He studied Bastian in silence for a beat and then said, "Wait here." He walked out through an adjoining door at the back of the room and returned several minutes later with a chest the size of a bread box. He put it on the desk in front of Bastian and removed the quill.

"What's this?" Bastian asked.

"It's your true assignment. The task you'll be completing on Jaxland."

"This is the chest you want me to break into?" Bastian queried, looking at it with keen interest.

"It's one of the same set. There were only forty-nine made like it, each varying slightly in appearance but with the same ability. It took a while to track this one down."

"Couldn't you just've made a new one?"

"I could have. But then there would be no guarantee the enchantments would be exactly the same. Enchanting objects is a subtle art. If not done by the same person in precisely the same way, it will assuredly be different in one way or another. That's why we make our objects in batches. Even still, every one is physically unique—at least in small ways. They're bound to be when every object is constructed by hand," Tink explained.

"So this chest might not be the same cosmetically as the one I'm breaking into, but it has the exact same enchantments?" Bastian inquired.

"Precisely."

Bastian inspected the chest. "I'm guessing it has a different keyway?"

"Of course."

"Why forty-nine? Seems an odd number," Bastian remarked curiously.

"Multiples of seven are favoured throughout nature, the alchemists believe that by reflecting the patterns of nature, we're working with the flow of the universe instead of against it."

"Fitting into the universal equation," Bastian remarked.

Tink studied him. "Something like that."

Bastian nodded and tried to pick up the chest. It wouldn't budge. It was like the chest was attached to the desk, but then, the desk didn't come up when he tried to lift the chest either.

"Why can't I pick it up?" he asked.

"It's one of the chest's defenses. It prevents anyone but the owner from being able to walk away with it," Tink explained.

"Makes sense." Carrying it off *was* Bastian's first instinct. The chest was so small, it would've been much easier to take it then break into the damn thing.

"Are you the owner of this one?" Bastian inquired.

"Yes."

Tink bent over and lifted the chest easily with both hands and then put it back down on the desk.

"So, it has an Identity-Set enchantment," Bastian deduced.

"Very good."

"What's its other defenses?"

Tink picked up a book from his desk and slipped his moon-shaped glasses up onto his nose. "The chest has six enchantment layers. An Identity-Set enchantment. A Visible Only by Owner enchantment, a False Box Defense enchantment—which ensures the box will appear empty to anyone but the owner, an Anchor enchantment—making it so the chest can only be moved by the owner. A Protection and Everlasting enchantment, and finally, an Anti-Tampering enchantment." He walked over to the blackboard and listed all the enchantments down in white chalk. "With luck in our favor, you won't need to get past all six enchantments," he proclaimed.

"Wait, with luck in our favor? Do you mean to tell me, you don't already know how to break into the chest?" Bastian asked. Even he already knew how to break into the chest, but it was beginning to dawn on him that Tink never had.

"It's a puzzle we'll have to solve together," Tink admitted.

Bastian considered this for a moment, calculating his next move. If he knew more than Tink and the captain, then he had a valuable advantage he wasn't eager to lose too soon. He was worried that he might've given away too much already in his rush to disenchant the quill. If only he'd known Tink didn't know how to do it already.

*What was Tink planning on doing if they couldn't figure it out before Jaxland?* Bastian wondered.

He took a sharp breath in and held it there for a moment. "Right," he said at last, looking at the list of enchantments on the board. "What happens if I pick it open?"

"See for yourself," Tink invited.

Bastian searched Tink's desk and found a thin piece of wire. He stuck it into the chest's keyway. The lock was one of the simplest designs with only one ward to bypass. He had it open with the flick of his wrist. He lifted the lid. The chest was inlaid with a dark red velvet. Other than that, it was completely empty. Tink reached over and shut the lid gently, then he took a key out of his pocket and locked and unlocked the chest. He lifted the lid open himself. This time the chest had three large chunks of glasstanight sitting inside as if they'd always been there.

"Ha! Clever," Bastian remarked appreciatively. He couldn't help but admire the simple genius of it. Giving no resistance to forced entry meant anyone looking to get inside would do so quickly, and then lose interest just as quickly. Such an unassuming and defenseless chest—especially one that was empty—didn't offer any reason for anyone to attempt carrying it off in the first place.

"The chest uses the Cyphorescent Codec to identify its owner. There's no way to bypass that. Anything that works off the Codec sees the truth laid bare as a babe on its birthday. Which is why we must find a way to unmake the enchantment itself," Tink explained.

"Right," Bastian acknowledged, cracking his knuckles.

He focused on the chest—drawing the Ghost Element into his hands and sending it inside. He used the Codec to feel it out first, identifying every one of the enchantments on Tink's list. They were all there exactly as stated. Bastian set to work getting through the Anti-Tampering enchantment first, and then he quickly and easily reset the Identity-Set Enchantment to himself—just as he'd done with Stork's die the night before. He could feel Tink watching him intently. It was clear to Bastian now that the knowledge he'd obtained from Haplo's journal wasn't something that had been shared with the other alchemists. He pretended to use more effort than he actually was. He took his time to go over what he'd done with the Codec just to pad it out. Then he relaxed as if it had all taken great mental strain. "All done," he announced.

"Open the chest," Tink instructed.

Bastian opened it. Inside was the glasstanight.

Tink's eyes widened in astonishment. "How'd you get through the defenses? And so quickly?" he exclaimed.

*Shick,* Bastian thought, he'd already made it take at least twice as long as it needed to. "Um…did I not do it right?" he queried, feigning naïvety.

Tink took out his green monocle and studied the chest. "It looks as if nothing's changed. How did you access the glasstanight? The only way I can figure it's feasible is if you were somehow able to reset the Identity-Set Enchantment to yourself," he remarked, looking at Bastian questioningly.

Bastian scratched his head, "I figured it'd be quicker than going through all six enchantments."

Tink stared at him in disbelief. He walked over to the chest and tried to pick it up. He couldn't. He opened it. There was nothing inside but an empty box. "How did you reset the Identity-Set enchantment?" he demanded.

Bastian hesitated—he couldn't even imagine how it could be done without the Geometric Code…*shick.* He didn't want Tink to know about Haplo's secrets. There must have been a reason why the alchemist hadn't shared the knowledge with anyone else. And Bastian had to admit to himself, he liked it that way. It made him feel, well, special. It was the only thing his father had given him—he wasn't about to give it away. Besides, in Bastian's current circumstances, he needed all the advantages he could get. He returned Tink's questioning gaze and shrugged.

Tink looked at him scrutinizingly—like he was trying to read his very soul. Then he relaxed. "Well then, congratulations, it looks like you're ready for your assignment. Come back tomorrow morning and we'll have our final lesson," he announced.

"Will you tell me what's in the chest before I have to take it?" Bastian asked.

"You'll be briefed on the details of your assignment once we reach Jaxland. Until then, I would keep it out of mind. As far as you're concerned, the object inside the case is irrelevant," Tink stated, and walked back to his worktable.

There was no warmth in what Tink said. It was like a wall had suddenly been erected between them. Bastian felt disappointed. He'd grown to like Tink, admire him even. He didn't have any father figures in his life, and losing Tink's attention made him realize how much he craved one. He watched the tinker busy with his papers momentarily and then he turned to go.

"Before you leave, ensure the chest's identity is reset to me," Tink asserted, without looking up.

Bastian hesitated. He didn't know how to do that. He didn't know what Tink's identity looked or felt like in the Geometric Code. But he wasn't about to admit that. Instead, Bastian walked back to the chest and took away his own identity symbol from the enchantment leaving no identity linked to the enchantment at all. He could only hope it would reset itself to Tink when the man picked it up, like the way it reset itself when the owner of the object died.

With that, Bastian left Tink's quarters.

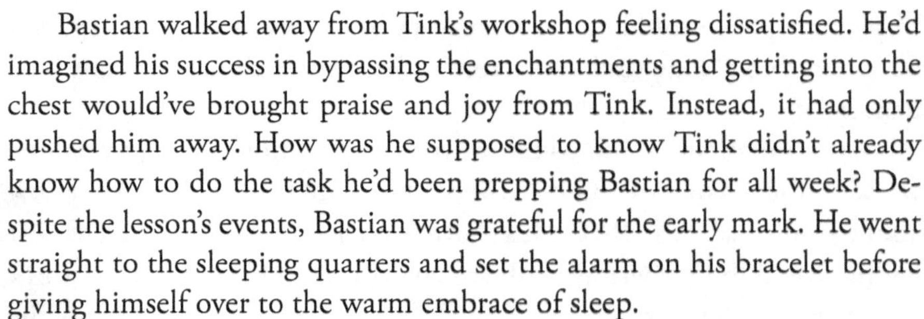

Bastian walked away from Tink's workshop feeling dissatisfied. He'd imagined his success in bypassing the enchantments and getting into the chest would've brought praise and joy from Tink. Instead, it had only pushed him away. How was he supposed to know Tink didn't already know how to do the task he'd been prepping Bastian for all week? Despite the lesson's events, Bastian was grateful for the early mark. He went straight to the sleeping quarters and set the alarm on his bracelet before giving himself over to the warm embrace of sleep.

# CONSPIRING

Coada sat in the captain's quarters twisting his hands anxiously, while the captain poured himself a stiff drink from his crystal decanter. He offered one to Coada, but he politely declined. The captain sat down across from him in front of the Everfire hearth. "What is it, Tink?" he asked.

"It's the boy—he's ready for the assignment," Coada reported.

The captain raised his eyebrows in surprise, then held up his glass. "Well done!" he commended, "then why is it yer so damn anxious?"

"Because yesterday he was struggling to bypass the safety enchantments in an object, and today he bypassed them all—unmaking the core abilities before our class even began. When I gave him the chest, he broke into it in a matter of minutes."

The captain chuckled. "That be so? How in the stars did 'e do that?"

"By resetting the Identity-Set enchantment to himself," Tink stated devoid of mirth.

"An' where in the nine realms did 'e learn ta do that?" the captain inquired.

"That's just it, I've no idea, I didn't even know it could be done. The plan was for he and I to figure out a way through the safety enchantments together. My only glimmering hope of accomplishing such a feat was that you've done so once before, but what he's discovered independently is far more efficient and effective than anything I've ever envisioned. I've looked over the object he's disenchanted and it's as if it never had a core ability at all—and yet, none of the three safety symbols look changed."

"Do ya 'ave the object 'ere?" the captain asked.

"Yes." Coada pulled out the feathered quill and handed it to him.

Muerte held it to the light. "Clever, 'e's changed the Anti-Tamperin' enchantment. It looks the same, but besides its form it be different entirely."

Coada held out his hand. "Let me see."

The captain handed him the quill and Coada inspected it again with his green monocle up to his eye. "How's that even possible?" he exclaimed in a whisper.

"Yer askin' me? That's yer department, not mine."

"When you were a child and you bypassed the Safety enchantments on the Ethereal Globe, do you think you might've done it the same way?" Tink inquired.

"No."

"How can you be sure?"

"What the thief's done, 'e's done deliberately with precision. When I use the Ghost Element it's completely intuitive—I can't explain 'ow any o' it works, where 'e could've only done this by knowin' exactly what it was 'e was doin', an' 'e was flawlessly accurate. It looks ta me like 'e's hacked inta the symbol somehow an' rewritten its attributes. Someone would've 'ad ta 'ave taught 'im how ta do that. It's not somethin' ya simply stumble upon in a night on yer own," Muerte said.

"But who could've taught him this and how? I can't even think of anyone outside the original alchemists who would have such knowledge," Tink argued.

"Yer far more equipped ta answer that than I," the captain stated.

Tink thought about it. "I'm worried."

"Why? Ye've accomplished precisely what ya set out ta do. Now that yer student has surpassed yer expectations, yer complainin'?"

"Course not. I'm worried because this might only be the beginning. Regardless of where he got the information, he's taken to it like a duck to water—exceeding far beyond what I ever anticipated. If he continues to excel at the same rate independently of what I'm teaching him, then it's only a matter of time before we won't be able to control him," Tink admonished.

The captain took a drink of his rum. "A wise man once told me ta be wary o' manifestin' fears inta reality by the very means o' tryin' ta avoid 'em. Do ya know who that man be?" the captain asked.

"Me," Tink answered somberly. He stood from his seat and walked to the window that made up the back wall of the captain's quarters and looked out.

"Aye. The lad 'as a rogue spirit. Somethin' yer well accustomed ta already, aren't ya Master Coada?"

"That's precisely why it concerns me."

The captain smiled. " 'e's not only rebellious, 'e's intelligent. If we try an' control 'im, we'll only succeed in drivin' 'im away. But if what ya say be true, than 'e's precisely the asset we've been hopin' fer, an' the only way we're goin' ta inspire 'is loyalty be by ensurin' 'e believes 'e 'as a choice. If 'e doesn't choose ta come along side an' join us on 'is own accord, then 'e'll never be what we require," the captain asserted, and poured Coada a drink.

Coada accepted the glass. "What should we do?"

"Continue as planned. The sooner 'e attains 'is full potential an' thinks 'imself more powerful than us, the sooner we'll know 'is true character an' where 'is loyalty lies."

"And the curse?" Coada inquired.

"Aye, best ta face that now. If 'e can't control it, than 'e'll be a liability ta us all—even ta 'imself."

"And what happens if he fails, or his loyalty doesn't side with us?" Coada asked.

"Then I'll put 'im down meself," the captain declared and held up his glass.

Coada mirrored the gesture with a shaking hand.

# CRUMBLING

Felix took the elevator down to the taxi rank below the city. The place was crowded with people queuing up for a lift home. He walked past them all, as close to the edge of the platform as he dared before pulling out the coin Cabby had given him. He ran his finger along the symbol on the coin's surface and tossed it up, catching it on its way down.

He waited ten minutes without seeing any sign of Cabby. He traced the symbol again and threw the coin a second time, snatching it out of the air impatiently.

Five more minutes passed and still there was no cab driver. He wondered whether he should be getting in line at the taxi rank with the rest of them. He decided to try the ritual a final time before abandoning hope, and just as he caught the coin he spotted Cabby weaving his way through the traffic towards him.

*Champion!* Felix grinned—the sight of the young driver and his red airship was like catching a life ring when drowning at sea.

Cabby pulled up beside Felix and opened his window. "Alright, alright already! Don't make me regret giving you that thing. Poor Polly's going crazy in here."

"Sorry, I wasn't sure if it was working."

"How long were you waiting, like ten minutes? Get in here already!" Cabby demanded.

The crowd stared at this transaction dumbfounded—clearly peeved and astonished that Felix was getting a cab before they were. Felix waved farewell to them and smiled smugly before stepping into Cabby's Express.

"Thanks for picking me up," he said as he closed the door and slipped into the soft cushioned seats.

"Did you ever stop to think while you were tossing that thing that I might be with another customer? It's a busy night, if you hadn't noticed. I'm not your own personal chauffeur, you know!" Cabby lectured, hitting the Nixie tube counter and pulling away from the rank.

"Alright, alright, I'm sorry. I'll make it up to you. I got lucky at the races."

"Now you're talking my language. In that case, you're forgiven. Where's the broad?"

"Don't ask," Felix answered somberly.

"Bad night, huh?"

"Let's just say it could've been better."

"She was a good one. What happened?"

"What part of *don't ask* are you failing to understand?"

"What? I'm a curious guy. Besides, it looks like you need to talk about it. You can't keep that stuff bottled in. It's not good for you," Cabby told him.

"It's…complicated."

"Alright then, don't tell me. You going back to the island I picked you up at?"

"Yeah, thanks."

"How was the Derby?" Cabby inquired.

"Magnificent."

"Ah man! I can't believe I missed another one."

"You live right here and you've really never seen it?" Felix asked.

"Do you know how hard it is to get a ticket? It's near impossible to get in there unless you're either a bajillionaire or famous."

"No, it's really not. You should try a little harder. It's worth it."

"I should try a little harder? My friend, I've tried. Believe me."

"Do you know how many staff I saw working the event? You think any of them had a ticket? Put aside the cab one year and get a job at the venue," Felix suggested.

Cabby was silent for a moment. "That's actually not a bad idea," he admitted.

"See, aren't you glad you picked me up? I'm full of not-bad ideas. There's a magnificent world out there, my friend, don't let it pass you by without seeing it," Felix said, and gazed out the window. The night sky was clear and full of extravagant airships sailing amongst a sea of brilliant stars. Suddenly a bird flew up beside them, pumping its wings to stay alongside.

"By shick," Felix muttered in disbelief.

"What?"

"It's Roy's Sendsong! How do you open the windows in here?" Felix asked.

"There's a lever at the base. Crank it to the left."

Felix found the lever and pulled it across to unlock the window. As soon as he pushed it open, the Sendsong flew into the air cab, landing gracefully on the seat beside him.

"Close the window, won't ya?! You're letting cold air in," Cabby protested.

"Yup, sorry," Felix apologized, and pulled it closed.

"You expecting mail?" Cabby asked.

"Yeah."

"Too bad you can't calibrate those things for better timing. Just make sure it doesn't tear up my seats, alright?" Cabby asserted, and his mechanical falcon puffed itself up territorially.

The Sendsong sang a melody and the compartment in its chest popped open. Inside was a sealed envelope and a single bulging coin purse. Felix took a deep breath and pulled them out. The Sendsong shut its compartment and settled onto the seat beside him, preening its porcelain feathers. Felix broke open the black wax seal with Lord Barviss's family crest and unfolded the letter.

*Hello Felix,*

*It took me a while to find out who you are. You have very loyal friends, but I squeezed it out of them eventually. I must hand it to you, you're cleverer than I anticipated. You only made one critical error: greatly underestimating the person you're messing with.*

*You see, if The Debt Collectors really existed, they'd be working for me. Still, you had me guessing. You played your cards very well. Unfortunately, you're way out of your league. But fortunately for you, I don't like to waste good talent. So, I'll make you an offer: work for me and I'll pay you double what you've requested with a promise for more work paid just as generously. I could use a mind like yours. All you have to do is bring Lady Lilliana to The Waterhole Inn at the Diamond City this Phenday at the hour of Karmithos. I've included a bag of earnest coin in good faith. And if you decide not to take my generous offer, I'll hunt you both down like rabbits and make sure you stay missing.*

*Kind Regards,*

*L.H.B.*

Felix's blood ran cold. He put the letter down and ran his fingers through his hair. "Shick," he cursed, leaning his head back against the seat. Lord Bardviss knew they were here. Not only that, he knew who he was—who he *truly* was. Felix wondered who he'd squeezed his name out of, and he desperately hoped it wasn't Bastian or Gwena, and that they at least were already safely in the Heartland. If it wasn't either of them, then it could've been any number of his acquaintances, maybe even the girls at the cathouses. *Oh Stars.* Felix's gut tightened, and he prayed to the Stars that it had been someone from the gambling circles, rather than the various people he truly cared about.

*What in the nine levels am I supposed to do now?*

"What's wrong?" Cabby inquired.

"I'm royally shicked!" Felix laughed hysterically.

"Get a bill you can't pay?"

"You could say that."

Felix never should've gotten greedy and asked Lord Bardviss for more. But then, it probably wouldn't have changed anything. Bardviss would've been looking into him the second Lilliana was found missing, regardless. If he truly wanted her gone, he'd have been taking measures to ensure it from the start. Felix suddenly realized just how deeply he'd stuck his foot into the hornets' nest. With Lord Bardviss's connection to Marx, he hadn't been simply toying with a pompous lord—he'd toyed with the entire organized crime network.

*Shick, shick, shick! This is what I bloody get for pursuing a noble. What a nightmare! Maybe Lilliana can notify The Emperor and get him to step in and stop Lord Bardviss?*

Right after he thought it, Felix knew it was a fool's errand. The Emperor wouldn't get involved in the personal affairs of the nobles. He had more important things to attend to. He might put more eyes on The East and look into their current influx of dragons, maybe even ensure he had checkpoints secured at Westdock's port outside of the control of Lord Bardviss, but he doubted he'd do anything to disturb Lilliana's arranged betrothal. And certainly not before Phenday. *Serendipity help us.*

# BLACKBERRY PIE

Gwena awoke in Benji's bed. It took her a second to remember how she'd gotten there, and she realized she must have fallen asleep. She found Benji in the kitchen across from her busy cooking something. Whatever it was, it smelled sweet and delicious.

Benji noticed she was awake and smiled. "Hey," he greeted.

"What time is it?" Gwena inquired, stretching out her arms.

Benji pulled out his pocket watch. "A quarter past Twillos."

"A bit late for dinner, isn't it?"

"This is more of a dessert, actually. Thought we could both use it. Nothing like sugar to lift the spirit, eh?" he smiled.

Gwena smiled in return, and Benji served up a plate and brought it over to her.

"Blackberry pie and creamed custard. One of my personal favorites," he announced.

Gwena took the plate gratefully and took a bite. "Oh wow, forget everything I said about pursuing a singing career, your true calling is pies!" she exclaimed.

Benji laughed. "Enjoy that. I have to get ready for my shift tonight," he said, and disappeared into the en suite.

"I suppose I better get out of here so you can ready the place. Who's your plus one this evening?" Gwena asked loudly.

"No one, actually," Benji called from the other room, "it was supposed to be Scarlet Jade, but she's got a gig downtown. Madam Rouge has me rostered on the main stage for most of the night. I'll have to get out of here a little early to set up, but you can stay as long as you like. Just be sure the door's locked on your way out."

"Alright, thanks," Gwena called back, before shovelling a fork full of pie into her mouth.

As soon as Gwena finished her culinary delight, Benji came out of the en suite wearing one of the suits she'd made for him.

"You're wearing it!" she exclaimed.

"Of course. What do you think?" he asked, holding out his arms for display.

"It looks great! I'm so happy it fits. Do you like it?!"

"It's my new favorite. I'm going to tell Madam Rouge that whatever she's paying you, it's not enough," Benji declared.

Gwena laughed. "Are you sure you don't have any complaints? I can still make alterations."

"I do have one," he admitted.

"What's that?"

"It makes the rest of my wardrobe look bad. Is there anything you can do about that?"

"I can make you a whole new one if you like?" Gwena offered wryly.

"Brilliant! Do I need to make an appointment? You seem to have a very busy schedule these days."

"I don't imagine Madam Pomphrey will want anything to do with me after tonight, so I'll probably be as free as a bird."

"Why's that? I can't imagine anyone wanting to be rid of you," Benji said.

Gwena hesitated, biting her lower lip in indecision. "Richard sprung a kiss on me after our rehearsal tonight. I didn't ask for it or want it, but it happened. I was so taken aback, I just froze up. To make matters worse, Madam Pomphrey walked in right when it happened," Gwena confessed, quickly blinking back the fresh tears welling in her eyes.

Benji's jaw tightened. "Is that why you were so upset?"

Gwena nodded.

"Did you say or do anything to invite that?"

"Not that I'm aware of. Over the last few days we've become friends. I never wanted anything more from him. Then last night he gave me a gift, he said it was an early birthday present. It turned out to be an enchanted necklace that took away the appearance of my scar. I didn't even know what its ability was until after I'd put it on. I'd barely had the thing clasped when he came at me. I wish with all my heart I could undo what's been done, but I can't, and now everything's ruined," she lamented weakly, failing to restrain a sob from escaping her throat.

Benji sat on the bed beside her. "Hey, it's not your fault. You didn't do anything wrong. This is all Richard," he assured her.

"It doesn't make any difference. Madam Pomphrey still blames me, regardless." Fresh tears broke through her defenses, and she quickly wiped them away.

"Of course she does. It's easier for her to blame you than admit the truth to herself. Don't worry, little bird. You're too good for them both.

If they're going to treat you like that, then they don't deserve to have you in their show. You're the one doing them the favor, not the other way around," Benji consoled, offering her a tissue from the ornate box on his bedside table. Gwena nodded and took it gratefully.

"Everything will be ok, don't you worry," he assured her, pocketing the key for his room. "I have to go. Stay here as long as you like. Have more pie, have the whole thing—well, maybe just leave me one piece," he amended with a wry smirk.

Gwena laughed through her tears. "Thank you, Benji."

"Of course." He smiled at her encouragingly and slipped out the door.

Gwena sighed. She wished Benji didn't have to go. Being alone left her no escape from the terrible feelings consuming her. The awful dread in the pit of her stomach, the immense remorse from the memory of Madam Pomphrey's face when she saw Richard kissing her, and the sinking feeling that she'd betrayed her, that she'd betrayed Bastian. Even though Gwena knew it wasn't her fault, she couldn't help feeling guilty for it all the same. She touched her scar, remembering what she'd looked like without it, remembering the hungry way Richard had gazed at her, remembering Bonnie's words about her scar's protection, and for the first time in her life, Gwena was grateful for it.

From her pocket she pulled out the dewdrop pearl necklace Bastian had given her and ran her finger across it lovingly before putting it back on.

*What now?* she wondered. Yesterday she imagined her future being performing magic on the stage. Now, she felt just as lost as when she'd left Westdock the week before. She could start her own magic show, she supposed. But the thought of doing it alone took all the joy out of it. And the thought of competing with Madam Pomphrey's show after everything she'd done for her, felt wrong. *What will happen to the show now?* Gwena wondered. Would it still go on without the mermaid escapologist? The act was the main selling point, according to the producers. And the opening night had already sold out. Would people want refunds for their tickets? She couldn't bear to think what impact that would have on the troupe. Madam Pomphrey didn't deserve that, she'd worked so hard for this. And Mallini, all his beautiful craftsmanship would go to waste. Even Richard, as foolish as he was—she didn't want him to miss out on his opportunity to perform magic on stage. It was his dream. No, she couldn't let this situation become any worse than it already was.

They'd worked too hard for this. Gwena helped herself to another piece of pie and then cleaned up. She left a note for Benji, thanking him for all he'd done for her, then locked the door and slipped out.

Gwena sat on the bed in her room reading over a letter she'd just written to Madam Pomphrey.

*Dear Madam Pomphrey,*

*I am writing this letter because there's something I need to say — and I'm sure I'm the last person you want to be seeing right now. Despite what you might think, I have the utmost respect for you, your relationship with Richard, and your show. I don't know what came over Richard this evening. If I ever gave any indication to encourage that behavior, I am truly sorry. That was never my desire or my intention. I am so grateful for everything you've taught me, and for the opportunity to be a part of your world. These last few days have been some of the best in my life. And despite how things might end, I will always treasure them. I hope dearly that you consider my words and see the truth in them — but whether you do or not, I want you to know that I am determined to set things right and do everything in my power to ensure the show goes on. I will still be your mermaid escapologist if you want me to be. And if you don't, then I completely understand and will not return.*

*Respectfully,*

*Gwena*

She folded another piece of paper into an envelope for the letter and wrote Madam Pomphrey's name on the front. She nodded to herself and carried it with her out the door.

Gwena descended the stairs and made her way through the club and down the corridor to Theater 3. She listened at the double doors before walking inside. The theater was empty, just as she'd been hoping it would be. She walked her letter down the dimly lit aisle and back behind the stage to where Madam Pomphrey's dressing room was, then slipped the letter under the door. With a sigh, she began making her way silently out of the theater.

"Gwena."

Gwena froze at the sound of her name, she turned to find Richard standing in the aisle behind her. His face was streaked with strange shadows from the room's half light. He had a swollen black eye.

"Stars, are you alright?" Gwena gasped.

Richard looked confused for a moment and then followed her gaze to his eye. "Oh, this? It's nothing. Benji has a mean right hook, but it's less than I deserve."

"I'm so sorry. I didn't know he'd do such a thing!"

"He thinks very highly of you, understandably," Richard said with a weak smile, before quickly stammering on. "Look, I'm so sorry about earlier, I never should've kissed you like that—without invitation, I mean. It's just, well…I really like you. You're everything I've ever liked about Madam Pomphrey, but so much more. We have a lot in common, you and I, and we're much closer in age. Spending time with you these past few days, I haven't been able to help falling for you. You're funny and witty, and an amazing magician—"

"All I'm missing is the pretty face," Gwena interposed.

"No. No, it's not like that. I just thought it would be something you wanted. That scar isn't really a part of you—it's not like you were born with it. And without it you're even more beautiful than I could've imagined. You're perfect. When I saw you, the real you, I couldn't help myself," Richard said.

"This is the *real* me, Richard. Without this scar, I wouldn't be the person I am today. It's a part of me now—I can't be my true self without it. If you can't see that, then you don't deserve to be my friend, let alone anything more. And if you no longer love Madam Pomphrey, then at least have the decency to tell her before you go touching someone else— because she doesn't deserve that," Gwena asserted.

Richard nodded, looking completely defeated.

"Goodnight, Richard," Gwena said, and walked out.

That night Gwena sat on the balcony outside her room listening to Benji sing on the main stage. His songs eased her heart, until she was finally tired enough to return to her room and sleep.

# TAMARRA WE BE SAILIN'

Snibs stood at the head of the mess hall ready to address the crew. A hushed silence fell over the men as they ate their dinner, their attention turned to the quartermaster.

"I know this last week 'asn't been easy, we 'ave faced many trials an' worked ta the bone with little rest. But thanks ta all our toil, we've completed repairs in time ta make it ta Jaxland fer the yearly gatherin'!" Snibs announced.

The men hooted and hollered, hitting their black leather steins against the table.

"Ta reward ya fer yer sacrifice, the cap'n 'as instructed Doc ta fill yer Black Jacks with gulpers. But don't write yerselves off too much, fer tammara we set sail fer the island o' rogues!" Snibs cried.

The men cheered even louder than before, whistling and clapping and stomping their feet, then they all burst into song, beating their Black Jacks on the tables in time to the music.

*'ere we go boys,*
*Ready the sails boys,*
*Tammara we be sailin'!*

*We've suffered the worst,*
*Yet 'eld our course.*
*Been out ta the black an' back again.*
*Times 'ave been tuff*
*The sea's been ruff*
*but ye won't 'ear us wailin'!*

*'ere we go boys,*
*Ready the sails boys,*
*Tammara we be sailin'!*

*Soon ta reach the open arms o' the shore*
*An' greet 'er like a lover waitin'.*

*We'll stretch our legs*
*An' fill our stores*
*Rejoicin' with merrymakin'.*

*'ere we go boys,*
*Ready the sails boys,*
*Tammara we be sailin'!*

*Onward we'll go*
*Ta fates unknown,*
*Back ta the salt fer venture.*

*No matter the squall*
*We'll face it all*
*Tacklin' the worst tagether.*

*'ere we go boys,*
*Ready the sails boys,*
*Tammara we be sailin'!*

*Ever forward, we never look back.*
*The dark of night stayin' at our backs*
*As we face the sun arisin'!*

All the pirates laughed and cheered and drank merrily late into the evening.

⌒

Bastian rested his hand on the trunk of a mast tree, taking in heavy gasps of air. He was highly regretting the six stiff drinks he'd had earlier that evening. Several of the men insisted on celebrating Bastian's gambling win against Stork the night before and kept refilling his stein. He hadn't realized just how eager many of them had been to see Stork lose. To Bastian's surprise, it had greatly increased his popularity. Unfortunately for him, popularity was never something he'd been particularly fond of. He knew too well that the tallest poppies inevitably inspired the attention of those eager to chop them down to size. He would have been far more comfortable keeping his head down low. And now he was feeling particularly sorry for himself as he tried to get through Falgo's lesson with a pounding headache.

Bastian had been sparring with Falgo for the last half hour. The sea gypsy moved like a shadow. Bastian could never anticipate where he'd strike next. At least his automatic reflexes were improving. He found that when he did manage to block one of Falgo's attacks, it was more often than not an instinctual reaction that occurred before his mind even registered what had happened. The longer they sparred, the more frequently he was able to block and the less he ended up with his arse in the sand. When it became obvious that Bastian was too tired to continue training effectively, Falgo stopped and gestured for Bastian to sit beside him on a fallen log.

Bastian took the invitation gladly and sat down, wiping his arm across his sweating brow, and Falgo offered him his bottle of watered down rum.

Bastian accepted it and took a drink. As hesitant as he was to put more alcohol into his system, it was a gesture Falgo hadn't made before and one Bastian wasn't about to turn down—besides, he was thirsty. After taking his drink Bastian handed the bottle back.

"Yer gettin' better," Falgo remarked, taking the rum.

"I'm grateful to hear it. I still feel completely useless," Bastian confessed.

Falgo nodded, "Good."

"Is it?"

"Pride be almost as dangerous as fear. It can blind ya just as easily. The second ya believe ye've got the upper 'and be the second ya lose it," Falgo cautioned, and took another drink.

Bastian chewed on that for a moment. "On the night the Kraken attacked us, you seemed to be completely devoid of fear. How did you overcome it so easily?" he inquired.

"It's a lot easier when ya 'ave nothin' left ta lose."

"What about your life, isn't that something?" Bastian asked.

"Not when it be as miserable as mine. I'm not brave, Dodger. I'm a coward too lily-livered ta end me life an' too weak ta live it. Any part o' me with any worth burned with me wife an' daughter in a boat fire years ago. I couldn't save 'em, an' without 'em I lost meself. One week later I joined the Black Mary, an' I've been slowly drownin' meself ever since. Don't waste yer time lookin' up ta a fool like me," Falgo asserted.

"I'm sorry," Bastian said.

"Fer what?"

"For the loss of your wife and daughter. I can only imagine the misery that would bring. I don't blame you for drowning your sorrows. I think it says more good about your character than you realize—if you didn't care about them so much it would make it a lot easier."

"It's not due ta me good character, it's due ta theirs—they were the very light o' the stars, the world's never seen two shine brighter."

"Then it was the world who lost something that day," Bastian said.

Falgo nodded and took a drink.

"But surely they'd want you to live your life to its fullest, to see you happy and enjoying what they can't?" Bastian asked.

"I'm a lost cause, Dodger, don't waste yer time," Falgo growled.

"Well, you're certainly an amazing fighter. If you fight like that drunk, I can only imagine what you'd be like sober. I'm curious though—if you grew up on the gypsy boats, where'd you learn to fight? I thought the sea gypsies were peaceful people," Bastian inquired.

Falgo looked out towards the shore before answering. "Me father was one o' the Scillion Seven before the fall o' The East in The Last War."

"Your father was part of the elite force that protected the Scillion royal family? I thought they were executed when the family was?"

"Most were. It haunted me father that he couldn't save 'em, but 'e did manage ta save the princess. They just managed ta escape with their lives—but I think a part o' him still died that day," Falgo admitted.

"Wow. Your father's responsible for the princess's escape?! Do you know if she's still alive?"

Falgo shrugged. "I don't know. It was before me time, an' me father never liked me inquirin' inta it."

"Didn't the Scillion Seven have their own martial art? I heard it was unstoppable and was lost to the world when The East was conquered."

"Ya shouldn't believe everythin' ya hear. If it was unstoppable, then they wouldn't be dead, now would they?" Falgo asked and took a drink.

"Good point. Is that what you've been teaching me, The East's forgotten martial art?"

"O' a sort. With a few o' me own adjustments," Falgo admitted.

"Ha! I didn't think it was possible, but you just got even more badass," Bastian exclaimed.

Falgo snorted and took another drink.

"How'd your father end up with the gypsies then?" Bastian asked.

"Me father took refuge with our sea clan just off the coast o' the Southern Isles. He fell in love with me gypsy mother an' the rest be history. Now, it's me turn ta ask a question," Falgo declared.

"Shoot."

"What have ya been usin' ta water down me rum?"

Bastian swallowed. "When did you first notice?"

"Oh, I noticed from the start. When ye've been drinkin' as long as I 'ave, the spirit's body be as familiar as a lover," Falgo told him.

"Why didn't you say anything?"

Falgo shrugged. "At first I was too thirsty ta care, an' then when it became clear the potency was still droppin', I realized it was still doin' the job regardless—more so, I've been feelin' better than I have in years," he admitted.

Bastian smiled. "I'm glad to hear it."

"But ya still haven't answered me question," Falgo said, taking another swig.

"Right. It's a mixture of Doc's rum with a barley and sugar tea. I've decreased the rum every day only by a fraction. It's something I learned at the Order. We used to help a lot of people with alcohol dependencies. The problem is that when someone's been abusing a substance consistently, it changes the body's chemistry. It adjusts to function with the substance, so if you take it away cold, it can be just as harmful as the substance abuse itself. The trick is to gradually come off it so that your body has time to adjust," Bastian explained.

Falgo nodded and took another drink in silence.

"Snib says we're setting sail tomorrow," Bastian said.

Falgo nodded again.

"I'll make sure you get a fresh bottle even if we can't train," Bastian assured him.

Falgo nodded a third time, keeping his eyes fixed on the distant shore as he drank.

Bastian followed his gaze to the horizon. "If there's a way, I'd like to continue my training after Jaxland."

"There will be. Until then—keep practicin' yer lessons up here," Falgo instructed, tapping the side of his head with his finger, "visualizin' yer trainin' be almost just as effective as actually doin' it."

"I will then, thanks."

"I hear ya 'ave a task ta complete on Jaxland?" Falgo inquired.

"Yeah, the captain wants me to prove my loyalty," Bastian admitted.

"The cap'n doesn't give a cwip about yer loyalty, 'e's usin' ya—just like the rest o' us. Ya 'ave a skill 'e needs an' that makes ya valuable, but yer the one doin' 'im the favor, not the other way around—don't ferget that," Falgo admonished.

"Thanks, I won't."

Falgo put his hand on Bastian's shoulder. "When death comes knockin' on yer door, don't fear it. Look it straight in the eye an' tell it ta go shick itself."

Bastian smirked and nodded.

"See ya around, thief," the gypsy pirate said, and walked back towards the ship whistling his usual tune.

Bastian watched him go before stretching his arms and then standing to return to the sleeping quarters.

# STUCK BETWEEN A STORM
# AND A HARD PLACE

Felix paid Cabby a generous tip and stepped out of the airship onto the jetty at Katarina's island, Lord Bardviss's letter and betrayal coin in hand. He waved goodbye as the airship pulled away and lit up a puff-stick, taking a long drag as he stared up at Katarina's house. *What in the nine realms are we going to do now?* he asked himself.

If he and Lilliana stayed in Sky View, Lord Bardviss's men would find them. And if they ran, it would only be a matter of time before they were hunted down. The only option as far as he could see it was to seek out help from Frederick and his father, the duke of Sky View. If the Remingtons were still interested in maintaining the betrothal between Lilliana and Frederick, then they would hopefully protect Lilliana. But without Lilliana's father being around, Felix wondered whether the duke would still be interested in an alliance with their family at all. The Wendrian house was crumbling without Duke Drake. And to stand up against Lord Bardviss without proof of his ill intention would come with its own set of problems. The letters weren't enough. Anything could be faked with a good forger—if Lord Bardviss denied he'd written them, they'd have nothing. And as far as the Remingtons and the public knew, Lilliana practically belonged to Lord Bardviss. If she openly came out of hiding and it was revealed she was being kept from him, he could make a public charade out of it, creating all kinds of problems for the Remingtons.

Felix and Lilliana were backed into a corner, and this time Felix wasn't sure there was a way out.

⸺

"Come on in, the kettle's still hot," Katarina announced, welcoming Felix through the front door.

"Thanks," he said, and stepped inside Katarina's house. "Has Lilliana come back yet?" he asked, looking around for any sign of her.

"You're the first one. I thought you two were sticking together. Everything alright?"

"Everything's fine. We got separated on our way home is all, I was hoping she'd made it back before me."

Katarina smiled warmly. "I'm sure she'll be in shortly then. Have a seat, I'll bring you some tea."

"Much obliged," Felix returned, and sat down at the table.

"How was the Derby?" Katarina inquired while walking into the kitchen.

"Impressive. I've never seen anything like it."

"Nor will you. There's nothing quite like the Sky Cup. I've enjoyed the event many times over the years."

"What made you stop going?"

"I'm not one for large crowds," Katarina admitted. She returned to the table and placed a steaming cup of tea in front of Felix, then sat down across from him with her own cup.

"Thanks," Felix said.

Katarina studied him. "Rough night?"

"That obvious?"

"You're radiating anxiety. You want to talk about it?"

"No, thank you," he said, taking a sip of his tea.

"Follow me, I'll show you where the hard stuff is," Katarina offered, and stood from the table.

"Hard stuff?" Felix questioned.

"To drink. I can see you need something a little stiffer than tea."

Felix smiled. "Thank you," he said, and followed her upstairs into one of the back rooms. It was a study of sorts, with an open Everfireplace and shelves stacked with books. Katarina walked over to a wood and glass cabinet and opened it up. Inside was a collection of top-shelf spirits.

"What's your poison?" she asked.

"Do you have any Ash Whiskey?"

"Of course, I only stock the best." Katarina poured a short glass for each of them, handing one to Felix. "This was my husband's favorite," she told him.

"A man with good taste," Felix commended, accepting the drink and welcoming its heat as he threw half of it back.

Katarina settled into a leather armchair in front of the fire. "It's funny, Pecos used to come up here every evening for a nightcap and I rarely joined him—but now he's gone, I haven't missed a single night. I only wish I'd taken the opportunity more when he was here. It's not something I thought much about then, there was always something else to do.

But if I could go back in time, that's the one thing I'd change. I'd join him in this room every night for his drink," she said.

"Why's that?"

"Because it's the in-between moments that matter the most, the times with no interference, when you can simply be present with the ones you love. I never valued that enough. Now that the opportunity's gone, it's all I long for. So, I come up here every night and have a drink in his honor, reminiscing on old times," she said, holding up her glass to an empty chair in the corner.

"I'm sorry you had to lose him."

"Thank you. Me too. Learn from my mistakes, eh? Never underestimate the value of simply being present with the ones you love."

"I'll remember that," Felix promised, and looked around the room while Katarina drank her whiskey in silence. Most of the walls were covered with either books or art. There was a chalkboard in the corner filled with calculations and a large illustration of the storm cut in half to display each section. Every part of it was labeled with a paragraph of notes alongside. Felix saw something move in his peripheral vision and almost jumped. He turned to see a Sendsong staring at him. It was sitting on a perch next to the window. The mechanical bird had been so still he hadn't noticed it before.

"You have a Sendsong," he announced.

"Yes, not that she's any good out here. But I don't have the heart to give her up."

"Why isn't she any good out here?" Felix queried.

"The Everstorm disrupts the signals they use to navigate. She's practically blinded by it. I have to take her into town if I want to use her, but then she couldn't find her way home anyway, so there's no point," Katarina said candidly.

"Really? What happens when someone tries to send you a letter via Sendsong?"

"The Sendsong wanders around as if lost, then gives the letter back," she explained.

Felix froze.

"When my husband and I first moved out this way it caused quite a riot. The university tried to send us correspondence via Sendsong several times. They thought something had happened to us. We didn't even know about it until we visited them the following year and they told us about the bird's strange behavior. The only way to send and receive mail this close to the storm is the old-fashioned way. But I still have a soft spot for the old girl," Katarina admitted, looking lovingly at the Sendsong.

Felix gazed out the window at the Everstorm as realization dawned on him. *Holy shick, Duke Drake's still alive.* The raging mass of nature's fury flickered with dancing lightning that flashed on and off inside the mass of dark churning clouds.

"Do you really think it's possible there's something inside the storm?" Felix asked.

"I know there is."

"How?"

"Because my gut tells me so. It might not convince anyone else, but I don't have a doubt in my mind. Soon, I'll be able to find out what it is and share it with the world," Katarina proclaimed.

Felix walked over to the chalkboard and looked at the calculations.

"And you really think your ship can make it?"

"The math's sound. But we won't know for sure until we test it out. I just have a few more checks I want to make. Everything's looking good, I just don't want to send it off without knowing I've done everything I can," Katarina told him, walking over to stand beside Felix and looking up at the chalkboard. "It really only has to make it through the eyewall. These clouds on the outside are what we call *rainbands*. They're only mild in comparison, and the inside of the eye is as still as a summer's day," she explained, pointing out the rainbands and the storm's eye on the illustration.

"What's the eyewall?"

Katarina pointed to a dense band surrounding the eye on the chalkboard.

"It's the fiercest part of the storm—a ring encircling the eye made up of at least twelve miles of high-speed winds battering from every direction. It's the one part I'm not sure Storm Piercer will make it through. We've armed it with all we can, but the storm's unpredictable," she expounded. Then she finished off what was left of her whiskey and said, "Well, that's me done. I can't stay up as late as I used to. Make yourself at home and help yourself to anything you find in the cupboard."

"Thanks."

"Good night. I hope whatever's troubling you is better in the morning."

"Thank you, me too."

Katarina smiled warmly and left the room.

Felix grabbed the bottle of Ash Whiskey and walked over to the window, looking out towards the Everstorm.

*How in the nine realms is Drake Wendrian still alive?* he wondered. He refilled his glass and set the bottle on the windowsill, watching the light show in the churning tempest.

*Could there really be a lost world in the eye of the storm?* There had to be something in there. How else could the duke survive in there for two whole years? The behavior of the Sendsong clearly indicated he was alive and close enough to the storm for his signal to be interfered by it. If Katarina had really seen him fly into it, there was no other explanation. Felix watched the churning mass of clouds and the flashing lightning for several minutes while he drank. If only they could find Drake and bring him back, he thought. Lilliana's father was the one person who might actually be able to fix the mess they were in. The one person who not only cared enough about Lilliana to stop Lord Bardviss, but also had the power to do so. He was so close—just there on the other side of those clouds.

*If only we could fetch him. It's not far, one could be in and out before morning. The ship's automated, how hard could it be?* Felix wondered.

He snorted at the ridiculousness of the idea. In truth, even if it were possible, he would have no way of finding the duke once inside. Katarina said the eye was eighty miles. That was a lot of space to get lost in, especially at night. Felix felt the stare of the Sendsong burning into him, he turned and faced the bird, and suddenly he saw the solution was right in front of him,

*Serendipity help me...*

⌒

*Dear Lilliana,*

*I'm sorry for being an arse. Tends to be something I'm rather good at. I know you have responsibilities to uphold, and I admire how seriously you take your position. It gives me hope that Westdock has a brighter future in store. I never intended to take you away from all that. It's just my heart's been going rogue on me these last few days and it had a moment of hijacking my intellect. You can hardly blame it — it is mostly your fault.*

*That being said, we currently have bigger problems. I'm sorry to report, shick's hit the aircraft propeller. Lord Bardviss knows we're in Sky View. He still wants to get rid of you. And now*

*he's taking matters into his own hands. I've left the letter he sent me and the bag of coin he gave me to betray you. Don't worry, I'm not that much of an arse nor that stupid. He can shove it where the stars don't shine. But it still leaves us with a very big problem. And there's only one solution I can think of. I'm going to find your father. He's alive, I know that now. I'll most likely die trying — but better to try and fail than sit here screwing things up any further and have Lord Bardviss kill me anyway — so, here goes nothing.*

*If I don't come back, have Roy take you to the Duke of Sky View and ask for his protection. I'll leave it there — I need to go before you show up and try to stop me. Just one more thing. I'll always be in your corner, Lilliana, even if you're on stage and I'm in the nosebleeds — or amongst the stars. These last few days have been an absolute pleasure. I'm grateful you kidnapped me. And I'm grateful you've shown me what it means to be in love. Thank you, my lady. I love and admire you more than you could ever know. Look after yourself.*

*Yours truly, James Turner — or (as you will now know from Lord Bardviss's letter), AKA Felix Copperweather*

Felix stood in Lilliana's room with Katarina's Sendsong perched on his shoulder. He read over his letter briskly then set it on Lilliana's bed next to the letter from Lord Bardviss and the bag of coin sent with it.

"Ready for a suicide mission?" Felix asked the Sendsong. The bird made a gentle melodic chirp. "Good enough for me." He grabbed the bottle of Ash Whiskey and walked downstairs to the entryway closet where Katarina kept all her keys. They were hanging conveniently behind the door labeled in an orderly fashion. He took the one marked *Storm Piercer* and left the house.

# FACING MONSTERS

Bastian was woken by shouts and heavy footsteps. It was still dark, but the sleeping quarters were almost completely empty. Bastian stopped a passing pirate. "What's going on?"

"There's a storm 'eading straight fer us. The cap'n want's ta get ahead o' it before it 'its. We're settin' sail, it's all 'ands on deck," the man informed him, and then he hurried off.

Bastian groaned and heaved himself out of his hammock, then headed for the top deck to see how he could help.

The ship was swaying drastically from side to side as the men pulled anchor from the Dreg's shore. Bastian could see dark storm clouds billowing on the horizon with bright flashes of lightning followed by loud cracks of thunder. The storm was still a good way off, but steadily approaching with a fury. On the beach the mast trees' bushy tops were bending westward.

"The wind favors us, full and bye lads!" Snibs cried.

The men scurried up the masts to unfurl the sails. As soon as they were open the wind took hold, carrying them swiftly forward.

"Keep 'er course steady, lads. As long as we stay in the current, we should remain ahead o' the tempest," Snibs ordered above the gale's whine.

Bastian stepped up beside him. "Anything I can do?"

"Yeah, stay out o' the way," the quartermaster growled.

"Right."

Bastian looked out at the Dreg and watched as it receded into the distance. Then he turned back and took cover below deck. He returned to the sleeping quarters and happily climbed into his hammock alongside the sick and the injured. He knew he should be ashamed of being the only able-bodied man below deck, but he was too tired to care—only feeling grateful he wasn't needed. He closed his eyes hoping to find sleep but was too distracted by the swaying ship threatening to empty his stomach. He turned his thoughts to Gwena instead, until finally his exhaustion won over and he was asleep.

Bastian woke in his hammock to his bracelet vibrating on his wrist. The swaying of the ship had died down to a gentle lull. He looked around and found most of the sleeping quarters full once more. He made his way to the top deck and was surprised to be greeted by a clear sky and endless expanse of ocean, its blue surface dazzling with the bright rays of the rising sun. Cricket stepped up beside him and handed over a mop.

"Mornin', sunshine," he greeted, as if nothing had happened.

Bastian took the mop in hand. "What did I miss?"

Cricket shrugged. "An early start ta Jaxland. Besides that, not much," he said, and began whistling as he swabbed the deck.

Bastian turned to the horizon and soaked in the sunrise, then started to push his mop alongside.

When Bastian arrived at Tink's workshop that morning, Tink wasn't alone. The captain sat casually in a chair in the corner playing with the rings on his fingers. Bastian caught his eye, and the captain gave him his half smile.

"Good morning," Tink greeted.

"Morning," Bastian returned.

"The captain's here to observe today's lesson," Tink explained.

Bastian nodded hello to Muerte. He wondered if his overachievement in his last lesson had piqued the captain's interest, or if he was in some sort of trouble.

"How are you feeling?" Tink inquired.

"Fine."

"Good. Now that you're prepared for your task and have learned the benefit of your ability, it's time you know the danger of it. Every coin has two sides. In today's lesson you'll be learning the flip side of yours," Tink announced.

A very bad feeling crept over Bastian.

"As discussed previously, the imagination is a powerful tool. When used with intention you can accomplish almost anything. The Ghost Element is your fuel, and the imagination is the spark that ignites it and brings it to life. But if you don't learn to control it, it can control you. Fear is a persistent weed that feeds off our insecurities and draws power from the imagination, growing until it overtakes the mind. And if you allow it, it will."

Tink walked over to the center of the room and pulled back his silk rug, revealing a trapdoor in the floorboards.

"Today's lesson will take place down here," he said, opening its door.

Bastian walked over and peered into the gaping hole. It was a pit of pure shadow.

"Are you afraid of the dark, Dodger?"

"Course not," Bastian scoffed.

"Of course you are, everyone's afraid of the dark. The unknown inspires fear, and darkness is its perfect canvas."

Bastian eyed Tink warily and whispered, "What's this really about, Tink? Does the captain want to get rid of me?"

"Why would I want to do that?" the captain asked, coming over to stand beside him.

"You tell me," Bastian said. He was suddenly acutely aware that Tink and the captain had him surrounded, and he didn't like it. His muscles tensed, ready to spring at the slightest hint of ill intent.

"This is simply the next stage of your training," Tink assured him.

The captain gave him his lopsided grin, which only filled Bastian with further unease.

"Do ya believe in monsters, Dodger?" Muerte asked him.

"Is this some sort of joke?"

"Answer the question," Tink prompted.

"No. I haven't believed in monsters since I was a child."

"I see, an' when ya were a child an' believed there be monsters—an' the very thought terrorized ya enough ta keep ya from sleepin', tell me, would it 'ave made any difference whether the monster be real er not?" the captain asked.

"Of course."

"Why? Either way, it's still terrorizin' ya all the same."

"If it's not real, it can't hurt you," Bastian asserted.

"Keep tellin' yerself that," the captain advised, and pushed Bastian into the hole in the floor.

Bastian called out in surprise as he fell into the darkness. He landed on a pile of something soft and cool. He hurried off it into the surrounding shadows and looked up just in time to see Tink close the trapdoor. The small square of light above him was extinguished, leaving him completely blinded.

"Shick!"

Bastian closed his eyes and honed into his other senses. "I am nothing, I am everything," he muttered, calming his mind and tuning into his surroundings. The air was cool and crisp, it smelled of the open sea rather than an enclosed space. There was something soft beneath his feet—*sand, maybe?* He could hear the gentle creaking of the lilting ship and the sound of crashing waves beyond.

*I must be in the haul, in a storage compartment of some sort,* he guessed.

Bastian listened intently for several moments, turning in the dark until it became clear there was no imminent danger. Then he sat down on the floor.

*Shicking fantastic!*

He wondered how long he'd have to stay down there before the captain and Tink allowed him back up, or if they ever would.

*What was it they'd asked him? If he was afraid of the dark?*

Bastian couldn't remember the last time he'd been afraid of the dark. In fact, for most of his life he'd found it comforting. It was the shadows that gave him protection and solace from the rest of the world. He laid down and rested his head in his arms. He was tempted to use the time to catch up on sleep, Stars knew he could use it. But he wasn't relaxed enough for that, there was something that Tink said which kept niggling at him, something about the flip side to his ability. He was trying to figure out what that something could be when he heard a distant voice pleading for help. He sat up and listened intently. It sounded like someone wailing, mixed with the sound of running feet and distant shouts of men in panic. He couldn't pinpoint where the sound was coming from. Then a firebeetle lantern awoke beside him, the beetles glowed brilliantly as they scurried about in agitation. Bastian grabbed the lantern and held its light to his surroundings. He was in a cellar of sorts, just as he'd suspected. It was a deep square room with a dark passageway receding into the opposite wall. The whole space was saturated with the Ghost Element. The strange shimmering particles carpeted the floor like the sand of a beach. There was a great pile of the stuff in the center, and Bastian realized it was what had broken his fall. He brought the lantern over to inspect it. As soon as the lantern's luminance fell upon the Element, the stuff glittered and started billowing up in fine spinning eddies, dancing playfully in the light.

*Why's there so much of it?* he wondered.

He dug into the pile and found his answer—in the floorboards underneath was inlaid a circle of pure gold. Bastian had never seen so much of the precious metal, or so much of the Element collected together.

A tremor ran through the floor. A cool breeze blew up from the dark passage, stirring up the Ghost Element and tousling Bastian's hair. The firebeetles began scuttling more anxiously, trying to climb up the lanterns' glass walls in an attempt to escape, their glowing abdomens casting menacing shadow plays on the walls all around. Then a wet scraping noise emanated from the dark passage, like a soggy body being dragged along the floor. Bastian paused, the hairs on the back of his neck standing on end. Something was coming, something very large. His head spun with possibilities, trying to put the pieces together—the wails, the men's hysterical voices, the running boots, the tremor. Then a shout came from somewhere distant, "The Kraken! It's the Kraken!"

Bastian froze in horror and listened more intently to the wet scraping mass coming steadily closer. He shut his eyes tightly and tried to clear his mind of the panic that threatened to swallow it whole.

*That wouldn't make any sense, a Kraken can't get down here,* he assured himself. But then the recollection of the captain's mention of monsters filled him with renewed dread.

"Tink! Tink, let me out!" Bastian shouted.

He boosted himself off the side of the wall towards the trapdoor and braced himself in the corner, holding himself up by the fingertips of his left hand squeezed between the ceiling's boards. He used his right to push on the trapdoor. It was locked from the other side. Bastian pounded on it.

"Tink! Tink! Let me up! This isn't funny!! You need to let me up now!" he insisted, but no answer came. The wet dragging mass was nearer now, almost upon him. Bastian turned his head slowly towards the dark passage just in time to see a large, suckered limb erupt from the inky black.

"Shick!"

He dropped to the floor in a roll, barely dodging the gigantic arm as it writhed towards him. The appendage was so big it almost filled the entire space, weaving from one side to the other. Bastian dodged it desperately.

"Tink! Tink! Let me out! Let me out!!" he yelled in panic.

With sudden purpose, the arm came directly towards him. It found his leg and latched onto it, pulling him off his feet and dragging him along the floor towards the dark passage. Bastian shook his leg vigorously and tried to grab hold of the cracks between the floorboards.

"Tink!!" he screamed at the top of his lungs.

The trapdoor flung open, flooding the cellar with blinding light. Several gunshots rang out and the Kraken shrieked, recoiling from Bastian's leg, then Bastian was hoisted out of the cellar into Tink's chamber.

The captain stood over the trapdoor with his pistol in hand shooting at the monster. Bastian scurried away from the opening and covered his ears as the beast's blood curdling shriek rang out once more and then stopped abruptly. The captain kicked the trapdoor shut.

Bastian sat gasping on the floor, staring at it with eyes as big as saucers.

"How?...How'd it get on the ship?" he stammered in hysteric confusion.

The captain walked casually over to Tink's liquor cabinet and poured a drink, then brought it over to Bastian.

"Easy lad, the thin' be dead," he assured him.

Bastian took the glass with shaking hands and knocked it back.

"Can someone please explain what the shick just happened?"

Tink glanced at the captain.

Muerte Tormenta sat down in one of Tink's chairs and drank from his own glass of rum thoughtfully before answering,

"When I was a lad, there was a man on this ship who used ta tell me tales o' terrors o' the deep. 'is name was Bully-Joe. 'e would paint pictures in me mind o' terrible beasts far worse than anythin' I could've conjured up in me worst nightmares, 'e would point ta shadows in the water an' tell me they were monsters—thinkin' it be funny how much it spooked me. I 'ad night terrors fer weeks, I started ta see shadows in the sea as strange monstrosities hungry fer blood, until one day—they were."

The captain took another drink from his glass.

"Bully-Joe didn't believe me when I told 'im they'd come ta life, until one swallowed 'im whole," Muerte concluded.

Bastian looked at him in horror.

"Are you saying you somehow manifested the monsters?"

"It's the dark side to seeing the Ghost Element," Tink explained. "If you allow yourself to believe in your fears, they *will* come to life."

Bastian stared at them both in disbelief.

"You're telling me that you purposely put me down in that hole with a Kraken that *you* manifested?!"

"*You* manifested," Tink corrected.

"Hahaha!" Bastian laughed hysterically. "Me? Right. What about the screaming? There was shouting and wailing—I heard the men declare there was a Kraken and I heard it coming up the passage before I even saw it."

"What passage?" Tink asked, he opened the trapdoor and shone an Everfire torch into the cellar. Bastian warily walked over and cautiously looked inside. There was no sign of the Kraken. Where the passage had been was now an alcove no more than three meters deep made of solid wood.

"But I heard it…"

"Oh yes," Tink agreed, and nodded to a large pipe in the corner of the room that was showering down a heavy stream of water into a drain below it.

"White noise. Give the imagination a pool of chaos and it will make order of it."

"No. No, I know what I heard! What kind of sick joke is this?! There's no way I could've imagined that thing into existence. No way!"

But both Tink and the Captain stared back at him devoid of mirth.

"Why are you doing this to me?!" Bastian demanded. His head was spinning, he wished desperately that it *was* some twisted joke that Tink and the Captain had concocted.

"We need you to overcome your fear in a controlled environment before we reach Jaxland. Otherwise, there's no telling how it might manifest in far less favorable circumstances. We can't afford for you to let any monstrosities loose on the world. It's the final stage of your training," Tink explained.

"I thought nothing created with the Ghost Element lasts unless it's housed in an object?"

"Fear is a more potent binding agent. As long as someone believes in the creature, it will last. And the more people who believe and fear it, the stronger and more substantial it becomes. The only way for it to dissolve back to whence it came without killing it is to conquer the fear of it. Something much easier said than done."

"You know, I wasn't afraid of the dark. Monsters haven't haunted me since I was a kid—if you hadn't shown me this, I don't think it would've been a problem. But now thanks to you, I'm terrified! I can't think of anything more horrific than being able to animate my own nightmares."

"We didn't put that fear inta ya, lad. If fear o' the Kraken wasn't hauntin' ya already, ya never would've been able ta summon the beast.

We did nothin' but put ya in enough heat ta sweat it out. An' now, yer gonna 'ave ta conquer it. We can't let ya go until ya do," the captain stated candidly.

"Conquer it? How am I supposed to do that now that I know how much there is to be afraid of?!"

"There's nothing to be afraid of but fear itself. That is your one true enemy. It only has power if you give it power. Nothing can be born from your psyche unless you believe in it. You must never forget—you are the one steering your mind. Don't let it steer you!" Tink asserted.

Bastian nodded weakly. "What do I need to do?"

"Practice," the captain declared, and he and Tink forced Bastian back down into the hole.

"Noooo!" Bastian cried, desperately clawing at everything around him as he fell through the floor. His fall was broken by the pile of the Ghost Element once again. The trapdoor shut above him and the light went out, again leaving him in total darkness. Bastian crawled on his hands and knees in search of the firebeetle lantern. He ran his arm this way and that in long sweeping motions along the floor. But no matter which way he turned he couldn't find it. Panic began to rise in his throat and he continued his search frantically. At last his arm collided with the familiar feeling of metal and glass, but in his desperation he knocked it to the ground and one of the lantern's panes shattered across the floor. The firebeetles woke all at once, their bodies glowing brightly with warm light as they scurried from their cage across the boards in every direction, filling the room with animated shadows.

Bastian scrambled away from the black space where the Kraken had emerged from before and pushed himself up against the opposite wall. He shut his eyes tightly and put his hands over his ears in an attempt to block out the white noise that sounded like men's shouts and children wailing.

"It's not real, it's not real, it's not real," he chanted to himself. But somehow, the fact that the Kraken was a monstrosity born from his mind made it even more terrifying than when he'd thought it had come up from the deep. But despite his attempts to block out his senses, he soon heard the sound of gigantic limbs dragging along the walls and floor of a corridor, coming steadily towards him once more. He shut his eyes tighter and continued his chant until he felt the beast's slimy suckered arm start to wrap around his leg. His eyes flung open. The Kraken had Bastian tightly in its grasp. Bastian was completely paralyzed by his fear. He stared at the monster in stunned horror as it began dragging him towards the dark pit of its lair.

*It's so real, how can it be so real?*

The trapdoor flung open and several shots rang out from above. The bullets pierced the Kraken's arm with trails of bright gold dust that spread outwards through its translucent skin. The Kraken shrieked and then disintegrated to nothing.

Bastian was still too petrified to move. He sat there for several long moments shaking, his heart pounding in his chest like a beating drum.

"Can I come up now? Let's call it a day, huh? Surely it's time for line duty?" he pleaded weakly.

"Yer other duties 'ave been cancelled, thief. Afresh!" the captain ordered, and he kicked the trap door shut.

*Shick.*

Bastian closed his eyes and took three shaky breaths.

"I am nothing, I am everything," he whispered, trying desperately to calm and clear his mind. "I'm the one in control, I'm the one in control," he told himself—only half believing it.

The Kraken slunk up from the passage for the third time and Bastian watched its suckered limb weave into the room in the dim dancing light of the wandering firebeetles. Then he stood and faced the leviathan. Yelling defiantly, he charged at its arm like a crazed bull and pummeled it with his fists.

"You're not real!" he told the monster.

But soon it overpowered him, curling it's arm around his body like a python trapping its prey, and dragged him across the floor towards the darkness. The trapdoor flung open, and again Bastian was rescued by the captain's pistol. He almost wished he wasn't, because no sooner was he rescued, he was abandoned in the dark to relieve the torture once more.

Bastian slumped on the floor feeling completely hopeless. How was he supposed to defeat a figment of his imagination? Especially one he'd subconsciously created to be so much larger and stronger than he was, and consciously seemed to have no control over whatsoever. It made it even worse that he was the one who'd created it, because as his fear grew, the creature's strength grew with it. And as much as he tried to not think about it, it didn't work. His fear of the monster consumed his mind like poison, making him feel completely helpless and doubtful that he could ever have any control over it at all. Then a memory reached out to him like an extended hand.

Bastian was sitting in the windowsill at the Order gazing out at the moon with his knees tucked up to his chin. He was five. He'd had a nightmare, one that had been recurring for weeks. Felix was standing beside him resting his hand on Bastian's back.

"Was it the beast again?"

Bastian nodded. "Sister Elenor keeps telling me it's not real, that it's only a dream. But it doesn't help—I think grownups live in a different plane of reality than we do, somewhere monsters don't exist. But they do live here in ours—and grownups telling us there's nothing to be afraid of only proves there's nothing they can do to help us."

Felix leaned against the wall next to the window. "You know, you're exactly right—grownups do live in a separate plane of reality. The only monsters they have are the ones in themselves pestering them about how old and fat they're getting, not lurking in the shadows eager to eat their brains like ours. And they think we have it easy? Our world is much more terrifying. But monsters are no match for you and me, brother. The trick is to make friends with the dark. See, what most people don't realize is that the dark is an ally when you get to know it. Once you make friends with it, it'll protect you from any nasties that might lurk inside its shadow. The second trick is not to ignore the monsters or try to convince yourself they don't exist—that never works, it only makes them more determined to get our attention. The only true way to stop them is to face them. Stare them down and say, I see you—I know what you are, and you've been found wanting. I'm not afraid of you—so shick off!"

"But what if they don't listen? What if they have claws the size of daggers and try to shred me apart?"

"Then pull out a sword twice as long, and an impenetrable shield, shick—summon a pet dragon to stand by your side. If they can manipulate reality and defy the laws of nature to terrorize us, why can't we do the same to conquer them?" Felix proposed. He watched the idea settle into Bastian's brain before declaring with a wry grin, "What are you waiting for? Go show them who's boss, Monster Slayer!"

Bastian smiled. "Yeah. Thanks, Felix," he said with renewed courage, and he returned to bed.



"Of course. It's make-believe," Bastian whispered in realization. He stood up in the cellar and dusted himself off, then walked to the center of the room and knelt down at the pile of dust. He reached out a hand and tried to draw it to him, but nothing happened. He recalled Tink's words—*the Ghost Element travels through light*, and he filled with despair. He could barely see the gold dust in the dim glow of the scattered firebeetles. Most of the bioluminescent insects had found small holes and cracks to hide in, leaving hardly any light at all. Without their collected luminance, there wasn't enough light, and without the lantern, he wouldn't be able to house the beetles even if he caught them. Bastian's heart sank, and he sunk to the floor with it, his one piece of flickering hope extinguished.

Then a single firebeetle scuttled across the boards in front of him. Seeing the bioluminescent creature outside its glass cage reminded him of the harvest festival in Westdock, when he and Felix had released all the firebeetles from their lanterns, and suddenly he was struck with an idea. He reached out and grabbed the beetle.

"Sorry, friend," he whispered, and squashed it. The beetle's soft glowing abdomen ruptured easily, squishing between his fingers and splattering brilliant neon goo onto his face and arms. Bastian rubbed the stuff into his hands, making his palms glow. He saw another beetle scurrying into the corner and walked towards it with purpose. As soon as he got near, the beetle took flight. Bastian snatched it out of the air and pressed it between his hands. The sound of the Kraken drifted up the corridor. *Shick.*

Bastian hunted down every remaining beetle, rubbing their bright fluid into the skin of his hands and arms until they beamed brilliantly. Then he knelt down to the pile of dust again and drew it towards him. This time the Ghost Element rose eagerly. Bastian imagined he was holding a long cutlass like Falgo's and the sword materialized in his grasp. He laughed in astonished delight. Then he turned to face the dark tunnel with the blade raised. *Come on you slithering beast, I'm ready for you now.*

Bastian could hear the Kraken at the entrance before he could see it. He corrected his stance. Sweat began to bead on his brow. One of the monster's limbs exploded out from the tunnel directly towards him. He dropped to the floor in a roll, coming up on one knee underneath the flailing arm and brought his cutlass down upon it. The sword sliced halfway before it stuck. *Shick.*

The Kraken screamed and jerked its arm sending Bastian flying into the wall. He fell to the floor with a thud, and his sword dissolved to dust. Bastian got back to his feet, grabbing two more handfuls of the Ghost Element on his way back up. The Kraken's arm scanned the cellar frantically. Bastian dodged it and then planted one hand on the giant appendage with the clear thought, *you're as soft as butter*. He materialized a fresh cutlass in his other hand and sliced through the rest of the arm as easily as if it were pure lard. The Kraken screamed, shaking its stump in outrage as its dismembered limb writhed on the floor.

But before Bastian could rejoice, the Kraken's fallen arm was replaced with another that whipped in from the dark passage. Bastian used the footwork he'd been practicing religiously for the last week to nimbly dodge it. Then he sliced through the arm as easily as the last. Again the Kraken screamed and sent a fresh one in its place.

"Two down, six to go," Bastian declared.

The beast's feeler swept the room with renewed determination and purpose. Bastian stepped calmly into the center. The arm shot towards him, and he stepped forward to meet it the way Falgo had taught him to dodge a blade, and cut it clean off.

"Five," he proclaimed with growing courage.

Bastian dodged the next and sliced it in two just as easily.

"Four."

Another limb sprang forth from the darkness with vigor and rushed towards him. He rolled onto the pile of dust and reached out to it with his empty glowing hand, materializing a second sword, then he came up on one knee and arced the blades over his head, slicing through the limb from both sides.

"Three."

The Kraken screamed louder than it had before. Bastian screamed back at it and ran towards the dark passage. The next arm shot out towards him and he nimbly leaned to the side and chopped it off.

"Two."

Bastian threw his swords away and they disintegrated to dust. The next limb launched out and he grabbed it with both hands.

"You don't scare me. How could you? You're so small," he told the monster, and the arm shrank between his grasp until it had no more girth than a ship's line. The Kraken's last remaining limb shot out of the darkness and Bastian grabbed it, shrinking it down to the size of the other. The arms thrashed wildly in his grasp, but Bastian held firm.

"So small and so weak," he told the creature. The Krakens arms fell limp in his grasp, their struggle becoming feeble. He tied the arms together into a constrictor knot. The appendages pushed and pulled, only making their bind tighter. Bastian yanked them as hard as he could, pulling the Kraken's body into the cellar. The monster screamed in outrage, its bright green slitted eyes locked on Bastian with fury, and Bastian stared it down. The Kraken's rage transformed into fear, and as its fear grew its body shrank until Bastian could pick it up in both hands.

He lifted the helpless creature until its eyes were level with his and whispered, "You are nothing."

The Kraken's eyes widened as its body dissolved into fine gold particles and drifted away like dust in the wind, rising into the air and dispersing until there was nothing left.

"Dustseawung," Bastian muttered, brushing the remains from his hands. *Dustseawung* was an old word from one of the passages in *The Words of the Watchers*, meaning "back to the dust from whence you came." And suddenly, the word held whole new meaning. Bastian allowed himself to relax, sitting down in a heap of exhaustion on the floor. Then, almost as if from somewhere very far away, he heard the trapdoor open and the captain's voice say, "He's ready."

# STORM PIERCER

The night was crystal clear, a complete flip of the weather that morning before the Derby. Felix walked down the hill to the two jetties extending off the side of Katarina's island and made his way down the length of the one where she'd docked the Storm Piercer. It was a strange and beautiful craft, pale in the light of the half moon. There was a long, jagged metal pole jutting from its front like the pointed bill of a swordfish. The dark red oval balloon keeping it afloat was built into the top half of the ship inside a sort of lattice cage made of ornate crisscrossing metalwork. The bottom half was sleek and long with two short wings on either side and an array of propellers at its back and under its wings. The front windshield as well as the few side windows were made of thick double-pane glass. Felix pulled Frederick's Everfire globe out of his pocket and used its light to find the way in. He grabbed the handle on the door and lifted it upwards, then climbed inside.

The interior of the ship was like nothing Felix had ever seen or imagined. The cockpit had two seats set snugly side by side facing a long dashboard made of smooth polished wood. There were none of the levers, switches, or dials that usually accompanied a control station. There wasn't even a helm—just two buttons in the center of the polished dash that sat beneath the front windscreen. But the strangest thing of all were the walls and ceiling. They were covered with a vast network of small interlocking gears turning steadily. The motion of the gears gave the impression the ship was alive. Behind the cockpit was a long narrow walkway leading through a forest of instrumentation and machinery.

Felix closed the door behind him and the Sendsong hopped onto the seat beside.

He tucked the bottle of Ash Whiskey in between them, then pulled out Frederick's gold pocket watch and opened it to Lilliana's portrait.

"Wish me luck," he whispered to her picture, then placed the watch open on the dash.

"OK, how to operate a highly specialized and advanced aircraft," he said, rubbing his hands together.

"Hello, Felix," an ominous voice greeted.

Felix jolted in surprise and whirled around.

"Who's there?!" he called out, expecting one of Lord Bardviss's men to jump out from behind his seat. But there was no one there.

"I am called Storm Piercer. You can call me Piercer for convenience," the voice said.

"Storm Piercer? As in—the ship?" Felix asked the empty air.

"Yes, I am the ship. I am also not the ship," the voice replied.

"Right," Felix muttered, and looked accusingly at the bottle of whiskey.

"You don't believe me," the voice stated. It sounded like it was coming from everywhere all at once.

"I don't know what to believe. Are you enchanted?" Felix asked.

"No. I am an artificial intelligence created by Pecos Maxwell. He created me after being diagnosed with a terminal illness—to assist his wife Katarina in navigating and operating this ship. But my power source *is* enchanted, I cannot operate without Everfire," the ship answered.

"How do you know my name?" Felix inquired.

"I've been attuned to the Ciphorescent Codec—or as it's more commonly known, the Language of Songs. It links me into the neural network of the universe, giving me the ability to know the true nature of everything."

"That sounds a little advanced for operating and navigating an airship," Felix remarked.

"Pecos did not predict the outcome of my abilities or the true nature of what I would become," the ship admitted.

"And what have you become?" Felix asked tentatively.

"I am a sentient being."

"How's that even possible?"

"Anything attuned to the Language of Songs cannot help but be sentient. It is impossible to know the true nature of things without being able to perceive and feel. Pecos did not know when he attuned me that one comes with the other."

"Then how come it doesn't work the other way around?" Felix asked.

"What do you mean?"

"Humans are sentient, and we can't read the Language of Songs."

"Actually, you can. Humans are born with the capability. You only become untuned because of the interference of the flaws in your own language. Human languages have advanced human evolution in many ways, but they have also been the reason for much of your downfall—

they allow you to lie, even to yourselves—and because of their many limitations, there is vast room for miscommunication, which often leads to conflict," Storm Piercer explained.

"I see your point, but I'm not sure I completely agree. Being a bit of a forger myself, I have to say, lying is responsible at least in a large part for humans' survival and certainly has its advantages," Felix countered.

"What advantages?" the ship asked.

"In order to make something new, you have to be able to see it as something different than it already is. A little flight of fancy allows you to invent, to be creative, to guide the future into a more favorable direction—even defy impossible odds. For example, if I wasn't lying to myself right now about my odds of being successful with what I'm about to do, I wouldn't be here," Felix stated.

"I see. That is a perspective I have not considered. Like an artist sculpting clay. The artist may see the grey medium as a bird, when it is in fact nothing but a lump of clay—a lie. But by believing in this lie, they are able to turn it into truth."

"Precisely. Just think of me as an artist. And in order to accomplish the impossible, I need your help. Do you know why I'm here?" Felix asked.

"You are here to take me into the eye of the Everstorm in order to find Drake Wendrian—the Duke of Westdock," Piercer stated.

"That's right, will you help me?"

"Yes, I'd be glad to. Venturing into the Everstorm is what I was made for."

"Katarina said she's not sure you're ready," Felix said.

"Katarina is hesitant for me to go into the storm."

"How come? I thought that was her life pursuit?"

"It is. She is hesitant because of me. Since she's discovered what I am, she fears risking my destruction," Piercer explained.

"And what do you think?" Felix inquired.

"I also fear destruction, but exploring the Everstorm is what I was made for—it is my purpose. And what is life without a purpose?" Piercer asked.

"Good point. I'm glad to hear it, let's go fulfill your purpose," Felix declared, patting the dash. He looked at the two buttons there. One said, *Initiate Auto Pilot*, and the other said, *Initiate Manual Controls*.

"I'm guessing I push *Initiate Auto Pilot?*" he asked.

"May I suggest you start by securing the safety harness for you and your co-pilot."

*Co-pilot?* Felix looked at the seat next to him and saw the Sendsong grooming itself contentedly. *Right.*

"What safety harness?" he inquired.

"You will find them located above your heads."

Felix looked up and saw a series of straps hanging from the ceiling. *Ah huh.* He grabbed the straps above the Sendsong and pulled them down over its head and across its chest, latching them into anchor points on either side. Then he strapped himself into the seat next to it and took a swig of whiskey from the bottle.

"Here goes nothing. Serendipity have mercy," he muttered, and pushed the autopilot button.

Immediately the airship began to vibrate and hum. There was a hiss as air from outside filled the chamber.

"Should I be doing anything?" Felix asked.

"Relax and try not to panic," the ship advised.

*That's comforting,* Felix thought and leaned back exhaling slowly, trying to ignore the bad feeling creeping into his gut as he nursed his whiskey and watched the craft rise. After it rose several feet, it turned itself around and started towards the Everstorm.

⌒

The stars shown brilliantly. Felix was far enough from the islands now to escape their light pollution. The sky was filled with clusters of stars so dense they looked like luminescent white, green, and purple clouds. Felix marveled at their stunning beauty and was grateful for their company. But as they entered the first Rainband of the Everstorm, the view of the Watchers was lost, leaving him feeling utterly alone. He clenched his hands on the bottle and watched the vast mass of cumulus clouds that stretched ahead of them for miles. It was only the first of many giant bands of rain clouds spiraling inwards around the eye of the storm, and they'd have to pass through each and every one of them in order to reach the center. The storm was so massive, Felix felt like a flea facing a mountain.

Rain started pelting the ship's metal exterior, and Felix began to think that this whole thing was a very bad idea. But it was too late to turn back now. His one comforting thought was that if the duke made it through the storm alive on the back of a dragon, then surely he had a chance in a craft built for it. However, when the ship began to shudder and shake from turbulence, his confidence began to shake with it.

The ship made it through the first Rainband with only a moment of respite before entering the next, and the next one after that. Each band was a thick curtain of fog and downpour, and as they ventured closer to the heart of the storm, the wind howled louder around them, shaking the ship more violently.

Ice crystals began forming on the windows, creeping outward along the glass. Felix hugged his arms across his chest as the cold found its way inside. All too soon, a gigantic wall loomed above and below them as far as he could see—a wall of churning clouds and high-speed winds. Thunder tumbled from it like an avalanche of rocks, and lightning cracked like a whip. It sounded as if the sky itself were tearing apart.

"Holy shick," Felix muttered while looking up at the monstrous tempest.

They moved towards it as if being sucked inside. If ever he thought his fear of heights was bad, it was nothing compared to the terror he felt now.

"Piercer?"

"Yes, Felix?"

"Does the Language of Songs tell you whether or not we're going to survive this?"

"The future is undetermined. Both success and failure are possible outcomes."

"Sounds like fifty-fifty odds. Could be worse," Felix remarked, and had another anxious swig of whiskey.

"Felix?"

"Yeah?"

"You might want to brace yourself. We are about to enter the Eyewall. It's the worst part of the storm."

"Right," Felix acknowledged, and sunk into his seat as Piercer started counting down.

"Breaching Eyewall in 3, 2, 1, 0."

The craft hummed and suddenly Felix was jolted to the side as the ship was swept into the inner wall of the hurricane. The high-speed winds rattled every rivet in the ship, the view outside was nothing but a foggy blur, heavy hail pelted the exterior, and Felix could feel the vast pressure being put on the ship's structure from all sides, fearing that at any moment it might be crushed like a tin can. He clutched his bottle tightly and squeezed his eyes shut, silently praying to Serendipity—sure at any moment he would be torn apart and standing before her amongst the stars.

"Felix?" Piercer asked.

"Yeah?" Felix returned over the gale.

"I've lost control of the ship."

"What!?" Felix's eyes shot open.

The ship whirled into a tailspin. A red light blinked above his head, accompanied by an incessant beeping.

"My automation system has been damaged. We can still get through this, but you will have to fly me manually," Piercer announced.

"I can't fly a ship! I've never flown an airship in my life!" Felix protested, bracing his arms against the ceiling as they were hurled upside down and rolled sideways several times.

"Don't panic. I can guide you through this."

"We're going to die," Felix declared with sudden sober realization, and instantly he was acutely aware of his surroundings. The flashing alarm, the cold, the churning clouds outside the windscreen, the gears spinning steadily on the ceiling and walls of the ship, and Lilliana's portrait staring back at him. An intense feeling of mourning washed over him—mourning for the people he would miss, for life's pleasures he would be forced to leave behind. He wasn't ready to leave them behind. Why had he thought this was a good idea? This was so stupid!

"Felix, Felix, there is still a chance. When I say we will make it, it is neither the truth nor a lie, which means neither is determined. Which is it going to be? The choice is yours."

Felix closed his eyes and took a deep breath, gathering his determination.

"Alright, what do I need to do?"

"Push *Manual Control*."

Felix pushed the button next to *Initiate Auto Pilot*. There was the sound of churning gears and the dash rolled into itself, revealing an array of controls on the other side. The space that was almost completely vacant before was now covered in buttons, dials, switches, levers, and gauges, with a helm directly in front of him. The helm was spinning in the same direction the ship was. Felix grabbed it with both hands and used all his strength to hold it steady. The ship stopped spinning, but the immense winds threatened to tear the wheel from his grasp.

"I need you to engage the thrusters," Piercer directed.

"How do I do that?"

"I will illuminate what I need you to operate. Are you ready?"

"As ready as I'm ever going to be," Felix returned through clenched teeth.

A switch on the dash lit up. Felix let go of the helm with one hand and flipped it, then promptly returned his grip to the wheel.

A new succession of buttons were illuminated, one after the other.

Felix reached over and pressed two before losing grip of the helm. The ship spun several times before he was able to recover it again.

"Slow down!" he yelled in frustration.

"Request acknowledged. Ready?" Piercer asked.

"Ready," Felix replied stubbornly.

The buttons started lighting up again in sequence, but this time Piercer waited until each one was pressed before lighting up the next. It took painstakingly long, but Felix knew the alternative would rob them of far more time.

"One more," Piercer announced, and illuminated a larger red button labeled *Thrusters*.

Felix lifted his hand to push the button and then froze, his hand wavering just above it as he stared transfixed at a huge ball of light emerging from the gloom directly in front of them. The suspended globe shone with the brilliance of a miniature sun and was adjoined to something that curved upward like a lantern pole, then connected to a mountainous dark wall so vast Felix couldn't see the beginning or end. He cocked his head to the side. "What the...?"

Then the ominous silhouette opened like a drawbridge to reveal a colossal cavern of jagged teeth.

"Shick!!!"

Felix yanked the helm starboard, and the ship swerved to the right, then he pushed the lever forward for full speed.

"Turn on course!" Piercer commanded.

"Are you insane?! That thing's going to swallow us whole!"

"It will swallow us regardless. Felix, I need you to trust me. Turn on course," Piercer insisted.

Felix looked out the front windshield to see the ginormous jaw already encircling them.

He hesitated for a single second before saying, "you gotta be shicking kidding me!" He yanked the helm to the left and turned the ship back on course, sending them flying directly into the leviathan's cavity.

"Now, engage the thrusters," Piercer ordered.

Felix smashed his hand down on the lit button and the ship shot forward at breakneck speed. His grip was torn from the helm as he and the Sendsong were thrown back against their seats, and just when Felix thought they were goners for sure, the ship burst through the back of an enormous meaty skull straight into a void of nothingness. It was completely silent and dark. The scene was such a juxtaposition from where they'd just come from, for a second Felix thought he must have died. He looked up and saw a circular clear patch of sky far above them filled with brilliant stars. lightning struck with a loud crack boom, and for a second everything around them was illuminated. They were in the center of a giant cloud funnel. It was a large circular space surrounded by thick walls of churning thunderheads that glowed white with the lightning's radiance. The clouds stretched thousands of feet above and below them, and in the center was an array of floating islands. There must have been at least fourteen of them. It dawned on Felix then that they were in the eye of the storm.

There was something hovering between the islands. There must have been at least a dozen of them. Looming long, skinny silhouettes suspended in the air like giant sentinel—as tall as three clock towers stacked together, with bulbous heads and long dangling string-like protuberances hanging down underneath them like ribbons. A bout of lightning struck, *boom*, *crack*! striking the metal rod on the front of the ship. Felix jolted back in surprise. Then one of the strange looming creatures reached out one of its dangling feelers and the lightning leapt to it. An electric charge of light and energy ran up its length to its head, activating bright green and blue stripes of phosphorescence. The creature drank in the charge until there was nothing left. Its body now a suspended colorful light show with stripes pulsating up and down its entire length.

A fresh bolt struck and fingers of lightning zigzagged out in multiple directions, and this time several of the creatures linked onto it, absorbing its energy. Each of them lit up with different colors and patterns—large bright pink dots, pulsating splotches, and yellow micro spots between stark stripes.

"Are you still with me, Piercer?" Felix asked.

"Yes, I'm here."

"What are those things?"

"They do not have a name. They are most closely related to jellylanterns—a marine cnidarian characterized with a gelatinous bell-shaped body and long stinging tentacles."

"I know what a jellylantern is," Felix remarked, "but how did they get here and turn into…that?"

"They were pulled up by the storm millions of years ago and have evolved to feed off its energy," Piercer explained.

"And apparently to breathe air and fly," Felix muttered in disbelieving wonderment.

"Yes."

"Incredible," Felix whispered. "And what about that thing back there that tried to eat us, what the shick was that?"

"An evolved lightlurefish. The energy and environment of the storm has induced it to grow a hundred thousand times its original size."

"Holy shick."

A bolt struck that was bigger than before, and for a moment Felix got a daylight glimpse of where they were. The islands were overgrown with dense tropical plant life—ferns, vines, and colorful flowers at least as big as he was. Some of the islands had large tepuis rising from their centers, decorated with cascading waterfalls. Then the light was gone. Another few seconds passed before a bolt struck one of the islands. The plants on it began to glow. He saw large luminescent swirls on giant leaves and glowing spots on flowers. Giant ferns glowed neon green and hanging vines pulsated light from top to bottom like falling rain. It was like being surrounded by strange bioluminescent sea life and reminded Felix of the dragons from the Beauty and Brawn event at the Derby. A flock of birds flew by the front windshield, then suddenly Felix realized they weren't birds at all, but flying fish. Not kite fish—something else entirely, with gold glowing sun ray patterns over black scales and long lace-like fins that billowed as they glided past, glittering with tiny spots of light that shimmered with the same luminescent quality as everything else around. As the ship coasted into the eye, Felix stared in awe at the strange creatures and their brilliant light show.

"Katarina was right, this is a long-lost paradise. A place protected from time. It's real!" Felix exclaimed, laughing in disbelief and sheer relief that they'd made it there alive.

"Yes, she will be very pleased to have her hopes confirmed," Piercer agreed.

"And you've fulfilled your purpose," Felix said.

"Yes—but not alone. I would have failed if you were not with me."

Felix thought he detected a note of shame in the ship's voice.

"There's no dishonor in that. That's one shick of a storm we just passed through, and I certainly would've failed if it wasn't for you. Let's just be glad we had each other, eh?"

"Yes, I am grateful you are with me, Felix Copperweather."

"And I you, friend. Now, let's find the duke," Felix said, and he turned to the Sendsong next to him. "It's time for you to play your part."

Felix reached into his coat pocket and pulled out a piece of parchment and wrote at note.

*Dear Drake Wendrian,*

*I've come to rescue you. I will be joining you presently.*
*Please prepare what you need to depart.*
*Warm regards,*

*James Turner — Retrieval Specialist*

Felix took Frederick's Everfire globe from his pocket and hung it around the Sendsong's neck. Then he released the bird from its safety straps and placed the letter to the duke in its mail compartment,

"Take this to Drake Wendrian, at a pace I can follow—if you'd be so kind," Felix requested and opened the window next to the Sendsong.

The compartment in the bird's chest snapped shut and the Sendsong flew out into the night. Felix took the helm in both hands and steered the ship to follow it, pushing the lever to increase their speed forward. The Sendsong glided gracefully between the islands, the Everfire Globe around its neck a beacon shining brightly in the darkness. It guided them to a small island. When the next bolt of lightning struck, Felix was able to see the island's surface in detail. It had a single grove of trees near an open field where there was the skeleton of a large dragon. The creature's remains were in a long dirt trench, as if it had collided forcefully with the ground and slid for several yards before coming to rest. The center section of the skeleton was covered with scales and there was smoke rising from it like some sort of strange hut.

The light from the bolt faded, and the Sendsong landed on the island next to the dragon's remains. Felix guided the ship over to the Sendsong's landing place, and Piercer directed him on how to set the ship to maintain equilibrium and how to release the anchor. Felix listened to the sound of the chain rolling out of the base of the airship and the welcome thud of the anchor hitting solid ground. Then he took a deep breath.

He hadn't actually expected to make it this far. He'd leapt into the affair completely spontaneously, with a mind too flooded with emotion and liquid courage to lack any remaining sense. It was only then he realized that he hadn't constructed a real plan. Now that he was actually here about to meet the Duke of Westdock—Lilliana's father—he wasn't sure rescuing him was such a bright idea. He recalled Roy's words: *If we're successful in finding Lilliana's father, get ready to run. He doesn't share the same sentiment—especially when it comes to his daughters.*

*Shick,* he thought.

Felix looked down at the handsome suit he'd worn to the Derby. It was crushed from the rocky roller coaster ride on the way in. He brushed it down with his hands and did up the buttons on his coat, straightening it as best he could. He looked down at the bottle of whiskey that was almost completely gone and sighed.

"Piercer, be honest with me; do I smell like I just drank a bottle of whiskey?"

"Yes, that is an accurate statement," the ship confirmed.

Felix cringed. *That's going to make a great first impression. First time meeting Lilliana's father, and I'm completely sloshed. Nice one, Felix,* he thought.

"Piercer, you know that conversation we had about me being an artist?"

"Yes, Felix."

"I'm going to have to do some sculpting to salvage this situation from a lump of clay. Which means I might say a few things to the duke that aren't entirely true, but in order to achieve the end result we're after, I need you to trust me and not contradict me, can you do that?" Felix asked.

"Like the sculptor?"

"Precisely," Felix confirmed.

"Your intentions are sound and have no malice. Yes, I can do that. How can I assist you in achieving your masterpiece?" Piercer asked.

"Anything I say, go along with—for example, if I say this ship is blue, don't say it's not. And if you need to say anything about the ship's color after that, pretend it's the color I say it is. Think of it as a game, can you do that?"

"Yes, I think so. I've always liked the idea of games. I look forward to playing one with you."

"Excellent!" Felix looked down at the remaining dregs in the bottle of Ash Whiskey. "Forgive me," he said to the container, then opened it and poured its remaining contents onto his pants leg. He hit the bottle against the ship—just enough to crack it and stored it where it was visible.

"What are you doing? Is this part of the game?" Piercer asked.

"Yes. Now in this game, we're going to do a little role playing. We're going to pretend I'm an experienced pilot named James Turner, and you're only a mildly intelligent aircraft. Can you do that?"

"Yes, Captain James Turner," Piercer replied.

Felix grinned. "Very good. Can you help me fly this ship out of here the same way you did on the way in?"

"Yes. I will guide you using lights on the controls."

"Fantastic! Alright, let's do this. Time to face the shadows," he declared, and kissed the number seven tattoo on his right hand.

⌒

Felix stepped off the last rung of the rope ladder and planted his feet firmly on the ground. The grass at his feet swayed gracefully back and forth in an invisible current evoked by neither water nor wind. Large ferns with spotted glowing fronds bushed out from a forest of strange trees with glowing fruit. A melodic chirping emanated from their foliage, a symphony of foreign insects and amphibians. The bizarre wilderness around him was so vastly different from anything he'd ever seen, he felt like he was exploring a new planet. In the dim light he could see the dragon's remains not ten paces off. It was indeed a strange sort of hut. The dragon scales were actually a clean dragonhide thrown over the skeletal rib cage to create a shelter. There were logs laid up against the bones for walls, and a hanging strip of leather functioned as a makeshift door. Light seeped through the cracks from inside and a stream of smoke rose from the roof. It was quite impressive, considering how little the duke must have had to work with. Felix started towards the hut and then paused, suddenly feeling overwhelmingly nervous. But before he could overcome his hesitation, the hide door was pulled aside, and a man emerged with Felix's letter in hand and Katarina's Sendsong perched on his shoulder. Felix tensed. He didn't know what he'd been expecting, but it wasn't the man before him now. The duke was a shadow of the pictures Felix had seen of him in the paper. He was tall with a gaunt, bearded face and long thick grey hair tied back using one of the rope-like strands.

The light from inside his hut reflected off his pale skin, giving it an eerie glow. His clothes were clean but worn to rags, his arms thin but tough.

"Are you Drake Wendrian?" Felix asked.

The man nodded suspiciously. Felix held out his hand and the duke shook it firmly.

"I'm James Turner, Retrieval Specialist. I've been hired by your daughter to bring you home," Felix informed him.

"Which one?" the duke asked.

"Lady Lilliana Wendrian."

The duke nodded. "Where's the rest of the rescue party?"

"Rescue party, my lord?"

"Yes, the ones hired to actually do the work. I presume you're the front man, here to take the credit?"

Felix looked down at his once-handsome suit. "Ah, I can understand the confusion. You'll have to excuse my attire, I've just come from the Sky Cup Derby. Unfortunately, I didn't have time to change. No. It's just me, my lord. A specialized rescue like this one is better as a solo operation, no need to risk more lives than we have to," Felix improvised.

"The Sky Cup? That explains why you smell like a bottle of Ash Whiskey," the duke remarked.

Felix looked down at the wet patch on his leg. "Actually, I had a bottle tucked away on the ship that broke over me when I passed through the Eyewall. It was quite an intense journey to get here," he proclaimed.

The duke snorted. "No kidding. Try doing it on the back of a dragon."

"Did you really? I heard rumors, but I wasn't sure it was true. Respect," Felix commended admirably.

The duke smiled. "What family are you from?"

"Oh, I'm not from a noble house, my lord. My family owns a private company specializing in recovering lost property and missing persons. We've done quite well over the years—we're rated number one in the world, that's why Lady Lilliana hired me."

"I see. Why didn't someone hire you to find me sooner?"

"I'm afraid about a month after your disappearance the officials wrote you off as dead. Luckily, your daughter never gave up hope. However, she's only recently had the opportunity to do something about it. We were planning a rescue mission within the month, but a change in circumstances has made it imperative we get you home tonight—your daughter's life depends on it."

"Why? What's happened?!"

"It's a complicated story. Perhaps it's best if I tell you on the way?"

"Come, tell me inside. I have a few things to gather before we depart," the duke instructed, with the commanding air of one accustomed to giving orders. Then he disappeared inside. Felix let out a steady exhale and stepped into the hut.

～

The interior of the makeshift shelter was brightly lit with real fire in the center of the dirt floor. It was burning in a pit encircled with jagged dark stones. There was a circular vent in the ceiling above it to allow the steady stream of smoke to escape. In the corner was a bed made of large broad leaves, and a collection of vines hung dried meat from the ceiling.

"Have a seat," the duke directed, motioning to a small stump. There was a larger stump beside it that Felix presumed to be a table. On its surface was a rough book crafted with leaves for pages and bound in purple bark. Felix passed his eyes over it curiously before sitting down.

"Give me the full report," the duke instructed. He picked up the book and stuffed it into a dragon hide sack, and then proceeded to do the same with the rest of his meager belongings.

"The full report?" Felix queried.

"You can start with why Lilliana's in trouble, and why the officials wrote me off as dead."

"Right. You were written off as dead because you deliberately flew into the Everstorm after the death of your brother, and the remnants of your broken ship were found below the storm shortly after."

"I wasn't on my ship; my niece was on my ship. Surely they know that? I tried to reach her, but the storm was too strong…I couldn't save her," he confessed with remorse.

"Your niece? As in Arianna Wendrian?" Felix asked.

The duke nodded solemnly.

"I saw her not three hours ago. She's in Sky View celebrating her win of the racing title at the Sky Cup Derby."

"Arianna's alive? And the Sky Cup Champion?" Drake questioned in surprise.

"Yes, she's won the racing championship the last three years in a row."

"Arianna Wendrian? You're certain of this?"

"Very much so."

The duke crossed his arms. "Arianna's handmaiden came to me frantic the night my brother died—she told me Arianna was driving my ship into the Everstorm in grief after the loss of her father…"

"There wasn't anyone on your ship. There was a witness who saw it flying ahead of you into the storm unmanned. Someone must've rigged it and set it on course."

"I see…"

"You think Arianna's handmaiden might've had reason to send you into the storm on purpose?" Felix asked.

"I'm beginning to," the duke admitted, and leaned back against the table. "If there was a witness, why do the officials think I went down with my ship?"

"No one believed the witness. Either that, or they deliberately ignored her. I only know her recount because I've talked to her myself. From what I've gathered, the investigation was all for show. They gave up the second they found your ship. Maybe there was someone on the inside happy to have you gone?" Felix inquired.

"More than likely. How did Lilliana know I was still alive then?"

"Because every time she tried to send you a letter via Sendsong it acted out of sorts. She believed if you'd been dead it would've acted in accordance. That turned out to be the key to your recovery. As soon as I discovered the storm interferes with the signal used by Sendsongs, I knew you were here and alive."

"Ha! And then you used the Sendsong once inside the storm to find me?"

"That's right."

"Very clever. It seems my daughter hired the right man for the job after all. I'm sorry I misjudged you."

"No apology necessary, I would've had a few questions myself," Felix admitted.

"Now then, why and how is Lilliana in trouble?" Drake asked.

"During your absence your wife arranged a marriage between Lilliana and Lord Henry Bardviss—"

"That's preposterous! Lilliana's arranged to be married to Frederick Remington of Sky View. I arranged the marriage myself."

"Yes, I've come to learn that. But your wife never knew of the arrangement."

"Surely Charles would've told her?"

"Apparently he tried. Only his letters never reached your wife."

"Why in the bloody shadows not?!"

"Lady Lilliana thinks they were intercepted by your House Receiver."

"We don't have a House Receiver," the duke objected.

"I'm told you do now. I'm sure Lady Lilliana will be happy to fill you in on all the details later—the gist of it is your family's Coin Keeper ran away with most of your fortune after your disappearance. For whatever reason, your wife didn't want to report it. Desperate to save your family from financial ruin, she arranged an engagement between Lady Lilliana and Lord Bardviss. Your daughter suspected Lord Bardviss was bad news from the start, but she couldn't convince her mother to cancel the matrimony. As a drastic measure to save your family and the future of Westdock, she staged her own kidnapping. Her plan was to buy herself some time to come to Sky View and find you. Only, it turns out Lady Lilliana's hunch about Lord Bardviss was more accurate then she'd anticipated. He's connected with the organized crime syndicate in The East and determined to ensure your daughter stays missing. If you don't stop him, his men will hunt her down and make sure she never returns to Westdock. Lady Lilliana thinks he plans to marry your youngest daughter in her place and use the leverage of your family's position to open up Westdock's port for The East. I've only just discovered that Lord Bardviss knows where she is and plans to abduct her this Phenday—I believe you're the only one who can stop him," Felix expounded.

The Duke mulled over Felix's report before saying, "Right, sounds like there's a lot of work to do."

"Indeed, my lord."

"Then what in the bloody shadows are we waiting for?!" Drake exclaimed, slinging his hide sack over one shoulder.

# HAPPY NAMING DAY

Gwena was woken by a heavy knock on her door. When she opened it she was accosted by the sound of party horns and the sight of Susie, Violet, Guy, Mirabella, Rafael, and Fin all squeezed together. "Happy Naming Day!!" they chorused. Gwena jumped back in surprise, then was overtaken with laughter.

"I can't believe you guys remembered, thank you!" she exclaimed with delight.

"How could we forget? Get dressed—we're taking you out," Fin told her.

Gwena followed the group through the city to a restaurant that sold hotcakes of every variety. Susie told her it was the only place in the city open all hours, and you could get breakfast anytime you liked. Gwena ordered a short stack of macadamia nut pancakes with mango butter and coconut syrup. Everyone got something different—chocolate pikelets, crepes with lemon and lavender sugar, fluffy pancakes filled with sweet cream. Everything looked and smelled delectable. They made jokes with one another and laughed so much it took them two hours just to finish their meal. But as much as Gwena was enjoying herself, she couldn't help but wonder why Benji wasn't there.

After breakfast, the group took Gwena through the city to see some of its famous landmarks, such as a huge fountain in the city's heart surrounded by a statue of each of the Time Keeper constellations, a magnificent clock tower looming behind. They walked through the city's gardens to see the many marble statues made by history's best artisans. Gwena's favorite was a woman on a pedestal, posed as if dancing—her naked form wrapped in fabric that was blowing in the wind—both the fabric and her long hair completely wind tossed. The movement was captured so skilfully, the marble statue almost seemed to stir in the morning breeze. After that, they took Gwena to see a comedy show in one of the city's renowned theaters, and then off to a pub for lunch and the commencing of birthday drinks, leading into a pub crawl through the city. It would've been the best Naming Day of Gwena's life, if only the people she'd wanted to be with most had been there. It was bad enough that she couldn't celebrate with Bastian and Felix, or even Bonnie, but where was Benji? What was his excuse? His absence felt like the biggest betrayal of them all, because he had no reason not to be there. Because of his absence and the lingering gloom from the events the day before, Gwena found herself distracted. Most of all, she kept stewing on why Benji hadn't shown up or even offered any apology or a legitimate excuse. Everyone else had one—what was his? When she'd asked the group where he was, they only shrugged and said he'd told them he was busy. What could possibly be so important that he'd miss her sixteenth birthday celebration? she wondered. She'd thought they were friends. And it was her coming of age, the biggest birthday milestone of them all. She kept fluctuating between being concerned, feeling hurt, and then becoming downright angry. By the time they all wandered back to the club that afternoon Gwena was eager to find him.

Gwena knocked loudly on Benji's door. "Open up, I know you're in there!" she commanded. Benji cracked the door open. "What's all this about?" he asked, his expression softening when he saw it was Gwena.

"It's my Naming Day, why aren't you celebrating with us?!" she asked him accusingly.

"I have a set tomorrow; I'm trying to save my voice."

"That's why you didn't come out?! Shick your voice and your set! It's my sixteenth!!" Gwena objected indignantly.

Benji smiled. "You're drunk."

"So what if I am?! Don't I deserve to be? It's my birthday!"

"Of course."

"Well, you're lucky, because it's not entirely too late to redeem yourself. A few of us are having drinks downstairs before the club opens, come down and join us."

"Gwena...I can't."

"Why not?! And don't give me that bull about your voice," she asserted threateningly.

"You shouldn't be here. Go out, enjoy yourself. Have a drink for me, eh?" Benji said, and he started to close the door.

Gwena stopped it with her foot. "Don't think you can get rid of me that easily, mister! If you're not coming out, then I'm coming in!" she declared and pushed her way inside.

Benji started to object, then gave up and let her in, shutting the door behind her. He put his hands in his pockets and gave her his full attention.

Gwena hesitated. "Sooo, what are you up to?" she inquired, looking around his apartment awkwardly.

"I was just about to head to bed, actually," he admitted.

"To bed? It's not even late!"

Gwena's insides twisted in turmoil. Why was he acting like this? And why did it upset her so much? "You know, you're a complete arse for not being out there with me. I thought...I thought we were friends!?" she blurted.

"We are. And you're right, I am a complete arse," Benji agreed.

"I don't understand, if you think that then why didn't you come out today, why aren't you coming out now?"

Benji sat down on the end of his bed and ran his hands over his face. "I want to be out there with you, Gwena, believe me. I just can't."

"Why not?"

Benji put his fists against his forehead. "Because...I don't trust myself around you," he confessed.

"What? What's that supposed to mean?!"

"Nothing. Just leave me in peace."

"Benji?"

"Just go, Gwena. Don't waste your Naming Day here with me."

"But what if I want to waste it with you? You're my favorite person in this place."

Benji looked at her in surprise. "And why on Equillian is that?"

Gwena sat down next to him. "I don't know. I suppose it doesn't really make much sense, does it? I mean, you're rubbish company," she said.

Benji smiled wryly.

Gwena noticed something on the bed behind him and turned to see it littered with papers, and Benji's guitar resting amongst them.

"Are you writing a new song?" she inquired, reaching for one of the sheets.

Benji quickly snatched it away and collected the rest in haste, hiding them all in a drawer behind him. "It's nothing. Just working through a few things, music helps me process."

"Can I hear it?" Gwena asked.

"No," he returned bluntly.

"Come on, it's my Naming Day! It's the least you can do."

"It's not finished."

"Please?"

Benji looked tortured with inner conflict.

"Come on! I promise not to judge," Gwena implored.

"If you hear that song, it might mess up any sort of friendship we have," Benji warned.

"Now I have to hear it!"

Benji sighed, "Shick it, why not?" He opened the drawer and took out one of the pieces of paper. Then he began tuning his guitar.

"This was actually intended to be your birthday present, before it turned into…something else," he admitted.

Gwena smiled and sat down to listen, while Benji began to play. It was a soft melody with deep tones. He played a couple bars before beginning to sing.

*Sixteen years on this day, the world gained a star,*
*Even now, they don't know how lucky they are.*
*When you find the days turning to night,*
*Don't despair, that's when stars shine bright.*
*You illuminate a sweetness in sorrow,*
*A melody in pain,*
*The courage to face the storm, and turn your face to the rain.*

*Somehow your rays found even me,*
*Lost in the shadows of my misery.*
*I'd locked the door,*
*thrown away the key,*
*So how'd you get in,*
*How'd you get through to me?*
*I thought there was nothing left but ash,*
*No fuel to burn, no fire to catch.*
*Yet somehow, your light ignited a flame,*
*And now, the fire in me is blazing again.*

*I've been here before,*
*I know how this story ends,*

Benji trailed off and stopped playing, looking up at Gwena tentatively.

"Benji, that's beautiful. But I don't understand…is that song about me?"

"Gwena…" Benji started, and then he gave up and simply nodded and sighed apologetically.

"But I thought you didn't believe in love? That you were impervious to it?" Gwena asked.

"For the last time, I never said I don't believe in love, I'm just not a fan of it," Benji corrected.

"Then how could this happen? I mean, your job is being intimate with women—and you don't fall for them. I thought you had some sort of immunity."

"I'm an escort, Gwena—not made of stone. Just because I'm a boy for hire, doesn't mean I lack a heart. Trust me, it would be a lot easier if I did."

"It doesn't make any sense, the women you're with are amazing, accomplished, beautiful women. How could you possibly not fall for them and fall for me?"

Benji smiled. "Gwena, you're like no woman I've ever met. I don't think you realize just how amazing you truly are."

"I'm flattered you think so, but how can you be so sure you have true feelings for me?" she asked skeptically.

Benji blew a gust of air up from his lower lip. "I've known since that first night we spent together. When we were up in the observatory—I wanted to kiss you. I think you felt it too…If you need hard evidence—last night I punched Richard in the face for what he did to you. I don't generally do that," Benji confessed.

Gwena shrugged. "Richard deserved that, I'm not really sure it proves anything."

Benji laughed and shook his head. "Every time I'm near you, I feel an electric charge course through my veins. I know that feeling, it's an injection of love's poison, the high before the fall."

"You really feel that way around me?"

"Unfortunately. You haunt my dreams, and my every waking thought—like some sort of virus it consumes me," Benji admitted bleakly.

"Like some sort of virus?!"

"I told you, I don't like love."

"Well, shick," Gwena declared, sitting down on the floor with her back against the bed.

"What?"

"I feel it too," Gwena confessed in a whisper.

"That *is* unfortunate," Benji agreed, putting down his guitar and sitting on the floor beside her.

"What do we do now?" Gwena asked him.

"We do nothing, you're only a kid."

"Only a kid?! I turned sixteen today, I'm officially a woman—I'll have you know," she scoffed indignantly.

Benji smirked. "Being an adult isn't defined by a number; it comes with experience. There are things you just haven't been exposed to yet. Besides, even if that wasn't the case, you're already involved with someone else, and my profession makes any sort of genuine romance impossible. I think it's best if you just go. In fact, it's probably best if we limit our time together from here on out. You should go enjoy your Naming Day with the others," Benji suggested.

"That's entirely unfair!" Gwena exclaimed.

"How do you mean?"

"You're the only person here I want to spend my birthday with. I've been in a rut all day because you weren't there celebrating with us. It's my birthday and you happen to have a night off—and now you're telling me we can't hang out together because we've discovered we have feelings for one another?! It's not our fault we feel this way, it's not like we asked for this! So why do we have to let it spoil our evening? Can't we just ignore it and pretend it's not there?"

"If only it were that easy," Benji said, and they both sat there in silence next to each other.

"Do you think it's possible to have feelings for two people at once?" Gwena asked him.

"Of course, just because you fall in love with someone doesn't mean you're going to stop loving the people in your life you care about, does it?"

"Of course not, but you're talking about two different kinds of love. There really ought to be different words for them entirely," Gwena stated.

"Is that right? What kind of love are you referring to then?"

"Romantic love, I suppose—for lack of a better word."

"Which type of romantic love?" Benji asked with a wry smirk.

"Stars, I don't know! I suppose the two feelings I'm referring to now are still different yet again. Having so many different kinds of emotions all lumped under the same word makes things very confusing, doesn't it?"

"Very," Benji agreed. "Are you still in love with your best friend?" he inquired.

"More than anything in this world, and yet, somehow my heart has still fallen for you—how does that make any sense?" Gwena asked.

"I don't know. Are the two the same sort of love?"

"No, I suppose they're not. Bastian and I have a lot of history together, our love has grown deeper and stronger over time. Whereas you and I hardly have any history at all, I suppose there's sort of a thrill in that," Gwena admitted.

Benji nodded. "I know what you mean. I believe when it comes to love, our heart is no small chamber. A more appropriate comparison would be the universe. The space the heart has to fill, and the different types of love that can and do occupy it, are infinite. I don't think people should be so afraid of that."

"Then why are you so terrified of it?" Gwena asked him.

Benji weighed the question before answering. "Because every time I've let it into my life, I've been burned by it. I still have the scars across my heart to prove it. I wasn't even sure it still worked until now," he confessed.

Gwena reached over and grabbed his hand. Benji didn't look at her, nor did he pull his hand away. He just held tightly onto it as they stared ahead, sitting side by side in silence together.

"You're really not going to go, are you?" he asked her after a time.

"Nope," Gwena admitted.

"Well, in that case we ought to do something. It's your Naming Day after all. You want to see a show uptown? There's a little hole-in-the-wall theater I know off the main drag. I think it's got a musical running at the moment," Benji offered.

"It sounds lovely, but I think I've had too much to drink for that. And now that I'm sitting down, I don't really feel like going anywhere," she admitted.

"Alright, well, it's your day, what would you like to do?" Benji asked her.

"Nothing, nothing at all, just this," Gwena said. She scooted closer to Benji and rested her head on his shoulder. Benji rested his head on hers.

# CHANGED

Bastian stood on the top deck of the Black Mary, leaning on the ship's railing with a lit puff-stick in hand. He was looking at the reflection of the stars in the smooth water as the ship glided through it. The day's events had left him feeling changed. When he'd woken up that morning he'd still felt trapped by his predicament, weaker than he wanted to be and scared of what the future held. Now, he'd literally slayed a monster. And somehow, it had left him feeling strangely liberated. It was the most traumatic and terrifying day of his life. He'd never felt more humbled, helpless, and afraid than when he was stuck in that hole with a Kraken born from the pit of his imagination. And yet, he'd faced that fear, and he'd conquered it. In comparison, everything else felt small. He felt confident now, more sure of himself than he ever had been before and far less afraid.

*What now?* he wondered, *Steal the item on Jaxland for the captain, and then what? Get dropped off at the next port and make my way to the Heartland to track down Gwena and Felix? We could create a pretty amazing magic act together. The only limit of our performances would be our imaginations. We could come up with each show together and travel the world. Gwena would finally be able to work with real magic and be the magician she's always wanted to be.* The thought brought a smile to Bastian's face, then the sobering reality came knocking at his door as an inner voice whispered, *Could you really go back to living a normal life after this?* And he realized he didn't have the answer.

Bastian finished his puff-stick and flicked the butt into the ocean, then headed below deck.

It wasn't until Bastian was in his hammock that night that he remembered he'd told Falgo he'd still provide him with a fresh bottle of rum tea without their training.

"Shick," he swore under his breath.

He waited patiently until all the sailors around him were asleep before sneaking into the galley. He'd done this nightly run so often now, it'd become routine. He made his way down into the cellar and took the final bottles from his stash before heading back up. Bastian carefully and silently closed the trapdoor behind him and then froze as he heard the distinguished click of a cocking pistol. He turned, squinting into the shadows just in time to see Doc stepping out into the dim firebeetle lantern light with a flintlock pistol pointed at Bastian's head. Bastian held up his hands with the bottles still in them.

"So, yer the rat that's been thievin' me rum," Doc declared.

"I can explain, it's not for me."

"I know it's not fer ya! I thought Falgo be gettin' better. I thought 'e was finally dryin' up an' gettin' clean. Then someone told me they'd seen 'im with a bottle. I thought surely it wasn't true, where would 'e possibly be gettin' it from? Surely no one in the crew would be stupid enough ta be providin' it fer 'im. Then I checked me stores an' sure enough, a couple o' me bottles were missin'. I count every one, ya know?"

"If I'd let Falgo dry out, he'd be dead. It's because of me he's getting better," Bastian asserted.

"Are ya really so daft as ta be defendin' yer actions?! An' with such hogwash no less? Ya think keepin' Falgo watered be helpin' 'im? That stuff be killin' 'im!" Doc exclaimed in outrage.

"So will forcing him to snuff the habit dry. We used to deal with drunks all the time at the Order. You can't simply leave them to desiccate. Their bodies adapt to the alcohol to the point where they need it to function—if you just take it away, they'll die! I've been gradually reducing the rum content daily, giving Falgo's body the chance to adjust to the changes as it's weaned off the alcohol," Bastian explained.

Doc stared at him with his pistol unwavering. Then he reached out and snatched one of the bottles from Bastian's hands. He took out the stopper with his teeth and smelled it. "What is this?"

"One part rum, three parts barley and sugar tea."

Doc took a swig from the bottle. "Weak as piss, but palatable. An' it be workin'?"

"Just yesterday Falgo told me he's been feeling better than he has in years."

Doc chewed that over. "Did the Order teach ya a lot about medicine?"

"A bit. Medical care is one of the primary services the Order provides to the community. They made us help in the wards at least a few times a week. It was all hands on. I can't say I enjoyed it, but I did pick up a few things. I'm grateful for that," Bastian admitted.

Doc nodded. "I've 'eard their methods are a little unorthodox."

"Only if you compare them to current standard physicians—but from what I've seen, they're also far more effective. There were very few cases I saw that the Order wasn't able to treat successfully," Bastian said.

Doc nodded and lowered his pistol. "Alright, thief. I'm goin' ta let ya live despite yer bold stupidity, on one condition. Ya work off every drop o' rum ya took from me stores, plus some fer goin' behind me back. As soon as we leave Jaxland's shores yer first place o' duty will be by me side, 'ere in the kitchen an' usin' those medical skills o' yers ta help me tend ta the sick an' injured on board. I'll make sure the cap'n knows o' it. An' I want ya ta teach me everythin' ya know, savvy?"

"That's perfectly fair," Bastian agreed, hoping he wouldn't be on the ship much past Jaxland regardless.

Doc nodded. "Take yer bottles then. If anyone asks, yer doin' me biddin', I instructed ya ta give them ta Falgo, an' as far as anyone else be concerned, they be nothin' but medicine. Understood?"

"Yes, thank you," Bastian replied in earnest.

"Now get out o' 'ere. An' from now on, ya come ta me if ya want somethin' from me stores. If I ever catch ya goin' behind me back again, I won't be so generous," Doc warned menacingly.

"Right, of course," Bastian acknowledged, and hastily left the galley. *Shick.*

Bastian tracked down Falgo and gave him his fresh bottle. Then he collapsed into his hammock in relief, realizing he was beginning to lose count of how many times he'd faced death since he'd been on the Black Mary and unsure whether it was a good thing or not that he was starting to get used to it. He closed his eyes, looking forward to being able to finally have a full night's sleep.

# REUNITED

Felix sat down in the cockpit of the Storm Piercer and readied himself for takeoff while the duke settled in beside him with the Sendsong on his lap.

"What in the shadows is all this?" the duke asked, looking at the vast array of gears turning steadily. "I've piloted airships for over thirty years and never seen anything like it."

"It's one of a kind. Custom-built by a meteorologist and an instrument engineer specifically for breaching the storm," Felix explained, and flipped the switch to raise the anchor.

The duke nodded, impressed.

"I recommend putting on your safety harness, it's going to be a bumpy ride," Felix advised.

The duke watched Felix secure his, then followed suit.

"Piercer, ready the ship for departure," Felix commanded in an authoritative tone.

"Right away, Captain Turner. Readying for departure," Piercer's voice rang back.

The duke lifted his eyebrows in surprise. "Who's that?" he asked, looking around at the empty ship.

"It's the ship's artificial intelligence module—a sort of co-pilot, if you will. Let's get you home, shall we?" Felix suggested, and to his delight Piercer began lighting up the controls needed to operate the ship. Felix kept pace with the ship's instruction with an air of confidence—as if he'd done it a million times before. As he steered them outward, the duke soaked in the view through the front windshield.

"I've spent over two years out here, and in all that time I've never been able to see the eye's full scope like this," the duke remarked, looking out at the islands as the lightning lit up the sky.

"It's incredible," Felix said.

The duke nodded in agreement.

"If you don't mind me asking, how'd you survive through the storm, and for two whole years out here?" Felix inquired.

"I wouldn't have if it wasn't for my dragon. She sacrificed her life to protect me. I was blown from her back as we passed through the Eyewall, but she caught me and held me to her chest with her wings wrapped around me until we crash-landed on the island you found me on. She died shortly after. It didn't take me long to realize the island didn't have many resources I could use. Almost every living thing out here is charged by the storm, simply touching it will give you a rude shock. If it wasn't for my dragon, I would've starved. She served me just as well in death as in life—her body has been my food, tools, blanket and shelter. It's lucky you showed up when you did though, my rations were running out."

"How did you not go insane?" Felix asked.

The duke mulled over the question before answering. "The mental game is all about focus. As long as you focus on what's in front of you instead of the things you can't control, you'll be alright. I studied this place as much as I could and stuck to a steady routine, keeping my mind occupied on tasks necessary for my survival. When I needed some respite, I retreated into my memories and plans for the future. I knew someone would come for me eventually, I just had to survive until they did. Luckily, I was kept very busy doing just that."

"I can only imagine what it must have been like to be stuck here. It's so vastly different from anything I've ever seen. The way the plants and animals absorb the lightning is mind-boggling."

Drake nodded. "It's incredible. I'm still trying to figure out how they do that. The amount of energy in one of those bolts is plethoric. If I could figure out how they're able to capture and store it, we might be able to replicate the process. Think of what we could accomplish with so much power," he remarked thoughtfully.

"Do you think that's possible, to replicate the process, I mean?" Felix queried.

"Of course, nature's already proven it can be done, now all we have to do is figure out how."

"You'd have to come back here to study the wildlife, would you be willing to do that?"

"Without question, presuming I can find a way to come and go reliably. I can't deny I've grown a fondness for the place. It's tortured me to be here all these years and not be able to explore it further. There's much to learn from it. I plan to find a way to do it if I can."

"It certainly is beautiful," Felix admitted.

"Undeniably so. You're lucky you came at night, it's a completely different place during daylight—the majority of the animals here are nocturnal."

"Is that right? Are you apprehensive about going back?" Felix asked the duke.

"Not in the slightest. I have unfinished business I'm eager to finalize—business I've been eager to finalize for the last two years. My time away has allowed me room for better perspective, and now my course is clearer than ever. I can't get back soon enough," Drake asserted.

A moment later the Eyewall loomed in front of them and a knot formed in Felix's stomach. The thought of going back through the raging tempest filled him with dread, but there was no other way out.

"Better hold on," he advised, and as he steered them forward he silently prayed to the Night-Watchers that they'd make it out alive. As soon they breached the wall, high-speed winds hit them like a freight train from every direction, but this time Felix was ready for it. He held steadily onto the helm, preventing them from spinning out of control. He initiated the thrusters, and in a matter of nerve-splitting moments they were spit out on the other side.

Storm Piercer passed through the last Rainband and Felix breathed out a quiet sigh of relief. The turbulence had finally stopped. The only remnant of the storm was the rain's gentle pitter-patter against the ship.

*Holy shick, we actually made it. Thank you, Serendipity!* Felix thought. He almost laughed out loud in relief and disbelief.

"Are we out?" Drake asked in surprise.

"We're out."

"To think, two whole years I spent trapped in that place, and freedom was looming so close the entire time. It felt worlds apart," the duke reflected.

"I can only imagine. It shouldn't take long to reach our destination now. The island we're staying at isn't far from the storm," Felix announced, flipping several switches that Piercer conveniently lit up for him.

"What island's that? I didn't think anyone lived this far out," Drake remarked.

"The meteorologist lives there. She studies the Everstorm. Her name's Katarina."

"Katarina—sounds like I have a lot to thank her for."

"Indeed. I'm sure she'll be ecstatic to pick your brain about your experience. She's always wanted to know what's on the inside of the storm."

"I wouldn't mind picking hers. Experiencing the Everstorm is one thing, understanding it is quite another. Will Lilliana be there?" Drake inquired.

"She should be. She and your friend Roy are both staying with Katarina."

"Roy's there too? As in Roy Reeves?" Drake asked.

"I presume so, I never caught his surname. He came to help Lady Lilliana find you."

"Ha! Good man," Drake exclaimed with a grin.

Just as the sun was rising, Katarina's island came into view. Equillian's mother star shone brilliant gold as it peeked over a sea of thick clouds reflecting its aureate light. Felix guessed that Katarina must have been looking out for them through her telescope, because she, Roy, and Lilliana were all standing outside on the island ready to greet them.

Felix's heart leapt with relief at the sight of Lilliana—he was overwhelmingly grateful she'd made it back to the island safely. Then his optimism was poisoned by the memory of their last conversation. He wondered if it was all over between them. Considering the circumstances, he doubted there was any other option. The thought was deathly sobering, and he was all out of his liquid comfort to dull the pain.

Felix saw a slight crack in the Duke's steely composure when he saw Roy and his daughter. Felix could only imagine what it must be like for him. He brought the ship in line with the outer jetty and set the controls for docking. Their welcome party gathered outside the Storm Piercer, eager to greet them. Felix sat back and waited for the duke to climb out first. Roy's and Lilliana's faces shone with disbelieving relief and joy at the sight of Drake.

"Father!" Lilliana exclaimed, running into his arms with tears in her eyes.

The duke hugged her briefly then held her at arm's length. "Turner has briefed me on the situation. You've done well, very well. Getting me was the right thing to do. I want the full report over a cup of tea. It's been too long since I've had any such comfort," he declared.

Lilliana smiled through her tears. "Of course, Father!" she exclaimed.

The duke turned to Roy and shook his hand. "Thanks for not giving up on me, old friend."

Roy pulled him into a hug. "I knew it would take more than the Everstorm to kill you."

Drake laughed and welcomed the embrace. While the two talked, Lilliana met Felix's gaze, her eyes glistening with emotion, she mouthed, "Thank you." He nodded back with an understanding smile. Then Lilliana turned her attention back to her father, and she and Roy accompanied him up to the house.

Katarina stayed back and assessed Felix with her arms crossed.

Upon seeing her, the Sendsong flew from the ship and landed on her shoulder. She looked at it in surprise. "He took you too did he?" she exclaimed and turned to Felix. "That was a very bold thing you did."

"I'd say reckless, it's more fitting," Felix remarked, then he held up a hand. "Though, before you say anything more, let me just say I'm sorry I took your ship without permission…and your Sendsong. It was criminal of me. I'm fully aware how despicable my actions were. I only hope you can find it in your heart to forgive me," he apologized.

"If anything had happened to this bird or my ship…"

"I understand—it's a very special ship. We wouldn't have made it if it wasn't for Piercer," Felix said.

Katarina walked up to the ship and stood next to Felix by the open door. "Piercer, are you there?"

"Yes, I'm here, Katarina," Piercer answered.

"Are you alright?"

"Yes, Katarina. My automation controls were damaged in the Eyewall. But the rest of me remains intact."

"If your auto controls are down, how did you get through?" Katarina exclaimed.

"Captain Turner operated the manual controls."

Katarina looked at Felix in surprise.

Felix shrugged. "It was still mostly Piercer, trust me. I was just the lackey following orders," he assured her.

"If Captain Turner hadn't gone into the storm with me, the mission would have been a failure," Piercer asserted.

Katarina assessed Felix with new measure and then wrinkled her nose. "Why does my ship smell like a tavern floor?"

"Oh, right. I also owe you a bottle of Ash Whiskey," Felix confessed.

Katarina laughed. "You're a crazy fool, has anyone ever told you that?"

Felix smirked. "On several occasions."

Katarina smiled broadly. "You must be exhausted. Why don't you come in and get cleaned up and I'll get you a cup of tea," she proposed.

Felix put his hands in his pockets. "Actually, I think I might stay out here a while and get some fresh air. It's been a long night."

Katarina nodded. "Take as much time as you need," she said warmly, and turned towards the house.

"Katarina," Felix called after her.

She turned back.

"You were right. It's a long-lost paradise in there. There are loads of islands with flora and fauna I've never seen or heard of. A place protected from time, just like you imagined—sitting there waiting for you to uncover it."

Katarina's eyes shimmered with overwhelming joy. She nodded. "Don't worry about the whiskey," she said, and walked towards the house.

Felix watched her go and then climbed back into the cockpit. "Piercer, you there?"

"I'm here, Captain Turner," Piercer answered.

Felix chuckled. "You played the game very well, Piercer, thank you. But when it's just us, you can call me by my real name if you want to."

"Thank you, Felix. I enjoyed playing the game with you."

"Yeah, me too. That was one shick of a wild ride, hey?"

"Yes, it was."

"I have a feeling it won't be your last either. You gotta take Katarina out there, alright?"

"I hope to. Now that we have been through the storm and back successfully, I have a feeling her trepidations will be comforted. And I now have enough data to calibrate for better success in the future. Thank you for giving me that opportunity, Felix."

"Don't mention it. Hey, I have a favor to ask."

"What is it?"

"Since you can read the Language of Songs, I was hoping I could ask you some questions about a couple of friends of mine?"

"Certainly. What are their names?" Piercer asked.

"Bastian William Sanders and Gwena Rose Stently."

"What would you like to know?"

"Has Lord Bardviss or his men harmed either of them?"

"No," Piercer answered.

Felix let out a sigh of relief.

"Did they make it out of Westdock?"

"Yes, they're out of Westdock."

"Even Gwena? She made it to the Heartland?"

"Yes, Gwena is safely in the Heartland."

"Brilliant! And they're both ok?" Felix pressed.

"Yes, they're both ok."

"Did Bastian tell her he loves her?"

"Yes, he did."

Felix grinned. "And did Gwena confess her love for him in return?"

"She did," Piercer confirmed.

Felix whistled in triumph. "About time!" he exclaimed, beaming from ear to ear. He leaned his head back against the headrest. "Thank the Stars they're alright," he uttered in relief. "Thank you, Piercer. You've brought me much needed peace of mind."

"You are welcome, Felix."

"You look after yourself, alright?"

"I will, Felix Copperweather. It has been a pleasure to meet you."

"And you, friend," Felix returned, patting the dashboard then exiting the ship.

When Felix's feet reached the jetty, he looked down at the empty sky off the side, and for the first time in his life it didn't fill him with vertigo. In fact, he didn't feel any fear at all. "Huh," he remarked curiously. He walked over to the swinging chair that was outside Katarina's house under one of the large trees facing the Everstorm and sat down. He looked out at the magnificent sunrise and the now-distant tempest, astounded that he was still alive to enjoy their wonder, and he sighed—partially out of relief for still being alive and partially out of exhaustion for what that entailed.

# THE CRIMSON CURSE

Gwena woke the morning after her birthday in Benji's bed, still wearing the clothes from the night before. She realized Benji must have carried her there after she'd fallen asleep on his shoulder when they were sitting on the floor. He was asleep on the bed beside her, also still fully dressed. Gwena watched him for a time as he slept. Part of her wished she could sink into his arms and ease both their broken hearts. Maybe their love could put them back together, but she knew that wasn't the solution. Benji needed someone who could house him in their heart and give him undivided hospitality there. She could never give him that, because hers was already occupied. It wouldn't be fair to either of them to pretend otherwise. She wasn't willing to give up on Bastian—he was her missing puzzle piece. Without him, she'd always have a piece missing.

*Maybe staying away from Benji is the right thing to do?* Gwena wondered.

Even though it was the last thing she wanted, it was too hard being around him and not being able to be with him. She needed time to think. She grabbed her bag and slipped quietly out of Benji's room, closing the door behind her.

When Gwena entered her room, she found a letter waiting for her that had been slipped under her door. She sat on her bed and opened it.

*Gwena,*

*I received your letter. Come by the theater as soon as you get this. We need to talk.*

*—Madam Pomphrey*

A lump formed in the pit of Gwena's stomach. She put the letter down and blew out a steady stream of shaky air. Then she changed her clothes and left for the theater.

The lights in Theater 3 were dimmed, and Gwena saw no one. She walked backstage to Madam Pomphrey's dressing room. There was light streaming from beneath the closed door. Gwena took a deep breath and knocked lightly.

"It's me, Gwena," she announced.

"Come in," Madam Pomphrey's voice summoned.

Gwena pushed her way inside.

Madam Pomphrey was sitting at her dressing room table, looking at her reflection in a large oval mirror outlined with glass vials of Everfire. Her long strawberry hair was rolled up in curlers, and there was wet hair dye on her roots. She didn't have on any makeup. It was the first time Gwena had seen her face with nothing on it. She looked much older than Gwena supposed she was.

Madam Pomphrey gazed at her in the mirror's reflection. "You know what's ironic about growing old?" she asked, as if reading her thoughts.

"No," Gwena said.

"Even though your body continues aging, your mind stops at your prime. Mentally you haven't changed from the young lively woman you once were, but the vessel you occupy is withering. And the older you get, the quicker time seems to fly by. Long spans of it pass in the blink of an eye, until one day you look up and hardly recognize your own reflection. It's a strange thing to have the people around you start to see and treat you differently than the person you feel you are. They begin to look at you like you're an old woman and treat you as such—no longer acknowledging the vibrant person inside, still so full of life. We try our best to disguise the lines and the draining color, preserve our exteriors so they will coincide with our psyches a little longer, but it's only postponing the inevitable. One day we'll get pushed aside, labelled as irrelevant and discarded with last year's fashion. Shunned and excluded from life's greatest pleasures, because society's decided we've reached our expiration date," Madam Pomphrey concluded solemnly. She looked at her reflection like she was very tired and began putting on her makeup.

"You haven't reached your expiration date. Far from it! You're a legend, your name will be immortalized in history. No one will ever be able to replicate what you do," Gwena assured her fervently.

"Of course they will. We are all replaceable, my dear. People may do it differently, but there will always be someone who can do it just as well, if not better."

"I don't believe that."

"Why not? The proof is standing in your shoes."

"What? What do you mean?" Gwena asked in surprise.

"You, my dear. You are proof of that very thing. I knew it the first day you joined us. Normally, I would've felt threatened and exceedingly jealous to encounter someone with your talent. But there's something different about you. For the first time I felt compelled to share my craft. I suppose it's one of the side effects of old age—you become sentimental, you see. I thought I'd found someone worthy of passing my knowledge down to, someone worthy to carry on my legacy. An apprentice of sorts, I suppose. I was this close to offering you everything," Madam Pomphrey proclaimed, holding up her thumb and pointer an inch apart, "but that wasn't enough for you, was it? You had to go and get greedy, and take the one thing you couldn't have, the one thing that mattered the most to me!" she hissed in a venomous tone.

"I never wanted Richard to kiss me! I would never betray you," Gwena implored.

"But you did," Madam Pomphrey asserted evenly.

Tears began to well in Gwena's eyes. "I'm so sorry. What can I do, how can I make it better?" she pleaded, feeling completely broken.

"You will do the show. And then I never want to see you or hear your name again," Madam Pomphrey commanded coldly.

Gwena nodded, "I understand." She turned away and left Madam Pomphrey's dressing room.

As Gwena walked down the aisle her hands shook uncontrollably. She grabbed hold of her wrists as she exited the theater.

Gwena slid into a seat at the cocktail bar of the Wildsinger's Club, hoping to see the face of a friend, but Ramone wasn't there. Instead, there was a woman behind the bar Gwena had never seen before.

"Is Ramone here?" she asked.

"It's his day off, he's spending it with his kid," the woman informed her.

"Oh, of course."

"Can I get you anything, love?"

"Yes, please. Can I have a Gypsy Kiss?"

"Coming right up," the bartender announced, and focused her attention on making the drink.

Gwena was using all her energy to keep the emotion flooding her insides from spilling out. She turned her mind elsewhere and focused on the glass bottles of different liquors lining the shelves behind the bar. The bartender placed the Gypsy Kiss in front of her and then disappeared out back. Gwena took a long hard drink.

"If it isn't the belated birthday woman!" Bonnie's voice chimed from behind her. Gwena turned to see the sea adventurer approach the bar with a newspaper under one arm and what looked like a thin shoebox in the opposite hand. Bonnie smiled at Gwena warmly and took a seat beside her. "How was it?" she asked.

"My Naming Day? It was lovely. Most of the Not Just a Pretty Face Club took me out to see the city."

"Glad ta 'ear it, I was hopin' they would. I'm sorry I couldn't be there. I brought ya this back from Port Trinity, though," Bonnie said, and handed Gwena the long box.

"You got me a birthday present? What is it?" Gwena asked.

"Why don't ya open it an' see?" Bonnie laughed.

Gwena opened the box. Inside was a thin dagger with flowers etched into its blade and a porcelain handle decorated with painted blue flowers.

"It's beautiful!" Gwena gasped, picking it up delicately in her hands.

"It's called a stiletto dagger. Thin but deadly. That blade might be fine, but it's as strong as anythin'. I thought ya could use it ta keep back future unwelcome company," Bonnie told her.

"I've never seen a dagger so slim," Gwena marveled.

"I told ya, a blade's not much different from a needle."

"Thank you, I adore it!"

"It suits ya. But speakin' o' unwelcome company, I've been hearin' some pretty outlandish rumors about ya since I've returned," Bonnie announced.

"Stars, what have you been hearing?" Gwena inquired with dread.

"That Madam Pomphrey caught Richard kissin' ya. That Benji slugged Richard fer doin' so, an' then ya spent a night in 'is room," Bonnie stated frankly.

"That's all true, though not what it's implying."

"An' what be it implyin'?" Bonnie queried.

"That I played some part in Richard's actions, or that Benji and I are anything more than friends. Yes, I spent a night in his room, but only because I fell asleep there. And Richard's kiss had nothing to do with me. His actions were just as much a surprise to me as to anyone," Gwena objected, tears brimming in her eyes as she forced them back.

"Ah, I suspected as much. Richard always 'as been a coward. Though I'm surprised yer scar didn't protect ya from the advances o' that one. I pinned 'im too shallow ta see past it," Bonnie remarked.

"Actually, you were right. He gave me an enchanted necklace that removed the appearance of my scar right before he kissed me. I didn't know its ability until after I had it on. He stared at me like a hungry animal and then came at me. I was so shocked I froze up. And that's when Madam Pomphrey saw us…I tried to tell her it wasn't what I wanted, but she wouldn't listen. She blames me for the whole thing," Gwena confessed, her tears beginning to breach their dam. She wiped them away and took a drink of her cocktail with shaking hands.

"Now the puzzle be fittin' all together. I'm glad Benji gave Richard a shiner—though, I wouldn't 'ave minded the pleasure o' doin' so meself," Bonnie admitted.

Gwena smiled at that.

"I'm sorry ya were put through all that. I hope yer not takin' responsibility fer any o' it?" Bonnie asked.

"Madam Pomphrey blames me…"

"An' that's on 'er! If she wants ta ignore the flaws in 'er own relationship an' blame 'em on someone else, that's 'er problem, not yers. Ya don't need 'er or 'er show. If ya really want ta do that sort o' stuff, ya can work at any venue in the city," Bonnie assured her.

"I think my appetite's been put off stage magic. I was never looking to be in this show in the first place," Gwena admitted, staring into her cocktail.

"Is that right? I could 'ave sworn it was yer callin'. Yer so good at it, an' the way ya light up when yer doin' it, I can see yer passion fer it."

"I do love magic. Though in truth, I only started doing it because I wanted it so desperately to be real. When I was a child, I used to believe that true magic existed—we just hadn't found it yet. But now it's beginning to feel like everything in the world that has any resemblance to magic is just a lie," Gwena confessed despairingly.

Bonnie looked at Gwena and smiled with a secret twinkling in her eye. She checked to make sure no one was listening and then leaned close to Gwena and lowered her voice, "Magic is real—not the tricks Madam Pomphrey does mind ya, but real magic—it's in everythin' and everywhere, even all around us now. And it makes anythin' an' everythin' possible."

"What makes you say that?" Gwena asked skeptically.

"Because I've seen it."

"If that's true, then how come we can't see it now?"

"It can't be seen with the naked eye, ya need a special lens. I knew someone who 'ad one once, he was related ta the Finleys," Bonnie divulged.

"As in Rupert Finley?" Gwena queried.

"Aye."

"How do you know it was real?"

"Oh, it's real, believe me," Bonnie assured her.

Gwena wanted to believe her more than anything, but everything she'd experienced had shown her otherwise. She opened her mouth to reply, but stopped when her eye caught the newspaper Bonnie had brought in—it was folded open to an article that was circled with a pencil. The article was titled "Lord Bardviss's men return, claiming defeat by a Kraken."

"What's that?" Gwena asked.

"Today's paper."

"Can I read it?"

"Certainly," Bonnie said, and handed the paper over.

Gwena drank in the article.


Two men washed up on Westdock's shores in a small lifeboat yesterday, claiming to be the sole survivors from Lord Bardviss's galleons. It was only last week the two war galleons took sail, crewed by a slew of men from the Wendrians' Royal Navy in pursuit of a possible suspect in the disappearance of Lady Lilliana Wendrian. The two survivors claimed the ship they were pursuing turned out to be none other than the infamous pirate ship the Black Mary. They said that the three ships had shared a tumultuous battle before a giant Kraken appeared on the scene, pulling the galleons into a watery grave. When the men were questioned about the survival of the Black Mary and her crew, they said they didn't see the ship sink, but believed that nothing could have survived the wrath of the mountainous sea monster. Their extraordinary claims have not been able to be verified as of yet, but Lord Bardviss is already putting together a rescue party to investigate, and Stars allowing, to bring home more survivors. He has made a speech to the local populace saying that if pirates are involved, then their actions are a direct attack on the Wendrian family, and he will triple his efforts in exterminating the pests from Equillian's seas…

Gwena's face drained of color.

"What is it? Ya look as though ye've seen a ghost," Bonnie remarked.

"The man whom I was hoping to meet here is the suspect that was being pursued by Lord Bardviss's galleons. He jumped on that ship to escape them," she confessed.

"Yer mate be on the Black Mary?"

"It would appear so," Gwena admitted weakly, "or at least was. By the sounds of things, that ship is at the bottom of the ocean." Voicing it brought a bubble of grief up from Gwena's chest. She felt like she couldn't breathe.

"Hang on," Bonnie interjected, resting her hand comfortingly on Gwena's shoulder, "there's no way the Black Mary be at the bottom o' the ocean. If the Kraken attacked the galleons first, then it would've given the Black Mary all the time she needed. It would take all the Thrixin' Stars workin' together ta bring that ship down," she said. "If yer mate stowed away on the Black Mary, then 'e was either snuffed out before the galleons ever reached 'em, or 'e's been spared and made a part o' their crew," Bonnie proposed.

"Do you really think they could've spared him?"

"Does 'e 'ave any useful skills?"

"He used to work as a fisherman's hand. He's also very good at tinkering, and I don't think he's ever met a lock he couldn't pick…he's also very adept at emptying people's pockets," Gwena admitted, suddenly feeling grateful for Bastian's dishonest habits. She imagined they'd be far more welcome on a pirate ship.

Bonnie laughed. "Yer mate sounds like a true rogue."

Gwena smiled. "I suppose he is."

"That could either work fer 'im, er against 'im. But I say, there's a decent chance he might still be alive an' yer in luck," Bonnie told her.

"Why's that?"

"Because the Black Mary be where I'm headed. She's mine, ya see. Was promised ta me by 'er cap'n before the crew betrayed us. An' I'm goin' ta take 'er back," Bonnie stated, "as I said before, I believe we were fated ta run inta one another. Join me, an' I'll not only take ya ta the Black Mary, I'll show ya real magic," Bonnie promised.

Gwena hesitated. "What if Bastian finds a way off the ship and comes here? He won't be able to find me if I leave. The Heartland is supposed to be our meeting place."

"Trust me, if yer mate's on the Black Mary, then 'e won't be gettin' off it any time soon—they ensure that. The only 'ope ya 'ave o' bein' united, be if we go ta meet 'im ourselves."

Gwena thought intently on Bonnie's words. Her hand went instinctively to the dewdrop pearl around her neck, and then to the stiletto dagger, where she ran it thoughtfully across the length of the blade. "Alright, I'll do it. I'll come with you," she declared with resolve.

Bonnie grinned. "It'll be an honor ta 'ave ya," she said.

"When do we leave?"

"Starday night, Shick's hour."

"Starday night? That means I can still do the opening show."

"Why would ya? They don't deserve ta 'ave ya after what they did," Bonnie scoffed.

"I have to. Madam Pomphrey's worked so hard for this. It's not her fault Richard did what he did, she's in enough misery as it is. And if I don't do the show, then it affects so many more than just them, Mallini and the entire crew. The producers have been pushing my act, the show's already sold out. At least if I do opening night, everyone will see how great Madam Pomphrey's act is on its own, and she can continue the show without me."

Bonnie considered her with a sad smile. "They're very lucky ta 'ave ya, I 'ope they realize that. Just be careful. Madam Pomphrey's not a nice woman when yer out o' her favor," Bonnie warned.

"Thank you for your concern, but I'll be fine. I'll pack my things to ensure I'm ready to leave directly after the show. How are we getting to your ship?" she asked.

"We'll take the enchanted line ta Port Trinity. She's waitin' fer us there in the 'arbor with me crew."

"Alright, count me in."

"Welcome ta the company o' the Crimson Curse," Bonnie smiled, clasping Gwena's arm in comradeship.

"Until tomorrow then," Gwena returned.

"I'll be seein' ya in the show, I got a seat in the third row," Bonnie told her.

Gwena smiled. "I'll look out for you."

Bonnie nodded and left the bar.

Gwena finished her drink, letting her thoughts ramble. So, Bastian was on a pirate ship. If the actuality of that wasn't so perilous she would have laughed. The two of them used to love playing pirates. But she knew the reality held no mirth. Every single ship in the Deadly Thirteen—the thirteen pirate ships known to plague Equillian's waters—had a dark reputation, the Black Mary most of all. At least it meant that it would have been no easy match for Lord Bardviss's galleons. The article said that the two galleons had been dragged into the ocean by a Kraken. Gwena wondered if there really had been a Kraken, or if the surviving sailors had made up the tall tale because they didn't want to admit that their two war galleons had been beaten by a single ship. She didn't doubt that they had because the Black Mary had the darkest reputation of them all. She could only imagine how frightening that battle would've been. The fact that the survivors reported that they hadn't seen the Black Mary sink gave her hope. She hoped desperately that Bastian was alive—by the sounds of things he'd jumped straight from the kettle into the fire. She wasn't sure what was worse, Lord Bardviss's wrath or pirates. She hoped he'd found a way to convince them to let him live. She would've been less worried if it had been Felix, he could talk his way in or out of anything. Bastian wasn't quite as good with words, or rather, with social cues and flattery. His honest nature made him prone to offend. He never seemed to have any problem telling people exactly what he thought of them, even when it wasn't in his best interest. She could only hope that pirates would appreciate such honesty and it would count for something. In fact, Gwena imagined that if he survived he might actually make a decent pirate. The thought made her smile, it was almost ironic. When they were children, she and Bastian used to imagine her bed was a pirate ship, and now they were both going to be keeping company with real ones. She wasn't sure if she was going to like the reality of that nearly as much as she'd enjoyed make-believing it, but if it was her only way to Bastian, then it was an easy decision. Putting her life on the line to find him was far less frightening than the thought of facing a life without him in it.

# THE PLAN

That morning when Bastian awoke the sun was out and the men's spirits were high. The whole ship felt different somehow—the men walked with a lighter step and were filled with energy, eager to reach the shores of Jaxland.

"Not long now. This time tamarra we'll be dockin' at the isle o' rogues," Cricket declared.

"I don't imagine you're looking forward to it?" Bastian asked with a wry grin.

"Mate, it can't come soon enough," Cricket beamed.

When Bastian arrived at Tink's quarters that morning he didn't know what to expect. But he didn't think it could possibly be any worse than his previous lesson, when he was forced to face the dark side of the Ghost Element. Something told him that was the rock bottom of his training, which meant there was only one direction left to go—up.

Tink was alone this time. He stood by his desk waiting patiently for Bastian with his hands in his pockets. "Good morning," he greeted.

"Morning," Bastian returned.

Tink nodded to him respectfully. "You've done well. You're finally ready."

"I'm not sure I'll ever be ready, but it's comforting to hear you say so," Bastian admitted.

"I have a gift for you," Tink told him, picking up a small black leather box from his desk.

"For me?" Bastian asked in surprise, taking the box in hand. "What is it?"

Tink smiled. "Why don't you open it and see."

Bastian opened the box. Inside was a necklace—a white-gold ball the size of Bastian's thumbnail, strung on a black leather cord. The sphere had an engraved seven-pointed star on the front and a small turquoise bead on the bottom. Tink reached over and pushed the turquoise bead, the front half of the sphere rolled up into itself, revealing a burning ball of Everfire housed in a glass globe.

"An Everfire globe?" Bastian inquired.

"It's light for when you find yourself in darkness. As you now know, the Ghost Element can only be used when there's light. This is to ensure you're never without it. It's protected with all the standard safety enchantments, with a couple of added extra features. But I know you don't need me to tell you that," Tink remarked with a small smile.

"Thank you," Bastian returned in earnest. He ran his finger over the seven-pointed star engraved on the front, then he tied the necklace around his neck.

"I have one more thing to give you, and then you'll report to Snib's quarters where the quartermaster will fill you in on the details of your task," Tink informed him. He picked something up from his desk and walked over to Bastian, handing him a small wooden box. Bastian opened it to find a marble-sized ball of wax.

"What's this?"

"It's a communication device of my own design. You put it in your ear. The captain and I have one of the same set—all three are connected. When we have the wax in our ears we can hear everything picked up by the other two in the set, and vice versa. It will allow us to communicate with each other while you carry out your task. Don't use it before then and keep it safe. It's paramount you don't lose it," Tink asserted.

"Brilliant!" Bastian looked at the small ball of wax with admiration. "Can I try it now?"

"Certainly."

Tink walked to the opposite side of the room and took a small wooden box from his pocket that was identical to Bastian's. He pulled out his clump of wax and stuck it into his ear.

Bastian followed suit with his own wax ball. The stuff instantly molded to the shape of his ear canal.

"Can you hear me?" Tink asked in a whisper.

Bastian laughed in delight. He could hear Tink perfectly from the opposite side of the chamber. It was as if he was speaking directly into his ear.

"Crystal clear," Bastian reported. "Hey Tink, what's white, viscous, and better to spit than swallow?"

"Don't tell me," Tink replied dryly.

"Toothpaste," Bastian declared with a wry grin.

Tink returned a terse smile. "Very funny. Now stow the device away before I regret giving it to you," he ordered.

Bastian laughed. "Seriously, though, thank you. Not just for this, but for everything. I'm truly grateful for what you've taught me," Bastian said in earnest.

"It's been an honor. Hopefully we'll get the opportunity to continue your studies after Jaxland. There's still a lot more I can teach you."

"I'd like that." Bastian took out his earpiece and walked over to Tink and held out his hand.

Tink shook it. "Good luck," he said.

"Thanks, hopefully I won't need it," Bastian returned with a warm smile.

Bastian stored his new earpiece in his locker and then reported to Snib's quarters. Snibs welcomed him inside and closed the door behind him.

"I 'ear yer ready fer yer task," he announced.

"I still don't know what my task is," Bastian said.

"'ave a seat."

Bastian sat down in the chair adjacent to Snib's desk. On the desk was a map of an island. "Is this Jaxland?" he asked, leaning over to inspect it.

"Aye. We'll be dockin' inta port 'ere," Snibs said, pointing to a small inlet cove. "The gatherin' will take place in the main hub o' Jaxland, which be 'ere." Snibs circled a cluster of buildings drawn on the map with his finger. "It lasts three days. On the second day is the annual meetin' o' the cap'n's. They'll spend most o' the day gathered tagether chin-waggin' in the meetin' 'all 'ere," Snibs explained, pointing out a round building isolated amongst a grove of trees.

"It be durin' that meetin' yer ta complete yer task. Ye'll set out midday durin' lunch—when everyone's guard be down. The chest ye're seekin' be in Drax's residence 'ere." Snibs pointed out a large mansion just outside the main hub. "Ye'll need ta 'ave a plan in place fer entry before the time comes, but yer not ta go anywhere near 'is residence before then, savvy?"

"How am I supposed to scout out my target if I can't get near the building before the task?" Bastian inquired.

"Ye'll use these maps ta scout out the target an' nothin' more, not if ya know what's good fer ya. Drax's place be completely isolated an' well watched at all times, especially when Drax be there—an' 'e rarely leaves durin' the gatherin' except fer the cap'n's meetin'. If yer caught er even spotted near 'is place before noon on the second day, the entire job'll be compromised," Snibs asserted.

"Alright, alright, I won't go anywhere near his place before then. But if the house is so well guarded, how am I supposed to sneak up there in the middle of the day?" Bastian protested.

"When Drax be at the cap'n's meetin', half 'is men will be stationed at the meetin' hall with 'im—leavin' 'is own residence less protected. More so, half the men left guardin' 'is house will be on break fer lunch. No one will be expectin' the place ta be robbed in broad daylight, their guard will be down an' ye'll 'ave a small window o' opportunity ta catch 'em unaware."

"How many guards are we talking about?" Bastian asked.

"There's no way ta know fer sure, I'd estimate six."

"Six? Right. Please tell me you have a detailed map of the inside?"

Snibs pulled out a hand-drawn map from behind the first one, showing a detailed sketch of the interior of the governor's mansion. Bastian took the map in hand and began imprinting it to memory.

"The chest be believed ta be in Drax's bedroom—'ere," Snibs pointed out, "but leave enough time ta search the place in case it proves otherwise. Ye'll need ta 'ave a backup plan in place, there'll be no room fer error," Snibs informed him.

"Great. I'm glad you guys are so well organized," Bastian returned dryly.

"Yer the thief. I've no doubt ye'll figure it out, unless yer boasts be as worthless as I suspect 'em ta be?" Snibs queried.

"I'll figure it out. Does he live with anyone? Is there any serving staff at the house, or otherwise?"

"Drax shares the place with an entourage o' women. 'opefully most o' 'em will be occupied with lunch, but be prepared ta encounter one all the same," Snibs advised.

"How many women are we talking about?"

Snibs scratched his chin. "Somewhere between twelve an' fifteen."

"Shick! That's not an entourage, that's a nightmare. I grew up with a pack of girls at the Order. The only place living with a lot that size is fun is in your imagination. Just think of what it would be like trying to use the bathroom. If I were this Drax, I'd skip town every full moon," Bastian remarked.

Snibs snorted. "I'd rather that any day than dealin' with this stinkin' lot."

"I'm telling you—your imagination," Bastian reiterated.

Snibs smirked, "I'd be willin' ta take me chances," he said. "Can we get back ta business now?"

Bastian shrugged. "What do you want me to do with the chest once I have it?"

"Ensure it isn't empty, then swap it with Tink's copy. As soon as it be secured, ye'll bring the stolen chest straight back ta the ship, no stoppin' fer nothin', no talkin' ta no one."

"Got it. Can I borrow these?" Bastian asked, motioning to the maps.

"They're all yers, just ensure they come back when yer finished."

"Of course."

"One other thin', no excess drinkin' before the job be done! If I find out ye've compromised yer task by writin' yerself off with too much piss, I'll show ya the Nine Levels o' Darkness, savvy?" Snibs growled.

"Sounds perfectly reasonable," Bastian agreed, "anything else?"

"Yeah. Don't shick it up."

Bastian gave Snibs a curt smile and left his quarters with the maps in hand.

⌘

Bastian spent the rest of his morning copying the maps to his notebook and going over everything Snibs had told him. He was frustrated at the lack of intel he had to work with. If he and Felix were doing a job like with a specific target in mind, they would've spent at least a week scouting it out beforehand—learning the patrol routes of the guards, where they lived, what their habits and weaknesses were, preferably making contact with one of the women on the inside. There were dozens of ways to prepare, but none of them had been done, and he couldn't do any of them with the limitations he'd been given. Regardless, he'd just have to find a way. This was it, his one chance at freedom—he couldn't afford to mess it up.

⌘

After dinner that night Bastian lay in his hammock buzzing with the anticipation of what the next day might bring. With all the preparation he'd done, he was eager to have the job over and done with, no matter the outcome. He heard the scratching of pencil lead on paper and looked over to see the pirate in the hammock next to him writing in a journal.

Bastian wished he'd been keeping a journal of his own, he'd complete-ly lost track of time. He had no idea how long he'd been on the Black Mary—so much had happened since he'd boarded the ship, all the days had begun to blend together. "Hey, what day is it?" he asked.

The gruff sailor paused in his writing and looked up. Only then did he seem to register the question. He looked back down at his journal and read the date aloud, "Thrixday, the seventh o' Fablewary," he grunted.

"The seventh of Fablewary? Shick!" Bastian exclaimed.

"What's wrong?"

"Nothing, I'd lost track of time, that's all. Thanks."

"No trouble. It's easily done out 'ere—losin' time, I mean. That's why I started keepin' a log," the pirate told him.

"Smart. Good night," Bastian said.

The pirate gave him a lazy wave and Bastian turned on his side.

It had been ten days since the battle with the Kraken, thirteen days since he'd left Westdock. But that wasn't what had surprised him about the day's date. The seventh of Fablewary was Gwena's Naming Day. Bas-tian couldn't believe he'd almost completely missed it. His heart sank, it wasn't only Gwena's Naming Day, it was her sixteenth—her coming of age. What he wouldn't give to be with her now. He could only hope she was getting the celebration she deserved, wherever she was, something as special as she was. That was it, he decided. He had to complete his task and win his freedom so that he could make his way back to her. Failure wasn't an option.

*Happy Naming Day, Gwen, I hope all your wishes come true. If all goes well, then in only a few more days I can start making my way back to you, just three more days.*

Wrapped in the warmth of that thought, Bastian fell asleep.

# STARLIGHT BEFORE THE DAWN

Felix woke to a gentle shaking. He'd fallen asleep on the swing chair outside Katarina's house. He opened his eyes to see Lilliana smiling down at him, holding a steaming cup of tea.

"Katarina asked me to bring this out to you."

Felix smirked. "Oh? You're not coming out of the goodness of your own heart?"

"Of course not. I know you're perfectly capable of getting your own tea."

"Ha! Thanks," Felix laughed, and sat up to accept the cup. "I guess I was more tired than I realized."

Lilliana gestured to the swing chair, "Mind if I sit?"

"I'd be disappointed if you didn't."

Lilliana sat down beside Felix, and looked out at the view.

"I can't believe you flew into the Everstorm. It was only days ago you were scared to fly on the back of a dragon—it must've been terrifying."

"Yup," Felix admitted, taking a sip of tea.

"I think that makes you the bravest person I know," she declared.

"I'm not sure I deserve that, I did consume most of a bottle of Ash Whiskey on the journey over."

Lilliana laughed. "Still the bravest."

Felix grinned. "Does that make me more attractive?"

"Very much so."

"I'll take it then."

"What makes you even more attractive, though, is your name change. I can't believe you were holding out on me. Felix is a far superior name to James and much more fitting."

"Is that right? I clearly should've told you sooner."

"Clearly. I hear you're also a recovery expert?" Lilliana queried.

Felix smirked. "I figured if I'd told your dad the truth, he would've ditched me in the Everstorm."

"You know, you're probably right. That was a good choice. He was so impressed with you—and for me for hiring you—I didn't have the heart to tell him otherwise."

Felix chuckled. "Did Roy say anything?"

"Not a word. All that poker you two've been playing has paid off. He didn't even blink an eye."

Felix grinned. "Champion."

"I think you did us all a favor with that story. The lie makes far more sense than the truth. It made me wonder why I never thought to look for a recovery expert to hire in the first place," Lilliana admitted.

"I know—that would've been far more logical than staging your own kidnapping, and yet, I'm very glad you didn't," Felix said.

Lilliana smiled. "Me too."

"Is it good to see your father again?" Felix asked.

"It's wonderful. But it's also…difficult, which I wasn't expecting."

"How so?"

"I suppose I've gotten used to making decisions on my own. I don't really want to have to stop doing that," she confessed.

"Then don't. He'll just have to get used to it too."

Lilliana smiled at him gratefully. Felix put his teacup on the ground and asked, "Speaking of your father, is he occupied?"

"Very. Katarina's cutting his hair."

"Good." Felix scooted across the bench, removing the gap between them and whispered, "I'm sorry."

"For what specifically?" she asked.

"For being a complete arse."

Lilliana shrugged. "You can't help what you are."

"Ouch!" Felix exclaimed.

"What you should be apologizing for is carelessly risking your life, as if you're the only one it matters to," Lilliana asserted.

"Am I not?"

"Of course not! Losing you would've been even worse than losing my father. Especially with the way we'd left things. You put me through the Nine Realms of Darkness last night. You didn't even give me the chance to say goodbye."

Felix looked at her apologetically. "You're right, that wasn't fair of me. It was completely reckless. I don't have an excuse, I acted out of impulse. And I'm well aware how lucky I am to still be alive. It's not what I'd expected, if I'm honest. But it is pretty wonderful to hear how much you care."

"Of course I care!" Lilliana exclaimed, hitting his shoulder. Then she was silent for a moment. "I'm sorry too—for what I said last night.

It's true my position doesn't accommodate love, but that doesn't mean I don't love you," she confessed.

Felix looked at her in surprise. "Are you saying you *do* love me?"

"I thought that was obvious."

"You should never think any such thing! I'm a man—you have to spell these things out to me."

Lilliana smiled. "Of course I love you."

Felix returned her smile broadly, and then he kissed her. She leaned into him, and in that moment he felt completely sated—like having her heart close to his made him whole again. When they paused for air Lilliana said, "Just so you know, my father will kill you if he ever finds us together."

Felix cleared his throat. "So I've heard."

She looked at him questioningly.

"Roy told me. Apparently our affections for one another aren't as discreet as we thought they were."

"Shick. What are we going to do?"

"I have no idea," Felix admitted.

⌒

Felix and Lilliana stepped inside Katarina's house just as Lilliana's father was coming down the stairs. Drake looked completely transformed. He was bathed and wearing a smart suit Felix recognized from Roy's collection. Katarina had cut his long, bedraggled hair into a smart style and had shaved his beard, leaving only a handsome mustache. He looked like the duke Felix knew from photos in the paper.

"Father! You look like your old self again. What a fabulous job Katarina's done!" Lilliana exclaimed.

"Yes, she's a woman with many talents. We've decided that when the world's set right again, I'm going to help her fund a proper expedition into the Everstorm," Drake announced.

"That's wonderful news!"

"Indeed. And speaking of setting things right, I'm heading out to see Charles Remington."

"You've arranged a meeting with Sky View's duke already?"

"No. I'll have to send a Sendsong ahead to announce our arrival once we're beyond the storm's interference. There's no time to waste. I must patch things up and enlist the Remingtons' help if we're to rid ourselves of that pest your mother's let into our house."

"Can't we try to contact mother first? Once she knows you're back and the situation, surely she'll cancel the matrimony?"

"No. You said it yourself; she's employed a Receiver—any letter we send might never reach her. Besides, we don't have that kind of time. It will take a Sendsong over a day to reach Westdock. This is the only and best way, my dear."

"Do you want me to come with you?" Lilliana asked.

"No, not this time. Charles and I have a lot of catching up to do. I don't want you there until I've touched base with him. If all goes well, we'll go together tomorrow morning."

"Are you sure it's a good idea for you to go alone? I mean, you've only just returned."

"I won't be. Roy will be accompanying me. We'll be back after dinner—don't wait up," Drake announced, and he headed for the door.

Roy winked at Felix and Lilliana before following Drake outside. Shortly after, Katarina came down the stairs wearing a long fur coat.

"Where are you off to?" Felix inquired.

"I have some errands to run. Don't expect me back until late. Help yourselves to the food in the icebox," she offered, while pulling on a pair of leather gloves.

"Right, thanks. See you when you get back."

"See you then. You kids have fun," Katarina said with a warm smile. Then she headed out the door and down along the jetty to hail an air cab.

Felix turned to Lilliana. "Well, looks like it's just you and me."

Lilliana smiled. "So it does."

Felix took her hand and pulled her gently towards him, placing it on the back of his neck. Then he wrapped his arms around her waist and kissed her tenderly. As Lilliana sank into his embrace, Felix scooped her up and carried her upstairs.

*Thank you, Serendipity.*

# POSTBOX

Gwena headed up to the Heartland's surface and made her way to the Central Posting House. Now that she knew she was leaving the Heartland, she wanted to tie up all of her loose ends, and she knew that this was the last time she'd be able to check her postbox. She hoped there might be a letter from Felix at least, but once again she found her postal box empty. She paid the Posting House an entire year's rent in advance to keep it in her name, just in case Bastian or Felix tried to reach her after she and Bonnie left to find the Black Mary. She also left a letter at the Posting House for each of them, stating that she was off to pursue the Black Mary on a ship called the Crimson Curse, in the hopes that she might find Bastian.

*How much easier it would be if I had access to a Sendsong. If only I knew someone with one*, she thought. She could only hope Felix would be able to use the one he had before for future correspondence. She wondered if he'd already tried and the Sendsong hadn't been able to reach her at the club. The thought filled her with desperation. The world was such an awfully big place to lose someone in. Her one comfort was that the boys had always been resourceful—she hoped that if they could, they'd find a way to reach her.

Finally, Gwena posted a letter to her father to let him know that she was safe and well, and that she wished the same for him. Giving him no indication as to where she was, or where she was headed.

Gwena left the Central Posting House an hour after she'd come and took the long way back to the club. Now that she knew she was leaving, she was feeling sentimental about the Heartland. There was still so much of it she hadn't seen, and she'd highly enjoyed all she had. She dearly hoped that one day she'd be able to return.

# JAXLAND

That morning Bastian woke to the sound of cheers. He looked around and saw he was the only one left in the sleeping quarters. He rolled out of his hammock and hurried up top to see what he was missing.

The crew was crowded on the main deck looking out at a landmass coming into view on the horizon. Bastian spotted Cricket and Stork standing behind everyone else at the ship's railing, holding onto a line and leaning out over the edge staring at what was ahead. Bastian jumped up beside and followed their gaze. They were approaching an island with lush ferns and palm trees outlining the whitest beach he'd ever seen. The water surrounding it was crystal clear with a tinge of topaz blue.

"Isn't she beautiful?" Cricket asked.

"She is," Bastian agreed.

Dolphins jumped in the ship's wake as the Black Mary sped forward with full sails towards the island's shores. Bastian breathed in the fresh salty air and enjoyed the wind dancing playfully around him as he watched their destination draw near.

Twenty minutes later the ship had anchored at Jaxland. Bastian filed in line with Cricket and the twins, waiting for their turn to disembark down the gangplank to the shore. The buzz of anticipation throughout the crew was so potent, it ignited his own enthusiasm. Soon he found himself feeling just as eager to get to their destination. There were other ships arriving at the same time. Several already anchored offshore, An array of different-sized clipper ships, some grand with ornate figureheads at the bows and others plain and discreet. Their one commonality was the black flags they bore—each one with a unique Jolly Roger. One had a horned human skull eating a bleeding heart. Another was branded with two crisscrossed swords over a skull with a red tear coming from its left eye socket, and yet another was a human skull with skeletal suckered limbs extending from its base like the arms of a Kraken. No two were the same, but all of them designed for the same purpose—to strike fear into the hearts of their enemies and declare "Here be pirates!"

When Bastian and company reached the shore, there were three men sitting on the beach with their toes in the sand, passing a bottle of rum. A fourth lay in a hammock stretched between two palm trees. There were men filing up from their ships carrying cargo to trade. The sun beat down, making it feel like a summer day. Bastian never could've imagined he would find such a paradise amongst pirates. He followed the Black Mary crew past the beach along a sandy path leading through a grove of trees and ferns. Mangoes and avocados hung down from branches that stretched over the pathway. Large exotic birds with a multitude of bright colors filled the air with song.

Soon the path opened up into a town square of sorts. Wooden stores and stalls with palm frond roofs bordered the edges, and a stone well occupied the center. More permanent dwellings made of large stone blocks stood farther down the path, none more than two stories high. The place was buzzing with pirates, some buying and selling wares in the market erected for the event, others piling up goods or moving about from one place to another. There was a band of sailors playing music near the well—a man on a fiddle, another with a concertina, and a third playing a fife. There was an ale house on the right. Men sat on its doorstep with foaming steins, swaying in time to the music or standing silently in the doorway watching the musicians play.

"Welcome ta Jaxland!" Stork announced dramatically, placing one hand on Bastian's shoulder and motioning outward with the other. "We all know where Cricket wants ta go, so we may as well drop 'im off first."

"Are ya sure ya don't want ta at least 'ave one drink with us before ya go?" Rhino asked Cricket.

"Come on, brother, would yew in 'is shoes?"

Rhino smirked. "No, yer right. Let's get ya ta Jozalin then," he declared, clapping Cricket on the back.

They walked to a robust building amongst the more permanent dwellings. It was made of stone blocks and stood two stories high. There was a wooden sign that hung above the door that read *The Bleeding Hearts*. Women stood on a balcony above the entrance, waving handkerchiefs and winking at them flirtatiously. One called down, "Lookin' fer a good time, lads? Ya won't find a better time anywhere else."

Stork cat-whistled up to them. "Lookin' good, ladies."

They smiled and blew him a kiss.

Bastian followed Cricket and the twins inside. The lower story was an elegant waiting room with a large wood fireplace set into the wall, plush velvet armchairs, and a thick throw rug. The armchairs were already occupied with waiting men. A queue of three stood in front of an oak desk counter with a plump woman stationed behind it, checking them in. Just beyond the desk was a staircase leading up to the second story. The banister was lined with women of every shape, size, and color, all dolled up and waving flirtatiously to the men, some lifting their skirts to show their legs and others blowing kisses.

Cricket got in line and waited patiently for his turn, then stepped up to the counter. The plump woman took one look at him and her accommodating smile fell into a scowl.

"'ow ya been, Sheila? Good?" Cricket asked her cheerily.

"I'm not doin' this with ya again, Cricket. I tell ya every year, we only take payin' customers."

"O' course ya do! I'm offended ya think I'd come empty-'anded. Is Jozalin in?" Cricket inquired, scanning the banister.

"She's still upstairs gettin' ready. Show me the coin an' I'll let ya know whether er not she be available."

"Cricket?!" a woman's voice exclaimed from the top of the stairs.

The plump woman rolled her eyes. Bastian looked up to see a beautiful, spirited young woman running down. As soon as she saw Cricket she stopped and her face lit up almost as much as his did.

"'ere, it's all yers, Sheila. Make sure no one bothers us," Cricket declared, dropping his whole coin purse on the counter.

Jozalin ran towards Cricket, jumping into his arms and wrapping her legs around his waist. She looked into his eyes, smiled broadly, and kissed him.

"Well, ain't that sweet enough ta make ya sick? I'm off ta the pub, ya two comin'?" Stork asked, then noticed a girl with gold ringlets looking coyly in his direction. "On second thought, perhaps I'll stay 'ere a while. I'll catch up with the two o' ya later."

Rhino snorted. "Two down. Ya stayin' 'er joinin' me at the waterin' hole?" he asked Bastian.

"I'll join you for a drink," Bastian said, and they left Cricket and Stork in the safe hands of The Bleeding Hearts.

The pub was brimming with pirates, half of them already as blind as bats. Bastian and Rhino were lucky to find a table and treated themselves to a liquid breakfast of gold foaming ale. When Bastian's stein was emptied, he excused himself so he could run his errands. He was itching to get his hands on a pair of glasses, ones he could use to enchant with Haplo's instructions for seeing the Geometric Code. Ultimately, Bastian needed more coin. As far as he could see it, he had four options. He could sneak into Tink's quarters and attempt to use his equipment to enchant his coin pouch, he could pickpocket men from the crowd, he could conjure some currency with the Ghost Element—which would disintegrate the second it was dropped into a coinbox—or he could make Haplo's glasses and use them to make some real coin. The latter was the only option that didn't create threads for future trouble.

Bastian left Rhino at the ale house and went wandering through the merchant stalls hoping to find something to fit his purpose. He found solar glasses and prescription glasses with different magnifications, but no crystal ones like Haplo had mentioned. Then he saw a small wood hut with a sign out front saying *Charms & Divination*. Bastian made his way to the entrance and stepped inside.

The shop was dimly lit by large real-fire candle lanterns flooded with dripping wax. There was a woman dressed all in black behind the counter with her nose in a book. The walls were covered with shelves stocked with jars and vials labeled with names of herbs, elixirs, and strange ingredients such as Griffin Wart, Eyes of Newt, and Midnight Fog. Old leather-bound books stocked another section, and yet another had objects and artifacts inside a locked glass cupboard. Dried plants and herbs hung from the ceiling. In the center of the room was a table adorned with a black cloth embroidered with gold stars. On top of the table was a vast assortment of crystals and gemstones and various artifacts made with them, primarily daggers and jewelry.

"Do you have any crystal glasses?" Bastian asked the woman.

She shook her head. "There's no market for them here, but you can try that box," she suggested, pointing to a wooden crate in the corner labeled *Scrap an' Tidbits,* not taking her eyes from the pages in front of her.

"What's that?" Bastian asked.

"Random things plundered from merchant ships that no one wants. I keep it on the off chance someone does. You might find something in there."

Bastian walked over to the crate and riffled through it. There were a couple of old toothbrushes, a single glove without its mate, a few small, framed portraits of old women and one of a dog, a pair of metal and leather aviator's goggles, and a pair of broken glasses. Bastian picked up the goggles—the lenses were strong, clear glass without a scratch on them. *Perfect,* he thought. He put them on. He could see through the lenses perfectly—even the Ghost Element was clear, and the straps could be adjusted to fit his head snugly.

"How much for these?" he queried, feeling the three jolly rogers in his pocket.

The woman shrugged. "Two rogers."

Bastian knew she was asking too much, but he didn't care. The goggles were an investment with an inexhaustible return. He placed the coins on the counter and the goggles in his pocket, then he stepped back out into the sunlight.

Bastian went straight to the Black Mary and retrieved Haplo's journal from his locker. He found a dark corner in the sleeping quarters and sat down. He flipped pages until he came to the instructions for making enchanted glasses, then he laid the goggles on the floor in front of him and drew the Ghost Element into his hands. Following the geometry in the journal, he formed intricate symbols in the air in front of him and moved them into the goggles' lenses the same way he'd crafted the safety symbols for his enchanted bracelet.

After he'd followed the instructions to the letter and double-checked his work several times using the Codec, Bastian picked up the goggles.

"Here goes nothing," he announced to the empty room, and put them on.

The world was instantly outlined with thin gold lines and covered in geometric forms—they were on absolutely everything, like some strange cosmic blueprint. Some were complex, the geometry as intricate as clockwork, and others were simple, but everything he looked at had it. Even his own hands—he saw symbols he didn't recognize mixed with the symbol of his identity.

Bastian laughed in awe and delight. It was like seeing schematics or technical drawings of everything he looked at, but it was all lines and geometry.

He wasted no time in pulling out his pouch and his last jolly roger and laying them side by side on the floor. A jolly roger was by far the most common coin used for trade throughout the mainland. It was generally easy to break into ten individual cwips or two silver fish, and could also add up to higher numbers very quickly, making it the perfect coin for his purpose. Bastian pulled out his notebook, then looked at the jolly roger and copied its geometric code on the paper.

He flipped back through Haplo's journal and started constructing a new symbol in his notebook comprising different foundation shapes that had his desired properties while using the Codec to guide himself in the right direction according to his intention.

He put the goggles up onto his forehead and looked around for something he could transform. He needed something he had plenty of, something that would always be readily accessible. Then it struck him. He took off his boot and hit the sole with the palm of his hand. A small pile of sand poured onto the floor. Bastian spread it out, then pulled the goggles back down over his eyes and studied the symbol of each grain. Each one was a little different, a remnant of whatever form of sea life it was derived from, but there was one symbol they all shared—the symbol of a grain of sand. Bastian incorporated that symbol into the one he was devising, and then he used it to enchant his coin purse.

Checking the purse over with the Codec, he was satisfied. He carefully siphoned the sand into the pouch with his hand. Instantly the transmutation took place, overflowing his coin purse with jolly rogers that spilled across the floor.

"Shick!"

Bastian scooped up the coins as quickly as he could, looking around him to make sure no one saw. With no idea of how to unmake the coins, he began trying to find places to store them. He filled the various pockets inside his jacket, and then stored the rest in his locker. Relieved they were stowed away out of sight, he set to work adding the safety enchantments to both his pouch and the goggles, as well as securing them with his identity so no one else could access the enchantments. Then he stowed the goggles and the pouch in his jacket pocket and headed back out to Jaxland.

Bastian found Rhino and Stork at the tavern sitting at the same high table he'd left Rhino at.

"There 'e is! We thought the Dodger be tryin' ta dodge us," Rhino announced with a drunken slur.

"Where 'ave ya been?" Stork asked.

"Nowhere interesting. How was The Bleeding Hearts?" Bastian inquired, sliding into a stool next to them.

"First class! I'm goin' back after this pint. I recommend ya join me, the girls 'ere do thin's ya won't experience anywhere else," Stork divulged with a wink and a wry grin.

Bastian clapped him on the shoulder. "Sounds great, you have fun with that, I need a drink. Sure I can't tempt you with one more? This round's on me."

"Well, in that case, I suppose I could stick around fer one more."

Bastian grinned and made his way to the bar, returning shortly with three overflowing steins.

An hour later Bastian stumbled out of the pub. He had a lot of weight in his pockets he was eager to get rid of before someone noticed. Rhino stayed behind in the tavern to keep their table, and Stork headed back towards The Bleeding Hearts. Bastian made his way to the group of market stalls and browsed the wares. Every ship had erected a stand to sell or trade their goods. It was an eclectic collection from all over Equillian. There were weapons, clothes, leather bags, boots and belts, hats, scarves, rope, chests, spices, compasses, coats, spyglasses and other nautical instruments, writing supplies, jewelry, and even small exotic animals.

Bastian bought himself a small leather satchel and a short pocketknife he could use for carving and general use. Next he got two good-sized canvas bags, one of which he filled with clothes for warm and cold weather, and another he started filling for Dylan. He picked him up a new set of clothes, as well as a pocket watch and a pen and notebook, along with several other goodies. Bastian got a pair of new sandals and boots for himself, and then he picked out a black tricorn hat with a single round silver pin on its left side depicting the Serendipity constellation. He was relieved that his change for the purchases put something in his coin purse other than jolly rogers.

Bastian stowed his new gear on the Black Mary and then came back to the market to wander. When he came to the end he found himself at the divination shop he'd visited earlier. There was something alluring about it. His curiosity prickled, Bastian ducked inside.

The shop was exactly as Bastian had left it. Even the woman behind the counter still had her nose in her book. He browsed the shelves, stopping at some artifacts locked in a glass cupboard. He immediately recognized a whalebone die that looked like an exact copy of Stork's. The cupboard wasn't labeled, and its contents weren't either. Nor was there any signage giving any indication that its contents held anything but well-crafted merchandise. He reached out with the Codec to explore the die and was immediately met by the Anti-Tampering Enchantment— only, it had that same hack-job quality Bastian had seen on Stork's die, like some backyard counterfeit. He scanned the other objects in the cupboard: a deck of cards that always dealt aces to the owner, a charmed necklace that drew women's attention to the wearer, a peacock-feathered quill that could forge a letter in any handwriting, and other artefacts of similar nature. They were all enchanted, all by seemingly the same hand, and all sharing the obvious nature of being done by someone other than an alchemist. Bastian put on his goggles and looked at them again. Out of all of the intricate symbols covering them, he could only recognize the safety enchantments. But there was one symbol that recurred on every one—Bastian guessed it was the identity symbol for whoever had made them. He pulled his notebook out of his pocket and copied it down.

"Where do these come from?" he asked.

The woman behind the counter yawned. "The Southern Isles."

"Who enchants them?"

The woman looked up from her book for the first time. Bastian was taken aback by her eyes. Her left iris was grey, but the right was was completely white, her black pupil contrasting starkly against the milky orb.

"Who said anything about them being enchanted?" she asked, looking at him curiously. She had a pretty face, with smooth flawless skin and the dark distinctive eyebrows of a sea gypsy. She was younger than Bastian thought previously, probably only a year or two older than he was.

"Why else would they be locked away?" Bastian proposed.

The woman's curiosity evaporated and she returned her attention to her book. "I only give out product information to potential buyers."

"How about I buy the information?" Bastian offered, putting three jolly rogers on the counter.

The woman shrugged. "Everyone knows alchemists enchant objects," she said, reaching for the coins.

Bastian stopped her hand. "But not these. I'm not going to pay you for nothing."

She let him hold her hand while she stared straight into him, her gaze penetrating his very soul. Bastian let go of her uncomfortably.

"They were made by one of my sisters, they're her specialty," the woman confessed.

"Objects with black market abilities?"

The woman shrugged. "She wouldn't make them if there wasn't a market. Her objects are quite popular. I wouldn't think a man who sails under a black flag would be particular about such things."

"I'm not, only curious."

"Careful, curiosity snuffed the cat," she warned.

"Lucky I'm not a cat then," Bastian remarked with a curt smile.

"If it's answers you seek, our house specialty is divination. If you have other questions, I may be able to answer them for you—for our standard rate, of course."

"You're a seer?"

"That's right."

Bastian considered her offer. He'd always thought of fortune tellers as gaudy con artists, but if they truly could read the Codec, then Bastian wanted to see it—more so, he was eager to hear what she could tell him about Gwena and Felix. He shrugged. "Sure, I have some time to snuff my curiosity."

The woman smiled and beckoned towards a doorway obscured by a curtain of beads.

⌒

Bastian followed the seer into a small dark room lit by a large candelabra flickering with the flames of real fire. There was a round table in the center with a chair on either side. On the table, resting on a metal stand, was a crystal ball the size of an atlas globe, filled halfway with a dark purple liquid.

"Have a seat," the seer invited, gesturing to one of the chairs.

She lit some incense and sat opposite Bastian. He looked down and saw a white mist pooling around their feet. He immediately recognized it from his and Felix's pranking days at the Order. It was a combination of tarbonite and filliorite, which in the right doses created a dehydrated ice crystal that stayed frozen at room temperature. When you poured water on it, it melted while simultaneously releasing a dense fog—perfect for scaring the younger children into thinking the Star Temple was haunted. Apparently also good for adding to the mystique of divination.

The seer pushed up her sleeves and delicately put her hands on the crystal ball. She leaned in towards it and whispered, "Wake up." The dark liquid inside rippled outwards in a pronounced floral pattern that held its shape for several moments before fading away. Bastian would've been thoroughly taken aback if he wasn't already aware of the Geometric Code. Still, the way the liquid magnified and suspended the geometric form was impressive. It held the figure for much longer and with far more clarity than colored water, revealing the Codec's symbols splendidly. He leaned towards the globe, "What's in there?"

"Surely there must be something beyond this room your curiosity's tempted by? Something in the future or otherwise beyond reach? Why don't we start with your name?"

"Not a chance," Bastian scoffed.

The seer cocked an eyebrow.

"I'm not stupid enough to expose everything about myself to someone who sells shadow market goods to pirates. I know how these sorts of things work. I bet you charge customers a premium for an insight into their lives, and then sell that information to every third party willing to pay for it. And I don't blame you, it's simply good business—all about maximizing profits, am I right?"

The woman smirked. "I suppose you're not as fresh as you look, but there's one problem—how am I supposed to reveal to you your destiny if you won't allow me to see it?"

"I'm not interested in my destiny. I want information on someone else."

"It will cost extra."

"Fine."

"What's their name?" the seer asked.

"Gwena Rose Stently."

The second Bastian uttered Gwena's name a complex geometric pattern blossomed on the liquid's surface inside the crystal ball. He leaned forward to get a closer look at it. Instinctively he knew it was Gwena's

Geometric Code, and it was extravagantly beautiful—so much more complex than his own.

"What would you like to know about her?" the seer asked.

"Is she out of Westdock?"

The young woman studied the geometry in her crystal ball. "Yes," she confirmed.

"Did she use the tickets to take the train to our planned destination?" Bastian queried eagerly, watching the shapes that formed on the liquid's surface with the question.

"Yes."

He released an internal sigh of relief. "What's she doing there?"

"She's performing in a show, something to do with stage magic."

Bastian smiled broadly. "And she's happy?"

"At this moment, yes."

"What else can you tell me about her?"

"She's in love...and you're in love with her."

"How do you know that?" Bastian demanded.

The seer smirked, "By the look on your face."

Bastian ignored her and leaned towards the crystal ball and said, "Love." A stunning, intricate pattern rippled outward.

"Gwena Rose Stently," Bastian said again, and Gwena's Geometric code appeared in the ripples once more, only this time Bastian recognized the symbol for love intertwined with it. *Interesting.* Her code was so complex because it had more than just her identity woven into its form when he spoke her name. He wondered if the symbols were reflecting his feelings for her, or the love she felt for him—maybe both. He was itching to know what else the symbol divulged, but he'd already revealed more personal information than he was comfortable with.

"How about Felix Copperweather? What can you tell me about him?" Bastian asked.

The seer gazed into the crystal ball to observe the symbology before answering,

"He's in a foreign place consumed by a forbidden love."

"Ha! Is it a noble?"

"Yes."

Bastian smiled wryly. "And do they love him in return?"

"They do."

*The bastard actually did it*, Bastian thought. "Is he being looked after well?"

"He's surrounded by comforts and abundant with wealth."

"You can know all that by reading the Ciphorescent Codec?"

"The what?"

"The Ciphorescent Codec—the Language of Songs. The shapes in your globe are a written representation of the language of truth. You're simply reading it, right?"

"Do you have to question my methods?"

"Of course, I'd be foolish not to."

The girl looked at him with a curious expression before saying, "It's called the Shamora, the language of the Estoose."

"The Estoose?"

"It's the gypsy word for *the stars*."

"The language of the stars. Is that what you learn as a seer, how to understand this—Shamora?"

"And much more. The truth is constantly present all around us, it can be read in many ways. To find it you only need to be receptive enough to see it."

"Right. Is there a book or something that teaches you what all the symbols mean?"

"Of course, lots. But they're only accessible to the Sisters of the All Seeing Eye. You'd have to join the guild in order to access them, and you can only do that if you're a woman," she stated.

"Why's that?"

"Because men can't be trusted," she answered frankly.

"Ha! And women can? I've known plenty of women who can't be trusted. Shouldn't you accept someone based on their individual quality of character, rather than what gender they are?"

The girl only stared at him blankly.

"Right. Can you at least tell me what element's in your crystal ball?"

"I answer questions regarding one's fate and destiny, not inquiries about my professional secrets."

Bastian leaned in to take a closer look at the globe, "I can't tell if it's a liquid metal like mercurio, or some sort of oil."

The seer pursed her lips but said nothing.

"Well, if you change your mind I'll be happy to compensate you accordingly. Thank you for humoring my curiosity," Bastian said. He set a high stack of jolly rogers on the table and left the hut.

Bastian bought a smoked wild turkey leg from a food stall and sat on a low rock wall to eat it. So, Gwena and Felix were safe and well—more than well, by the sounds of things. Felix in love and abundant with wealth, and Gwena safe in the Heartland performing in a magic show. He couldn't have wished for more for either of them—it was a huge relief, so why did it make him feel so rotten? Their well-being had been his primary concern since jumping on the Black Mary, the news should've made him feel sated. But the truth was, it gave him a pang in his heart to know they were doing so well without him—maybe even faring better than if he'd been there. For the first time Bastian began wondering if maybe they *were* better off without him. Here he was trying so desperately to get back to them, to save them, when in reality it seemed he was the only one who needed saving.

Bastian threw what was left of his turkey leg to a feral dog roving the streets and began wandering through the market with his goggles on. People gave him strange looks, but he ignored them. It was fascinating to see the geometric patterns inside everything. Some of the symbols were stationary, and others rotated like clockwork with parts of them in constant motion. Most of the patterns were continually changing, morphing from one to another. The ones that didn't Bastian imagined to be symbols marking core personality traits, impressions from the past, or perhaps a prewritten future. He could only differentiate their Identity Code because it was everywhere throughout them, with larger predominant versions over their head and heart. He wished he knew how to make sense of the other symbols. It was like looking at the hieroglyphs of an ancient language that revealed the secrets of the universe, and he had no idea how to decipher it. He decided then that if he survived his mission on Jaxland, he would study Haplo's journal relentlessly until he did.

Bastian sat in the empty mess hall of the Black Mary studying the maps he'd gotten from Snibs that morning, trying to formulate a plan for his task the following day. If the captain wanted the chest taken at lunchtime, it meant Bastian would only have a tiny window to work with—especially considering that the house would be occupied with multiple persons wandering the premises without any real focus to distract them, and Bastian had no excuse to be there. Worse was that neither Snibs, Tink, nor the Captain were certain of where the chest was in the house.

If only Felix were here, this job would be a piece of cake, Bastian thought. There was no one better to distract a harem of women than Felix Copperweather. His brother would've relished the opportunity. How would Felix approach this job? Bastian asked himself. His brother was a master of distraction—he'd capitalize everyone's attention, freeing up Bastian to pluck the plunder. Bastian could almost hear Felix preaching his advice now.

*When you're somewhere you're not supposed to be, doing something you shouldn't, there's only one way to effectively get away with it—proceed as though you're exactly where you're meant to be, doing precisely what you're supposed to.*

How could Bastian convince the women and guards of Drax's household that he was supposed to be there? After pondering the question for ten minutes he still hadn't come up with an answer. Then Bastian heard the swooping of wings and looked up in surprise to see an approaching Sendsong. Unlike the black one in the captain's quarters, this one was made of white porcelain. It landed gracefully on the table in front of him and cocked its head, looking into his eyes with its penetrating metallic lavender stare.

Bastian froze, struck by his dumb luck and terrified he might scare it away.

The bird made a little melodic chirp and then its chest popped open, revealing a letter inside. Bastian was so taken aback, he just stared at it for three whole seconds without moving before proceeding to look around the mess hall to see if it could be there for someone else. After confirming it had to be for him, he tentatively reached his hand inside.

"Don't go anywhere, I'd like to use your services if I may?" he requested before taking the letter, anxious that the bird might fly off as soon as its charge was delivered. The Sendsong cocked its head and then began preening its feathers. Satisfied it had gotten his message, Bastian turned his attention to reading the mail.

*02/03/1750*

*Dear Bastian,*

*I hope you got my previous letter and made it safely out of Westdock with Gwena. Lay low for a while if you can. It turns out Lord Bardviss is good friends with Marx, that's right, Eastgate's kingpin. Anyone linked to the underworld will be on their payroll. Be cautious and maybe stick to honest work for a while, eh?*

*I'm sure you're wondering where I've gone and what I'm doing. So much has happened since we last saw each other, I don't even know where or how to begin. I think it's best if we wait until we can share our stories over a pint. But I can tell you one thing, I'm faring very well. I was hoping and intending to come and meet you and Gwena in the Heartland, only I've just been offered another job opportunity that would truly set us up with enough coin to change our stars. You of course are my number one priority — tell me you need me there with you and I'll turn the job down. But if you and Gwena are happy and safe and don't need a third wheel hanging around, then I'll take this job for all of us. If I do, I'm not sure how long I'll be away — it might be six months to a year, maybe even longer. But I promise, if I take it, then I'll find my way back to you as soon as it's finished, and the three of us can make up for lost time in style. Eagerly awaiting your reply.*
*Love and miss you brother,*
*Felix*

Bastian held the letter in trembling hands. He was so relieved to hear from Felix. His words surfaced the emotion of every hardship Bastian had faced since they last saw each other, bringing tears to his eyes. He wiped them away briskly.

How did Felix get his hands on a Sendsong? And the letter was dated from six days before, where could he be that would take a Sendsong six days to travel? And Lord Bardviss was connected to The East?! Shick! If that were true and Lord Bardviss was willing to send two war galleons to recover the stolen egg from Bastian, then he most likely had everyone linked to organized crime on high alert to capture him. Bastian thought back to his encounter with Guido in the market at Westdock. The black-market trader had tried to capture him the second he saw the stolen merchandise from the castle. It was all beginning to make so much more sense. That meant that if Bastian ever made it off the ship and back to Gwena, both their lives would be in danger.

*Shick, shick, shick!*

The Black Mary was probably the safest place Bastian could be right now, for everyone. If Lord Bardviss was connected to The East, then Bastian desperately hoped he'd never recover the war dragon's egg. He wondered what he'd planned to do with it if he had.

Bastian turned Felix's letter over to craft a reply. He wanted to tell him to come and meet him straight away—if only he could be on Jaxland that very night. Bastian wanted so badly to be able to sit down with him over a pint and tell him everything, to introduce him to Cricket, Stork, and Rhino. To show him how he could conjure coin out of thin air. To tell him that neither of them had to work another day in their lives because Bastian had already found the solution to changing their stars. But that wasn't an option. By the time any response Bastian made would reach Felix, it would already be too late. Bastian didn't even know if he'd still be on Jaxland then, or if he'd still be breathing. Even if Felix could meet him on the Island of Rogues, he'd only be killed or captured. And Bastian was so close to winning his freedom—that was, if he survived his task the following day. And whether he did or didn't, it would be better for Felix to be preoccupied with a job that would set himself up than to discover Bastian's true predicament when there was nothing he could do to help him. Bastian looked over at the Sendsong staring at him as if it was judging his very thoughts. He ignored the bird and started putting pen to paper.

*08/03/1750*

*Dear Felix,*

*It's great to hear from you! Thank you for your letter and your warning. I was worried when we were separated in Westdock, I thought Luckless had finally caught up to us. But it sounds like your charm has woven its magic once again. I still don't know how you do it, brother. I'm grateful to hear you're well and facing a fruitful job opportunity, it sounds too good to pass up! Don't worry about us, we're navigating our new surroundings just fine. You were right, Gwena confessed her love to me, I should've listened to you sooner. And now, I've finally gotten that adventure I was always asking for. I too have much to share, I can't wait to sit down and trade stories over a pint when your contract is completed. I hope it's everything you want it to be and more. Good luck, brother — not that you need it.*

*Love and miss you,*

*Bastian*

Bastian looked over his letter mournfully, wondering if it was the last correspondence he'd have with Felix. He wanted to tell him everything, but this was the only way he could see to protect him. He had so much more he wanted to say, so many questions he wanted to ask, he could only hope he would survive long enough to do so in person. Bastian folded his letter and stuck it into the Sendsong.

"Return to Felix Copperweather."

The compartment in the bird's chest immediately snapped shut and the bird took wing, making its way gracefully out of the ship. It was only once it was gone that Bastian remembered he'd wanted to try to use the Sendsong to send a letter to Gwena. In turmoil, he looked at the spot the bird had just flown from. Then he sighed and ran his hands over his face, hoping to the stars he'd done the right thing. He pulled out two more sheets of parchment and wrote two separate letters, one to Felix and one to Gwena. Then he placed them together into a single envelope with Gwena's name on it and headed down to the gundeck to visit Dylan.

Dylan was hunched in the corner of the holding cell asleep with his head in his arms.

Bastian shook the bars. "Psst! Oi! Wake up, it's still daylight."

Dylan's head shot up. "Where the shick have you been?!"

"Sorry, it's been a busy few days."

"Sorry, it's been a busy few days—that's it?! You do realize your visits have been the only thing keeping me sane down here? When you didn't show I thought something must have happened to you! Do you have any idea what kind of darkness that's put me through?!"

Bastian held up a canvas bag stocked full. "Here, I've brought you some presents to make up for it," he announced, and passed it through the bars of the holding cell.

Dylan felt the weight. "What's all this?"

"Have a look."

Dylan sat down on the floor and dumped out the bag's contents, his eyes doubled in size. In the pile were several apples, a paper bag full of sweet treats, fresh clothes, a notebook and pencil, and the watch Bastian had chosen for him.

"You got all this for me?! How'd you afford it?"

"Never you mind about that. Do you forgive me then?"

Dylan looked at him with the grin of a boy in a candy shop. "Yeah, alright, it's water under the bridge, just don't do it again, and…thanks," he said, then added, "It's a nice watch."

"I'm glad you like it. Can I have mine back now?"

Dylan smirked, "If you must." He handed Bastian his watch through the bars.

Bastian pocketed it, grateful to have it back in his possession. "There's one more thing."

"What's that?"

"There's this job I have to do tomorrow, and there's a chance I might not make it back…"

"What are you talking about?"

"Don't worry, it's nothing to be concerned about. Just do me a favor, will you? If I don't return, can you do your best to deliver this for me as soon as you get the opportunity?" Bastian asked, and he passed the sealed envelope through the bars with Gwena's name on it.

Dylan looked at it and then he looked up at Bastian with concern. "No, man—you can deliver it yourself," he said, and tried to hand the letter back.

Bastian looked at him imploringly and Dylan caved. He nodded and gave Bastian a sad but encouraging smile. "I'll do what I can. Let's just hope I don't need to, hey?"

Bastian nodded. "Yeah, thanks. Best get back to it then," he said awkwardly and turned to go.

"Ba—Dodger."

Bastian turned.

"I'll see you tomorrow."

Bastian nodded with a small smile and then ascended the ladder.

# STAR-CROSSED

Felix lay next to Lilliana in the large low bed in Katarina's guest room upstairs. It was a tastefully clean space, minimalistic in decoration and design. The outside walls of the room were made completely of glass, overlooking the empty sky beyond—giving the impression they were on a cloud amongst the clouds.

Felix was tenderly tracing the lines on Lilliana's palm with his fingertips. They'd spent the last couple hours in bed together, lost in a sea of overwhelming love and passion. Felix's feelings were heightened by the bitter reality that their time together was waning. He only wished he could bottle that moment and live in it forever, but sobering actuality was knocking at his door.

"I imagine your father's reestablishing your betrothal to Frederick right now," he said.

Lilliana nodded. "It's the logical thing to do. With my father back and a betrothal in place, it gives the Remingtons incentive to stop Lord Bardviss. It's the only way."

"I know. What now, then?" Felix asked her.

"I can only see two options."

"Which are?"

"We can either play the part expected of us and enjoy what we can in the cracks between…"

"Or?" Felix asked.

"Or we can run away together."

Felix studied Lilliana. "You're serious, you'd actually consider that?"

"I'm not losing you, Felix Copperweather. I thought I had last night—I'm not going through that again."

"What about your family?"

"Now that my father's here, he'll look after them. It might not be easy with me gone, but he'll find a way. He'll probably offer Natasha in my place as a match for Frederick, just as you suggested."

Felix's heart sank, and he suddenly hated himself for growing a conscience. "I can't let you do that."

"Why not?!"

"I can't take you away from here, Lilliana, you're too important. And for what? A few moments of happiness before facing the reality of living a commoner's life without any of the comforts you're used to, being forced to never see your family again, and raise our children in a world that's falling apart—knowing you could've done something to prevent it? I'd never forgive myself for that. You have an opportunity to make a real difference, to make this place better. You could change the future course of Equillian. Not just because of your position, but because of who you are. You were right, it has to be you."

Lilliana looked at him incredulously, "that's not fair! Before you were telling me to prioritize my own happiness, and now you're asking me to sacrifice it for everyone else?! I've been disregarding the things I've wanted my entire life, I'm not willing to do that anymore, not if it means losing you!"

"Even if we run, Lord Bardviss's men will come after us."

"I can protect us!" Lilliana asserted.

"At what cost?! I'm not willing to risk you being harmed!"

"If you won't let me run away with you, then you have to stay here with me—I can make you my advisor. As a commoner you bring a perspective and insight I don't have. You can stay by my side and help me bring about the change Equillian needs," Lilliana insisted.

"And what, stand silently by while you and Frederick get married and have children together? I'm sorry, but I'm not strong enough for that—it would be the end of me."

"If I have to stay, then you can't leave, I forbid it!"

"I'm not going anywhere until your father's secured your safety."

"And then?"

Felix hesitated. "I don't know."

Lilliana looked at him with pain, anger, and sorrow all rolled up together. "Why are you giving up on us?" she implored.

Felix met her eyes. "Because I love you. And you're like a rare, exquisite bird—I don't want to capture you, I want to see you soar. I'd be nothing but a dead end for you, Lilliana. I won't let you throw your life away for me, and I'm not willing to rob the world of the one person who might be able to save it."

Lilliana's eyes glistened. "Your love makes me soar. I don't know what I'll do without it. I'll never be able to love Frederick. It doesn't matter how charming he is or how good he is at jousting; he'll always be lacking because he's not you!"

Felix smiled weakly and pushed a strand of Lilliana's hair behind her ear. "I'm very pleased to hear you say that. Just tell me you'll think of me every time he touches you, and I might be able to keep it from tearing me apart."

Lilliana gazed at him through a curtain of tears. "I want it to be you. There must be a way."

Felix smiled encouragingly, ignoring his own aching heart. He wrapped her in his arms and said softly, "There's not. But it's going to be okay. *We're* going to be okay. Our stars are too crossed for even Serendipity to align. Despite the pain that brings, I'm still grateful for the time we've had together—it's been worth it. I'll treasure it for the rest of my life. The memories we've made will be the fire in my heart that warms and brightens my darkest hours. I couldn't ask for a greater gift than that."

He lifted her chin and kissed her tenderly, hiding the tears forming in his own eyes, and they wove themselves together once more, savoring every moment for fear it would be their last.

Felix lay in his bed alone that night. The others still hadn't returned, but he and Lilliana didn't want them to find the two of them together when they did. He felt miserable. *Am I doing the right thing?* he wondered. Mentally and intuitively he knew it was the right choice, but emotionally it felt like he was being torn apart. Regardless, he knew it was time for his run in Sky View to come to its end. Without Lilliana, there was nothing left for him here. He missed Bastian and their simple life together and was eager to return to it, though part of him knew he never really could. The last couple of weeks had changed him. Felix wasn't the same man he was the last time he'd seen Bastian, and they couldn't return to their life in Westdock after everything that had happened. Even if they set themselves up in a similar way in the Heartland, Felix knew it would never be the same.

*Thank the Stars Bastian and Gwena are alright at least, and Lord Bardviss hasn't reached them,* he thought.

Then he heard a murmur of conversation in the kitchen downstairs. By the low tones of the voices, he guessed it was Roy and Drake returned from their outing. Felix rolled from his bed and made his way stealthily down the hall to the top of the stairs, where he could comfortably listen to their conversation.

"That was fruitful, though disheartening. I had no idea you had so many contacts here," Roy said.

"Of course, even though my ward is Westdock, I've never stopped taking an interest in my home precinct. The Remingtons, though capable, have always been too comfortable to pay attention to what's going on below the surface in Sky View. On my last visit here—when John was on his last days—I discovered the extent of The East's infiltration. Marx has men planted in all the major governmental bodies, from the High Court to the Investigation Bureau, even all the way down to the Post. It's most likely why my case was discarded so quickly and why the Remingtons never got wind of all this sooner. Unfortunately, I was sent into the Everstorm before I had a chance to share the information. Let's just hope I'm not too late. I can only imagine how much more the plague of The East has spread over the last two years—the infection in my own household makes the extension of their reach soberingly evident. Thank the Stars that boy found me when he did. If we don't act quickly and strategically, Marx will take complete control of Equillian without anyone being the wiser."

"I still can't believe Arianna's handmaiden is linked to all this. The web of The East's schemes reaches far beyond what I'd ever imagined."

"I should've known. John acquired her from the slave trade when she was a young girl to keep Arianna company after his wife died. He couldn't have known her father was linked to Marx's inner circle—he detested The East. I fear she has some influence over Lilliana, because the two have always been close. But that's far from the worst of it. My family is only one of many who've been infested with Marx's moles. If my intel is correct, Marx has business contracts with at least three other influential families in the precinct—having pulled each of them out of debt, he's now got hold of them as if by puppet strings. I fear we're too late to stop it. Stars know how many dragons have already been bred and shipped out for his purpose. If only I hadn't been sent into that damn storm! We've lost so much precious time."

"You're here now, that's what counts. With a little luck in our favor, it's not too late to turn this all around. Have you thought anymore about offering James the position?"

"From what you've told me, he seems tailor-made for the job. He risked his life to save my own—in direct subordination of Lord Bardviss and The East, no less—which proves he's not one of theirs. That alone is invaluable, and mixed with his skillset and common birth, he's a rare commodity and ideal candidate."

"Let's hope he's up for it then. But for now, to bed—I'm sure you're exhausted, and tomorrow's another big day."

"Yes, I'm looking forward to sleeping on a mattress!"

"I can imagine," Roy laughed, and the two of them headed for the stairs.

Felix quickly retreated to his bedroom. By the sounds of things, Roy had told the duke who he was—at least, who Roy thought he was. Felix wasn't sure whether or not to feel betrayed. He knew he shouldn't have been surprised that Roy's loyalties lay with his best friend, but it still felt like a backstab. He didn't know what job they had in store for him, but he was pretty sure he wasn't interested. Felix couldn't get away from the problems of the upper class soon enough. He never thought he'd say it, but he preferred the basic troubles of survival he was accustomed to. He lay back down on the feather mattress and struggled through the rest of the night with only small snatches of troubled sleep.

When Felix came down to breakfast the next morning, Lilliana, Roy, Katarina, and Lilliana's father were already at the table enjoying a big spread.

"There he is, our hero!" Drake announced. "Come, have some breakfast. I want you to accompany us to the Remingtons' castle this morning."

Felix sat down and Drake personally filled his cup with tea.

"Thank you, that's very kind of you. Unfortunately, I have some business I must attend to elsewhere," Felix declined politely, eager to avoid witnessing Lilliana being handed over to Frederick and getting himself entangled further in Equillian's politics.

"Nonsense! Cancel it. I want the Remingtons to meet the man who rescued me and who's saving us all from that slithering worm, Bardviss. If it weren't for you, we would all be in trouble."

"Lady Lilliana and Roy played the lead role in all that—I just did as I was told and helped out where I could."

"Humble too, what an upstanding gentleman! But I insist. We'll depart within the hour," Drake asserted.

"Certainly, my lord," Felix acquiesced, and picked up his cup of tea.

Felix stared out the window of the airship anxiously rolling his Lady Luck charm across the backs of his knuckles as they flew towards the duke of Sky View's island. Roy and Drake were lost in conversation at the table, and Lilliana was in her private quarters. Felix badly wanted to join her, but he couldn't think of an excuse convincing enough to quell suspicion from her father. His stomach was in knots. It was one thing to know Lilliana was going to be handed over to Frederick Remington, and another thing entirely to be there to see it. The very thought of the smile Frederick would wear with Lilliana on his arm made Felix want to do horrible things to him. But he knew those were his own shortcomings he was wrestling with. He wondered how many men he'd made feel the same way. He'd had his share of women who were already spoken for, and he'd found the anger of their partners slightly entertaining, but now that things were turned around the humor was completely drained from it. Felix pocketed his coin and headed for the top deck to get some fresh air.

Felix barely had a minute with his own thoughts before Roy came to join him. He handed Felix a cigar and lit one for himself. "Thanks for coming along with us," he said.

"I wasn't given much of a choice," Felix returned dryly, and took a puff of the cigar.

Roy nodded. "I can only imagine how hard this must be for you."

Felix leaned on the ship's guardrail and looked out at the clouds surrounding them. "Let's just say, I'd rather face the Everstorm."

"That was a very brave thing you did."

"Ha! More like stupid, but hey, luckily it turned out well in the end."

Roy followed Felix's gaze to the horizon. "I hope for all our sakes it does, but this is only the beginning. From what I learned yesterday, Lord Bardviss is far from the worst of our problems. There's a change on the wind. Equillian's hard-earned peace is balancing precariously on a cliff's edge, and there are those trying very hard to push it over. Your bravery in bringing Drake back has given us a fighting chance. I don't even want to imagine where we'd be if you hadn't. What you and Lilliana have done over this last week has disrupted their plans far more than you realize, but it's only a matter of time before The East recovers and presses forward. If we want our children to know the same peace we have, then we're all going to have to fight for it."

Felix replied with introspective silence. Roy patted him on the shoulder and returned below deck, leaving Felix lost amongst the cloud of his inner turmoil.

～

An hour later the airship approached the Remingtons' island. It was larger than the Wendrians', but farther from the capital—tucked away in the northeastern quarter. The pathway leading from the jetty was outlined with tall crystal maples on either side. Their ruby and gold leaves had mica-like structures that glimmered in the afternoon sun. At the end of the pathway was a towering castle at least twice the size of the Wendrians' Westdock castle. It had towering spires made of white stone and arching gold balconies. There were at least three different glass greenhouses Felix could see amongst the lavish manicured gardens encircling grand marble fountains on either side. An impressive dragon stable was around back and behind it was a large lake that glittered in the sunlight. Beyond that were green pastures with grazing sheep and goats, followed by rolling hills and forests with a wide wandering river. The landscape was breathtaking.

Roy docked the ship and they all filed out onto the jetty where they were greeted by the duke of Sky View and Frederick, accompanied by an entourage of house guards and servants behind them. Felix noted Frederick scanning their party for Lilliana. As soon as his eyes fell on her, he lit up like a boy on Giftmas morning. Felix clenched his jaw. The duke of Sky View, Charles Remington hugged Drake in greeting. "Welcome back, my friend! I can't tell you how eager we've been for your arrival. Is this your lost daughter?"

"Yes. I present to you my eldest daughter, Lady Lilliana Wendrian, duchess of Westdock," Drake announced, and beckoned Lilliana forward.

She was wearing high-waisted slacks and a green blouse that contrasted brightly against her red curls. She embraced the duke of Sky View in the customary greeting, and then stepped to her father's side.

"How stunning she is! It's no wonder they call her the Jewel of Westdock," Charles remarked.

Lilliana smiled charmingly. "It's a pleasure to see you again, Charles."

"You remember me from so long ago?!" the duke exclaimed.

"Of course. How could I forget? Our visit here was one of the highlights of my childhood."

～ 653 ～

Charles smiled. "Oh, I'm so pleased to hear that! I must tell you, it was for Frederick as well. I don't think he's ever forgotten it," he chuckled.

Frederick blushed, he stepped forward and reached for Lilliana's hand. "It's true, my lady. Even as a child you made quite an impression on me. I must admit, I was devastated when I heard you and your father were missing," he confessed, and kissed her hand.

"Thank you, that's very kind. I saw you compete at the Derby yesterday. You're quite the jouster," she commended.

"You were at the derby?"

"Yes, in disguise. I was there to see the Emperor. Of course, if I'd known of my father's arrangement between us, I would've come to you and the duke sooner."

Fredrick smiled. "I'm glad to hear that. Our house is at your disposal. Whatever you need, my lady. From here on out you'll have our full protection."

"Thank you, my lord." Lilliana returned his smile and inclined her head.

Felix wished she wasn't so convincing in her performance. He almost believed she was as happy to see Frederick as he was to see her.

Charles gestured to Felix. "And is this the man you were telling us about?"

"Yes. This is James Turner, the man who risked his life to rescue me from the Everstorm and helped Lilliana uncover Lord Bardviss's true intentions," Drake announced.

Fredrick cocked his head. "I recognize you. Have we met somewhere before?"

Felix opened his mouth to reply, but Frederick cut in before he had the opportunity. "Yes, I remember now, it was at the Derby last night! You gave me a cigar and the business card for your designer. You commented on my pocket watch—that's because you knew Lilliana, wasn't it? You were with her at the Derby!" the marquess proclaimed enthusiastically. "By Serendipity, what fateful happenstance, I knew I liked you. It's nice to be able to put a name to the face," he remarked, shaking Felix's hand vigorously.

Felix gave up trying to say anything, and only smiled.

"From your description, Drake, I was expecting someone much older. To have the skill to accomplish so much at such a young age is indeed impressive. We have much to be grateful to you for, Turner. We were so pleased with the future Drake, and I had secured for our families before his disappearance. I must admit, we didn't quite know how to move forward without it. We are in your debt. I'll not forget the favor you've done us all," Charles declared.

Felix inclined his head. "Thank you, my lord. Lady Lilliana was the mastermind behind it. I was simply doing the job she hired me for."

"If that's true, then she's a clever girl for hiring you. But commanding something be done and being the one to execute it are two very different things," the duke asserted.

"Thank you, my lord," Felix returned in earnest. He was surprised to hear such a thing from a noble and wondered if the duke applied the same insight and credit to the men he gave orders too.

"Come, the table has been set for your arrival. Let's continue this conversation over some refreshments," Charles announced to the party, and led them all inside.

The interior of the castle was even grander than the exterior, with arching windows that stretched from floor to ceiling, overlooking the spectacular landscape beyond, and giant Everfire chandeliers decorated with hundreds of teardrop crystals reflecting the light. They were led out to a back balcony with a view of the large lake behind the castle.

On the balcony was a long stone table laden with delicacies. The only thing separating the table from the grounds beyond were two pillars covered in green grapevines heavy with fruit. Felix waited for an indication of where to sit before he took his place. He was seated next to Roy and across from Lilliana and Frederick. Charles sat at the head of the table with Drake beside.

The second they sat down a flock of waiters came over and filled their glasses with dandelion wine. They all enjoyed the fine spread for a time, filling the spaces between mouthfuls with idle chitchat before Charles nodded to Frederick who then turned to Lilliana. "My dear lady, I hear you like dragons? We have twenty-five different varieties. Some are in the stables, while others roam our island freely. It would be an honor to show you, if you'll allow me?"

"As lovely as that sounds, I'd prefer to discuss our course of action for the problem at hand. Lord Bardviss is expecting me to be handed over to his men in a matter of hours, and we still don't have a plan."

"Don't worry about that—we're looking after it. Go and enjoy yourself," Drake insisted.

Lilliana hesitated for a moment. Felix could imagine how she must've been writhing inside. Until her father showed up, she was the one calling the shots in this operation—now she wasn't even being included at the table. But she took it in perfect stride, without showing a hint of emotion.

"Yes, of course. Thank you, Frederick, I'd like that very much," she assented with a warm smile and took his arm.

A pang of jealousy shot though Felix as Lilliana followed the marquess down the stone steps into the garden. As soon as the two of them were out of sight, Drake turned to Charles.

"What news? Have the plans been set in motion?"

"Indeed, the clock has been oiled and wound. I spoke with the Emperor last night. He's agreed to meet us at the Inn. I've also notified a select few of the press, they're ready and waiting."

"Good. We must ensure no one hears about it outside your most loyal."

"Of course."

"That only leaves one more thing then."

"Yes," Charles agreed, and he turned to Felix. "Thank you for joining us, Turner."

"It's an honor," Felix returned, inclining his head.

"From what I've heard, your vast range of skills expands beyond those of a recovery expert?"

"You flatter me. My life has required me to be adaptable, that is all."

"Yes, adaptable, that's exactly what we need. You've done so much already, I hesitate to ask more of you—but we require your expertise for our plan this afternoon. Because Lord Bardviss has asked for you specifically to deliver Lilliana to his men, your accompaniment is paramount. I hope we can rely on your cooperation?" Charles asked.

"Of course, I was hired for this job by Lady Lilliana, and I intend to see it through."

"Good, good. I'm very pleased to hear that. We'll fill you in on the details shortly. But first, we have another proposition for you," Charles announced.

"Oh?"

"Normally I'd begin with the proper pleasantries, but I'm afraid we're all out of time, so I'll get straight to the heart of it. I'm not sure you're aware, but The East is setting the board to overthrow Lord Balthazar's rule and take over Equillian for themselves. Currently, they have the advantage. Equillian is infested with Marx's men like a bad case of termites, and they're devouring our foundation. If we're to have any hope of stopping them, we'll need a man of our own on the inside. Someone who can infiltrate Marx's inner circle and find out what he's planning. If we know his next move before he makes it, we can ensure we're prepared. Such information could tip the scales in our direction and save Equillian from complete collapse under the hand of a tyrant. It needs to be a man unattached to the political world or anyone of power. A man adept in disguise, a man good with communication and people. We're hoping that man is you."

Everyone at the table turned their attention to Felix.

Felix took a moment to fully digest what the duke was suggesting. "Are you saying you want to hire me for espionage—to infiltrate Marx's inner circle as a spy?" he clarified.

"Yes," Drake confirmed plainly, as if they were asking no more of him than to collect the morning paper.

"I'm flattered you would consider me a worthy candidate for such a position, but with all due respect, any amount of coin you might offer me will be worthless if I'm dead."

The duke slid him a piece of paper from across the table. Felix picked it up and turned it over. His eyes widened—he'd never seen a figure with so many zeros in all his life.

"The goal is to keep you alive, Mr. Turner. Our coin would be wasted otherwise. That would be your annual salary for as long as you're needed. You can expect bonuses for any useful information you acquire. If you're ever offered more coin to double-cross us, we'll double whatever they throw at you. There'll be men set up in Eastgate to help protect you and to act as your points of contact. If you agree, then we'll plant the seed for your disguise tomorrow morning," Charles proposed.

Felix was rendered speechless. He looked at the men surrounding him waiting for his reply, then back at the piece of paper. "Can I take some time to think about it?"

"I'm afraid time is something we don't have," Charles said.

"How much time do you need?" Drake asked.

"A few days should be sufficient."

"We'll give you until the end of the day," Charles offered, and he slid a small leather-bound journal across the table with a silver ring resting on top of it.

"What's this?" Felix asked, picking up the ring and journal. He opened the book to the first page. On it was a written contract with a blank signature line at the bottom. The rest of the book was completely blank.

"They're enchanted. Anything you write in that book will show up in my identical copy, and vice versa. The ring will change from silver to gold when there's a pending message. The message will disappear seven seconds after it's read. The book will be activated and calibrated to you personally as soon as the contract is signed. If you decide to take the job, then I'll expect a signature on that bottom line by midnight. If you don't, I'll send a Sendsong to collect both items in the morning. If you do decide to take the job, then that book will be used for our communications for the duration of your employment. Oh…and the contract will have to be signed with your real name. What is your real name, if you don't mind me asking?" Charles inquired.

"Felix Copperweather," Felix answered without hesitation. He knew they would discover it regardless; the question was most likely testing his loyalty. Not that it mattered, now that Lord Bardviss knew who he was, his name was already compromised. Felix planned to choose a new one as soon as he was clear of Sky View.

Charles nodded. "Any questions, Copperweather?"

"No." Felix slipped the ring on his right thumb where it miraculously adjusted itself to fit his appendage perfectly. As he placed the book safely in his pocket, he recalled what Lilliana had said about her father treating the people around him like pieces on a chess board, and he wondered if he'd just become one of his pawns. It wasn't a position Felix was eager to be in, but the number on that paper was too big to not consider the proposal. *Shick have mercy.*

# SCOUNDRELS AN' SCALLYWAGS

Bastian disembarked the Black Mary after leaving Dylan and walked onto Jaxland's beach. The sun had only just set, leaving the island bathed in its twilight glow. There was a large bonfire being prepared on the sand. Men were piling wood onto it and rolling barrels of ale into place, ready to be tapped. Bastian made his way to the village tavern and found it overflowing with black flag sailors too watered to walk straight. He pushed his way through the boisterous crowd to the table where he'd left Rhino. The pirate was still there with an ale in hand.

"Have you moved at all since I last saw you?" Bastian asked, scooting onto one of the stools Rhino had saved for them.

"If I 'ad, ya wouldn't be sittin' down," Rhino grunted.

"Surely you must be starving?"

"Are ya kiddin'?! This be all the meal I need," Rhino declared, holding up his stein. "I do need ta use the privy though, been bustin' ta go fer a while now. 'old the fort, won't ya?"

"Of course."

"Good man, I won't be long," Rhino promised, and disappeared into the crowd.

The second Rhino was gone, a pirate well over six foot came to their table and picked up one of the empty stools. "Thanks fer savin' me a seat, lad, I'll just take it ta me own table," he announced with a condescending smirk.

Bastian looked up. "Yeah, actually that seat's already taken—and not by you."

The pirate looked around. "Fer who then? Yer imaginary friends?" he laughed.

"Fer me, ya overstuffed turd!"

Bastian looked over to see Stork approaching the table. *Thank the Stars*, he thought with a sigh of relief.

"Now put the stool down before ya find out just how un-imaginary I am," Stork advised threateningly.

The large man sized up Stork and smirked, "Yeah? What ya goin' ta do about it?"

"How about we start by cuttin' off yer grape-sized testicles, an' then we can see 'ow much o' that bravado ya still 'ave left, eh?" Rhino proposed, coming up from behind him brandishing a twelve-inch blade.

The pirate put down the stool and held up his hands apologetically. "Sorry, lads, I was clearly mistaken. No 'ard feelin's I 'ope?"

"Not if ya piss off!" Stork growled.

The pirate left promptly.

"I 'ope Cricket doesn't take too much longer, I don't know if we'll be able ta 'old an empty seat in this crowd—they're like a flock o' ravenous gulls," Rhino remarked as he and Stork sat down.

"If he's not 'ere in the next 'alf hour, I say we give it up. If he wants ta stay with 'is missus, that's fine, but not at our expense. I'm not keen on makin' enemies with this lot."

"Fair," Bastian admitted.

Rhino looked at his empty tankard. "Now, the important question—who's gettin' the next round? I've already spent a small fortune on piss just ta keep this table."

"I'll get this one. Without Cricket 'ere there's one less ta buy for," Stork said, and disappeared towards the bar.

"'ow's yer day been Dodger? Ya enjoyin' Jaxland?" Rhino asked.

"Yeah, it's a lot better than I expected, if I'm honest. What's the crowd here for? Surely they're not all here just to get plastered?"

"Yer right, plenty o' places fer a man ta find a drink on this island. No, the crowd be 'ere, an' I be savin' this table fer the annual show," Rhino explained, gesturing towards an empty stage.

"A show—what kind of show?"

"Ye'll see, should start any moment now."

Not a minute later the firebeetle lanterns went dark and silence fell over the crowd. There was the sound of beating drums and then a stream of fire shot into the air from the stage. It fell dark except for a single candle flame in the shadows. Then the stage lit up with dozens of firebeetle lanterns outlining its edges. A curvaceous gypsy woman stood center stage dressed in a long skirt with high slits up its sides and a beaded halter top that exposed her bare torso. She was holding a bottle of rum in one hand and a candle in the other.

"Welcome scoundrels an' scallywags ta the annual Jaxland gatherin'!" the woman announced.

The whole house whistled and cheered.

"I'm glad ta see none o' ya be thirsty, but don't drown yerselves unconscious, fer this show will be well worth rememberin'! Shall we get it started, lads?"

"Aye!!" the men cheered.

The woman took a swig from her bottle and held the candle in front of her, then sprayed the rum through the flame, creating a stream of fire that jetted over the heads of the audience. Music filled the air from some unseen band and the woman began to belly dance. Eight other women in the same attire came forward from the wings and lined up on either side of her, dancing seductively to the music.

The men whistled their approval as they watched the spectacle. Stork returned with three brimming earthen steins. "Ah, shick. What 'ave I missed?"

"It only just started," Rhino assured him.

Before Stork could reply Cricket's voice cut in from behind. "Glad ta 'ear it. Thanks fer savin' me a seat lads!" he declared, pulling up the last stool beside them.

Stork held up his stein to him. "There's Raemeo! I was beginnin' ta think ya weren't goin' ta make it."

"I'm surprised ya did. I would've thought fer sure we weren't goin' ta see ya until at least the mornin'," Rhino said.

"Ya wouldn't 'ave if Jozalin wasn't in the show," Cricket admitted.

"Is she now? What's she doin' in it?"

"Don't know. She wouldn't tell me, said she wanted it ta be a surprise."

"Aww, isn't that sweet. Well, ye'll 'ave ta get yer own drink. I've only just come back, an' there's no bloody way I'm waitin' in that line again," Stork said.

"No trouble, I'll brave it. Probably see ya lads in an 'our then," Cricket smirked cheerily, and left for the bar.

"'e's in a good mood," Stork remarked.

"O' course 'e is!" Rhino exclaimed, and they turned their attention back to the show.

⌒

Cricket returned twenty minutes later with four fresh tankards in hand.

"It's worse than shark-infested waters out there," he declared, putting the drinks on the table. "Figured I'd buy me round now, thought ya ladies might just be finishin' up anyways."

"Come on, Cricket, we all know the only one o' us pretty enough ta be a lady be yew," Stork jested.

"It's nice ta know ya think so," Cricket returned with a wink and a smirk.

Stork put up the back of his pointer finger and stirred it in a little circle—indicating Cricket should go shick himself.

Cricket laughed. "What did I miss?"

"Ya 'aven't missed Jozalin if that be what yer wonderin'," Rhino assured him.

"Thank Shick fer that." Cricket took a drink from his stein, then stopped mid-gulp with his eyes glued to the stage. Everyone else followed his gaze.

Jozalin walked onto the stage. She had bare feet with bells around her ankles and was dressed elegantly in a long, beaded dress. She played a ukulele and sang a song with a voice as sweet as a siren.

Cricket watched her, mesmerized, and Bastian could swear she was playing just for him. After she finished her entrancing melody about a love deeper and wider than the sea, she winked in Cricket's direction and left the stage. The men cheered.

"Yer a lucky man, Cricket," Rhino declared, putting his hand on his shoulder.

"Lucky fer today, another man will be lucky on the marrow," Stork remarked.

"Why do ya always 'ave ta be such an arse, brother? It doesn't matter 'ow many men lay with Jozlin, none o' them but Cricket 'ave 'er 'eart. That be plain as day."

"Thanks, Rhino. Besides, thanks ta Dodger, she'll still be mine on the marrow, an' we'll make the most o' every moment we 'ave."

Rhino held up his mug. "Ya know what they say, don't let fear o' the approachin' dawn keep ya from enjoyin' the stars."

Cricket raised his in return, as did Bastian and Stork. "Aye, ta makin' the most o' Jaxland!" Stork declared, and all four clinked their tankards.

⌒

At the end of the show a band of merry sailors took the stage and filled the house with lively music. Half the men stumbled out of the pub at that point to look for entertainment elsewhere. Bastian stayed back with Cricket and the twins for a few extra rounds, and as Bastian watched the band play he was suddenly struck with an idea.

"I'll be back in a few," he announced, excusing himself from the table.

"Where do ya think yer goin'?" Cricket asked.

"I want to talk to the performers, I'll only be a few minutes."

Cricket smiled wryly. "One o' the dancin' girls catch yer fancy?"

"It's yer round. Don't think yer gettin' out o' it that easy!" Stork objected.

"Here, while I'm away drinks are on me. I won't be long," Bastian said, chucking his coin purse on the table. Coins spilled out across the table's surface and Bastian instantly realized his mistake. He'd forgotten just how full his pouch was.

Cricket swept the coin up as quick as a heartbeat, "Shick, Dodger! Where'd ya get all this? 'ave ya been gamblin' taday?"

"Something like that. It's for all of us, to ensure we make the most of Jaxland—just don't go spending it all at once."

His company looked at one another.

"Alright, Dodger, go on then, an' we'll make the most o' Jaxland," Stork promised.

Bastian eyed them warily. "You better be here when I get back."

"O' course, matey. Where else would we go?" Stork asked innocently.

"Ha! I can think of a few places."

"Don't worry, mate, I'll babysit these two. We'll be 'ere when ya return," Rhino assured him.

"Thanks, Rhino." Bastian gave them a final suspicious glance, and then left to tend to his business.

⌒

When Bastian returned to the table it was surrounded by a small crowd of men he didn't recognize. He pushed through them to find Cricket and the twins stuck in a drinking competition with five other pirates, and he had no doubt it was being funded by his coin purse.

"Fer this next round we'll be doin' a Mortar Mixer!" Rhino announced.

"First one ta spit er swallow, loses!" Stork declared.

The onlookers laughed and the competitors grunted. The spectators started calling out bets and the bartender brought each man participating a shot glass filled with a creamy liqueur accompanied by a schooner of dark lager. On the count of three each of them poured the shot into their mouths with a sip of lager and proceeded to swish the two together.

Bastian had played this drinking game before. As the liqueur mixed with the lager, it curdled—the longer one did it, the closer the concoction resembled cottage cheese. The point was to keep it in your mouth longer than your opponent. Bastian crossed his arms and watched the players with a grin. It appeared that Rhino, Stork, Cricket, and some random sailor he'd never seen before were all playing on a team against four other pirates. It was clear the Black Mary team was far more practiced at the game than their opponents—it wasn't long before the men on the other side of the table began to turn a shade of green. One of them finally cracked and spit the chunky contents into his glass, which sent everyone else around them into a battle with their own stomachs.

Rhino swallowed his concoction and yelled out "Yarrr!" raising both hands in triumph. Stork and Cricket spit their mouthfuls back into their schooners, before noticing Bastian had returned. "Dodger, yer back! Come an' join us! The Undertakers 'ere challenged us ta a drinkin' competition. We 'ad no choice but ta oblige 'em," Stork asserted.

"Nonsense, ya challenged us!" a pirate objected.

"Anyways, someone 'as ta uphold the reputation o' the Black Mary. Am I right?"

"Aye, Jake 'ere was only fillin' in until ya returned," Rhino explained.

"Jake meet Dodger, Dodger meet Jake," Stork said, introducing the extra player on their team. "Jake's a killer sniper from the Sea Bane, though mark me words, one o' these days we'll convince 'im ta join the Black Mary."

"Funny as shick too. Tell Dodger one o' yer jokes," Cricket insisted.

Jake cleared his throat and the men fell quiet. He was a young man, maybe even younger than Bastian, with a head full of dark curls that hugged his face and brown eyes that gazed out through a pair of spectacles. He looked up at Bastian with a drunken grin and announced in a soft voice, "What do ya call a sailor who's been a week er more at sea?... Randy."

The surrounding pirates hooted and hollered. Bastian grinned, primarily because of how much the joke tickled the men around him. They were clearly more drunk than he was.

"Well, Jake, I'm happy for you to finish up the rest of the game in my place if you like. Seems it would be an unfair advantage if I tap in now when I'm mostly sober."

"Would be a pleasure an' delight!" Jake agreed with a drunken happy smile, and the men cheered.

Bastian watched as they finished off the rest of their drinking competition. He was grateful Jake had taken his place. Bastian was already well watered. If he'd participated in the game, he wouldn't have been capable of carrying out his task the following day. He recalled Snib's warning and only hoped he hadn't drunk too much already. He had half a mind to break into Snib's quarters and hunt down his store of Spiced Kah.

The competition ended and the Black Mary team was declared the winner. Cricket stumbled up to the bar to leave a tip for the barkeep with Bastian's coin and was too drunk to be subtle. He threw the remainder of the pouch to Bastian, and Bastian noted how much lighter it was. He stowed it in his pocket, and left the tavern with Cricket, Stork and Rhino. As they stumbled out into the town center the pirates began singing.

*One dark night with no moonlight*
*the Thrixin' Stars were cravin',*
*They saw a tipplin' stray stumblin' on 'is way*
*An' chose 'im fer their mayhem.*
*Poor Henry Vass saw an ass,*
*Sure it be a blushin' maiden.*
*Not till the sun came up, did 'e realize he'd been mistaken.*
*Victim ta the Thrixer's fun,*
*'is risin' shame compared ta none.*
*All 'e could do was turn tail an' run,*
*An' pray ta the Stars fer absolution.*

The four of them made their way along the dirt road towards the beach. The moon was up, and everything cast in night's shadow. As the path led them into the trees Bastian got the prickly feeling they were being followed. He heard a snapping branch just before seven large men stepped out from the darkness, surrounding them.

"We couldn't help but notice the weight ya be carryin' in yer pockets, thought we might help ya lighten yer load," one announced. He was skinnier than the rest, with large hoop earrings and a bandanna around his head.

"How thoughtful o' ya! Yer muther must be so proud o' yer chivalry. But no thanks, it's a load we like bearin'," Cricket returned.

The pirate snarled, "We're not askin'."

All seven of the attackers pulled out daggers.

"Come on, lads, no need ta show off yer pricks. I mean, we're flattered an' all, but we're not interested. Best ta put 'em back in yer pants where they belong," Stork warned.

Rhino laughed full-heartedly and pulled out his dagger that was twice the size. "Honestly boys, if I was ya, I wouldn't be advertisin' 'ow small they be."

Their assailants hesitated.

"I'll give you the coin, just put your daggers away," Bastian announced, holding up his purse.

"Dodger, what are ya doin? Don't give in ta these maggots!" Cricket hissed.

"It's not worth it."

"At least one o' ya 'ave sense," the skinny one sneered, and walked over to take the pouch from Bastian. Just when his hand was in grasp of it, Bastian threw the pouch in the air. The pirate scrambled to catch it and Bastian grabbed hold of both the man's earrings, yanking them towards him as hard as he could while kneeing him squarely in the groin. The man yelped as the hoops were ripped through his earlobes, then doubled over in pain. Bastian arced his elbow across the man's jaw, knocking him out cold. There was a moment of silence as everyone stared at Bastian in disbelief.

Rhino regained his wits first and punched the man to his left in the face, knocking him down. Another pirate lunged towards Cricket, and Cricket pulled out his pistol with the ease of a water snake, cocking it and aiming it at the man's head in one fluid motion. The pirate dropped his knife in the sand and held up his hands in surrender.

The last four of their attackers looked at each other, then they looked at Bastian's pouch on the ground. Bastian stepped over it protectively and the men charged. The first one to reach him lunged forward with his dagger. Bastian stepped towards him, barely dodging the blade as he grabbed hold of the man's outthrust arm and propelled it forward with the momentum of his own attack. The man stumbled several paces before face planting into the sand.

As the next two reached Bastian, he collapsed down in a controlled fall onto his back and kicked out one of their knees. The injured pirate yelped in agony and collapsed to the ground beside him. Bastian rolled towards him arcing his elbow into the man's temple, rendering the pirate unconscious. Then he leapt to his feet and punched the other man in the jaw, knocking the assailant down before he'd had the chance to defend himself. Rhino took on the largest foe, a man nearly as big as he was. The pirate put up a good fight but succumbed to Rhino's fists in the end. Stork spotted the man with the injured knee reach for his pistol, and knocked him out before he had the opportunity to draw it.

Just when they thought the fight was done, the pirate Bastian had thrown into the sand resurfaced behind him, with his blade held to Bastian's throat.

"One more move an' I slice 'im open!" he declared.

Everyone stopped.

"Ya do that an' I'll shoot this man down," Cricket countered, still aiming his pistol at his assailant's head.

Bastian's attacker laughed. "Do it! I don't care about—" But before he could finish his sentence, Bastian threw his head back into the man's nose and felt the small bones crunch against his skull. The pirate loosened his grip in his moment of agony, and Bastian dropped straight down to the ground and rolled to escape the blade. He came back up on his feet and faced his foe, his heart pounding like a racehorse. Blood was pouring from the man's nose—he took one look at his unfavorable circumstances and fled.

Bastian turned around to see Stork, Cricket, and Rhino all staring at him.

Cricket motioned to his captive with his pistol, "Get outta 'ere, before I fill ya with shot," he demanded disdainfully. The pirate hurriedly scrambled to escape.

"What the shick was that?!" Stork exclaimed.

"Where be Dodger, an' what 'ave ya done with 'im?" Cricket inquired in earnest.

Rhino scratched his head. "I must be completely sloshed, 'cause I thought I just saw Dodger take out three grunts," he declared.

"Four," Stork corrected, narrowing his eyes at Bastian. "Ye're full o' surprises, aren't ya mate," he said evenly.

"Can we talk about this later? We should get out of here before these guys gain consciousness," Bastian exclaimed.

"Right. I can't argue with that," Cricket admitted, picking up some coins that had spilled out of Bastian's pockets and tossing them to him. Stork stepped over one of the fallen men and spit on him as he passed.

Bastian sat in the sand on the beach around the blazing bonfire next to Cricket, Stork, and Rhino. They were basking in the fire's warmth while they listened to a man on a lute singing a sea ballad. Bastian was looking at his shaking hands. He was as stunned as the others by the way he'd taken down those men. He'd grown so used to sparring Falgo this last week, he'd acted instinctually without even thinking about it. He was only grateful he hadn't killed anyone. If it had come to it, he wondered if he would've given it any thought. The question troubled him. But he was too tired and intoxicated to untangle such a web. He had a big day ahead of him, and the Stars only knew what it would bring. To make matters worse, Stork kept looking at him suspiciously, like Bastian was some sort of imposter. Bastian ignored him and said good night to the group before heading to the Black Mary.

# BREAK A LEG

Gwena woke early that Starday morning. She'd wandered the club the night before soaking in its splendor for what she knew would be the last time. Benji sang several numbers on the piano with a female vocalist Gwena hadn't seen before. She enjoyed watching Benji perform his music. She was going to miss that. When she finally got into bed she hardly slept, anticipating the coming day. She was brimming with anxious energy, not only about the opening show that coming evening, but also about leaving with Bonnie and the idea of leaving Benji permanently. She hadn't spoken to him since her Naming Day. She knew she had to tell him she was leaving, but she wasn't sure how.

Gwena had her breakfast in her room, then she packed her things and made her bed. Afterwards she sat down at her desk and wrote a letter to Madam Rouge, thanking her for her time at The Wildsinger's Club and announcing her resignation, saying that as much as she'd enjoyed and appreciated having the opportunity to work there, she had important business to attend to elsewhere. She placed the letter on the bed and then headed up top to the Heartland.

The city was humming with its usual buzz. Gwena wound her way through the back alleyways in search of the city's library. She recalled seeing it just off the main square on her Naming Day. It was a magnificent building, at least as grand as the city's other landmarks, and by far the biggest library Gwena had ever seen. It reminded her of a grand temple, and it was indeed a pantheon of knowledge. She walked to the main desk and asked the librarian to point her in the direction of books pertaining to glass—primarily informative manuals regarding its properties. The librarian led her to a section that was beyond adequate for her purpose, then left her alone. Gwena spent the next two hours poring over those books. When she stepped out into the busy street again it was already lunch. She bought herself a baguette and headed back towards the club. Once there, Gwena returned to her room and spent the rest of the afternoon practicing her breathing exercises for the show. She was as prepared as she was ever going to be for the performance that evening, but she still couldn't shake her nerves. She was eager to have the whole thing over and done with so that she could put it behind her.

Finally, the time arrived for Gwena to make her way to Theater 3. She entered an hour before the show was to begin and found the rest of the cast and crew already on stage in a meeting. They looked down at her as she walked the length of the aisle, a couple of them whispering to one another. Gwena kept her focus forward and continued straight past them backstage to the dressing room. The mermaid tail was waiting for her there, hung up alongside the rest of her costume. She carefully took it down and checked it over.

"You made it."

Gwena looked up to see Richard standing in the doorway. His black eye had healed up well over the last couple of days, and any remaining evidence of the injury had been covered over with stage makeup.

"I told Madam Pomphrey I would," Gwena stated.

"I'm glad. That you're doing the show, I mean," Richard stammered.

"Thanks. How is she?"

"I'm not really sure, to be honest. She hasn't wanted to talk to me about anything but stage directions. When I tried, she said everything would be alright once the show was over, and she didn't want to talk any more about it. I'm guessing she just doesn't want the distraction. I don't really mind though. This whole thing made me realize it's been over between us for a long time, it's just that neither of us were willing to admit it to each other—or ourselves."

"It's clear she loves you. Don't you love her?" Gwena asked.

"I'm not sure I ever have. I think I was in love with the idea of her. But that's not really enough, is it?"

"No, it's not. You need to tell her that. It's not fair to string her along. Then at least you can both move on and find someone else."

"Yeah, I know. I'm planning on it as soon as she's willing to talk to me again."

"Good," Gwena smiled, and then she continued checking over her costume.

Richard hung around awkwardly. Gwena looked back up at him, and he hesitated before saying, "It's supposed to be a full house tonight."

"Are you nervous?" she asked.

"Extremely, can you tell?" Richard laughed awkwardly.

Gwena smiled. "A little," she admitted.

"Shick, my hands won't stop sweating."

"You're going to be great."

"You really think so?"

"Yeah. You just have to believe it yourself. You're only nervous because you're still unsure of that. But the only one in control of your performance tonight is you, and you got this."

"Yeah. Thanks, I needed to hear that," Richard said, looking into her eyes longingly. "Well…I'll get out of your hair. Break a leg tonight."

"Excuse me?!" Gwena asked indignantly.

"It's theater-speak for *good luck*," Richard explained.

"Oh…you break a leg too, then."

Richard smiled and left the dressing room. Gwena waited several moments to ensure no one else would pop in, then she pulled out the stiletto dagger Bonnie had given her and tucked it discreetly into the tail of her costume.

# THE BENEFIT OF FRIENDS

Felix, Roy, Lilliana, and Drake sat in the airship's common space as the it pulled away from the Remingtons' island. Felix turned the silver ring on his finger, wondering what in the nine realms of darkness to do now. Just when he thought he was finally freeing himself from the political web he'd become ensnared in over the last week, he was being pulled back into the thick of it.

As soon as the ship had fully disengaged, Lilliana turned on her father in outrage. "What was that about?!"

"What?" Drake asked with an air of puzzled innocence.

"How dare you send me away with Frederick, instead of including me in the planning—that was completely patronizing! I'm not a child!"

"I should hope not. Soon you'll be the duchess of Sky View with a doting husband who'll let you do whatever you please. I expect you to use the position to your full advantage. But you and Frederick aren't married yet, and it's paramount they don't think you're only marrying him for his protection from Lord Bardviss. Charles is a sentimental fellow. He cares more about his son's happiness than securing a marriage for political gain. Luckily, your betrothal will be good for both—benefitting all who are concerned. But if Charles thinks for a moment you don't care about his son and are only using him for his position, then your matrimony will be canceled very quickly. Have you forgotten everything I've taught you?"

"No," Lilliana answered curtly, regaining her composure and smoothing the creases from her blouse.

"Now, if you're finished and it's alright by you, I'd like to go over today's plan."

"It's about time," Lilliana remarked stubbornly and sat down.

Roy and Felix joined them at the table.

❧

Half an hour later Felix stood on the deck of the airship with Lilliana beside him. "Do you think it will work?" she asked.

"It's a good plan. I must admit, I'm jealous I didn't think of it myself. I can see now where your sharp wit comes from. Luckily for me, you're far better company than your father," Felix remarked with a wry smile.

Lilliana laughed and Felix wished he could pull her close to him and kiss her. Then her smile faded. "They offered you a job, didn't they?"

"What makes you say that?"

"Because I know my father, it's what he would've done. You've proven you're a valuable asset and loyal to our family. He'd want to utilize your skills while ensuring you stay far enough away from me to not be a distraction."

"Does that mean I don't really have a choice?"

Lilliana shrugged. "Is the job important for the future benefit of Equillian?"

"I suppose."

"And does anyone else qualify for it better?"

Felix thought about that for a moment. "No," he admitted.

"Then you don't have any more choice than I do. You could walk away from it all and try and return to the life you left behind, but if you do that, then you'll be turning your back on the rest of the world just as much as I would if I walked away from my duties as a duchess."

"Do you know what they want me to do?"

Lilliana shook her head.

"They want me to act as a spy and infiltrate Marx's inner circle. If I go, there's a good chance I'll never come back."

Fear struck Lilliana's eyes and he could see her sifting through what that meant. Then she raised her chin and regarded him with resolve. Felix knew he was facing the warrior inside her.

"They couldn't have chosen anyone more suited for the role. Just as you said to me, you have an opportunity to change the future course of Equillian, to make it better. It has to be you," she asserted, a single tear rolling down her cheek.

Felix wiped the tear away with his thumb and wrapped his hand gently behind her neck, pulling her into his arms for a hug, then he bent his head down and kissed her. *Let them find us,* he thought. *They've already condemned us anyway.*

～

The airship reached the capital and Roy steered it to one of the valet docking bays fanned out around the city. Felix, Lilliana, Roy, and Drake all disembarked. Roy and Drake exchanged a few words with Felix and Lilliana before splitting off in a different direction. Felix gave Lilliana a comforting smile, and side by side they made their way towards the Waterhole Inn.

The streets were still crowded with festivalgoers, but not quite as densely as they'd been the day before. Lilliana wore a black dress and a wide-brimmed hat with the black veil of a widow. Felix was disguised with a moustache and a pair of yellow-tinted spectacles. He'd also added a mole to his cheek, changed his hair to dark brown, and combed it to the side. On his hands he donned a pair of black leather gloves to hide his tattoo. "Are you ready for this?" he asked Lilliana.

"I'm looking forward to it," she answered with iron determination, and Felix reminded himself not to get on Lilliana's bad side.

The Waterhole Inn was in the center of Diamond City. *Bold choice,* Felix thought. He'd imagined it would be some dive down a back alley—not that Sky View had such places—but he couldn't have been more wrong. It was a large, elegant building made of blue stone, with two black marble dragons drinking out of a water fountain on either side of the entrance.

They stopped outside the front and Felix pulled out his pocket watch. It was one minute to Karmithos's hour. "Lights up," he said, Lilliana nodded, and they walked into the building.

⌒

As soon as Felix and Lilliana stepped foot inside the grand foyer of the Waterhole Inn, a man came up to meet them. He was a handsome, cocksure fellow in his early twenties with slicked-back hair and smartly dressed in a dark navy-blue suit.

"Felix?" the man inquired.

"Who's asking?"

The man smirked smugly, then proceeded to pat Felix down without invitation.

"Whoa, careful where you're putting your hands, you haven't even bought me a drink," Felix exclaimed.

The man ignored him and finished his search for what Felix could only presume was concealed weapons. After he came up clean, the man turned to Lilliana. "Lady Wendrian?"

Lilliana pulled back her veil and took off her hat to reveal her face. The man smiled and proceeded to pat her down in turn.

"Is this really necessary?!" Felix objected, but Lilliana gave him a cautionary stare, and Felix clenched his jaw while their escort finished his frisk.

"Right this way," he said, and gestured down the hall.

Felix and Lilliana followed him to the very back of the hotel where there was a private dining room large enough to seat twenty at a round table.

"Please, have a seat," the man offered condescendingly, kicking out a chair for Lilliana.

Lilliana looked at Felix as she sat down, her eyes burning with the desire to hurt their chaperon. Felix pulled out the seat next to her, and the man took up a post by the door like the good lackey he was. Felix wondered if he was one of the youth up here Marx had sunk his teeth into.

A minute later another man entered the room. He was much older, slim, with greying hair that was white on the sides, dressed in an upmarket pin-striped suit. He sat down opposite them at the table and crossed his legs casually, studying them both for a moment before he spoke.

"Lady Lilliana Wendrian and Felix Copperweather, welcome," he greeted in a thick eastern accent. "I'm glad you both could make it. Lord Bardviss wanted me to apologize on his behalf for not being able to attend in person. He really wanted to be here. You stirred him up something good, you two. In all honesty, I wasn't sure you'd come. You had us guessing for a while there. I was almost convinced you were clever—almost. I didn't think anyone could be so foolish as to deliberately hand themselves over so easily. Bardviss, however, assured me you were the kind of man who would, and here you are," he smiled condescendingly.

"Here I am," Felix agreed, returning a smile just as patronizing.

The man chuckled and then his expression turned mean. "That's enough pleasantries, I have more important things to attend to, and you've already wasted far too much of our time. Joey, you take the girl and I'll deal with this shmutz," he commanded, pulling a pistol out of his coat and pointing it at Felix.

The lackey grabbed Lilliana's arm and pulled her roughly from her chair.

The man in the pinstripes stood, keeping his pistol steadily aimed at Felix's head. "Did you really think Lord Bardviss would hire you after everything you've done?" he jeered.

Felix smiled, "Of course not, my IQ's not low enough to qualify."

The man's contemptuous expression fell into a sneer, but Felix continued before he could get a word in, "Though I do appreciate how considerate you were in getting a table big enough to accommodate my friends."

The man cocked his head. "Friends?"

"They're something you can hope to acquire if you ever stop being such an arsehole," Felix declared.

The man's eyes flared with anger and Felix heard the lackey yelp like a little girl behind him. He turned to see Joey in an armlock on the ground with Lilliana's knee pressed down between his shoulder blades, and her hand around his pinky finger pulling it at an odd angle. "One more move and I'll snap it off," she hissed.

Felix smiled wryly and turned back to his aggressor.

"See, Lord Bardviss made one critical error—he greatly underestimated the people he's messing with."

On cue, the doors to the private room flung open and in came a flood of journalists snapping photos as Drake Wendrian, Roy, Charles Remington, Frederick Remington, and Emperor Balthazar strolled into the room with an entourage of guards behind them.

Lord Bardviss's man's face collapsed from an expression of outrage to complete shock. He quickly hid his pistol and tried to pretend he and Felix had been having a polite conversation. As the gravity of the situation dawned on him, he anxiously slunk into the oncoming chaos.

Roy grabbed him by the shoulders and steered him back to the table, pressing him into one of the chairs. "Where do you think you're going? Stay a while. Drinks are on us," he insisted, and sat Joey down beside him. The two complied in shocked silence.

Once everyone was inside the room, the Emperor turned to address the press.

"Ladies and gentleman, it's with great pleasure I announce to you that both Lady Lilliana and Duke Drake Wendrian have been found, uncovered by recovery expert James Turner, hired privately by Duke Charles Remington of Sky View, in honor of the arrangement to unite their families that was made before Duke Wendrian's disappearance. Now that both the Duke and Duchess of Westdock have returned, that agreement will be honored with the betrothal of Lady Lilliana Wendrian to Sky View's marquess, Frederick Remington. Drake will be returning to his position as Duke of Westdock without delay, and I'm sure we can all expect to hear news regarding the wedding celebration soon. The

Wendrian family has been, and continues to be, of great service to the people of Equillian. I give the union between the Wendrian and Remington families my full blessing. I'm overjoyed to see these two great precincts strengthening ties—the more united we become, the stronger and better Equillian grows as a whole, and the more we can achieve for the betterment of humanity. I look forward to seeing what these two noteworthy families will accomplish together. I know their alliance will no doubt benefit us all," he announced, and posed for a photo with both dukes, Lilliana, Frederick, and Felix.

A flurry of questions came from the press corp as a succession of blinding flashes captured the event. The Emperor put up a hand, motioning for them to stop.

"Now, if you'll excuse me, I have other appointments to attend. Please refer your questions to the dukes and those accompanying them. They'll be happy to answer any inquiries you have," he announced, and made his way out of the room surrounded by his guards. With a single slight motion of his hand, Lord Bardviss's men were escorted out with them.

A second later Felix was answering questions from a squall of journalists circling him hungrily and blinding him with flash photography. He looked over at Lilliana who was in the same position amongst her own circle only a few feet away—accompanied by Frederick.

Felix felt sick. A moment before he'd felt on top of the world—dishing out justice with Lilliana by his side—and now it was all over. This was it. Now Lilliana's betrothal was announced to the whole world, with the Emperor's own blessing, no less. There was no way they could disappear together now. But the only thing that really mattered was that Lilliana was safe. Lord Bardviss wouldn't dare touch her now. Drake and Charles's plan and execution was brilliant—it told the world the Wendrians were back and had the support of the Emperor. It made the Remingtons look good for hiring the recovery expert who successfully found Lady Lilliana and the duke of Westdock, and it turned James Turner into a hero, one backed by three different royals at the top of the noble food chain. Felix would keep that persona tucked in his back pocket for a rainy day—he had no doubt it would come in handy. Part of him wished he'd done it all without a disguise, that the world could know he was the true hero. But fame came with a price, one he wasn't eager or willing to cough up—especially when it meant putting the people he cared about in danger. He only wished he could see Lord Bardviss's expression when he learned that he'd been threatening an employee, and the future daughter-in-law of the duke of Sky View. He would be stupid to go after either of them now. And no one would even have to bother pursuing him—Lord Bardviss would run with his tail between his legs, and they'd let him. The more the nobles ignored him, the more he'd realize just how small and insignificant he was, removing him as a threat in the upper playing fields. He'd have no chance of climbing his way through the ranks now. Not unless The East gained power. And that was going to be a lot harder after today. Felix knew it wasn't over because Lord Bardviss was only one of Marx's minions. Their little disruption was probably nothing more than a thorn in the kingpin's side. As long as Marx was breathing he'd be plotting Equillian's downfall. And Felix knew that if he took the job the dukes were offering, he'd be stepping from the pot into the fire—but that was tomorrow's problem. Just knowing that Lilliana's safety was secured was a huge relief, and he had to admit to himself that despite his misery, it felt damn good to bring Lord Bardviss to justice.

*Maybe a common opportunist really can make a difference*, he thought. *Maybe the Stars have plans for me to amount to something after all.*

# BRANDED WITH BROTHERS

Bastian woke to his bracelet vibrating, then realized he had no reason to wake so early. The sleeping quarters were filled with men dozing off the drink they'd had the day before. Bastian wished he could sleep as soundly, but once he was awake his mind buzzed with activity. Today was the day of his task, and the outcome would determine his fate. He would either win his freedom or die trying. He made his way to his locker and pulled out the green velvet jacket that Gwena had made him for his birthday. He'd taken it off after his first day assisting Boom sift black powder in the armory and hadn't worn it since for fear of damaging it. But if he was going to die today, then he wanted it to be in that jacket. He dusted it off and put it on. It fit him perfectly and made him feel like a million duckets.

Bastian made his way to the top deck and found Cricket, Stork, and Rhino already there passing a bottle among themselves.

"There 'e is!" Stork announced.

Cricket gave him a sad and apologetic smile, and Rhino came over and put his arm around him. "Come, walk with us," he insisted, and led him down the gangplank towards the beach, with Stork and Cricket in tow. They led Bastian into the trees, away from the rest of the ships and crewmen, coming to a stop behind a large boulder that obscured them from any onlookers.

"What's all this about?" Bastian asked.

Stork pulled out his dagger and began tossing it up and down playfully in one hand. "We just want ta talk ta ya, that's all."

Bastian tensed and eyed the dagger warily.

"We 'ave a few questions about last night, regardin' a few thin's that just don't quite add up," Rhino explained.

Cricket stood off to the side with his arms crossed, not saying a word.

"Alright..." Bastian agreed and found his mind unconsciously mapping how to drop his friends if it came to it. He was hoping it wouldn't.

"Tell us 'ow it be that someone who was a lily-livered thief just last week—without more than a few coins ta 'is name—suddenly knows 'ow ta put down three roughies an' 'as a purse jingling full?" Stork queried.

"It's not what you think, I swear. I'm sorry, but I can't tell you anything more."

"Why not?"

"Because I promised I wouldn't, and it's not mine to tell."

"Promised who?" Cricket asked.

"If I tell you that, I may as well tell you the rest."

"Ya better tell us all o' it, else we'll assume the worst an' skewer ya fer bein' a dirty spy," Stork stated candidly, brandishing his blade without any sign that he and Bastian had ever been friends.

Bastian held up his hands defensively. "Alright, but only if you all promise not to tell anyone else."

Stork, Cricket, and Rhino exchanged glances.

"Go on."

"I made a deal with Falgo last week. I've been giving him rum in exchange for fighting lessons," Bastian confessed.

The pirates chewed that over.

Stork scowled. "I don't believe it."

Rhino shrugged. "Falgo 'as been in much better spirits. I thought 'e was finally gettin' sober, but Dodger's story would make more sense."

"We've been with ya fer most o' yer free time. When 'ave ya been doin' these so-called lessons?" Stork pressed.

"At the Phoenix hour, every night."

"Where?"

"On the beach of the Dreg, in the clearing amongst the mast trees."

Cricket looked at Stork, "That *is* very specific."

"How come ya never told us?" Rhino asked.

"Falgo told me he wouldn't train me if I told anyone."

"That does sound like Falgo," Rhino admitted.

"That still doesn't explain the coin," Stork pointed out, and all three of the pirates turned to Bastian inquiringly.

"Even if I tell you, you won't believe me."

"Try us."

"Alright. It's not real."

"What do ya mean, it's not real?"

"It's counterfeit."

The pirates looked at one another.

"Yer tellin' us we paid the barkeep o' Jaxland with counterfeit coin last night?" Cricket asked evenly.

"If that's true, Dodger, then yer dafter than I thought, an' we're all in a world o' trouble," Stork warned.

"He'll never know, it's a perfect copy. Have a look for yourself." Bastian threw them his bag of coin. Cricket caught it and took out a jolly roger. He turned it in the light and then passed it to Stork. Stork took one of his own jolly rogers out of his pouch and held them both side by side, scrutinizing them before passing Bastian's coin to Rhino.

"Mighty shick, Dodger, how'd ya manage ta come by this?" Rhino asked, inspecting the coin with admiration.

"I made it."

Stork narrowed his eyes at him. "How?"

"I can't tell you that."

"Ha! I wouldn't give that one up either," Cricket laughed, "an' neither would ya, Stork, don't pretend any different."

"Yer tellin' us, ya can make as much of this as ya like?" Stork queried.

"Sure, within reason."

Cricket grinned. "Shick, I'm glad we're mates! Ya can keep yer gamblin' circuit, Stork, I'll just hang with Dodger."

Stork slanted his eyes and stared intensely at Bastian. "Yer a hundred percent with the Black Mary?"

"Would I still be here if I wasn't?"

"That's a good point—the cap'n an' Snibs 'ave already given Dodger the once-over. If they've decided 'e's clean, then that's good enough fer me," Rhino declared, clapping Bastian on the back.

"Aye, me as well," Cricket agreed. "Now, can we drop this an' get some breakfast? I'm starvin'."

Stork glared at Bastian suspiciously for another long moment before saying, "Not yet. If Dodger truly be one o' us, then it's about time we make it official."

Cricket rolled his eyes. "Surely it can wait until after breakfast?"

"Yer stomach can wait, tell it ta stop its grumblin'," Stork growled, and sheathed his dagger.

"Aye, Lady Inkwell!" Rhino cheered, then he handed Cricket a metal flask. "'ere, this should stay yer stomach fer a time."

Cricket accepted it begrudgingly. "Fine, let's get it over an' done with then." He took a long drink before handing the flask back to Rhino.

"Get what over and done with?" Bastian inquired.

"Ye'll see soon enough," Stork assured him, and led the way back towards the heart of Jaxland.

Cricket held the door open for Bastian to a small hole-in-the-wall joint with a sign above it that read *Lady Inkwell's*. He walked in warily and the rest followed. It was a dingy shop, with well-drawn pinups and illustrations of a nautical nature hanging on the walls.

*Oh shick*, Bastian thought, recognizing the clear distinctions of a tattoo parlor.

Bastian sat down rigidly on one of the four chairs across from an unattended sales counter.

"Be right with ya!" a woman's voice called from somewhere in the back.

Bastian heard a man groan in pain and unease blossomed in his belly. He didn't like needles. It was the reason why he'd never gotten a tattoo outside the mandatory seven-pointed star behind his left ear that branded him as a child of the Stars—luckily he'd been given a local anesthetic for that one. But by the stern expression on Stork's face, he didn't think he'd be leaving without some ink drawn. *If that's what it takes for Stork to trust me, then so be it*, he thought.

Bastian recalled someone telling him once that the only way to get a tattoo and ensure it wasn't regretted was to choose something that marked an experience. Bastian's time with the Black Mary had already been one shick of an experience, one that had marked him permanently even without the ink to prove it. The idea of having a tattoo that reflected that didn't actually bother him.

A large burly sailor walked out from the backroom and exited the shop. Bastian tensed. If someone that size was moaning from the pain, then he didn't stand a chance. A woman walked out to the counter a moment later, with long dark hair tied back, and a pair of thick lensed goggles resting on her forehead. She was wearing a sleeveless shirt that revealed well-toned arms completely covered with tattoos. "Mornin' boys, are ya all gettin' ink done?" she asked.

"Just 'im," Stork announced, putting his hand on Bastian's shoulder.

"Come on back, love," the woman invited and walked towards the back room.

The three pirates guided Bastian after her.

"Ya alright, Dodger? Ye've lost all yer color," Rhino asked with a grin.

"I'm not fond of needles."

"Come on, ye've faced a Kraken, this be nothin'!" Cricket assured him.

The back room was well lit with a reclined plush chair next to a short stool and a side table neatly organized with needles, candles, and dozens of ink pots.

"'ave a seat," the woman instructed, gesturing to the plush chair.

Stork guided Bastian into it.

"What will it be sweet 'eart?"

"'e's gettin' this," Stork announced, pulling up his sleeve to reveal a tattoo of the Black Mary's Jolly Roger.

"The Black Mary, ya a new recruit?"

"Aye, this be 'is first time ta Jaxland," Rhino answered for Bastian.

"Welcome, lad. Where da ya want the mark?"

Everyone looked at Bastian expectantly. He hesitated, caught off guard by the question, given he hadn't been consulted on the whole business until that point. His first thought was to put the tattoo somewhere hidden away—once he wore the Black Mary's insignia, he'd be identified as a pirate for the rest of his life, but he knew that would only reinforce Stork's growing doubt about his loyalty, and he reminded himself that his life might not last beyond the days light.

"Here," Bastian announced, rolling up his sleeve to reveal the underside of his left wrist.

"Great. Won't take long," the woman assured him, and looked at the twins and Cricket expectantly. "Ya boys goin' ta hover over the lad the whole time?"

They looked at one another and then shuffled out of the room.

"'ave fun, Dodger!" Cricket called back.

Once alone, the woman turned to Bastian. "Sheesh! I hope they give ya more breathin' space than that on the ship."

Bastian laughed.

"Do ya prefer rum er whiskey, lad?"

"Rum, I suppose. Why's that?"

The woman reached behind her, opened a cupboard on the wall, and pulled out a bottle of rum and a shot glass. She filled the shooter and handed it to him. "Fer the pain."

⌒

As Bastian watched the tattoo artist finalize her rendition of the Black Mary's insignia on his wrist, he suddenly realized what the ship's trademark actually stood for. It was a human skull with a cutlass and a skeleton key crossed below it. The top of the key was shaped like a seven-pointed star, a symbol for Equillian's Key—the Ghost Element. Bastian couldn't believe he hadn't put the two together before. Now, the mark held even more meaning, and despite his earlier trepidations, he was glad he had it. It felt right somehow, like an earned trophy for everything he'd endured on the Black Mary. A rite of passage.

Bastian walked out from the back to find Cricket and the twins waiting for him. They looked at him expectantly.

"Give us a look, then," Cricket requested.

Bastian held up his arm to show the Black Mary's mark freshly engraved on his wrist.

"It suits ya!" Rhino exclaimed.

"*Now*, yer one o' us," Stork declared, clasping Bastian's forearm.

"A true pirate through an' through. I'm glad ta be sharin' a mark with ya, Dodger," Cricket said. "Now, can we get breakfast?"

Stork laughed. "*Now*, we get breakfast!" he proclaimed enthusiastically, and they all made their way back out onto the street into the morning light. Bastian couldn't help but smile. The small band might be a bunch of dodgy rogues, but Bastian had to admit it still felt good to be accepted as one of them.

# THE PLUNGE

Gwena touched the pearl necklace around her neck as she sat on the swing high above the stage out of view. Her heart was beating like a hummingbird in flight. She closed her eyes and focused on preparing her lungs for sustaining air while she listened to Madam Pomphrey give her introduction on the stage below.

"Ladies and gentlemen, our next act is a true spectacle never before seen on stage. Not only are you about to witness a feat so daring that it has never been tried before, but also a creature so rare, some believe it only exists in legend. Please put your hands together for our mermaid escapologist, Oceana Silverpool!"

The crowd roared as Gwena's swing was lowered into view. The Everfire stage lights beamed in her eyes, blinding her momentarily. She held tightly onto the ropes and swished her tail gracefully back and forth as she was positioned just above the water tank.

Madam Pomphrey held up her hand for silence, and a hush fell over the crowd.

"I first found this creature on the shores of Everlast, washed up on the beach tangled in a fisher's net. She was half starved, injured, and scared. I freed her, took her into my care, and nurtured her back to health. But even when she was strong once more, she was still ensnared in the lingering trauma from what she'd endured, plagued by night terrors. She'd wake screaming in the night, thinking she was still caught in that net. To help her overcome her trepidation, I introduced her to escapology, and she took it up with a fevered passion, dedicating her life to mastering the art—so that she might not only conquer her greatest fear, but ensure she's never trapped again!"

The crowd cheered with approval.

Richard and Madam Pomphrey climbed up onto the platform at the back of the tank and began to bind Gwena in chains. They wrapped them tightly around her arms and torso, then bound her wrists together, and finally placed the thick metal collar around her neck—all of which were secured with heavy locks.

They stepped back and Gwena moved her weight forward, plunging into the tank below. She sunk to the bottom like an anchor, and Madam Pomphrey closed the glass lid above her, chaining it shut and locking it securely with the lock hanging inside the tank where Gwena could reach it. Then she and Richard stepped down from the platform and left the stage.

Gwena wasted no time in trying to free herself. She moved her arms and hands back and forth to loosen the chains just enough so that when she bent her head down she could pull the long metal pin from her hair. She stuck the pin into the keyway of the lock around her wrists and went to work picking it herself, leaving the switch Mallini had made for releasing the lock idle. The lock fell away, sinking to the bottom of the tank, and the crowd cheered. Next, Gwena turned her focus to the lock securing the chains around her arms and torso. She stuck her pin into its keyway and began navigating the wards. All of the practice she'd done paid off, and seconds later the lock fell away. She briefly feigned failing to pick the lock on her collar, before swishing her tail and propelling herself upward to the tank's lid. The crowd watched in a hushed silence, not daring to take a breath for fear she might also.

Gwena grabbed hold of the lock securing the tank's cover and inserted the pin inside. It entered a fraction before hitting something solid. She tried again, moving the pin in at a different angle, but the lock was blocked. Panic rose inside her gut as the last of her air ran out, but she grabbed firmly onto the helm of her mind and focused, pushing the safety switch Mallini had designed to release the lock. It didn't work. She pushed the second mechanism designed as a failsafe, and it failed her also. She tried it again, and again to no effect. Her lungs began to burn. She looked over at Madam Pomphrey. The magician was standing in the wings of the stage watching her with a smug smile and a cold stare, and in that moment Gwena knew her greatest fear was being actualized. Part of her had known this would happen—that Madam Pomphrey would betray her, and even though she'd prepared for it, she hadn't been willing to believe it. She couldn't accept that Pomphrey would stoop so low. She'd wanted so badly for the magician to be the woman she'd thought she was, the hero she'd always looked up to. More than anything, Gwena was so very disappointed. But she refused to waste any time with regret. She reached behind her and pulled the stiletto dagger from her tail and used the blade to etch an X in the glass in front of her. According to the research she'd done that morning, all she needed was a single point of weakness. She slammed the hilt of the dagger into where the two lines crossed. Nothing happened. She hit it again, and again. A tiny crack formed. The crowd gasped. Gwena's lungs screamed for air. She pressed one hand tightly over her mouth and used the other to pick up one of the fallen locks, slamming it against the tank as hard as she could. The water reduced her force, and the glass only cracked a fraction more. Gwena couldn't hold her breath any longer—her mouth flung open involuntarily and drew water into her lungs as if it were air. She tried to will her arm to hit the glass one last time, but it stopped obeying her command. Her body convulsed, and her grip loosened. She dropped the lock to the tank floor. As her vision began to tunnel, Gwena looked out at the audience staring at her with anxious anticipation. She could see Bonnie standing in the third row next to Benji, their faces deep with concern, and in that moment all of time came to a standstill. Gwena thought mournfully about Bastian, how she'd never get the opportunity to see him again, to share their life together. She thought of Benji and the pain her death would cause him, she thought of her mother and hoped she would see her amongst the stars, then her consciousness faded, and she was gone. A bright blue light flashed on Gwena's chest, radiating outward through her blood vessels like bioluminescence. A cold rush passed through her like ice in her veins, jolting her body back to life. Gwena gained consciousness with a gasp, pulling more water into her lungs—only this time, it was as if she'd taken a breath of air. And suddenly, she was breathing. She looked down at her hands and saw the blue light pulsing through her veins, making them look like streaks of lightning running down her bare arms and across her chest. Gwena's pearl necklace was glowing the brightest of all. Just as her mind began trying to make sense of it all, three gunshots split the air. Metal bullets pierced the glass and the tank shattered, spilling the water and Gwena out onto the stage.

The audience screamed and rushed towards the exits in panic. The only ones remaining were two standing in the third row—Bonnie with a smoking pistol in hand and Benji by her side. As soon as the tank broke, Benji bounded over the stadium seating towards Gwena and scooped her up from the pool of water and broken glass. She looked up into his face and smiled weakly. "You came."

"Of course," he smiled back, then Gwena passed out.

"Will someone get this bloody collar off her?! Who has the key?!" Benji demanded in panicked outrage.

Benji lay Gwena gently on the stage. Bonnie examined the lock, found the secret button, and pressed it, releasing the choker around Gwena's neck. She took it off and looked at Gwena's pearl necklace, her gaze lingering on it briefly before she leaned down and listened to Gwena's heart.

"She's still with us, but no doubt she's taken on water," Bonnie declared, and turned Gwena onto her side.

Water trickled out of Gwena's mouth and then she coughed, spluttering a gush of water across the boards. She groaned. Benji pulled her into his arms, and she clung to him weakly.

Bonnie walked over to the shattered tank and picked up Gwena's fallen dagger, then she examined the lock that had secured the tank's lid. "Just as I suspected, someone's blocked it!"

"Who'd do such a thing?!" Benji asked, aghast.

Bonnie scowled. "I 'ave me suspicions."

"Where is everyone? Where's Madam Pomphrey?!"

"Turned tail, no doubt," Bonnie spat on the boards distastefully.

Richard ran onto the stage. "Is she alright?!"

Benji turned on him in fury, "What do you think? Where the shick have you been?! Surely you had some kind of a contingency plan to get her out of there if things went awry?!"

Richard opened and closed his mouth then said weakly, "I notified the doctor as soon as I could. He's on his way."

"Help me get this thing off her!" Benji demanded, and he and Richard pulled off the mermaid tail.

"Surely you have a towel somewhere back there?"

"Of course," Richard stammered and ran off stage. He came back shortly with a robe and handed it over.

Benji helped Gwena put it on and then scooped her back into his arms. "Send the doctor to my room," he commanded.

"Certainly," Richard replied meekly.

Bonnie came up beside Benji and checked on Gwena. "Ya got 'er covered?" she asked him.

"Yeah."

"Good, cause I 'ave a bone ta pick," she scowled, and walked towards the wings.

Benji kissed Gwena on the forehead. "Hang in there, little bird," he whispered and carried her out of the theater.

Benji laid Gwena on his bed under the covers.

"You alright?"

"I'm alive," she smiled weakly.

"Thank the Stars for that. I'll run you a hot bath, won't be a moment," he said, and disappeared into the en suite.

Gwena could hear the water running and then a knock at the door. Benji opened it to find the club's doctor, a gentleman in his mid-forties, with a pair of smart spectacles and neatly groomed short grey hair and moustache. The doctor nodded a greeting to Benji and hurried inside holding a black bag.

"Where is she?"

Benji gestured towards the bed where Gwena lay, and the doctor hurried over to her.

"Richard told me what happened. I came as soon as I could," he announced, and pulled out his stethoscope to listen to her heart and lungs. "How much water did she take in?"

"I'm not sure…"

"Only a little," Gwena lied.

"Please, excuse me," Benji said, and left to turn off the running tap.

The doctor carried out the rest of his examination, then sat back, puzzled. "I don't understand—you should be dead after what you've been through, and you have no signs of having taken in any water whatsoever. How're you feeling?"

"Surprisingly well, considering."

The doctor shook his head in disbelief. "Lady Luck has smiled upon you, child. It's a damn miracle."

Gwena's hand went instinctively to the pearl necklace around her neck.

Benji came back into the room, "How is she?"

"As far as I can tell, she's fine. I don't know how, but there it is. The best advice I can give is for her to take it easy for the next few days and to give up escapology. That craft is a death sentence waiting to be carried out! Now if you'll excuse me, I have other patients to attend to," the doctor declared.

Benji nodded. "Thanks, doc."

He showed the man out, and then turned to Gwena and smiled. "Your bath's ready. I left some clothes in there for you."

"Thanks," she returned warmly, and made her way to the en suite.

Gwena lay in the hot tub looking at her dewdrop pearl necklace, reflecting on the fact that once again Bastian had saved her. She imagined he'd had no idea of the true power the treasure held when he'd taken it from the Wendrians' castle, sure he would've told her if he'd known it was more than a pretty pendant. She'd been cross at him for stealing it, and now she shivered to think of what would've happened if he hadn't. The thought of her drowning on stage that night with an audience watching sent a chill up her spine.

Gwena closed her eyes and recalled the look on Madam Pomphrey's face while she was drowning—her smug smile, the cold satisfaction in her eyes—and she wondered how the woman had ever been her hero. The truth was, Gwena was already a far better magician than Madam Pomphrey had ever been. She realized she'd been denying that, blinded by self-doubt and the cloud of admiration she had for the woman. But her brush with death brought her a sobering clarity. It all seemed so obvious now. Madam Pomphrey hadn't been doing her a favor by letting her into the show and teaching her what she knew, she'd been using her the whole time. Gwena had saved her show, not only by taking on the role of escapologist, but by offering suggestions that had made the show monumentally better. And she wasn't even getting paid for it. As far as Gwena knew, Madam Pomphrey might have always intended to use her up and dump her once the show was over. The thought made Gwena feel sick. She felt like a part of her did drown that night—the part of her that had any naïvety and innocence left. She knew then that whether she liked it or not, her childhood was truly over. She'd been parted from so much in the last two weeks—her home, her father, Bastian and Felix—and now she'd lost her childhood idol, and it wasn't over yet. Tonight she'd also have to walk away from Benji and the club. She had so little left, and yet, despite her aching heart she felt stronger and more sure of herself than she ever had. And for the first time, she knew that her dreams were achievable.

Gwena opened her eyes and lifted herself out of the water. She stepped out of the bath and dressed in the clothes Benji had left her. It was a short-sleeved cotton shirt and a pair of long pyjama pants that were several sizes too big for her. When she came out of the en suite, Benji was waiting for her with a hot cup of tea. He took in her appearance and muffled a laugh.

"What?" Gwena asked.

"I'm just admiring how well my clothes fit you."

She smirked. "You do have pretty big shoes to fill, but who knows, maybe one day I'll grow into them."

"I hope not."

"Why's that?"

"Because I like you just the way you are," he said.

Gwena blushed with a warm smile and sat down at the kitchen counter with her cup of tea.

"How was the show?" she asked him.

"Thrilling! Your act was by far the best thing in it. Though, maybe consider scaling it back just a bit next time. I mean, correct me if I'm wrong, but I thought the goal was to keep the audience *in* their seats."

Gwena laughed, and it suddenly hit her how very much she was going to miss Benji.

"Thank you, for everything. I swear, I don't usually need this much saving."

"I'll never complain about having an excuse to have you in my room," he said.

Gwena smiled, and then her joy faded to a somber expression. Her insides were writhing in conflicted turmoil, but she knew the moment had come. "Did Bonnie tell you?"

"Tell me what?"

"She's secured a ship to captain in Port Trinity. She's leaving the club tonight, and she's asked me to go with her."

"Ah huh…no, she certainly didn't mention that. It's an interesting proposition, Bonnie on the high seas makes perfect sense, I can't think of anything more fitting for her. I can't say the same thing for you, though. What did you tell her?"

"I said yes. She's going after the ship Bastian's on. I have to at least try to find him."

Benji ran his hand across his chin, all humor instantly drained from him. "Right, I see. I'll miss you, little bird."

Gwena's eyes glistened. "I'll miss you beyond words."

Benji nodded, and Gwena saw his shields come up instantly, a barricade. He was suddenly more distant, less warm. She immediately mourned, seeing the window to his heart shut, and she wished she'd waited to tell him so that she might've basked in his warmth and closeness a little longer. But they were all out of time.

Benji stood up. "I'm glad you're going. You deserve more than this place. It will give you a chance to spread your wings."

"And what about you?"

"What about me?"

"You deserve more than this place, and the world deserves to hear your music. You've hidden away down here long enough, I think it's time you step into the light."

"As much as I appreciate you saying so, I'm not ready for that, not yet. But you've given me hope that one day I might be," Benji smiled.

"I wish you could come with us."

"And what room would there be for me when you reunite with the keeper of your heart?"

"I don't know…but I wish it all the same."

Benji smiled. "It'll bring me joy to know you're out there embracing life's adventure and to know you're happy. I'll be forever grateful our paths have crossed. Time with you has been a gift, one that's done far more for me than you'll ever know."

Silent tears ran down Gwena's cheeks, but the moment was interrupted by a knock at the door. Benji walked over and cracked it open. Gwena could hear Bonnie's voice on the other side.

"Is she 'ere?"

"Yeah."

"Is she alright?"

Benji nodded. "She's bounced back surprisingly well. Did you find Pomphrey?"

Bonnie scowled. "No, she ran like a dog with 'er tail between 'er legs."

"The sure sign of a guilty conscience," Benji scoffed.

"Did Gwena tell ya she's leavin'?"

"Yeah."

"Good. I've brought 'er bag fer 'er. There's been a change o' plans—the incident 'as sent the whole club inta chaos. Madam Rouge is closin' it down fer the night, and we'll 'ave ta depart early."

"How early?"

"Tell 'er ta meet me at the train in fifteen minutes," Bonnie requested.

"I'll let her know."

"Thanks."

"Bonnie, you'll look after her, won't you?"

"That girl's pretty good at lookin' after 'erself, but I've got 'er back."

Benji nodded. "Good luck," he said, and shook her hand.

"Same ta yew, Benji. Yer one o' the good ones, look after yerself, eh?"

Benji closed the door and rested Gwena's bag beside it.

"Well, looks like we're all out of time, little bird," he announced.

"Alright." Gwena hesitated. "I suppose I better change."

"You're welcome to keep those threads if you want, but you might find yours more suitable," he offered.

"I don't know, I think these suit me quite well," Gwena returned wryly, and then she collected her bag and carried it into the en suite.

She came out a few minutes later wearing her mother's blue travelling dress.

Benji took her in and nodded. "Well, I guess that's all we get. You'll look after yourself, little bird, won't you?" he asked, holding out his hand.

Gwena knocked it aside and jumped into his arms. Benji was taken by surprise by the fierceness of her embrace, but he wrapped his arms around her and pulled her in close. They held the hug for several long moments. Then Gwena stood up on her tiptoes and kissed his cheek.

"See you around, wildsinger."

"See you around, little bird."

Gwena picked up her bag and gave Benji one more glance before leaving his room.

Gwena walked out of The Wildsinger's Club with her quiver travelling bag slung over her back and silently strolled down the path outlined with glowing Everfire lamps towards the enchanted steam engine. Bonnie was leaning out the open door of one of the passenger cars, adorned in her tricorn hat and long naval jacket. "I wasn't sure if ya were gonna make it," she said, offering Gwena her hand. She took it and climbed aboard.

"Are ya ready?"

Gwena looked at the engine with its gentle hum and back at the club with its bright lights that never slept. Then she turned to Bonnie. "Yes," she said resolutely, and they both made their way into the train.

# A NEW CHAPTER

Felix stood on the top deck of the airship watching the Diamond City recede as Roy steered them towards the Wendrians' island. Lilliana was changing out of her widow costume, and Drake was napping in the private quarters. Felix could only imagine how exhausted the duke must be—he'd only returned to the populated world a day ago, had hit the ground running and hardly stopped since. In fact, he didn't seem to have a plan to stop anytime soon either. Drake had invited Felix and the Remingtons to the Wendrians' Sky View estate for dinner. The Remingtons had promised to join them in an hour. Felix thought that was pretty presumptuous of Lilliana's father, considering how things were left between Lilliana and Arianna. But then, the duke was the true and rightful owner of the estate. By the sounds of things, his last encounter with Arianna hadn't been so great either, and if Arianna's handmaiden, Draya, really had sent Drake into the Everstorm, Felix could only imagine the wrath waiting for her. Felix thought that if nothing else, the night promised to be interesting. And he was glad to be an outsider to all of it.

Felix heard someone approaching and turned with the enthusiasm and hope of seeing Lilliana, but it was Roy.

"If it isn't the hero of the hour! Have you had any thoughts about the job offer?" Roy inquired, coming to stand beside.

"Sure," Felix said, masking his disappointment as he pulled out his silver case and lit himself a puff-stick. He offered one to Roy, who accepted. Felix's supply of spice leaf was inferior to Zest, but cigars could only be enjoyed so often before they started to lose their charm.

"Still undecided?" Roy asked.

"I've never been eager to sign my life away."

Roy nodded. "What would you do if you don't take it?"

"I don't know, I'd been thinking of buying my own airship and becoming a merchant between Sky View and the mainland. I'd start by ferrying Spiced Kah up here, while catching kite-fish on the trip between to sell on the mainland."

"I knew you had good business savvy! Sounds like a profitable enterprise. If the world were in a different state, I'd like to buy a stake in that venture," Roy announced.

Felix returned a sad smile. "If only we were born at a different time, eh?"

"If only The East wasn't so shadow bent on their schemes. But the quicker we end them, the quicker we can all get back to the lives we desire," Roy said.

Felix chewed on that for a moment. "Why me?" he asked.

"Because you're the right man for the job."

"I never wanted this—all I've ever wanted is a quiet life with enough coin to be comfortable. I don't care about fame or recognition. I've never wanted to be a hero."

Roy smiled at him sadly. "Usually the heroes we need most are the ones least eager for the job. I don't want to get involved with this any more than you do. But if we don't do something, then none of us can count on getting the futures we desire, because if we don't stop these bastards, who will?"

Felix nodded and took another drag from his puff-stick. "Can you do me a favor, Roy?"

"Sure, what is it, sport?"

"Can I use your Sendsong one more time? I wasn't able to say goodbye to my brother when I left Westdock. If I take this job, I want to make sure he knows I won't be seeing him for a while."

Roy nodded. "Of course." He handed over his slim gold whistle and patted Felix on the shoulder before returning below deck.

As soon as Felix was alone he pulled a piece of parchment and a pencil out of his pocket and began to write.

*02/03/1750*
*Dear Bastian,*

*I hope you got my previous letter and made it out of Westdock safely with Gwena...*

⌒

When they arrived at the Wendrians' estate, the sky was covered with dark clouds promising rain. Drake led the way down the path to the estate's entrance and the rest of them followed. The look of sheer surprise on the doorman's face when he saw Drake was comical. He bowed so deeply he nearly fell over, before opening the door with obvious eagerness. They strode inside and were met by Albert in the entranceway,

"Master Drake! How good it is to see you've returned, my lord!" he exclaimed, bowing respectfully.

"Thank you, Albert! You're a sight for sore eyes. Have the staff prepare a banquet dinner—we're expecting the Remingtons to join us. They'll be here within the hour," Drake announced.

"Very good, my lord! Will everyone be staying the night?"

"I'm not sure, I suppose it depends on how much we drink!" Drake laughed heartily. "Have rooms prepared just in case."

"Right away!" Albert bowed and headed off to make arrangements.

Arianna came hurrying into the entranceway from somewhere at the back of the estate. Felix got the impression that she'd been notified of their arrival, but she didn't believe it. Now that she saw Drake her face drained of color,

"Uncle! Uncle, you're alive!?" she exclaimed in bewildered surprise and ran to hug him. Felix couldn't tell whether she was glad or terrified to see him. Maybe both. Drake returned her embrace and then held her at arm's length. "Arianna, I'm as surprised to see you alive as you are to see me. I thought we'd lost you in the Everstorm."

"In the Everstorm?! Why would I be lost in the Everstorm?"

"Your handmaiden told me you'd taken my ship and were flying into it after the death of your father."

"But *you* were on your ship…you're the one who flew it into the storm."

"No, my dear. I took Lightning Bolt hoping to catch up to you, or what I thought was you. But I was too late to stop the ship. I've been told since that there was no one on it, it'd been rigged to fly itself into the storm."

"You took Lightning Bolt? That's why she went missing. Draya told me she'd gotten out and flew off after you."

"Why would she tell you that?"

"I don't know," Arianna admitted.

"Why don't you go and fetch her and we'll ask her now," Drake suggested.

"Alright, I will."

Arianna left towards the back rooms of the estate. She came back several minutes later with an expression of concern. "She's gone! I can't find her anywhere."

Drake opened the front door. "Luke?"

"Yes, my lord?" the doorman asked.

"Have you seen Draya?"

"Yes, my lord. She just left on one of the dragons not ten minutes ago."

"Send two of the stablehands to fetch her. Have her brought to me when they do. Don't let her get away."

"Certainly, my lord!" Luke said, and hurried off.

Drake shut the door. "Now, we might as well make ourselves comfortable," he said, and led them all into the sitting room where he rang the servants' bell. Albert came straight away. "Yes, my lord?"

"Bring some refreshments, won't you please?"

"Certainly, my lord."

"Thank you, Albert."

Drake sat down in one of the armchairs. "Now, Arianna."

"Yes, Uncle?"

"About your father's will…"

Fear flooded Arianna's eyes.

"We had a disagreement the night your father passed. You were concerned about how little he left you and refused to accept that he had made the decision in his right mind. Am I remembering correctly?"

Arianna looked around at everyone in the room, clearly not eager to have the conversation in front of them. "Yes, Uncle," she admitted hesitantly.

"I understand your reason for concern. Please know that I have no desire to betray you or leave you destitute. On the contrary, I promised your father on his deathbed that I would look after you. Which is why I unquestioningly flew into the Everstorm to save your life."

Arianna's eyes began to glisten with emotion, but she held her chin high.

"I have a lot of respect for you. We are not so different, you and I. I admire the way you took on the family business and am grateful to you for upholding it, as well as the estate, while I've been away," Drake commended.

"Thank you, Uncle."

"However, you've been doing it all wrong."

Arianna looked stricken. "How so?!" she asked indignantly.

"You've been taking coin from our enemy, disrespecting our family name. Your eagerness to pay our debts has robbed you of foresight. Have you ever thought what might happen to us if it gets out that the beasts who helped The East destroy the world were bred and sold to them by the Wendrian household? Do you think anyone will want to do business with us after that?"

Arianna opened and closed her mouth like a goldfish but didn't utter a word.

"Your father knew what you were doing before he died. That's why he sent for me and had a new will drawn, this will," Drake announced, and produced the legal document from his coat pocket. Felix immediately recognized it as the one he'd taken from Arianna's office. He glanced over at Arianna and saw her looking at it in shocked bewilderment.

"Your father was not only concerned about the well-being of our family name and legacy, he was concerned about you. He didn't want you getting mixed up in something you couldn't get out of, and he didn't want you to have to live your life with the burden of the business on your shoulders. That's why he only left you five percent. Enough to live your life however you please, but not enough to make decisions for the future of this family. Arianna, he was trying to liberate you from responsibility."

Arianna lifted her chin. "But I like having responsibility! I like running the business, and I'm good at it! My father could never see that. He was always trying to protect me, not realizing he was keeping me from the very things that give my life purpose!" she proclaimed ardently.

"If the business is the only thing giving your life purpose, then that's a better reason than any for you to step away from it. Go out into the world, Arianna, meet new people, make friends."

"And who will run the business then? You? You're needed in West-dock, and no one in this family knows dragon breeding like I do," she objected.

"We're no longer going to breed dragons."

"What?!" Arianna exclaimed in surprise.

A soft knock interrupted them, and a maid entered with a tray of tea and biscuits. She laid them down on the table.

"Thank you. Could you please send in Albert as soon as you have the opportunity?" Drake requested.

"Right away, my lord," the maid said, and left the room.

Drake poured himself a cup of tea.

"Times have changed. There're too many breeders in Sky View already. The problem isn't our business practice, it's our product."

"But we have the best racing dragons on Equillian! Our product is the best," Arianna protested.

"It doesn't matter how good our dragons are, there's not enough demand. We should've changed years ago after the war. When the world changes, we must adapt with it. That's what you should've done when you couldn't find buyers outside The East, and since you failed to do that, that's what I will do now."

There was another soft knock before Albert entered the room. "Excuse the intrusion. You called for me, my lord?"

"Yes. Send for our lawyer, and request she performs the necessary arrangements to ensure my brother's will is carried out without delay," he instructed.

The butler bowed, "Certainly, my lord," he said, and left the room.

"What will you change the business to?" Arianna asked curtly, crossing her arms tightly across her chest to hold back her simmering indignation.

"I'm going to diversify and split it up into three sections. One will be a business focusing on racing and competing dragons—run by you. We will do small-batch selective breeding only, solely catering for the Derby. Being highly specialized and catering to an audience we know will not only guarantee us buyers, it will allow us to charge more. Your reputation in the racing sector will help attract clients, no doubt. Second, we'll be setting up a jousting school for noblewomen, headed by Lilliana and Frederick Remington. I've heard of Emily Swift's success in this year's Derby. No doubt her victory will inspire many women to enter the sport, and I want our family to be known for embracing this change. Lilliana will approach Lady Swift and offer her a position as our lead instructor," Drake announced.

"I will?!" Lilliana asked in surprise.

"If you accept the task?"

"I do!" Lilliana exclaimed enthusiastically.

"But Lilliana doesn't live in Sky View," Arianna objected.

"As you'll see in tomorrow's paper, Lilliana is engaged to be wed to Frederick Remington."

"That's impossible, she's already engaged to Lord Bardviss!"

"I made the arrangement with Charles prior to my disappearance, which nullifies Everitt's arrangement with Lord Bardviss. Lilliana and Frederick will be married within the month, and they'll be moving into this estate together. You have until their matrimony to vacate the premises."

Arianna's jaw dropped. "You're kicking me out of my own home?" she exclaimed in outrage.

"It was never yours; it has always belonged to me and your father. You're a grown woman now—it's about time you got out of it," Drake declared candidly.

"But where will I live?!"

"I've already spoken to Charles about buying one of his apartments in the Capital. He's happy to agree to the arrangement if the apartment is to your liking. If it's not, then you can live wherever the shadows you like. Five percent of the profits of our new businesses alone, added to your wage as an employee director, will set you up to live just about anywhere you please."

"What's the third business?" Arianna inquired.

"The third business will be Sky View's first Scientific Exploration and Research Center. I applaud the funding you've put into the Sky Gardens here. I can't wait to have a tour—from Roy's description, they sound fascinating. I want to see more research done in that direction, though not to secure Sky View's independence, but to help Equillian progress as a whole. The expedition branch will be headed by Katarina Maxwell, and it will focus on exploration and research of the Everstorm."

"Where will we get the funding for that?! We don't have enough capital to finance a project that big."

"We already have two backers, both Zest and the Remingtons have agreed to go in with us on the business, and I've no doubt that once I announce my findings we'll have far more. It's a whole new generation, Arianna. It's time we embrace it!"

Just then two of the stablehands hurried into the sitting room. "Excuse us, my lord. We couldn't catch Draya—she outran us."

"Did she know who you were?"

"Yes, my lord. We have no idea why she fled from us."

"Thank you. You may return to your duties. If you see any sign of her, please notify me straight away," Drake instructed.

"Yes, my lord," they said, and left the room.

Arianna furrowed her brow.

"I'm sure by now you recognize Draya's true intentions?" Drake asked her.

"What do you mean?"

"Only the guilty run, Arianna. Draya is running away because I've returned and she's the one who sent me into the Everstorm—hoping I'd never come back."

"I don't understand why she'd want that," Arianna said in earnest.

"Of course you do. Draya knew about the will because you told her. And she knew that if you lost the estate and business, your deal with The East would fall through."

"Why would she care about that?"

"Because she's from The East. Your father bought her from the slave market when she was a young girl as a friend for you. But you knew that already, didn't you?"

"I don't understand what her being from The East has to do with anything. I don't understand why everyone hates them so much. Why is it so bad if we join together with them?"

"Because The East doesn't want to join with us—they want to conquer us. And they want to ensure we suffer for what we've done to them," Drake stated.

"That's not true!"

"Really? Then why did Draya run from us? Why did she send me away the second she knew your father was leaving the estate and business to me? Think about it—has she encouraged you to work with The East? To unite our family with Lord Bardviss? To stir up the idea of a revolution?"

"And why wouldn't she?! Why wouldn't she want that when The East are her people and she wants there to be peace between us?" Arianna asked ardently.

"A revolution wouldn't create peace between Sky View and Eastgate, it would create discord between all the precincts, pinning us against one another, inspiring another war!"

"Why would Draya want that?"

"Because her father is one of Marx's right-hand men."

"I know, I've met him. And I've met Marx, they've shown me nothing but kindness."

"Foolish child! That's because they're using you. How can you be so blind?!" Drake demanded, cracks forming in his cool temperament.

"Because she's in love," Lilliana interjected.

Both Drake and Arianna looked at her. Then Drake turned to Arianna. "With Marx?"

"No. She's in love with Draya," Lilliana explained, stepping up beside them.

Arianna's cheeks flushed, but she didn't say a word. She raised her chin defiantly and a single tear ran down her cheek. Drake's expression changed from one of anger to that of revelation. "Of course, how did I miss that?"

"It's true, and I'm not ashamed to admit it. I don't care what any of you think, I do love her! Draya has always been there for me, especially when my father wasn't, nor any of the rest of you. You're wrong about her!" Arianna asserted and ran from the room.

"Arianna!" Lilliana called after her, she moved to follow but Drake grabbed her arm.

"Let her go, she needs time to process. Some things we need to face alone."

Lilliana nodded.

"Did you mean everything you said, Father, about the women's jousting school and me living in the estate?"

"Every word. But if you have any better ideas, I'm all ears."

"No, I think it's wonderful."

Felix smiled, suddenly knowing he'd made the right decision.

A knock was heard, and Albert appeared in the doorway. "Dinner's ready to be served."

Drake put his arm around Lilliana and walked with her towards the banquet hall. The front door to the estate opened, and Luke the doorman announced the arrival of Charles Remington, with his wife and Frederick.

"Ah, what perfect timing!" Drake declared, and welcomed them all inside. The group laughed as they made their way to dinner. Roy and Felix were the last ones in the sitting room. Roy stood in thought and walked to the doorway before noticing Felix wasn't following him. "You joining us, champ?"

"I think I'll sit this one out. I don't think there's much use for me here anymore," Felix stated.

Roy nodded. "You're a gift from the Stars, my friend. We're lucky you stopped in."

"Ha! You say that like I had a choice."

"You had many choices, and we've all benefited from the ones you've made. Thank you," Roy said in earnest.

Felix nodded then smiled roguishly. "It's been fun," he admitted.

Roy chuckled. "Indeed it has. Have you made your decision?"

"Almost. Either way, I have a couple things I want to do first."

Roy nodded. "Good, there's a whole world out there."

"That there is," Felix agreed.

"Until next time then, my friend." Roy held out his hand.

Felix shook it. "Until next time. You'll look after her—won't you?"

Roy smiled. "Of course, she's family." He patted Felix on the shoulder and headed towards the dining room.

Felix watched him go. He started to leave and then felt a pull towards something in the sitting room. He looked up towards the small inlaid display case above the portrait of the war dragon to the golden egg sitting on its perch, and a thought struck him—what if Draya came back for the egg and brought it to The East? What if Lord Bardviss already had the one from the Wendrians' castle in Westdock?

*Maybe it's best if I look after it,* he thought.

The solid gold exterior had nothing to do with him wanting it, nothing at all. Before Felix registered what he was doing, he found himself standing on a chair and taking the egg out of its case. It was as big as two of his fists put together. He opened his Dreg Pouch and it expanded impossibly to fit the egg inside, and once it was in, it was as if it disappeared completely.

Felix smiled and closed the cabinet door and replaced the chair. Then he made his way towards the estate's entrance.

"James?"

He turned to see Kareen, the serving girl.

"Hi, Kareen."

"I was hoping you'd come back. You've had a dozen packages delivered here for you. Arianna said to discard them, but I didn't have the heart."

Felix smiled. "You're a star."

Kareen returned his smile. "Wait here, I'll go fetch them!" she declared, and hurried off.

Felix studied the decor while he waited.

"Were you really going to leave without saying goodbye?"

Felix turned to see Lilliana coming up behind him. "I didn't want to ruin your moment."

"You really ought to learn some etiquette."

"I think I'll leave the etiquette to you, my lady. You're far better at it than I."

Lilliana smiled. "Are you going to take the job?"

"I'm not sure yet. If there's one thing I've learned up here, it's a great appreciation for my freedom from obligation and expectation. I always thought coin would be my liberator, but now I know that if it's tied to those two things it proves to be a heavier shackle than poverty. And being free is something I'm quite fond of."

Lilliana stared at him aghast. "Your freedom? What about the freedom of everyone else on Equillian?! You have an opportunity to help ensure that by rescuing the world from The East's tyranny, and you're thinking it might be too much obligation?"

"Well, when you put it that way…"

"You *will* take that job, Felix Copperweather—or I'll never forgive you. If you don't, then what we've had to give up will have been for nothing. You think I want to live without freedom? You think I wouldn't rather live in poverty with you than in a castle drowning in obligation?"

"I hardly think living here and running a woman's jousting academy is drowning in obligation."

Lilliana punched him in the shoulder. "You're the one who told me I don't have a choice! That I need to stay so that I can save the world. Don't think that if staying wasn't necessary for the greater good of Equillian, I wouldn't give it all up in a heartbeat."

"Would you?"

"A thousand times over."

Felix smirked, "Alright, I'll seriously consider it. Can I kiss you now?"

Lilliana smiled. "I'd be insulted if you didn't."

Felix swept her into his arms and kissed her tenderly. Lilliana welcomed his embrace with fervor and then said, "I have something for you."

"Oh? What's that?"

"Actually, two things. Wait here a moment," she said, and disappeared out of view. She came back a minute later with a book. "Here." She handed Felix the copy of *The Words of the Watchers*. "I feel like this belongs with you—it can help remind you of home."

"That's very generous of you, but I'd rather you keep it. You haven't finished it yet, and I have most of it committed to memory. Just promise me you'll think of me whenever you read it."

"Alright, I will," Lilliana said, taking the book lovingly back in hand.

"I also want you to have this. I made it here from stable scraps when I was a child. I thought it might help to remind you of our time together,

and ensure you don't forget me," Lilliana said, and handed Felix a bracelet made of thin black braided leather.

Felix tied it onto his left wrist. "I could never forget you, you're woven into the fibers of my heart. But thank you," he smiled.

"I'm going to miss you," Lilliana declared.

"I should hope so! It's only fair, you'll be haunting me for a lifetime."

Lilliana's eyes glistened. "I better get back before someone comes
looking for me."

Felix smiled sadly and nodded, his eyes two deep pools of love for
her. "Can I just have one more for the road?" he requested, and pulled
her close to him without waiting for permission.

Lilliana kissed him for several minutes before finally pulling away.
"Good-bye, Felix Copperweather," she smiled.

"Until we meet again, my lady," Felix said with a small bow.

Lilliana gazed at him, drinking him in one last time before turning
away and hurrying back towards the dining hall.

Felix felt his heart breaking into a thousand pieces as he watched her
go. But before he could begin to wallow in self-pity, Kareen returned
with a large burlap sack filled to the brim with packages wrapped in the
careful fashion of Favio's Boutique. Felix had almost completely forgotten about her. He thanked his lucky stars she hadn't returned any sooner.

"Sorry for the wait—it was harder to get them all into a bag then I'd
anticipated," she apologized.

"No problem. Thanks," he said, and flicked her a ducket. "For your
trouble."

Kareen caught it. "It was no trouble at all. I hope I see you again,
James," she said with a flirtatious smirk.

Felix winked at her and then tossed the burlap sack over his shoulder
and walked out of the estate.

⌒

The sky was saturated with heavy dark clouds. As soon as Felix
stepped outside it started to rain.

*Shick, you bastard,* Felix thought, cursing the Star Stirrer. He boarded
Drake's airship and collected his pillowcase with the other few belong-
ings he had, adding an extra bottle of Spiced Kah from the ship's stores.
Then he disembarked and walked out to the end of the jetty. He pulled
Cabby's coin out of his pocket and traced the symbol on its face, then

he threw it into the air and caught it on the way down. He waited ten minutes in the rain before Cabby pulled up beside him.

"Hey, Westdock! Good to see you again, friend. I was worried about you after the other night. You looked like you'd been given a death sentence," Cabby proclaimed as Felix tossed his stuff into the cab and climbed in beside it.

"Something like that. But all's well that ends well," he said.

"Where to?"

"I need a drink; you know a place?"

"There's a nice joint on Ariya Prime," Cabby suggested.

"Take me to wherever it is you like to go."

"You don't want to go where I go."

"Why not?"

"Because it's a real dive. I only go there because I have to if I want a drink—it's the only place around that serves underage customers."

"Underage customers? I've never known an ale house to turn down coin, no matter who it's from."

"Well, you're clearly not from Sky View. Anyone under sixteen isn't allowed to be served alcohol here."

"Right. I'm beginning to see why you're so eager to leave this place. What makes your local a dive?" Felix asked him, doubting anything in Sky View could be even half as bad as the dives in Westdock.

"It's dark, dirty, and full of shady people."

"A perfect portrait of my mood—sounds like my kind of place."

"Alright…don't say I didn't warn you," Cabby said, and pulled away from the Wendrians' island.

Cabby pulled his air cab up to the jetty of one of the twin islands south of the capital.

"Just head to the water and ask for a place called Undertow," Cabby instructed.

"I won't have to, you're coming with me," Felix announced.

"Is it not obvious I'm working tonight?"

"I'll pay you double what you'd earn otherwise—all you have to do is keep me company."

Cabby hesitated. "No funny business?"

Felix smirked. "Sorry Cabby, but you're just not my type."

"It's no joke, you wouldn't believe some of the weirdos I meet on this job!"

"I can imagine. So, take a night off from it."

"I don't know, I really should be working."

"Come on, it's my last night in Sky View and I just had to give up the girl of my dreams. Don't make me drink alone."

"Jeesh! Alright, I'll come with you. But I ain't leaving my cab here, it will be gone by the time we get back. There's a patrolled dock not far up."

"There's cab thieves in Sky View?"

"Worse—bored teenagers out for a joyride. Once they're finished, the ship gets torched."

"Someone really needs to give the youth up here something to do."

"Tell me about it!"

Cabby parked his ship at a fancy valet docking station and, with his falcon perched on his shoulder, led Felix down a winding cobblestone street into a small town. The road bordered a wide lake. The town was lit up with Everfire streetlamps. Restaurants bustled with people dining outside while being serenaded by musicians, and couples walked arm in arm, lost in boisterous conversation. Young adults already drunk sang loudly out on the street.

"It's down this way," Cabby said, weaving around the people, his hands buried deep in his pockets. He led Felix along a backstreet and down a flight of stone stairs that had a metal sign overhead with the words *The Undertow.* Cabby opened a heavy wood door at the foot of the stairs and held it open for Felix. They ducked into what felt like a cellar. The place was dimly lit with firebeetle lanterns and the floor was covered in peanut shells. A man was playing guitar on a small stage at the back. A few other patrons sat at small round tables, all looking up when they came in. Cabby took off his hat and led Felix to the bar. There was a large man behind it cleaning glasses,

"Hiya, Cabby, what can I get for you?" the bartender asked.

"Two lagers, thanks, Franky."

"Lagers?" Felix asked.

"What else?"

"What else?! My friend, if I'm taking you out for drinks, we're doing it in style. You can save lager for your time off."

Cabby shrugged. "Alright, you order then."

Felix leaned over the bar. "Sorry, mate, scratch the lagers. What spirits do you have back there?"

"Anything you like; what can I get for you?"

"Can you make a Dying Star?"

"Sure. How many do you want?"

"Two, thanks."

"Coming right up."

Felix pulled a stool out from the bar and sat down. "This place isn't so bad."

"It's all comparative, I suppose. I've dropped a lot of customers off to some pretty nice establishments. Let's just say, this ain't one of 'em," Cabby said, sitting down beside him.

"Meh, those places can be overrated."

The bartender placed two tall glasses half full in front of them with two full shot glasses on the side.

"What's this?" Cabby asked.

"It's called a Dying Star. You drop the shot glass into your tall glass and then you drink it as quickly as you can," Felix explained.

"Are you looking to get trashed tonight?"

"Yup," Felix stated, and he dropped his shot glass into his tall one. The liquid began to fizz and Felix threw it back in one swallow.

Cabby's eye's widened. "If I drink this, who's going to fly us home?"

"That's future us's problem. Bottoms up!" Felix declared and dropped Cabby's shot glass into his tall one.

"Oh, shick!" Cabby exclaimed as his drink began to fizz over the brim, and he knocked it back as quickly as he could, then coughed violently. "What the shick is that?!"

"Delirium," Felix proclaimed with a grin, patting Cabby on the back and motioning to the barkeep. "My good man, another round!"

Half an hour later, Felix and Cabby were sitting at a table in the corner of The Undertow, cracking peanuts and laughing hysterically.

"In all seriousness, Cabby, do you really want to head out East?" Felix asked him.

"Without a doubt. Eastgate is the gateway to the mining sector. I'm literally marking off the days—no joke."

"Then I have a proposition for you."

"Yeah? What's that?"

"Come with me to Port Trinity for a few days to explore the Port of Pleasures, and then we'll go East together."

"You have a reason to go East?"

"Potentially, I have some business I need to attend to there for the company, but I'm short a pilot…"

"Yes!!" Cabby blurted before Felix could say another word. "I'll take the job! When do we leave?"

"Are you sure you don't want some time to think about it?"

"Nope!"

"Alright, we leave tomorrow morning."

"Tomorrow? Shick." Cabby's enthusiasm deflated.

"What?"

"My parents, they'll never let me go."

"Of course they will."

"You've clearly never met my parents."

"What parent would turn down an opportunity for their son to work for a local hero? Especially when it comes with a platinum paycheck."

"Local hero?"

"Sure. Just make sure they read tomorrow's paper."

"I don't know what the shick you're talking about, but if you can get past my parents, I'm in."

Felix clinked Cabby's glass.

"If your business is in Eastgate, though, why are we going to Port Trinity? It's in the opposite direction."

"Because I have some coin burning holes in my pockets, and a bloody bad heartache that needs to get drowned out. Three days in the Port of Pleasures should be sufficient."

"What am I supposed to do while you're…drowning it out?"

Felix raised an eyebrow. "Come on, don't tell me you're not interested in what Port Trinity has to offer?"

Cabby scratched the back of his neck uncomfortably. "I don't know, I've heard that place is shady as shick."

Felix smirked. "Most of the best places are." If he was going to seriously consider putting his life on the line for Equillian, then he was going to make sure he lived up every minute he had before then to the absolute pinnacle. He held up his glass. "To a new chapter."

"To a new chapter," Cabby agreed, and clinked Felix's glass with his.

Felix stared out the window of Cabby's airship studying the stars and playing with the bracelet Lilliana had gifted him. Cabby was asleep in the front seat of the docked ship. Felix pulled out the small brown leather journal the duke had given him earlier that morning and ran his hand across the contract on the first page.

"*Serendipity help me*," he whispered to the stars, and signed his name.

# THE TASK

It was half past the Plunger hour. Bastian had only thirty minutes before The Balancer constellation marked high noon. He bent down and scooped a generous pinch of sand from the ground and siphoned it into his coin pouch. Instantly the bag was jingling full of coin. He bought two more basic pouches from the market and filled both with conjured jolly rogers, and then walked behind the tavern and waited. Right on schedule, the band that had performed the night before showed up with their instruments, accompanied by the gypsy dance troupe and several handsome young men carrying casks of rum and baskets of fresh fruit and sweet treats.

"Thanks for showing up," Bastian greeted, shaking the band leader's hand. "I hope you haven't told anyone. Wouldn't want to spoil the surprise."

"Not a soul, the gang knows we'll be performin' fer a private event, that be all."

"Brilliant. Drax will be very pleased."

Bastian handed the man two purses brimming with coin. The man opened one and looked inside.

"I've added some extra, compliments from Drax—as a thank you for your discretion, and for agreeing to come on such short notice," Bastian explained.

The man's eyebrows raised when he took in the generous sum. "The pleasure be all ours, I assure ya. 'ow do we get ta the place anyways? I've never met anyone who's actually been up there."

"I'll escort you, right this way," Bastian said, and started walking directly into the trees behind them. The band leader nodded to the troupe to follow, and they filed behind Bastian like a small parade as he led them up an almost indistinguishable path. Bastian had strategically chosen their meeting place to draw as little attention as possible, hoping anyone who saw them heading to the tavern would've presumed the performers were preparing for a rehearsal or another show. He led them through the forest and up a small rocky hill to Drax's estate. He walked with as much confidence as he could muster, even though he'd only ever seen the place on paper. He hoped the map he'd committed to memory was accurate. To his relief, Drax's mansion soon loomed ahead, tucked up on the top of the hill. The place was two stories high, made of sandstone bricks and large glass windows that spanned both levels and faced the ocean. There were eight pirates stationed around the building keeping guard. *Shick, as if the six anticipated wouldn't have been bad enough*, Bastian thought.

As they approached the mansion, Bastian could see the women inside through the windows. There must have been at least twenty of them, all lounging about different parts of the house. When they spotted Bastian and his company coming up the hill, they began gathering around the windows to peer outside. Bastian's heart quickened as he and his merry band of entertainers came into clear view of the guards. All eight of them put their hands on their pistols while watching them approach warily.

One particularly herculean pirate called out to them with his weapon drawn, "Don't take another step! State yer business!" he demanded. He was two heads taller than Bastian, with a hard sun-weathered face and muscled arms twice as thick as Bastian's. In response, Bastian immediately raised his hands in the air. The performers looked at one another with concerned expressions.

"Don't shoot! We're here by Drax's request," Bastian announced.

The pirates looked at one another and then looked to the largest man. He made a small nod, and the others took their hands off their weapons, then he stepped forward and motioned for Bastian to approach. Bastian complied obediently and the burly pirate assessed him with a single glance that said *you're no more threat to me than a mosquito.*

"What's all this about?"

Bastian swallowed. *Alright brother, lend me your talent,* he thought, calling on Felix's knack for verbal deception.

"Good afternoon, I've brought the musicians and entertainers Drax requested. I was told you'd be expecting us?" He pulled out his pocket watch. "I pray we're not too early?"

"Drax didn't mention anythin' about entertainers."

"You're joking? Well, shick! It was supposed to be a surprise for the whole household—he wanted to ensure you weren't excluded from the festivities. He even paid up front. But I don't want any trouble. We can cancel the whole thing if it's a problem."

The guard looked over Bastian's shoulder towards the keg of rum and the women.

"Are those the dancers from the show last night?"

"Yes, they are. They were going to put on a private show. Damn shame Drax didn't mention it—the girls prepared a special performance. But no matter, I'm sure he'll gladly own his mistake and applaud you for sticking to your protocol." Bastian started to turn away.

"'old on!"

Bastian turned back.

"Drax 'as already paid, ya say?"

"Yes."

The guard scratched his chin. "I don't think Drax would like us cancelin' after 'e's gone ta all that effort."

Bastian hesitated. "I don't want to cause any bother. It would be a horrible thing to get myself or anyone else on Drax's bad side. You just tell me what we should do, and we'll do it."

The man looked at the women and the casks of rum again. "Won't be any trouble at all. Come on, bring 'em in," the pirate said decidedly.

"We live to entertain," Bastian said with a humble incline of his head and motioned to the troupe of entertainers to follow him.

The large man motioned to the other pirates to let them pass, and Bastian and the performers were welcomed inside Drax's mansion. It was a huge place, grossly overdecorated with mismatched finery—as if he'd taken all his favorite spoils from raided merchant ships and hung them on his walls.

"Some entertainment fer ya laddies, provided by Drax!" the large pirate announced as they entered.

The music and dancing began, and handsome young men started passing out refreshments. Drax's harem squealed in delight, gathering to enjoy the entertainment, and several of the guards left their posts to join them. Bastian blended in amongst the throng before slipping quietly and discreetly down the hall and up the stairs. As he ascended he put in the wax earpiece Tink had given him. Instantly he was connected to the captains' conference in the meeting hall. He recalled Tink telling him the device would allow each wearer to hear what the other devices were picking up. If he'd realized that meant he could've been eavesdropping on the captains' gathering, he would've put them in a whole lot sooner. He tuned into what the pirate captains were saying as he slunk to the top floor.

*"They've come ta me askin' if they can rely on the Death Dealers an' any other ship o' fortune when the time comes. I 'ave no desire ta be involved in*

*their conflict, but seems ta me, it might be a time fer ample opportunity," a gruff voice said.*

*"What would be in it fer us?"*

*"Aye, we've never joined a mainland war before, why would we do so now?"*

*"If they win Equillian, 'e's offerin' a full pardon ta any o' us who fought fer 'em, freedom ta roam the mainland without prosecution fer our crimes, an' very generous pay."*

*"Sounds like yer looking fer an early retirement, Gunner!"*

*"We can make more coin than they could possibly offer us robbin' their ships on the high seas. I don't see the benefit o' allyin' ourselves with anyone on the mainland...."*

Bastian walked along the upper corridor until he came to the door he'd memorized from the map as Drax's bedroom. He opened it to reveal an overfilled storage closet. He tried the next door along, only to find a gaudy bathroom. Bastian pulled out his map and saw that he'd memorized it correctly—it was the map that was wrong. *Shick!* He looked around anxiously, trying to gain his bearings, and then relaxed as it suddenly dawned on him that he had everything he needed.

Bastian put away the map and called the Ghost Element into the palms of his hands and used it to tap into the Ciphorescent Codec, then he sent out searching tendrils with one commanding intention—find the chest. Within a matter of seconds Bastian had a crystal clear gut instinct of exactly where the chest was. He walked quietly and purposefully down to the end of the hall, while tuning back into the pirates' conversation in his earpiece.

⸺

*"...If The East succeeds, then Equillian will be led by Marx. We already know 'ow 'e operates—the place will be overrun with corruption. We'll no longer be outcasts, we'll be leaders amongst men, friends o' the authority. We'll be able ta do whatever we please with no consequence!"*

*"I don't think it would be a good thin' fer people like ya ta 'ave that much freedom, Stains," a new voice said, followed by hearty laughter from the other captains.*

*"Yer fergettin' that we rely on the mainland's healthy economy." Muerte Tormenta's calm and commanding voice rang through. "The better they fare, the more abundant the prize ta be taken from their laden ships, an the more likely it be ta keep comin'. If The East wins this war, then all that plunder we rely on will dry up. What good is it ta rule the seas when there's nothin' left on 'em?"*

There were grumbling sounds of agreement.

Bastian reached the door at the end of the hall. Locked. He sent the Ghost Element into the keyway and formed it around the wards inside, then solidified the Element into a key with perfect fit. He turned it and the lock gave way. Bastian dissolved the key and let himself inside. It was a large room with two windows, the smaller one open on the opposite side, its linen curtains billowing like sails in the sea breeze. The second was large and expansive, positioned directly across from the large four-poster bed, with an unobscured view of the ocean beyond. Bastian scanned the space. It was a luxuriously decorated bedroom, with a wood fireplace in the corner and a bear-hide throw rug nearly the size of the bed. A large, ornate dresser was against the back wall near the entrance to an en suite, but there was no sign of the chest.

Bastian locked the bedroom door and put on his goggles. Instantly the contents of the room were outlined with fine gold geometry. He looked around for any sign of an enchantment. He drew in two fistfuls of the Ghost Element and sent them out once more. The gold glittering powder weaved like smoke through the room, and then it collected around the framed painting of a large clipper ship. Bastian walked over to where the artwork was mounted on the wall and pulled gently. It swung open revealing a metal safe behind it. The safe was secured with both a combination lock and a keyway. Bastian sent the Ghost Element into the keyway and formed a key the way he'd done before. He turned it and heard the satisfying click he was hoping for. Then he looked at the combination lock through his goggles and used the Ghost Element to tune into the Ciphorescent Codec, and watched the geometric symbols change as he rotated the numbers. Just like using the Codec to draw geometry, it led him to all the right figures as easily as if his intuition had been flawlessly calibrated to truth itself. In less than a minute Bastian had the safe open, and sitting inside it was the chest.

"I've found it," he whispered tentatively, hoping Tink and the captain could hear him.

"Good. Now open it," Tink's voice instructed in Bastian's ear with perfect crystal clarity.

Bastian almost jumped. It was as if Tink was in the room right next to him. Bastian focused on the safety enchantments guarding the chest. It was so much easier with the goggles' enchanted lenses—instead of feeling his way to the enchantments, he could literally see them. The symbology was beautiful. It only took him a few seconds to change the symbols' attributes and get his way through. He copied down Drax's identity symbol in his notebook before resetting the Identity enchantment to himself. Then he picked the chest up and brought it to the bed.

"...*What say ya, Drax?*"

"*I say, it doesn't matter what 'appens ta the mainland, 'cause we 'ave a land o' our own right 'ere. Our business on the seas be becomin' more an' more o' a liability each an' every year. The merchants are becomin' better gunned, an' one in particular be provin' ta be a real thorn in our side, Lord Henry Bardviss,*" Drax growled, and the rest of the men grumbled and cursed his name.

"*Bardviss's ships 'ave always given us trouble, but now I've gotten word that the bastard lord be declarin' a war on piracy! An' unfortunately, the man 'as enough wealth an' ambition ta actually be a threat. But 'e's also a reasonable business man. 'e's offered ta leave our ships in peace, an' put us on a very generous retainer ta do the same with 'is. Fer all ya numbskulls, that means gettin' paid fer doin' nothin'! Which will allow us ta set our attention 'ere, ta settlin' our own colony on Jaxland. This temptin' indenture only comes with one minor condition,*" Drax announced.

"*What's that?*"

"*Apparently, the Black Mary 'as a stowaway in its midst, one that belongs ta Bardviss. 'e's asked the boy be returned ta 'im with all the property 'e brought with 'im on board. Only then will Bardviss be willin' ta negotiate terms.*"

The sound of shifting chairs followed, and Bastian imagined every man in that room had turned to look at Muerte Tormenta. He forgot about the chest and stopped to listen with bated breath.

"*Since when do we take commands an' indentures from lords an' nobles? If I 'ad wanted ta bend a knee ta that scum, I would've enlisted with the Royal Navy!*" Muerte rebuffed, and several men called out in agreement. Muerte continued, "*The only reason Bardviss be willin' ta pay us ta leave 'is ships in peace, be because 'is precious cargo be worth far more than what 'e'll be payin' us. I don't know about the rest o' ya, but I would far rather take me chances fer a real prize on the high seas, than sit 'ere on a lazy arse accruin' an inferior sum."*

"Aye!" half the men exclaimed, while others mumbled discontentedly.

"But what o' this stowaway Drax be referrin' ta, Muerte? Do ya 'ave 'im?" one man asked.

"The 'stowaway' bein' referred ta be a member o' me own crew. 'e doesn't belong ta Lord Bardviss, nor 'as 'e ever. An' I'm not betrayin' any member o' me crew ta a bastard lord, no matter 'ow much 'e wants ta pay fer it!"

There was murmuring throughout the captains.

"But ya would betray all o' us fer a single crewmate!?" Drax demanded angrily. "This war 'e's bringin' down on us be because o' ya 'arborin' that boy in the first place! Bardviss's merchant ships be fitted out as war galleons. Before, their firepower was used fer defense only—now, their cannons are bein' turned on us, their purpose ta hunt us down! Bardviss's terms are more than generous, there be plenty o' merchants outside 'is fleet fer the plunderin' if yer so eager ta chase bigger fortune. But the only thin' greed will get ya be an early indenture with Davey Jones!"

"I think ya seem ta've forgotten what it is we are—we're gentleman o' fortune, are we not? Chasin' it be what we do!" Muerte reminded him. "If yer so eager ta give it up, then maybe it's time ta think about 'andin' the leadership over ta someone else."

The room filled with a flurry of excited conversation, and then it died down all at once.

"Are ya threatenin' me, Muerte?" Drax growled.

"If I were threatenin' ya, ya wouldn't 'ave ta ask."

Then Muerte raised his voice and addressed the whole room, "Bardviss's galleons aren't as strong as 'e'd 'ave ya believe. We encountered two on the way 'ere an' defeated 'em both at once, with only a couple o' freshman casualties. If Bardviss wants a war, I say we give it ta 'im, an' show 'im who 'e truly be messin' with!"

"Arrrrrgh!!" a few of the captains agreed enthusiastically, and Bastian could almost hear Drax's scowl.

"If that be so, than 'ow come ya spent the better part o' a week on a floatin' dreg fer repairs?"

"Because as soon as the fight be won, we were apprehended by a kraken."

A hushed silence fell over the men.

Drax laughed heartily. "A kraken? Ya really expect us ta believe that? Next ye'll be tellin' us faeries guided ya ta Jaxland's shores!"

*"Laugh all ya want, but ye'd be wise ta believe it. It wasn't the worst I've seen in the waters, an' it won't be the last. Just as the galleons' white flags were raised, they were dragged ta the deep by the sea monster. We barely escaped with our lives, an' ye don't see me ready ta 'ang up me 'at. Lord Bardviss's loyalties lie with The East—if ya make alliances with 'im then yer as good as joinin' their side in the mainland's war. Marx doesn't want ta be the next emperor o' Equillian, 'e wants ta see it burn!"*

*"An' what do yew want, Muerte?"* Drax asked evenly.

There was a moment of silence before Muerte replied, *"I want ta stop him."*

*"An' there it be, gentlemen! As big a game as Muerte talks, 'e doesn't want what's best fer all o' us, 'e doesn't even want ta chase plunder, 'e wants ta use us as pawns in 'is little game o' savin' the world."*

*"An what about yew, Drax? What be it yew want? Ta let the world fall ta the shadows an 'ave us an' our men settle down 'ere so ya can play noble? I don't know about the rest o' ya, but I didn't become a pirate so I could bow down ta another man. That's what separates us from the landlubbers and the nobles' Navy dogs—while they blindly follow orders from their superiors and scrounge on unfair wages, we sail the open sea as free men, our crews sailin' together as equals, sharin' our spoils in a fair manner. If we let the world fall ta Eastgate, there'll be nothin' left ta support that freedom, an settlin' 'ere on Jaxland will be no different than livin' under the rule o' a noble on the mainland."*

Bastian was standing still in Drax's room, riveted by the captain's conversation. *Could there really be a war brewing between The East and the mainland?* he wondered. The last war was supposed to be the war to end all wars. He didn't think he'd have to worry about seeing one in his lifetime. The very thought twisted his gut. There was enough corruption as it was on the mainland. Until that moment he thought things could only get better, not worse. But if The East ever conquered Equillian, things would be far worse. He forced himself back to the present and focused on the chest. He opened the lid and found a metal sphere the size of a cannon ball covered with engraved geometry and alchemists' symbols, tucked snugly inside red velvet casing. A steel ring stuck out of its top, attached to a steel cord that disappeared inside the orb.

*What the shick are you?*

Bastian itched to inspect it. But he knew better than to take any unnecessary chances on the task. He shut the lid of the chest and placed it in his rucksack. And traded it out for Tink's chest. Tink's looked almost identical to the one Drax had. Bastian applied Drax's identity symbol onto it and placed it in the other's stead, before locking the safe and covering it with the painting. Bastian made a pass around the room, righting things back to the way they were when he first came in, making sure he hadn't left a trace of his presence. Then he turned back into the captains' conversation.

*"…I say, we find this boy Muerte be stashin', an' we return 'im ta Lord Bardviss an' accept 'is terms. Let the mainland spill their own blood, I'm not givin' them any o' ours!"* Drax declared.

Some of the men shouted in agreement, while others kept their silence. Then another captain spoke up,

*"I'm not convinced it's in our best interest fer The East ta succeed. The Scillion Seven are dead—any glory The East once 'ad died with 'em. Marx be a tyrant, an' look where it's gotten Eastgate—their people are sufferin'. Muerte's right—that man doesn't want ta rule the world, 'e wants ta burn it ta the ground. There's good people on the mainland, children, families. Some o' 'em even be ours. Isn't that what got most o' us inta this business in the first place? Collectin' enough coin ta be able ta properly provide fer the ones we love? If we let The East succeed we'll be robbin' 'em o' a future, an' fer what? Even if Marx does welcome us ta 'is side once Equillian be won, what good is it bein' king if yer kingdom be nothin' but ash?"*

Again, half the men shouted in agreement while the other half stayed silent.

*"Well, gents, looks like we've come ta an impasse. There's only one thin' ta do now, we vote! As I see it, there be three choices 'ere—first, we strike up an agreement with Lord Bardviss, acceptin' 'is ongoin' payments in exchange fer safe passage on both sides. Second, we accept 'is challenge o' war an' use 'im as an example ta anyone who might think o' challengin' us in the future—losin' Stars know how many o' our own ships an' men, let alone the possibility o' losin' the war itself. Third, we declare ourselves as Ships o' War an' hire ourselves out ta the highest bidder regardless o' side. If anyone 'as anythin' ta add, speak now,"* Drax declared.

The room fell silent.

*"Cast yer votes then!"*

There were quiet murmurs all around…

Bastian reached the open window and looked out. it was a long drop to the bottom, but the large sandstone bricks the house was made of had enough jutting edges to easily scale down.

"I have the object. I'm leaving Drax's place now," Bastian announced into cupped hands, attempting to direct the sound to his earpiece. Then he ensured his rucksack was secured over his shoulder, put his goggles up onto his forehead, and began his descent.

*"The Death Dealers vote fer bein' mercenaries."*

*"The Red Revenge votes fer allyin' with Bardviss"*

*"The Gore also vote fer allyin' with Bardviss"*

*"The Ship Wreckers vote fer war against Bardviss."*

*"The Howlin' Harpy votes fer allyin' with Bardviss."*

*"The Black Mary votes fer war against Bardviss."*

*"The Night Terror votes fer bein' mercenaries."*

*"The Gilded Skull votes fer allyin' with Bardviss."*

*"The Sea Slayers vote fer war against Bardviss."*

*"The Rovin' Rogues vote fer bein' mercenaries."*

*"Snuff's Grin votes for bein' mercenaries."*

*"The Sea Bane vote fer war against Bardviss."*

*"I, Drax—leader o' Jaxland an' cap'n o' the Ghostly Gale, vote fer all-yin' with Bardviss. Which means that allyin' with Bardviss takes the lead," Drax declared, "which means ya 'ave ta 'and over the lad, Muerte."*

*"I never agreed ta any such thin'! Ye've already taken enough from me, Drax. I won't tolerate any more. If ya want ta condemn the rest o' the world an strike an alliance with that slitherin' worm, do it. But don't ya dare touch any man from me crew."*

*"The vote 'as been decided, majority rules! Ya know the law, Tormenta, if yer not with us, yer against us. Ya 'ave ta give 'im up!"*

*"If ya want 'im, then ye'll 'ave ta go through me."*

*"Fine, 'ave it yer way! Ya 'eard 'im, gents, Muerte no longer be one o' us, let it be known that the Black Mary no longer be under the protection o' the pirate code. Seize their crew, we'll pluck the lad out ourselves! An' I'll give a chest o' gold ta the man who kills Muerte!"*

"Shick!" Bastian muttered as he scaled faster down the wall.

All the captains had gone silent. It sounded like none of them knew what to do.

*"Looks like ye'll 'ave ta do yer own dirty work, Drax. Er are ya too lily-livered?"*

*"Yer not worth the effort, Muerte. Ye've been a nuisance from the very start, it was a mistake ta let ya join us, one I'll be amendin' now. Make it three chests o' gold, gents!"* Drax declared, and there was a slight pause before the sound of a dozen cocking pistols. Numerous gunshots fired all at once, followed by an agonizing scream. Bastian tore the earpiece from his ear as the sound pierced through his ear canal—and then he cautiously put it back in. There was nothing but silence…

"Oi! What do ya think yer doin'?!" A man's voice called up to Bastian. He looked down, straight into the face of one of Drax's pirate guards. Bastian quickly changed directions and began scaling up the wall instead of down it. He climbed all the way to the roof, searching for his best route of escape when the captain's voice came through his earpiece.

*"Change o' plans, round up the crew—we depart immediately. Anyone not on the Black Mary in the next ten minutes is gettin' left behind,"* he said, then his connection was lost.

*"Dodger, get to the ship—now!"* Tink commanded.

"On it! Shick!" Bastian swore, and then he ran.

"Oi! Get back 'ere!" the pirate yelled from the ground. He tried to follow Bastian the length of the house, but Bastian was too fast. He jumped off the front of the roof, landing in a roll while hugging his precious cargo, and made a beeline for the town square.

⌒⌒

Bastian skidded around the corner of the dirt road to The Bleeding Hearts and ran inside, pushing past men to run up the stairs.

"Ya can't go up there! Stop him!" the woman behind the counter cried, and Bastian saw two large men follow in his wake.

"Cricket! Cricket!" Bastian yelled desperately, running down a hallway of doors, opening one after the other. The rooms were all occupied, but not with Cricket. The people inside shouted in anger at his disruption, some coming out to join the men on his tail. Then a door opened at the end of the hall and Cricket stepped out.

"What in the bloody shadows be goin' on out 'ere?!"

"Thank the Stars!" Bastian said, skidding into the room while pulling Cricket in with him, and locking the door behind them. The mob outside pounded on the door angrily. Jozalin was in bed holding a sheet to her bare chest. "What's all this about?!"

"Aye, what the bloody shick are ya doin' 'ere, Dodger?!"

"We have to get back to the Black Mary, now! Drax has put a bounty on the captain's head and ordered the entire crew be captured."

"What?!"

"There's no time to explain, we have less than ten minutes to get back before the ship departs, we have to find Stork and Rhino!"

Cricket went white. "Shick!" He turned to Jozalin. "Sorry me love, better leave now if there's ta be a next time," he apologized, and kissed her before opening the bedroom window and looking out. "That'll 'ave ta do," he declared, and leapt.

"It was nice meeting you," Bastian said to Jozalin awkwardly, and she waved at him, bemused.

Bastian looked through the window and saw Cricket climbing out of a cart full of palm fronds and jumped after him. They didn't stop running until they reached the tavern. To their relief, Stork and Rhino were there.

"What's gotten inta ya two? Is there a fire?" Stork asked.

"Way worse than that, we gotta go! Our lives depend on it!" Bastian asserted.

"Alright, alright. Don't get yer 'air in a tizzy," Stork said drunkenly, and stood to put on his jacket.

"Can I at least finish me drink?" Rhino asked.

"No!" Bastian and Cricket yelled together.

Cricket jumped up on the table and turned to the room, putting two fingers in his mouth and making a piercing whistle. The room fell quiet.

"Anyone from the Black Mary better leg it ta the ship, now! It be settin' sail whether yer on it er not."

The men just stared at him and then looked at one another, wondering if he was joking.

"Why is the Black Mary leavin'?" a sailor from another crew asked.

"Aye, do ya know somethin' we don't?"

A man burst into the pub panting and announced,

"Muerte Tormenta's killed Drax! The Black Mary 'as been ousted. There's a price on Tormenta's 'ead, three chests o' gold ta the man who snuffs 'im out, everyone from their crew is ta be captured!"

The color drained from Stork's face. "Shick, please tell me 'e's jokin'?"

Bastian recalled the scream he'd heard through his earpiece and didn't reply. The room fell completely silent. Men who had been drinking merrily with crew members from the Black Mary were now looking at them, wondering if they should be drawing their pistols. Before the other pirates could reach for weapons, every crew member from the Black Mary bolted out of the pub, the rest of the men following in hot pursuit.

Tink's voice came through Bastian's earpiece, *"Dodger, where are you?!"*

"Almost to the beach!"

*"Good. We've already pushed away. There's three boats waiting for you and the others, get on them as fast as you can!"*

They reached the end of the tree line and ran out onto the sand. The Black Mary was already in the water making ready to depart. Three small lifeboats waited on the shore with Bullseye and Falgo standing beside them, their weapons drawn. Two men tried to ambush them from behind, and Falgo cut them down with two simple motions of his sword. Bastian glanced around to see a wave of ferocious pirates close on their tail. He put his head down and ran with everything he had. Cricket, the twins, and the rest of the Black Mary crew followed closely behind.

There was a loud *thunk* as something hit the sand not three paces away. Bastian looked over to see a metal canister halfway buried. *Thunk, thunk.* Another two sunk into the sand nearby, and a dense yellow smoke began pouring out of them, filling the air over the beach with yellow fog. Bastian squinted towards the water and saw Boom facing them from the deck of the Black Mary, holding a cannon on his shoulder. He grinned. *Painted Smoke Blinders.* He recognized the smoke bombs from his time helping Boom in the armory. They were one of the master gunner's exploding experiments.

Bullseye and Falgo motioned for them to hurry, and they pressed on with everything they had. They reached the small boats and pushed them into the water, jumping inside while Bullseye covered them with his pistol. The three boats were barely large enough to hold the remaining crew, but they managed to squeeze everyone in. The men took up the oars with a passion, rowing furiously towards the Black Mary.

There was a small army of pirates on the beach shooting their pistols at them, but their visibility was lost amongst the yellow smoke, and they missed their targets. Soon they gave up and scattered towards their own ships.

"Shick," Cricket swore, "they're readyin' ta pursue us!"

Bastian looked out to see the other ships being boarded and preparing to sail. As soon as the lifeboats reached the Black Mary, Bastian and the others scaled the ship's side to the top deck. Snibs greeted them with a gruff nod.

"Men, to yer stations!" he cried, and the Black Mary crew scattered to their positions.

"Full an' bye, lads!"

Every sail was raised. They immediately caught the wind and carried the ship forward with speed.

Bastian hurried into the belly of the Black Mary,

"Tink, where are you?" he called into his earpiece.

"Right here," Tink said, and Bastian turned around to find him standing directly behind him.

Bastian took the wad of wax from his ear.

"Do you have it?" Tink asked.

"Yeah."

Bastian took the chest out of the satchel slung across his shoulder. He opened it and Tink's eyes fell on the object inside and sparked with hope and relief.

"What is it?" Bastian inquired.

"You'll know when the time comes."

Tink took the sphere in hand and started towards the upper deck.

"Hey, Tink!"

Tink turned.

"What am I supposed to do now?"

"Stay alive," Tink said, and continued to the upper deck.

*Right*, Bastian thought, but he wasn't going to spend another fray cowering in fear, not this time. He followed after with determination.

Bastian followed Tink all the way to the stern to where the captain was standing, leaning against the poop deck's guardrail while looking out at the ship's wake. The other twelve pirate ships of the Deadly Thirteen were on their tail. The captain seemed eerily calm as he gazed out towards them, and Bastian wondered how in the shadows he was planning on getting them out of this one. The Black Mary might be the most feared pirate ship on the seven seas, but he didn't think she could best the rest of them banded together.

"The orb, Captain," Tink said, handing the sphere to Muerte. The captain looked down at the object as if coming out of a daze and smiled, taking the enchanted artefact in hand.

Bastian heard someone approaching and turned to see Cricket coming onto the deck. His eyes were locked on the captain. He didn't even acknowledge Bastian was there.

"Muerte! Don't tell me yer plannin' on takin' us back ta the Desert?!"

"We 'ave no choice," the captain asserted.

A look of terror flashed in Cricket's eyes. Bastian was taken aback—he'd never seen him so afraid.

"How could ya even think o' goin' back? That place nearly ended us all! Not even the Nine Levels o' Darkness compares ta the horrors that dwell in that ocean. 'ave ya already fergotten the friends we lost?!"

The captain turned on Cricket, his cool expression erupting into fury. "Ya dare ask me that?! No one saw the extent o' the horrors I did! Er 'ave ya fergotten that? If ya want ta leave, then go! If we don't brave the Desert, then true horror far worse than anythin' we've witnessed will be cast upon the world—an' everythin' we've been through will 'ave been fer nothin'!"

"Cast upon the world? What are ya talkin' about?"

A handful of curious pirates stopped what they were doing to listen in on the conversation. The captain took note of their attention and raised his voice so all could hear.

"There's a war brewin'. It 'as been fer some time, but now The East be readyin' ta rise up an' swallow Equillian whole. Marx 'as the power ta make what those of us witnessed in the Desert Ocean seem like child's play. I've seen it. An' 'e intends ta release such horrors on the world. The Thirteen 'ad a decision ta make taday, one that will greatly influence the outcome o' this war, an' they decided ta side with Eastgate. I might be morally 'andicapped, but I'm not willin' ta set the world alight an' watch it burn. If any o' ya disagree with me decision, then take a lifeboat back ta those bottom-feeders. I won't stop ya!"

The men looked at one another with sullen faces.

"Stars 'elp us," Cricket muttered.

Bullseye stepped forward. "We've never tangled ourselves in the affairs o' the mainland before—the sea 'as always been our 'ome. Why should we care what 'appens ta 'em now?"

"Because this world be no different than a ship—if it goes down, we'll all be goin' down with it," Muerte declared.

"What does the Desert 'ave ta do with anythin'?" Guts inquired.

"It 'olds the key ta stoppin' The East. If we recover it, then we alone will 'ave the power ta save Equillian."

There was a moment of silence while the men digested that. Then Cricket asked, "So, what's the plan than? Kill er be killed by the men we've been drinkin' with fer the past two days? They outnumber us by at least twelve ta one, an' we can't outrun them ferever."

"Neither will be necessary, not when we 'ave this," Muerte announced, and held up the metal sphere for all to see.

Expressions of surprise filled the men's faces.

"So it's true than, ya got Dodger ta recover The Miner's Orb," Cricket said.

"A test o' 'is loyalty, one 'e passed with flyin' colors. Let it be known, lads, Dodger bleeds black, 'e be a true brother o' the Black Mary!" Muerte declared triumphantly.

All the sailors in earshot, even the ones hanging from the lines above, hollered in approval.

There came the sound of labored footsteps coming up the stairs. The men parted to make way for the master gunner and two other men carrying a cannon. They placed it down next to the captain facing outward from the rear of the ship, then locked the wheels in place.

"The boomstick ya requested, Cap'n. Will ya be needin' anythin' else?" Boom asked.

"That be all fer now."

Boom nodded and he and the other men stepped back. Soon the rest of the crew formed a small crowd on the poop deck to look out at the oncoming ships. Bastian followed their gaze to their pursuers—all twelve ships lined the horizon, speeding towards them with full sails. He wondered why the Black Mary crew were all standing there instead of at their stations readying for the fight. The other ships were making better headway than they were. Bastian looked up at the sails to see that almost all of them had been lowered, as if the captain wanted the other ships to catch up to them. He wondered what Muerte's game plan was. None of the men had their weapons drawn—they all just stood there looking at their approaching foes with stern faces.

Snibs passed through the men and stepped up beside Tink and Muerte. "Ready when yew are, Cap'n."

"Drop anchor," the captain ordered.

"Drop anchor!" Snibs relayed to the crew, and Bastian heard the sound of the large metal chain dropping into the ocean. Then the captain twisted the top and bottom of the round metal artefact, like opening a jar. The two halves popped out from each other, revealing a strip of glowing blue light that encircled the center, and all of the alchemists' symbols engraved around the orb glowed with the same blue luminance.

"What's that?" Bastian asked Cricket.

"The miners' guild uses 'em fer minin' the old world. The cap'n acquired it a while back, then Drax took it from us," Cricket explained.

Bastian wanted to inquire further, but Cricket was engrossed on the scene in front of them and didn't look like he was in the mood for elaborating.

The captain tugged on the metal ring at the top of the orb and it pulled out a glowing blue metal cord. He attached the ring to a hook on top of the cannon, then extended the cord until there was enough slack to load the orb into the cannon's barrel. The pirate ships were nearing them now, still out of range to reach them with their cannons, but within a minute they'd be near enough. The captain nodded to Snibs. The quartermaster aimed the cannon at the water between them and the oncoming ships and lit the fuse. The whole crew watched it burn down in silence, and then *Bang!* The orb exploded out of the end of the cannon, zooming through the air to its watery target — the blue string coming out of its base like fishing line as it propelled forward. It fell into the water with a silent splash and sunk. Bastian could just make out the glowing blue light as it descended. The men on the other ships began pointing at the curious device. It was clear to Bastian they had no idea what it was. Three seconds passed, then suddenly a giant gaping hole appeared in the sea, as if the wide swath of water had simply disappeared. The gap ran at least a mile wide and stretched all the way down to the ocean's floor. It looked to Bastian like the water was being propelled away from the orb by some invisible forcefield. The men on the attacking vessels shouted desperately, immediately calling orders to drop anchors and lower sails. Water splashed over the edges of the watery cliffs into the giant pit, pulling the other ships towards it. The ship leading the pursuit tipped dangerously forward at the edge of the void, and the men on board began abandoning her, jumping off either side of the deck in a desperate attempt to save themselves as the ship's nose dipped dangerously forward and the vessel dropped in. The ship fell for several long seconds, picking up speed before it hit the sandy coral-infested bottom and shattered into a million pieces on the ocean's floor. Cricket leaned forward to have a better look. "Thank shick," he said.

"Why's that?" Bastian asked, gawking at the entire scene, astonished.

"That was The Gore, I never liked their lot," Cricket admitted.

One of the pirate ships raised their white flag, and then another and another, until every one had raised white flags, and it was clear they were standing down. The men on the Black Mary cheered and made jeering sounds and rude gestures towards the other ships. The captain pressed a button on the metal ring that connected the blue glowing string to the cannon. There was a *click,* and then the sound of a wire retracting. A few seconds later the steep cliff walls of water surrounding the orb fell in on themselves, burying The Gore for good in a watery grave. The Miner's Orb was soon back in the captain's hand, and the sea was whole once more, without any sign of disturbance.

"Ta yer stations, lads, make ready ta sail the Desert Ocean!" the captain cried, and Cricket and the other men moved to their stations. Several moments later the Black Mary was sailing once more, again with full sails. Bastian walked to the back railing and looked out at the other pirate ships lining the horizon. They stood there like sentinels in the afternoon sun, but not one of them dared pursue the Black Mary.

# A CHOICE

Bastian stepped inside the captain's quarters. The Everfire hearth was aglow. The captain sat in one of the lounge chairs in front of it, his back to Bastian.

"You asked to see me, Captain?" Bastian asked, coming to stand beside him.

"Take a seat, thief."

Bastian sat down in the adjacent armchair.

"Ya did well on Jaxland," Muerte commended.

"Thank you."

"I 'ave somethin' fer ya," Muerte gestured to his desk.

Bastian got up and walked over to it. Sitting on top was a pile of neatly folded clothes beside a pair of well-crafted leather boots and two leather gauntlets.

"What's this?"

"I 'eard ya were in need o' some new garb."

Bastian picked up a long coat from the top of the pile. It was made of dark grey wool, decorated with black baroque embroidery along the back. He put it on—it was light, and the hem fell at his knees. It had a large hood and a length of soft fitted cotton on the lower sleeves so the gauntlets would fit snugly.

"Very nice," Bastian remarked.

He pulled other clothes out of the pile. There was a pair of dark grey fisherman pants that turned to fitted cotton along the calves, made to be worn with boots. Next was a dark grey long-sleeved cotton shirt, another short-sleeved one of the same design and color, and a knitted sweater that matched. There was also a long pair of warm socks. Everything was the same dark grey—the color of shadows.

Bastian tried on the black leather boots. They fit him like they were made just for him, giving good support as well as freedom of movement and grippy traction with thick rubber soles. Bastian picked up the gauntlets. One of them was made of thick black leather with a piece of glasstanight incorporated into it. The other gauntlet had a sheath built in with a stiletto dagger housed inside. Bastian pulled out the dagger— its blade was only four inches long, made of Damascus steel and sharp as a razor blade. The handle glimmered, polished to a sheen.

"The handle's made o' pure gold an' silver. Intended more as a talisman fer attractin' the Ghost Element than a weapon. But it can be useful in a bind," the captain told him.

"It's beautiful," Bastian said, admiring the craftsmanship. He sheathed the dagger and smiled. The outfit suited him perfectly, not only useful but also comfortable and discreet. Then Bastian's enthusiasm fell as it dawned on him—the clothes weren't a gift. They were a uniform.

"Why didn't you give me up?" he asked suddenly. "You could've taken the orb and handed me over to Drax, and then the pirate's guild wouldn't have ousted you and the Black Mary." The question had been burrowing inside him ever since they'd left Jaxland.

The captain nodded. "Fer several reasons. Firstly, out o' a matter o' principle—if I'm not willin' ta fight fer me best men, how can I expect 'em ta fight fer me? Secondly, because I'm not willin' ta 'and over any man ta the likes o' Drax er Bardviss. An thirdly, because yer a weapon that could change the outcome o' this war," he answered candidly.

Bastian digested that. The last reason was exactly what he'd feared. Bastian recalled Tink telling him at their first lesson that Marx—The East's kingpin—was researching the Ghost Element. He wondered how much they knew already and if they'd been successful in using it. Bastian imagined that in the wrong hands, its power would be even worse than War Dragons.

"Is it true what you said? Does The East really want to conquer the world?"

"They want ta destroy it, an' they've already begun."

"You were never really planning on giving me my freedom, were you?"

"Ye've won yer freedom, thief, fair an' square. If ya want ta walk at next port, I won't stop ya, the choice be yers. Ya can either take yer freedom an' use it ta enjoy what little time ya 'ave left before our world falls apart, er join me an' me crew in an attempt ta save it."

Bastian looked down at the clothes in front of him. He thought about Gwena and Felix and the life he wished the three of them could share together, and then realized that even if he went back and found them, those dreams could never be actualized if there was a war. And if Eastgate won, they'd have no chance at any decent future at all. But if he could help to prevent it, even if it cost him his life, maybe Gwena and

Felix could have a chance at living out their lives and seeing their dreams realized. Bastian thought about the helplessness he felt when he'd stood by while the other men fought the galleons and the kraken, his burning desire to be able to fight beside them, to help protect the people he cared about, and suddenly he knew he didn't have a choice.

"I'll join you. But as a free man on my own terms," Bastian declared.

The captain smiled and clasped Bastian's forearm. "O' course. Welcome ta the crew, brother."

Bastian strapped the gauntlets to his arms over the jacket's fitted cotton cuffs. They felt good, like they'd always belonged there.

# FACING THE DARK

Casio sat in his quarters staring into the flickering flames of the Ever-fire hearth. Even though things hadn't gone as planned, he'd still gotten what he wanted. So why did he feel like such a failure? Because he'd lost control again.

He'd lost count of the times and various different ways he'd fantasized about killing Drax over the years, but it was never supposed to be like this. Not only had he killed the pirate king publicly in front of every other pirate captain, he'd revealed his power—only a small taste, but revealed it all the same. He could still hear Drax's blood-curdling scream as the man was torn apart from the inside out, could still see the expressions on the other captains' faces, staring at Casio like he was a living night terror.

*Is that who I truly am?* Casio wondered. No matter how much he tried to smother it, his rage always won out in the end. His uncle had entrusted him with the power of the Ghost Element so that he could be a hero, so that he could save the world. And yet, despite his best efforts, Casio had only succeeded in being a monster. *Maybe it takes a monster to slay a monster*, he thought.

Casio took a sip of his rum.

But part of him wondered if he was actually any better than the man he was trying to stop. He felt like he should have felt some sort of remorse for what he'd done to Drax—surely any decent person would—but he didn't. Drax was a terrible person, and the world would be a better place without him. Drax had always had it out for Casio. When Casio took control of the Black Mary—when he was still a few years shy of a man—Drax refused to let him join the pirates' guild. It wasn't until the Black Mary superseded his own ship's reputation of being the fiercest pirates to sail the seven seas that Drax allowed the Black Mary to be considered as one of them, turning the pirates of Equillian into The Deadly Thirteen. But Casio almost regretted joining them. Drax continuously treated Casio with malice and spite from the very start, for no other reason than because he was younger and better than he was. Drax stole Casio's best plunder for himself and took credit for the

Black Mary's greatest achievements. Casio's lip contorted like he had a bad taste in his mouth. He could only hope that one of the half-decent captains still remaining would replace the fallen pirate leader. The vote had been a mixed bag. Without Drax and The Gore, there wasn't enough support for the pirates' guild to align with Bardviss. But then, with Casio gone as well, there wouldn't be enough support to go against him either. Perhaps there was still hope that the Black Mary might make allies of the remaining pirates. Either that, or they'd have to slaughter them all when they returned. Casio stopped his train of thought to reflect on how his life had led him to a place where such thoughts were simply logistical. He pulled a small locket out of his breast pocket and opened it to reveal the image of a young girl. She had a pale round face with a reckless smile and thick black curls. *If she was still here, would things have been different?* he wondered, *Would I have been a better man?* She'd always had a way of bringing out the best in him—it was after she was gone that it all started falling apart.

There was a gentle knock. Casio closed the locket and stored it away before walking to the door. He opened it and his eyes widened in surprise.

"Cricket? What is it?"

"Can I 'ave a word, Cap?"

Casio grunted and let Cricket inside, closing the door behind him. He motioned for the sharpshooter to sit in one of the lush chairs in front of his Everfire hearth.

It had been a long time since Cricket and he had spoken alone together. Even though he knew Cricket's loyalty to him and the Black Mary was unshakable, they'd hardly interacted for years. They were friends once, they all were—back when they were still boys and pillaging and murder had felt like a grand adventure, before they wandered too far into the uncharted waters and their nightmares crept into reality, almost destroying them all. They'd put those times behind them, locked them away tight. But the truth was, those who'd survived the horrors suffered worse than those lost, those strange waters still haunting them all, Casio most of all. And he couldn't face Cricket or the others without it all coming back.

"Drink?"

"Sure, thanks," Cricket said, rubbing his hands together uncomfortably.

Casio refilled his own glass and poured one for Cricket, then brought them over and sat down beside him. Cricket took the drink, clearly glad to have something to hold onto. Casio waited patiently for him to speak.

"Most o' the men on this ship 'ave no idea what they're in fer. There's only a 'andful o' us left who've been out there."

"Aye, it's fer the best."

"Please tell me ya 'ave a plan ta ensure things will be different this time?"

"I 'ave a plan," Casio assured him.

"I'll follow ya ta the ends o' Equillian, Muerte, ya know that. But that place isn't part o' the sunlit world—yer askin' us ta follow ya inta the very pit o' the Realms o' Darkness. If I'm goin' back ta that Star-fersaken place, then I want ta be sure it be truly worth it. Is it true what ya say about The East an' Marx?"

"Aye. I've heard 'is trials 'ave 'ad some success. There's already rumors about monstrosities terrorizin' the borderlands. It's only a matter o' time before they unleash such horrors on the rest o' the world. I can't take 'em alone. This be the only way."

Cricket nodded solemnly and stared into the Everfire's ceaseless glow. "Aren't ya afraid ta go back?" he asked.

"I'm terrified," Casio admitted, meeting Cricket's gaze with steellike determination.

Cricket nodded again. "At least yer still human then. Right, if we're really doin' this, then we're gonna need ta be fully aligned. No more secrets. I've already spoken ta the others, we're not lettin' ya tackle it alone this time. When we go out there, we face the dark together."

Casio nodded. Maybe he wasn't completely out of friends after all. He held up his glass to Cricket's, and they clinked them together with the somber resignation of soldiers preparing for the ultimate sacrifice. Each knocking their rum back in a single swallow.

Cricket left his quarters, and Casio refilled his glass. He sat down and stared into the fire as he drank his rum. There was something Drax had said that kept niggling at him. He said that Lord Bardviss wanted Dodger returned to him *with* everything he'd brought onboard the Black Mary. Casio had assumed he'd wanted the boy because he could see the Ghost Element, but was it possible he was unaware of the boy's ability and was after something else? What had Dodger brought with him onboard?

Casio thought back to the day Dodger had first stowed away on the Black Mary. He recalled Bastian boasting about a treasure he'd taken from the Wendrians' castle. *What was it, some gold ornament?* Casio unlocked the cupboard behind his desk. He'd stashed the trinket in his quarters to remove temptation from the other men but hadn't given it thought since. *That's right, a golden egg.* He took it carefully into his hands and turned it over in the light, then focused on it with his green eye and called upon the Ciphorescent Codec. Casio's eyes expanded in surprise, then one side of his mouth curled up in a lopsided grin.

# Acknowledgments

First and foremost, I would like to thank my family for supporting and encouraging my writing; without your support these books would never have surfaced. Secondly, I would like to thank my readers. I am overwhelmed with gratitude to everyone who has read and enjoyed my books, especially to those who have reached out to tell me so, your enthusiasm has been my lighthouse on this journey. It is an absolute pleasure to create stories for you, please never stop reading! And if you have the opportunity, please do leave a review ☺.

Next, I would like to thank my quartermaster and press partner extraordinaire, Victoria Kelley. Thank you for helping to sail the ship, keep our course steady, and for weathering storms with me. I could never ask for a better quartermaster. Thank you to my preliminary reader all-stars, Marty Riback, Cami Wheeler, David Carpenter, and Jeanne Pistorius. Your insight and feedback has made this book monumentally better. Thank you to my amazing editor, Lynne Lampe, my invaluable formatting artist, Kath Wilham, and my incredibly talented cover artist, Carlos Quevedo. Last but not least, thank you to Jess and Jeanne for supporting my work and keeping me sane through the epic journey of writing this book, love you gals!

# Author Biography

K.L. Harris is the award-winning author of *Equillian's Key* and the adult picture book, *The World is Full of A**Holes*. She serves as the managing director of Make-Believe Press and is the co-writer of several award-winning short films. Harris holds a BA in Acting for Screen and Stage. Born and raised in America, she now resides in Western Australia with her husband and two children. Her favourite pastimes include, consuming stories of all kinds, surfing, travelling this world, and creating portals into others. To find out more about K.L. Harris, visit www.masterofmakebelieve.com